To

Favor

Viking
Daughter

by

Jay Palmer

Books by Jay Palmer

The VIKINGS! Trilogy:
             DeathQuest
             The Mourning Trail
             Quest for Valhalla

Jeremy Wrecker, Pirate of Land and Sea

The Magic of Play

Website

http://JayPalmerBooks.com

Cover Artist

Katarina Sokolova

Viking Daughter

To Karen, my life, my love, and my devotion ...

The beauty of Freyja
The strength of Thor
The wisdom of Odin
My Valkyrie ... and more

Jay Palmer

Viking Daughter Sagas

Saga 1

Viking Daughter

Chapter 1

"I will not marry Jarl Austmaðr!" Hávi screamed.

The flying, feathery dust slowed and stilled in the single bright beam of sunlight slicing through the dark paneled room. Mother and daughter glared at each other like berserkers.

"How dare you!" Helga seethed. "Jarl Austmaðr is chief of the wealthiest clan in the Skåne, leader of the viking!"

"And if I refuse ...?"

"Women can't refuse marriage."

"Why not?"

"We don't have the right."

Mother and daughter stared, irresolute, jaws set so hard that teeth drove into gums.

"So ... I've been sold?" Hávi sneered.

"Consider yourself lucky," Helga scowled. "Jarl Hersir insisted that you be married ..."

"What?" Hávi shouted. "Austmaðr wished me ... *without marriage?"*

Worry-lines slackened; Helga lowered her eyes.

"You'd give me to a man who'd use my honor as privy-straw?" Hávi asked.

"The decision wasn't mine ..."

"Jarl Hersir decided this? Mother, how could you ...?"

"Jarl Hersir is our clan-chief ...!" Helga shouted, but suddenly she faltered, choked, and grasped her throat.

"Mother ...?" Hávi hesitated, then she worriedly took her mother's hand and helped her to sit on an ornate wooden bench.

"It's the same in every clan," Helga gasped, clearing her throat. "Lindisfarne! Lindisfarne! The men shout it as if it's Ragnarök."

"What do you expect?" Hávi asked. "What kind of fools hoard golden cups and crosses in a castle defended only by men wielding books?"

"Lindisfarne was a monastery," Helga said. "Those were holy books."

"Their gods are fools," Hávi said.

"They have only one god, and don't doubt his power," Helga warned. "France, Italy, Spain, Germany, and England

2

have been conquered by this Christ. They thought that no one dared attack their holy men, these ...," Helga searched for the word, "priests."

Hávi glanced about, lost in the unfamiliar extravagance. Jarl Hersir's mansion boasted more rooms than she had fingers, each more opulent than the last. The bed beside them was art, its fancy headboard and footboard exhibiting fantastical sea dragons, finely carved and painted, with fanned bat-wings and long intertwined tails encircling rows of spiral seashells. Thick, colorful quilts lay stacked upon the bed, vivid reds and bright yellows upon snow-white in intricate patterns, looking warmer than anything that Hávi and Helga owned. The dark-stained doorways appeared as the gates of Valhalla, carved with ravens and wolves, their lintels in the shapes of swords. Even the sole window gleamed ornate, its oiled lambskin translucent, almost clear in direct sunlight. Its bright sunray fell upon a sea-chest of polished rowan bearing bearded faces capped with iron, painted amid intersecting wood-burned rows of magical runes.

Hávi bowed her head, wiped tearful eyes, and recited a charm against evil.

> *"Frigg, who beseeches flower and dew,*
> *Baulder's blessing now prove true,*
> *By Odin's secrets, living and dead,*
> *Your protection on my head."*

Tightly they held each other. Outside of that decorated door, Hávi would no longer be her mother's daughter; Hávi would be the intended bride of Jarl Austmaðr.

"When must I ...?"

"Tomorrow," Helga said. "It won't be so bad; you won't have to milk goats any more ..."

"I'll have to milk an old codger's babies!"

3

"Dry your eyes," Helga said. "You must look fair for your husband-to-be."

Helga stood, then pulled Hávi in front of a large copper mirror in an oval redwood frame carved with seals chasing dolphins in an endless race around the brightly-polished metal. Outside of the sunbeam, the copper mirror reflected darkly, but both knew how Hávi looked: Hávi stood tall, nearing her father's height, but she had inherited her mother's sharp chin, a heart-shaped face centered around an aquiline nose, eyes brighter than a cloudless midsummer sky, and cascades of sun-yellow hair spilling to her waist. Clearly Hávi was her mother's daughter, although a finger's length taller, not yet bearing Helga's lines of age or her gray-white streaks. Helga brushed Hávi's thick hair with her fingers, trying to straighten her obstinate curls.

Handsome young men, fierce and brave yet kind and gentle, hollered protests from the depths of Hávi's imagination; *they'd never marry her now.* The Norn witches had woven the thread of her life; Hávi had seen too many tear-streaked brides to believe that she'd be rescued. She'd witnessed marriage vows frequently interspaced by pathetic whimpers and sobs, and once a fainting, yet those vows and speeches had always continued, and before the unconscious bride had awoken, the ceremony had been completed.

They could not avoid the dark-stained doorway forever.

Every eye turned as Hávi emerged from the mansion's front door into the bright sunlight. Spring had come early; birdsong cheeped and twittered from every blossoming tree, chipmunks darted nervously around Law Rock, and the sky stretched blue and wide, dotted with towering, billowy clouds. Villagers stood about, enjoying the first warm day without the thick, heavy cloaks that they'd clutched tightly about them throughout the bitter winter. Cloakless, Jarl Hersir waited on his doorstep, tall and broad-chested, with wide, muscular arms, his left hand missing courtesy of a Saxon axe when he was but a boy. Jarl Hersir possessed friendly eyes and a hooked nose, but the rest of his face was hidden by shaggy black hair and a beard so thick that a shadowy bush seemed to have grown atop his shoulders. His rich scarlet raiment, rare, coarse auroch fleece with a pine-green hem, collar, and cuffs contrasted his rugged appearance. Hávi spied many familiar faces furtively watching her while pretending to be busy attending chores or gossiping in small groups; *why couldn't Jarl Hersir have talked inside rather than parade her on his doorstep?*

"You honor us, the whole Hersir clan," Jarl Hersir spoke softly to Hávi, his deep voice reminiscent of her dead father. "You're too young to understand, but someday you'll bless this union."

"Why me?" Hávi asked glumly.

"Hávi!" Helga snapped.

"Peace, Helga," Jarl Hersir nodded knowingly, his large hand reassuringly comforting Helga's shoulder. "Girls Hávi's age don't marry old men willingly. Hávi, I hope that no other holds your heart, for Jarl Austmaðr was smitten with you yesterday when he saw you pass by. His wife died a month ago, and for him to ..."

"A month!" Hávi exclaimed. *"One month?"*

"It's never too soon to remarry," Hersir said sadly. "Dearly the Austmaðr clan has earned its wealth; all of the clans need tall, strong sons ..."

"Is that why I was chosen?" Hávi demanded. *"For my height?"*

"And your beauty and youth," Jarl Hersir finished. "Hávi, we need this marriage. Clan Hersir barely has enough food to endure a mild winter."

"Is that what I am being traded fo...?"

"Hávi!" Helga scolded.

Jarl Hersir bowed his shaggy head.

"What would you have, Hávi?" Hersir asked. "Don't you want to marry?"

"I ...," Hávi fell silent, uncertain. She didn't *not* want to get married, but ...

"Your friends will all be married before the first snow, if enough men live," Jarl Hersir said. "Jarl Austmaðr just hastened your ceremony. You'll be happier than your friends; you'll be the chieftess of clan Austmaðr. You'll have servants and a house that dwarfs mine ..."

"What about Mother?" Hávi demanded.

"Helga will also marry," Hersir said, and Helga nodded obediently. "As an older woman with her own ranch, she'll have first pick of those who come home alive, assuming that she hasn't chosen one before they leave ...?"

Jarl Hersir glanced at Helga questioningly.

"Three months make little difference in men," Helga said. "I can't afford another dead husband, no one to teach my sons to fight, and I've no desire to spend the winter bearing a dead man's infant."

"Very well," Hersir sighed, "but I want every maid birthing before this time next year."

"You do your tasks, *and come home*, and we'll do ours," Helga promised.

"We need sons, not daughters ..."

"We'll chant the proper charms and prick the women with nettles, but Frigg alone chooses the fruits of the womb."

Jarl Hersir nodded resignedly, then slowly and deeply, he bowed to Hávi. Hávi stepped back, shocked by his gesture of respect.

"Tomorrow you'll be Chieftess Austmaðr," Jarl Hersir smiled. "You'd better get used to it."

Jarl Hersir and Helga walked away in silence, although Hávi knew that they'd start discussing her wedding as soon as they stepped out of earshot. Hávi considered eavesdropping, but then she heard fast-skipping feet and a repressed giggle.

Völu ran up, yellow-brown eyes wide, dark-red pig-tails flopping and swatting her head, freckled cheeks glowing like roses, barely-concealed laughter about to burst from her tightly-grinning lips. Hávi blushed, grabbed Völu by the arm, and hauled her off at a run around the other side of the building, stopping between a large herb garden and an empty horse pen. There Völu exploded.

"Did ...? Are ...? Do ...?"

Hávi frowned. "Austmaðr claimed me."

Völu shrieked with childish delight, an effusive, piercing note of unbridled joy.

"Close it!" Hávi muted her, smothering Völu's round mouth with her hand. "Are you daft? Do you want everyone to know?"

Völu pushed aside Hávi's muzzling fingers.

"But ... everyone knows!"

"What?!?"

"The whole clan knows; probably both clans!"

"How?"

"You can't keep this secret!" Völu laughed. "The plans for the wedding started this morning, and everyone knew that Austmaðr wasn't here just to negotiate for sailors."

"Why didn't you tell me?"

"Why didn't you insist that the sun would rise?" Völu argued. "Besides, you've been with your mother all morning, and when she took you into Hersir's house ... well ... it wasn't hard to guess. Hávi, you're going to be rich!"

"Women are property no matter who owns them," Hávi retorted. "You'll know that soon enough."

"Well, I'd rather ...," Völu began, but then she startled. *"What ...?!?"*

"All of the maids will be married before the first snows," Hávi said. "Hersir said so."

Völu squealed, but her delight was mixed with worry. *"Who ...?"*

"That depends on who survives the viking," Hávi said. "But I wouldn't get your hopes up. Widows like Mother, women with land, will get first choice, and there may not be enough men to go around."

Völu paled. *"I-I could get ... left out?"*

"Don't you get it?" Hávi shouted angrily. "You'll be married to whomever ...!"

"I get it!" Völu defended herself. "Whomever Hersir chooses! I'm not stupid! Just because I don't have your big ...!"

Völu's insult never leapt past her lips; without warning, Sleitu came around the corner of Jarl Hersir's house.

"Is this a private conversation?" Sleitu asked, a wry, sarcastic smile on her boney face. "If so, then why are you shouting so loudly that all of clan Hersir can hear?"

Taken aback, Hávi and Völu swallowed hard; *how loud had they been talking?* Sleitu grinned smugly. Of all the girls in clan Hersir, Sleitu alone matched Hávi's height, but she was skinny as a steel needle, blueberry-eyed, her strawberry-gold hair long and straight, her thin face pointed like a bird's,

8

and her long nose resembled a sharp raven's beak. She seldom spoke to anyone, bumptious, aloof, and in a crimson pouch on her belt Sleitu always carried a hickory frame holding a palm-sized tin mirror, which Sleitu claimed was silver but which she polished twice a day to keep from rusting.

"*Chieftess Hávi!*" Sleitu chuckled. "How droll! Well, you are moving up in the world, aren't you? What will this make you: *Austmaðr's fourth wife?* You know how old men get; after three real, wealthy wives, he probably just wants a demure plaything."

"*Loki-cursed harridan!*" Völu screamed, but Hávi seized her shoulders and held her back.

"Austmaðr wants *live* sons," Hávi sneered, and Völu let out a little shriek and cupped her mouth. Sleitu glared, but evidenced no other sign of discomfiture.

"Don't worry," Sleitu hissed, narrowing her eyes. "I'm sure that *you* won't end up like Austmaðr's last wife ... or *be* his last wife."

With a murderous glare, Sleitu stormed away, gone in an instant. Völu gave Hávi an equally-deadly stare.

"Are you mad?" Völu demanded. "Do you want Frigg to curse you?

> *Baulder's weakness, blind Hod's cast,*
> *By entrails of Loki held fast,*
> *Serpent's poison, ground quakes,*
> *Bind this evil and all it makes."*

Hávi said nothing as Völu recited her charm three times, then spat on the ground. Blessed Frigg, Odin's wife and goddess of mothers, cursed women with infertility for far less than she'd said, but Hávi couldn't help it; Sleitu had tormented all of the clan-girls with her early marriage to Mikli, a large, handsome youth, only a year ago. Sleitu had already been pregnant by spring when Mikli sailed off on his first viking, but Sleitu had miscarried shortly afterwards and Mikli had been slain by an arrow on his first raid.

"Let's get out of here," Hávi said.

They ran along the thin wooded trail, avoiding as many clansfolk as they could, but Hávi noticed that everyone that they passed eyed her and smiled widely. They circled the millwright's, slipped through the loud, open smithy, getting yelled at only once, and then reached the trail around the fjord, ignoring the boys who called to them as they polished clan Hersir's three sleek dragonships. They ran past several more startled people, almost caused one man to spill two buckets of fresh water, and then dashed toward the sandy dunes between tall brown weeds whose spring-green leaves were newly-budding.

The wide, long beach lay deserted save for the crashing waves and seagulls. They ran out into the open, reveling in the commodious free space, the strong briny wind, and the constant thunder of the sea. Hávi kept running.

"Hávi, come back!" Völu shouted. "Don't you want to talk?"

"No!" Hávi shouted. "Married women can talk! I want a strange ship to sail up and take me away!"

"You'd flee?" Völu gasped, running after her. *"You'd disgrace our whole clan?"*

"If I had somewhere to go I would."

"You'd end up a servant or a whore! You'd be raped and left to starve!"

"Why do you think I'm not jumping into that ocean and swimming away?" Hávi stopped and lowered her head, breathing hard from running. *This wasn't a bad dream. This wouldn't be forgotten in a week.* "I'm ... I'm going to be married, aren't I?"

"It won't be so bad," Völu tried to calm her. "You'll be rich, and we ..."

"You'll be here," Hávi said. "I'll be on the other side of the inlet."

"We ... we'll still see each other ...!"

"How?"

"It's not that far! Men travel from clan Austmaðr all the time!"

"Right: *men travel.*"

"You'll be chieftess! Surely ...!"

"Völu," Hávi said softly, "we'll never see each other again."

"I won't let that happen!" Völu said fiercely.

Hávi suspected that Völu was wrong, but said nothing. Tomorrow Hávi would no longer be part of clan Hersir; her place would be across the inlet.

"What happened to Jarl Austmaðr's other wives?" Hávi asked, and Völu frowned.

"Sleitu was right," Völu admitted. "Austmaðr's wives have always been wealthy."

"Until now."

"His first wife died during the gasping sickness; that was when we were only four. His second wife he divorced; Austmaðr had to fight a war to keep her dowry. Austmaðr's third wife never bore any children and ... well, she just got sick and died. Some said that she was poisoned, but no one dared accuse Jarl Austmaðr."

"Daughter of Loki!" Hávi exclaimed. *"What manner of man owns me?"*

"You're getting married, not purchased."

"The distinction is as tiny as a baby flea," Hávi scowled, and she picked up a smooth stone and cast it into the sea.

"There you are!" cried a squealing voice, and Hávi and Völu startled to find six girls almost upon them, racing across the sands, their bat-pitched laughter carried off by the strong wind. Þongull led them; she was the oldest and swiftest of the unmarried village girls, followed by five younger cohorts. Ørrabein trailed slowly behind; Ørrabein had fallen down a rocky hillside as a child and limped ever since.

"Congratulations!" Þongull shouted, and the other girls chorused her merriment.

Hávi accepted their congratulations and oaths of envy, but Völu quickly told them about Jarl Hersir's plans to wed every man who returns from the viking, and the squealing girls virtually forgot about Hávi, gossiping about their own impending marriages. Völu kept them jabbering for almost half an hour, and then she over-spoke them all.

"*Sleitu!*" Völu shouted. "Frejya's necklace! Sleitu doesn't know!"

"We should find her!" Þongull shouted, and the other girls agreed.

"Go ahead!" Völu urged. "We'll catch up!"

As quickly as they'd appeared, the laughing girls ran off, slapping feet kicking loose sand in every direction as they raced back toward the dune-trail, their giggles quickly lost in the gusty wind.

"Good luck, Hávi!" Ørrabein shouted as she hurriedly limped after them.

Hávi eyed Völu slyly ... and then thanked her profusely.

"You deserve to enjoy your last free day," Völu said. "Besides, Sleitu irritated me ... and we might as well send one set of irritants after the other."

Laughter erupted from both of their mouths, and suddenly Hávi crumpled onto her knees on the gritty, dry sand. Hávi wept unabashedly, Völu's comforting arms tight around her.

"Come, let's get you home," Völu said, although no comfort tinged her voice. "Dry your eyes; we can't get to your house without passing through the village ... and you don't want Jarl Austmaðr seeing you weep before your wedding."

"What ... what if I begged him ... to set me free?"

"Then Jarl Hersir will marry you to a poor man before the snows and you'll bed the winter in a barn under poorly-cured goat-skins," Völu said. "Some girls will get stuck with Dala and Hálmi, who're older than Jarl Austmaðr. I know that it seems impossible, but you're better off suffering now than later."

Sleitu stood in front of Jarl Hersir's house, Þongull, Ørrabein, and the younger girls surrounding her, as Völu escorted Hávi through the village. Several wives and widows stopped and congratulated Hávi, who politely thanked them for their blessings, deferring to their elderly status; discourtesy was unforgivable in clan Hersir. Völu stood by silently, then escorted Hávi home.

Hávi and Helga lived with two surviving grandparents, Jorgen's father and Helga's mother, who'd bedded together since before Hávi was born. Gamli, Jorgen's father, had slowly ceased talking over the years, and would've died if Hlöðu hadn't taken care of him, seen that he ate, and put him to bed. Gamli watched over their flock of goats, or so everyone assumed. Hlöðu dressed him and led him out onto their hillside every morning, although he seemed as uninterested in the goats as in anything else. Every day Gamli stood silently on their hill, rain, snow, or shine, until Hlöðu brought him back into the house.

Jorgen had built their home in the traditional longhouse style like the barracks that he'd grown up in. Their home

13

wasn't decorated with ornate furnishings like Jarl Hersir's magnificent mansion: their low, sod-roofed longhouse was half-buried, which made it warmer in winter, with a wide trench around it to direct the rainwater away. Floored with clay, down its center ran seven feet of sturdy table, built into its frame, with benches on both sides. Five kegs and three wash barrels pressed against the wall to the right, a stone fireplace and four polished chairs to the left. Four small chests of clothes and six shelves of curing cheeses lined the walls before the two great beds, one for Gamli and Hlöðu, the other for Hávi and Helga, over which their winter cloaks hung on pegs. A large sack of flour sat under the cheeses, a regular gift from Jarl Hersir; Helga made the best goat-cream pie in the clan, and she always made an extra for Jarl Hersir. Behind the beds, a thick curtain hid the goat's pen, the second half of their house, where the beasts sheltered when winter ice buried everything.

When they reached her door, Hávi begged Völu's forgiveness but confessed that she wished to be alone. Völu tenderly kissed her cheek, then made Hávi promise that she'd comfort her in the fall if she got stuck marrying Dala or Hálmi.

Helga arrived soon afterwards and broke the news to Hlöðu, but unlike Helga, Hlöðu frowned at her granddaughter.

"That's why she's so sour!" Hlöðu said. "Came home with that red-headed girl an hour ago and hasn't budged from that bench since."

"Leave her be," Helga said. "Some girls take longer to get used to being married."

"Married!" Hlöðu spat the word like a curse, then leaned over and hugged Hávi. "I remember what being young was

like. Hávi, have you even talked to Jarl Austmaðr?"

"No."

"Ever seen him?"

"Yesterday ... from a distance."

"Well, you're better off than I was," Hlöðu said. "I was pushed up beside a man whose name I didn't even know: your grandfather."

"It's not fair," Hávi said.

"Fairness is a dream," Helga said. "Life's real."

"Young girls need dreams," Hlöðu said.

"Dreams are insidious," Helga retorted. "The bigger one dreams, the harder they're crushed."

Hávi whimpered while Hlöðu scowled.

"Jarl Austmaðr's a wealthy clan-chief," Helga said derisively to Hávi. "Did you think that you'd marry a young prince?"

Only Hlöðu's glare answered Helga, who lifted their black cauldron, still shiny from a recent oiling, set it under a water-keg, and turned its tap. The sound of splashing water mixed with Hávi's muted sobs. Hávi wiped back her tears, knelt down before the fireplace, and picked some kindling out of the box.

"I'll do that," Helga said.

"But I always ..."

"I don't want you dirty ..."

"I wash before supper!"

"Leave her alone," Hlöðu said. "Let her have one last night of peace."

"Mother, go bring in Gamli," Helga said sharply.

In a huff, Hávi started the fire, ignoring her mother's objections. Helga boiled gruel in goat's milk, added cubes of cheese and flour to thicken it, and then surprised everyone with a large loaf of fresh bread, a gift from Jarl Hersir, which proved tasty when dipped into the gruel. Nonstop Helga and Hlöðu discussed Hávi's wedding and what it meant to their family and clan, but Hávi ignored them. Only her fear of rape and starvation, or of being hunted down and carried back, kept her from fleeing into the night.

Chapter 2

All of clan Hersir arrived for Hávi's wedding. Everyone that Hávi knew mingled in the center of the village, garbed in their brightest finery. Jarl Hersir and Jarl Austmaðr stood centermost, not far from the front of Hersir's mansion, before Law Rock, both smiling, although teeth were hard to see behind Jarl Hersir's thick tangle of black hair and beard. Völu and Sleitu had both pushed to the front, Völu bouncing excitedly on her toes, Sleitu coldly frowning, her slender jaw set. Even Hlöðu had come to witness the joining, although her smile wasn't as bright as Helga's, who walked with her head so high that Hávi mused it might pop off and fly into the clouds. The fragrant, early-flowering rhododendrons sprouted bright pink blossoms beside Law Rock, which clan-boys loved to scale and slide down its back side despite its rough edges that frequently scuffed holes in tunics and trousers. The boys didn't dare slide down the rune-covered face of Law Rock; breaking a single rune would curse the whole clan, and they'd be punished for even contemplating such a risk. Fortunately the gray, cloudy sky spitted a misty rain, not enough to stop the ceremony, but which Hávi hoped would shorten her nightmare. Save for the light drizzle, it was Völu's dream-wedding, and Hávi only wished that Jarl Austmaðr had fancied her excited best friend instead.

Hávi shined in the new clothes brought to her house early in the morning by Jarl Hersir's servants: a fine, newly-woven yellow paisley dress trimmed with baby fox, softer than anything that Hávi had ever worn, over a chemise of white silk reputedly from Odin's birth-land, Asa, the legendary lands where the sun rises in the distant east, all held together by a wide leather belt decorated with steel rings and oval plates that looked like silver. Everyone congratulated Hávi, spouted effusive praises, and some even bowed. Hávi blushed to each compliment and gesture of respect; two days ago she'd been just another village girl, a plain goat-milker ignored by the adults unless chores needed to be done. Today she was the center of their universe. Hávi fought back her tears and glanced skyward, wondering if Thor would spare her a lightning bolt, or anything that would slay her before she was sold, a tall baby-maker exchanged for winter food, but Hávi bowed her head forlorn; the gods, who'd never before spared any bride, seemed unlikely to change their immortal ways.

Jarl Austmaðr stood before a line of armored warriors holding spears that towered over everyone's heads. Hávi had never seen him up close before; Jarl Austmaðr stood taller than Jarl Hersir, his thinning black hair brightly-streaked with gray, his aged beard shaggy and long, although not as thick as Jarl Hersir's. Under his spidery gray brows shined keen eyes, focused even from a distance, as if gifted with Heimdal's godly sight, a wide musk ox nose, and sagging ears drooping halfway to his shoulders; they seemed too large for his head. Faded scars crossed one cheek as if it'd been repeatedly slashed just above its gray hairline, yet his most prominent adornment hung around his neck; numerous thick chains reflecting the dim light too brightly to be brass: *gold, the magical metal! No wonder Jarl Austmaðr had lived so long!*

Jarl Hersir waved them forward. Helga squeezed Hávi's right arm and Hlöðu gripped her left; Helga's face was rigid, determined, as if she'd force this ceremony by will alone. Hlöðu looked sad, clutching Hávi possessively. But Hávi had no desire to be a squealing lamb carried to slaughter; Hávi stopped before the whole Hersir clan, which hissed a sudden, subtle gasp, and Hávi firmly extricated her arms from Helga and Hlöðu; she wouldn't live her last moments of freedom bound like a thrall.

Helga and Hlöðu fell in behind as Hávi marched forward unescorted. Hávi bit her tongue to keep from trembling as she looked closely at Jarl Austmaðr, whose face was covered in tiny wrinkles and whose smile displayed half of his teeth faded yellow-brown, the other half missing. Jarl Austmaðr looked older than Jarl Hersir, perhaps older than Gamli.

Every muscle knotted to hold Hávi still. Here was the altar of her honesty, the sacrifice of her virgin maidenhood. Hávi wrinkled her nose and blinked, struggling to fight back her burgeoning tears. Jarl Austmaðr bowed deeply to her, his long earlobes slightly jiggling as he lowered his head; a silent scream tore through Hávi's clenched heart. Under her breath she whispered a chant.

> *"Lift the cat and drink the sea,*
> *Devour all the food that be,*
> *Thrice rent valleys in the Earth,*
> *Courage, now prove thy worth."*

"A glorious day!" Jarl Hersir shouted loudly, his voice booming over his gathered clan. "A blessed day! A wedding day!"

Cheers arose from the clan, Völu's shrill shriek piercing the clamor. Brass-encrusted cow horns rose and blasted forth deafening notes, each a unique, consonant pitch, drowning out the jubilant voices. Rawhide drums hammered and high-piping whistles and flutes tinkled on the tips of the celebratory tumult. Hávi grimaced. Eventually Jarl Hersir waved to his men and their instruments fell silent.

"Odin!" Jarl Hersir cried, looking up into the rainy sky. "We seek only to please you! Look down upon this joyous union, not only of two people, but of this joining of mighty clans! See this union strengthen those who already sacrifice to you, whom you have made strong! Odin, grant them the wisdom to find strength in each other! Frejya, grant them joy! Frigg, grant them countless sons! Thor, grant them firm, solid roots! Tyr, grant them courage! Loki, grant them cunning! Heimdal, grant them, your children, the endless sight of each other which only your eyes can see! Sygn, grant them devotion, and may this union endure for all the years of their lives yet to be counted!"

Again cheers erupted, horns blasted, drums pounded, and flutes piped. A single fat, unbidden tear rolled down Hávi's cheek. Her stomach began to cramp.

Jarl Hersir's wife came forward holding out a living circlet of early tulips and daffodils woven amid baby oak leaves and bound by fresh ivy. Jarl Hersir took the circlet and held it up before everyone, then lowered it onto Hávi's head, crowning her sun-yellow hair, and Hávi choked, afraid that she'd vomit. The soft foliage caressed her scalp. Its leaves gently rustled around her ears. Its weight almost crushed her.

Hersir recited the ancient words, a tongue so old that few could translate it. Hávi caught the old names of the gods, Wotan instead of Odin, Fræj instead of Freyja, but she paid scant attention to the rest, feeling only a numbness creep up her limbs as her nausea spun. Jarl Hersir's words became a discordant, monotonous drone, a reverberating cave's echo in her ears. Her temples were pounding.

Hávi had never seen torture, but stories abounded. *Did torture feel like this?* She seemed to be slipping away, floating, leaving her sickness behind, but only for a moment. Then her stomach twisted, her head pounded, and she felt more ill than the Crushing Cough that had bedridden her for three weeks.

Sand was sprinkled into her hair while Jarl Hersir kept speaking. Hávi glanced at Jarl Austmaðr, who smiled his missing-tooth grin at her, calmly shifting his weight from one foot to another as if his whole life wasn't changing, collapsing, decaying before his eyes.

Something scratched her arms; Helga and Hlöðu were slowly circling her, brushing the *'happy couple'* with boughs of pine and spruce: blessing a non-existent love to remain evergreen. The rough needles scraped like sharkskin; Hávi was being bagged like a sack of ground-wheat ready to be sold.

Sprinkles of fresh spring water wet her tear-streaked face. Jarl Hersir dipped his fingers into the bowl, then flicked at Jarl Austmaðr, who ignored him, and then stifled a yawn. Hávi staggered; *he yawned at their wedding! She was dying and he was bored!*

"Hávi?" Jarl Hersir asked.

Hávi noticed her name.

"Repeat after me," Jarl Hersir repeated. "I, Hávi Hersir, daughter of Jorgen and Helga, pledge my love and obedience

..."

Jarl Hersir continued. Hávi barely listened, mumbling inaudibly, but Jarl Hersir ignored her and spoke as if Hávi had recited every word loud and clear. Slowly Hávi became aware that she was still mumbling as Jarl Austmaðr began reciting his unheard marriage vows, promises of loyalty and faithfulness, defense and support; the vows of a master, not the bondages of a slave.

The broom was brought forward like a headman's axe. Death hovered before Hávi's feet, a yawning precipice that Hávi prayed would drop her into Niflheim. Hávi took a deep breath as something seized her fingers, lifted her hand, and together they jumped over the broom into oblivion.

Cheers cascaded, hollow and mocking. Music thundered storm-sea bleak. Jarl Austmaðr raised Hávi's hand and turned her to face the whole Hersir clan. Völu leaped wildly while Sleitu laughed darkly.

Bile rose too fast to restrain. Hávi vomited.

Drenching-wet cloths plastered Hávi's face.

"Just the excitement," Helga's voice was followed by Hlöðu's scowl.

"Get her hair," Völu's voice echoed as fingers squeezed tighter on her arm. "There, by her sleeve."

Where was she? Blades of grass became visible. A wooden wall, an empty trough; Hávi was beside Hersir's house, near his herb garden. The wet cloth was removed, water splashed, and then it returned, flooding her face. Hávi coughed and sputtered.

"Hávi?" Völu asked. "Feeling better?"

At first Hávi thought *'my stomach feels better', 'my head isn't pounding',* and then the ground dropped beneath her, the earth split open, and Hávi crumpled into its pit. Her right hand splashed into the water bucket as she toppled forward: *Hávi was married.*

Hollow consolations filled her ears for minutes as Hávi struggled to compose herself. Hávi was sold, her dreams traded for horrors, her virtue lost. Hávi was a slave having never spoken to her master.

"Leave her be," Hlöðu said.

"Chieftess Austmaðr," Helga said proudly.

Slowly Hávi turned to face her.

"It had to be done," Helga said. "For the good of the clan ..."

"You're not my mother!" Hávi screamed.

Helga's hand slapped hard. Hávi almost fell, but Völu held her tightly, cradled Hávi against her chest, and shouted angrily as Helga and Hlöðu began arguing so vehemently that none of their words could be discerned. Hávi clung to Völu desperately. *This couldn't be happening; there had to be a mistake!*

Slowly her bodice tightened: Hávi was breathing. Hávi was alive.

Hávi was married to a total stranger.

"Hávi, the wedding feast's started," Völu said softly.

Hávi entered Jarl Hersir's house as she'd approached her wedding, Helga and Hlöðu behind her. Jarl Austmaðr and Jarl Hersir both stood and raised their drinking horns as Hávi appeared inside the doorway, and the whole Hersir clan raised the thick rafters with their cheers.

Hávi stepped across the hall alone and circled the head table to the only empty chair. Jarl Austmaðr, husband and stranger, bowed deeply, then motioned for her to sit beside him. She tried to avoid meeting his eyes; *she was his wife.* It was her lot, a woman's burden, the doom of her sex. Hávi sat like a condemned prisoner before the axe, keeping her eyes lowered.

A rough hand touched the back of her head. Hoary fingers closed. Her spine snapped rigid, her muscles fighting not to shudder or pull away. Even Hávi's body was no longer hers; the hand upon her neck turned her head. Jarl Austmaðr's wrinkled face swam into her vision. Aged lips pursed and approached. Hávi closed her eyes; the old jarl kissed her, and the deathscream of countless dreams died in her ears. Horror and disgust washed over her, but the entire clan was watching, cheering, and she sat helpless, stunned beyond disbelief, every eye watching her eagerly. Hávi shuddered: *worse than his kiss was to come!*

Hávi picked at her food, fearful of upsetting her stomach again, glad for the hollowness consuming her. Course after course was served, even kalops and köttbullar, Hávi's favorite foods, but she couldn't stomach a bite. She nibbled at the salad and pepparkakor, but the rich cake's contrast of honey and pepper dripped tears upon her cheeks. She left them unwiped and attended to her drink: hot, sweet, cinnamon-flavored wine.

"Careful," Jarl Hersir warned her. "That glögg's very strong."

Hávi listened to his words and drank deeply.

Musicians played between the courses, even after the sweet hot saffron buns were served fresh from the ovens. Hávi ate one, its steamy warmth barely a memory to her chilled, stiff body. Hávi had sat heedless through their conversations; Jarl Austmaðr and Jarl Hersir discussed trades of food and arms and destinations for the viking, ideas for finding more men, and problems dealing with the increasingly-guarded churches protecting Europe. Hávi glanced across to see Helga, Hlöðu, and Völu watching her from the women's tables at the far end of the hall; even Jarl Hersir's wife sat with the women.

Drummers took over the evening's entertainment. Logs flamed in the large, stone-circled fire pit in the center of Jarl Hersir's hall. Men jumped up and danced before the clapping clan to hammering drumbeats, formed a leaping, gyrating ring encircling the fire, and the younger men took turns leaping over the rising flames. Half-drunk, some stumbled as they jumped, evoking howls of laughter as they kicked sparks into the air or fell onto their faces. Jarl Austmaðr laughed the loudest, obstreperous, craggy laughter, and Hávi cringed at the sound.

The gods were sadists or madmen; *did they create mortals because they enjoyed causing suffering?* It didn't matter if a man was good or evil, kind or cruel; *why hadn't the gods included fairness in the nature of the universe?*

Eventually Jarl Austmaðr stood and reached down to her. Hávi trembled. Her hand seemed to lift of its own accord and strong, clammy fingers grasped hers. Hávi rose slowly to his firm, steady grip. Jarl Austmaðr was her husband; *her doom had been decreed.*

Hávi didn't even look at the women's table as she passed it; she didn't want to see Helga's triumph, Hlöðu's compassion, Völu's excitement, or Sleitu's cruel grin. Hávi had grown up raising goats, watching countless billies and nannies mate: Hávi knew what was coming.

Jarl Austmaðr led her to the very same ornate room where her mother had revealed her doom. She entered, eyes locked on the opulent bed as if staring at her coffin. It gleamed resplendent in the candlelight, the bed which had shined so brightly in the daytime that she didn't dare touch it.

Suddenly Jarl Austmaðr pulled her into his arms and tried to kiss her, but Hávi couldn't. She struggled against him and, surprisingly, he released her.

"I'm no fool, wife," Jarl Austmaðr said, speaking to her for the first time, his voice deep, his missing teeth making him lisp slightly. "You don't get to be as rich as I am without brains; young girls don't dream of old men. To tell the truth, I didn't want to get married. But here we are: I'm your husband, you're my wife, and here's our wedding bed. My dishonor's yours now; this marriage must be consummated or I'll be disgraced."

Hávi looked up into Jarl Austmaðr's aged face, into his dull, moose-brown eyes under wrinkled, shaggy gray brows.

"Why me?" Hávi asked.

"Why do you breed your strongest cattle?" Jarl Austmaðr asked rhetorically.

"My family owns goats," Hávi said.

"You're *my* family now," Jarl Austmaðr said. "You're my wife, and you own hundreds of goats, cattle, oxen, and half of the Skåne."

"Women own nothing."

"Legally, perhaps," Jarl Austmaðr said, "but no husband's perfect, and a rich husband isn't the worst. I've sent hundreds of Austmaðr clanswomen to husbands that they didn't know, and none of them ever died for it. Many found happiness, as I hope you will. I'll give you comforts that this backwater clan's never seen, and you'll never know hunger or cold. But, for this, you must submit to your wifely duties."

Hávi shuddered and closed her eyes. Jarl Austmaðr began to chant.

"Frigg, blessed queen of the womb,
Freyja, before whom all men swoon,
Gefion, Eir, Sif so fair,
Make a son to be my heir."

The silence that followed was broken by muted cheers from the hall; they were still celebrating her ruin, the whole Hersir clan, even the women. Hávi choked.

"Let's not make this any harder," Jarl Austmaðr said softly. "Undress."

Unable to move, Hávi stood sobbing. Strong, hoary fingers reached out and gently pulled upon her rich new belt, carefully unfastened its silver buckle, and let it fall. Her dress tugged awkwardly about her and a coarse hand firmly grabbed her wrists and lifted them high. Her dress and chemise wrenched and tightened about her shoulders as they were lifted; Hávi made no effort to help or resist, although she wanted to. She should fight, flail her fists and defend herself, but to what avail? She was married, owned, and it was a husband's legal right ... *no, she couldn't even think it!*

Finally both of her garments pulled free. No thunder boomed as loudly as her soft new clothes falling onto the floor. Naked, nothing remained to shield her now. Hávi stood before him, bared, helpless. *She couldn't allow this! She had to do something!*

Hands reached out and touched her, unfamiliar fingers probing forbidden places. Hávi's doom was heralded only by tears.

Jay Palmer

Chapter 3

Dead inside, Hávi stumbled out of Jarl Hersir's house, one limp hand hanging over Jarl Austmaðr's thickly-muscled arm. She'd done nothing, allowed him to ... Hávi still couldn't say it, not even recall it, although she'd be eternally pained by his invasion, his violation of her honor. She felt like a dead leaf blown about by irresistible winds. Her prayers to the gods had gone unheeded. Jarl Hersir loudly congratulated Jarl Austmaðr and slapped his back, smiling, and Hávi, again in her wedding dress, was grateful only for the thin mists, hoping that they'd hide her shame. She couldn't even raise her eyes to face Jarl Hersir; she didn't want him seeing her haggard, tear-streaked face.

"Good journey!" Jarl Hersir said.

Hávi's ears perked alarmingly.

"The tide will do most of the work, if we catch it," Jarl Austmaðr said. "We'll be home before nightfall. If your supplies don't arrive within five days then send me a messenger, but I wouldn't worry about it."

"I'm not worried," Jarl Hersir grinned. "I'm sure that all debts will be settled ... before we join your fleet."

Jarls Austmaðr and Hersir laughed loudly. Together they marched down to the water, and there Hávi saw ten strange warriors waiting upon the dock beside a huge, sleek dragonship. *Where were they going?* But she kept silent, her shame on public view. She couldn't force the horrible memories of her wedding night from her mind. Jarls Hersir and Austmaðr shook hands one last time, and all but two of the men jumped aboard the ship, and then Jarl Austmaðr escorted Hávi out onto the dock, handed her down to two of his warriors and, with all three men helping, Hávi stepped awkwardly down into the dragon, barely able to see its deck-planks through her blur of tears. The wooden dragon tilted and rocked dangerously beneath her feet; she'd never before been on any ship. Jarl Austmaðr jumped aboard with surprising ease, shaking the ship, and the last two men pushed off, and then they recklessly jumped aboard at the last moment. Hávi gasped as the ship bobbed free in the water; she instinctively grabbed as she foundered. Her finger's closed around her new husband's arm.

"Don't worry, we're safe," Jarl Austmaðr laughed, and then he spoke loudly to his men. "Oars out! Take us home!"

Timbers scraped and long oars splashed into the water. Soon the snarling, wooden dragon's face surged forward, farther from shore with every stroke. As they reached midstream, their prow turned toward the sea. Terrified and helpless, Hávi watched Jarl Hersir and her familiar home-shore slowly dwindle behind her until it was gone forever.

Many ornate chests lined the deck, set in rows. Each rower sat upon a chest, alone manning an oar. Jarl Austmaðr sat Hávi upon a vacant chest in the rear and masterfully untied a rope until a wide plank beneath the spiral-carven dragon's tail splashed into the water, and then Jarl Austmaðr seized upon a stout curved pole and held it firmly, sitting in the very back of the boat.

"Oars up!" Jarl Austmaðr shouted. "Raise the sail!"

The sail was a vast red-and-white striped square wider than Hávi's house. As men pulled on the ropes, the sail rose to a frightening height. Hávi worried that its weight would break the slender mast, but these sailors knew their business; the sail billowed in the wind and pulled their ship out of the inlet onto the wide crashing ocean. The roar of the surf filled her ears as acrid, briny gusts blew her blonde curls across her tear-drenched face. On the breakwater, their ship bucked like a wild horse, tossing them up and then crashing down, and Hávi shivered; she'd just passed farther from her house than ever before. Hávi was clan Hersir no more; Hávi was clan Austmaðr.

Sailing was a nightmare; at first Hávi had been afraid that they'd flip over or break apart, and then Hávi realized that she was alone with strangers and had no idea where they were taking her. Hávi was a poor swimmer; the waters here were all icy and she didn't like their chilling tingles, so Hávi had ignored the other kids when they ran toward the countless lakes and streams that filled their countryside. *If the ship sank ...!*

Hávi stared at the wide coastlands; she'd never seen such sights. They passed by more lands and inlets than she'd known existed, and not just lands; thick forests abounded, nestling many small villages. Wide farms combed every field with long rows of newly-planted crops, and many hillsides were terraced, clustered around unfamiliar houses where Hávi spied strange men on horses, other men pulling plows, and unknown women hanging freshly-washed bedding and tunics. Small boats floated everywhere; fishermen cast and pulled back thin nets, sometimes straining under the weight of their catches.

"Well?" Jarl Austmaðr asked. "What do you think of the Skåne?"

"This ...?" Hávi asked hesitantly. "This is the Skåne?"

"My half," Jarl Austmaðr said proudly. "Clan Hersir lives on the other half ... with four other clans."

Hávi stared at the wide coastlands. *All of this ... belonged to Jarl Austmaðr? Her husband ...?*

Hávi had once seen a wood-carved map of the whole world from its northern ice-flows to the southlands of England, but her teary eyes gaped, amazed for hours as they sailed past more coastlands than she'd ever seen, spied the far sides of mountains that she'd never expected to view, and glimpsed high, distant peaks that she'd never imagined existed. Villages grew larger as they sailed north, and the sun slid toward the icy western mountaintops, crossing from civilized Sweden to the barbarous Norwegian lands.

Suddenly a village larger than Hávi had ever seen appeared around a bend, visible only through a narrow inlet. Buildings as tall as trees, dwarfing Jarl Hersir's mansion, loomed closer as they sailed through the inlet into the fjord. Countless smaller buildings hid behind a forest of naked masts of dragons, knarrs, and fishers, some billowing bright-striped sails as their sailors hurried about, others lowering flapping sheets as they glided toward crowded docks in the deepening sunset. One amazing sight glowed brighter than any other: a sparkling white road, straight and steep, leading from the farthest center of the fjord up a long hill topped with the largest building of all.

"Welcome to Skadi," Jarl Austmaðr smiled at Hávi. "Welcome home."

Disbelieving, Hávi stared. Of all the stories that she'd ever heard only fabled Asgard matched this magnificence.

A loud horn blew from the city, and a crowd bigger than clan Hersir gathered as they approached the wide, sturdy dock, each pylon thicker than the roof-beam of her longhouse. Their sail lowered and Jarl Austmaðr masterfully steered their dragon, by drift alone, alongside ancient pylons. Torches flared in the growing darkness, and a great cheer arose as Jarl Austmaðr climbed up onto the dock. Tall men in exquisite finery stepped forward, but everyone stopped as Jarl Austmaðr held out a hand and assisted Hávi up onto the sturdy dock beside him.

"People of Skadi, behold!" Jarl Austmaðr shouted, holding her hand high. "Behold Hávi Hersir Austmaðr, my new bride!"

A short, uncomfortable silence met this announcement, and then a tall, slender man with bright red hair and a jutting, angular chin clapped his hands, and instantly many applauded, and joyous shouts followed. The tall red-headed young man stepped forward and bowed deeply to her.

"Welcome to Skadi, Mother," he said, but his voice was harsh, sarcastic, and no smile brightened his face.

Mother? Hávi stared incredulously, abashedly aware of her tear-streaked face. *Mother!?!*

Fear crept up Hávi's spine as they walked up the hill. Every footstep crunched; beneath her soft shoes, the bright white road was paved with countless broken seashells, fragments of oysters, clams, mussels, and scallops, and the chorus of their grinding underfoot gritted her teeth. Dozens of strangers followed her and her new husband up to their huge, magnificent new home. The strangers crowded around them; their brightly-dyed wools looked as if they'd just come off the loom, pinned with large, exquisite iron and brass broaches, many bearing polished stones, all far fancier than the finest clothes that most of the people in clan Hersir owned. Rapid, shallow breaths caught in Hávi's throat; Jarl Austmaðr's huge house wasn't built of wood, but of massive stone blocks, surrounded by a stout fence of sharpened tree-trunks nine feet high and frighteningly formidable. Its gate wide enough for six men to walk through shoulder-to-shoulder, and they entered through the largest doors that she'd ever seen. Warriors in bright, expensive mail, wearing swords and wielding spears, saluted Jarl Austmaðr as he approached, and then they stood aside, stealing only furtive glances at Hávi. The closer that she walked to the huge mansion the more impressively it towered, and the more Hávi struggled to breathe, to walk, to keep from vomiting as she'd done at her wedding. More warriors awaited them before its huge doors, and older men in strange matching robes rushed to open more doors as Jarl Austmaðr approached. Uncountable candles lit the small room inside, not clay grease-lamps: actual tall, white-wax candles, yet Jarl Austmaðr pulled Hávi past them without a sideways glance.

Hávi's soft shoes skidded on the polished stone floor as she froze, eyes wide, so stunned that Jarl Austmaðr had to steady her, upholding her arm to keep her from falling. They entered a hall bigger than Jarl Hersir's whole mansion. Walls twenty feet high towered in every direction, and teams of horses could race around the many-trunked columns supporting the massive ceiling, each column bearing four bright, flaming torches. Every man, woman, and child in the

Hersir clan could house in this one gigantic room. Every wall was hung with colorful tapestries and brilliant banners, and built into the far wall were three high, thin windows that opened upon other rooms.

Her eyes followed the decorations to their farthest point, past the countless rows of tables and benches; on a dais, three feet above the rest of the room, stood a long high-table, and behind it rose another dais, towering over the high-table, and upon it stood two matching high-backed, gold-polished chairs; one for Jarl Austmaðr and ... one for ... Hávi forced her gasping breaths, swallowing air: *one for her.*

"A feast!" Jarl Austmaðr cried. "A wedding feast for my new bride!"

Cheers exploded all around them, and a dozen servants dashed toward small doorways in the side-walls. Jarl Austmaðr pulled Hávi forward; men bowed and maids curtsied deeply before him, but he paid them no attention, and merely bustled past. They circled around one end of the impossibly-long table, climbed several steps onto the lower dais, and then slid behind the long high-table to its two massive center chairs, equally well-made and polished, their tall backs topped with rounded points like inverted walrus tusks. Jarl Austmaðr pulled out one chair and invited Hávi to sit upon it, but she only trepidatiously glanced behind the high-table at the high-backed, gold-polished chairs on the taller dais behind them.

"Overwhelmed?" Jarl Austmaðr asked. "Don't worry; you won't have to be here long."

Jarl Austmaðr sat on her right. The clamor of footfalls made Hávi look around; strange people had followed them up onto the lower dais, and others circled around to the other side. Even more people took seats upon the benches at the foremost tables. Strangers streamed in through every door, some still adjusting colorful cloaks and fastening huge, finely-wrought clasps, a hundred strange faces, but every eye stared at her. Hávi wished that she could hide.

A great musk ox horn was set before Jarl Austmaðr, beer-suds spilling over its rim, gold-chased and jewel-encrusted with an inlay of a silver crown upon a golden rising sun between ebony ravens and a black wolf's head bearing red eyes. The horn had attached twisted-iron bars forming a stand around it. Jarl Austmaðr seized the great horn, drank deeply, and suddenly cheers echoed distressingly. The whole hall seemed to shake, and Hávi clutched at the thick table desperately.

"My people!" Jarl Austmaðr shouted as he set the heavy horn back onto the polished oak high-table. "I left you a sad widower, but return a joyous newlywed! I've taken a bride of clan Hersir, and in token, Jarl Hersir has promised us all of his dragonships and three hundred warriors!"

Cheers erupted as Hávi gasped. Ships and warriors; *was that what she'd been sold for?*

"Behold Hávi Hersir Austmaðr, daughter of Helga, a noblewoman of clan Hersir, now my bride, now your queen!"

Expecting the explosion of cheers, Hávi forced a troubled smile, but wished that everyone would stop staring. Jarl Austmaðr motioned forward a skinny old woman with tightly-bound gray hair, and she immediately approached the high-table and curtsied with unexpected grace as she reached a small open space; she wore a spotless white dress with a deep green apron consisting of two long rectangles of fine cloth, one hanging down the front and one hanging down the back, connected by heavily-embroidered wide green straps over her thin shoulders. Large circles of domed brass, etched with spirals and rings, were pinned to her apron with long needles thick enough to knit with; the needles looked dangerously sharp.

"Hávi, this is Mjóvi, chief lady of my household," Jarl Austmaðr said, gesturing to the old woman. "Mjóvi, take my bride to my chambers. Let her rest for an hour, no longer, and then dress her in Austmaðr colors and bring her back to the feast."

Mjóvi bowed only slightly, but reverently, and then she circled the long table and took Hávi by the arm. Desiring to run, Hávi walked slowly, letting the thin old woman guide her behind the crowded chairs and then through a wide doorway in the back wall. The doorway led to a long, narrow, barren room with two wide stone staircases, one going up, one going down, and many closed doors. Mjóvi led her to the stairs going up, but Hávi resisted, warily placing one foot on the lowest step, testing its strength to hold her; several staircases existed back in clan Hersir, but only in barns, and they were all wooden and slick, with boards that bent beneath her weight. These stones didn't budge.

"Come," Mjóvi commanded gruffly, and Hávi followed.

At the top of this stair was another stair flanked by two bored-looking guards, but neither attempted to stop them. Tremulous as they reached the top of the second stair, Hávi stood parallel with the tops of tall trees outside these stone walls, but without hesitation Mjóvi pulled her into a room more magnificent than she could conceive. Wall-mounted weapons hung over fancy chairs and a thick scroll-covered table, all heavily decorated, paling her wedding-night-room in Jarl Hersir's house. Their final destination, through another door, was a large warm bedroom filled with tall ornate wardrobes, a massive bed which had bedposts carved in the shapes of fierce horse-heads, and a big fireplace with a display of huge swords over it, and two other closed doors. Piled logs blazed in the fireplace, lighting the tapestry-covered stone walls, the emblem of crown, sun, ravens, and wolf's head that she'd seen on Jarl Austmaðr's massive drinking horn painted, carved, and embroidered everywhere. The wooden furniture gleamed as if made of metal, the wood itself yellow; Hávi had never seen golden wood before.

"This is your bed-chamber," Mjóvi said dryly, as if speaking to a child.

Hávi looked at her disbelieving; Mjóvi wasn't the oldest woman that she'd ever seen but she looked more imposing than Jarl Hersir's wife. Mjóvi wasn't nearly as tall as Hávi, skeleton-thin, and had eyes that could make baby goats flee in terror. She bore the deep wrinkles on her face like men bore battle-scars, and Hávi could only imagine the challenges that she'd faced and the servants that she'd cowed by glare alone. Her eyes were green like a spruce tree, the skin of her eyelids and face heavily-crinkled, but her gaze was fixed and penetrating.

"Please ...!" Hávi said. "I ... I'm ..."

"*Scared?*" Mjóvi asked harshly. "You should be. Every woman in Skadi, from wealthy widows to shameless young vixens, would kill to be in this bed-chamber ... and you'd be wise to fear their ambitions."

Mjóvi's voice stabbed through the air as if gutting a boar, and sharp needles prickled Hávi's skin, uncertain whom she most-feared: these dangerous unknown women ... or Mjóvi.

"*Please ...!*" Hávi pleaded.

Mjóvi fixed an unblinking stare upon her.

"Wait here," Mjóvi said. "Sit upon the bed, or lay, if you like; it's *your* bed. I'll send my child to wait on you."

Mjóvi exited through the door that they'd entered, and

closed it firmly.

Alone, terrified, Hávi glanced around at the rich, unfamiliar finery and unsettling fire-flickering shadows. A large shuttered window graced the far wall, and two closed doors stood side-by-side on the left wall, and tall wardrobes loomed menacingly. Hávi reached out and touched the bed; its new-looking quilt lay thick and soft, so inviting that Hávi pulled her hand back, fearful of being punished for touching it. Her breath quickened; *what she wouldn't give for a chill, foggy morning and a complaining old nanny goat to milk!*

"Mistress Austmaðr?" asked a timid voice.

Hávi jumped. In the doorway stood a small rowan-haired girl, her light-brown tresses tinted holly-berry red, and as she stepped into the firelight the red grew stronger, as if her hair couldn't decide which color it really was. A few years younger than Hávi, neither plump nor thin but well-boned, with a round, cherub face and bright, pale-azure eyes, she stood hunched as if frightened, but her full height couldn't reach Hávi's shoulders. She timidly closed the door behind her, holding out her hands toward Hávi but seeming afraid to come closer.

"Are you ... unwell?" she asked.

"I'm sorry," Hávi said. "I'm just ... just ..."

The young girl smiled.

"I understand," she said. "It's too wonderful, isn't it? Being queen? What an honor! You must be so proud!"

She came forward, took Hávi's arm, and pulled her beside the bed, pushed her against it, and knelt before her. Hávi recoiled from the poisonous touch of both the soft quilt and the kneeling young girl, trapped between them.

"What're you doing?" Hávi cried.

The young girl gaped up at her, thunderstruck.

"T...taking off your shoes," she stammered. "Y...you don't want to wear your shoes in bed, do you?"

"In this bed?!?"

The young girl looked frightened.

"It's ... *your bed.*"

Hávi realized that she must sound like a madwoman, her eyes ablaze, and the serving girl cowered before her.

"You ... you're Mjóvi's daughter?" Hávi asked.

"Daughter? Oh, no; I'm her niece. My name's Tryggvi."

"Tryggvi," Hávi said. "Do you ... wish ... that this was ... your bed?"

"Me?" Tryggvi looked horrified. "Me, a simple servant? Oh, m'lady, I wouldn't dare dream so high!"

Tryggvi shuddered as if stunned with incomprehension, then bent to the ground and untied the laces on Hávi's shoes.

"I can do that ...," Hávi offered, but Tryggvi ignored her.

"No, m'lady, you can't touch your own feet!" Tryggvi insisted, and Hávi gaped, uncertain what she meant. Moments later Hávi stepped out of her shoes, her bare feet touching cloth.

"What's this?" Hávi asked, unable to rise any higher than her toes without jumping onto the priceless quilt. "A tapestry on the floor?"

"Why, no, m'lady; it's a carpet," Tryggvi laughed. "Don't they have carpets in clan Hersir?"

Hávi felt foolish; she'd stood on carpets before, but only atop dirt, and never so thick and warm. She'd been so amazed by the other furnishings that she hadn't noticed the rich carpet. Suddenly Tryggvi rose and flung back the prized quilt so absently that Hávi gasped.

"F-for you," Tryggvi gestured, confused by Hávi's reaction.

Hesitantly Hávi sat upon the soft snow-white sheets. The

straw inside the mattress felt spiky, uncrushed: new. Tryggvi grabbed Hávi's legs and lifted them onto the bed, then pulled the soft quilt over her and gently eased Hávi down until her head rested on furry lamb's skin pillows filled with feathers, their softness caressing her long blonde curls.

"There," Tryggvi said with satisfaction. "Can I get you anything, m'lady? Some wine or cheese?"

"N-no," Hávi tried to smile.

"I'll just let you sleep then, m'lady," Tryggvi said, bowing and stepping backwards toward the door.

"No!" Hávi cried. "I mean: no, don't leave. Would you ... sit with me?"

"Me, m'lady?" Tryggvi asked, surprise widening her eyes.

"Yes," Hávi said, "and please, call me Hávi."

"Oh, m'lady, that wouldn't be proper!" Tryggvi gasped.

"Look, Tryggvi," Hávi said, mustering courage that she didn't think she had, "I don't know what you've heard, but I'm no noblewoman. Two days ago I was a goat-milker on a tiny ranch that my mother owned ..."

"What?" Tryggvi gasped.

"That's right ..."

"That can't be!"

"It is ... or it was."

"Your ... mother ... *owned* ... a ranch?" Tryggvi asked incredulously.

"Wha...?" Hávi gaped. "Yes, mother owned ..."

"Women in clan Hersir can own property?"

"Well, she inherited it ... when Father died."

"How long has she owned it?"

"Four years."

"That's unlawful!" Tryggvi said. "In Skadi, a widow must surrender all that she owns to a man within four months of her husband's death. Surely you have a man in the house, someone who actually owns it ...?"

"No, well ..., Gamli, my grandfather ... but he's old, not right in his mind ..."

"Still, he's a man, the lawful owner," Tryggvi said. "At least I assume so, begging your pardon, m'lady. That's the law."

"What a terrible law!" Hávi said, wondering if it were true. Helga and Hlöðu had always cared for Gamli meticulously, constantly wary of his health even though he couldn't speak or feed himself ... and sometimes soiled his own trousers. "Please, come sit beside me."

Hávi scooted over to make room for her to sit and Tryggvi complied, although she settled nervously upon the very edge of the bed.

"Now, tell me about Jarl Austmaðr," Hávi said.

"M'lady!" Tryggvi jumped to her feet. "I can't!"

"You've lived here all of your life!" Hávi insisted. "I know nothing about him!"

"M'lady, please, it's not my place ...!"

"Tell me!"

Tryggvi's round face paled, making her hair look more auburn than light-brown. She glanced fearfully towards the door. Hávi thought that she might bolt, but Tryggvi only bowed her head.

"M'lady, I've never spoken to the jarl ...," Tryggvi confessed.

"Neither have I," Hávi said. "Until yesterday, I'd barely heard of Jarl Austmaðr."

"How can that be?" Tryggvi asked. "Are ... are you jesting? Please, m'lady; I'll be punished if I speak wrongly!"

"No one will hear you but me and I'll say nothing," Hávi assured her. "Please ... I need your help."

Tryggvi trembled, then took a deep breath and cast another fearful glance at the door.

"B...because you order it, m'lady," Tryggvi stammered. "J...Jarl Austmaðr is a gr...great man."

"Why?" Hávi asked. "What's he done that's so great?"

"He rules half of the Skåne!" Tryggvi exclaimed. "He's a great king and a mighty warrior! Men from all over Sweden flock to his banner!"

"That's why he's so great?" Hávi asked. "Because men flock to him?"

"I can't think of a better reason," Tryggvi said. "Frigg knows we need them."

"Need who?"

"The men, of course."

"Why?"

"Why ...? *m'lady, you're teasing me!*"

"I'm not!" Hávi insisted. "Why do you need men?"

"For the women, of course," Tryggvi hesitantly explained, as if afraid she'd insult Hávi.

"For the women?" Hávi asked. "Why do women need extra men?"

"Extra?" Tryggvi exclaimed. "M'lady, clan Hersir may have plenty of men, but clan Austmaðr's dangerously short. There's not one unmarried man for every five maids!"

"What happened to them?"

"The vikings: the summer raids to the south-lands. Every year they bring back more wealth and fewer men."

"But ... then ... why did Jarl Austmaðr ... marry me?"

Suddenly Hávi sat up in the rich bed: *clan Hersir's men; that's why Jarl Austmaðr had married her! She was the price for three hundred men!*

"But why?" Hávi demanded. "The men of clan Hersir will

go home after the viking ..."

"Not if Jarl Austmaðr pays them to stay," Tryggvi said. "He'd welcome them, gift them with farms, young wives, and three serving girls apiece; that's what he did with the warriors from clan Dúfunef last year; we gained at least fifty, and not-nice men they are; their serving girls are as pregnant as their wives."

Many footsteps approached; doors opened and closed.

"Oh, m'lady, please say nothing ...!" Tryggvi said as she jumped up and bowed before the door opened.

"Tryggvi, have you been bothering Mistress Austmaðr?" Mjóvi demanded in her icy tone.

"I ... I begged her to sit with me," Hávi interrupted what was sure to be a scolding.

"Mistress Austmaðr does not beg!" Mjóvi frowned, and then she summoned a troop of six women into the room. All of them were carrying thick cloths and buckets of steamy water.

"Come," Mjóvi said to Hávi. "We need to get you cleaned up for supper."

"I bathed this morni...!"

"Mistress Austmaðr bathes before every presentation," Mjóvi said, and she stepped past Tryggvi and yanked back the warm quilt.

Hávi stood unresisting, and suddenly Tryggvi and the other women encircled her, unbuckling her belt and untying her dress-laces.

"Hey!" Hávi complained, but no one heeded her.

"Stand still or it'll take longer," Mjóvi said forcefully.

Seconds later, Hávi stood self-consciously naked amid the chorus of strange women. Hot wet rags pressed and rubbed her from every direction, soapily scrubbing every inch of her, even places where only her mother and Hlöðu had ever touched, and then only when Hávi had been very young. Brazen unfamiliar hands lifted her arms, widened her thighs, and held her head still as her face was scrubbed. Hávi stood shocked, appalled, uncomprehending why she couldn't bathe herself. One at a time, her feet were lifted, and even her soles were washed. Then fresh rags dipped in other steamy buckets, and Hávi was scrubbed a second time, the clean, rose-fragrant water even hotter than the soapy, and Hávi wondered why anyone needed to be washed twice at once, let alone twice in one day. Then thick, dry wools visited everywhere that the wet rags had ventured, making Hávi's eyes pop, constantly replaced by new wools until she was dry as a dead tree on a midsummer's day. Then the ladies all stepped back except Mjóvi, who'd only observed the intrusive bathing, and who stared at Hávi, naked on the carpet, as if sizing up the worth of a prized billy goat.

"Dress her," Mjóvi ordered.

Jay Palmer

Chapter 4

Hávi entered the great hall in finery more extravagant than her wildest imaginings, fabrics soft and shiny, so rare that she didn't recognize its cloth or weave. An embroidered black raven decorated each of her large breasts, a silver crown over a rising sun between them, a sable wolf's head bearing red eyes over her stomach, all on a gown of magnificent deep-lake blue. Entwined gold and black ropes composed her belt and soft gold-leather slippers snugly encased her feet. Silver chains hung from her ears and around her neck, each dangling tiny studs of many different beautiful stones, dark-red garnets the only ones that she recognized. Upon her head rested a weave of silver wire that Mjóvi had called a tiara, a fragile silver spider web with tiny faceted gems gleaming like miniature stars.

Silence fell as Hávi stepped through a side-door into the great hall. Every man stood and faced her as all of the servants retreated.

"Walk to the center of the room," Mjóvi whispered from behind her.

Worriedly Hávi stepped forward, out of the side door, between an empty table and a full one.

"Turn to face the high-table, walk to your husband, and curtsy before him."

Hávi obeyed, but she only bowed; she didn't know how to curtsy. Every eye watched Hávi as she approached Jarl Austmaðr, who stood before his plate, her empty chair upon his left, the tall red-headed young man upon his right.

"Welcome, Hávi, my wife," Jarl Austmaðr said, and then he turned to the tall red-head. "This is Sterki, my eldest son and the next Jarl Austmaðr."

Hávi bowed deeply to Sterki, but he only scowled at her.

"Why, Father?" Sterki demanded. "You don't need more sons."

Gasps filled the hall and Hávi paled.

"No, but you need tall, strong stepbrothers," Jarl Austmaðr replied without hesitation, although his voice deepened warningly. "Captains to sail your dragons, generals to command your armies, rulers over distant lands that you've yet to conquer, brothers sworn to your empire ..."

Sterki frowned, and then he bowed stiffly, reluctantly, as if unconvinced. Hávi bowed again to him but only perfunctorily; she wanted to go home.

"Sterki's three older brothers, the eldest sons of my first wife, died honorably a'viking," Jarl Austmaðr said, and he gestured to the two younger men beside Sterki. The elder was short and thick with closely-cropped hair; the youngest was thin and pale-white: an albino. "This is Auðgi and Hvítvi, Sterki's younger brothers." Auðgi bowed quickly, shaking the high-table which his right hand rested upon, and Hvítvi bowed slowly and gracefully. Hávi bowed to both individually.

Seated beside Jarl Austmaðr, Hávi spent the rest of the evening being stared at, but no one spoke to her. They feasted past the midnight bell amid jugglers, minstrels, and a magician that instantly created flying birds from eggs, and mixed powders in a stone basin that smoked and finally burst afire with a few magic words. Beside her sat an old man with a frown chiseled from granite, a scraggily, completely-gray beard, and the top-half of his right ear was sliced cleanly off. Hávi tried to get his attention but he purposefully avoided her eyes. While the minstrels played, Hávi feasted on a delicious pie of shredded beef in sour cream, finely spiced, wrapped in a flakey golden crust, but she found it hard to enjoy anything.

"Time for bed," Mjóvi's voice finally whispered over her shoulder.

Hávi's heart sank, yet she stood, helpless, unnoticed by her husband. Obediently she followed Mjóvi back toward her room.

"What was that meat pie?" Hávi asked curiously.

Mjóvi suddenly looked furious.

"You don't know?" Mjóvi demanded. "It's Lihamurekepiiras, a Finnish meatloaf. The Mistress Austmaðr must know how to cook."

"I can cook," Hávi said.

"Cook what?"

"Gruel, goat-cream pie, oat bread ..."

"Peasant cooking," Mjóvi scoffed. "You must learn proper cooking."

"Okay, but ... don't the servants ...?"

"I didn't say that you'd cook," Mjóvi pointed out. "I said that you needed to know how to cook. I'll send Tryggvi to undress you."

"I can undress ...," Hávi began.

"You will wait for Tryggvi!"

Hours later, after Tryggvi had left, Hávi screamed as two guards abruptly awoke her, bursting into her room. Screaming for Helga, Hávi clutched the priceless white quilt protectively as the strange men entered her chamber; between them hung Jarl Austmaðr, almost unconscious, stinking drunk. The guards threw back the quilt, making Hávi scream again, futilely trying to conceal that she was wearing only a thin nightgown. Roughly they dumped Jarl Austmaðr onto the bed beside her, and then they left without a backwards glance. Hávi jumped out of the bed as Mjóvi and Tryggvi burst inside her bed-chamber.

"Be silent!" Mjóvi snapped at Hávi. "Are you trying to awaken all of Skadi?"

Hávi glanced at Mjóvi and Tryggvi, wide-eyed, horrified, cheeks drenched, hands trembling.

"Go back to bed," Mjóvi said firmly.

"B...but ...!" Hávi stammered, gesturing.

"Get into your husband's bed!" Mjóvi ordered. "And no more screaming!"

Hávi glared, disbelieving, but Mjóvi seized Tryggvi's arm, forced her out, and pulled the door shut behind them.

Tears burst forth and Hávi crumpled onto the carpet. *Surely Niflheim, the cold land of the dead, couldn't be this bad!*

Hávi awoke the next morning, still on the carpet, wrapped in a warm cloak that she'd borrowed from a wardrobe, cuddled before the fire that she'd expertly banked. Quietly, fearful of waking him, she returned the cloak and searched the remaining wardrobes, but the clothes that she'd arrived in were missing, so she selected a simple brown dress with only a little embroidery. Dressed, she made it out into the hallway unseen. Jarl Hersir would be furious, she hoped, if he knew how she was being treated. No more tears flowed; Hávi was past crying: *Hávi was angry.*

"M'lady!" Tryggvi gasped, coming out of a room with a basket of candles. "What're you doing?"

"Be quiet!" Hávi shushed her.

"M'lady, you can't be running about the castle before Jarl Austmaðr wakes!"

"Why not?"

"Why ... what if he awakens and ... *wants you?*"

"Then he can escort me to bed before midnight and not be carried into our bedroom before the cocks crow."

"M'lady!" Tryggvi gasped. "You can't say such things!"

"Listen, Tryggvi," Hávi said, "I don't know about you or clan Austmaðr, but I'm not used to jumping every time that a man snaps his fingers."

"But ... but ... weren't you ...? There must've been some man ...!"

"After my father died, only my mother and grandmother told me what to do," Hávi said. "I never liked it, but I'm starting to think that I owe them many thanks. I didn't want to get married and I didn't want to move here, but I'd like to see where I've moved to."

"M'lady, in clan Austmaðr, it's not your place ..."

"Is it your place to tell me my place?"

"No ..."

"Good."

"... Jarl Austmaðr gave that job to Mjóvi."

Hávi's glare subsided; she'd have to avoid Mjóvi.

"Tryggvi, I'm just going outside ..."

"You'll be recognized!"

"Nobody's awake yet ..."

"I've eaten breakfast, emptied chamber pots, and scooped two fireplaces!" Tryggvi said. "Mjóvi's eaten, inspected the maids and matrons, yelled at the laundresses, and ordered your breakfast prepared."

"Where's she now?"

"Mjóvi went to the kitchen, last I saw, about ten minutes ago."

"Good," Hávi said. "Then I'll be outside before she notices ..."

"M'lady, no!" Tryggvi said. "In that dress, you'll be recognized from across the courtyard!"

Hávi looked at the frightened servant girl and smiled wickedly.

Minutes later, Hávi and Tryggvi hurried down the stone steps; Tryggvi had dressed her in servant's clothes: a faded, light gray-green dress with rectangular white aprons, front and back. Tryggvi had also covered both of their heads with folded white scarves tied under their chins. Each of them carried a wash-bucket half-filled with wet rags, and they lowered their heads and tried to look inconspicuous.

"Not that way!" Tryggvi whispered at the bottom of the stairs as Hávi turned toward the huge hall, and they slipped down the long corridor and through several doors before footsteps startled them.

"Scrub!" Tryggvi hissed.

Both women fell to their knees onto the hard wooden floor, hurriedly slopping water and sliding wet rags back and forth. A nearby door opened and five men streamed out into the hall arguing something about saddles, and they passed the floor-washing women without noticing them. Both women waited, scrubbing long after they'd left, and then they headed in the direction that the men had vanished in and finally emerged into the back of a stable. Tryggvi led, and soon she and Hávi walked out onto a wide dirt yard; they were outside of the castle, but still inside the wooden palisade.

"You were peasant-born!" Tryggvi exclaimed.

"I told you so," Hávi smirked.

"You'd have had that whole floor scrubbed in ten minutes," Tryggvi said.

"That's nothing," Hávi smiled. "Try milking a nanny-goat when her newborns are running wild across the hillside."

Tryggvi led Hávi around and pointed out everything to her, mostly the many windows of the castle and what was inside each. Outside of the castle stood six longhouses where lesser castle guards slept, but they couldn't go inside those, and Tryggvi blushed when a guard whistled at them. Hávi bristled at the guard.

"Ignore them!" Tryggvi warned. "We're not supposed to be here!"

"I'm not supposed to be here," Hávi reminded her. "You live ..."

"I haven't been here since I was thirteen."

"What?" Hávi exclaimed. "But ... you live in the castle!"

"Inside; I don't come outside unless I have to."

"You don't leave the castle?"

"I was thirteen when my breasts grew," Tryggvi said. "One of the guards thought that I was old enough ... he ..."

"Raped you?"

"No," Tryggvi said. "I ran back inside ... and stayed."

"How old are you?"

"Almost seventeen."

"You ... you've been hiding indoors for four years?" Hávi gasped.

"Better than the alternative."

"Jarl Hersir would never allow that," Hávi said, but then she remembered; Jarl Hersir had allowed exactly that, to Hávi, knowing that it was against her will. The memory of her ghastly wedding night moistened her eyes but Hávi didn't want to start crying again, so she forced herself to keep looking at everything inside the palisade.

"Jarl Austmaðr isn't ...," Tryggvi started, but then she gasped, horrified. *"M'lady, forgive me! I didn't mean it!"*

"I want you to be honest," Hávi said. "I need to know about my husband ... especially the bad stuff."

"M'lady, I can't ...!" Tryggvi began, but she wilted under Hávi's stare. Tryggvi looked nervously about, but no one was close enough to overhear, so she lowered her voice to a barest whisper. "I dare not speak, m'lady, but there are others who will: ask Jarl Illingr."

"Who?"

"Jarl Illingr," Tryggvi hissed, casting fearful looks in every direction. "The old man who sat beside you at feast last night."

"The one with only half an ear?"

"The one with only half of two ears."

"Really? I ... I never saw his other ear."

"M'lady, please!" Tryggvi begged. "I dare say no more!"

"How can a man get identical cuts on both ears?"

"From your husband," Tryggvi whispered, and then she hurried on.

Castle Austmaðr was three stories, like stone houses stacked atop each other. Hávi learned that there were also two floors deep underground, one under the kitchen, where food was stored in summer, which Tryggvi said was always cold, and another underground chamber existed, but Tryggvi had only heard of it and didn't even know where its entrance was; only men went there, and some never came out.

Eventually they circled around to the front. Hávi wanted to sneak out of the gate, but Tryggvi insisted that the guards wouldn't let them pass without knowing their business, and she refused to fabricate a lie. Still, Hávi insisted that they walk past the gate so that she could see through it, but Hávi stopped as they neared the gate; outside, all along the spiked wall, a deep ditch had been dug. Tall weeds now filled the ditch so that it looked even with the rest of the lawn, but in the daylight Hávi spied thick, sharpened stakes driven into the ground, points upwards, almost hidden by the tall weeds. She hadn't noticed them in the darkness as she was led inside the gate, and she was glad that she hadn't tried to run then; one slip and she'd have fallen into that hidden ditch and been impaled. Outside of the gate, Hávi saw many distant buildings, but before she could ask Tryggvi about who lived in them, both guards glanced at them and they hurried away.

Large dogs roamed the courtyard and several came up to greet them. Hávi petted the friendly dogs while Tryggvi frowned and stayed back, and then they circled all the way around the back to the stables.

"Okay, that's it," Tryggvi said. "Let's sneak back in ..."

"What?" Hávi asked. "We haven't seen anything!"

"What did you expect to see?"

"Well ... something!"

"Everything important's inside the castle."

"Then why are we out here?"

"You ... said that you wanted to go out!"

Hávi glared at Tryggvi, and then burst out laughing. Tryggvi stared as if Hávi had gone mad, and then chuckled softly. Arm-in-arm they entered the castle, wound their way through the maze of doors and hallways, and they were still laughing when they finally ascended to the very top of the stone stairs, still carrying their rags and water-filled buckets.

"Where've you been?" Mjóvi's icy tone frosted them.

Menacingly she stood before the carved door to Hávi's bed-chamber dressed in a severe black dress pinned with huge silver broaches, their long, broad pins sharpened like dagger-blades.

Hávi and Tryggvi exchanged glances but neither replied.

"Jarl Austmaðr asked me where you were and I didn't know!" Mjóvi fumed, hissing. "I will always know where you are! *Do you hear me?"*

Hávi nodded meekly.

"Tryggvi, you'll be punished ...!"

"Tryggvi tried to stop me!" Hávi argued. "She told me not to leave ...!"

"And you found that servant's dress in your husband's wardrobe?" Mjóvi demanded.

Both girls bowed their head.

Pushed inside her bed-chamber, relieved of her bucket and rags, Hávi stood alone before Jarl Austmaðr's weary, bloodshot stare from their bed.

"Where were you?" Jarl Austmaðr deeply growled.

"I just ... wanted to see my new home ...," Hávi began.

"You were gone when I awoke!" Jarl Austmaðr angrily snapped. "Do you know how that makes me look?" Hávi stared at him uncomprehending. "I'm the leader of half the Skåne!" His volume rose dangerously. "People watch me for signs of weakness! My wife ... *leaving my bed ... on our first morning!"*

"*I ... I ...!"*

"*Do you understand what you've done?*" Jarl Austmaðr shouted.

"No," Hávi confessed. "I wish that I did ..."

"*My men will ...!"*

"No one knows," Hávi interrupted. "No one saw us."

Jarl Austmaðr stared at her.

"How can that be?" Jarl Austmaðr asked.

"We ... I went ... dressed like this ... as a servant," Hávi said. "Everyone dismissed us ... I mean, me ..."

"Us ...?"

"I ... I'd rather not ..."

"*Who?*" Jarl Austmaðr shouted.

Hávi lowered her head.

"Tryggvi," Hávi said. "Mjóvi's niece. Please don't blame her! I made her ...!"

"Come to bed," Jarl Austmaðr said sharply. Hávi startled, a quick inhale hissing past her teeth; she didn't want him touching her again. "Don't make me wait. I'm your husband and I married you to give me sons. You have to get pregnant as soon as possible."

"Is that all I am?" Hávi demanded. "Your son-birther?"

"I should've asked if you were stupid," Jarl Austmaðr shook his head. "Stupid girls are easier." Hávi stared, stunned to silence as her husband continued. "Hávi, who did you want to marry? Tall as you are, Jarl Hersir was certain to make you wed soon. Who would you have chosen?"

Hávi swallowed hard, silent and downcast. None of the boys in clan Hersir had seemed mature enough, the old men too mature. Most of the young men that she knew had died on their first viking. There were several boys that she'd liked, but not enough to let them ... befoul her.

"Hávi, come here."

Obediently Hávi stepped forward. She sat on their bed, facing the door that she'd entered, her back to her husband. She didn't know why she obeyed. He'd punctured her honesty and murdered her dreams; like the inside of a drum, nothing filled Hávi but air, as if he could turn her upside down and see hollow emptiness. *Had she been broken like a wild horse under a whip?*

Jarl Austmaðr's aged hand closed upon her shoulder and gently turned her to face him. His deep, grating voice strained to be soft and tender, defiant against his coarse, scarred appearance.

"I wish that I was young," Jarl Austmaðr whispered to her. "Tight, smooth skin wouldn't disgust you. If I wasn't the lord of clan Austmaðr then you'd flee from me ... but I am. I have duties that I must perform ... and so does my wife, but I don't want her sobbing every time that she sees me." Hávi realized that tears were leaking from her eyes despite her battle to restrain them. "Hávi, we have a baby to make and we can't wait on youthful desires that might never develop. I'll be a good husband, but you must be a good wife ... in public and in private. Bear me a son, and tolerate occasional public appearances without tears, and I'll give you what I can."

Hávi cringed; she had only two choices, to futilely resist until she was broken by bonds, whips, and starvation ... or willingly yield to the inevitable. No shame would mark her submission: he was her legal husband and she'd married him an honest maid, but he was still a stranger, aged, wrinkled, and Tryggvi's whisper about Jarl Illingr's butchered ears frightened her. Jarl Austmaðr seemed considerate in private. In public he seemed distant, yet she'd only seen him among his friends at the wedding feasts of two clans. Jarl Austmaðr was unquestionably wealthy and powerful; such men were reputedly generous to their friends, but what was he to his enemies?

"Wife, you know what we have to do," Jarl Austmaðr said. "You can take off your clothes yourself ... or I'll do it." He paused, taking a deep breath. "Don't make me call for my guards; I doubt if you'd like to be undressed by them."

Slowly, reluctantly, Hávi pulled off her servant's garb and then she sat back down, naked, unprotected. Jarl Austmaðr gently pushed her down, eased her head onto her soft, furry pillow, and then laid atop her and forced himself inside. Hávi gritted her teeth, this time more aware of her pain than her shame. Tears poured, but Hávi bit back her sobs, fighting to endure.

Wash-women reappeared moments after Jarl Austmaðr left, led into the room by Mjóvi. Hávi was curled on her bed, sobbing.

"Get up, you silly girl," Mjóvi said. "Stop that blubbering."

Hávi opened her eyes, unable to stop crying, wishing that she could see one friendly face, but the only friend that she had outside of clan Hersir was missing.

"W-w-where's T-Tryggvi?"

"Scrubbing chamber pots," Mjóvi snapped. "She'll return when she's learned her lesson. Now get out of that bed."

"It wasn't her fault ...!" Hávi spoke forcefully, but Mjóvi's voice cut through hers.

"Tryggvi's not your concern," Mjóvi hissed with the deadly sound and precision of a hunting arrow. "She's been forbidden to speak to you and she'll be punished again if I catch her. Now stand up!"

Long minutes later, scrubbed and perfumed, dressed in pinks and reds that reminded her of a blooming flower, Hávi was forcibly led downstairs into the kitchen. The kitchen was low-ceilinged, but one whole wall was hidden by sixteen large stacked kegs on a rack of oiled, lashed wooden beams. Pungent, acrid scents assaulted Hávi as she entered, making her eyes water, but the busy kitchen, for all its chaos, looked surprisingly clean. Everyone in the crowded kitchen attended their duties quickly and confidently with no bickering, no one getting in each other's way. A wide, round fireplace lay under an enormous copper funnel that rose into the ceiling, heavily-blackened from the smoke that wafted into it. Large beef portions hung from iron spikes over its flames, and one boy was turning the meat with a giant crank, keeping the grease-dripping cow-legs and thick slabs of ribs from burning. Another boy hung a large iron pot onto a hook, swung it low over the fire, and then used a small, long-handled shovel to scrape a pile of red-glowing coals around its base. A girl no older than ten was grinding cinnamon in the largest pestle that Hávi had ever seen. Six women sifted grain through shallow reed-baskets. A tall, dirty-white cloud suddenly plumed high over a wooden half-barrel as a huge bag of ground flour was poured into it by two men. A blood-splattered cook with a wide-bladed hatchet chopped large, skinned fish and tossed the pale-pink slices into a cauldron filled with a yellow-green broth wafting reeking fumes. A cart piled high with vegetables was being emptied onto a cluttered table surrounded by five women masterfully wielding sharp knives so fast that Hávi feared that severed human fingers would fly into the air.

"Look there," Mjóvi pointed at a woman stirring a huge barrel. "Those are herrings being pickled; pickling preserves fish longer than anything else. The viking expedition can eat them during rough seas when nothing can be cooked. Even four months from now, on their way home, if they don't open that barrel until then, the pickled herring will still be edible."

"Fine," Hávi said, pushing back her sleeves. "Where do you want me to start?"

"Start ...?" Mjóvi asked. "What're you talking about?"

"You want me to learn to cook ...," Hávi said.

"Learn, not do," Mjóvi said. "Mistress Austmaðr must know how to cook. Mistress Austmaðr doesn't soil her hands in a kitchen."

Hávi scoffed but fell silent at a glare from Mjóvi; arguing was pointless, and she didn't need someone else being punished. She was the stranger here; she had to learn how things were done and what behaviors were acceptable. Hávi hated to placate Mjóvi, who obviously didn't care in the least how she felt. Homesick already, Hávi bit back a caustic remark and hoped that Tryggvi was right about Jarl Illingr.

Hávi was hungry before Mjóvi finished uselessly parading her around the kitchen, explaining each person's duties in detail, often beratingly, as if the servants weren't there or couldn't hear her criticisms. She carefully described how food for the viking had to be stored and that perishables wouldn't be prepared until right before the sailing. The smoked salmon smelled irresistibly delicious. Hávi was no stranger to cooking, although she'd never seen so much food, but Mjóvi's biggest accomplishment in dragging her and half-a-dozen other ladies around the kitchen was to get in the way of the cooks and their helpers. Left alone, Hávi would've gladly proven that she could cut vegetables or sift grain, and probably would've learned more from helping the cooks than from listening to Mjóvi, but her opinions seemed irrelevant. In her own kitchen, Mjóvi would have her way.

After eating a tray of pastries and anchovy fillets in her room, Hávi was left alone with strict instructions to rest. Hávi's claim that she wasn't tired fell uselessly upon Mjóvi's inflexible insistence; Hávi stared at the door long after Mjóvi had closed it, feeling that her bed-chamber was mostly a prison. She tried to open the two other closed doors in her room only to find that they were locked, and she briefly wondered what was in them.

Two hours later, Mjóvi burst into her room and ordered her to follow. Sick of confinement, Hávi trailed Mjóvi down the stairs into a room that she'd never seen.

Coolness struck her as she entered; despite its worn, faded tapestries and swirling, polished crosshatchings covering every gray-stone wall, the small, fantastically-ornate chamber was uncomfortably cold, its wide fireplace stacked with unlit-wood. Even the torch sconces were intricately carved, the woodwork seemingly nailed to the colorful walls just to make the room look more-fancy, as if it desperately needed to be over-decorated. On the table stood two tall, brightly-glowing brass candelabras illuminating a tray of sweet pastries, a bottle of wine, a pitcher of ale, and several thick wooden mugs and silver goblets. Two young men were sitting at the table, silently facing her as she entered, the third rapidly pacing back and forth as best he could in the tight space, his red hair flashing in the torchlight. Hávi recognized the three men instantly.

"I don't want to do this!" Sterki shouted at Mjóvi.

"Your father commands that you and your brothers become acquainted with your new stepmother," Mjóvi said defiantly.

"I can converse with my own whores," Sterki snarled, and he glared at Hávi. She swallowed hard and tried not to react.

He'd called her a whore ...! In clan Hersir, Hávi would've punched the boy stupid ...!

"Forgive the future Jarl Austmaðr," Hvítvi, the albino, interjected softly.

"Don't interrupt me when I'm speaking!" Sterki snapped at his youngest brother.

"Excellent," Mjóvi said calmly, with a tone of sadistic satisfaction. "Mistress Austmaðr, I leave you with your sons."

"No!" Sterki shouted, but Mjóvi ignored him, as she did everything else, and departed.

The four stared at each other. Sterki continued his pacing, a tall, red-headed wolf angrily prowling his confinement. He avoided Hávi's eyes, intent only upon his blustering. He couldn't have been more than nineteen, scarcely older than Hávi, his dark eyes fixed, his cheeks colored by a short red scruff that would someday become a long beard, jerking his head as if locked in an unspoken argument.

"Perhaps our new stepmother would like some wine?" Hvítvi nudged Auðgi, breaking the locked silence.

"Good idea," Auðgi said, and he poured some wine into a goblet, ignoring Sterki's piggish snort.

As Hávi stepped forward to accept it, Hvítvi came around the table and pulled out an oaken chair with a deep red cushion upon it. Hávi smiled sweetly at Hvítvi and sat as directed, and then took a sip of the rich, tart wine. She faced her two younger stepsons and nodded graciously.

Auðgi plopped back down onto his chair hard, accidentally banging his youthful arm upon the table, which shook beneath his impact; Auðgi quickly grabbed the two empty goblets before they toppled, and then he blushed. Hvítvi chuckled at his brother's clumsiness.

"I'm afraid that my brothers have no manners at all,"

Hvítvi offered a wry smile and quietly returned to his seat.

Not one of Jarl Austmaðr's sons looked alike. Auðgi looked older than Hvítvi, but not by much; both close to her own age, showing yet no trace of beard. Unlike tall, red-headed Sterki, Auðgi was almost round, barrel-chested, yet no sign of fat showed except the puffy smoothness of his face. Hair just darker than wheat graced his head, and his jovial expression warned that he might break into laughter at any minute. Hvítvi was the strangest boy that she'd ever seen: an albino, snow-skinned and milky-haired with pink eyes that seemed to drill into her. Hávi had seen only one albino, an old woman of the Hersir clan who'd died years before, who'd borne a striking similarity to Hvítvi even on her deathbed. Slender, immaculately dressed and groomed, thin, with long snowy hair, Hvítvi moved with a grace that neither the wolf-like Sterki nor the bear-cubbish Auðgi could claim. Hvítvi alone seemed to be comfortable sitting still.

"So!" Auðgi piped up. "Welcome to Skadi!"

Sterki scowled, his pretended-ignoring blatant.

"T-thank you," Hávi said, feeling uncomfortable and self-conscious. As their new stepmother, Hávi tried not to blush; an onlooker could mistake them all for kids of clan Hersir, save for their overly-formal clothes.

"How are you related to Jarl Hersir?" Hvítvi asked pleasantly.

"I'm not ..."

Sterki laughed derisively.

"I knew it!" Sterki snapped. "A commoner, a whore, daughter of a dung-farmer ...!"

"My father was Jorgen the Slayer!" Hávi shouted as she jumped up, angrily challenging Sterki. He halted, then marched up and stared at her eyes-met.

"Never talk back to me!" Sterki shouted at the top of his lungs. *"You and your bastards won't live a day into my reign!"* With a curse, Sterki jerked open the door so fast that it banged against the wall, and then he strode imperiously out, leaving it creaking on strained hinges. All three stared at the doorway as he vanished, hard boots stomping down the hall.

"He should wear a musk ox's tail over his face so that people recognize what they're looking at," Hvítvi said softly.

Auðgi burst into laughter and Hávi foundered, unsure; she didn't dare agree that the next Jarl Austmaðr was an ass, but she couldn't deny it either. Neither younger brother seemed surprised at Sterki's outburst or departure, both chuckling as their outward styles decried, Auðgi boisterous, Hvítvi smooth and subtly. Yet Sterki's threat to kill her and her children had been serious; of that Hávi was certain.

"Don't mind him," Auðgi laughed. "Sterki lives in fear that someone might not think he's as important as he does."

"We're sorry," Hvítvi added. "We could've told you that this would happen. Father makes excuses for Sterki because he's the next Austmaðr, but he knows what he's like. Perhaps you should mention Sterki's threat to him."

"I ... I'll consider it," Hávi said non-committally.

"So, what did you do in Hersir?" Hvítvi asked.

"My family herded goats," Hávi said. Auðgi and Hvítvi exchanged unreadable glances. "My father died a'viking and we've struggled since then."

"Interesting," Hvítvi said slowly. "Do you know why ... forgive my impertinence ... why Father chose you?"

Hávi stared at them both, then lowered her head.

"For my height," she admitted. "And for clan Hersir's men and ships."

"The men and ships are why he married a Hersir," Hvítvi

said. "Unsurprising that he chose you for your height. Auðgi and I seem to be ... disappointments."

"No, I'm sure ...," Hávi began, but she broke off. Jarl Austmaðr prized tall sons; she could see why he favored Sterki over Auðgi and Hvítvi.

"It's no secret," Hvítvi assured her. "I feel sorry for Auðgi; he'd be a far better clan-chief."

Auðgi displayed an obviously-pained grimace that almost made Hávi smile.

"What of you?" Hávi asked Hvítvi.

"I?" Hvítvi laughed. "I'm the castle joke! I can't stand sunlight, my bones are brittle, and I nearly bleed to death every time I get cut. How could I lead men into battle? No, my short, stupid brother is better suited to be chief; clan Austmaðr would accept Auðgi. But me? Never!" Hvítvi chuckled softly. "It saves me from Sterki feeling that I'm a threat to him."

"Sterki's almost killed me twice," Auðgi said. "Accidents, he claims, but I don't go outside alone ... and never with him."

"Wise," Hvítvi said, "which is unsurprisingly rare for my brother."

After exchanging brotherly grins, Auðgi stood up, walked to the door, and had almost pushed it closed when Mjóvi burst inside.

"What happened to Sterki?" Mjóvi demanded.

"He was his usual charming self," Hvítvi assured her.

Auðgi burst out laughing, then stopped abruptly as Mjóvi glared at him.

"This audience is over!" Mjóvi cracked each word like a carriage whip. "Hávi, back to your room!"

Chapter 5

Silently trembling, Hávi's head rested on Jarl Austmaðr's arm, the sweat on his gray chest-hair glistening in the morning light. No more tears moistened Hávi's eyes; his frequent invasions of her body quickly became routine. She was his wife: complaints weren't proper and wouldn't change anything. Hávi closed off her mind, entered her dark place, and tried to ignore his haggard breathing ... and his rough hands where only tenderness belonged. Jarl Austmaðr always heaved off leaving her bruised and violated, but Mjóvi would have her washed right afterwards, and Hávi didn't dare voice her disgust.

"I want to meet clan Austmaðr," Hávi said warily.

"There's another feast in three days ...," Jarl Austmaðr offered.

"Not in the hall," Hávi interrupted. "I want to go outside ... to see the village."

"Why?"

"Mjóvi won't let me do anything."

"Mjóvi said that she's keeping you busy."

"Watching the cooks, but never cooking," Hávi said derisively.

"You want to work?" Jarl Austmaðr raised both eyebrows.

"I'm used to doing, not watching."

"Well, you are a unique Mistress Austmaðr," Jarl Austmaðr smiled. "My other wives only fawned over jewelry and rare cloths."

"I'd trade those jewels for a stubborn goat to milk."

"I'll see that you get one," Jarl Austmaðr laughed. "Mjóvi will have a fit, but she's got to learn that you're not my old wives."

"All I want is Tryggvi," Hávi said. "She was born here, and we'll be back before dark ..."

"You can't wander about Skadi with just Tryggvi," Jarl Austmaðr said. "I'll assign you a guard."

"How about Jarl Illingr?" Hávi asked.

Jarl Austmaðr's eyes widened.

"Illingr?"

"He sits next to me at feast, but we've never talked."

"Then I'll move him!" Jarl Austmaðr growled. "Stay away from Jarl Illingr! Don't talk to him! Don't trust him!"

"Oh!" Hávi exclaimed, taken aback. "I ... I'm sorry! I didn't know ..."

"I'm surprised that he dared to introduce himself," Jarl Austmaðr scowled. "Jarl Illingr's nothing but a tool that I occasionally need. Never speak to him!"

Hávi fell silent, afraid. *Who was Jarl Illingr? Why did her husband's voice fill with disgust at his name?*

Two hours later, washed and overly-dressed, Hávi bowed

to a frowning Mjóvi at the main castle door. Tryggvi and the guard who'd been posted to accompany them stood behind her.

"Tomorrow you'll learn a proper curtsy!" Mjóvi snapped, her thin brows furrowing deep lines across her forehead, her taut lips decrying displeasure.

Hávi nodded with a sickly-sweet smile. Jarl Austmaðr had been true to his word: *she and Tryggvi were going outside the castle!*

Tryggvi led Hávi down the crunchy-shell road to the center of Skadi, which Hávi had only glimpsed in the pale red sunset of her arrival. Mansions that she'd have considered huge before seeing Castle Austmaðr loomed everywhere. Pressed together, some sharing outer-walls, the steep-roofed, two-story buildings were mixtures of thick wooden beams, darkly-stained, mortared stones, and some substance that she couldn't identify but which looked like mud-pressed straw under a thick tan-white coating. Many buildings bore wide boards carved with pictures that resembled what Hávi assumed was the profession of its occupants: knitting needles and a ball of yarn over one door, a hammer and an anvil over a smithy, and a foaming ale-horn over another. She wondered why they were needed; in clan Hersir everyone knew each other, what they did, and where they lived. *Why would anybody need to carve a wooden plaque and hang it outside their house as some kind of sign?*

"I haven't been here since my mother brought me," Tryggvi said, absently looking around at the many wide dirt paths leading away from the white road, all lined with houses and shops. "This was a grand idea. Where do you want to go first?"

"Fresh bread!" cried a man pulling a strange cart: a large

wooden box on two big wobbly wheels.

"Ale! The finest!" another man cried.

The hammering coming from the smith's house was the only familiar sound, although back home the smith only hammered indoors in winter. The rest of the noise, especially the shouting, Hávi had never heard before. *Why were they shouting?* They seemed more bored than angry. Then a cry of warning made Hávi look up; several buildings away, a woman lifted a bucket out of a second-story window and dumped dirty water all the way down to the street.

Then Hávi spied something strange: three large wooden devices stood upon a small rise not far from a stone-circled well. Supported by a thick beam driven into the ground, each device bore three holes in its wide, stout wooden plank, a large hole surrounded by two smaller holes, and the center device had a small man standing inside it, his head and hands trapped inside of the holes. Hávi stood horrified, wondering why no one was running to help him.

"What's that man doing inside that board?" Hávi asked.

"He's a bad man!" Tryggvi said.

"What's he done?" Hávi asked.

"I don't know, but he's in the stocks for something," Tryggvi said. "Let's go watch the woodcarvers."

"Why's he in that ... *thing?*" Hávi demanded.

"That's a stock!" Tryggvi said. "He's being punished!"

"He can't get out?"

"Certainly not!"

"Does Jarl Austmaðr know about this?"

"Hávi," Tryggvi said softly, "those are Jarl Austmaðr's stocks."

Hávi stared at the trapped man; *her husband had put him in there?*

"Hávi, no!" Tryggvi shouted as Hávi started toward him. "Guard!"

Hávi glanced at their guard, a middle-aged man with a lo spear and a wide paunch that looked very bored behind his greasy beard. He seemed as surprised as Hávi by Tryggvi calling upon him.

"Madam?" he asked, wiping a dirty hand upon his heavil stained red tunic.

"Stop her!" Tryggvi ordered. "You can't let her go near a prisoner! It's dangerous!"

The guard looked perplexed.

"Is it dangerous?" Hávi asked the guard.

"Nobody in a stock is dangerous," the guard explained, "and that boy wouldn't be dangerous outside of one."

"Boy?" Hávi asked, and she determinedly stormed to an up the hill, Tryggvi crying out warnings behind her.

A sunburnt, exhausted face, too weak for its youth, glanc up at Hávi as she approached. He had long sandy hair and eyes that would've been brown had they not been fully bloodshot.

"Water!" he croaked desperately as she approached.

Hávi angrily turned to Tryggvi.

"How long has he been in there?" Hávi demanded.

"Five days," croaked the youth, his high voice cracking with the effort. "Please, I haven't had water since yesterday ..

"No!" Tryggvi shouted, grabbing Hávi's arm and pulling her back. "No closer!"

Hávi glanced at their guard, but he only shrugged and shook his head at Tryggvi's frightened warnings. Hávi looke back at the youth.

"What ... why did they ...?"

"I just wanted a sword!" the youth said. "I didn't steal

71

those bits!"

"What?" Hávi asked.

"He's a Dropper," their guard said.

"What's a Dropper?"

"He works for the smelters," the guard explained. "They smelt the ore into tall, narrow ingots. The good iron sinks to the bottom and the slag floats on the top. The boy carries the cooled ingots up to the top of a cliff and drops them off, then runs down and collects the shattered fragments. The smelters sort the fragments by their colors into different qualities of iron."

"So why's he in ... that board?" Hávi asked.

"The smelters said that he stole some of their best fragments."

"I didn't!" the youth insisted. "I made my own from rocks that I found!"

"How do you ... open this contraption?" Hávi demanded, looking closely at the stock.

"No!" Tryggvi insisted. "Your husband locked him in there! Only he can release him!"

"She's right," said the youth. "If you free me, Jarl Austmaðr will lock you beside me." Then he looked up at her questioningly. *"Husband ....?"*

Hávi bit her tongue before she said something wrong. Jarl Austmaðr had locked the youth in there, and dishonoring her husband would ruin what little relationship they had. He'd let her leave the castle and take Tryggvi; she didn't want her new freedoms curtailed. She glanced behind the stocks and saw a sight that she recognized: on the next hill, a larger hill, stood a great boulder covered with runes and magical symbols: Law Rock. This Law Rock was much bigger than the one outside of Jarl Hersir's house; she wondered who had gone there to

accuse this boy.

"Please, I just want some water ... and maybe a crust of bread ...," said the youth.

"They don't feed you?" Hávi demanded.

"My sister should be here before nightfall," the youth confessed. "She brings me food and water, what my parents can spare, but it's a long walk from our house. Please, just a handful from the well ...!"

Hávi glanced from the youth to the well and back again.

"Hrafna's tavern has good ale, better than well-water," the guard suggested, nodding his head toward a nearby building.

"What's a tavern?"

"A good place to spend an afternoon," the guard explained. "They'll feed the boy, if you request it."

Hrafna's tavern bore the sign with the foaming ale-horn. Inside, it looked like a longhouse, like the home that Hávi'd grown up in, save that it was twice as wide and its ceiling was flat, not sloped, and two long tables ran the length of the building leaving no room for beds. A stone fireplace divided the long walls on both sides and the far wall was almost hidden behind twenty highly-polished barrels stacked to the ceiling.

"Welcome! Welco...!" A burly man approached them, and then he stopped dead, his eyes wide, and suddenly he bowed deeply. *"Mistress Austmaðr!"*

"Mistress Austmaðr wants some food and ale sent to the youth in the stocks," the guard said, and he turned to Hávi. "Isn't that right?"

"Uh ..., yes," Hávi agreed.

"At once!" the burly man said. "Please, be seated by the fireplace! Brækir! Blönduhorn! Mistress Austmaðr has honored us!"

Footsteps on the ceiling preceded a large trapdoor opening, followed by two women quickly descending the rungs of a ladder built into the wall. One was lithe and youthful, reminding Hávi of Völu when she was fourteen, but her hair was long, straight, and blonde with mismatched braids. The other was older, slower, a thick wool shawl over her shoulders, with a kind face, but a hoarse, screechy voice.

"Stay there, all of you!" the older woman shouted threateningly, and the high voices of complaining children whined overhead. Youthful faces stuck down and peeked through the trapdoor, young boys and girls of all ages. Hávi watched the older woman descend until she stood beside the kegs, then she hurried forward, bowing. "Mistress Austmaðr! What a blessing!"

"Blönduhorn, pour an ale and run it out to the stocks," the burly man said. "Let him drink as much as he wants ..."

"Hrafna!" scolded the old woman.

"It's what Mistress Austmaðr wants!"

Both women paled, and moments later young Blönduhorn dashed past them and ran out the door, a foaming tankard in her hands. Their guard pulled out a bench right in front of the fireplace and offered it to Hávi.

"Yes, please sit!" the burly man said. "I'm Hrafna, and if there's anything that you desire you have but to ask!" he turned to the older woman. "Brækir, send Blönduhorn back out with some bread when she gets back, and bring our best grapes and some västerbotten."

"No, we don't want to put you out ...," Hávi insisted.

"Nonsense!" Hrafna laughed as if Hávi had said something funny. "You can't honor Hrafna's tavern without tasting our västerbotten!"

"What's västerbotten?" Hávi asked.

"It's cheese," Tryggvi said.

"Our best cheese!" Hrafna boasted. "Aged a whole year and stronger than any in Skadi! Just wait; you'll love it!"

"Mistress Austmaðr?" asked the guard. "It's not polite to leave without ..."

"Don't listen to him!" Tryggvi snapped. "He just wants a drink ...!"

"Forgive me!" Hrafna cried. "Brækir, ales for all our new, most-welcomed patrons! Oh, this honor has flustered me! Hurry!"

Brækir bustled off, and Hávi felt obliged to sit down. Brækir brought back a tray of three ales and set them before Hávi, Tryggvi, and their guard. The guard thanked Hrafna profusely as he raised his tankard to his lips.

"Anything else?" Hrafna asked, seeming overly generous. "Bread? Stew? I could cook something special if you like? Hog's head? Mutton?"

"You have hog's head?" Tryggvi asked.

"The butcher's not far away," Hrafna assured her. "Anything for Mistress Austmaðr!"

Hávi smiled but said nothing. Back home, it was customary to offer a guest something to drink, but expensive foods and aged cheeses? Even Jarl Hersir hadn't been so honored by Helga when he came over after hearing that she was baking goat-cream pies.

A board of pungent cheese and thin wheat wafers appeared, and Hrafna carefully cut a thick slice of cheese, tipped it onto a cracker, and offered it to Hávi. Hávi bit into it; it was a hard cheese, it crumbled as she bit into it, and it had a startling flavor, its piquant quite unexpected.

"Quite ... good," Hávi said, not sure if she was being

honest but not wanting to offend his generosity.

"Thank you! Thank you!" Hrafna effused.

Several minutes later, Blönduhorn returned and departed again with some fresh bread for the youth in the stocks, and then the door opened and several men timidly peeked inside.

"Come in, come in!" Hrafna called to them. "See who's sitting in my humble establishment!"

Men, women, and even some children of clan Austmaðr entered, and Hávi got her wish: Hrafna introduced her to each person by name. All of the men bowed deeply and spoke praisingly of Jarl Austmaðr, assuring her of how glad they were that Jarl Austmaðr had reunited them with such an ancient and respected clan as Hersir. Several women curtsied elegantly before her, reminding Hávi of Mjóvi's warning, noting the grace that all of these women possessed, a fluidity that Hávi's tall, ungainly body had always lacked. Tryggvi tried to silence her jokes, then paled aghast as Hávi detailed her humble lineage and expertise at milking goats. The Austmaðr clansfolk laughed, and one man swapped stories with Hávi about a cantankerous nanny goat that he'd raised. Her stories of daily chores earned howls of glee.

For over two hours they sat in Hrafna's tavern, longer than Hávi would've liked. Everyone seemed genuinely happy to meet her, and when she reminded Tryggvi that they had to be inside the castle at sunset and that she'd like to see the rest of Skadi, one man argued that everybody of importance was already there. But Hávi begged their pardon and Hrafna fawningly thanked her and begged her to return before she, Tryggvi, and their guard slipped out his door.

Seven children, from able youths to a girl barely older than four, busily worked on the exquisite rare woods in the next shop that they visited. The older boys sawed and chiseled, the older girls sanded, and the youngest kids wiped oiled rags over gleaming cedar chairs and oak chests. The woodwright ordered them all to stop working when the guard informed him who Hávi was, which made all of the children fidget, apparently unused to anything interrupting their chores. The woodwright introduced his whole family and his wife opened a fresh bottle of wine, but Hávi only sipped at her smooth wooden goblet as the woodwright displayed all of his treasured masterworks that sat unsold; much looked exactly like the heavily-decorated furnishings of Castle Austmaðr. Hávi smiled politely as he directed her attention to individual pieces, and she honestly complimented him on the fine craftsmanship of an impressive small ornate box made of six different woods. The woodwright thanked her effusively and then insisted that she accept the box as his gift. Hávi tried to refuse but Tryggvi accepted it for her, offering to carry it for her mistress. The woodwright seemed delighted and the guard asked for more wine.

A rug weaver's, a candlemaker's, and a smithy later, Hávi decided that she'd seen enough for one day. She asked Tryggvi to take her back to the castle, claiming that she was fatigued, although she actually just needed to escape all the fawning and generosity. Tryggvi's arms were loaded with gifts from the merchants of clan Austmaðr, each of whom seemed to think that Jarl Austmaðr's choosing Hávi was a gift from Freyja herself. Hávi doubted if she was important enough for a goddess to have decided her fate, but she saw all arguments as pointless. Their guard stumbled out of the last door too drunk to protect anyone.

A young girl, about twelve, ran up and fell to her knees in the mucky street, blocking their path. She bowed so low that her face almost touched the filth.

"Mistress!" she cried. "Bless you!"

"Who ... who are you?" Hávi asked after a confused moment.

"I'm no one, unimportant," the young girl said, "but I'm your servant forever, if you want me. My life is yours."

Hávi's eyes widened and she glanced at Tryggvi, who seemed equally surprised.

"Why ... why would you ...?"

"For your generosity to my brother," she said. "Bless you! Bless you!"

Hávi glanced up the hill to the sole figure of the young boy, still trapped in the stock, and then down at the tiny girl groveling in the mud.

"Hurry home, child," Hávi smiled. "I'll talk to Jarl Austmaðr about your brother."

Jarl Austmaðr ordered someone to release the boy during supper, again held in the main hall, but most of the tables sat empty. After Hávi had described her visit with clan Austmaðr, Jarl Austmaðr grinned a half-toothed smile.

"I'm glad that you made such a good impression," Jarl Austmaðr said. "After the things that I've had to do, it's best if I give them a reason to praise me."

"Why wouldn't they praise you?" Hávi asked.

"They could be just trying to curry favor," Mjóvi warned Jarl Austmaðr with a potent glare at Hávi.

"Peasants liking the royalty," Sterki mused nastily. "A wise ruler would find a way to exploit their favor."

"I disagree," Auðgi said. "Happy servants don't question authority; it's in our best interests that clan Austmaðr loves its leaders."

"Happy people hide less from tax collectors," Hvítvi

agreed.

"Fear makes peasants hide nothing," Sterki sneered. "Why should peasants hide anything? As clan-lords, demanding taxes is our right."

"This isn't England, Sterki," Jarl Austmaðr said. "Their savior-god grants Christian kings powers unknown in Sweden: excommunications, free tax-collecting, and religious protections against uprisings. You can't rule Swedes by fear; our people are too proud, too courageous. The jarl of Austmaðr must balance greed with generosity, cruelty with forgiveness."

"Like that thief today?" Sterki demanded.

"That boy just wanted to go viking early, just like yourself not too many years ago," Jarl Austmaðr smiled reminiscently. "He'd been sufficiently punished; it cost me nothing to set him free, and what did I get for it? My bride prized by two clans, and the favor of peasants whose obedience I need for the viking and our continued prosperity; in exchange for nothing, that's a bargain."

Sterki scowled loudly.

"It's not a woman's place to interfere with judicial decisions," Mjóvi said. "I don't care about the boy; I care how your people see you."

Jarl Austmaðr sat thoughtfully, and then he continued eating, ignoring all conversation. Sterki, Auðgi, and Hvítvi continued their brotherly quarreling non-stop. Hávi held her tongue and said no more. She was starting to hate Mjóvi; a true, profound hate. Hávi understood why men clung to the ancient ways; they owned everything, alone possessed rights, and married lifelong servants and free whores. Women married lustful masters ... and sometimes brutal overlords. Only women like Mjóvi had the strength to enforce change, yet they clung to their servitude tighter than anyone.

"Mjóvi was right," Jarl Austmaðr said as Hávi slid beside him under their fancy quilt. "I'd profit greatly from my people's adoration. All that I need to do is publicly argue with you to keep my people from thinking that I've gone soft."

"Publicly argue ...?" Hávi asked.

"Just a meaningless gesture," Jarl Austmaðr assured her. "Something ridiculous that you can suggest in front of others ... which I can resolutely deny, just enough to confirm that I rule Skadi."

"You want to ... publicly condemn me?"

"Only for show; then you can be publicly generous, like you did today with that iron-thief."

Hávi thought quickly.

"So ... I should suggest something like ... women should have the right ... to refuse marriage ... to a man that they didn't like?"

"Ha!" Jarl Austmaðr laughed. "That's perfect! Say that at the feast!" Jarl Austmaðr grinned, pushed back the quilt and rolled atop her. "You're proving a great asset!"

Hávi choked as he kissed her, but she clenched her teeth and forced herself to endure.

Chapter 6

Hávi's perfect curtsy before the high-table delighted Jarl
Austmaðr. Mjóvi pursed her lips but said nothing as Hávi
circled to assume her seat beside her husband.

True to his word, Jarl Austmaðr had moved Jarl Illingr
several seats farther from center. Downcast, Jarl Illingr never
looked up as Hávi scooted past him. She stole several glances
at him, especially noted the sliced-off tops of both of his ears,
and wondered why Jarl Austmaðr hated him so ... yet kept
him at his high-table.

Frequent cheers filled the crowded hall. The roar of
conversation drowned out the musicians playing in the corner.
Older pages helped the serving girls rush pitchers of ale to
every table while four jugglers in the center aisle dangerously
tossed knives and flaming torches high into the air, all
tumbling in circles of deadly steel and fire, delighting
everyone except those nearby. Three times the population of
clan Hersir sat before them, yet Jarl Austmaðr had told Hávi

that only a handful of clan Austmaðr would attend.

The over-filled hall was brightly lit, the fires roaring, the colorful tapestries almost glowing, and the red eyes of the black wolves on the Austmaðr crests seemed to watch everyone. Jarl Austmaðr wore a bright amber tunic today, Hávi in a dress that was made for a woman thrice her girth belted around her thin waist by a silver-chain. Mjóvi had scowled when she saw it, and before escorting Hávi down to the feast, Mjóvi had ordered Tryggvi to take certain dresses to the seamstresses.

After many days of watching the cooks, Hávi recognized all of the fancy dishes. The kalops steamed invitingly, cubed beef swimming in a buttery sauce of onions and bay leaves, the pickled beets gleamed, the baked köttbullar stuffed with grated onions and rusk crumbs mixed into its ground beef and pork and then rolled into tiny balls, baked layered in rich gravy and served with lingonberries. The delicious viltwallenbergare boasted minced meat and the bones of moose, roe deer, stag, hare, and fowl seasoned with celery roots, leeks, onions, garlic, white peppercorns, cloves, and juniper berries all splashed with red wine and encircled with wild mushrooms. Hávi's mouth watered seeing the stekt strömming, marinated herring caked with coarse rye flour, pepper, and hard red onions all fried in butter. Hávi held her wooden cup as a servant poured her glögg; the hot mulled wine steamed rich and spicy and warmed her heart as she drank deeply, armoring herself for what she was about to do.

Jarl Austmaðr rose to his feet and raised his jewel-encrusted drinking horn. Conversations failed as every bench scraped backwards and everyone ceremoniously stood and held their tankards high, every face turned toward the high-table.

"Fifteen days!" Jarl Austmaðr shouted into the sudden silence of the expectant crowd. "In fifteen days we depart upon the most-successful viking that clan Austmaðr has ever seen!"

Rafters shook from the deafening, tumultuous cheers, and then silence fell again as everyone drank. Awestruck, Hávi sipped her glögg while staring at her husband. *Fifteen days? He was sailing away? Why didn't anyone tell her these things?*

"Clan Austmaðr welcomes Jarl Dúfunef and all our friends of clan Dúfunef," Jarl Austmaðr continued, raising his voice but pausing for more cheers. "Clan Dúfunef is the first of six allies who'll arrive soon, allies that'll guarantee us plunder beyond our wildest dreams!"

A tall, strong, fierce-looking man beside Jarl Austmaðr raised his own ornamented drinking horn to the cheering hall, his rugged features youthful, but his thick black hair was streaked with gray like an aged wolf-pelt, and beside him sat an old greybeard, one of the few who hadn't risen, but whose age understandably excused him. Both wore pure white bearskin cloaks, and on the table before them was a long, straight, helical horn, obviously magical, with a thin sharp point, its twisted spirals heavily etched with symbols and runes. Three tables full of strange men, close to the high-table, cheered uproariously, each warrior wearing a sealskin cloak pinned with a sharp, carven tusk. Their swords rattled, their fists pounded on the tables, and their cups raised and emptied. Servants rushed to refill every mug.

A huge roasted pig, toasty-brown, came out of the kitchen to be greeted with a thunderous ovation. Behind it, servants streamed out with uncounted dishes and platters. Many servants crowded the already cluttered high-table, adding more delicious treats, but most slid between the long rows of tables, their platters accepted graciously. The pig was set upon a small table right below the high-table and carved by the chief cook, who personally served thick juicy pork slices to the entire high-table.

As the devouring began, the feast quieted enough to hear the musicians. Whole cows and barrels of stew filled the hall, divided between countless platters, plates, bowls, and mouths. Months of brewing poured down thirsty gullets, and everyone seemed delighted. Hávi sat silent, alone wondering what married life would be like all summer without her husband, and what would happen to her, Mistress Austmaðr, left alone all summer ... *with Mjóvi.*

Hávi couldn't hear a word of what Jarl Austmaðr discussed with Jarl Dúfunef, his face turned toward him, their heads leaned close together. Sterki sat on Hávi's other side, but he ignored her completely. Auðgi and Hvítvi occasionally leaned over their plates and exchanged smiles with Hávi, but the ongoing racket prevented conversation. Hávi mused silently, rehearsing the arguments that she'd carefully thought out. Jarl Austmaðr may think that her speech was mere show, but at least she'd be heard. Knowing beforehand that Jarl Austmaðr would refuse her made it hard; Hávi would be humiliated, but at least her thoughts would exist somewhere outside of her mind. Silently she mumbled a charm of protection.

> *"Odin, hold me in your eye,*
> *Ravens black, caw now thy cry,*
> *Gungnir, make them of you fear,*
> *Chase my foes, mighty Sleipnir!"*

Hávi took one last sip of glögg to steady her nerves, and then stood up. At first no one took notice, then a few heads turned toward her, several conversations faltered, and more took notice. Hvítvi nudged Auðgi several times before he, too, looked at Hávi. The noise in the hall dropped suddenly, a silence so abrupt that even Jarl Austmaðr and Jarl Dúfunef stopped talking.

"My dearest husband," Hávi said clearly, loud enough to be heard by the nearest tables, but not shouting so that the back tables could hear, "I have ... deeply considered a matter ... which I must bring to your attention."

No reply met Hávi's words, only surprise and curiosity. Even the servants had halted in midstep. Jarl Austmaðr spread his hands wide as if he'd no idea what his wife was going to say.

"F...for the good of our people," Hávi continued, "I feel ... it is right ... that women should have the right to ... to refuse a marriage that they do not want."

Shock painted every face before her, wide eyes, dropped jaws, and even a few loud gasps. One man laughed, and soon many joined in, treating Hávi as if she'd uttered a joke. Mjóvi glared death at her.

Jarl Austmaðr stood with a smile and held up his open hands to silence the mirthful hall. When everyone fell silent, he spoke.

"My new wife would change our ways, but this I will not allow," Jarl Austmaðr said loudly, his booming voice reaching every ear.

Cheers and the hammerings of tables met this declaration; the hall of warriors celebrated her rebuke.

Terrified but determined, Hávi stretched her fingers wide and held up her open palms. Silence fell again, every listener hoping for a public argument.

"More sons would be born of willing wives than of women forced into marriage," Hávi said loudly. "With the dread cost

of the vikings, for any man unwanted by one woman, ten
stand eager to marry. Frigg would be pleased. The right of
women to refuse a husband would produce stronger, healthier
sons."

No cheers met her words, only rapt attention as all eyes
turned to Jarl Austmaðr; his half-toothed smile had vanished.
Beyond him sat the younger Jarl Dúfunef, whose wry grin
tokened amusement. Mjóvi glared furiously. Hávi braced
herself, knowing that Jarl Austmaðr would deny her, that
she'd be made a laughingstock to assert his authority, but her
husband didn't reply to her.

"Jarl Illingr?" Jarl Austmaðr called, looking down the table
past Hávi. "Jarl Illingr, what says our laws about marriage?"

Shocked, Hávi stared at her husband, then slowly turned
to face Jarl Illingr; she'd never even heard his voice before.
Jarl Illingr rose slowly, his long gray beard masking a stern
face with knit brows. He turned and spoke directly to Jarl
Austmaðr, loudly so that all could hear.

"Thus speaks our laws," Jarl Illingr said, his aged voice
bitter and grainy. "Over wife, sons, and daughters, of all
promises, oaths, contracts, and marriages shall rule the father
or husband, and invalid shall be any promises, oaths,
contracts, and marriages without his approval. The father or
husband may determine and inflict reasonable punishments
upon his dependents for the making of any promises, oaths,
contracts, and marriages short of death or outlawry.
Repercussions of any illicit promises, oaths, contracts, and
marriages may be demanded at Law Rock and thereafter
arbitrated at the Thyngr. Following the death of the father or
husband, the wife will supersede until the sons are of chosen
age, whence the eldest living son of chosen age shall hold
jurisdiction over his family. Thus speaks our laws."

Jarl Illingr fell silent but he didn't sit. The hall erupted in cheers again, but not as loudly or long; all turned to Jarl Austmaðr.

"Thus say our laws, so shall it be!" Jarl Austmaðr said loudly.

Thunderous applause shook the hall. Smiling men clapped and stood, and many drew heavy daggers and pounded their pommels upon the tables in approval.

Hávi held out her hands again, prepared to continue with the rest of her argument, but Jarl Austmaðr seized her arms and lowered them.

"It's late," Jarl Austmaðr said forcibly, his meaning clear. "The glögg has flowed freely tonight. Retire to our chambers and await me there."

Hávi returned his glare defiantly, but she couldn't win. Any further argument would embarrass her husband and gain her nothing; the rights of women wouldn't be considered by a hall full of warriors. A firm hand gripped her arm, digging in with sharp nails; Mjóvi pulled her away, and as they slid behind the crowded high-table, more cheers erupted: *the hall was celebrating her defeat.* Hávi glanced up at the raised dais behind the high-table; under the thin window-slits, the matched tall, empty, straight-backed thrones dominated everything else in the hall. She still hadn't once sat in that chair.

"What were you thinking?" Mjóvi hissed as they exited the hall. *"How dare you? Are you mad?"*

Hávi said nothing. Perhaps she was mad. This was a world of men ... and some things would never change.

No bath came that night; every able servant was attending the hall of guests. Hávi changed into her nightgown alone, reset the logs in the fireplace, then got down on her knees and blew upon the red-glowing embers.

"What're you doing?!?"

The voice startled her, but it was Tryggvi, not Mjóvi. Tryggvi pushed into the room and tried to pull Hávi up. "Here, I'll ...!"

"I've been lighting fires since I was six!" Hávi shouted so fiercely that Tryggvi shrieked. "I'm sorry. I didn't mean ... I'm just ... just ..."

"Everyone's talking about it," Tryggvi interrupted. "Men are laughing; most think that it was a bad joke."

"What did you think?" Hávi asked.

"M'lady, *my* opinion hardly counts ..."

"If every woman says that then it'll always be true!"

"M'...m'lady, it always has been true. Are ... are you feeling ill?"

"I'm not sick," Hávi insisted. "Yes, I am: sick and tired!"

"Bed's the best thing for you," Tryggvi said. "Here, let me help ..."

Hávi didn't resist as Tryggvi threw back her quilt and then covered her up. Tryggvi quietly stoked up the fire and blew out the candles, leaving only the tiny dancing flames in the fireplace casting flickering horse-head shadows upon the walls. Hávi curled up and cried, ashamed, wishing that she was home in clan Hersir. *From now on she would be the joke of the Skåne.*

"You were wonderful last night!" Jarl Austmaðr said after Hávi's regular morning abusement.

Gasping from the after-pains of her morning violation, Hávi struggled to remain calm, to speak without saying what she felt.

"You ... you think ... so?"

"Oh, you were the talk of the hall," Jarl Austmaðr assured her. "Jarl Dúfunef was highly impressed."

"Really? What did he say?"

"He said women of strength are a worthy challenge, more fun than the docile cows in clan Dúfunef."

Hávi froze, appalled.

"Challenge ...? Cows ...?"

"Yes, yes," Jarl Austmaðr laughed. "I'm well-pleased."

"What do you mean: *'challenge'*?"

"You know ...," Jarl Austmaðr said. "Stern, formidable, harder to break ..."

"Break?" Hávi asked. "Is that what men want, *to break women ... like untamed horses?"*

"Well, some men ..."

"Is that what you want?"

Jarl Austmaðr paused, then rolled onto his side to look at her. His brows stretched thin, aged eyes askance.

"I told you what I want," he said softly. "I want new Austmaðr sons. I expect you to birth them."

"As often as we mate, it won't take long, Frigg willing," Hávi said. "I've recited the charm for sons until I'm sick of it. But I want to know what you thought of my argument."

"We argued?"

"Last night!"

"You were asleep when I came in ..."

"In the hall!"

Jarl Austmaðr looked puzzled, and then his eyes opened fully.

"That ... that nonsense about women refusing husbands?" he asked. "Hávi, you can't be serious!"

"Why not?"

"Why ... well, for one thing ... if you'd had that right, then you'd have refused me."

"There're plenty of women who'd kill to be in your bed!"

"Hávi, it's not that I couldn't find someone else, it's that I can't afford to be denied. If I allowed that, even once, I'd have to fight my own people to rule them. We're Swedes, not Germans or Frenchmen. I rule the Skåne because I protect my people from the Finns, the Welsh, and those cursed Norwegian barbarians. My strength is their belief in my courage. I can lose a war; I can't lose their belief."

"What about commoners' marriages?" Hávi asked. "They could ...!"

"If I didn't own land, what woman would want me?" Jarl Austmaðr asked. "What about all those other old men? We've lost too many to allow bachelordom. If we don't replenish the viking's losses then we risk invasion."

"Many women are desperate to marry because there are so few men," Hávi argued.

"I need every woman expecting: wives, scullery maids, shepherdesses, whores ..."

"You ... you've thought about this before!"

"W-why do you say that?"

"Your arguments are ... not spontaneous."

Jarl Austmaðr frowned at Hávi.

"You're too smart for a woman. Hávi, I'm sorry that I asked you to do this. Look, we don't have long before I sail south and I'll be busy until then. Perhaps you should dine at the women's table."

"No, I'm ..."

"Hávi, you will dine at the women's table."

Mjóvi tortured Hávi, rehearsing her curtsy and making her watch the cooks for hours before every dinner. All that she could think of, while trying to stay out of the cook's way, was Jarl Illingr. *If only she could talk to him ...!*

"Mjóvi, do you know Jarl Illingr?" Hávi asked.

Mjóvi momentarily froze, then slowly uncoiled like a serpent.

"Why?"

"I want to know more about clan Austmaðr ... and he's a jarl," Hávi said.

"What do you want to know?" Mjóvi asked.

"Well, Jarl Illingr seems to know a lot about laws ..."

"Women have no business learning law," Mjóvi insisted. "Mistress Austmaðr is obedient to Jarl Austmaðr ... and me."

"I was just curious ..."

"You will not talk to Jarl Illingr!" Mjóvi shouted, a seething poignancy to her voice, her eyes daggers.

That evening, after her third scowering of the day, Mjóvi led Hávi to the women's table. Mjóvi sat Hávi next to Tryggvi, then walked up and took her own place at the high-table. Jarl Austmaðr filed in with many others. Jarl Illingr came in through another door, seemingly unnoticed by everyone but Hávi. Silently he took his seat at the high-table.

Servants rushed out with platters, bowls, and pitchers. To Hávi's surprise, not one servant came near them; first the high-table, then every other table was covered with food, the men half-finished with their meals before the first dish was set on their table. To make it worse, the other women were talking animatedly about some wash-girl who'd suddenly gained weight, and how they suspected that she was pregnant, and some voiced suspicions of who the father was. Not one woman seemed bothered by their food's delay: not even a pitcher of stale beer sat on their table, yet these women accepted it without notice or complaint; it was a man's world, but not by their fault alone.

Vitkals-och lingonsallas and kalops finally arrived and the women shared them out. Vitkals-och lingonsallas, a cabbage and cranberry salad, was supposed to be chilled, kept in the under-floors beneath the kitchen where glacial ice was stored, but theirs was warm. The kalops, usually steaming, were barely warm inside, its thick gravy cold. Jarl Austmaðr had long finished eating, still talking to the two Jarl Dúfunefs, senior and junior, Mjóvi sitting next to Sterki, Auðgi, and Hvítvi. Jarl Illingr sat at the very end.

"Mistress?" Tryggvi asked hesitantly, holding out a bowl of cold stekt strömming.

Hávi took the bowl, then noticed as Tryggvi looked down, a sad frown darkening her face. "What's the matter?"

"Nothing, m'lady."

"What?"

"Nothing, 'ma'am."

"Tryggvi!"

Every woman at the table fell silent; Hávi hadn't meant to vent frustration, to raise her voice and draw the attention of the whole table. Tryggvi looked terrified.

"It's my fault!" Tryggvi said, her voice cracking, on the verge of tears.

"What did you do?"

"It's because of me, isn't it?" Tryggvi sobbed. "You were banished here because of me!"

"What?" Hávi asked. "Tryggvi, Jarl Austmaðr sent me here because I tried to press him about women refusing marriage!"

"I-I should've warned you ...!"

"Jarl Austmaðr told me to bring that up!"

"What?!?" asked several women, who seemed taken aback just by speaking to Hávi.

"Jarl Austmaðr wanted to publicly rebuke me," Hávi whispered to all of them, and then she described his plan to use her to gain clan Austmaðr's affection. The women hung on her every word, wide-eyed, amazed. Before Hávi finished, the women had shushed her several times, casting fearful glances about, and Hávi whispered her last sentence with all of the women leaning close. "So, once he realized that I was serious, he ordered me to eat here."

A young, pregnant girl, no older than fifteen, smiled brightly.

"Mother, I thought that you were very brave," she said softly.

"M-Mother?" Hávi startled, and she stared at the girl, disbelieving her ears.

The pregnant girl gasped, her hand covering her gaping mouth.

"You ... you didn't ... know?"

Eyes wide, Hávi shook her head. *Was this true? What was she to say?*

All of the women stared at her.

"They didn't tell you?" asked another woman.

"Mother ....?" Hávi repeated hesitantly, looking at the horrified girl.

"St-stepmother, actually," the pregnant girl said shyly. "D-didn't anybody tell you? I-I'm Breiðr, your stepdaughter."

Hávi stared open-mouthed. She turned to Tryggvi.

"I-I thought that you knew ...!" Tryggvi gaped.

Hávi stared at the young, pregnant girl. She was thin and tiny save for her round stomach, with green eyes and long, straight hair like fresh golden straw, but with a face unlike her father or her brothers, boasting a prominent, jutting, angular chin.

"Y-you're Sterki's s-sister?"

"A-and Auðgi and Hvítvi's," Breiðr nodded.

Hávi struggled to comprehend this claim.

"Are ... are there any others?" Hávi asked.

"I have two older stepsisters," Breiðr said, "and four younger stepsisters, the oldest of which is nine." Hávi gasped. "My two older stepsisters are married: Væna to Jarl Dúfunef, Drífa to Kaða from clan Jótun."

Hávi stared at her in disbelief.

"I-I-I h-have ... s-s-seven ... daughters?"

"I-I thought that you knew!" Tryggvi stammered. *"How could Jarl ....?"*

Tryggvi hung her head and started to cry. Hávi didn't know what to say. Shock colored every expression at the table.

"You're ... my stepdaughter ...?" Hávi said hollowly, stunned.

"I ... guess so," Breiðr said, blushing.

"Where ... where are ...?"

"In the nursery," Breiðr said.

"W-what are their names?"

"Fróði, Auða, Grái, and Hrogn."

"I-I guess I-I'd better ..."

"I'll ... take you there."

"No! I'm ... I mean ..., no, not yet," Hávi said, and everyone stared at her. "I-I'm not ready."

"How could you be?" Breiðr said. "Father should've told you!"

"He didn't even tell me about his sons, not at first."

"That's strange; his sons are his life, but his daughters?

Father doesn't even know his youngest daughters' names."

Hávi closed her eyes; *how could Jarl Austmaðr have done this? How could he marry her with no concern for her or the family that she'd inherit?*

"Wait!" Hávi said. "Your oldest stepsister's nine? I thought that he divorced his second wife because she couldn't bear him children!"

"His third wife bore him no children," Breiðr corrected. "His second wife bore him only daughters."

"W-what happened to his third wife?"

All of the women looked nervous.

"She got sick," Tryggvi said, but no conviction strengthened her voice. Closed-mouthed, Tryggvi bowed her head, her chin against her chest, avoiding Hávi's horrified stare. *What had Völu told her so long ago about her husband's three wives?*

Hávi glanced at the faces of the other women, most of whom she didn't know, but all of whom obviously knew what'd happened to Jarl Austmaðr's other wives; their silence spoke volumes.

"What ... what's going to happen to me?" Hávi asked softly.

Chapter 7

With bright, innocent faces, Hávi's four youngest
stepdaughters, Fróði, Auða, Grái, and Hrogn, stared up at
Hávi as Breiðr introduced them. Hávi greeted them warmly
while, in the back, Mjóvi scowled impatiently. Mjóvi saw no
purpose in this and Hávi had been surprised when Mjóvi
acquiesced, although she refused to allow it to take place in
the nursery and ordered Tryggvi to bring the girls to the small,
cold, colorful audience chamber where Hávi had first spoken
to Sterki, Auðgi, and Hvítvi. Reluctantly Hávi agreed to meet
them there; secretly she determined to find the nursery soon.

Fróði, Auða, Grái, and Hrogn were obviously sisters: their
matching dark-red hair and freckled cheeks reminded her of
Völu, evoking a pang of homesickness, although their eyes
were green, not yellow-brown. Fróði, the eldest, stood
protectively over her younger sisters, keeping them slightly
behind her, and she looked upon Hávi as all children do at
adult strangers. Auða, who had a skinned knee and a brown

bruise upon her forehead, constantly fidgeted, distracted by everything. Grái seemed very nervous, as if afraid that she'd done something wrong, and little Hrogn fussed, unhappy about being taken from her toys. Hávi wished that she'd brought sweets or presents, something to ingratiate her to the stepdaughters that she'd known nothing about. Breiðr finally picked up Hrogn, trying to delay the inevitable tantrum.

What should she do? She was their new mother, and she'd only just learned of their existence. The children seemed reluctant to talk, and after a few awkward *'hello's* and questions about what games the girls liked to play, there was nothing left to say. Mjóvi interrupted by ordering Tryggvi to take the children back to the nursery and insisted that Hávi follow her back to her bedroom ... where another surprise awaited.

"This is Hvassi," Mjóvi said, introducing Hávi to the largest woman that she'd ever seen. Hvassi was so round that Hávi, had she hugged her middle, couldn't have touched her own fingers behind the stout woman's back. Hvassi had penetrating brown eyes, long graying hair, and rolls of flesh around her neck that looked like stacked necklaces of chins. She was sitting in a sturdy chair before a frail wooden stand framing an arm's-length circle of cloth.

"Jarl Austmaðr said that you wanted something to do," Mjóvi explained, her displeasure barely concealed. "Hvassi is clan Austmaðr's chief seamstress ... and you can see why."

Hávi glanced at the framed circle of cloth and astonishment widened her eyes. Embroidered into the fine wool was a scene so detailed that it seemed to come alive. Two dragonships, their fanged reptilian heads alive and spewing fire, crashed together as tiny warriors aboard each ship flung long spears and shot arrows, many holding swords

98

over their heads. A bright banner over the battle-scene displayed many runes, each rune sewn with dozens of tiny stitches, and despite that Hávi couldn't read, it was highly impressive.

"Hvassi will teach you embroidery," Mjóvi said in a sharp, admonishing tone. "That'll keep your fingers too busy to complain."

Suddenly the impressive artwork threatened; Hvassi may be able to produce such masterworks, but Hávi doubted if she could ever fix a loose seam. Helga had tried to teach her knitting, but Hávi had ruined so much yarn that Helga finally gave up.

"You will not be milking goats!" Mjóvi sneered.

Subtly wasn't Jarl Austmaðr's greatest skill, Hávi thought, or perhaps he didn't care as much as she'd thought, but Hávi feared that she'd regret his repeating her complaints to Mjóvi. Mjóvi had undoubtedly reported Hávi's questions about Jarl Illingr; Hávi wondered if her husband would punish her. If she wasn't more careful, soon she'd make enemies of them both.

With a lessening of her etched frown that could've been mistaken for a sarcastic smile, Mjóvi departed, leaving Hávi alone with Hvassi. Hvassi smiled, a bright, friendly smile, but it was a fixed smile, the smile of one starting an inevitable chore.

"Have you ever embroidered anything?" Hvassi asked in a deep voice so husky that Hávi thought she sounded like a man.

"I ... I've never been able to thread a needle," Hávi confessed.

"Well, I guess that's where we'd best start," Hvassi said cheerily, but her eyes did a soft, exasperated roll.

Threading the needle proved impossible. Despite carefully trimming the loose ends of the thread and moistening them (Hvassi forcefully lectured that spitting on one's fingers wasn't acceptable conduct) and lining them up with the punctured end of the steel needle as carefully as possible, Hávi could no more thread a needle than she could milk a billy goat.

Half-an-hour later, Hávi pulled her first thread through the tiny eye with a faint squeal of delight. After innumerable tries under patient tutelage, fighting her own fat fingers, Hávi had thrice stabbed the thread through its eye, but fumbled it back out before she could grasp its tiny end. Hvassi was sighing with each breath; she'd demonstrated threading the needle a dozen times, but Hávi simply couldn't do it.

"I'm the worst student that you've ever had, aren't I?"

"A lot of girls take time ...," Hvassi began, but Hávi cast her a doubtful look. "Yes, you're the worst. But don't worry; we'll practice it every morning."

"I-I'm not sure ... I'm just not good ..."

"You'll learn quickly enough," Hvassi assured her with a gentle chuckle, her many chins jiggling under her paunchy jowls.

"Mjóvi's doing this to punish me," Hávi explained.

"Don't judge Mjóvi so harshly," Hvassi said. "I'm sure that she's doing what she thinks best. Her loyalty to your husband has been proven beyond question."

"How?"

"Countless ways," Hvassi explained, "although the greatest of which was marrying that cursed husband of hers, which she only did because Jarl Austmaðr asked her to."

"Who did she marry?"

"Didn't you know?" Hvassi asked. "Mjóvi is married to Jarl Illingr."

Jarl Illingr? Hávi paled so suddenly that Hvassi looked concerned.

"Dear, are you alright?"

"Mjóvi ... Jarl Illingr ... married?" Hávi gasped, horrified. *What would she do? She had asked Mjóvi about him! How could she have been so stupid?*

"What's the matter, child?" Hvassi asked.

Hávi closed her eyes and crumbled. No wonder Mjóvi had reacted so strongly! She must've thought that Hávi had known and was nastily slighting her! But perhaps Hávi was saved; surely Mjóvi wouldn't have told Jarl Austmaðr that Hávi had asked about her own husband!

But ... *was Mjóvi now a mortal enemy?*

Hávi looked at Hvassi, her enormous body was fully relaxed, her gaze clear; Hvassi was no timid servant like Tryggvi. Hvassi appeared to be a strong-willed woman, a master of her craft; surely she didn't fear Mjóvi.

"Who is Jarl Illingr?" Hávi asked.

"Ahh, Jarl Illingr," Hvassi said. "Jarl Illingr's a shamed man."

"Shamed ...?"

"Jarl Austmaðr made sure of it."

"He cut off Jarl Illingr's ear-tips."

"Oh, he did far more than that," Hvassi said. "I'm surprised that you didn't know; it was common gossip for years. Didn't you hear about clan Illingr?"

"Illingr's a clan?"

"Jarl Illingr was a clan-chief," Hvassi explained. "He and Jarl Austmaðr argued over the spoils of a viking. Jarl Illingr accused Jarl Austmaðr of cheating, of lying, and named him a thief at Law Rock. Jarl Austmaðr swore that the charges were false, but he didn't dare face Jarl Illingr at the Thyngr; Jarl Illingr's the most respected law-speaker in Scandinavia. So, on the eve of the Thyngr, Jarl Austmaðr quick-raised an army and surprised clan Illingr. Every tavern, barn, and farmhouse in clan Illingr was burned to the ground. Most of its men were killed and Jarl Illingr was captured alive. Most of clan Illingr was allowed to live, although forced to take oaths of no-reprisal, but Jarl Illingr's whole family was executed, even the women and children."

Hvassi stopped, looking at Hávi's horrified expression. Hávi swayed weakly and clung to her thick, horse-head-carved bedpost. *Jarl Austmaðr had killed women and children ....?*

"Perhaps I shouldn't have told you," Hvassi frowned.

"Why?" Hávi demanded. *"Why kill Jarl Illingr's children?"*

"Leaving vengeful heirs to grow to manhood is dangerous," Hvassi said. "Jarl Austmaðr's no fool; he made Jarl Illingr marry Mjóvi on purpose."

"But why ....?"

"Because Mjóvi's barren."

Barren? Hávi fell onto her bed. *Barren? The curse of Frigg! What had she said to Mjóvi? Had she ignorantly made any reference to being barren?*

"I'm sorry," Hvassi said. "I shouldn't have told you, but then, you'd find out soon enough. Everyone knows."

'Mjóvi!' Hávi thought. *'Mjóvi made certain that I knew nothing!'*

Worry crossed Hvassi's round face, but Hávi had to know.

"Why?" Hávi pleaded. "Why did he let Jarl Illingr live?"

"Dear, as I said, Jarl Illingr's the most-respected of all Law-speakers! Don't you know what that means? With Jarl Illingr in his control, no one dares challenge Jarl Austmaðr legally!"

"H-h-how could Jarl Illingr ... serve the man ... that murdered his family?"

"Perhaps you shouldn't know that ..."

"Please!"

"His ears," Hvassi said slowly, watching Hávi's pale, shocked face half-hidden behind unnoticed blonde curls and folds of her thick, soft quilt. "Those aren't the only marks that Jarl Illingr bears, but Jarl Austmaðr left him his manhood ... as long as he works for him."

"So ... Jarl Illingr can still have children ..."

"... not on a barren wife," Hvassi pointed out, "and every woman knows what would happen to her if she bore Jarl Illingr's bastard."

Hávi closed her eyes and sank into the soft, warm folds of her quilt. *A killer:* that's what she'd married, a murderer of women and children. Was clan Hersir so distant that news like this never reached it? No, surely Jarl Hersir knew, and many of the adults; why hadn't anybody told her? So that she'd marry him, of course; *Jarl Hersir, Helga, even Hlöðu must've known!*

Why not tell the village girls? Because then the girls might object to their arranged marriages, that's why. Who would obediently stand though their wedding ceremony if they knew that their husband was an evil man, a child-murderer? Brides would have to be carried to Law Rock bound and gagged while fighting to be set free, screaming for mercy, refusing every vow. Best to keep them ignorant than allow a fertile maid a chance to avoid a pregnancy, a possible son to fight for the clan. Brood-mares, that's what they were, hens to be caged with the rooster, nannies for any strong-horned billy.

Women did have a few rights: they couldn't be killed

outright and they could testify at a Thyngr, but little else. Hávi wished that she understood how their strange laws worked, but Jarl Austmaðr and Mjóvi would never allow it. But now she knew something else; Jarl Illingr was an expert law-speaker; he could tell her everything, and he had no reason to love Jarl Austmaðr, his torturer, or Mjóvi, his barren wife. *But would Jarl Illingr even talk to her?*

True to his word, as the viking approached, Jarl Austmaðr proved too busy for Hávi to approach during the day. He left after each morning's violation, which she was physically getting used to, although the more that she learned of her husband the stranger he seemed. During one morning's scrubbing and dressing, which still felt highly invasive and uncomfortable, Hávi faked a loud cough and some sniffles right under Mjóvi's watchful eye. After her bath, Mjóvi instantly ordered her to be dressed in her nightshirt and put back into bed, and then Tryggvi was sent to the kitchen to fetch steaming chicken broth and dandelion tea. Hávi objected as the wash-women filed out, but, as expected, her complaints fell unheeded. Mjóvi felt Hávi's forehead and announced that she didn't have a fever, but she refused to take chances.

"You'll stay in bed all day," Mjóvi insisted.

"Please, it's just a little cough ...!" Hávi argued.

When Tryggvi returned, Mjóvi examined the broth and tea and frowned deeply, the closest that she came to a gesture of approval, and then ordered Tryggvi to see that Hávi drank it all and didn't get out of bed. Tryggvi promised, and Mjóvi departed.

"Poor dear!" Tryggvi said to Hávi. "What first? Tea or broth?"

Hávi grinned wickedly, threw back her covers, and jumped out of bed.

"What I want," Hávi said commandingly, "are those servant's clothes that you got for me when we snuck out of the castle."

"Mi'lady! You're delirious!"

"I'm fine," Hávi said. "I just needed to get rid of Mjóvi."

"Mi'lady, this is unseemly!"

"Can you get the dress without being seen?"

"Mjóvi will beat me!"

"She'll never know."

"We can't go outside agai...!"

"We're not going outside."

"But ... where ...?"

"We're going to see Jarl Illingr."

Horror paled Tryggvi's round face, but Hávi stood determined; Jarl Illingr was her only hope, her only possible ally, an educated, unwilling prisoner in a castle full of frightened subjects loyal to a murderous king.

"Tryggvi, please, I have to!" Hávi insisted. "It won't take long, just a few minutes where I can speak to him alone ...!"

"Alone? That's improper!"

"I *have* to speak to him!"

"Jarl Illingr can't be trusted!"

"Neither can you," Hávi accused. "Why didn't you tell me that Jarl Illingr was Mjóvi's husband ... or what Jarl Austmaðr did to clan Illingr?"

"Mi'lady ... it's not my place ...!"

"You can apologize on the way to Jarl Illingr's ..."

"I can't!" Tryggvi whined. *"If we get caught ...!"*

"Are you my friend or not?"

Tryggvi resisted, but she was weak-willed; less than an hour after Mjóvi had left, concealed in a gray-green and white servant's dress and armed with buckets and rags, Hávi and Tryggvi carefully peered into the empty hallway before stepping out the door. Their faces downcast, tell-tale hair hidden beneath white scarves, they quick-stepped down the stone stairs and past a group of castle boys who sniggered at them as they passed, ignorant of whom they were speaking to. Fighting to keep from looking up, Hávi followed as Tryggvi led her into a part of the castle that she'd never seen, reminding her of how little she knew of her own home, but she didn't look about; *she was finally going to meet Jarl Illingr.*

Tryggvi led her to a dark, narrow, steep spiral staircase, and they ascended many steps until Hávi was sure that she was above her third-floor bedroom. She glanced out as they passed a narrow window-slit; they stood in a tall tower, but Hávi couldn't say which one. Far up, the stairs dead-ended into a wooden ceiling. Hávi stared confused at the stairs which led to nowhere, but Tryggvi motioned for silence and pressed an ear against the wooden ceiling, then whispered in Hávi's ear.

"This is Jarl Illingr's chamber, but I can't tell if he's in there or not."

"How do we get in?"

"The trapdoor: just push it open."

Hávi noticed the sawn rectangle as soon as Tryggvi had pointed it out.

"Five minutes!" Tryggvi warned. "We go back in five minutes!"

Hávi smiled; it was probably the closest that Tryggvi had ever come to giving an order. Was she growing a spine? Regardless, Tryggvi couldn't go back without her; they'd both get in trouble. Hávi put her hand against the low ceiling and pushed; the trapdoor was no heavier than a half-grown goat.

Hávi poked her head up to find Jarl Illingr's startled face staring at her. He was sitting in a chair before a tiny desk buried in scrolls, holding a book, but his widened eyes made him look comical, not learned.

"You!" he gasped. "Mistress Austmaðr, what are you doing ... *here?"*

Hávi wasted no time. She climbed up into his tiny round room, which was freezing cold, and closed the trapdoor behind her. Despite Jarl Illingr's expression, he looked the same as before, gray-bearded, old and crusty, save that he was wrapped in a thick, black cloak which covered him to the floor. Her gaze caught upon his severed ear-tips, sending shivers up her spine.

"Are you going viking?" Hávi asked.

Jarl Illingr said nothing, just stared as if she were mad.

"I take it ... that means that you'll be here over the summer?"

Jarl Illingr nodded.

"I need to meet with you," Hávi said. "We can't let anyone know; we'll have to be very discreet, if you're willing."

"Why?"

"They're keeping me in the dark," Hávi said. "Jarl Austmaðr and ... Mjóvi ... your wife."

Jarl Illingr looked askance at her but Hávi continued.

"If you don't want to, just say no, and I'll never bother you again. This meeting need never have happened."

Hávi wondered if he'd think her insane, but his deep-set eyes stared unblinking, his lean face impassive.

"To .... to what purpose would these clandestine meetings serve?" Jarl Illingr asked.

"I need information," Hávi said. "I need to understand

what's happening ... and why. I-I need to understand our laws."

"You ... a woman?"

"Women suffer the most under our laws."

"Ahhh!" Jarl Illingr nodded. *"'Rights for women to refuse marriage'?"*

"Yes."

"Our laws forbid it."

"Who made our laws?" Hávi asked. "Do they ever change?"

"Constantly," Jarl Illingr warned. "Usually not for the best."

"I need to know," Hávi said. "There's nothing that I can do for clan Illingr, but ..."

"If I'm caught teaching you then your husband will carve up more than my ears."

"You know that a woman's promises are empty," Hávi said. "Still, if there's anything that I can do for you ... within reason."

"There's nothing that you can do for me," Jarl Illingr said.

"Are you ... *happy* ... married to Mjóvi?"

Jarl Illingr smiled grimly.

"You have found my Achilles Heel."

"What's an Achilles Heel?" Hávi asked.

"Never mind," Jarl Illingr smiled. "You have to leave; it's not safe here. I'll say nothing of your visit."

"Will you meet with me? Just to answer a few questions?"

"I'll think about it, but not until after the viking; until then, it's too dangerous."

"Thank you," Hávi said, and then she shivered and glanced at the tiny, empty fireplace, the first that she'd seen without wood. "It's freezing in here! How can you stand it?"

Jarl Illingr reached down and lifted the folds of his cloak off the floor. Beneath his cloak shined a light: tight between his shoes, Jarl Illingr clenched a lit oil lamp, enclosed in glass, tiny wafts of smoke heating the folds of his cloak from the inside. Hávi stared at it, then nodded and opened the trapdoor.

"My servant's name is Tryggvi ..."

"My stepniece."

Hávi startled; *she'd forgotten about that.*

"Good day, Mistress Austmaðr."

"I'll see that you get some firewood," Hávi promised.

Hávi and Tryggvi hurried back down the spiral stairs and through the dangerously-crowded halls. Hiding their faces, they crept past several kitchen servants headed toward the main hall, and then hurried up the stone steps. They made it back with no one noticing them, pushed into Hávi's room, and shut the door behind them.

"Hurry, get out of that dress and back into bed," Tryggvi urged.

"Yes, do," said a husky voice.

Hávi and Tryggvi let out brief, startled screams.

Jay Palmer

Chapter 8

"Mjóvi sent me here," Hvassi said warningly from behind a pouty frown, her puffy, sagging jowls attempting a hint of tautness. "She seemed to think that I could provide you with some instruction even though you were so ill that you had to be bedridden." Hvassi gazed appraisingly at Hávi. "You don't seem to be nearly as ill as she described."

"Oh, I just took her ...," Tryggvi began.

"In a servant's dress?"

Tryggvi fumbled for an excuse, but any attempt to deceive Hvassi would only alienate her.

"Please don't tell," Hávi implored.

"Where were you?" Hvassi demanded, and Hávi and Tryggvi cringed and shifted their weight from foot to foot; Hvassi glared impatiently with stern, knowing eyes. "You can't expect me to risk my position hiding your secrets without knowing what I'm risking. Tell me what you're up to or I'll go straight to Mjóvi."

"No ...!" Tryggvi whined, but Hávi relented.

"We went to see Jarl Illingr."

"Mjóvi's husband?" Hvassi laughed suddenly. "You two must enjoy punishment! Surely you don't that think that he can protect you from Mjóvi."

"That's not why we went to see him."

"Why did you want to talk to Jarl Illingr?"

Hávi hesitated, cast a worried glance at Tryggvi, and then lowered her head.

"I had a question," Hávi answered, "a legal question."

Tryggvi's eyes flew open and she glanced at Hávi, but she quickly returned her stare to the thick carpet. Hvassi stared at both girls for so long that Hávi feared that she could penetrate their thoughts.

"Refuse marriage?" Hvassi finally asked Hávi, who nodded, and much to their surprise, Hvassi smiled. "I heard about your request at the feast; that was very brave. Jarl Illingr would know a way, if any exists, but you're taking a huge risk just speaking to him. If Jarl Austmaðr or Mjóvi finds out ..."

"Then I'll be locked up forever," Hávi finished pleadingly, knowing that she was right. "Tryggvi will be punished and we'll never see each other again."

"No more than you deserve," Hvassi snapped. "I caught you, and if I can catch you, as big and slow as I am, then anyone can. I won't tell on you ... this time, but if you two aren't more careful then the whole Skåne will know of your doings."

"We'll be careful," Hávi promised ardently.

"Thank you," Tryggvi said at the same time.

Hvassi refused to hear their repeated expressions of gratitude and waited impatiently while Hávi changed back into her nightdress and climbed into bed. Tryggvi poured the now-cold tea and chicken broth out the window and then took the tray downstairs. Hvassi waited until they were alone and then gave Hávi a penetrating stare.

"I know that you didn't want to marry Jarl Austmaðr," Hvassi began, her voice strong with conviction, "but ... *rights for women?* I admire your ambition, but don't be foolish; men will never grant us rights that overrule theirs." Then Hvassi smiled wickedly. "Besides, instead of the right for women to refuse marriage, why not let women choose the marriages ... and make men unable to refuse us?"

Hávi laughed brightly, but Hvassi only shook her head and refused to discuss it anymore.

"I'm not foolish enough to get involved in the fumbling antics of young girls," Hvassi said pointedly. "I'm not going to get blamed when you two get caught ... as you eventually will. Jarl Austmaðr wants you to learn needle-point and you'll learn it before he returns ... *or else!*"

Hávi cringed: Hvassi's threat now had as much weight as she did. Hvassi cleared her throat, shook her head slightly, and began talking as if Hávi had just entered the room, as if their whole prior conversation had never happened. Hvassi carefully described the two basic stitches, the cross-stitch and the chain-stitch, demonstrating each on a spare scrap of cloth, and for once Hávi devoted her whole attention to her lesson.

Hvassi gave Hávi a clean, blank circle of cloth in a round frame no larger than a handspan and pointed out the details of the weave, how the interwoven horizontal and vertical threads made tiny square patterns that would allow for straight lines, if carefully followed, and how the needle could be slipped between the threads rather than piercing them, which would make the embroidery even and artistic. Then Hvassi handed Hávi a distressingly thin needle and a skein of embroidery thread which was much thicker than normal thread, which Hávi had previously failed to pass through her needle. Trying to stab the thicker thread through the tiny eye proved impossible, yet Hvassi could do it with ease and once threaded it with her eyes closed just to prove that she could. Hávi would never equal this great seamstress; still, she tried very hard.

Tryggvi returned, her tray now laden with a pitcher of warmed ale, three mugs, and several plates of food; Hávi still hadn't managed to thread her needle. Hvassi sighed and showed Hávi how to store her needle in her cloth so that it didn't get lost, took back the skein of thread, and the three of them broke for lunch.

"I got all that I could," Tryggvi said, holding out plates of thin-sliced moose drenched in a thick sauce filled with large wedges of baked onions. "It wasn't easy; the cooks are preparing for the viking so they didn't want to give me anything."

"It won't be long now," Hvassi said. "All of the chaos and confusion will vanish once they sail."

Hávi voiced the question that she'd feared the most.

"Once the men are gone, will Mjóvi be in charge?"

"Mjóvi?" Hvassi chuckled. "What makes you think that Mjóvi will be in charge of anything?"

"Well, she ... she's in charge of me, isn't she?"

"Jarl Austmaðr assigned Mjóvi to supervise you," Hvassi explained. "As the wife of Jarl Illingr, Mjóvi's the highest-ranking woman in Skadi, next to you. Krókr runs the castle; he lets Mjóvi manage the female servants because he doesn't trust any man to do that."

"Who's Krókr?"

"Master Krókr is Jarl Austmaðr's chief seneschal," Hvassi

explained. "Master Krókr manages the castle and most of Skadi."

"Why haven't I met him?"

"Why should you? Krókr's a servant, Jarl Austmaðr's chief servant. He never sits at the high-table; he says that his presence there would undermine Jarl Austmaðr's authority."

"So Krókr rules the castle after Jarl Austmaðr sails south?"

"No, Hvítvi rules; Krókr serves Hvítvi until Jarl Austmaðr returns."

"The albino?" Hávi asked. "He said that he'd never be allowed to rule!"

"The warriors won't allow him to rule," Hvassi corrected, "but those men sail south for the summer. Hvítvi can't be a Jarl Austmaðr, he just holds the title until his father, Sterki, and Auðgi return."

Hvítvi, Hávi thought, remembering his strange milk-white skin and pink eyes: *Hvítvi could protect her from Mjóvi!*

Hávi endured Jarl Austmaðr's invasions of her body every morning, but he hurried off right afterwards, and Hávi seldom saw him again until he stumbled in late at night. Sometimes he absently asked how her day went, and other times he was so drunk that he just passed out on their bed. He always seemed exhausted and occasionally grumbled mysterious complaints about strange jarls and clans that Hávi had never heard of. Her days passed amid endless hours with Hvassi, with whom Hávi was starting to feel more comfortable; her company was infinitely preferable to Mjóvi's.

Hávi finally managed to thread her needle, after countless tries, and Hvassi started her on a square pattern using cross-stitch and chain-stitch. Hávi had great difficulty following the tiny lines of the weave. Sewing was frustrating, but she wanted

to avoid causing any trouble right before Jarl Austmaðr led
the viking south. Hvassi had been right; Hávi had been taking
too many risks.

Tryggvi also proved a great seamstress; once, after serving
their meals, Tryggvi picked up an extra needle and threaded it
with almost as much ease as Hvassi, and then began working
on a linen scrap, making a chain-stitch circle without an error
in half the time that Hávi could. Hávi cursed under her
breath and crossed her eyes, struggled to pierce her needle
between the woven threads, and stabbed her finger for the
third time that day.

Finally, after Hávi learned to sew relatively straight lines,
Hvassi took Hávi to the sewing room to sit with the other
seamstresses; about twenty lived in the castle, and for each
seamstress there were two small girls who combed and spun
wool all day. Hávi liked sitting among the other women
although she was clearly the worst seamstress; their basic
stitches were straight and even beyond anything that she could
manage, and a few nearly equaled Hvassi's skill. They sat in a
large room full of looms and spinning wheels, a warm fire
always burning, with thick old tapestries on the wall depicting
great dragons and wolves and famous scenes from legend.
Along one wall was a huge loom for making sails and three
women worked together on it every day. Their gossip was
comforting and reminded Hávi of living at home while Helga
and Hlöðu blissfully argued over the unimportant doings of
their neighbors. Breiðr, Hávi's eldest stepdaughter, sat among
them daily, endlessly knitting thick scarves and stockings for
the viking. Breiðr brought Hávi's youngest stepdaughters to
their room several times, much to the delight of the women,
and Hávi always had Tryggvi fetch sweets from the kitchens
for the occasion, which appeased the young girls and silenced

even little Hrogn's tantrums.

Mjóvi frequently came and surveyed Hávi's education, but usually she only scowled.

"I hope that you plan to teach her to sew a straight seam," Mjóvi once snapped at Hvassi while staring over Hávi's shoulder at a pathetic square of interlocking chain-and-cross stitches.

"All in good time," Hvassi smiled, sickly-sweet against Mjóvi bitter tone. "Proper sewing takes time to instruct ... just like goat-milking."

Mjóvi departed furious, and all of the women muffled their laughter as she slammed the door behind her.

Breiðr was a delight, much like her stepbrother Auðgi in humor, quick to smile and always ready to laugh, although more like Hvítvi in her delicateness. Breiðr needed help moving the smallest spinning wheel, could never have budged the heavy chairs, and was shocked when Hávi assisted her by picking up a large spinning wheel and lifting it clear over a couch with no visible effort.

"In clan Hersir, the girls grow up wrestling the boys," Hávi proudly explained. "The boys won't admit it, but there're some girls that they won't wrestle because they'll lose."

"How can a girl wrestle a man?" Breiðr asked.

"You have to know where to knee them," Hávi explained with a swift-demonstrated knee-kick, and all of the seamstresses laughed.

For the first time, thoughts of clan Hersir didn't overwhelm Hávi with homesickness. Hávi marveled at this but, sitting among the other women, she felt accepted. Despite her pitiful needlework, Hávi relaxed for the first time since Helga had told her that she was going to be wedded. Mjóvi's increased absence, save for her morning and evening

baths, relieved Hávi greatly. Most of the women dined with
Hávi in the great hall; they rose as a pack and headed to the
women's table, although Hvassi always stayed away; the
kitchen maids would bring trays for her and the other elders.

"Why does Mjóvi sit at the high-table?" Hávi asked Breiðr
as they waited to be served at the women's table.

"Jarl Austmaðr insists," Breiðr whispered. "Jarl Austmaðr
made Jarl Illingr marry Mjóvi, and he wants her at the high-
table whenever he's there to constantly remind everyone of
the power that Jarl Austmaðr wields."

"But Mjóvi never sits next to Jarl Illingr," Hávi said, and
some of the women giggled.

"We'd never eat if they did," Breiðr whispered, smiling.
"Jarl Austmaðr can tie two musk-oxen together, but he can't
stop them from fighting."

All of the women laughed, but Hávi silently recalled how
Jarl Illingr had reacted to his wife's name during their brief
meeting; Mjóvi might prove a valuable tool in gaining her
husband's help ... as long as she never found out about it.

Mjóvi appeared in the sewing room the very next day.

"Jarl Austmaðr summons his wife," Mjóvi said darkly.

All of the women froze, and Hávi paled. What had they
discovered? She'd finally felt welcomed in Skadi; was she
doomed to be locked in her room from now on?

Obediently Hávi rose and followed. Mjóvi tried to walk
quickly, stiff and aloof, but Hávi's long legs matched her pace
with ease. Mjóvi led Hávi to the great hall, which was full of
men, but no one was sitting; the tables had all been moved
against the walls and servants were hurrying to heap platters of
hot foods and drinks upon them.

"Hávi!" Jarl Austmaðr cried as Mjóvi brought her forward.

Jarl Austmaðr said nothing else, just motioned to his left. A tall, ragged-tangle of black hair above a crimson tunic met Hávi's eyes; Jarl Hersir grinned at her. Hávi squealed with delight and threw her arms around the familiar face from home.

"Hávi!" Jarl Hersir cried and he hugged her tightly. "Jarl Austmaðr's told me how happy you've made him."

Hávi's eyes widened; *she made him happy?* He so seldom told her anything that she wasn't surprised that he'd never told her this. Or was he just being polite?

"I have tried to ... honor clan Hersir," Hávi said, trying to speak properly, laying a familiar hand on Jarl Austmaðr's arm. He rubbed her shoulder affectionately.

"You have," Jarl Hersir assured her.

"How's Mother?" Hávi asked.

"Actually, I have lots to tell you," Jarl Hersir said, "but perhaps we should find someplace where we can talk privately ..."

"I know just the place," Hávi said, and then she turned to Jarl Austmaðr, bowing slightly, "with your permission, my husband?"

"Of course!" Jarl Austmaðr laughed. "I need to arrange docking for the ships coming tomorrow. Have fun!"

Jarl Austmaðr and Jarl Hersir embraced warmly, and then Jarl Austmaðr headed off toward a side door with a dozen retainers trailing, all desperately trying to ask questions while being studiously ignored. Mjóvi remained glaring at Hávi, her arms tightly folded; she'd never leave them alone and there was nowhere that they could go inside the castle without her following them.

"Come," Hávi said to Jarl Hersir, and she took his arm and pulled him toward the main doors.

"Where are we going?" Jarl Hersir asked.

"A place that you'll love," Hávi smiled, speaking loudly enough for Mjóvi to clearly hear. "Hrafna's tavern."

"Hávi!" Mjóvi exclaimed, and both turned to face her, arm in arm.

"Jarl Hersir is my old clan-chief," Hávi said sharply to Mjóvi. "He's been like a father to me. Surely you don't think that I could have a better guard in Skadi?"

A nanny goat with the expression on Mjóvi's face would produce only sour milk.

Hrafna's tavern was packed, but when Brækir spied Hávi standing in the doorway, she let out a startled scream which silenced half of the tavern. Instantly she bowed, apologized, and welcomed Hávi back to her tavern so quickly that her words tumbled over each other. Hávi waved her silent and motioned to Jarl Hersir, using their sudden attention to be heard.

"Brækir, this is Jarl Hersir, clan-chief of my birth-family," Hávi said.

Brækir tried to bow and curtsy at the same time and almost fell over. Many men quickly stood and bowed as whispers ran down the tables.

"Mistress Austmaðr!" Hrafna ran up, virtually dropped a tray of ale mugs upon a crowded table, then bowed deeply, wiping his hands on a greasy apron. "Blönduhorn! Fresh ales and västerbotten!"

Hávi repeated her introduction and Hrafna paled, then bowed more deeply than Hávi had imagined his paunchy stomach would allow.

"Jarl Hersir!" Hrafna exclaimed. *"What an honor!"*

"Always glad to meet a tavern master!" Jarl Hersir said

brightly.

Several men gladly offered Hávi and Jarl Hersir their seats. Hrafna insisted that they sit beside the fire, but Jarl Hersir explained that he and *'Mistress Austmaðr'* had family matters to discuss, and then he handed Hrafna two silver coins to buy drinks for every man in the tavern, and the cheer that followed this request shook the rafters. Soon the tavern returned to its previous noisy jubilation as ales, crackers, and västerbotten were placed before Jarl Hersir and Hávi, who sat beside each other on a bench at the very end of the table. Jarl Hersir smiled, sliced off a wedge of the zesty cheese, and slid it in between his thick black mustache and beard.

"Helga sends her love," Jarl Hersir said, "but the news isn't all good."

"What's happened?"

"It's Gamli," Jarl Hersir said. "He's been ill. Hlöðu's been taking good care of him, but Gamli's health is failing. I fear that your grandfather won't be there when I get back."

Hávi staggered, recalling her grandfather playing with her when she was young; a happy, laughing man, not the silent, withered shell that couldn't take care of himself. Then she remembered what Tryggvi had said.

"So ... Helga and Hlöðu will lose our ranch?"

"I'll see that she gets married so that she can keep her house and goats. She has four months after his ... failing."

"Isn't there some way that she could keep the ranch without marrying?"

"Why wouldn't she want to marry?" Jarl Hersir asked. "Our laws give women four months to allow for the viking to return."

"I've learned so much here," Hávi said, "but I'm confused; why can't a woman own property?"

"Because that's our law," Jarl Hersir shrugged. "It's always been that way."

"But don't laws sometimes change?"

"Yes, but I'm no expert," Jarl Hersir said. "I'm a jarl because I'm a clan-chief, but I'm not that good remembering specific clauses. But don't worry about your family; I couldn't live without your mother's goat-cream pies!"

Hávi forced a laugh; Jarl Hersir wouldn't appreciate her ambitions, and if he wasn't a legal expert then he wouldn't be able to help.

"I miss home," Hávi admitted.

"Has Jarl Austmaðr been treating you well?"

"He's been ... kind," Hávi said, not wanting to speak ill of her husband in public.

"He says that you're beloved by his people," Jarl Hersir smiled. "We're very proud of you back home."

"How's Völu?"

"Who?"

"Völu, my old friend? Red-head, pig-tails, ...?"

"The one with all the freckles?" Jarl Hersir said. "She's fine. She was at your mother's house the last time I visited, helping take care of Gamli, I think."

"I miss her terribly," Hávi said. "Is there any way that Völu could come here, even for a visit?"

Jarl Hersir frowned. "Völu is very important back home. She's young, healthy, and pretty; if I brought her here then she'd bear Austmaðr sons." Hávi frowned deeply at these words. "I ... I could send for Sleitu, if you want ...?"

Hávi shuddered. Sleitu: she'd miscarried her first-born so Jarl Hersir would let her go, but not Völu. *Did all men see women foremost as breeders?*

"No," Hávi said softly. "Thanks, but ... Sleitu and I ...

never got along."

Jarl Hersir began describing the planting of all the farms in clan Hersir, detailing obvious gossip about people that Hávi had known since birth, but soon a tall, richly dressed warrior stepped up and bowed to both Jarl Hersir and Hávi. He introduced himself as the son of a clan-chief that Hávi had never heard of and Jarl Hersir invited him to join them. Soon Hávi felt abandoned in their conversation of warriors, dragonships, and their prospects for the viking. Afterwards, a steady stream of warriors stepped up to introduce themselves, and while each bowed deeply to Hávi, none spoke more than a formal greeting. Hávi began eating the spicy västerbotten on the hard crackers, trying to think in the raucous tumult of warriors toasting and boasting. The man sitting next to her was careful to give her plenty of room on the bench, probably fearful of touching her, but everyone else crowded around, eager to hear whatever Jarl Hersir said; apparently clan-chiefs didn't often drink with commoners.

Suddenly Blönduhorn let out a tiny shriek. Some men laughed, but Hávi jumped to her feet. Everyone, even Jarl Hersir, stopped and stared at her.

"Blönduhorn, did one of these men just grab you?"

Blönduhorn blushed and glanced at an old bearded warrior, who paled and looked guilty, but Blönduhorn shook her head.

"No, Mistress Austmaðr," Blönduhorn said, although her cheeks glowed crimson.

"That's good," Hávi said firmly, and the men exchanged wary glances. Blönduhorn hurried back toward the kegs and the warriors quickly shifted to give her room to pass.

Conversations slowly returned to normal. Afterwards, Blönduhorn avoided meeting Hávi's eyes; Hávi suspected that

Blönduhorn was afraid of getting punished just for objecting to lewd touches. Yet none of the warriors dared touch Blönduhorn again.

"Jarl Austmaðr will expect me back soon," Hávi said an hour later after she'd finished the västerbotten, some ginger pastries, and half a plate of sweet grapes.

"Of course," Jarl Hersir said to Hávi, but for ten more minutes they were forced to wait while every warrior within reach stood and shook Jarl Hersir's only hand. Hrafna came back a final time, having checked on them at least five times in the last hour, vowing welcome anytime that Jarl Hersir and Mistress Austmaðr wished to honor them. They exited from Hrafna's tavern to cheers for clan Hersir.

"Perhaps tomorrow you'll come to the docks," Jarl Hersir told Hávi. "You know most of our men."

"I'll try," Hávi promised, clinging tight to his thick, comforting arm. "I just want to hold close for a moment ... and feel like I'm home."

Little was said as they strolled through the crowded streets of Skadi. Bonfires on the beach illuminated the low clouds, making them flicker a dull red as if the sky were aflame. The burning sky eclipsed the first sliver of a new moon, the sight of which disturbed Hávi, although she couldn't think why. Gathered for the viking, hundreds of warriors cheered, chanted, and sang by their ships while others explored Skadi in small groups. Seeing Hávi, some whistled and approached.

"This is Mistress Austmaðr!" Jarl Hersir warned, and at his tone even the fiercest warriors paled and fled into the evening shadows. Jarl Hersir would kill any of clan Hersir that insulted a noblewoman of clan Austmaðr; doubtless the other clan-chiefs would, too.

"Jarl ...," Hávi confessed, "Jarl Austmaðr scares me

sometimes."

"Has he hurt you?"

"No, but he's hurt others."

"So have I," Jarl Hersir said. "It's the viking way; nothing defeats as quickly as fear. When we're abroad, savagery is required to make men flee before us or throw down their arms. Warriors contest to murder more brutally; it makes our enemies quaver. We never leave anyone alive who isn't terrified, and we spare only those who cower so that they can spread their frightened tales. We can't afford mercy; the more our enemies fight back, the more we die.

"But the vikings can't last forever. Already many churches are heavily-defended. New churches are being built like stone fortresses. The Catholics can't afford our endless raids; in the end, it'll be us or them. We must conquer all of Europe ... or Europe will conquer us."

"Who'll win?" Hávi asked.

"The one with the least fear," Jarl Hersir said seriously. "That's how you win, Hávi: *never fear.*"

Jay Palmer

Chapter 9

Never fear!

Mjóvi stared at her, but Hávi stood unflinching as the servants stripped her shoes, overdress, and finally the thick towel that she was wearing. Then Hávi jerked suddenly. She seized the wrists of the older woman, startling her and the women holding their washcloths and buckets of warm, soapy water. Dark feelings cascaded over Hávi beyond any that she'd ever known: her world tilted, blackness closed in, lights flashed before her eyes, and she managed to keep from falling only because every muscle in her body seized in the same instant. Hávi had worn a towel every dark of the moon since she was twelve. Tonight had been the new moon ... but the towel was clean. Hávi stood stunned, but fought to keep her voice even.

"*N-n-n-no b-blood,*" Hávi stammered, looking up at Mjóvi.

"You ... expected ...?" Mjóvi began.

"I-I always b-bleed under moon-dark," Hávi said. "I ... I

always ..."

"You're pregnant?"

"I-I d-don't know," Hávi said. "I've-I've never missed a-a bleed before."

"Jarl Austmaðr must be told."

"I'd like to tell h..."

"I'll do it," Mjóvi said, and she strode from the room in three paces, slamming the door behind her. Too late Hávi moved to stop her, but, naked, Hávi couldn't chase Mjóvi down the stone stairs. Fear was one thing, modesty another, but Hávi's dislike of Mjóvi intensified; *Hávi wouldn't fear her again!*

"Wash me," Hávi ordered the servant women, "but put that nightshirt away. Ready my best dress and find me some jewelry."

Dressed in the fanciest gown in her wardrobe, a golden gown that sparkled of silver studs and pale green stones, dangling earrings, and capped with her silver-spiderweb tiara, Hávi strode out of her bedroom door just as Mjóvi reached the top of the stairs. The two stared imperiously at each other.

"Jarl Austmaðr commands your presence," Mjóvi said.

Hávi nodded defiantly; she'd intended to go whether summoned or not.

Cheers erupted as Mjóvi led Hávi into the hall. Mjóvi dutifully stepped aside as Hávi approached the high-table and performed a perfect curtsy before Jarl Austmaðr. While everyone else stood and clapped, Jarl Austmaðr remained seated, then motioned for everyone to be quiet. Finally Jarl Austmaðr rose to his feet and faced Hávi.

"I need to hear it from your lips," Jarl Austmaðr said.

"This quickly, right before the viking, news like this can warm an old man's heart."

Bearing the whole hall's focus, reveling in the anxious silence, she looked up at Jarl Austmaðr and, for the first time, saw her husband in a new light. Jarl Hersir's words echoed inside her; her husband had to act brutally in public, but he had never once hit her. She performed a second perfect curtsy, delighting in her slow movements amid the tense silence.

"My beloved husband," Hávi spoke loudly, projecting her voice to every ear in the hall, "I believe that your next child, hopefully your new son, grows within me."

Thunderous cheers exploded as Jarl Austmaðr raised both of his arms to the ceiling, fists clenched in triumph. Hávi stood still, not taking her eyes off her husband, as boots stamped the hard flagstones, fists pounded on thick tables, hands clapped, and shouts echoed throughout the great hall. Jarl Austmaðr accepted their applause, and suddenly Hávi noticed a presence beside her. Hvítvi appeared, ghostly-pale; slowly he bowed to her, and then he held out his hand. Hvítvi gently escorted her to the end of the high-table, up the three steps, and along the narrow space behind the high-table. She spied Auðgi easily lifting a stout chair over the heads of many, hurrying forward; the new chair was placed beside her husband. Jarl Austmaðr hugged her as she reached him and then he helped her to sit onto the chair beside him. She sat smiling; *Hávi had returned to the high-table.*

Older men, stern and gruff, sat around her. Sterki, Auðgi, and Hvítvi had been slid to one end of the table, Sterki looking furious. Mjóvi took a chair not far from them, Jarl Illingr seated at the very opposite end of the table. Everyone at the high-table seemed to be a jarl or clan-chief save for Mjóvi and Hávi's stepsons and, of course, herself. Jarl Austmaðr often wrapped his thick arm around her shoulders and hugged her, and twice Hávi received a sloppy, beer-wet kiss on her cheek. Hávi smiled. Once, the rare affections of her husband would've disgusted her, but now the old man's touch was familiar, if not loving; in time she might actually like him.

Later that evening, after the huge feast had been eaten, Jarl Dúfunef was the first to stand.

"Well, if we're going to get an early start tomorrow then I'd best get going," Jarl Dúfunef said.

"It's still early!" Jarl Austmaðr complained.

"Being a fierce, snarling captain all summer takes a good night's sleep," Jarl Dúfunef smiled.

Many other jarls and clan-chiefs excused themselves shortly afterwards, retiring from the table, while others moved to chairs closer to Jarl Austmaðr, determined to drink all night. Soon less than half of the high-table chairs were occupied; Jarl Austmaðr sat and laughed with his remaining guests. Jarl Hersir took the empty seat beside Hávi and she turned to talk to him, but was interrupted as her husband asked Jarl Hersir if he had any extra sails for a ship whose rigging had broken.

Sitting between her old jarl and her husband, Hávi kept silent, thinking how ironic it was that the day when she'd finally accepted her husband was the day before he left for the summer. Perhaps she was bewitched by the magic of impending motherhood; Jarl Austmaðr had never appealed to her before. Now he'd be gone and she'd be alone ... without his protection. Mjóvi had warned Hávi that other women would kill her to take her place, never mentioning that Hávi's biggest threat was Mjóvi. Hvítvi would be her only hope of surviving Mjóvi until Jarl Austmaðr returned.

Hávi glanced at her husband, who was laughing, gesturing animatedly, and widely smiling with all of his remaining teeth. Perhaps if she was a better wife then he'd be more like the husband that she'd dreamed of. *How could she do that?* Provide for his needs, she realized, but she didn't like lying underneath him, letting him penetrate and bruise her; he was her husband but they shared no love. *What other needs did he have?* He'd need to get up early the next day, but she couldn't insult her husband by suggesting, before his allies, that he needed rest.

Hávi swallowed hard, took a deep breath and calmed herself, then laid a firm hand on Jarl Austmaðr's arm.

"My husband, the nights will be long until you return," Hávi said, fighting to keep her voice even. "I'll await you in our chambers."

He kissed her hand as she rose, but Hávi didn't go straight upstairs. Hávi wandered slowly down the hall and, on an impulse, strolled into the kitchen. Several cooks and servants startled as she entered, and then they bowed or curtsied.

"Don't stop on my account," Hávi told them. "Just ignore me; your tasks are more important than ceremony."

Leisurely Hávi toured the busy kitchen, carefully avoiding getting in their way, as the cooks and servants stoked the ovens, ground wheat, and kneaded huge rolls of dough. Baking smells filled the warm kitchen, and on wide shelves Hávi found over seventy loaves of bread, many still steaming from the oven, ginger or cinnamon heavily sprinkled over them before they cooled. Two cooks wearing padded mitts were hastily pulling hot saffron buns out of an oven and setting them beside a deep basket piled to the brim with thin gingersnaps. Over the largest fire, half of a cow was spitted and being slowly turned by a young boy who looked exhausted; Hávi stole a gingersnap and gave it to him, much to his surprise. Hávi observed a row of men slicing cooked meat, then handing the slices to others, who spitted each on a metal fork and then held each slice right into the fire, quick-searing both sides so that they'd last longer. Hávi smiled at them, which made them look nervous, and then she finished her walk past two men sealing small barrels of strong-smelling smoked salmon and pickled herring. She exited into a different hall, glanced down a corridor that she'd never explored, considered it, and then turned back toward the familiar stone stairs. Soon enough she'd explore every part of the castle, and then all of Skadi, and even Mjóvi wouldn't stop her, but now wasn't the time; she'd told her husband that she'd be in their chamber when he arrived, and she'd be a poor wife to embarrass her husband the night before the viking.

Pregnant! I'm going to be a mother!

Tryggvi rose as Hávi entered.

"Good evening," Hávi said brightly, a wide smile on her face.

"Mistress?" Tryggvi asked hesitantly. "Mistress, are you well?"

"Friend, not Mistress," Hávi corrected her.

"Mistress?" Tryggvi asked again.

"Help me undress," Hávi said, "then hurry down and fetch a bottle of wine ... no, two bottles, and bring some cups as well."

"Yes, Mistress."

"Friend!"

Wearing a warm green nightshirt, Hávi leaned back against her soft, furry feather pillow, more relaxed than she could recall. Tryggvi reappeared with two cold bottles and two cups. She set them on the bedside table and poured one cup full.

"Fill both cups," Hávi instructed.

Tryggvi obeyed, and then tried to hand both to Hávi.

"That one's for you."

"Mistress?"

"My name's Hávi."

"Beg pardon ...?"

"I want you to call me Hávi."

"But ... Mistress, ..."

"Say it."

"But ..."

"Say it!"

"Hávi."

"That's better."

Hávi drank deeply, then glared at Tryggvi until she nervously sipped at her own wine. Her timidity made Hávi smile; if she could make Tryggvi into a strong-willed woman then there'd be hope for every woman.

"I admire you, Tryggvi."

"Thank you, Mistre..., I mean, Hávi."

"Don't you want to know why?"

"If it pleases you."

"Because I think that you'll make a great mother."

Tryggvi startled, then started to protest.

"No," Hávi said determinedly. "I've decided to ask Jarl Austmaðr to assign you a husband when the men get back."

"But Mistress ...!"

"I won't even listen unless you call me Hávi."

"Mis... Hávi, you can't!"

"Are you going to stop me?"

"No, but ...!"

"Then you'll be married this fall."

"But ..."

"I'll insist that he is young and strong," Hávi assured her. "Handsome, if I can manage it, but we'll see."

"Mistress ...!"

"It's decided."

"But why?"

"Because we need strong sons, and I want them raised by good mothers," Hávi said.

"Mistr..., I mean, Hávi, please! I'm only a servant! No man will want me, and forcing a man to marry me will only cause hate. He'll beat me! I'll ..."

"No one will beat you," Hávi promised. "You're the best friend of Jarl Austmaðr's wife; no warrior will risk his displeasure."

"It's not my place ...!"

"Even the lowest scullery maid deserves some respect."

"I ... I can't marry!"

"Why not?"

"No man will want me!"

"Women have to marry whether they want to or not."

"A woman forced to marry a man becomes his servant," Tryggvi explained. "A man forced to marry a woman becomes her master; a resentful master."

"You could make any man happy."

"Please, Mistress, don't do this!"

"You're afraid?"

"No, not afraid ..."

"What would you call it?"

"I ... prefer choices ... with the least risk ..."

"That's the same thing."

"No, it isn't ...!" Tryggvi argued, then suddenly she gasped. *"Oh, M'lady! Forgive me!"*

"Forgive ... what?"

"I-I ... contradicted you ...!"

"So?"

"I can't ... shouldn't ...!"

"Tryggvi, that's what I want!" Hávi said. "I want you to argue with me! How can I trust you if you won't argue with me? I'm used to doing for myself and now I've got a castle full of servants; I don't need another handmaid! What I need is a friend, a trustworthy friend who isn't afraid to tell me when I'm sticking my hand into a fire ... before I get burned!"

"M'lady, I'll always warn you ..."

"Even if you think that I might get angry?"

Tryggvi gulped and lowered her eyes, breathing heavily.

"Yes, Mistress."

"My name is ...?"

"Hávi."

"Good, " Hávi said. "Now understand, Tryggvi: you're my friend and I'll do everything I can to protect you, but somebody's got to do something. This can't go on."

"What can't go on?"

"The way men treat us!"

"You or me?"

"Both of us! Women, all women!"

Tryggvi raised her eyes and stared at Hávi. Her lips trembled, and the cup in her hand shook.

"Mistress ...," Tryggvi said hesitantly, sweat beading upon her forehead, "Hávi ..., you ... *you're sticking your hand into a fire ... and you're going to get burned."*

"Hávi!" Jarl Austmaðr beamed, almost chuckling as Tryggvi hurriedly took the nearly-empty cup from Hávi's hands and swept the tray from the room. "I've never felt as confident before a viking! We've got over a hundred dragonships, many knarrs, and the eastern shores won't be expecting us this early."

"That's wonderful," Hávi said supportively, although she knew next to nothing about the raids.

"We'll make our enemies regret their births this summer," Jarl Austmaðr promised delightedly. "Churches; that's our key. That's how we're going to win."

"Churches?" Hávi asked. "Those halls of holy men?"

" *'Priests'* they call themselves," Jarl Austmaðr said, "but they won't be alone; every year more soldiers are guarding them. Churches have been the sites of some of our worst losses."

"Then why ...?"

"As Jarl Hersir said, it's these Catholics or us, and this year it's going to be us," Jarl Austmaðr said eagerly. "The eastern empires survive because of the financial support of their churches, most of which are wood; this year we've agreed to torch every church after we raze it. The Catholics won't feel so devoted to their god when they see what we can do to his palaces. Once their churches fall, their kings will lose the majority of their taxes, and then they won't be able to support large armies or fleets. Eventually their empires will crumble, and then we'll sweep in; the fertile farmlands of the Rús will be ours!"

"I'm sure that they will."

"And you," Jarl Austmaðr smiled, "bearing my son!"

"Hopefully."

"It's a boy," Jarl Austmaðr smiled proudly. "I can feel it. I'll come back laden with the plunder of nations to find a new son!"

"Sons take longer than a summer to grow," Hávi reminded him.

"Oh, of course," Jarl Austmaðr laughed. "Well, hurry it up if you can; I'll want another son right after this one."

"Yes, my husband."

Jarl Austmaðr glanced at his reflection in the mirror, then started unbuckling his wide, brass-decorated belt.

"Husband, who rules Skadi while you're away?"

"Hvítvi keeps things going. Not much to do, really; Krókr manages most of it. The only thing that Hvítvi has to worry about is settling minor disputes or delaying them until I get back. Hvítvi doesn't even have to worry about defense; Hafr has three ships this year. He'll be sailing up and down the coast."

"Hafr?"

"My half-brother," Jarl Austmaðr said. "Big guy, great fighter, but not too bright. Very loyal, though; you needn't worry about him. Hvítvi knows how to handle Hafr."

"You must trust Hvítvi greatly to leave him in charge."

"Oh, Hvítvi would've been a great leader if he hadn't been born cursed," Jarl Austmaðr said. "Hvítvi thinks circles around most men, and he's subtle; you never know from his face what thoughts are spinning inside of his head. If Hvítvi had been born in Hafr's body then he'd be stiff competition for my throne."

"Sterki and Auðgi compete?"

"Constantly!" Jarl Austmaðr laughed. "It's good for them; makes them tough. I fought with my brothers every day, and

Sterki and Auðgi are both stronger for it. Sterki will make a great Jarl Austmaðr and Auðgi will make a great fleet captain."

"Beloved," Hávi said hesitantly, "Sterki ... threatened me. He said that ... if something happens to you ..."

"Then your child will be a threat to him?" Jarl Austmaðr finished. "Don't worry; I'll talk to him, make him understand. He'll need stepbrothers to rule wisely. Besides, I'll be back this fall; I wouldn't miss the birth of my own son, and it'll take more than a few Rús cavalry to hurt me."

"Sterki frightens me."

"I taught him to be frightening, trained him to be demanding and intolerant," Jarl Austmaðr said. "It's all an act. Trust me, when Sterki assumes my crown and command of the viking then you'll be glad that he's feared."

"He said that he'd kill my child ..."

"I said that I'll talk to him!" Jarl Austmaðr snapped, his voice suddenly deep and gruff.

This discussion was done. She truly believed that Sterki would kill herself and her child, but there was nothing that she could do about it.

Jarl Austmaðr slid into bed beside Hávi, who cringed as he snuggled against her. She knew that he'd been drinking and had hoped that he might pass out, but as his rough hand closed upon her breast, Hávi knew what was coming. He kissed her temple, making her shut her eyes. *Was this the same man that she'd thought so highly of in the great hall?* Jarl Austmaðr treated her like a favorite nanny goat, a pet to be brushed and smiled at, but whom you slapped when they peed just as you started to milk them. Had she really begun to care for him or was she slowly accepting his mastery, bowing to marital subservience? What'd happened to the strong, tall Hersir girl who at thirteen had pinned a boy her own age in front of Law Rock and held him while everyone laughed? *Had a few months of arranged marriage broken her like a wild stallion succumbed under a whip and halter?*

One last night, Hávi thought, gritting her teeth as he pushed inside of her. Tomorrow Jarl Austmaðr was leaving, and before he got back, things would change. No more Hávi Austmaðr: *Hávi Hersir lived again.*

Saga 2

Viking Wife

Chapter 10

In the harbor-adjacent Norse city of Skadi, Hávi Hersir Austmaðr walked excitedly, arm-in-arm with her husband, down its wide main street, which was paved with crushed oysters, clams, and seashells that crunched loudly beneath her feet. Seventy naked masts filled her vision. Throughout the Skåne, the largest province in Scandinavia, today was the great sailing day, when the warriors left their homes for the summer viking. Jarl Hersir stood before the three dragonships of his clan, a tall man whose black hair and beard were so bushy that little of his face could be seen. Hávi smiled when she saw him; she'd been born in clan Hersir, but she'd married the leader of clan Austmaðr.

"Hávi" cried a familiar voice from the cluster of fierce-prowed dragons.

"Bifru!" Hávi shouted, and she almost bounced on Jarl Austmaðr's arm.

"Hávi!" chorused the whole group of young Hersir men.

"Back to work, boys," Jarl Hersir growled at them, but his gruff tone wasn't reflected in his smile as he faced Hávi's husband. "Good day, Jarl Austmaðr."

"Best day!" Jarl Austmaðr grinned.

"Good morning, Hávi," Jarl Hersir bowed slightly.

"Good morning, Jarl Hersir," Hávi curtsied brightly, and several of the younger men laughed.

"Mind your work!" Jarl Hersir barked, and this time his acerbic demeanor paled the Hersir boys' faces.

Hávi grinned; once she'd wrestled some of those boys to the ground, but now, as Jarl Austmaðr's wife, they couldn't whistle or throw sand at her. She and Völu could run past them shrieking and they couldn't give chase anymore. Hávi glanced around; she'd explored the streets of Skadi with Tryggvi, her maid, but the only other time that she'd been this close to these docks was the day after her horrific wedding when she'd been stolen from her home, the day that she couldn't stop crying. Back then, only a few dozen ships had filled the harbor, mostly small fishing boats. Today the harbor was ringed with huge dragonships, dozens of carven, painted prows: wooden eyes and ivory fangs, nightmare serpents to frighten their unsuspecting enemies across the sea.

Bright flags and banners flapped in the wind on ropes tied to tall masts upon which great striped sails would soon be hoisted. Many clan-chiefs and ship captains milled about on the shore, some wearing mail so bright that it had to be newly-forged, each shirt worth a fortune. Two thousand warriors stood ready, eagerly awaiting the viking.

Once Jorgun, Hávi's father, had waited for a viking like this, but his ship had been lost without survivors. Hávi glanced at the warriors aboard the Hersir ships and wondered how many of her clansmen wouldn't return.

"May I say good-bye?" Hávi whispered.

"Of course," Jarl Hersir replied.

Hávi stepped up onto the dock before her old friends, who were polishing the dragon and shifting cargo, but they barely looked at her.

"It's me, guys," Hávi said.

"Yes, Mistress Austmaðr," Bifru said distantly.

Hávi glared at him; none of the boys met her eyes with theirs.

"Bifru!" Hávi scolded. "All of you! It's me! Bifru, you once chased me all the way home with a snake! The rest of you threw me in a lake!"

"No," Bifru whispered coldly. "We did that to Hávi Hersir; we could joke with her. We'd be killed if we offended Mistress Austmaðr, even by accident." Bifru bitterly glanced up at her. "Sorry, Hávi, but you're not ... *you* ... anymore."

Hávi stared at Bifru and the others, overwhelmed by conflicting feelings. Bifru and she'd played together since they were little, before the boys stopped playing with girls. They'd wrestled, tossed rag-balls, and climbed trees together. A hundred dreamy, half-forgotten childhood memories flooded her, but it was as if they belonged to another life, someone else's life, unrelated to the reluctant-newlywed that Mjóvi, the ranking prune-faced castle shrew, had forced to curtsy and sew. Sadly, they were right; Hávi wanted to kick Bifru in the shins, but she couldn't; kicking a soldier on the first morning of the viking wasn't dignified, would insult her husband, and Bifru really could be killed for disgracing both Jarl Austmaðr and Jarl Hersir. The lives of her childhood friends depended on her, on how she acted in front of them. She'd never be allowed to joke with them, not like she used to, and they couldn't even talk to her in private.

"Just don't forget, Bifru ...," Hávi leaned forward and hissed her words through gritted teeth, *"... I can still stand you, or any of these other milksops, on your heads ... anytime that I like!"*

Hávi stormed back and seized Jarl Austmaðr's arm as he spoke to Jarl Hersir and several other men, but other than patting her hand gently, Jarl Austmaðr took no notice.

"Clan Ríki's just arrived," one man said to Jarl Austmaðr, pointing out across the harbor at several striped sails visible upon the sea. "They're waiting for us; no point in beaching now."

"Well, we can't wait for the others," Jarl Austmaðr said. "Hvítvi knows where we're going and he can send them. The rest of the fleet's waiting at Logsly's."

"We're just waiting on the sacrifice," Jarl Dúfunef said.

Jarl Austmaðr smiled and Jarl Dúfunef, Jarl Hersir, and the other jarls nodded. Hvítvi stepped out of the crowd and held up a huge sword; it was brightly polished, curved, wider than a handspan, and looked frighteningly sharp. Jarl Austmaðr absently took the heavy blade, and then all of the men walked toward a large pile of wood.

A horn was blown and men from every dragonship lifted

their heads. Some moved closer to their shield-mounted rails. One man walked toward the large woodpile leading a massive bull on a tether. The bull seemed reluctant, but the man held some turnip greens in his other hand, and the bull followed the treat.

"*Odin! Odin!*" some of the men started shouting, and soon every man took up the roaring chant. "*Odin! Odin! Odin! Odin! Odin! Odin!*"

Jarl Austmaðr stepped up beside the massive bull and raised the huge, gleaming sword high over his head. The shouts of *'Odin!'* escalated, a deafening roar echoing across Skadi. Jarl Austmaðr raised his voice and shouted to the sky.

> *"Gods of our fathers, I call upon thee,*
> *Grant us riches or Valkyrie!*
> *Gods of Asgard, by fire and ice,*
> *Accept now this sacrifice!"*

Jarl Austmaðr took a firm grip on the wide, raised blade, flexed muscles seldom seen on a man his age and, with a frightening scream of fury, Jarl Austmaðr slashed downward. In one stroke he decapitated the bull; its head plopped onto the sand as a gush of blood spewed seven feet, instantly painting the ground. The men cheered joyously.

Jarl Austmaðr held high the bloody sword, accepting their cheers, and then Hvítvi stepped up beside him. Jarl Austmaðr handed him the bloody sword as Hvítvi smiled.

"Good omen!" Hvítvi said, nodding at the red, foamy pool. "Look how far it goes!"

"A very good omen," Jarl Austmaðr agreed, beaming as all the jarls nodded. "Well, son, take care of the Skåne. Make sure that it's still here when I get back."

"Farewell, stepmother," Auðgi grinned, exaggerating with a comical bow.

"Farewell!" Hávi smiled at him.

Hávi stood watching as Jarl Austmaðr and Auðgi strode away from her without another word as a hundred others climbed aboard their ships.

"Husband!"

Jarl Austmaðr turned suddenly, as if surprised to find Hávi still there. Hávi fought to keep from feeling offended, took a deep breath, and right there upon the sand, Hávi executed a perfect curtsy. Jarl Austmaðr grinned, and then approached her in rapid steps, wrapped his arms around her, and hugged her tightly right in front of all of his men. Then he kissed her.

"Have a good summer," Jarl Austmaðr said. "I'll miss you every night."

Hávi said nothing, merely nodded, feigning obedience. Half of the viking was staring at them; she couldn't disgrace her husband by insisting on prolonged last-minute words. Jarl Austmaðr released her, walked the length of the dock, and stepped over a rail with practiced ease.

"Sail!" Jarl Austmaðr cried to his fleet.

Lines were hauled in and oars splashed out. Every man seemed busy except Jarl Austmaðr; he raised a hand and a great cheer arose. Hávi glanced behind her: Hvítvi and over a hundred townspeople stood there, all cheering. Many children ran forward, all the way to the water's edge, waving good-bye to fathers and brothers, but only Jarl Austmaðr waved back until all of the oars were in place and steadfastly rowing. Then a few raised one hand and waved as the mighty dragonships slowly pushed across the harbor toward its distant, narrow mouth. All too soon the last ship sailed through the gap and out to open sea. Hávi watched until every ship vanished from sight around the bend.

"They'll be fine," said a soft, cultured voice. "Father's only happy when he's fighting. Shall we go home?"

Hávi looked at Hvítvi's albino, smiling face, which almost looked frosted in the bright morning sunlight.

"Do we have to go back to the castle?" Hávi asked.

For the first time since Hávi had met him, Hvítvi looked surprised.

"Where would you like to go?"

"Hrafna's tavern," Hávi said hesitantly, but at her suggestion Hvítvi grinned bright, even, snow-white teeth.

"I'd love some västerbotten," Hvítvi smiled.

"Hey, Hvítvi," Hrafna said softly, casually, as they entered.

"Hi, Hrafna," Hvítvi waved absently as he escorted Hávi to benches near the fire. A few elders, men too old to go viking, sat drinking at a back table near the kegs, but all looked up as Hvítvi and Hávi sat before the cold blackened stonework.

"I'll get it!" Blönduhorn said, and she rushed forward and grabbed some kindling and threw several handfuls into the fireplace, and then she tried to lift a large log one-handed while holding the kindling in place.

"Here, let me," Hvítvi said, but Blönduhorn startled and she pushed his hand aside with her hip.

"No, m'lord!" Blönduhorn cried. *"You'll get cut!"*

Blönduhorn grunted as she lifted the log and then tossed it atop the kindling. It crashed into the fireplace, raising a cloud of gray ashes. Hávi was impressed; Blönduhorn was skinny as a starving snake, but stronger than she looked. Blönduhorn ran back for a lit candle, her long yellow mismatched braids flopping, again reminding Hávi of Völu, her childhood best friend still in clan Hersir. Blönduhorn returned with one hand protectively cupping her flame, which she then held under the dry kindling until it caught, crackled, and smoked.

Blönduhorn glanced at Hvítvi as she leaned back, away from the smoke, and Hvítvi give her a wink. Blönduhorn blushed and hurried back toward the kegs.

"A friend of yours?" Hávi inquired.

"Not like that," Hvítvi scowled, but he couldn't wipe the smile from his face. "Blönduhorn's a good girl; I've known her since I was seven and she was four."

"She's very pretty," Hávi noted.

"There're plenty of whores in Skadi, if you know where to look," Hvítvi said. "Tavern wenches abound throughout the Skåne, but I don't want Blönduhorn becoming one of them; she's like my little sister."

"She doesn't look at you like a sister."

"No."

"Why not? Because she's a peasant?"

"Now you sound like Sterki," Hvítvi said. "No, because I couldn't do that to Blönduhorn."

"Do what?"

"Curse her with a child like me."

Hávi stared at Hvítvi.

"You're joking."

"I'm not," Hvítvi said. "I wouldn't do that to Blönduhorn."

"It doesn't work that way," Hávi said seriously. "We had an albino in clan Hersir; she bore six children and none of them were albinos."

"Really? Not one?"

"And none of her grandchildren are albinos."

Hvítvi stared into the fire, his expression relaxed, but his hands clenched tightly. Hávi could tell that he was thinking hard, though his face remained impassive. She made a mental note; *never assume that you know what's going on inside Hvítvi's mind.*

"Blönduhorn looking good now?" Hávi asked softly, smiling.

Hvítvi sighed heavily.

"Hávi ... Mother ... Stepmother ..."

"Hávi."

"Hávi, I've had one child and he was as white as I am, didn't live long, and killed his mother in childbirth."

"That's ... terrible," Hávi said, absently touching her lips with her fingertips, futilely attempting to cover her shocked, open mouth.

"It was two years ago," Hvítvi said. "It was ... unthinkable."

"I'm sorry," Hávi said tenderly, placing a comforting hand on his arm. "I've never heard of that happening. But that's no reason to think that it'll always happen ..."

Hvítvi's face remained emotionless but his fingers trembled. He stared at the rising flames, and then he reached into the kindling box and pulled out a large handful of tiny sticks to throw onto the fire.

"No!" Blönduhorn gave an exasperated shout, and she rushed forward.

"I can feed a fire ...!" Hvítvi complained.

"Not in my house!" Blönduhorn insisted, and she seized his hand, upturned it, and dumped the kindling onto the floor.

"Blönduhorn, let him be!" Hávi ordered.

"Mistress, has Hvítvi told you what happens when he bleeds? The last time that he picked up a knife my mother pressed every clean cloth that she had against his finger for over two hours ... and he was still bleeding! By the time that it clotted he was whiter than ever and had passed out; they had to carry him home."

"I was twelve!"

"It was just a little cut."

"*I don't need another mother!*" Hvítvi snapped, and he pulled his hand from her grip.

"No, you don't," Blönduhorn agreed, but from her tone she implied that he needed something besides a mother, but Blönduhorn was careful not to finish that sentence. She knelt down before the fireplace and gingerly swept the spilled kindling into the tiny flames, and then she slid her hands around the flames to pull out some old, charred, blackened fragments, which she piled masterfully over the flames so that their fiery tongues flicked between their cracked, once-burned remains. As the flames began to ignite the dry coals, Blönduhorn stood up, her fingers blackened from handling the charred chunks.

"Would you like some breakfast? Mother's minding the children, but I can fry some goose eggs ..."

"That'd be nice," Hvítvi said exasperatedly.

Hávi grinned; Hvítvi may be able to control his expression but his voice belied his embarrassment. As Blönduhorn fled out a small door beside the kegs, Hávi smiled at her stepson.

"She cares for you," Hávi said.

"We're not going to discuss Blönduhorn," Hvítvi said with undisguised finality.

"I have a request," Hávi said.

"What kind of request?"

"A small one."

"Goats?"

"No."

Hvítvi grinned and Hávi almost smiled.

"Mjóvi," Hávi said.

"*Ugh,*" Hvítvi's face twisted as if he'd tasted fetid goat-cream.

"I agree."

"A most insufferable woman."

"Is there some way that you could ... unassign her to me?"

"I was hoping that I wouldn't have to," Hvítvi said. "Every summer I have to come up with something to keep her out of my hair. One year it was a garden, and then I had her set up a house for healers, and one year I sent her out to inspect our other castles; that almost caused a revolt. I don't dare send her out of my control."

"We have other castles?"

"Why, yes."

"I hate that."

"You hate ... other castles?"

"I hate being ignorant of what everybody else knows. Mjóvi's purposefully keeping me uninformed; I only recently found out that I had stepdaughters. Why do you *dare not* send her away?"

"Mjóvi knows every wealthy woman in the Skåne."

"Wealthy women?"

"Oh, yes," Hvítvi said. "Every house must have a man, but not all households are run by their husbands. Several of our wealthiest families wouldn't have a single copper if their wives didn't manage their households. Those husbands give their wives free-reign, but the wives can't be seen managing their family's finances without disgracing their family, so they prop up their husbands in public. Most are like Mjóvi, curses that husbands tolerate only to be rich ..."

"Isn't there one who's smart and nice?"

"Probably," Hvítvi admitted, "but that's the problem: the smarter they are, the less likely anyone will suspect who's running their households. I only know of a few for certain, the rest are just suspicions."

"How can you tell?"

"When one of clan Austmaðr's wealthiest men is obviously a drunkard or doesn't have enough sense to keep his own mouth shut about illicit dealings ..."

"Interesting," Hávi said, wondering who those women were and if they'd support her.

"... and Mjóvi's spent decades currying their favor," Hvítvi finished.

"Oh," Hávi groaned; perhaps she was better off avoiding them.

"Summer's their favorite time," Hvítvi said. "While their husbands are viking, the women can do anything; go check out the woodwrights, if you want proof."

"The woodwrights?" Hávi asked; she didn't know that there was more than one.

"The woodwrights work all winter just for the week after the viking sails. They won't have a polished table-leg left by the end of the week; the women will buy up everything and commission them with work to last the summer."

"What about Mjóvi?" Hávi asked.

"She'll be in the thick of it, of course. She hasn't got any money herself, but she keeps her ear to every keyhole and knows every secret; her wealthy women-friends often reward her for providing valuable information. She knows all of the gossip, who's in favor and who's not, and those wealthy hens peck at every tidbit. I'd love to send her away, but she stirs up hatred everywhere that she goes; Father would come home to find riots in Skadi."

"Couldn't you ...," Hávi pleaded, *"couldn't you give her some project ... other than me?"*

Hvítvi chuckled; a warm, inviting sound.

"I'll see what I can do."

Hrafna came by and checked on them, his face beaded with sweat, his breathing labored. He brought them fresh ales, explained that he was outside chopping firewood, and Hvítvi assured him that they had all that they needed. As they spoke, Blönduhorn came up bearing two plates of steaming eggs and sizzling bacon and laughed when her father looked longingly at the food.

"I'll make you some, but don't tell Mother," Blönduhorn whispered to her father.

"Bring it outside when it's ready," Hrafna whispered. "I've got lots to do today."

Left alone to eat in peace, Hávi and Hvítvi slowly ate their breakfasts, their backs to the crackling fire. Hávi stole glances at Hvítvi; his white skin was womanly-smooth, his long, thin hair like strands of snowflake, his pink eyes strange beyond description. He caught her gaze and she quickly looked away, but he only smiled; if he was amused or just teasing her Hávi couldn't tell.

After eating, Hvítvi drew two coppers out of a tiny doe-skin pouch on his knotted-wool belt and left them beside their dirty plates, and then he escorted Hávi all the way back to the castle. They walked in silence, save for the crunches beneath their feet; Hvítvi showed no outward sign but he seemed lost in thought; Hávi wondered what he was thinking, but feared to ask: *how would she know if he was telling the truth?* They entered the great hall, and Hvítvi thanked her for sharing breakfast with him, and then, just before he turned away:

"So, this albino woman of clan Hersir," Hvítvi asked softly, his voice almost a whisper, "not one of her children was pale?"

"No, nor were her fourteen grandchildren."

With a polite bow, Hvítvi strode off toward a side door.

Servants mingled about the hall, some sitting at tables, one musician holding a lyre, but he was polishing it, not plucking it. Two older boys were lifting and moving tables back to their customary symmetry and placing benches around them, and some younger kids were playing with a puppy that was yapping shrilly, but Hávi ignored them all, wondering what Hvítvi was thinking.

Mjóvi; if Hávi didn't hide someplace then Mjóvi would find her. With Jarl Austmaðr gone for the summer, Mjóvi would lock her in her room, probably never to get out, until summer ended.

"Excuse me," Hávi said to one of the pages, who seemed startled to be addressed by Mistress Austmaðr, "Can you show me where the nursery is?"

"Y-yes, Mistress," the boy stammered. "This way."

"Let's stop by the kitchen first," Hávi said. "I want to pick up some sweets for the children."

Determined to make friends with her young stepdaughters, Hávi followed the boy to the kitchen, but her mind kept returning to Hvítvi's haunting image and pale-pink eyes; Hávi wondered if she'd finally found a friend.

Chapter 11

"Did you hear me?" Mjóvi shouted. "Get out of that bed!"

Hávi groaned weakly, lifted a dizzy, fuzzy head which slowly spun around in her tilted bedroom; the effort drained her.

"She's sick!" Tryggvi's voice echoed distantly.

Hávi's stomach knotted and twisted, and then she jumped up; hands tried to hold her down but Hávi knocked aside the unseen figures, leapt out of bed, and made it halfway to the door before she fell and puked upon the carpet. Women screamed in the distance ... *or right in her ear?*

"Excellent!" Mjóvi said.

Even amid vile retching, this odd pronouncement struck Hávi.

"Get her off the floor!" Mjóvi shouted. "Clean up that mess! Scrub Mistress Austmaðr and put her back to bed."

"What's wrong with her?" Tryggvi asked.

"Morning sickness," Mjóvi said. "She's pregnant, all right.

We'll have to keep her in bed all summer."

"No," Hávi groaned and spat.

"Go down to the kitchen ...," Mjóvi began.

"No!"

Hávi spat again, then lifted her head; a long, disgusting line of drool stretched from her lower lip to the soiled rug.

"Go," Mjóvi hissed.

Hands grabbed Hávi and lifted her up. Weakly, fearing that she'd faint, Hávi pulled upon the helping hands until she staggered upright. A wet cloth tasting of soap slid over her face; Hávi sputtered, slightly gasping. Her damp nightshirt was pulled off. Strength returned slowly; puking had made her stomach feel better. Morning sickness: Hávi had seen it but never guessed how awful it felt; *she really was pregnant.* But, as the familiar, warm wet rags swabbed her from toes to hair, two women knelt by her feet, cleaning the carpet. Then Mjóvi's face swam right before her.

"No," Hávi said firmly, putting all of her remaining strength into her voice. *"I won't spend all summer in bed."*

"You'll do whatever Mistress Austmaðr must for the sake of Jarl Austmaðr's son," Mjóvi seethed, delight in her voice.

Hávi inhaled, trying to draw enough strength to defy Mjóvi. She shook her arms free of the hands struggling to hold her upright and seized the wrist of a hand sliding a wet cloth over one breast. Hávi forcibly pushed the hand back.

"Keep washing her," Mjóvi ordered. "She's got to ..."

As the wet rags returned, Hávi felt her balance restore. She was taller, younger, and stronger; firmly she placed a different hand on two of the wash-women's chests and pushed them backwards, each with controlled shoves that left no doubt that she could shove harder. Shocked, the remaining women retreated.

"I won't stay locked up in this room all summer!" Hávi said, a threatening growl deepening her voice.

"You'll do as I say!" Mjóvi snarled.

Hávi rose to her full height and closed the distance between them in one step. She glared down at Mjóvi, Mjóvi's taut, thin, wrinkled chin hovering between Hávi's large nipples.

"Make me ...!" Hávi sneered challengingly.

Mjóvi returned her glare with equal intensity.

"I will," Mjóvi hissed. *"Be certain of that."*

The *bang!* of Hávi's door against the stone wall blasted her ears. Hávi waited until Mjóvi was gone from her outer room, and then she felt herself sway, the last of her strength expended.

"Tryggvi?"

"Yes, Mistress?" Tryggvi's voice quavered.

"Wash and dress me," Hávi said. "No, let the others; go get Hvítvi."

"Hvítvi?"

"Hurry. Run. Tell him that I need him ... right away. Go! Now!"

Tryggvi hesitated, then hurried out the door.

The soap-washing was finished, the rinsing nearly done, when hard footsteps echoed from the next room. Even the women scrubbing the rug glanced up. Two armed guards appeared at the door and glanced inside; the elder women screamed and flung themselves to block the men's view; Hávi gasped and covered her nakedness with her hands.

"What goes on in there is none of your business!" Mjóvi's voice shouted. "Mistress Austmaðr is sick and can't be allowed to leave her chambers. *Don't let her out under any circumstances!* Do you understand?"

"Yes, Mistress," both deep voices replied.

"Mjóvi!" Hávi screamed.

Mjóvi stepped into the doorway, triumphant delight etched on her face.

"Yes, Mistress Austmaðr?"

"Mistress Mjóvi," Hávi said formally, "as the wife of a jarl, you are the highest-ranking woman in this castle, aren't you?"

"Yes, Mistress Austmaðr, I am."

"But I'm Mistress Austmaðr, wife of Jarl Austmaðr, and I out-rank you."

"Most true."

"Then I order you to send those guards away."

"Your husband placed you in my care. I wasn't placed in your care. You'll do as I ..."

"What's going on here?"

Hvítvi appeared behind Mjóvi, his pale pink eyes staring into the room. One of the washer-women tore the thick white quilt off the bed and flung it over Hávi's shoulders. Hávi glanced to note which of the old women had covered her; *she owed her.*

"Why are these guards here?" Hvítvi demanded. "Who ordered them ...?"

"I did," Mjóvi spoke up. "They're required."

"Why?"

"Mistress Austmaðr's ill."

"No, I'm not!" Hávi shouted, and she would've stepped forward but the washer-women held her back.

"She's ill!" Mjóvi insisted, pointing to the stained carpet. "She vomited on the floor and now she wants to run around; in her condition that could threaten your father's child."

Hávi started to argue, but Hvítvi slapped the back of his own hand suddenly, a soft, single clap, but it drowned out all other sounds. Hvítvi stared at Hávi, then at Mjóvi, and then at the washer-women, and finally at the guards. Meeting the guards' eyes, he jerked his head irritably, causing his white hair to flash across his shoulders; both of the guards bowed and departed in haste. Then Hvítvi nodded slightly to the washer-women and politely stepped aside, leaving them a clear path to exit, which they did as quickly as they could, two stopping to help the women who'd been scrubbing the carpet to stand. All sped past Hvítvi bowing, keeping their eyes averted. Soon Hávi stood alone, wrapped in her thick quilt, staring at Hvítvi and Mjóvi.

Hávi opened her mouth to speak, but Hvítvi gestured her silent before a single word escaped her lips. Jarl Austmaðr's youngest son stood like a marble statue, hidden thoughts racing behind his calm facade. Hávi blanched; *he's more patient than I'*. She had to wait no matter how difficult it was, no matter how badly she felt.

Slowly Hvítvi walked across the room, stopping right before the darkened wet spot, which now bore soap bubbles from the half-washing that it'd received. He looked down at it as if it were a curiosity, then he lifted his eyes and stared at Hávi.

"Are you sick?"

"Just morning sickness," Hávi said.

"I see," Hvítvi said.

"Pregnant women always ...," Hávi began, but again Hvítvi cut her off with a gesture.

"Are you concerned for her health?" Hvítvi asked Mjóvi.

"For the health of Jarl Austmaðr's unborn son, your next stepbrother," Mjóvi said icily.

Again Hvítvi fell silent, slowly turning his head left, then right, carefully viewing everything in the room; the two locked doors, fireplace, window, and bed ... and both women. No smile brightened his snowy face. Hávi tried to keep from shuddering; *if he decided against her then Mjóvi would lock her in this room until fall.*

"Hávi, what do you want of me?" Hvítvi asked.

"Nothing," Hávi said, taking a deep breath and trying to compose herself; she couldn't afford to appear childish. "I just want to be free, in my own home, to go where I want and do what I wish."

"Mjóvi, is Hávi's request unreasonable?" Hvítvi asked.

"Jarl Austmaðr instructed me to insure that Hávi doesn't dishonor him or clan Austmaðr," Mjóvi said.

"Has she dishonored clan Austmaðr?"

"No, I ...," Hávi began.

"I didn't ask you," Hvítvi interrupted Hávi, and then he turned toward Mjóvi, patiently awaiting her reply.

"Yes," Mjóvi said. "She's insulted Jarl Austmaðr several times." Mjóvi stopped as if concluding a speech, but Hvítvi kept staring expectantly at her until she continued. "She left Jarl Austmaðr alone on her first morning before he awoke."

Hvítvi stared at Mjóvi, then turned to Hávi.

"Is this true?"

"I was a new bride; I didn't know any better. Now I do."

"Well, Mjóvi obviously knew what you should've been doing that morning, didn't she?"

Hávi stared into Hvítvi's pink orbs; she didn't want to admit anything, but his silent patience demanded an answer.

"Yes-s-s."

Hvítvi turned back to Mjóvi.

"Has Hávi repeated that mistake?"

Mjóvi stared back impatiently.

"No."

"Has Hávi done anything else?"

"You heard her!" Mjóvi said irritatedly. "Challenging her husband at feast! Before guests! Insulting him before the whole Skåne!"

Hvítvi looked back at Hávi.

"That was Jarl Austmaðr's idea," Hávi said defiantly. "Jarl Austmaðr wanted the people of Skadi to like me, but he needed to publicly rebuke me, so he told me to say that. We discussed it beforehand."

An expression finally dawned on Hvítvi's insufferably placid face: amusement. Mjóvi scowled.

"How do we know that's true?" Mjóvi hissed.

"I'm not here to judge truth," Hvítvi said, strength issuing from his soft voice. "I'm here to keep the peace until Father returns, and I can't do that while the guards and servants are shirking their duties to gossip about you two having public spats!"

After a long, uncomfortable pause:

"Hávi, are you endangering my unborn brother by getting out of bed while sick?"

"No," Hávi insisted. "In clan Hersir, some women work in the fields until the day that they birth, and their children are stronger for it."

"Mjóvi, is this true?"

"I don't know or care what they do in backwater clans," Mjóvi scowled.

During another long pause Hvítvi stared around the room again, taking in everything from the floor up, his pink eyes slowly traveling, seldom pausing on anything. Hávi clutched her thick quilt tight around her shoulders and endured the dreadful waiting.

"Mjóvi, who's lived here all of her life and knows

everything about clan Austmaðr, is surely more qualified than any newcomer to know all of the local customs; isn't that true, Hávi?"

"*Yes,*" Hávi answered although the word burned her tongue.

"Hávi, who is the highest-ranking woman in this castle, has learned from her one mistake and has assisted Jarl Austmaðr in his dealings, even at the cost of her own dignity; isn't that so, Mjóvi?"

"Her dignity isn't ...,"

"*Isn't that so?*"

"*Yes...,*" Mjóvi said disgustedly.

"Hávi is free to do as she pleases, within reason," Hvítvi said. "If she does anything to dishonor her family or clan, then Mjóvi will report it to me and I'll curtail those freedoms."

Hvítvi turned and strode out of the room without a moment's hesitation.

Dumbfounded, Hávi and Mjóvi stared at the empty doorway, Hvítvi's receding footsteps all that remained of him. Then Hávi and Mjóvi looked at each other, unsteadiness and uncertainty masking both of their faces. Suddenly Mjóvi's brows knit and she swept out the door, stomping as hard as her slight, aged frame could manage. Mjóvi slammed both doors behind her so hard that Hávi winced at the bangs, but otherwise she stood stunned. The thick, white quilt slipped from her trembling fingers and fell off her shoulders, collapsing into a mound of softness entrapping her ankles.

What had just happened? Had Hvítvi ... just freed her ... from Mjóvi?

Hávi forced herself to recall Hvítvi's words precisely and struggled to determine their ramifications. *Was there any way that Mjóvi could twist Hvítvi's words?* Mjóvi would, if she could; of that Hávi was certain, but as the words replayed in her head ... his last command had saved her. Mjóvi could do nothing to Hávi but report her actions to Hvítvi, and what did that matter?

It mattered because Mjóvi wouldn't take this easily; Mjóvi wasn't going to bow down and let Hávi win. Hvítvi or not, Mjóvi would be watching Hávi like a starving, vengeful cat stalking a tiny mouse, itching to devour her foe.

Hávi tried to calm down and quell her complaining stomach. Mjóvi couldn't catch her dishonoring clan Austmaðr if Hávi didn't do anything that she shouldn't be doing. All that she had to do was behave herself.

Dressing herself was more difficult than Hávi remembered. Even the least-fancy clothes in her wardrobe had buttons and sashes or required broaches to be pinned on just so; Hávi hadn't realized how well her dressing women knew their job. Or had she gotten so used to being dressed that dressing herself now felt tedious? Or was her morning sickness making it harder than it should've been? Hávi suspected the latter; several times she had to lean against her horse-head bedposts for support, breathless and labored.

Dressed save for her belt, which she couldn't bear the weight of upon her stomach, Hávi climbed down the stone steps more carefully than she'd ever descended anything. She staggered into the kitchen, tapped a young girl hard on the shoulder, and then stole her stool as the child jumped off in fright.

"Goat milk," Hávi breathlessly gasped at the child. "Get me ... goat milk."

The child vanished, and moments later the chief cook ran up to Hávi holding out a large wooden cup. Hávi seized the vessel and drank deeply; familiar comfort poured into her like a gift from the gods. Its taste was strange, a little bitter, but the sweet hominess of goat milk brought back memories of sitting in her old house, Helga gossiping while Hlöðu fed Gamli, Hávi eager to finish her chores so that she could sneak off and find Völu. Finally her stomach relaxed; pain diminished to a mild annoyance.

"Mistress Austmaðr?" the pudgy cook asked. "Are you ill?"

"Of course she's ill!" one of the old women snapped. "Look at her; she's having a baby! Come, dear, we need to get some food into you. Porridge with butter, that's what you need, just don't eat it too fast; you need to learn what foods your baby likes. A few teas help morning sickness; I'll see that some is brought to your room every morning. Karl, get a decent chair in front of that table. Come, my dear, let's get you someplace more comfortable."

With the cook and the old woman helping, Hávi made her way to the table just as a young man ran into the kitchen with a large heavy chair. The chair had a thick red cushion on it; Hávi was grateful as she sat down. Her lump of butter quickly melted atop the steaming boiled oats; Hávi was left alone as the old woman shooed everyone away and the cook barked his customary orders. The food settled her stomach right away, leaving Hávi feeling like her old self, but she'd seen women with morning sickness; *tomorrow it'd return.*

With a deep breath, Hávi pushed up. Women were slicing bacon into thin strips and chopping vegetables, men shoveling grain and kneading dough on a table layered in flour, and one little girl was grinding cinnamon in a granite pestle that weighed more than she did. Hávi picked up her empty cup, gave it to the little girl, and sent her for more goat's milk. As soon as she left, Hávi picked up the mortar and started grinding the spice. Strong as she was, the pungent brown, rolled-bark strips, imported from distant lands by the vikings, quickly crumbled, yet she continued pounding them into dust, evoking a scent so strong that Hávi coughed in their spicy, perfumed cloud.

"*Mistress!*" cried the cook. "*You needn't do that!*"

"You don't learn to cook by watching," Hávi said. "Back home I didn't eat until my chores were done. I want to learn how to bake cookies, too; when my husband returns, I want to present him with a dinner I made myself."

"*B-b-but M-mistress ...!*"

"You *will* teach me how to cook!"

The cook wasn't a brave man; his fat, dumpy face whitened to a near-Hvítvi pallor and he acquiesced, bowing and promising to do his best. Hávi spent her first fun day in the kitchen, despite her many visits; she ground sea-salt after the cinnamon, and then assisted the women in slicing vegetables for a hearty pie, although they chopped with a mastery that it'd take her months to attain. Hávi finished by kneading a mound of dough so heavy that the cook chastised some of his male-helpers, pointing out how Hávi had no problem with loads that they frequently grumbled about. Hávi grinned at their embarrassed faces; the whole lot of them couldn't hold a billy goat down and shave it. Even the girls in clan Hersir could out-wrestle them.

Bright yellow hair askew, locks straggled, and covered in brown flour and cinnamon dust, Hávi wiped her hands upon the apron that she'd borrowed, thanked the nervous cook, and headed out of the kitchen.

"*Hávi!*" wailed a hysterical voice.

Sobbing, Tryggvi burst out of a side-door and flung herself at Hávi, falling to her knees on the hard flagstones. She wrapped her arms around Hávi's legs so tightly that Hávi feared she'd topple.

"Tryggvi!" Hávi shouted, but she doubted if Tryggvi could hear her over her own pitiful weeping. "Tryggvi, what's wrong?"

"S-she's going to ... send me ... to a brothel!" Tryggvi wailed, tears soaking her cheeks.

"What?" Hávi cried, noticing many people running out into the hallway at the sound of Tryggvi's cries. *"Brothel? Who ...?"*

Hávi's questions went unanswered as Tryggvi collapsed into a tumble of tears. Hávi stared at all of the shocked faces watching them, and tried to take hold of Tryggvi's head without falling over, but she only managed to rub the top of Tryggvi's scalp reassuringly. Then Hávi realized her meaning: Mjóvi! Mjóvi was punishing Hávi *by inflicting pain on Tryggvi!*

"You're not going to a brothel!" Hávi shouted to be heard over Tryggvi's wails. Then she turned to several of the washer-women who bathed and dressed her, who'd arrived to investigate the commotion. "Help me get Tryggvi upstairs."

"No!"

Mjóvi walked into the hall, as tall as her slight frame could manage, stiff and slow as if in a formal procession. Tryggvi screamed, but Hávi squeezed the top of her head, trying to quiet her. Under Mjóvi's stare and the curious eyes of dozens of guards and servants, Hávi stood protectively over Tryggvi.

"Leave her be!" Mjóvi commanded.

"Tryggvi will not leave my side," Hávi warned.

Mjóvi smiled triumphantly.

"Mistress Austmaðr agrees with me!" Mjóvi announced to everyone watching. "From this day, it's my wish that Tryggvi becomes the handmaiden of Mistress Austmaðr, a fact which I would've revealed had the silly girl not fled in tempers."

Hávi stared warily; Mjóvi may be as hard as the point of an iron nail, but she wasn't stupid.

"Where came this talk of brothels?" Hávi demanded.

"An idle threat, should she displease her mistress, as the foolish child would've learned, had she stayed to listen," Mjóvi smiled like a cat with a trapped mouse. "As if I could condemn my dearly departed sister's daughter to such a foul occupation! So, Mistress Austmaðr, *do you accept my niece as your personal handmaiden?*"

Hávi hesitated; normally she'd have accepted delightedly, but Mjóvi's sly, oily voice reminded Hávi of the treats-game that Hersir boys loved to play on young girls: *'Close your eyes and put your hand into this bag'.* Usually it contained a lizard.

A frightened hand clutched at her thigh; Tryggvi was staring pleadingly up at her. *How could Hávi refuse?* Worse, what would Mjóvi do to Tryggvi if Hávi refused her publicly? A brothel might be a lesser fate than whatever evils Mjóvi could devise.

"Tryggvi is my handmaiden," Hávi said.

"Excellent," Mjóvi said ... and Hávi could almost see the tip of an imaginary mouse's tail slip into Mjóvi's cat-satisfied grin. "Get up, you silly girl! Hurry your mistress upstairs. Her ... appearance needs tending."

Mjóvi smiled as Hávi realized it: she was Mistress Austmaðr and she was standing before her own people covered in flour with her tight sleeves shoved up past her elbows, looking more disheveled than any servant would dare appear in public. Mjóvi had arranged this dramatic scene at just this time, knowing that everyone in the castle would hear about how ragged Hávi had looked; perhaps enough for Mjóvi to report to Hvítvi that Hávi had disgraced Jarl Austmaðr by her peasantly appearance. But, just as Hávi was about to speak, Mjóvi spun around and vanished through an open doorway, her disappearance so sudden that her departure startled several onlookers.

Hávi pulled Tryggvi to her feet with a strength that made Tryggvi cry out. Together they ascended the stone stairs; the voices behind them were softly murmuring even before they reached the first landing. Mjóvi had masterfully maneuvered this public farce: whatever it was, Mjóvi's trap was set.

Chapter 12

Smiling as if the universe were hers, Tryggvi escorted Hávi down the stone staircase. Bathed by Tryggvi alone, which took much longer but was infinitely more private, Hávi walked with even, measured steps into the great hall. Hávi wasn't worried about Mjóvi anymore; what could Mjóvi report? That Hávi'd helped out in the kitchen rather than watch and do nothing? That Hávi was more useful than any of Jarl Austmaðr's other wives? Hvítvi would be delighted ... and Mjóvi couldn't do anything without Hvítvi's approval.

No one challenged Hávi as she slid behind the high-table and took a chair midway between the center and the end. Few were seated at the high-table, just castle elders, most of whom Hávi knew on sight but had never spoken to; dignified men too old to go viking but too respected to have that pointed out, and Hvítvi, whose face was turned away, his snow white hair nearly matching the aged gray hair around him.

The old man whispering to Hvítvi stood up, patted the

albino's thin shoulder familiarly, and then slid his way behind the high-table toward Hávi. Suddenly she recognized his trimmed ears: Jarl Illingr. Hávi sat very still, frozen as he slid past her and the barest whisper escaped his lips.

"Come to my tower after the midnight bell."

Hávi froze; she'd forgotten his promise! But what if Mjóvi caught her now? *How could she possibly explain being caught with her husband's hated rival in his private chamber in the middle of the night?*

Throughout her meal, Hávi sat in quiet, nervous indecision. Her rosemary-flavored salmon with dill sauce and quail-stuffed sweet pies, filled with vegetables that she'd helped chop, tasted great, making Hávi remind herself to compliment the cook, but she was too torn to concentrate on eating. Only after the small honey-loaves were served steaming-hot did Hávi glance at Hvítvi, who was talking animatedly with men on both sides of him. Mjóvi, Hávi noted, was halfway down the table on the other side of Hvítvi. What Hávi needed most was strong friends; not cowards like Tryggvi, whom Hávi loved but who could never stand up to her aunt. Hávi needed women like Hvassi, stronger, older women whom Mjóvi couldn't intimidate.

Hávi glanced across the hall to the women's table, noticing that the servants were still carrying food to it after everyone else had nearly finished. Hávi recalled eating at that table: all of its food was cold and flavorless. With a glance down at her plate, and then a sly check to make sure that no one was watching, Hávi stuffed her last few morsels into her mouth, rose from her chair, and quietly slid past Jarl Illingr as he was just finishing his salmon. As she stepped past him, Hávi seemed to stumble, bent her head, and whispered into his ear.

"I'll be there!"

So much for staying out of trouble, Hávi thought.

A youth, carrying another tray of steaming honey-loaves fresh from the oven, walked into the hall as she descended the steps.

"I'll take that," Hávi said to him.

"Mistress?" the boy asked, confused.

"Go back into the kitchen and get another tray," Hávi ordered, and the youthful boy timidly surrendered the hot tray.

Hávi carried the tray straight to the women's table, and their expressions as she set the steaming plate on the table before them were pure delight. Hands instantly seized the sweet, hot loaves, some squealing with excitement as they gingerly dropped the honey-sticky bread onto their plates.

"Tryggvi, have a loaf," Hávi insisted as Tryggvi started to rise.

The women's table celebrated, so much that many men glanced curiously over to see what all their laughter was about. Hávi decided that she'd done all that she could for now, formally ordered the women to keep Tryggvi there until she'd finished her honey-loaf, and then headed out a side door toward the stone steps. Hávi reached the first step when a smooth voice called her back.

"Hávi!" Hvítvi said, not loudly but clearly, giving her no chance to pretend that she hadn't heard.

He was standing in the hall, and at a subtle wave of his hand, the old men near him bowed slightly, then walked away.

"At your service ... Jarl Austmaðr? Stepson? I'm sorry; I don't know what to call you now."

"Try my name," Hvítvi smiled. "What happened over there ... at the women's table?"

"Oh, I just brought them a tray of honey-loaves."

"Don't the servants do that?"

"Eventually, after everyone else has been served. That tray of honey-loaves was the first hot food to hit that table since I came to Skadi."

"Really?"

"I'm not complaining, but the high-table gets food while it's hot," Hávi said, trying not to sound insulting. "I ... don't think that anybody does it on purpose."

"Does the cook know?"

"I've never talked to him about it."

"Talk to him tomorrow," Hvítvi said. "Tell him that I told you to mention it and ask him to do what he can."

"I will," Hávi smiled. "Thank you."

"No, thank you," Hvítvi said. "I heard about your busy day."

"I enjoyed it," Hávi assured him. "I don't think that Mjóvi approved."

"There's so little that Mjóvi approves of that it's hard to tell," Hvítvi smiled. "I've been trying to find a summer task for her ... besides you, but nothing's inspired me."

"Your effort's appreciated."

A long moment passed, and then Hvítvi wished Hávi a good night and walked off down the long hall. Hávi watched him go, wondering where he went during the day, what he did, and who he saw. Hvítvi was still an enigma to her, but then, everything had seemed enigmatic since she'd left clan Hersir. That would change: Hávi would learn from Jarl Illingr things that no woman knew.

On the way up to her room, Hávi quietly slipped across the hall on the second floor. She carefully pried open the door to the servant's quarters, wincing as its rusty hinges loudly creaked, and finding it empty, she hurried inside. She rushed to the wardrobe, pulled open its doors, seized the first servant's dress that she saw, snatched an apron and a white scarf for her head, and then fled from the room. She climbed the last flight of stairs two steps at a time; Hávi pushed into her room, hurried to her wardrobe and stashed her stolen gown inside of it. She wouldn't be punished for stealing the gown, but if anyone guessed what she was going to do with it then it could mean her death.

In the silence of midnight, the hinges on the trapdoor creaked worse than the door to the servant's room. Hávi gritted her teeth, almost trembling, but she couldn't turn back now. As she pushed up the thick, heavy boards, Hávi lifted her head into the small, round room at the top of the tower. Light from the fireplace momentarily blinded her; it was brighter in here, at midnight, than during her first visit in the middle of the day.

"Welcome," Jarl Illingr said.

Hávi glanced quickly around the tiny tower room. She felt stupid; the dress that she'd stolen was too large for her, not big enough for Hvassi but for a rounder, shorter woman. Hávi looked ridiculous but she didn't dare go back and try to steal another while Tryggvi and other servants slept in there. Again she nervously scanned the tiny round tower chamber, filled with a small bed, a cluttered desk, and shelves of scrolls and papers, all illuminated by flames burning brightly in the fireplace.

"Looking for someone?" Jarl Illingr asked. "My frigid wife's asleep; this chamber's now warmer than her bed's ever been. Oh, yes: *thank you.*"

"Thank ... me?" Hávi asked hesitantly.

"I know that your servant, my chubby little stepniece, has

been leaving firewood on my steps every night," Jarl Illingr smiled. "I've watched her do it. This is the first time that this room's been warm since I came here."

Hávi blinked, trying not to react. *Tryggvi? Firewood? Every night?* Hávi remembered saying something to her about it long ago but she'd never guessed that Tryggvi had been so diligent. She'd have to thank her later; Hávi climbed into the tiny tower room and lowered the trapdoor behind her.

"Are you sure that nobody will come?" Hávi asked.

"No," Jarl Illingr grinned, "but no one's been here since you and your servant snuck up here a month ago. No one ever comes here."

"Why do you stay if it's so cold?"

"Because your husband makes me," Jarl Illingr hissed, not bothering to conceal his disgust.

Hávi smiled; this man hated her husband; *he had no need to lie to her.*

"Thank you ... for seeing me."

"Don't waste my time," Jarl Illingr said. "What do you want?"

"I ... want to learn ..."

"Yes, learn about our laws," Jarl Illingr said. "You want women to have the right to refuse a marriage. How will learning our laws help you do that?"

"I don't know," Hávi said. "I guess ... that's what I need to know first."

"A sad thing it would be to get caught here," Jarl Illingr warned. "Your husband would kill me. What he'd do to you wouldn't be much nicer. Is the risk that we're facing worth the reward that you seek?"

"I don't know the risk, so I can't say," Hávi said.

"If we're caught then I'll be killed and you'll be locked in this tower and women will never gain the right to refuse a husband."

"Don't laws change?"

"Yes, but only when there's no alternative. When the choice is between starting a feud or changing the law, or to avert a civil war, only then do laws change. They don't change just because someone wants them to, not even if that person's a jarl or a clan-chief, and certainly not when that person's a woman."

"Why not?"

"A good question," Jarl Illingr smiled. "The right question; it took you long enough to ask it. Learning law isn't just memorizing endless stanzas; learning law is about arguing, using words as weapons. Just having laws does nothing. You have to understand laws, to respect laws, and to wield laws as a warrior wields a sword. Laws are the weapons of political warriors, and you'd better have steel swords to back up your arguments or you'll lose everything."

"As you did?" Hávi timidly asked.

Jarl Illingr frowned.

"You know what your husband did to me."

"I've been told a few things but I don't know if they're true."

"Your husband murdered my family," Jarl Illingr said, his voice filled with bitterness. "My wife, my sons, my daughters, even my infant grandchild, and most of my clan. He burned all of our houses and drove my people in different directions, ragged, weaponless, carrying nothing but their babies. Then he claimed all of my clan's territorial lands and gave them to his own warriors, and put to death any of my people who came back to their farms. *I was a clan-chief ... and your*

husband destroyed my clan."

Jarl Illingr glared with a hate deeper than Hávi had ever witnessed, a hate that even Mjóvi couldn't manage. Hávi inhaled deeply and tried not to tremble: she couldn't appear afraid; he'd send her away if he suspected cowardice.

"I'm sorry," Hávi bowed her head.

"He had no legal right," Jarl Illingr continued, growling behind each word, his frustration glaring from red, vengeful eyes under heavy, furrowed brows. "Our laws forbid what he did, but he attacked us unawares in the middle of the night with sword and flame. My men were fighting for their lives while their wives and daughters screamed from inside their burning houses. My whole clan was murdered the night before the Thingr ... *over two lousy chests of gold!"*

"Chests?" Hávi asked, surprised. "Jarl Austmaðr has chests of gold?"

Jarl Illingr stopped his tirade and stared at Hávi, suddenly distrustful. His breath was ragged, as if he were on the verge of violence. For a moment, Hávi wondered if she should fear him; she saw no weapons, but they could be hidden anywhere. Jarl Illingr looked like an old ragged man, but he'd been a clan-chief, probably a warrior; *killing wouldn't be new to him.*

"Why are you here?" he asked suspiciously.

Hávi hesitated warily. "I ... told you ..."

"You have doors in your bedroom, don't you?" Jarl Illingr demanded. "Other than the one you go in and out through?"

"Yes, but they're always locked."

"And you've no idea what's in them?"

"No," Hávi admitted, wondering for the first time what was in them. The only time that she'd noticed them was her first night in the castle, and then she'd been too preoccupied with her own fright to worry about brooms locked in closets.

"You really have been kept in the dark," Jarl Illingr sneered. "Perhaps I shouldn't teach you, as ignorant as you are."

"P-perhaps," Hávi stammered, fighting to sound brave, "perhaps I should have Tryggvi stop bringing firewood."

"I survived without it before ... and it'll be summer soon."

"I'm trying to get Hvítvi to send Mjóvi away."

Jarl Illingr stared at her silently, and then he slowly smiled.

"If you can get rid of my wife then I'll teach you anything that you want to know," he said.

"If I can get rid of your wife then I will ... whether you teach me or not," Hávi said.

Both smiled conspiratorially. Their mutual hatred of Mjóvi bonded them, even if nothing else did. Hávi swallowed hard and then asked the question that she'd been dying to ask.

"What happened to your ears?"

Jarl Illingr's smile vanished.

"Your husband couldn't risk anybody challenging him for killing off my whole clan. If I was dead, any jarl could've made the challenge. As long as I breathed, only I, chief of clan Illingr, could legally condemn Jarl Austmaðr for his atrocity. But he made sure that I couldn't: he cut off the tops of my ears with a white-hot knife. By dawn, the morning of the Thyngr where I was to challenge him over the two chests of gold that were legally mine, I was writhing in agony; unable to speak, let alone testify. Jarl Austmaðr parades me at his table to insure that everyone can see that I'm free, but his guards have orders to kill me if I dare step one foot outside of this castle. I've threatened to kill myself, which would leave the other clan-chiefs free to challenge him, but none of the other clan-chiefs would promise to, so my death would be pointless. I demanded a bride to replace my murdered wife; I'd hoped for a new son to avenge clan Illingr. Jarl Austmaðr forced me to marry Mjóvi knowing that she was barren, but I didn't learn about her useless womb until a year after our wedding, not that she's given me many opportunities to seed her. I'd kill myself to avenge my clan but ...," Jarl Illingr hesitated, "no opportunity to hurt your husband has yet manifested."

"You'd kill my husband?" Hávi asked hesitantly, wondering at her own protectiveness.

"Gladly," Jarl Illingr assured her. "He knows it. That's why I'm not allowed to carry a knife or touch a sword. He punishes me if I defy him."

"He hurts you?"

"He confines me to my bedroom ... *with my wife.*"

Hávi shuddered. "If you hate my husband so much, why teach me law?"

"To hurt your husband," Jarl Illingr smiled as if this were obvious. "Women can't bring challenges at a Thyngr, so having Mistress Austmaðr equipped to argue laws will cause him nothing but trouble."

Jarl Illingr smiled wickedly at Hávi. He had nothing to lose by teaching her laws. *Women couldn't challenge at the Thyngr?* If not, then what good was learning law?

"Shall we begin?"

Hávi stared at him, fearing his smile.

"Will you swear," she asked, "swear upon the honor ... and the memory ... of clan Illingr ... that you'll teach me the truth ... not set me up with lies?"

"Of course," Jarl Illingr smiled. "But you must swear also, upon whatever you hold sacred, swear that you'll be utterly honest with me; there must be no deceptions between a master and his student."

"I swear," Hávi said hesitantly, "upon the clan of my birth, clan Hersir."

"And I swear as well," Jarl Illingr smiled widely. "If I taught you wrong, then you'd be dismissed as a fool. The more that you understand and argue our laws correctly the more trouble you'll cause for your husband. I swear that I'll help you cause that trouble."

Hávi bowed her head. She was being an unfaithful wife. She shouldn't be learning this. She would only hurt herself in the end. *She should open that trapdoor and flee back to her room.*

"Swedish laws derive, as all European laws do, from an ancient civilization called Rome," Jarl Illingr said without inflection, as if reciting a well-rehearsed speech. "Rome was founded in Italia, conquered most of the known world, and lasted for centuries. Roman law was absolute; Rome was ruled by Caesars, men wielding powers greater than kings. Caesars claimed to be gods and changed Roman law by will alone. But the Roman people had legal representatives: a senate, the marvel of the ancient world. Even back then, the world was too big to be ruled by any one man. Caesar used the senate to rule sections of Rome for him. The senate enforced the laws made by Caesar. Those laws made Rome strong.

"Roman law, as ours is today, was based upon fealty; each man owed fealty to his clan, each clan-chief owed fealty to his military governor, each governor owed fealty to his Caesar-appointed senator, and all of the senators owed fealty to Caesar. Each family member, wives, daughters, and sons who hadn't yet been declared warriors, or legionnaires, as they called them, owed fealty to their father. Roman fealty was absolute: a father could kill his wife and daughters as long as he claimed that he did it for the glory or security of Rome, and it was perfectly legal. Killing a son was more difficult; Rome needed its sons to populate its legions, armored armies that marched from the far corners of Byzantium through North Africa all the way to Hadrian's Wall in England."

"Where's ... Byzantium?"

"I'll cover geography later."

"What's geography?"

Jarl Illingr's smile grew wider.

"Don't worry; I'll teach you everything that you need to know."

"Will this knowledge help me change our laws?"

"Laws change slowly and only in time of great crisis," Jarl Illingr said. "Sometimes it takes a lifetime. When you're holding the key to changing our laws, you'll know it."

"What key?"

"The key that you'll have ... someday."

Firewood lay stacked on the bottom step of the tower; Hávi stepped over it and quietly slipped through the silent, candlelit hallways, carefully inspecting each passage beforehand, then hurrying through as fast as she could; her baggy servant's gown wouldn't disguise her for long. A dog barked from the great hall as she reached the bottom of the stairs and Hávi hitched up her skirt and ran up the stone steps, slipped into her room without being seen, threw off her disguise and hid it in a corner of her wardrobe, and then dressed in her abandoned nightgown and slipped into bed. It was early morning; soon the sun would rise and the cocks would crow, and she hadn't slept a wink. She snuggled under the still-cold covers, trying to warm them up, and thought about all that she'd learned. Rome; Jarl Illingr had laughed when she'd asked if Rome was as big as Skadi. Hávi would've thought that he was joking, but when he brought out maps of the known world and told her that more world existed outside its borders that still hadn't been explored, pointed out the tiny patch that was all of Sweden and the dot that was Skadi, and then all of the lands conquered by Rome, Hávi shivered. How could such a great empire have fallen? Was Rome real or just a legend? When Jarl Illingr described the vast wealth stolen from a hundred kingdoms, including an even more-ancient empire called Egypt, Hávi doubted him; it sounded like a children's tale, but she had no evidence to deny his words. Hávi glanced across her bedroom at the two locked doors; *what was behind them?* What secrets were only three feet away from the foot of her bed, and where were their keys?

Hvítvi would know ... but would he help her?

Cold. Wet.

Hávi groaned as a sickening wave of nausea swept over her. Her stomach cramped and her world tilted uncomfortably.

"Easy, m'lady," Tryggvi said, and she snatched the wet rag off of Hávi's forehead, took it by one corner and spun it around very fast in the air, then refolded the damp cloth and laid it back on Hávi's forehead; it was cold again. Hávi whined and tried to push it away. "Please, Mistress, lay still. Its morning sickness; it'll pass. Just try to sit up a bit. Have some tea: that'll ease the pain."

"Let me be," Hávi groaned.

An hour later, Hávi felt much better. The tea and dry

biscuits that Tryggvi had forced down Hávi's throat had seemed torturous but quickly calmed her stomach and cleared her head. Several times Tryggvi had lifted a small wooden bucket, fearing that Hávi'd be sick, but Hávi held it off. Hávi had seen other women sick from early pregnancy but never imagined how awful it felt; a pang of guilt stabbed that she hadn't been more sympathetic. She couldn't tell Tryggvi that part of her misery was from being awake most of the night; Mjóvi would force it out of Tryggvi and ruin everything. Hávi would have to space out her future lessons carefully, especially in light of her fragile condition.

"You look much better," Tryggvi smiled.

"Yes, but I don't think I'm up to working in the kitchen today," Hávi said glumly.

"What about visiting the sewing room?" Tryggvi suggested. "Or the nursery?"

"Perhaps," Hávi said, and then she glanced across the room. "Tryggvi, do you know what's behind those doors?"

"No, m'lady," Tryggvi said as if noticing the doors for the first time.

"Who'd have the key?"

"I don't know," Tryggvi said. "Jarl Austmaðr could have taken it with him, or Seneschal Krókr could have it, or Hvítvi."

"Where's Hvítvi?"

"Just down the hall. At least, that's where his rooms are."

"Help me up," Hávi said. "I want to see him."

Washed and dressed by Tryggvi alone, Hávi followed as Tryggvi led the way down the narrow upper hall. Inset into the hallway wall, beside a closed door, was a large fireplace, a roaring fire crackling inside it. It seemed an odd place for a fireplace: in the middle of an empty, narrow hall.

"Why is this fire lit?" Hávi asked.

"I don't know, Mistress," Tryggvi said. "There's often a fire here, but I've never asked why. These are Hvítvi's chambers, right through that door, but I haven't been in there since I was a little girl and ordered to wet-dust his outer-room."

Hávi considered listening at the door just to make sure that she wasn't interrupting anything, but how could she explain having her ear pressed against his door if Hvítvi suddenly opened it? Hávi rapped on the wood with her knuckles, which seemed swollen; she wondered if her pregnancy would swell her like a full wine-bladder. But no one answered the door.

"Do you know where Hvítvi goes during the day?" Hávi asked.

"I seldom see him," Tryggvi replied, lowering her eyes. "To be honest, no one does. At least, whenever I've heard anyone ask what Hvítvi does during the day all of the elders shush them. Most of the servants aren't even allowed at this end of the hall."

"I wonder why ..."

Suddenly a soft, anguished cry permeated the thick wooden door.

"What was that?" Hávi asked.

"Mistress, I think that we should go ...," Tryggvi said warningly.

Suddenly another painful moan echoed from within. Hávi reached out and grasped the door latch; Hvítvi's door swung open with the slightest touch.

"Mistress, no!" Tryggvi cried, but Hávi ignored her.

"Someone's hurt in there," Hávi said.

"You'll get in trouble!" Tryggvi warned.

"I'll be fine," Hávi assured her. "But you ... well, you should go back to my room."

"Mistress!" Tryggvi lowered her voice to a whisper. "You ... *you're going to burn your hands again!"*

"Perhaps," Hávi said, "but I'm going in anyway."

Chapter 13

Hávi stepped cautiously into Hvítvi's room, feeling quite the imposing stranger. Hvítvi's outer-chamber wasn't a bedroom; two wide loungers were layered with thick cushions and piled with thick quilts, and an uncluttered table pressed against the wall. The room's brightness struck Hávi the most; Hvítvi's outer-chamber was stark white: quilts, pillows, white-washed walls; the polished wooden ceiling and floors were dark grained, but almost everything else was as white as Hvítvi. Hávi was surprised; she'd have suspected that Hvítvi would want colors to contrast his paleness. Another roaring fireplace burned just inside the door, radiating sweltering heat, although no one was there to enjoy it. As with the fireplace in the hallway, Hávi wondered why it'd been lit.

Two doors offered promise. Hávi chose the closest, the door beside the blazing fireplace. To her amazement, as she first touched the latch, she instantly pulled back her hand; its wooden latch was unexpectedly hot, and as she touched it, steam hissed out of the loose gap around its handle. Curious, Hávi pulled the door open; white wisps of steam escaped from all around the doorframe in cloudy puffs. Hávi wondered where all the steam was coming from and peeked inside.

The room was not as bright as the outer-chamber, lit only by a single candle, but it was even whiter; all that Hávi saw was thick, swirling steam. Hávi had heard of such rooms; Jarl Hersir had a sweat lodge that he called his hot-fog house. She peered into the deep mist, opened the door wider, and stepped inside. Hávi warily entered into another world, blinded so badly that she couldn't tell how big the room was, bathed by intense heat and dampness. Everything was fog-white.

A human figure emerged in the swirling mists, growing slowly visible, so white amid the steam that he was barely discernable. Hvítvi was naked, lying on his chest on a long, low bench, his head leaning over its edge, his wet, long white hair covering his face and hanging to the floor. His thin, pale back and skinny legs brandished his albinism worse than ever. Hávi wanted to flee; she hadn't expected to find Hvítvi naked, but Hvítvi was trembling, writhing on his bench. Both of his hands clutched his head, pushing as if he were trying to squeeze his ears together.

"Hvítvi?"

Hvítvi jerked his head up at the sound of her voice, but then he winced in agony, shuddered, and collapsed weakly back onto the bench.

"Go ...," Hvítvi hissed like a dying breath.

"Hvítvi, what ails you?"

Hvítvi responded no more than a corpse. Hávi stared about, horrified; Hvítvi was undoubtedly sick, possibly dying.

Why was he alone? Where were the healers? *Why was he writhing unattended in a room full of steam?*

Like everything else, the floor was drenched, but Hávi quickly knelt upon it. Hvítvi seemed powerless to move his own limbs, but Hávi had cared for many sick goats and Gamli; Hvítvi might be a better patient than either, for he was conscious enough to assist in his own ministrations. Firmly she lifted and set him fully upon the bench so that his head didn't droop.

"W-what ... are ...?" Hvítvi asked, each breath an effort.

"Taking care of you," Hávi said in a voice that tolerated no argument. "How long have you been like this?"

"All-all my life."

Hávi hesitated and stared at him.

"You're not as sick as I thought."

"Headache," Hvítvi hissed. "Happens ... often. Steam ... helps."

"Oh!" Hávi said, and she glanced at the wall; she could see the backs of both fireplaces from inside the room, which explained why it was so hot, and underneath the bench she saw, from her stooped position, a bucket half-filled with water, a large ladle handle sticking out of it. Hávi ladled out a full measure of water and flung it at the back of the fireplace where it splashed upon the mortared rocks with loud sizzles and pops. Steam rose thickly off the hot rocks.

Hvítvi whined softly. Hávi ignored his protests and set her fingers to Hvítvi's temples, gently massaging as she'd often done for Hlöðu, who'd been terribly allergic to cats. Hvítvi groaned under her massage, but she ran her strong fingers back and forth, squeezing into the shape of his skull, forcing her fingertips hard and deep into the crevices of his bones, under his ears, and around the back of his head, and then she firmly worked her way back to rub his temples. Hvítvi groaned and twisted under her unrelenting pressure, but slowly he relaxed. Hávi kept it up, kneading his scalp until Hvítvi collapsed, his breathing slow and even; Hvítvi had fallen asleep, the best medicine that anyone suffering from a headache could enjoy. Hávi continued until she was certain that Hvítvi wouldn't reawaken, and then she gently slid her hands from the white mussed hair intertwining her fingers, considered his prostrate form for a moment, and then warily slipped from the steamy room. The idea of leaving poor, weak Hvítvi alone bothered her, yet how could she explain being alone with her naked stepson?

Checking to make sure that the hall was empty, Hávi hurried to her room and slammed her door behind her; all that she needed now was for Mjóvi to spot her sneaking out of Hvítvi's steam-chamber soaking wet. Tryggvi stripped her down and dried her with towels, redressed her, and then insisted that Hávi sit still so that she could comb out her wet, tangled hair.

"You're doing much better, a clear improvement," Hvassi beamed, her meaty hand motherly patting Hávi's shoulder as she examined Hávi's latest attempt at needlepoint.

Hávi had stitched a rectangle thirty rows thick, which was originally supposed to be a square, which was so small that she could cover it entirely with the palm of her hand. Hvassi could do better in half the time, probably while asleep, but it was the best needlework that Hávi had ever done. Today the women didn't care; Hávi had carefully taken the cook aside as soon as she came downstairs, whispered to him about her conversation with Hvítvi, and he seemed honestly shocked and loudly promised her that none of his dishes would be served cold to anyone anymore. Every servant in the kitchen had heard him, and within minutes, the gossip was racing throughout the castle. The women in the sewing room heard about it before Hávi arrived, and every one of them applauded Hávi's entrance and thanked her graciously. Hávi smiled and accepted their thanks, and later that afternoon, on her way to the privy, Hávi startled when two guards, who'd wisely never acknowledged her presence before, bowed respectfully. Apparently the guards were sick of eating cold food, as were the elderly and people like Hvassi who ate in their chambers. Hot food for everyone; *Hávi was the hero of Castle Austmaðr.*

Hours later, the young servant girl from whom Hávi had taken the task of grinding cinnamon appeared in their doorway. She quickly bent-then-straightened her knees, a childish imitation of a curtsy, and addressed everyone in the sewing room.

"Pardon me, ladies," she squeaked mousily. "Jarl Hvítvi requests Mistress Hávi to join him at supper ... now."

The timid girl looked around apprehensively, repeated her pathetic curtsy, and then fled from the room, leaving the door open in her haste. All of the women glanced at Hávi, some smiling, others looking concerned. Hávi feared what this might be about but dared not reveal it to anyone; she wondered if Hvítvi would punish her as he'd threatened to if she dishonored clan Austmaðr, but she forced herself to smile, set her needlework aside, and departed as gracefully as she could.

As she entered the great hall, Hávi froze: Jarl Illingr was seated at a lower table. All of the elders who usually sat at the high-table were by him or scattered about the hall. Upon the long, raised dais, seated alone in the center of the high-table, sat Hvítvi, a pale, solitary figure. Even at her forced-wedding, Hávi had never felt so self-conscious. Several eyes glanced momentarily at her, but most ignored her totally, although their awareness of her was undoubted; their silent indifference only made Hávi's attendance more obvious.

Hávi climbed the steps onto the dais and stared at Hvítvi. Normally she didn't sit beside him, but today, *how could she refuse?* To sit near one end would seem shocking; everyone in the castle would watch them sit apart in silence throughout the whole evening meal, just the two of them, alone at the high-table. Hvítvi stared straight ahead, unmoving, not even glancing at her, not giving her any sign. Hávi's courage, on which she'd always prided herself, failed; Hávi stood trembling, looking pointlessly foolish.

A derisive snort, barely audible but almost echoing in the strangely silent great hall, stabbed at Hávi's ears. Mjóvi was seated far from her husband, alone at the women's table. Supper was being served early tonight, another sign that something was amiss. But Hávi couldn't ignore Mjóvi's rude, pointed snigger; she couldn't show weakness in front of everyone while the nanny-bitch laughed. Hávi took a deep breath and paced off every step until she was standing behind the chair beside Hvítvi. *Curse him for not looking at her!* Slowly, having no choice now, she pulled out the chair beside him and sat down.

Hvítvi glanced at her as if surprised.

"Oh! Hávi! A pleasure to see you again."

Damn his calmness!

"Good day to you," Hávi replied courteously.

Hvítvi reached for a steaming cup, lifted it to his lips, sipped it, and then set it back down. Eventually a servant came up and placed a goblet of red wine in front of Hávi, who didn't know how much longer she could bear the tediousness. Hávi seized the thick, hearty wine, gulped too much, choked and coughed loudly, her distress echoing embarrassingly, and still no one in the huge hall looked at her. Mjóvi smiled wickedly.

"I hope that today finds you in good health," Hvítvi commented politely when Hávi's coughs subsided.

Hávi snapped her head to the side and glared at Hvítvi. Jarl or not, leader or not, ruler of the castle and Skadi or not, *Hávi wasn't going to put up with this nonsense!*

"Actually, no," Hávi said. "I think I'll finish my supper in my room."

Hávi started to get up.

"I wish you to remain," Hvítvi said softly but with a commanding tone, a firmness to his voice that she hadn't heard before.

Hávi sat back down.

"I received an unexpected visitor this morning," Hvítvi said coolly. "It was quite inappropriate. I was not ... ummm..., dressed for company."

Hávi clenched her jaw and forced herself to remain silent. She raised her hand toward her goblet to take another drink, saw her fingers trembling, and quickly hid both of her hands in her lap.

"You can imagine how surprised I was," Hvítvi continued.

"I would really rather eat in my room ...," Hávi said.

"This visitor helped me a great deal. That was also quite unexpected. Sadly, my ability to thank the visitor was severely hampered. You understand, while I was grateful to them, what might have happened if someone else had stumbled upon us ... together, in my ... unmentionable state, it could have been ... an embarrassment to all of clan Austmaðr."

Hávi's breath caught. Hvítvi had carefully chosen the words that he was using, was saying things casually that he couldn't say blatantly. Gossip, fueled by Mjóvi, could seriously disrupt the whole Skåne, from clan Hersir in the south to clan Dúfunef in the north. Hvítvi's position would be in jeopardy: Hávi had become a threat to him.

"I'm sorry," Hávi whispered.

"Sorry?" Hvítvi asked. "Why? You weren't there."

"Oh, yes," Hávi agreed. "I meant: I'm sorry that this ... visitor ... disturbed you."

"You may finish your supper in your room," Hvítvi said in his unexpectedly firm tone.

Hávi stared at him, but Hvítvi sat staring forward, looking at-ease, as if he'd been resting. *Hvítvi had just dismissed her, disgraced her in public, just as Jarl Austmaðr had done!* Hvítvi was displaying his authority over her before all of the elders of the castle. This was all a setup, purposefully-planned, a device to embarrass her. *Hávi had thought that Hvítvi was her friend ...!*

Sobbing hysterically, Hávi collapsed onto her bed. Betrayed, humiliated, friendless, Hávi cried, wishing with all of her heart that she was running off down a sandy beach with Völu, playing games and making snide comments about Sleitu and the other village girls, hoping that the adults wouldn't catch them and assign them chores. How badly she missed those chores, her mother, Hlöðu and Gamli, even her goats; the simple life of clan Hersir! She was doubly-trapped: no guard would let her out of the castle, no boat would carry her back to her lands, and they'd track and capture her if she fled. How far could she get, pregnant and suffering from morning sickness? They wouldn't allow Jarl Austmaðr's child to escape their control. Hávi was a prisoner bound by the child growing inside of her even more than by the stark, sharpened palisade around the castle. *If only she'd had the right to refuse marriage!*

Her aches the next morning were even worse, and Tryggvi's bucket had to be used before Hávi's stomach finally quieted. Hávi announced that she wished to stay in her room, but Tryggvi shook her head.

"I'm sorry, Mistress, but you can't," Tryggvi said. "We're going into Skadi today."

"What? Why?"

"I don't know, Mistress. A guard came to me this morning while I was carrying your tray up from the kitchen. He said that he was assigned to me for the afternoon so that you and I could go into town."

"I-I ...," Hávi stammered. She couldn't deny her desire to go into Skadi, to get out of the castle, but this was so ... unexpected. "Who assigned the guard? Was it Hvítvi ... *or Mjóvi?"*

"It was Seneschal Krókr," Tryggvi explained. "The guard wouldn't have asked why; servants don't ask those questions."

"But ... why?" Hávi asked although she didn't expect an answer. *Ordered into town? Whose trap was she walking into now?*

Midmorning passed before Hávi felt well enough to get out of bed. Tryggvi got fresh buckets of hot water and then washed Hávi thoroughly and dressed her in a simple light-blue gown. Together they descended the stone stairs, found their guard, a younger man than the last time, tall with long brown hair and a comically bushy mustache overlooking a

beard only half as thick, who seemed annoyed at the prospect
of escorting two women. He bowed gruffly to Hávi and
ignored Tryggvi, not bothering to conceal his mustache-buried
frown, and the women preceded him out the door.

The bright sunlight warmed their skin like sweet wine on
thirsty tongues. The day was clear, the blue sky shined
gloriously, bright billowy clouds floated on fragrant briny
winds, and a chorus of birdsong tweeted amid the raucous
cries of gulls and the laughter of playing children. The first
day of summer had arrived; no more huddling under heavy
cloaks, no more freezing nights. The promise of spring was
revealed in its glistening triumph: a perfect day.

Dogs barked at the castle children running about the
courtyard; no hiding in nurseries today. Breiðr, her swollen
belly reminding Hávi of what she'd be facing in six months,
stood watching Fróði, Auða, Grái, and Hrogn play among the
other children, each squealing with delight. Hávi felt bad that
she hadn't gotten to know her stepdaughters as well as she'd
have liked. They'd grown accustomed to her presence ever
since she'd started bringing them sweets, but they tolerated
her more than looked upon her as a mother. Hávi wondered
if the child in her womb would love her as she'd loved Helga
or if it'd be as indifferent to her as Sterki.

The people of Skadi cheered when Hávi appeared on
their streets, and many bowed deeply to her as she slowly
walked down the crunchy white sea-shell road. Some hurried
forward to greet her, and Hávi thanked them for their
courtesy, but she refused everything offered to her except one
of the sweet ginger cookies that the baker had a bowl full of
on his cart. The village children ran about, jumping and
playing, young boys chasing each other with sticks, baby girls
toddling about carrying rag dolls, all laughing and trying to

keep up with the older kids. Sunlight filtered through each leaf of the countless, distant trees; the thick woods beckoned to Hávi, and briefly she amused herself thinking of the pandemonium that she'd cause by slipping away from Tryggvi and her thick-mustached guard and exploring the wooded hills, but she couldn't; Mjóvi would hear of it and Hvítvi would confine her.

Hvítvi; Hávi rolled his name around inside of her head like a foul taste in her mouth. Hávi could wrestle him one-handed and break all of his fragile bones. *How could he treat her so badly after she'd helped him?*

The buildings of Skaði looked bolder, brighter in the sunshine. Hávi spent the morning inspecting all of the local shops again, now used to everyone fawning over her, but only a few offered gifts and Hávi stoutly refused them. The stocks, Hávi was glad to notice, stood empty, and Hávi wondered if Jarl Austmaðr would have them torn down if she asked ... probably not; Hávi didn't need to make herself mute by suggesting the impossible.

Beyond the stocks rose the tall hill upon which stood Law Rock; Hávi wondered if its carved runes read the same as the Law Rock in clan Hersir; she'd have to ask Jarl Illingr. She considered walking up to look at it but suspected that she'd better not.

At noon, the castle bell tolled. Many stopped and looked up; the castle bell always rang at sunrise, sunset, and midnight, but never at noon. Even Tryggvi looked up, startled.

"Let's go," their guard said sourly.

"Go?" Hávi asked. "Where?"

"To Hrafna's tavern; when the noon bell rings, that's where I'm supposed to take you."

"According to who?"

"Krókr gave me my orders; that's all I know," the tall guard said, scratching his wide, bushy mustache and trying to stare at them intimidatingly.

Hávi's stomach tightened; this couldn't be good, but the guard didn't seem inclined to ignore his orders, and again, *how could she refuse?*

No cheers came as Hávi entered Hrafna's tavern. The familiar hall was silent save for the children laughing outside. Hrafna, Brækir, and Blönduhorn were working silently by the kegs in the back. All glanced nervously at Hávi as she entered, but no one said a word or made any movement toward her. Save for them, Hrafna's tavern was empty.

No, not empty; near the fireplace, which was burning unusually hot for such a warm day, sat a single figure in a thick brown hooded cloak, warming himself before the high flames.

"Won't you join me, Hávi?" asked the smooth, familiar voice.

Hvítvi slid back his brown hood, his bright, snow-white locks revealing his identity as if a glowing lantern had been placed on his shoulders.

"What an unexpected surprise," he grinned. "Come, sit beside me, for real this time. We need to talk."

Hrafna, Brækir, and Blönduhorn all looked away when Hávi glanced toward them. She felt a hand familiarly touch her back; with a gentle effort Tryggvi pushed her forward, although from the look of shock on her round face, Tryggvi hadn't known about this, either. Their tall guard leaned back against the closed tavern door, strongly pressing his weight on it, suddenly looking more fearsome than comical; no one was entering or leaving uncontested; Tryggvi stayed beside him. Hávi made her way to the fireplace, and sat down in the same place that she'd sat in the last time that she'd sat here, the morning that the viking had set sail. Hvítvi stared at her, his strange, salmon-pink eyes oddly unnerving.

"What were you doing in my mist-hall?" Hvítvi asked, for the first time speaking bluntly.

"I ... I came to see you ... about something else, and I heard you cry out," Hávi said. "I didn't know that it was you ... I just heard someone in pain."

"That's very dangerous," Hvítvi warned. "There's a place in the castle, you need not know where, where Father puts people that he wants to suffer."

"Why would ...?"

"That's not a safe question to ask," Hvítvi interrupted. "What Father does to keep the Skåne under his control won't avail you to get involved in. You'd be wise to avoid places that you don't know. But I didn't ask you here ..."

"You ... asked me?"

"I told my guard to say that Krókr sent him. This *'chance meeting at Hrafna's tavern'* must be explained as coincidence. You and I caught alone in any room, especially when one of us is wearing nothing, isn't acceptable. Our family has powerful enemies; we aren't so secure that we can afford a scandal."

"No one saw me ..."

"The latch on my mist-hall slips if it's not properly secured," Hvítvi said. "My healer's servant found it open and asked who'd been with me. That's why I had to publicly admonish you last night: if you'd been seen ... Mjóvi would know about it by now."

"Mjóvi?"

"Mjóvi!" Hvítvi almost spat her name. "Surely you guessed? Mjóvi has spies among the guards, the servants, the elders, and the nobility; that's why I had to arrange our meeting like this, and why my guard's keeping your handmaid by the door where she can't overhear us."

"Tryggvi?" Hávi asked. "Tryggvi's loyal ..."

"She's Mjóvi niece."

"Yes, but ..."

"Do you really think that she could keep secrets from Mjóvi, if pressed? Look at her; she'd crumble from a single harsh word."

"I trust Tryggvi."

"Mjóvi would break her in minutes," Hvítvi said.

"Tryggvi never told Mjóvi about my meeting with ..." Abruptly Hávi bit back her words so hard that she choked.

"You mean ... *your meeting with Jarl Illingr?*"

"How ... how'd you know?" Hávi asked incredulously.

"I didn't ... until right now," Hvítvi shook his head. "You see what I mean? You two think that you're clever, that the things you're doing aren't being seen, but this castle has lots of eyes, and most of them tell someone everything. I have my own informants, some whom I trust and some that I know whisper secrets to several masters. Tryggvi's been spotted carrying firewood in the middle of the night, and firewood's been noticed on Jarl Illingr's stairs, then gone in the morning. It's not difficult to link her actions to you ... and you just confirmed it, very amateurishly, I must say. You'll have to get a lot better at this game before I share my secrets. Trust me; I've been raised on politics since birth, and since I wasn't allowed outside like my brothers, I've witnessed more than my share."

"Does Mjóvi know?"

"I doubt it. Tryggvi delivers the firewood every night after the midnight bell, so I've had my guards empty the corridor to

Jarl Illingr's tower and then leave that area unguarded to clear her way."

"Why?"

"Secrets are only valuable when no one else knows about them. If Mjóvi knew, as I'm sure she would have, then she could've used the information to make Tryggvi spy on you, or me, or she could've revealed it to many, and then my knowledge would be worthless. And Mjóvi isn't the only elder in this castle with motives of her own."

"But, what are you going to do, since you know ...?"

"I'm going to find out why ...," Hvítvi said, "from you, right now."

"What ....?"

"Why are you giving Jarl Illingr firewood?" Hvítvi demanded, suddenly gazing straight into her eyes. "Father put Jarl Illingr into that frozen tower on purpose. Tell me why you're rewarding him or I'll put an end to Jarl Illingr's heat. What are you getting from him?"

Hávi bit her tongue to keep from speaking, trying to sort out all of her confusion in an instant. *Would Hvítvi be deceived by a hastily-concocted ruse?*

"We ... just ... talk."

"What about?"

"About ... stuff."

"Tell me!"

"About ... laws."

"Really?" Hvítvi asked, and his stare softened. "You do know ... women can't become jarls?"

"I guessed it," Hávi sneered, although she'd never really considered it. "Women have no rights ..."

"That's not true," Hvítvi said. "Women can't be killed or raped ..."

"Unlike Roman times ..."

"You have been talking to Jarl Illingr."

"Women have no legal voice."

"Actually, they do," Hvítvi said. "Women can give testimony at Thyngrs. Perhaps Jarl Illingr isn't teaching you as well as ..."

"Women can't make an accusation."

"That's true," Hvítvi said. "But tell me: once you understand our laws, what do you plan to do?"

"I don't know," Hávi lied. "I just ... don't like feeling helpless."

Hvítvi's brows knit.

"Helplessness I understand," Hvítvi said hesitantly. "For the good of our clan, I can't condone secret meetings with another woman's husband, especially not for my father's wife. If you're caught, then I'll have to claim ignorance and publicly punish you, and it won't be pleasant. And Jarl Illingr will have to be punished, too, very severely, for his part. You can't tell him or anyone that I know about your ... lessons, as I assume that they are; mind you, other people may not be so generous in their assumptions. Even evidence that you've learned our laws will be suspect; you'll have to feign ignorance if the subject is ever broached. It's both of our duties to see that our clan isn't disgraced."

"I understand."

Hvítvi stared at her, his posture, tone, and manner radiating a strength that both of them knew that he didn't have; *he pretended well.* Long seconds ticked by uncomfortably.

"I ... I just wanted to say ... that I appreciate ... what you did for me," Hvítvi said, turning away from Hávi to stare into the fire, a snarl twisting his lips, his tone resentful. "Those headaches ... sometimes they last for days. How did you ...?"

"I didn't do anything," Hávi said.

"I was mostly oblivious, but I felt your fingers," Hvítvi said. "At first they hurt; I thought that you were purposely torturing me, but then it ... softened."

"My grandmother suffered like that whenever a cat got inside of our house," Hávi said. "I've been massaging heads since I was a child."

"You could be a healer," Hvítvi said, "if you weren't ..."

"... a woman," Hávi finished.

"I know how you feel," Hvítvi said. "Even when Father's away I can't be Jarl Austmaðr, even though I'm smarter than all of my brothers ..."

"Sterki and Auðgi," Hávi finished.

"They're just the survivors," Hvítvi said. "We had three older brothers, but they're all dead, killed in the vikings. Neither Sterki nor Auðgi were Father's favorites, but they're all that he's got left."

"Why not you?"

"Look at me!" Hvítvi seethed. "I'm cursed, almost a ghost. As a child, every time that I fell down my bones broke; they strapped pillows to me while I learned to walk. The slightest cut bleeds me dry. During every harvest, I sneeze my head off, and every spring I suffer indescribable headaches. Some foods make me sick; Stekt strömming almost kills me."

"But that should be easy," Hávi said. "Don't eat stekt strömming."

"It's not that simple," Hvítvi said. "I can eat all the herring and onions that I want. Sometimes I can eat bread without getting sick; other times it makes me violently ill."

Hávi paused and considered.

"What about the butter?"

"I don't put butter on fish."

"Stekt strömming is fried in butter," Hávi explained. "And
... sometimes you put butter on bread ..."

"And sometimes I don't!" Hvítvi gasped, his pink eyes
widening. "That could explain it ... but it won't matter. Father
can't make me his heir; the men of the Skåne won't accept
me: I can't lead the viking. I can't even fight a child."
Bitterness filled Hvítvi's voice, almost breaking his vaunted
control. "You don't know what it's like; I'm a grown man but
I've never grown a beard. Everyone treats me like a three-
year-old: *'Don't run!', 'Don't touch that!'.* Even Blönduhorn.
Father's ashamed of me."

"I can't believe that."

"Oh, he'd never admit it," Hvítvi said. "Father talks to me,
just not about anything important. Father only insists that I
join him for dinner so that my brothers show up. When I was
a kid, Father always drug me along when he took my brothers
someplace, but only because he was trying to prove that he
wasn't embarrassed of me. I couldn't go hunting because I
couldn't keep up or carry a blade, but Father used to take me
fishing, and not for my sake. My body can't take extreme
cold, and he'd drag me out before dawn to some chilly lake
where I'd almost freeze to death, but he hardly noticed; he
was too focused on my older brothers to pay attention to me.
In most ways, Father and I are total strangers. Look at my
brothers; even a blind man could tell that they're related to
Father. They talk alike. They share the same opinions. I was
always kept nearby but not one of them; Father parades me in
front of his friends, but in private we hardly speak."

Men are strange, Hávi thought. Jarl Austmaðr wasn't
stupid or subtle; nothing was as important to him as strong,
healthy sons. Hvítvi could probably see motives in him that

Jarl Austmaðr didn't even know that he had. *But how can a child excuse a parent for a lifetime of neglect?*

"I'm sorry," Hávi said.

"I've already experienced more than one life's worth of pity," Hvítvi sighed. "The gods cursed me and I can either live this way or entertain them by ending my life. That wouldn't be very difficult; they probably made me this way so that I could kill myself more easily. But I haven't so far ..."

"And you're not going to."

"How do you know?"

"Because I need at least one stepson that I can be proud of."

Hvítvi smiled at her, and Hávi's heart warmed like the swirling steam in Hvítvi's mist-chamber, a permeating balminess that surged throughout her; despite that Hvítvi was in no way like Tryggvi, openly deceptive and wholly secretive, Hávi felt that she'd finally found a trustworthy friend.

Chapter 14

"Tynwald," Jarl Illingr said. "Tynwalds are how Sweden is ruled. Clan-chiefs and kings can call themselves anything that they want, but decisions that affect the whole country must be agreed upon by the Tynwald, our highest council, the closest thing that we have to a government. After the Tynwald comes the Thyngrs, our loose system of law-making and administration, which were once called Þingvöllur, or Thing-Vollr, which translates to *'assembly field'.* The Thingvollr was an open-air assembly of free men in which laws were made and quarrels were settled. From the ancient Thingvollrs, the Tynwald was formed to prevent wars and feuds.

"Only a gathering of clan-chiefs can command a Tynwald. When a Tynwald starts, everyone stands silently as a blood-stained sword is brought in to remind everyone of why they're there: to prevent feuds. Then accusations, made at Law Rock, may be safely repeated by Law-speakers, and the council of jarls hears testimony from every man and woman who wishes to speak, and then they debate each matter. Their decision is the one absolute in Swedish law; no one can accuse the council or any member of collusion after a Tynwald decision's been reached. Decisions of a Thyngr, which any jarl can command, can only be challenged at a Tynwald.

"Do you understand what I just said?" Jarl Illingr asked.

"I ... I think so," Hávi said.

"Then you're not thinking enough," Jarl Illingr snapped. "Would a warrior wield a blunted sword or a spear with a cracked haft? Your survival in political circles depends upon your understanding our system of government. Even Swedish kings don't dare defy the decisions of a Tynwald council; that's why Jarl Austmaðr killed my whole clan the night before a Thyngr; he couldn't afford to be challenged in public. Do you understand?"

"Yes."

"So what does that mean?"

"It ... it means ...," Hávi stammered.

"It means," Jarl Illingr overspoke her, "that if you want women in Sweden to have rights, new rights, then Jarl Austmaðr can't force it outside of his half of the Skåne, and even in his own lands he can't make his law-changes permanent. Even convincing a Thyngr council isn't enough. Only a Tynwald decision can't be overruled."

"I see," Hávi said. "If I want my law-changes to last, then they have to be ruled upon at a Tynwald."

"Ruled favorably," Jarl Illingr corrected her. "Never forget: councils can rule against you, and if that happens at a Tynwald, then your last hope is lost."

Hávi sat in rapt attention. Jarl Illingr smiled at her.

"You're a good student, Hávi," Jarl Illingr said. "I almost regret teaching you; it's going to cause you trouble."

"You haven't taught me any laws yet," Hávi said.

"But these are laws that I'm teaching you," Jarl Illingr explained. "Laws exist in a society like fish in the sea; if you take fish from their water, they die. Take laws from its society, civilization crumbles. You can't know the laws unless you understand how they're made ... and who has the power to change them."

"But what *are* our laws?"

"The good of the common man is the supreme law," Jarl Illingr said. "What is neither just nor equitable cannot be the law; it is for the equity in the law that laws are accepted."

Hávi stared uncomprehendingly.

"You see?" Jarl Illingr said. "All that you understand of laws is that rich men make them and powerful men enforce them ... or ignore them."

"Everyone knows that," Hávi said.

"Yes, but everyone's wrong," Jarl Illingr explained. "Laws aren't made by the rich and powerful for dealing with peasants; they have armies for that. Laws are made so that rich and powerful leaders can deal with each other, otherwise they'd waste their armies fighting over every tract of land. Kings and jarls can't afford to waste expensive armies fighting amongst themselves: the enemies of Sweden would slaughter us. Jarls need a process for arbitrating disputes peacefully, so we have laws. But armies are made of peasants, and if the peasants don't trust their king, if he treats them unjustly, then they'll desert him and fight in someone else's army. Kings and jarls earn the respect of the peasants by obeying the laws; that's where the real power of law comes from: the respect and loyalty of the common soldier."

"No, that can't be," Hávi said.

"All laws shall be applied with wisdom," Jarl Illingr quoted, "because the greatest justice is also the greatest injustice, and mercy must be included in all justice. The good of the common man is the supreme law; and therefore, what is found useful for the common man shall be deemed the law even if the words of any written law would seem to order otherwise."

"Is this really the law?" Hávi asked.

"That depends on how you choose to perceive laws," Jarl Illingr said. "Many laws have been decreed, in many places, covering many events. What our laws say stands unquestioned. What our laws mean is always questioned. Which laws apply to which situation is eternally arguable, and the one who argues best prevails on which laws apply or take precedence."

"How will that help me gain rights for myself?" Hávi asked.

"You can't get rights for yourself," Jarl Illingr said. "Classes have rights, people don't. Jarls have rights. Clan-chief have rights. Men have rights. Even women have some rights. No one's ever named in the law; no one person has special rights. If you want a right then you must assign it to a class that you belong to; in your case, women."

"But how can I ...?" Hávi asked.

"No one can give another a better right than he has himself," Jarl Illingr said.

"But ... doesn't that mean ... that I can't give women rights ... because I don't have them myself?"

"Yes, it does."

"Then, no matter how well I learn the law, I can't ever change it."

"That's true."

"Then I'm wasting my time," Hávi said, looking up at Jarl Illingr's fatherly face, and then she noticed his wide smile. *"What?"*

"I've only once been in the sewing room, but I've seen the loom that goes along one whole wall," Jarl Illingr said. "That's a big loom."

"It's for making sails," Hávi said.

"How can one woman weave a whole sail?"

"One can't," Hávi said. "It takes a lot of women to weave a sail."

"The same is true for laws," Jarl Illingr said. "You can't make accusations that no one on the council's ever heard of. Why should they listen to you? You have to give them reasons to support you before you make the accusation."

"But I can't make an accusation!" Hávi said.

"That's why you can't do it alone," Jarl Illingr grinned. "Does it matter who makes the accusation?"

"Oh, so I need a man to make the accusation for me!"

"You need more than that," Jarl Illingr said. "A man who makes an accusation like *'rights for women'* will be disgraced unless he has enough backing to ensure that he'll prevail."

"Disgraced?" Hávi asked.

"Possibly executed," Jarl Illingr smiled wickedly. "Perhaps you should ask your husband to do it. Now that would be justice!"

"You look awful," Tryggvi said worriedly. "You don't look like you slept at all."

Hávi would've smiled if she hadn't felt so sick. She didn't dare tell Tryggvi that she was spending occasional nights in Jarl Illingr's tower. Hvítvi was right: Tryggvi would spill everything, yoke, white, and shell, under her aunt's mildest attack.

"You haven't planned my day today, have you?"

"No, Mistress."

"Good. I need more sleep."

Tryggvi stayed with Hávi all day, leaving her only to fetch food and hot drinks, leaving Hávi time to think. Jarl Illingr's lessons weren't what she'd expected, more a history and understanding of their legal system than what the laws were. *Could Hávi learn all the laws?* She'd marveled at skalds who quoted poems so long that hours passed while she listened. *Could women memorize countless stanzas?* Hávi'd never known one who'd tried, but then, women weren't allowed to become skalds. *Could a woman think as deeply as a man?* Hávi would've said no, but she'd grown up laughing at several idiotic boys who couldn't think their way to the surface if they were swimming underwater, but the plethoric challenge daunted her. Memorize all of the laws that Jarl Illingr knew? How could Hávi do that ... and how many insufferable, interminable years would it take?

Jarl Illingr's insistence that Hávi couldn't accomplish her goals quickly or alone flitted just outside of her grasp like an annoying hummingbird, not leaving her alone. Hávi wondered why he'd impressed those points so strongly. Hávi couldn't share her plans with anyone; the men would laugh at her and the women were as powerless as she.

Hvítvi wasn't at dinner when Hávi finally arrived, having made it out of her room only in the early evening. Her all-night excursion had almost made Mjóvi's wish come true; would morning sickness keep her confined to her room? Sleitu had carried her family's water buckets back from the stream every day of her pregnancy until right before she miscarried, yet Hávi had seen other mothers bedridden for months.

Mjóvi sat in a chair on one end of the high-table, Jarl Illingr at the end on the other side, and Hávi sat among the elders near the center, next to Hvítvi's empty chair. The elders made polite conversation, enquiring about her health, and then talking about the weather and the prospects of rain. One old man, whose name Hávi couldn't catch because he spoke with a strong, foreign accent, complimented Hávi on helping out in the kitchen, noting that it was nice to see *'a Mistress Austmaðr who was actually useful'*. Another old man with a large, ornate silver broach on his thick wool half-cape snorted disdainfully at this. Yet another old man offered to tell Hávi about the time that he'd seen a real sea-dragon, and before Hávi could accept or refuse, he'd started in on his tale, pointedly ignoring the eye-rolls and frustrated glances swapped by the other elders.

Hávi was sick again the next morning, but afterwards Tryggvi led her up a narrow stairs that she hadn't known existed to a door that opened upon the roof. Hávi let out a mild scream the first time that she looked over the thick-walled brink; never had she looked down from so high, especially not over such a straight drop.

The weather was glorious, the shining clouds so high that even the tallest mountaintops couldn't reach them. The wide green sea stretched out gleamingly bright; from atop the castle Hávi could see clear over Skadi's countless rooftops to its protected harbor and the trees that sheltered it. Hávi reveled in the free feeling of the wind, amused as the townsfolk of Skadi marched around their many streets, so tiny from this height that she couldn't identify anyone but the baker, and him only by his rickety cart. But beyond the vast planted fields and grazelands near the castle, the sight of deep forests made her want to weep; nothing would've made Hávi as happy as running off alone to explore those dark, strange woods.

Days passed into weeks. When able to, Hávi helped prepare evening meals, taking great pleasure whenever she spotted Mjóvi spying on her. Mjóvi was never alone, always busy talking to someone, but she consistently chanced to stop just outside of the kitchen's open doorway, from where she glanced at Hávi with an expression like a hobbled billy. Mjóvi always seemed to be nearby when Tryggvi took Hávi, covered in flour or grease, out of the kitchen and up the stone stairs to bathe and dress for dinner. The more disheveled that Hávi looked the louder Mjóvi scowled, but the cooks and helpers complimented Hávi twenty times a day. The chief cook boasted loudly that Hávi was the greatest gift that Jarl Austmaðr had ever given their clan.

When Hávi wasn't feeling well, if she could climb out of bed at all, Hávi would go to the sewing room. Her sewing was getting better; her chain stitch actually looked like a real chain, albeit badly-forged. Hvassi offered to teach her other stitches, far more complex, but Hávi wanted to get the basics mastered first, and the rectangle that she'd finished was now filled in with a shape that might've been a black wolf's head with red eyes.

Breiðr alone said that Hávi's wolf looked like a deathly-ill badger, which shocked the seamstresses but made Hávi and Hvassi burst out laughing. Breiðr was very kind to Hávi, several times bringing in Fróði, Auða, Grái, and Hrogn to see her. Hávi's youngest stepdaughters liked the sewing room now that they were familiar with it, and the old women enjoyed watching them play. Fróði and Auða were trying to do their first needlepoints although the older seamstresses had to thread their needles and Auða kept stabbing her fingers, then bursting into tears. Breiðr insisted on making the children formally present themselves before Hávi every time that they came in, and she presented herself to Hávi to show them how, reminding Hávi that Breiðr, who was now heavily-pregnant, was also one of Hávi's stepdaughters.

Hot foods changed Castle Austmaðr. Everywhere that Hávi went, guards and servants smiled at her. Blind indifference, or worse, people averting their eyes and trying to walk past Hávi without being noticed, which had started on her first day, was suddenly replaced with cheery greetings. Formal bows became customary from many of the guards. Inclusive smiles, even from chambermaids and laundresses, greeted Hávi wherever she went, and Hávi was delighted; not only was Castle Austmaðr becoming more livable and welcoming, Jarl Austmaðr had said that he wanted his people to love her, and save for a few bitter matrons like Mjóvi, Hávi had charmed all of clan Austmaðr. Breiðr reported that her youngest stepdaughters called her *'Mistress Sweets'* because of the cookies and smoked salmon that she always gave to them, and that all of the castle children had picked it up.

Hávi smiled often. Hávi still missed clan Hersir, her true, familiar home. She missed Helga, Hlöðu, Gamli, and, of course, Völu, but somehow Castle Austmaðr and Skadi had grown from a strange, frightening place into a semblance of comfort. For the first time since her wedding, Hávi felt at home.

One day, after breakfasting on the roof under a warm, hopeful sun, Hávi made Tryggvi show her as much of the castle as she could, everything that Hávi had never seen. Tryggvi led her through narrow, stone-walled, timber-ceilinged hallways that Hávi had only glanced down, where the wooden walls were rough and the floors hadn't been chiseled smooth, past rows of bedrooms for guests, elders, and special people like the chief cook, the master of the castle guard, and Master Krókr, and then Tryggvi actually walked her through a barracks cramped with too-many beds, and dark rooms where servants slept, in which some still snored, and where Tryggvi lowered her voice and used hand-signals to keep from disturbing.

The laundry room was large, filled with dozens of low, wide water-barrels, some soapy, some reeking of lye, and the whole chamber was strung with thin ropes upon which many blankets, tunics, and dresses were hung. The washroom was disturbingly noisy, filled with women gossiping, laughing, and arguing over loud splashes and slaps of wet clothes. As Hávi walked in, suddenly one young woman screamed, and the rest fell instantly silent. Everybody dropped their wet handfuls and jumped to their feet, most bowing or curtsying as best they could. Even Hávi was startled by their sudden reaction and stood dumbfounded, not knowing what to say.

"Please...," Hávi said, "please, don't let me interrupt ..."

"*What's going on in here?*" boomed a gruff, exasperated voice as a tall elder stormed into the laundry. "*Why aren't you working? What's ...?*"

The old man startled as he recognized Hávi, and then he quickly composed himself and stiffly bowed, respectfully but not deeply, for he was quite aged.

"Mistress Austmaðr!" he said. "Forgive me; I didn't expect you here."

Hávi had seen this man walking about the castle but had

never spoken to him; he towered almost a head taller than Hávi, built like a mountain, his wide hips and stomach sagged with age; he looked like he'd once been very strong. The laundresses knew him: many glanced worriedly at their castaway work, their hands uncomfortably empty.

"Forgive me, but who, might I ask, are you?" Hávi asked.

The old man seemed taken aback and many of the laundresses exchanged surprised glances.

"I?" asked the old man. "I'm Master Krókr, Seneschal of Castle Austmaðr and Skadi."

"Ahh!" Hávi smiled, and she performed a slight curtsy. "I've seen you but we've never been introduced."

"The honor is mine," Master Krókr said, repeating his slight bow.

"Please don't blame the ladies," Hávi said. "I asked my maid Tryggvi to show me the castle and I surprised them only moments before you arrived."

"Quite understandable," Master Krókr said. "With your permission, may they proceed with their duties?"

"Oh, please do."

Master Krókr smiled at Hávi, and then he turned and scanned all of the laundresses with a glare that needed no explanation. Water splashed from dozens of barrels as wet clothes and sheets were seized, twisted, and wrung free of water and suds. Some clothes were slapped against large, smooth rocks or upon the legs of the laundresses who raised their skirts to attend to their duties. The disturbing noise level returned, absenting only their voices, making Hávi understand why the women had been talking so loudly and why the sudden silence had summoned the attention of Master Krókr.

"Is there any way in which I may serve you?" Master Krókr asked Hávi, raising his voice to be heard over the splashing and slaps.

"Thank you, but Tryggvi knows the castle well enough to show me around," Hávi said.

"If I may, Mistress, I've witnessed you helping out in the kitchen," Master Krókr glanced at Tryggvi before returning to Hávi. "May I ask, begging your pardon, how long you expect to continue?"

Hávi fell silent, uncertain how to answer.

"Why do you ask?"

Master Krókr looked neither surprised not offended, merely subservient, almost fawning, but in an upright, dignified way. Already taller than she, Master Krókr held himself as high as he could, looking down his wrinkled nose past brown age-spots on both cheeks. His deep-set eyes, crowned with wiry white brows, glared steadily without blinking; distantly aloof, haughty and arrogant.

"I merely wished to schedule the helpers where they're most needed," Master Krókr answered. "The kitchen's not the only place for servant-work."

In the courtyard, Tryggvi let Hávi watch the blacksmith for ·almost an hour, keeping her distance as several overly-friendly dogs vied for Hávi's rapid-backscratchings. The smith in clan Hersir never let kids near his smithy; Hávi watched fascinated as the red-glowing lump slowly flattened under the smith's masterfully-wielded hammer.

"Is that going to be a sword?" Hávi asked.

"No, Mistress," the smith replied, his deep, gravelly voice sounding slightly amused. "This is just flat bar-stock; this'll be door hinges."

One of the smith's young helpers, a raven-haired boy covered in soot and furiously pumping a bellows with all of his might, smiled at Hávi's question, but the smith barked at him and he faced the ground.

There was more to see, the stables and the potter's, but Tryggvi insisted that Hávi, by the time that she'd been bathed and dressed, would be late for supper, so Hávi allowed her to lead her back inside the hall and up the stone stairs. After an annoyingly-harsh scrubbing, Tryggvi insisted that the courtyard was too dirty for Mistress Austmaðr. She dressed Hávi in her nicest yellow gown and they both went to supper.

Hávi sat among the elders again, who welcomed her warmly as she arrived. A bard was playing a lyre in the corner, singing softly, several tables listening in rapt attention. Hvítvi wasn't there, but Hávi knew better than to mention it. She sat among the elders and steaming platters were placed before her. The bard finished to scattered applause, but Hávi's attention was arrested by the sound of her name.

"Mistress Austmaðr?" asked a deep, familiar voice.

Hvassi came lumbering up from the women's table, followed by many of the sewing women, including several of the lady-elders, and Breiðr, who had Fróði, Auða, and Grái in front of her, and little Hrogn in her arms.

"What's this?" Hávi asked.

"We wish to present you with a gift," Hvassi smiled widely.

Smiles broke out on every face; Hávi stood up, wondering.

"With your permission," Hvassi said, and she stepped up to the high-table and lifted up a bundle of green cloth tied with a pink sash. The elders quickly pulled aside all of the dishes and pitchers of ale, clearing a clean spot on the table, and Hvassi set the present onto the table before Hávi.

"For you," Hvassi said, and she performed an awkward curtsy which, for her bulk, would've been comical, but Hávi knew the effort that it took her. All of the other women, even

Fróði and Auða, curtsied behind her.

Speechless, Hávi slowly untied the pink sash and unfolded the bundle, finally realizing that it was a new dress, dark green and so finely-made that Hvassi must've worked on it. Wide, beautiful white stitching adorned it everywhere, around its sharply-square collar, on both sleeves, even along its hem. Hávi gasped in amazement, her eyes popping as she stared at her new gown's craftsmanship, and suddenly cheers and applause broke out from everywhere. Even many of the men in the hall rose and clapped their hands. Tears burst from Hávi's eyes and she thanked them profusely, praising their incredibly-generous work and denying her worth of accepting it. As she stared blurrily through her tears, disbelieving the warmth that she felt inside, Hávi realized something that she'd never felt before: clan Hersir had always felt like home to her, but Hávi wouldn't leave Castle Austmaðr for anything.

Chapter 15

"Mistress!" Tryggvi cried. *"Hávi, wake up!"*

"Wha ....? Why're you ....?" Hávi stammered, bleary-eyed, the candle in Tryggvi's hand distressingly bright. "What time is ...?"

"It's the middle of the night," Tryggvi said, trying to soften her voice and speak up at the same time so that her words sounded like a loud hiss. *"Hvítvi, Mistress! Hvítvi summons you!"*

"Hvítvi?" Hávi asked. "Who? ... oh! What does Hvítvi want?"

"It's Master Kamban!"

"Who?"

"Master Kamban, the chief Healer," Tryggvi explained. "His boy was sent to fetch you! He says that it's urgent!"

"Let him in here."

"The boy?" Tryggvi gasped. *"In here?"*

"Yes," Hávi ordered, trying to lift her head off her pillow

with Herculean effort. She propped up on one elbow and winced as she peered past the glare of the candle while Tryggvi summoned the boy inside.

Hávi didn't recognize the boy but there were many of them, and not all worked in the kitchen. This lad was older than most, tall and lanky, that awkward stage where pimples covered his face and his too-long arms and legs made the rest of him look skinny. He looked terribly anxious.

"What is it, boy?"

"Hvítvi commands you to join him," the boy said, his squeaky voice humbled, almost apologetic. "Master Kamban sent me to fetch you."

"What does Hvítvi want?"

"You," the boy replied. "He wants you very badly."

"What for?"

"He's very sick."

Sick? Hávi threw back her warm quilt and jumped out of bed, then almost fell. The floor tilted wildly and the room spun.

"Hávi!" Tryggvi cried, and she barely managed to steady her before Hávi lost her balance completely.

The boy jumped back in surprise, then leapt forward and seized Hávi's other arm.

"Is she ill?" the boy asked. "I'm Master Kamban's attendant."

"No, she's pregnant."

"I'll be alright," Hávi insisted, clutching desperately to both of them, fighting to master her dizziness. "Take me to Hvítvi."

Despite Tryggvi's mumbled objections, still in her sleeping gown, Hávi was half-carried to Hvítvi's door. The fireplace in the narrow hall outside his door was burning brightly. The boy pushed Hvítvi's door open unceremoniously and then led them in; the white inner-room was aglow with candles but otherwise empty. The boy pulled open the thick side-door beside the other fireplace and Tryggvi gasped as steam burst out into the room.

"Stay out here," Hávi told both of them, and then she pulled free of them and entered the foggy chamber.

"This is completely improper!" growled a deep voice, and suddenly the tall head of Master Krókr appeared in the mists.

"Mistress Hávi, Jarl Hvítvi demanded you," said an even deeper, yet a younger voice coming from the bench. "Here, take my place. I need to watch this carefully."

A short, round-faced bald man with a long, wiry mustache that hung past his chin and made his face resemble a fat walrus stood and shuffled past in the small foggy room. Something *'thumped'* on the floor as he moved aside.

"You're Master Kamban?" Hávi asked.

"Yes," he said, limping aside. "Hvítvi told me of your healing touch upon his head; I'm afraid that I don't seem to have it."

Hvítvi was writhing in pain on the bench facing the other way, but he was otherwise exactly the same. Hávi sat down and closed her strong fingers upon his head. Hvítvi trembled beneath her touch, but she held him still and firmly squeezed and massaged. Hvítvi cried out but she ignored him.

"How long's he been like this?" Hávi asked.

"Three days," Master Kamban answered, leaning close and carefully observing her motions. "He hasn't had it this bad since he was nine."

Hávi worked her fingers hard, Hvítvi writhing and moaning beneath her ministrations, but she didn't give up. Long minutes passed and Master Krókr broke the silence.

"It's not working."

"Give it time," Hávi said. "This usually takes at least twenty minutes, but I've never known anyone to suffer so long first. Why didn't you get me sooner?"

No one answered her, but Master Kamban turned his eyes from Hávi's treatment to glare through the mists at Master Krókr, who ignored him completely.

For almost an hour, Hávi kneaded and flexed the smooth, tight skin upon Hvítvi's skull, occasionally working her way down his neck, squeezing tendons that felt like thin iron rods beneath his soft flesh, trying but quickly giving up on loosening the taut muscles of his skinny, pale shoulders. Hvítvi was wearing an undertunic that draped past his knees, probably put on him by Master Krókr or Master Kamban; his undertunic was soaked from the humidity but Hávi couldn't ask them to take it off him. She would've, so that she could work the muscles of his shoulders and back, if Master Krókr and Master Kamban weren't there.

Stiflingly hot, Hávi ladled the whole bucket at the dangerously-hot backs of the chimneys, making them crackle and fume, and the billowing steam grew so thick that it filled her lungs until she coughed. She could only see the men veiled through the swirling mists, Master Kamban's face eagerly watching Hávi's every movement, closely observing her hands as she pressed and squeezed into Hvítvi's flesh, dug into his thin, taut muscles, alternately rubbing and releasing, Master Krókr standing aside disdainfully, glaring with occasional scowls and sudden jerks of his head to look away, as if this was a great disgrace. *What would Hvítvi say now?* He'd warned her against disgracing clan Austmaðr; *what would Mjóvi do?* Hávi didn't know if helping Hvítvi would doom or bless her, but until he was better, she was too practical to care.

Eventually Hvítvi ceased writhing and slowly collapsed into an exhausted slumber. Hávi lightly slipped her tired, sore fingers from Hvítvi's skull, letting him sleep. She hung her head for a moment, weariness overcoming her; dealing with any crisis was taxing, and having been awoken in the middle of the night, her pregnancy only made it worse. Hávi rose slowly, motioned toward the door, and led the way out. In the white outer-chamber, Tryggvi and Master Kamban's attendant, the boy who'd come to fetch her, stood up as she came out. Masters Krókr and Kamban followed her into the room, bumping and thumping.

"There's too much steam in there," Hávi said to them. "Clear some of it out and let him sleep, but someone should watch him."

"I'll see to it," Master Kamban promised.

"Mistress Austmaðr," Master Krókr spoke angrily, "how did you learn to do that?"

"My grandmother suffered ...," Hávi began.

"And how did Jarl Hvítvi know that you could help him?" Master Krókr demanded, gruff and accusing. "How did you know what he needed? You showed no surprise upon entering a secret hot-fog chamber in the middle of a castle. How did you know about the young jarl's condition?"

Hávi froze; she couldn't answer without revealing information that she didn't trust Master Krókr not to use against her, and possibly against Hvítvi. Hávi slowly lowered herself onto a white divan, which she found was hard wood covered by a thick, white-wool blanket, breathing overly-hard, stalling, trying to compose herself, but Master Krókr glared from his great height, his gray-bearded jaw set. Hávi considered lying but wasn't sure which lie would save her and which would only make matters worse. With no recourse, she lifted her head and spoke clearly.

"When my husband returns I'll tell him everything; I don't answer to you."

Tryggvi gasped and Master Kamban raised both of his eyebrows high, but Master Krókr stood frozen as if she'd slapped him, yet the glare in his eyes intensified from angry to murderous. In a silence as deafening as a thunderclap, Master Krókr swept from the white outer-room, his heavy, stomping boot-clomps rapidly diminishing down the narrow hall. Hávi sighed; *she'd just made another formidable enemy.*

Master Kamban smiled widely at Hávi while Tryggvi looked horrified, and then he addressed his attendant.

"Attend Jarl Hvítvi," Master Kamban instructed the boy. "Lessen the steam and let him sleep as long as he can. If he asks to be carried to his bed, take him, and then come and get me. You know what to do."

"Yes, Master," said the boy, and he opened the door and vanished into the hot-fog chamber with undisguised familiarity. Then Master Kamban turned to Tryggvi.

"You understand," Master Kamban said to Tryggvi, seriousness lowering his already deep voice, "that you can't speak of this to anyone, ever, and no one must ever know about Hvítvi's health ... or that your mistress came here tonight."

"I won't," Tryggvi gulped.

"Wait for your mistress out in the hallway," Master Kamban ordered, and without a moment's hesitation, Tryggvi obediently stepped out into the hallway. She grabbed the door handle on her way out and pulled; she didn't need to be told that Master Kamban wished to be alone with Hávi.

Hávi glanced up at Master Kamban and her eyes widened. Master Kamban wasn't as short as Hávi had thought; the swirling mists had hidden most of him, and while Hvítvi was suffering she'd had no time to focus upon anything else. Master Kamban was steeply leaning over, grotesquely bent: *a hunchback*. A short, stout cane supported him, and the eyes in his round-face stared intently, his completely-bald head more stark than ever, giving him an odd, troubled appearance, his long, brown, wet mustache hanging like great tusks, still damp and dripping from the hot-fog chamber. Master Kamban looked more like a patient than a healer; his smile beamed friendly, but his many crooked teeth repulsed her.

"Don't be alarmed," Master Kamban said casually, "I know how I look. Sinister, wouldn't you say? *Monstrous?* I've heard it all. I've had to become an excellent healer to make up for it; few people trust anyone who's so obviously cursed."

Hávi bit her lip, uncertain what to say.

"Your touch-method is impressive. I've been trying for days to ease Jarl Hvítvi's pains. Just keeping him alive, making him eat and drink, has been difficult."

"Eat?" Hávi asked. "What have you been feeding him?"

"Just gruel," Master Kamban answered, his expression becoming inquisitive.

"Was there butter in it?" Hávi asked.

"I don't know."

"I think that butter makes him sick."

"Really?" Master Kamban's small, deep-set eyes regarded her suspiciously. "I don't suppose that you could tell me ... why you suspect that?"

"No."

"Ah. Well, don't worry: I won't try to force it from you," Master Kamban smiled. "I saw how much success Master

225

Krókr had; you don't like being ordered."

"I'm Mistress Austmaðr," Hávi said.

"So I gathered. I'm sorry that I haven't had the chance to meet you before, but as you can see, it's best if I remain in my room. Your husband faced stern opposition just allowing me to live inside his castle; many feared that my presence would curse the whole clan."

Hávi swallowed hard. Malformed infants were feared as an ill-omen throughout all of the clans. Few survived, and of those which lived, many were killed before they could curse their village. Thus deformities were rare, mostly beggars; Hávi never expected to see a hunchback inside Castle Austmaðr.

"I ... do hope that you'll share with me your secret for treating Hvítvi, for his sake," Master Kamban said.

"Of course," Hávi said, "but there's no secret: I just massaged his head."

"No charm?" Master Kamban asked, incredulous. "No incantation? No prayer?"

"No."

"Did you soak your hands in sparrow blood?"

"No!"

"Anoint your fingers with breast-milk from a one-eyed wet-nurse?"

"No! *Ick!*"

Master Kamban eyed Hávi expectantly.

"Just massage," Hávi insisted. "I could've used the charm against mistletoe, but I didn't think of it. I really don't know what mistletoe is, save that Loki fashioned a poisoned dart from it."

"*Really?*" Master Kamban asked sarcastically. "Mistletoe is a poisonous little vine with white, waxy berries, not native to the Skåne. Mistletoe often kills the tree that it grows on, but it's a weak, frail plant; how anyone could make a weapon out of it is a mystery. Well, if you'll pardon me, I'd best get back to my room. If you do happen to remember any charm that you might have used, do let me know."

Hávi started to speak when suddenly a sharp *'thump'* hit the stone floor as Master Kamban took his first lurching step away. She wanted to say something, to refute his implication that she was reserving some medical incantation, but each time that he stepped with his left leg, a resounding *'thump'* sounded, almost identical to his cane. Hávi stared at his long, worn gray robe, wondering if the hunchback even had a left leg, and if so, what caused the thump, or if he had only half of one leg with a cane strapped to it. But before Hávi could overcome her surprise, Master Kamban *'thumped'* out the door. Hávi stared blankly as he departed; *had she made a second enemy in one night?*

The sun had risen past its zenith and started to descend before Tryggvi helped Hávi out of bed. Earlier, Hávi had eaten a few bites and tried to rise only to be suddenly sick, and then crawl, stomach-churning, back into bed. She'd fallen asleep again, and then awoken hungry in the early afternoon.

The sudden knock upon their outer-door surprised them both, but Hávi settled back against her bed while Tryggvi went to investigate. Alarm pinked Tryggvi's cheeks as she hurried back.

"Jarl Hvítvi summons you!"

"Again?" Hávi asked. "Is he sick?"

"No, he's in the Hall of Audience."

A rushed bath and dressing later, Hávi hurried down to

the audience chamber where she'd first met her three stepsons. Tryggvi pushed open the door and held it wide.

"Good afternoon," Hvítvi said weakly. He was sitting at the table in a large, straight back chair, but even in the bright candlelight reflecting off the fantastically-painted walls, Hávi noticed that his pallor shone exceptionally pale; Hvítvi could fall naked into a snowdrift and no one would see him. Before him sat a small goblet beside an opened bottle of wine and a plate bearing an untouched loaf of brown bread.

"Hvítvi," Hávi said, performing a barest curtsy, at which Hvítvi managed a brief smile, but even that seemed to weaken him.

"You will address me as *Jarl Hvítvi!*" Hvítvi said very slowly but as harshly as he could manage, and then he locked his gaze on Tryggvi and stared until she sheepishly slunk from the room.

"As you wish, *Jarl Hvítvi,*" Hávi said, taken aback. *What had happened? Why was he angry at her?*

"You met Master Kamban?" Hvítvi demanded, his tone accusatory, the pace of his words spaced by exhaustion.

"Y-yes," Hávi couldn't lie; Master Krókr had been there.

"Go to your room and stay there," Hvítvi ordered. "The whole rest of today, and tonight, don't leave your room. Tomorrow you'll come here with Master Kamban at sunset. Bring your servant. You will teach him how you ... touch heads. Is that clear?"

Tears wetted Hávi's eyes. *How could he? She'd helped him when he needed her most!*

"Yes," Hávi said, half-defiantly, and she turned to obey him.

"*You will not leave this chamber before me!*" Hvítvi strained to shout.

Hávi glanced back. Hvítvi looked drained, but he slowly stood, squeezing out of his chair as if pushing it back required more strength than he had. Hesitantly, fighting for balance, Hvítvi imperiously stood and walked past Hávi as if he meant to ignore her, when suddenly his strength gave out; Hvítvi stumbled. Full onto Hávi he fell, grabbing at her to keep from falling, and she instinctively caught him, his thin frame so light that Hávi could lift him with ease. He pushed up, pressed against her, and suddenly whispered conspiratorially into her ear.

"This room has eyes and ears! Be at Hrafna's tomorrow at noon!"

He pushed off of Hávi, then glared angrily at her. The healer's assistant opened the door as Hvítvi banged his fist on it, and then he helped support Hvítvi and led him off down the hallway.

Hávi stared at Hvítvi until he vanished, Tryggvi staring worriedly from outside the door. *What had just happened ....? Eyes and ears ....?* More confused than ever, Hávi glanced behind her at the ornately painted walls, the empty high-backed chair, the wine and bread untouched upon the table. *Hvítvi had seemed so angry! Was this just another show?*

Hrafna's tavern? Did he wish to speak to her in private again? Then .... *he wasn't really mad at her!* Hope warmed Hávi's heart, but she stood worried; *what was going on to make Hvítvi take such extreme measures?*

Hrafna's tavern? Hávi was supposed to visit Jarl Illingr tonight. If they met, then she'd be in no shape to meet Hvítvi at noon. *Damn her morning sickness!* Hávi was eager to learn more about their laws, had formed legal questions to ply Jarl Illingr with, but Hvítvi might be risking more than she was by planning this meeting. *But how could she tell Jarl Illingr that she wouldn't be there tonight?*

Hávi felt foolish, standing alone in the cold audience room, puzzling over her predicament with Tryggvi staring at her from the doorway. If she went back to her room and stayed there, would Jarl Illingr be angry with her for not showing up? *She had to learn to change their laws!* The idea of countless little girls having to get married against their will stung her; she couldn't abandon them to her fate: *Hávi couldn't forget her terrible wedding night nor live with her own compliance.*

"Tryggvi, I need you to tell ...," Hávi started, but then she froze. *What had Hvítvi said? These walls have ears and eyes?* Suddenly Hávi glanced at the colorful room, its intertwining wooden decorations, yellow snakes and red cross-hatchings, and wondered if she was being spied upon. *Who would do such a thing? Mjóvi? Krókr? Kamban?*

"Tryggvi, I need you to go to the high-table during supper tonight," Hávi said clearly, wondering who might be eavesdropping on her. "Tell ... everyone ... that Mistress Austmaðr is very ill and will be spending all day and night alone in her room."

The same tall young guard arrived at her door shortly before noon. She examined him closely this time, wondering if he was so unlucky that he'd twice gotten chosen to escort Hávi into town or if he was someone's spy. A boy newly-grown into a man, his thick brown hair was unusually long and his comically-bushy mustache tried to make up for a youthfully-thin beard. He bowed gruffly to Hávi, frowning, and Hávi couldn't recall any other expression on his face.

"What's your name?" Hávi asked.

"Bíldr," he answered after an exceptionally frustrated grimace.

"Whom do you serve, Bíldr?"

"At the moment, you."

"Yes, but to whom do you owe your fealty?"

"To clan Austmaðr."

"Yes, but to whom do you report?" Hávi asked.

"I'm just a castle guard," Bíldr answered. "The captain, Master Krókr, Jarl Hvítvi, and Jarl Austmaðr, when he's home; are all lords to common guards."

"Yes, but to whom do your first loyalties lie?"

"To myself and my family," Bíldr said defiantly. "I'm a Swede."

Even the white shell-paved road into Skadi seemed darkened by the inclement weather. Heavily-cloaked, Hávi, Tryggvi, and Bíldr walked in silence save for the thick broken shells crunching in the mud beneath their feet and the pitter-pat of a light sprinkle. But midsummer had come; the trees were full and leafy and colorful wildflowers dotted the rain-washed hillsides.

"This way," Bíldr said, pointing to the woodwright's street.

"I thought that we were going to Hrafna's tavern," Hávi said.

"Not directly," Bíldr said. "Any meeting that you expect ... must be a coincidence."

The woodwright was delighted to have Hávi visit him again and he showed her a great chest that he was building. It hadn't been stained or polished yet but its craftsmanship was astounding: leaping seals played around its lid and it had many openings where doors and drawers would be fitted; the woodwright showed her the iron hinges and latches that would eventually hold it all together. Two wooden arcs topped each end, each roughly shaped with two serpent-heads facing opposite directions, a wide hole beneath each.

"Those holes are for the pole," the woodwright explained. "Two men will be able to carry this chest, fully-loaded, suspended from an oar."

"Fascinating," Hávi exclaimed, running her fingers along the intricate, looping knotwork carved into the flat top. "Who's this for?"

"No one ... yet," the woodwright smiled. "I'm sure that I can sell ..."

"I'd like this for Jarl Austmaðr," Hávi said.

"*Oh!* Um ... well ... yes, Mistress, as you command," he said hesitantly, looking disappointed.

"Oh!" Hávi gasped. "You need payment ...!"

"No, Mistress!" the woodwright stopped her. "I could never charge ...!"

"How much did you hope to sell this chest for?"

"Mistress, I cannot price my goods to you!"

"How much?" Hávi demanded, and as he started to object again Hávi slapped the top of the ornate chest with her hand. The noise startled everyone; all of the kids froze or ducked for cover, wide-eyed, and the woodwright's wife let out a stifled scream.

"For ... for anyone else, perhaps ... seven, I mean, ... *six silvers?*"

"Seven silvers," Hávi said, wondering where she'd get the money. "Finish the chest. Don't sell it to anyone else."

"Yes, Mistress."

"Thank you," Hávi said, and she turned to Tryggvi and Bíldr. "And now, since I've done what I came to Skadi to do, I'd like some västerbotten."

Three quick, explosive sneezes struck Hávi's ears as she entered Hrafna's tavern. Hvítvi sat cloaked before the fireplace, which was roaring flames so high that the worried looks on the faces of Hrafna, Brækir, and Blönduhorn could be discerned from a distance. They were gathered about him holding out small clean cloths with expressions of obvious concern. On a serving board sat a clay pitcher beside a steaming hot cup. As Hávi, Tryggvi, and Bíldr entered, all three of them turned and stared, but Hvítvi only sneezed again. Bíldr closed the door behind them and leaned with his full weight against it, and Hávi motioned for Tryggvi to remain with him, then crossed the room to Hrafna's fireplace. Brækir stepped back to make room for her, and Blönduhorn set down her cloths and hurried back toward the kegs.

"You should be in your steam," Hávi said as she sat down beside Hvítvi in the chair that Hrafna held out for her. Hvítvi looked awful, shadows darkening his milky pallor, his bloodshot eyes darker than his pink pupils, his nose rubbed raw from sneezing.

"Leave us," Hvítvi said dryly, his voice raspy, and Hrafna and Brækir instantly hurried back toward the kegs.

"You ... can't mention my hot-fog room," Hvítvi whispered, nodding his head toward the retreating trio. "They'd get into trouble just for knowing about it."

"I'm sorry," Hávi apologized. "I didn't mean to ..."

"I trust that you didn't meet with Jarl Illingr last night?"

"I stayed in my room ... as you ordered."

"Good," Hvítvi said. "Mjóvi suspects something; at midnight, two nights ago, Mjóvi showed up with half of her servants and demanded to see her husband. Master Krókr arrived by sheer coincidence just as my guards tried to object.

If you'd been there ..."

Hvítvi sneezed again, so violently that he almost fell off his chair, and Hávi reached out to steady him, tucking what she recognized as Brækir's thick wool shawl tightly around his cloaked shoulders.

"Why would I have been there?" Hávi grinned weakly.

"Very good," Hvítvi said. "But Master Krókr's angry; you can't redress him in front of servants. He'll be looking for any excuse to humiliate you, and he and Mjóvi are threats that you can't ignore. Don't be seen anywhere that you shouldn't; that includes my hot-fog chamber and any towers that you may enjoy visiting."

Hávi frowned. Not only was Hvítvi forbidding her from visiting Jarl Illingr for lessons but from coming to his aid when he was most ill. She couldn't see the sense in it: clan Austmaðr needed Hvítvi ... and she cared about him. *If she could ease his suffering then why shouldn't she be allowed to help?*

"Let me teach someone else," Hávi said. "How about that boy, Master Kamban's attendant?"

"Felian?" Hvítvi asked. "Why not Master Kamban ...? Oh, of course."

Suddenly Hvítvi's eyes narrowed and he glanced askance at Hávi.

"No, it's not like that ...!" Hávi insisted. "I mean ... *can Master Kamban be trusted?"*

"I trust him ... with my life ... daily," Hvítvi said coldly. "Master Kamban designed my hot-fog chamber. He's spent most of his life taking care of me. He's not bad, just deformed."

"I didn't know," Hávi said. "I didn't even know that Master Kamban existed until the day before yesterday."

"I'd like you ... to teach Master Kamban ... how you help me."

"I will."

"And ... I think you have a gift for healing," Hvítvi said. "In exchange for you teaching him, I've asked Master Kamban to teach you what he knows about healing."

Hávi stared wide-eyed at Hvítvi. *Was he mad?* Hávi was already struggling to understand Swedish law, cooking, and needlepoint. How was she, a lone woman, supposed to digest all of the information known only to experts like Hvassi, Jarl Illingr, and now Master Kamban?

Hvítvi sneezed again, rocking his head back and forth so hard that Hávi feared that he might snap his neck.

"You need to get back to Castle Austmaðr right now," Hávi said.

"In a ... moment," Hvítvi said, trying not to sneeze again. "You need to understand something that words can't prove. T-tell Blönduhorn to bring something ... over here."

Hávi glanced at the back of the tavern, then at Hvítvi's still-steaming tea cup.

"Blönduhorn, would you bring me some honey?" Hávi called.

"Please," Hvítvi corrected her.

"Please?" Hávi added, ashamed that she'd forgotten.

As Blönduhorn approached, carrying a clay jar of golden honey and a blackened iron spoon, Hvítvi spoke up.

"Master Krókr once shot Father with an arrow while they were hunting," Hvítvi said to Hávi. "It was an accident, a long time ago, but Father never forgot ... Oh, just leave the honey. Thank you."

Blönduhorn quickly set the jar and spoon onto the table beside them, and then hurried back to her parents.

"That'll do," Hvítvi said. "I'll go back now."

"Wait a minute," Hávi stopped him from rising. "What about Master Krókr?"

"What about him?" Hvítvi managed a barest grin, seeming strained by the effort. "As far as I know, Master Krókr's never been hunting in his entire life, and he certainly never shot anybody with an arrow."

"Then ... why ...?"

"You'll see," Hvítvi smiled. "In the meantime, is there anything else that you need?"

"Yes," Hávi admitted. "I sort of ... bought Jarl Austmaðr a new chest from the woodwrights. I promised him seven silvers for it, but I don't have a copper."

"Oh, that's easy," Hvítvi said. "I'll open the treasury."

"What treasury?"

Despite the pain that it caused, Hvítvi grinned sweetly.

"You really don't know what's right in front of you," Hvítvi smiled, and then he sighed from fatigue. "I forget about how much you ... don't know, not having been raised in ... Castle Austmaðr. Don't worry; I'll show you everything."

Chapter 16

In the audience room, Hávi stood as Master Kamban entered. His sudden appearance at the door was no surprise; Hávi could hear his leg and walking-cane alternately *'thumping'* up the hallway. Master Kamban wore greens today, a dark, forest mantle over a lighter, holly-green tunic. This tunic also reached to the hunchback's ankles, concealing his leg ... or whatever he *'thumped'* on. The glowing candles shined on his bald head which otherwise bore no trace of malformation, his skin nowhere near as white as Hvítvi's, but he was pale; he probably saw little sun, hiding his strangeness in his room. He stared at her, his ragged eyebrows rising as he saw Hávi standing, awaiting him, and after only a moment's hesitation he nodded, almost a bow, but Hávi said nothing, forcing herself to take no notice; she didn't care what gestures of respect he could manage; she didn't want his bad back to cause him to fall while trying to show her unneeded reverence.

"Good to see you again, Master Kamban," Hávi said warmly, gesturing to an empty chair.

"Thank you, *Mistress Austmaðr*," Master Kamban said sharply, stressing her title.

Hávi didn't reply, just stood very still as Master Kamban *'thumped'* across the floor and lowered himself onto the empty chair as Felian, Master Kamban's attendant, quietly secreted himself into the corner opposite Tryggvi, closer to the door. As he settled into his chair, Master Kamban's right leg stuck out very straight, allowing Hávi to spy the worn end of a stout stick poking out from under his tunic, seemingly strapped to the outside of his right leg.

"Jarl Hvítvi informed me that you'd reveal to me the secrets of your healing touch," Master Kamban said.

"I wish to," Hávi said, "but I can't tell you my secrets."

"You're not the only healer who jealously protects their mysteries," Master Kamban said, and he made as if to rise.

"I can't tell you because there's nothing to tell," Hávi said. "I'll have to ... *show you.*"

Master Kamban halted, then lowered himself back down into his chair.

"I'm not a healer," Hávi said honestly. "I don't have any secrets. I mean, I do know some charms, but just the ones that everyone knows, and I haven't used them while I massaged since I was a little girl. Everything that I know my grandmother taught me, and then only to treat her. All I need you to do is ... relax."

Hávi walked around the table toward Master Kamban. *She had to do this,* she kept telling herself. Touching a cripple wouldn't curse her; Hávi had played with Ørrabein the whole time that they were growing up, and Ørrabein was so crippled that she could barely limp around Hersir village.

Still, stories abounded of witches and trolls and dark elves casting spells on people, and those people always ended up cursing everyone that they came in contact with. Yet Master Kamban had been a hunchback since birth, had treated Hvítvi since he was a child, and had lived in the castle for years; surely if he was going to curse someone then he'd have done it by now. Still, Hávi had to fight the warning chills wriggling up her spine; those evil stories were told by master skalds trying to frighten their listeners, and Hávi shuddered, recalling chilly autumn nights under a bright orange moon in the middle of clan Hersir while a wild-eyed bard scared the children until they all screamed and fled to the safety of their eds.

"Close your eyes," Hávi ordered.

His mottled skin felt clammy beneath her fingers as she unwillingly laid her hands upon his scalp. Glancing to make sure that his eyes were closed, Hávi pressed harder, disgusted as his strange, clay-like skin flexed beneath her slightest touch. She wanted to draw back, but now that she'd started, how could she? She couldn't tell Master Kamban that she feared his curse. Normally she wouldn't have used a charm but Master Kamban's distrust bothered her, so she quietly mumbled the only healing charm that she knew.

> *"Hair of Sif, gold replaced,*
> *Mouth of Loki, healed face,*
> *Hand of Tyr, bitten away,*
> *Mistletoe, vanish today."*

Silently Hávi repeated her charm three times, each time letting her fingers dig deeper, push harder, drive into the crevices of Master Kamban's skull, roll over his sharp ridges, and slowly it seemed to help. Master Kamban's skin lost its clamminess and soon felt like everyone else's; she could feel his curse held at bay. She pushed strongly with her probing fingers, glad that Master Kamban had no hair as she molded the flesh of his scalp back and forth, his temples, his jowls, behind his ears, and the back and sides of his neck. Hávi shied away from touching his deformed, bent back, but Hvítvi couldn't blame her for taking reasonable precautions. She worked him as hard as she'd worked Hvítvi in his steam-room, and at first Master Kamban resisted her touch, flinching and wincing. Hávi couldn't blame him; although not in pain, she doubted if anyone had ever willingly touched him ... and never this much. Yet eventually she felt him relax, and half-an-hour later, when he was half-asleep, she slowly stopped.

"That ... that was most ... effective," Master Kamban said, breathing hard, seeming to come out of a restful nap. He sniffed, and then breathed in deeply through his nose. "Ahhh, my head has never felt so clear!"

"I ... I did use the mistletoe charm."

"I didn't hear any charm."

"I said it under my breath."

"Foolish girl!" Master Kamban grinned. "How do you expect the gods to hear when you mumble at them? Or worse, how are your patients supposed to believe in treatments that they can't see or hear?"

"My grandfather said that Odin could hear you whether you speak aloud or not."

"Odin, perhaps; he's the god of battles and master of magics, but the mistletoe charm doesn't call upon him, does it?"

"Oh! I never thought about that!"

"Regardless, the gods aren't invoked by charms alone. Often a patient's belief in your ability to heal them has a greater medicinal effect than anything that you chant. I'll show you; Jarl Hvítvi asked me to formally instruct you in the healing arts, teachings which no other woman in clan Austmaðr has ever learned, despite that some are very reliable healers. This is no small request; some in Castle Austmaðr won't take kindly to me teaching a woman, especially Mistress Austmaðr."

"Like Mjóvi and Master Krókr?"

Master Kamban delivered Hávi a seething stare.

"I wouldn't presume to name any of my suspicions, *especially not in this room,"* Master Kamban said in a raised voice, and he glanced about at the colorfully-painted walls and ornate carvings.

Suddenly Hávi recalled Hvítvi's words: *this room had eyes and ears.* Mjóvi and Krókr were sure to hear that she'd named them. Master Kamban may not be a friend but he was no fool, and he was taking a great personal risk by teaching her. Yet he obviously wasn't here willingly; *why here?* Nothing that happened in this room was a secret; soon all of clan Austmaðr would know that she was taking lessons from Master Kamban. *Why did Hvítvi want everyone to know?*

"I'm sorry," Hávi apologized. "You're correct, of course."

"Very well," Master Kamban said. "Now, tell me all of the charms that you know, and what you think each of them is for, and especially any healing that you've done."

Obediently Hávi recited every charm that she knew, describing when she'd used them, and included charms that she'd never used but had often heard. Master Kamban listened intently, often nodding his head and fingering the rounded top of his walking stick as Hávi talked. Hávi had actually done no healing; there were several healers in clan Hersir, most of them women, but Hávi didn't mention that.

Her list of charms was quite long and several times Master Kamban corrected a misspoken word or Hávi's poor pronunciation of some of the older names, but mostly he just listened. Finally Hávi gave up trying to remember any more.

"Very good," Master Kamban said when she was finished. "You seem well versed in basic charms, but you'll need to know twice as many before you call yourself a healer. Now, tell me what you know about herbs and potions."

"Nothing," Hávi said. "Sometimes Mother would send me into the woods to find certain flowers or leaves, or fresh spider webs, but then I'd get sent out of the house."

"Why?"

"Well ...," Hávi frowned and looked down, "to be honest, I ... accidentally ... knock things over ... a lot."

Master Kamban smiled.

"Perhaps we should end this lesson for today."

"I haven't learned anything ...!" Hávi complained.

"No, but I have," Master Kamban said. "I've learned what you need to learn, which is almost everything. I'll need to bring some herbs the next time that we meet; there's no point in telling you about herbs if you can't identify them. But if you want to learn something, answer me this: why did your mother ask you to fetch her fresh spider webs?"

"I don't know."

"Spider webs filter infectious vapors," Master Kamban said. "That's why it's healthy to keep live spiders in your house and always leave fresh spider webs undisturbed. Rolled into a large ball, fresh spider webs are used to cover bleeding wounds before you bandage them. A patient bandaged with fresh spider webs has a lesser chance of getting infected."

Master Kamban pushed up from his chair and struggled a moment, then regained his balance with familiar ease. Felian, his attendant, stepped forward and steadied him, and then Master Kamban attempted a low bow, seeming awkward and unbalanced, before he *'thumped'* out the door.

In Hávi's chambers, Tryggvi wasted neither time nor tongue disparaging Master Kamban.

"Nasty man!" Tryggvi hissed, her round face twisted with disgust. "Back bent like a horseshoe, a withered leg: the gods must've seen great evil in him to deform him so! I almost died when you touched his cursed flesh; I couldn't have done it, not for all the world. What was Jarl Hvítvi thinking, asking you to touch that horrible hunchback?"

"He's just a man," Hávi said, but her thoughts weren't of Master Kamban. Hávi didn't want to become a healer; she was interested in law. *Was Hvítvi trying to distract her, to take her attention away from the law, where women had little voice, and redirect her toward an interest where she could, at least, publicly claim credit?* While it was nice to be able to learn without having to sneak around, fearing getting caught, Hávi couldn't afford to be distracted; too many little girls would be forced to repeat her own torturous wedding night if she abandoned her goal.

Hávi glanced at Tryggvi, who was rattling on about Master Kamban's faults, and a strange thought came to her. She rolled the idea around in her mind, ignoring Tryggvi's babble. Then a dawning sensation flooded over her like a sudden deluge from thunderous black clouds: *Hávi understood!*

"Tryggvi, I need you to take a message to Hvítvi," Hávi said. "Tell Hvítvi that I need those silvers to pay for the chest that I bought. We're going into Skadi tonight."

Tryggvi pulled the door to Hávi's bedroom open wide and

performed a modest curtsy. Hvítvi stepped in, looking much better, and he bowed deeply to Hávi. Hávi slid off her bed and stood before him, then curtsied deeply.

"Good day, Mistress Austmaðr," Hvítvi said formally, his voice clear and warm. "I trust that your health is well."

"Good day to you, Jarl Hvítvi," Hávi said with equal formality. "I feel fine, thank you. I see that your health is equally well."

"Indeed, I am in delightfully excellent health today, and well-rested," Hvítvi said. "Mistress Austmaðr, forgive me, but I have business in this room," Hvítvi turned to Tryggvi. "Await us outside; this's Austmaðr family business."

Tryggvi and the several guards looked surprised but obediently stepped into the outer-room and closed the door behind them. Hávi glanced at Hvítvi; *the two of them alone in her bed chamber?* This would be the gossip of clan Austmaðr, if it got out. Mjóvi and Master Krókr would kill to hear news of this.

"We don't have long," Hvítvi whispered.

"Long for what?"

"You'll see," Hvítvi replied. "First, how was your lesson?"

"I finally understood *your lesson*," she replied, trying to glare reproachfully, although she couldn't help smiling.

"I thought that you might."

"Why cloak everything in riddles and mystery?"

"I have to be careful," Hvítvi said. "My leadership of clan Austmaðr, even during the summer months, isn't welcomed by all, and a poor leader I'd be to have Father ambushed by a rival clan-chief in his own city."

"There's such a thing as being too clever," Hávi said.

"Really?" Hvítvi grinned wickedly.

"You could just tell me what you want, plain and simple."

"I could ..."

"Don't you trust me?" Hávi asked.

Hvítvi's smile vanished, and for a moment he looked pained, as if his heart had suddenly paused, and his paleness grew. Then he sighed deeply, heavily, and bowed his head.

"I do trust you, *Mother*," Hvítvi said, and he paused as if straining to speak each word, "but I ... well, I'm not strong. It's ... not easy, being cursed; look at Master Kamban. People like us, we need to use what skills we have."

"So you exercise cleverness?" Hávi asked.

"Cleverness can protect against ... unexpected dangers."

Hvítvi raised his head hesitantly, his pink eyes driving right into Hávi's heart. Hvítvi was such a good young man; he didn't deserve to be cursed ... or treated like he was cursed. He was kind and gentle, strong in ways that only women understood. Hávi didn't think that she could bear life in Castle Austmaðr without him.

Suddenly Hvítvi grinned, reached into a pocket, and drew forth a small, strange silver object.

"Is ... is that a key?" Hávi asked.

"Haven't you seen a key before?"

"Yes, but never one so small."

"Come," Hvítvi smiled at her, gesturing her to follow him. "It's time that you learned what's behind these doors."

Hvítvi unlocked the first door. A small chamber was revealed, barely larger than a privy, but no foulness reeked from within. Weapons the like of which she'd never seen lay piled inside the tiny chamber, spears in front, and behind them stood crowded shelves upon which lay many helmets, barbutes decorated with circlets of brass ... *no, not brass!* ... Hávi slowly approached the door, disbelieving.

"Is that ....?" Hávi couldn't bring herself to ask. *"Gold?"*

"Some of it's gold, yes, and most of the inlay's silver, but there's a lot of brass and bronze, too."

Hávi stared, her gaze slowly sliding across the gleaming, intricate inlay on the heads of each spear: swirling tails of fantastical beasts, opened fanged mouths, and interwoven crosshatchings of designs so complex that even Hvassi would be impressed. On the other side from the helmets, hanging from iron hooks set into the ceiling, were at least eight coats of mail, steel-forged interlocked links: in clan Hersir, only Jarl Hersir owned such a valuable coat, and it was said to be invulnerable to swords. These coats shined, glistening as if oiled, and Hávi couldn't imagine what such treasures were worth. Only on the day that her husband, Jarl Austmaðr, had led the viking out to sea had Hávi seen several coats like these, and then only on jarls and clan-chiefs.

On the floor lay wooden chests, two large, many small, and several seemed to be over-filled, their lids unable to close; sparkles of gold and silver glinted from inside them. Gleaming brown bows and long quivers stuffed with arrows were piled atop the chests, and many handles of what looked like scabbarded swords stuck up from between the piled chests, large, bright, ornate brass pommels shining, bulbous counterweights bearing polished faces or decorated with precious colorful stones. Hávi stood and stared, speechless, but Hvítvi's hand gently pulled her back. He closed the door and relocked it, and then he unlocked the other door.

Hávi's breath caught in her throat. Huge crosses, cups, and chalices of gold and silver shined on crowded shelves alongside sparkling jewelry, platters, and plates, mostly silver, some gold, and radiant gems of all sorts facetted in dazzling multitudes of colors and grandeur, craftsmanship worthy of the gods, arm bands and bracelets and necklaces piled onto shelves like rusty tools, almost absently, as if hurriedly tossed in. More small boxes shined, polished and decorated brighter than Hávi had believed possible, some half-buried in mounds of untold wealth.

Hvítvi slid past her, bent, and lifted the lid of a large chest which must have pressed against the door when it was closed, and inside it were more coins than Hávi had believed existed.

"This is it," Hvítvi whispered. "The wealth and power of clan Austmaðr, the secret of our family's rule; this is plunder from seventy years of viking, wealth from all over the southlands, taken by my grandsires. You must never speak of this, Hávi. Take what you need, and a few extra coins, bronze and copper, to give out as you wish, but don't be overly-generous. We mustn't let others suspect the true wealth of clan Austmaðr or we'll have to fight every day to keep it."

Hávi staggered; all this time, mere feet from her bed, locked behind doors that she'd thought held clothes and brooms, lay wealth worthy of Asgard ... *and she'd had no idea!* Almost dizzy, Hávi wondered if it were a dream, and then she struggled to recall some charm that would protect her from enchantment, but what charm could be greater than the piles of wealth only a key away?

> *"Freja by her mighty swans pulled,*
> *Frigg of whom are women ruled,*
> *Sygn, Gullivig, Gefion, Rind,*
> *Send your blessings to me find."*

Hvítvi reached into the chest of coins, grabbed up a fistful, and with one pale finger scraped back all of the gold and most of the silver, and then he lifted the whole handful to Hávi, who gasped and clutched at the priceless coins. Never had immense wealth touched her, let alone clinked between her grasping fingers. Hvítvi drew her back, then closed and relocked the door. With difficulty, Hávi tore her gaze from her precious prize and looked up into his pale face, his infinite pink eyes.

"Hávi ...," Hvítvi whispered, but whatever he meant to say, Hávi never heard it. Hvítvi suddenly turned and swept from her room.

The woodwright graciously accepted Hávi's payment. He showed her the chest; it was still rough but he'd been working on it, and then he and Hávi thanked each other. Hávi excused herself and then headed straight for Hrafna's tavern.

Hrafna cheered when Hávi entered his tavern, and the tableful of men that he'd been talking to stood up and bowed respectfully. Hrafna approached, smiling widely and wiping his hands on his long apron. Hávi waited for him to reach her and then asked to be seated, with Tryggvi and her guard, at the table right next to the men. Hrafna looked momentarily surprised, and then he bowed deeply.

"Mistress Austmaðr may have anything that she asks for!" Hrafna declared, and he escorted her toward the table.

Hávi smiled at all of the men and they repeated their bows; Hávi recognized several of them but couldn't remember their names.

"Hrafna, I know that I've met these good men of Skadi before, but I'd be honored if you'd introduce us again."

"Gladly!" Hrafna said, and despite the look of surprise on their faces, Hrafna named each man and each head bowed deeply and fumbled a greeting, trying to sound courtly, failing entirely. Several were farmers, one a cobbler, two shepherds, and one a hunter.

"Moose, mostly," the hunter answered Hávi's question. "Elk, when I can get it."

"Elk's very dangerous prey," Hávi said to him.

"That's why their meat and hides are worth so much, begging your pardon," the hunter bowed.

With the farmers, Hávi talked about the early warm weather and prospects for a mid-summer harvest, which would mean two harvests in one season, a rare but priceless treat for a glacier-capped land where the growing season was short. While she talked, Hrafna fetched hot biscuits and honey, a bottle of wine, and a small plate of kryddost, a hard cheese spiced with caraway and cloves. Hávi had never tried kryddost before but insisted on eating a biscuit smothered in honey while it was still hot, and she ordered Tryggvi and her guard to try one as well.

Hávi kept one eye on her guard; she'd never seen this one before. She'd sent Tryggvi to ask Master Krókr to appoint a guard for her today, rather than asking Hvítvi, to insure that Mjóvi and Master Krókr got a full report. This guard was young, short, with long blonde hair that fell across his shoulders. He looked very nervous, slightly grim-faced, as if trying to appear sterner than his years merited. Hávi smiled at the farmers as she spoke to them but watched her guard out of the corners of her eyes.

Hávi asked the cobbler many questions and then promised to visit his shop and get measured for a new pair of shoes when Brækir and Blönduhorn arrived through the front door. Brækir carried a large sack of grain on each shoulder and Blönduhorn was carting a small but obviously heavy keg in both arms, and the men jumped to assist them.

The kryddost was so sharp that Hávi smacked her lips after her first taste.

"Brækir," Hávi said, "do you realize that, in all the time I've been here, I've never met any of your children except

Blönduhorn? I'd truly like to meet the others."

Brækir startled at her request, then sent Blönduhorn to fetch her brothers and sisters.

"They're not all mine," Brækir said. "Blönduhorn and her brothers are my sister's brood, but she passed away when her youngest was only a baby."

Soon all of the children had climbed excitedly through the trapdoor and down the ladder, then were forced to stand in a line. Blönduhorn was the eldest of six children, her brothers nine and ten. Brækir's two girls were six and four, and her son was barely two years old. Blönduhorn and her brothers had the same straight hair, both boys a darker blonde than Blönduhorn, while Brækir's children had inherited her once reddish-brown bushy locks.

Valla and Augi the older boys were named, and Hávi studied them carefully.

"Valla, has your father taught you any skills?" Hávi asked.

"I can press apples!" Valla said cheerfully.

"No, you can't!" Augi argued. "He can't turn the crank ...!"

"Yes, I can!" Valla shouted, and only Hrafna's swift buffets on their heads silenced them.

Hávi waited patiently until the boys stopped glaring at each other. She took a deep breath; *until now she could back out, but the time had come.* Hávi motioned the children back and then stood and faced her hosts.

"Hrafna, Brækir, I've been thinking very carefully about something, something that I must ask you, and something that you must feel free to refuse," Hávi said. "I need you to be honest with me, for what I'm about to ask you will be a request that even a close relative would hesitate to ask."

Hrafna and Brækir paled and the other men looked equally surprised.

"Mistress ... Austmaðr ...," Hrafna stammered.

Hávi held up a hand to silence him and then continued.

"As Mistress Austmaðr, it's my duty to see that my husband's needs are met. Wise advisors are always in great demand, but all of the best jarls are wizened; they won't be with us years from now. What I need are able, young boys to be trained from their youth, educated, so that the Skåne will never lack for knowledge of the den Skaanske Lov."

Brækir gasped and Hrafna looked upon her with disbelieving eyes. Everyone seemed stunned.

"I'll compensate you, of course, in silver," Hávi promised. "I know that this is a lot to ask, but I wish to insure that the knowledge of the jarls is passed down so that Jarl Austmaðr will always have wise Law-speakers to serve him."

"Do ... do you jest, Mistress?" Hrafna stammered. "You're asking ...?"

"For your oldest boys," Hávi said. "I'll arrange for lessons with one of the jarls; they'll become his apprentices ..."

"But, Mistress!" Hrafna argued. *"My family's simple taverners!"*

Hávi slowly smiled.

"Not anymore," Hávi said firmly. "Your sons will be Law-speakers."

Tryggvi stared at Hávi all the way back to Castle Austmaðr. Hávi kept smiling; all that was needed to make it work was Jarl Illingr.

Once inside Castle Austmaðr, Hávi thanked her nervous young guard, who hurried off. Hávi was sure that he'd run straight to Master Krókr and soon everyone in the castle would know what she'd done in town, as the whole town would hear; Hávi had made sure that her offer was witnessed.

"Tryggvi, I need you to do a favor for me," Hávi said. "I need you to take a message to Jarl Illingr."

Tryggvi's mouth fell open in surprise.

"Yes, Jarl Illingr," Hávi said pointedly, but she lowered her voice to a whisper. "Don't sneak up to his tower; I'm giving you a direct order and I intend for everyone to know about it. Tell Jarl Illingr that ... I would be delighted ... if he'd join me tonight, at the high-table, for dinner."

Dressed in one of her finest gowns, a bright yellow apron over a golden skirt, her long, wavy blonde hair brushed to perfection so that she almost glowed, Hávi entered the great hall early, thanked Tryggvi for her service, and then ascended the dais and slid all the way to the center chair. She sat down gracefully, calm and content, while the startled serving girls hurried to tell the cook that Mistress Austmaðr had arrived for dinner. They rushed out a glass of wine and some ginger rolls for Hávi, who asked them to provide some wine for Tryggvi, who sat alone at the women's table.

Soon most of Castle Austmaðr arrived, bustling into the great hall, many still fastening broaches and buckles, all curiously staring up at Hávi, who sat patiently alone until the elders joined her. A bard asked Hávi if he could perform for her, but she politely requested that he wait until after dinner, as she had important business to discuss. The bard bowed without complaint and sat at the closest table, straining his ears to hear every word.

Mjóvi arrived, her thin eyes warily observing everything, but she said nothing, just sat at the far end of the high-table where she usually sat. Master Krókr arrived moments later and he sat at the front table beside the bard, his frown deep and rigid, his eyes darting darkly about; Hávi pretended not to notice.

Hvítvi entered the hall, his blue jacket trimmed with white fur, unusually warm for this time of year. Hávi's breath caught; she'd forgotten about Hvítvi and wondered what he'd say. Clan Austmaðr could use two boys trained to advise, but Hvítvi could thwart all of her plans. Hvítvi casually ascended the dais and slid behind the seated elders and took the empty center chair beside Hávi, as he always did, but this time Hávi smiled brightly at him.

"Stepson, I have a surprise for you."

"Indeed?" Hvítvi smiled.

"Yes, but I must beg an indulgence," Hávi said. "There's another who must arrive before I can reveal it."

Hvítvi stared curiously but Hávi gave him a knowing smile.

"As you wish," Hvítvi said.

Jarl Illingr entered the great hall as always, his austere gray robe matching his long beard and remaining hair, but this time the whispers ceased instantly and a noticeable silence filled the hall. Jarl Illingr glanced suspiciously about, and then slowly ascended the dais to sit opposite his wife.

"Jarl Illingr," Hávi called softly, not having to raise her voice to be heard. "Jarl Illingr, would you come and sit beside Jarl Hvítvi tonight? Your wisdom is needed."

Frozen, one hand holding the chair at the farthest end of the table, Jarl Illingr paused, as if considering refusing, and then he reluctantly approached the center of the high-table, the elders scooting in their chairs to allow him to pass behind them. Jarl Illingr said nothing, just stepped up behind the empty chair beside Jarl Hvítvi and bowed slightly. Jarl Illingr's eyes briefly flashed from Hvítvi to Hávi, and then he sat in his chair.

"Thank you for joining us," Hávi said to Jarl Illingr,

carefully speaking loud enough to be clearly heard. "I've been thinking of things that I could do for my husband, devising gifts to present him with upon his return. Among the gifts that I would give him are two new servants, boys that I've purchased just this afternoon. These boys will be more than servants, not by the time Jarl Austmaðr returns, but by the time that they're grown men I hope that they'll be trained in the den Skaanske Lov, ready to serve my husband, and Sterki after him, for the good of clan Austmaðr. What I need now is a learned teacher for these boys."

Gasps followed this pronouncement, and though no one spoke loudly, whispers filled the hall.

"I will, at first, attend their lessons myself," Hávi said. "I need to judge if these boys are worthy of such teachings."

Jarl Illingr smiled, a smile that both she and Hvítvi clearly understood; Hávi would be attending all of the lessons. The boys were an excuse for her to be able to hear Jarl Illingr's teachings herself, and the whole castle could eavesdrop on her lessons and never suspect a thing.

"A most sensible precaution," Jarl Illingr said, nodding deeply, his eyes crinkled, "to insure that my wisdom does not die with me."

Hávi smiled; she'd done it, arranged to have regular lessons in law right in front of everyone, and no one could object. She glanced at Hvítvi, who was smiling; *this must be the way that he thinks.*

Chapter 17

"We know all about the law!" Valla jumped up and shouted, interrupting Jarl Illingr's first sentence.

"Valla, be quiet!" Hávi ordered, and Valla sat back down with youthful indignation while Augi poked him with a finger. Both boys were amazed by the colorful decorations of the audience room, and it'd taken some effort to make them sit still and pay attention. No point in telling them that they were being watched; both were too young to understand.

"Really?" Jarl Illingr asked Valla, staring into his innocent, piercing blue eyes. "What do you know about the law?"

"Law Rock!" Valla said proudly.

Jarl Illingr raised a wiry eyebrow. "What about Law Rock?"

"That's where the laws are made!" Valla said.

"Valla got in trouble for climbing Law Rock!" Augi added.

"Be silent!" Jarl Illingr shouted at both of them, his voice deepened by an anger that Hávi knew was only for the boy's benefit. "Don't speak again! You're fools and infants! One more word and I'll beat you both!"

Valla and Augi cowered as Jarl Illingr came toward them, one hand raised to slap, as if daring either boy to speak, his wrinkled face taut with fury, but Jarl Illingr's hand never fell. He held it raised for long, threatening moments, and then turned away.

"You will listen to me and do everything that I say," Jarl Illingr said. "You will not speak unless I ask a question. Do you understand?"

Both boys sat frozen save for involuntary shivers.

"Do you understand?" Jarl Illingr roared.

"Yes, sir!" they squeaked.

"Good," Jarl Illingr said. "Now, since you're both idiots, we'd best start with something simple: Law Rock. Every major town has one, and only one, Law Rock. Law Rock is identified by the runes carved into it, but laws aren't made at Law Rock. Accusations are made at Law Rock."

"You have to shout it three ...," Valla began, but he cut off as Jarl Illingr charged forward. This time Jarl Illingr's hand flew, but it was only a light buffet, mostly messing-up Valla's sandy-blonde hair.

"Be silent and listen!" Jarl Illingr shouted at Valla. "Law Rock is where legal accusations are made. Not anyone can make an accusation; women and children can't, and men can only make accusations that concern them. Where an accusation involves several men, only the oldest or the closest living adult male relative may make the accusation. If someone has the sole right to make an accusation, but is too afraid to voice it himself, then no accusation is made; the den Skaanske Lov makes no allowance for cowardice."

Jarl Illingr stopped and stared menacingly at both boys.

"Valla, who can't make accusations at Law Rock?" Jarl

Illingr asked.

Valla stared back, silent and terrified.

"Augi, what if someone is afraid to make an accusation at Law Rock?" Jarl Illingr asked, anger returning to his voice.

'Maybe this was a mistake', Hávi thought. Valla and Augi seemed nice enough, but they weren't the smartest boys. Would they be able to learn the den Skaanske Lov? Hávi frowned, *'Give them a chance; it's their first lesson'*. These lessons were really for her sake but it'd be nice if they could learn something. Jarl Austmaðr could use two young Law-speakers, and Hrafna and Brækir had been overjoyed at the prospect of having their sons taught the den Skaanske Lov. Still, as Jarl Illingr buffeted both young heads and started his speech again, the boys paid rapt attention and correctly answered his questions the second time.

"Very good," Jarl Illingr said. "I expect either of you to be able to repeat anything that I say during these lessons. I may ask you these same questions next week, or next year, and you'd better be able to answer them the same way. Do you understand?"

Both boys nodded their heads ardently.

"Now, accusations made at Law Rock have to be shouted loudly, clearly, and yes, three times, always in front of witnesses," Jarl Illingr said. "It has to be shouted three times so that each witness can memorize it and testify to the wording of the accusation at the next Thyngr. If someone is killed before they shout their accusation three times then the accusation wasn't legally made. However, an adult male next-of-kin, family elder, or clan-chief may afterwards make an accusation of murder against anyone who kills before Law Rock, which is considered an exceptionally-heinous crime. If an accusation is legally made, but its maker is killed before the

Thyngr, then any witness may bring forth the accusation to be deliberated by the council."

Jarl Illingr paused to ask each boy a question about what he'd just said, but each answered correctly, so he continued.

"Councils of a Thyngr are composed of leading men, usually ten, at least one clan-chief, a jarl, and the heads of prominent households; they judge the worth of each accusation. Councils deliberate upon their knowledge of the law, the testimony of all witnesses, and the reputations of those involved. Councils don't determine if the accusation was valid or not, only if it was validly made, and the circumstances of the case. That's an important point; councils don't determine innocence or guilt. People involved in a dispute have the matter arbitrated; sometimes one man pays the financial costs, not necessarily the plaintive, and sometimes costs are assigned to each, and fees are taken from every payment. A falsely-accused man may be rewarded handsomely from the possessions of their accuser, and the council takes a portion of each reward. Decisions of a Thyngr council may not be challenged at a Thyngr.

"At a Thyngr, the accuser, the accused, and any council member may call forth witnesses to give testimony, and Law-speakers whose expertise supports their case. Blood may not be spilt at a Thyngr; anyone legally accused of murder at a Thyngr faces the harshest punishments. A punishment, money, goods, livestock, land, or outlawry will be pronounced for every accusation.

"Outlawry is the worst punishment that a Thyngr council may grant. Outlawry deprives a person, man or woman, of legal existence. Stealing from a person who is outlawed is legal since a nonexistent person can't own possessions. Killing an outlawed person isn't murder; no relative can accuse someone of murdering a person who doesn't legally exist. Outlawed men may be tortured, outlawed women raped, and not even their fathers or clan-chiefs may accuse anyone for it without having to pay a hefty fine. No one may buy their way out of outlawry. Once outlawed, a person's only hope is to flee before they're captured or killed. Outlawry is given with a time period; killing a stranger is usually three years, killing a clan-member is usually seven years, and killing a relative is usually life."

'What would happen', Hávi thought, *'to the rape-seeded child of an outlawed woman? Would the child also be outlawed?'* But Hávi couldn't ask; she wasn't supposed to be learning law. *This arrangement wasn't as good as she'd hoped.*

Hávi sat impatiently while Jarl Illingr questioned both boys on what he'd just said, and then vehemently corrected their stammered, hesitant replies, always with the threat of a beating.

"But what if someone can't pay ...," Valla began, but he fell instantly silent as Jarl Illingr turned to him. But Jarl Illingr didn't hit; he regarded him coldly.

"Ask your question," Jarl Illingr commanded.

"W-what if someone c-can't pay the judgment of the ... um, uh, ..."

"What if someone can't pay the judgment of the council of a Thyngr?" Jarl Illingr finished. "A good question. If a fine can't be paid then the payer is outlawed, usually for one year. For a stranger or vagabond, that gives them sufficient reason to flee and never return. For a resident, their family or a friend may pay the fine for them, but then they are debt-bondaged to that person for whatever duration they agreed upon before payment was made. Some payments are delayed a year to give respective parties time to raise the sum, but all payments must be made. Accusations of failure to pay are commonly heard at Law Rock."

Hávi smiled; perhaps this arrangement would work, but she'd have to find a way to have her own questions answered. After another round of questions, making sure that the boys understood what he was saying, Jarl Illingr began reciting the same speech that he'd given Hávi, about how Swedish laws derived from Roman law, about the Tynwald, their highest council, and their loose system of law-making and administration, and how all decisions of a Thyngr could only be challenged at a Tynwald. He didn't describe the rights of women or how existing laws could be challenged; Valla and Augi had no reason to learn about the limited rights of women first.

The lesson lasted all day. Finally Tryggvi arrived to take Hávi to wash and dress for dinner, and Jarl Illingr quickly concluded the day's lessons. Hávi sent Valla and Augi back home after insuring that they'd return tomorrow to learn more of the den Skaanske Lov. Both boys repeatedly bowed and thanked Jarl Illingr, who mentioned a few ugly, arduous chores that they'd be doing if they failed to remember everything that he'd said today; Valla and Augi fled in terror.

All through dinner, questions riled Hávi. What if a wealthy man, even a clan-chief, was outlawed? Who could claim their lands and livestock, their ships, their villages and people? What would become of their wives and children? If an outlawed man was the head of a household, and he fled, then could anyone claim his house and throw out his wife and children? Since he hadn't died no one could inherit; could a title like head of household be transferred by means other than death? The more that she thought about it the more questions arose. Not asking questions would take her years longer to learn even the rudiments of law, but if she'd asked questions then everyone would know that the lessons were really for her. Valla and Augi might be good Law-speakers in ten years, but Hávi wasn't willing to wait.

Servants set steaming kalops and köttbullar, Hávi's favorite foods, before her. As the minstrels played and the elders around her gossiped and argued amongst themselves, Hávi regretted that Hvítvi wasn't there and hoped that he wasn't sick as she eagerly spooned the hot dishes onto her plate. Everything was finally starting to work out right.

She lifted her first hearty spoonful of stew into her mouth, then suddenly she choked, gagged, and coughed, spewing kalops all over the table. The mistral hesitated, then continued, uselessly trying to distract the hall, but the elders startled and rushed to help.

"It's the kalops!" Hávi exclaimed. *"There's something ... terrible in it!"*

The elders all glanced at each other, and then one man picked up a spoon and scooped some kalops off Hávi's plate, sniffed it, and then cautiously tasted it, just a bit. He paused, considered, and then shrugged his shoulders.

"It tastes fine."

"No!" Hávi insisted. "It's foul, bitter, like a ... it smells awful!"

"It's the baby," said an old serving woman. "The baby doesn't like kalops."

"What?"

"My second-born didn't like fish, any fish," the old woman explained. "I loved fish, especially salmon, but while he was inside me, all fish tasted like dirt in my mouth. Don't worry;

this'll pass after you birth ..."

"No more kalops?"

"Not a bite," said the old woman. "Babies can be very obstinate."

Carefully Hávi tasted the baked köttbullar before she risked a mouthful. The tiny meatballs stuffed with grated onions and rusk crumbs, layered in rich gravy, were delicious, and the lingonberries tasted as sweet as ever. But the bowl of steaming kalops, which one of the elders had moved several places down the table, taunted her. *Of all foods to dislike, why did her baby have to hate kalops?*

After eating, Hávi sat impatiently, watching from afar. The dishes now being carried to the women's tables looked as steamy as the ones that had been placed on the high-table almost an hour before; a long wait but their food was hot. When the women started eating, Hávi politely excused herself. She hurried back up to the room under hers and stole another servant's gown, this time checking to make sure that it fit. Then she slipped upstairs and hid the gown where Tryggvi wouldn't find it.

Legal questions kept mounting in her mind. Could a man defend his wife if she were outlawed? If a person was outlawed for a year, then returned home, could he reclaim his house if someone else had claimed it? When a wealthy person is outlawed, is there a mad rush to see who can steal his property first? Could a woman legally claim his possessions?

Long after Tryggvi had washed and put her to bed, Hávi slipped out from under her warm quilt, pulled on the stolen green servant's dress, and quietly opened her door.

Hávi crept up the spiraling wooden steps to the trapdoor.

Jarl Illingr was sitting at his desk in his big chair, wrapped in a blanket, his head slumped back, snoring loudly.

"Jarl Illingr ...?"

Jarl Illingr awoke with a start, wild-eyed, and his hand fumbled for a small knife on his desk.

"No! It's me!" Hávi said.

Jarl Illingr took a moment to identify her, and then he calmed himself.

"What do you want now?"

"I'm sorry for waking you," Hávi said. "I have some questions ..."

Jarl Illingr yawned loudly and wearily flexed his aged bones, then pulled his blanket tighter around his shoulders. Hávi stepped up into his tower.

"Where did you find those boys?" Jarl Illingr asked, still yawning. "It'd be easier to teach goats ...!"

"They're the sons of some friends of mine, a tavern master in Skadi ..."

"Ah, a tavern! How long it's been ...!"

"You drink wine at dinner ..."

"Drinking in the feast hall isn't the same as going to a tavern," Jarl Illingr said. "In a castle, the real drunks are thrown out, never get in, or have to stay in their rooms. Everyone's so formal and cautious that I never hear anything worthwhile. A tavern's different; hang around a tavern long enough and some idiot with more beer than brains will blab everything that he knows to anyone who'll listen. When I was clan-chief, I frequented every tavern in my villages just so that I knew everything that was going on."

"This tavern's not like that," Hávi said. "They're always respectful and ..."

"They're respectful because you're Mistress Austmaðr,"

Jarl Illingr said. "I'd get that treatment, too, if I walked in while the sun was up. But I always dressed in a ragged cloak, pulled my hood low over my face, and snuck in behind a group of farmers late at night. Then I'd order a jug of wine, wait for the drunks to beg for a mouthful, and soon they'd all be crowded around me, swapping gossip and laughing at my jokes. I had to appear stingy but I always let them drink as much as they wanted: the more that they drank the more they talked. I can't tell you how many feuds, which would've been exorbitantly costly, I stopped by hearing about them before they escalated. And the things that they said about me! I've sat hooded and listened to peasants berate my whole family. You'd be astounded by what people say behind your back."

Hávi had trouble believing that Hrafna would ever say anything unkind about her, yet she'd never know; Hávi could sneak out of her room late at night, but sneaking out of the castle was impossible.

"Jarl, about your lesson today, I was just wondering ...," Hávi said hesitantly, and then she began describing all her questions.

"Enough!" Jarl Illingr eventually stopped her. "Hávi, the law deals with all of this. A stranger can't just run up and claim the house of an outlawed man; the outlawed man belonged to a clan, and his clan-chief decides who gets it. Two clan-chiefs won't fight over a cattle-ranch; the cost of the men that would die would be worth three ranches. A Thyngr would arbitrate: one would get the ranch, the other the cattle. Even if it's something like a captured ship, arbitration occurs. Anybody can steal an outlawed man's sword, or clothes, but you've got to get them off of him first, and he may not give them up freely. When someone's outlawed, inheritance laws are used just as if they'd died, so wives can inherit, if they have no sons of age. Children born of rape are stepsons, legally below any child of an honest marriage, but children are never outlawed. Older children may be sold into the servitude of their clan-chief, but all are eventually freed.

"To be a jarl, you have to know these laws, but you're not trying to be a jarl," Jarl Illingr said plainly, almost plaintively. "You need to know how to affect change, gather support, and influence council members before they deliberate your issues. That's the hardest part of being a jarl, the politicking and leveraging of compromises, not just recalling precedents, but forcing others to acknowledge a precedent's worth. You can hire Law-speakers for trivial matters."

Hávi stared at Jarl Illingr, his worn, aged face, his wrinkles flickering as the candle-flame danced: he knew what she needed more than she did. Slowly Hávi smiled; *with his teachings, giving women the right to refuse an unwanted marriage will be easy!*

Jarl Illingr smiled back, his half-ear-to-half-ear grin warm and fatherly. Hávi recalled Jorgun, her father; tall, proud, and honest. Jorgun would've liked Jarl Illingr.

"Thank you," Hávi said.

"Thank you," Jarl Illingr returned.

"Why thank me?"

"A king who's lost everything is still a man," Jarl Illingr said. "I've spent the last two years rereading old scrolls; captured, trapped, forced to marry an unbearable termagant, I've been vainly gnawing at evil plots to recapture what your husband slew. Teaching has given me a new purpose, and even if Valla and Augi have heads like rocks, I'll drive the den Skaanske Lov into them. Perhaps, if taught right, they'll see to it that what happened to me never happens again. If not for you, I'd still be hopelessly trying to recreate a dead dream."

"I felt that way when I first came to Castle Austmaðr," Hávi said. "Forced into a loveless marriage ... convinced that my life was over ..."

"I had two granddaughters," Jarl Illingr said slowly, and tiny tears softened his eyes. "I'd like ... to think that ... if they'd lived ... they'd have grown up like you."

Gracefully Hávi spread her arms wide, stepped back, and performed a perfect curtsy. Jarl Illingr smiled and nodded respectfully, but then his smile failed. His jaw tightened and his face paled ashen-white; he motioned for Hávi to remain still, listening intently, and suddenly Hávi heard it, too.

Footsteps! Tramping up spiral stairs came the unmistakable clomps of many hurried boots. Hávi stared at Jarl Illingr: *they were trapped!*

"Hide me!" Hávi hissed.

"Where?" Jarl Illingr demanded, motioning to his tiny circular room. "There's nowhere to hide in a tower!"

"I can't be found here!" Hávi said.

"It's too late!"

"Seal the trapdoor!"

"No!" Jarl Illingr insisted. "That won't hold them for long. We're trapped, and for your sake, we're better off letting them march right in."

"Hvítvi'll kill me!" Hávi said.

"No," Jarl Illingr said coldly. "Hvítvi ... will kill me."

Hávi froze as his words penetrated her panic. Jarl Illingr was right: they wouldn't kill any woman bearing Jarl Austmaðr's son, *but Jarl Illingr ...!*

"No!" Hávi shouted. "I won't let ...!"

The trapdoor burst upwards and crashed against the stone wall. Two guards with sharp pikes poked their heads up into the tower room. Beside them stood tall Master Krókr, his aged face glowering, and Mjóvi, her wicked smile triumphant.

"What's going on up here?" Master Krókr demanded gruffly, his booming voice disturbing the quiet night. "Hávi Austmaðr, what are you doing up here in the middle of the night?"

"Conspiring!" Mjóvi shouted. "Hávi Austmaðr closeted with her husband's mortal enemy!"

Pushing aside the guards, fat Master Krókr and skinny Mjóvi stepped up into the tiny room. Four more guards and two servants poked their heads up through the trapdoor, unable to ascend into the crowded castle tower. Below them, other people seemed to be hissing and whispering.

"Well?" Master Krókr demanded. "Explain yourselves!"

"Disgrace!" Mjóvi shouted. "Disgrace upon our whole clan!"

"No!" Hávi shouted, but Jarl Illingr cleared his throat loudly, as if preparing to say something, and Hávi fell silent.

Jarl Illingr inhaled deeply, then slowly stood up as if preparing to make a speech. He motioned Hávi aside and she backed up against his desk.

"I am a jarl," Jarl Illingr said loudly, clearly enough that his voice traveled to everyone on the steps. "I do not answer to servants."

Gasps and whispers met this pronouncement, but neither Master Krókr nor Mjóvi flinched.

"Fine!" Master Krókr snarled. "Then we'll do it in public!" Master Krókr turned to one of the guards. "Go awaken Master Hvítvi. Tell him that Mistress Austmaðr has betrayed him!"

Angrily Hávi started to shout, but Jarl Illingr waved her silent, his cold eyes full of warning.

"Yes, tell him that," Jarl Illingr agreed, again loud and clear. "Let's get all of the lies spoken before we denounce them."

The guard hesitated, then his head slipped below the trapdoor, and grunts and complaints chorused as he pushed past others on the narrow spiral stairs. Hávi stared, horrified; *what would Hvítvi do? He'd warned her against starting a scandal!* She glanced at Mjóvi, who looked as smug as a hungry cat with a fat mouse trapped in her fangs.

"Come," Master Krókr ordered. "We'll discuss this in the Hall of Audience."

"No," Jarl Illingr said.

"Don't test my patience!" Master Krókr growled. "I'll ...!"

"You'll forcibly drag a jarl and Jarl Austmaðr's wife down three flights of stairs?" Jarl Illingr asked. "No, I don't think you will. Mistress Austmaðr and I are quite comfortable. If Master Hvítvi wishes it, then we'll meet him anywhere he chooses."

"You'll be killed for this," Master Krókr seethed.

"That choice, as well, won't be yours."

"How dare you?" Mjóvi hissed at Hávi. *"You've disgraced us all!"*

Hávi opened her mouth, uncertain what she was going to say, when Jarl Illingr interrupted her.

"Say nothing," Jarl Illingr advised.

Yet Hávi was sick of being abused, upbraided, downtrodden, spied upon, and plotted against.

" Your honor's as barren as your womb!"

Hávi's insult sang out clear and loud. Not a sound emanated from the startled, suddenly-silent crowd gathered below. Mjóvi's smile vanished; Hávi's insult would be the gossip of the Skåne. But Mjóvi's eyes narrowed; she'd caught

Hávi with her own husband alone up in his tower in the middle of the night.

"You're not one to speak of honor!" Master Krókr interjected, trying to intercede.

"Really?" Jarl Illingr asked. "Who are you to dishonor the wife of your master?"

"You dishonored her!" Master Krókr shouted.

"By talking to her?" Jarl Illingr asked. "By answering her foolish questions ... about rights for women?"

After many stunned, audible gasps, the sounds of fierce whispering and shuffling on the steps below them returned, and even the guards whose heads poked up through the trapdoor began whispering.

"Be silent!" Master Krókr shouted at them.

Jarl Illingr smiled and slowly sat back down in his chair. Hávi remained standing beside him, leaning against his desk. Master Krókr and Mjóvi glared at both of them, but not another word was spoken.

Footsteps approached; someone was rapidly climbing the stairs. *Hvítvi?* No, the hard stomps didn't sound like a brittle-boned albino who wore mostly slippers. The men on the steps squeezed together, and then a tall, youthful guard with long, thick brown hair and a comically-bushy mustache climbed up into the crowded tower: *Bíldr.*

"Master Hvítvi doesn't wish to be disturbed tonight," Bíldr announced. "He'll deal with this in the morning. I'm to escort Mistress Hávi to her room. The rest of you can go back to bed."

"But ...!" Master Krókr began.

"As Master Hvítvi commands, we must obey!" Jarl Illingr interrupted Master Krókr, but then he faced the tall seneschal. "Unless Master Krókr commands that we ignore

Master Hvítvi's rightful stewardship of Castle Austmaðr ...?"

Everyone looked expectantly at Master Krókr, but all knew that he couldn't denounce his master. Bíldr instantly pushed his way back though the trapdoor, holding out a hand behind him to assist Hávi.

Hávi tried to thank Bíldr on her doorstep, but he forcefully closed her door without a word, and then she heard his weight lean against her door from the other side; *she was locked in.* Hávi bowed her head; she couldn't blame Bíldr. Despite dire warnings, she'd been caught: *she'd undone everything.*

Chapter 18

"How stupid are you?" asked a smooth yet disgusted voice.

White as ever, Hvítvi was sitting on her bed, one hand leaning against a carven horse-head bedpost. A fearful charm chanted in her head.

> *'Dark-elves, gnomes, wicked trolls,*
> *Nidhogg's fangs and Garm's growl,*
> *Tricksy giants, dwarves, Black Surt,*
> *Summon back your spirits of hurt.'*

"I'm sorry," Hávi said.

"Sorry?" Hvítvi demanded. "You've insulted Father and all of clan Austmaðr! Mjóvi and Krókr will see to it that every clan in the Skåne hears about this!"

Hávi's cheeks flushed; she loved Hvítvi's voice, always so calm and controlled. Now a shrillness, an exasperated fury, seethed behind his urbane facade.

"I ...!" Hávi started, but she had nothing to say, no words

271

that could undo.

"Tell me everything," Hvítvi said. "Leave nothing out. A man's life depends on your words."

"It's my fault," Hávi said.

"That's obvious."

Hávi flinched from his rebuke but forced herself to go on, carefully choosing each phrase; one wrong word would doom Jarl Illingr.

"I had ... some questions, legal questions, from ... from the meeting ... the lesson that I'd arranged ..."

"With Valla and Augi," Hvítvi sneered. "Now they'll suffer for this, too."

"Oh, no! Please ...!"

"Continue with your tale."

"I ... I couldn't ask Jarl Illingr openly, so I ... went to see him ..."

"Alone, after I warned you not to?" Hvítvi demanded, his voice rising alarmingly. *"After I arranged for you to learn law in the open?"*

"You told me not to take Tryggvi ...!"

"I told you not to go at all!"

Hvítvi winced and leaned heavily upon a wooden horse-head, as if he'd collapse without its support. Hávi wanted to rush toward him, but the trouble that she'd caused already was worse than any physical pain.

"Jarl Illingr must die."

"No!"

"You want me to spare him?" Hvítvi breathlessly asked. "You'd condemn him ... to Father's retribution?"

"Retribution?"

"Torture."

"Jarl Austmaðr wouldn't ...!"

"*What do you think happened to Jarl Illingr's ears?*"
Hvítvi shouted. "A red-hot knife, pulled from the fire, cut off
both of his ear-tips. I watched Father do it; I couldn't eat for
days. What do you think he'll do when he gets home and
hears rumors that he's been cuckold by his oldest enemy ... in
his own castle? Father will have to kill Jarl Illingr by inches ...
or he'll be disgraced ... again!"

"*I'm ... sorry!*"

"So am I," Hvítvi said, and he deepened his voice to his
most imperious tone. "Mistress Austmaðr, you will remain in
your private chambers until Jarl Austmaðr returns."

Hávi gasped; *Hvítvi was confining her to her room for
months!* But what could she say? No excuse would justify
her crime.

With a deep breath, Hvítvi rose from her bed. He stared
at Hávi, his pale lips taut, and then he lowered his head and
swept past her.

"What about Jarl Illingr?" Hávi asked.

Hvítvi paused at the door.

"You decide," Hvítvi said. "I can give him a clean death
now or imprison him in the dungeon. *Think well on this!*
Once Father returns, you may wish that you'd killed him
while you could."

Hávi staggered: Jarl Illingr's life ... *in her hands?*
Immediate execution ... or months of imprisonment awaiting
unbearable agonies? A slow, extortionate torment, induced
excruciation beyond the value of living ... *or death?*

Hvítvi hesitated only a second; hearing no reply, he
departed.

Hávi flung herself onto her bed, weeping and wailing
unabashedly. Several times she cried out, heedless of who
might hear. She screamed and thrashed, beating her fists

against her precious warm quilt, the only thing left in clan Austmaðr that could give her any comfort. *Hersir!* Hávi prayed, wishing again that she could go home, but now she couldn't even leave her room. As Mjóvi had hoped, Hávi was now a prisoner; no more wandering the castle, needlepoint in the sewing room, or helping in the kitchen, never seeing her stepdaughters in the nursery, not even visiting Hrafna's tavern; no more västerbotten. *No more Jarl Illingr.*

"*Mistress?*" Tryggvi's voice, right beside her bed.

Hávi couldn't find the strength to lift her head. Finally she glanced at her only friend, her timid, cherub-faced handmaiden whose tear-streaked face matched her own; *the story had already spread throughout the castle.*

Hávi collapsed; she didn't deserve to be comforted, but she didn't have the heart to send Tryggvi away.

A strange clacking noise awoke Hávi, who couldn't recall falling asleep. Sunlight was brightening her shuttered windows but the strange noise seemed to be coming from the fireplace. Hávi glanced over; the fire had died. Tryggvi was cuddled on the carpet before the hearth wearing only her green-gray servant's dress, no blanket, shivering. Her teeth were loudly chattering.

"*Tryggvi!*" Hávi cried out, and she jumped from her bed and pulled off her warm white quilt, quickly wrapping it over Tryggvi's trembling body. Tryggvi awoke with a start and cried out as Hávi lifted her onto the bed. Hávi jumped in beside her, pulled the quilt tight around both of them and held Tryggvi until her teeth stopped clicking. Then Hávi tucked the quilt tight about Tryggvi and masterfully repiled the charred logs, wedged kindling into the crevices, and then she ran into her outer-chamber seeking a candle. As no lights showed, she grabbed a candle and pulled open her door; Bíldr was standing outside of it. He glanced questioningly at her.

"I need a light," Hávi said, and she held out her candle.

Bíldr silently took the candle, lit it from a sputtering wall sconce, and then returned it to her. Hávi stared at his youthful, mustached face.

"Are you here to keep me inside?"

Bíldr nodded.

"Can you tell me what's happening?"

Bíldr shook his head.

"Are ... are you allowed to talk to me?"

Again, Bíldr shook his head. He reached out, grasped her door ring, and Hávi was forced inside as he firmly closed her door.

After stoking the fire high, Hávi cared for Tryggvi until she was well enough to be scolded, but even then she barked very little; Tryggvi looked feebler than ever, as if a harsh word would crush her. Hávi didn't feel much better. The dry wood popped and crackled and soon the room grew very warm. Tryggvi pushed back the quilt, almost sweating under it.

"Now what?" Hávi asked.

Tryggvi glanced up at her.

"What ... do you mean?"

"I mean, now what do we do?"

"We?" Tryggvi questioned. "I should go downstairs and get your breakfast."

"I guess ... what I mean is, what should I do?"

Tryggvi frowned.

"Begging your pardon, Mistress, but I warned you: *'You're going to get your hands burned'.*"

"Hvítvi won't ever let me out, will he?"

"His job's to keep the Skåne from falling apart until Jarl Austmaðr returns. If he lets you out then people will question his right to rule. Master Hvítvi can't afford a revolt; he can't even lift a sword."

"So ... I'm a prisoner until Jarl Austmaðr returns?"

"Yes, Mistress."

"Hávi."

"Yes, Hávi."

Hávi's first day of captivity was self-made miserable. She kept running endless scenarios through her mind, blaming Mjóvi, Master Krókr, and even Jarl Austmaðr for not banishing everyone like them long ago. She even blamed Hvítvi, although guiltily, for caring more about gossip than her.

Of everyone that she'd met since coming to Skadi, Hvítvi confused her the most. Sometimes he seemed friendly, other times oddly distant. Master Kamban and Hvassi seemed the same: they understood the politics of Castle Austmaðr; Hávi should've enlisted their help; *wasn't that what Jarl Illingr had instructed her to do?*

The glow of her shuttered window failed as the unseen sky darkened. Hávi sat with Tryggvi, who'd brought up a baked chicken and some small cinnamon cakes, but the food sat cold and uneaten. Only the wine bottle was empty; Tryggvi had opened a second bottle to refill their glasses. In silence, they glared at everything, gnawing at the chewed ends of arguments and excuses that were all pointless. Their few attempts at conversation had dismally failed, and they even tried sitting in the windowless outer-room, admiring the shelves of scrolls that neither girl could read, and the maps that they didn't understand. Hávi had never seen much use in her outer-room; from it they carried two large chairs back into the bedroom and set the chairs before their fire.

Three days later, the boredom grew intolerable. Hávi kept pacing back and forth, loudly threatening to defy Hvítvi and walk out, not only out of her door but out of Castle Austmaðr and all the way back to clan Hersir. Tryggvi tried to shush her but Hávi snapped at her so fiercely that Tryggvi burst into tears and soon Hávi was blubbering with her, apologizing while they wept.

On the fifth day, a loud knock hammered on their door. Both girls jumped up, Hávi brushing out the wrinkles in her dress while Tryggvi tried to straighten out Hávi's hair, which Hávi hadn't let her brush because no one was going to see them, but Hávi sent Tryggvi to answer the door while she prepared herself as best she could.

"Out," Hvítvi's voice floated in from the outer-doorway, and then he marched into her bedroom. Hávi began an elaborate curtsy but he gestured for her to stop. "Breiðr's had her baby."

"Really?" Hávi asked. "Can I ... go see ...?"

"You know better than to ask."

"How's Breiðr?"

"Breiðr's fine; happy, although she'd hoped that it'd be a son, "Hvítvi said. "Her daughter seems very healthy; she's crying so loudly that you can't converse in the same room. Breiðr sends her love but she's one of the few. Castle Austmaðr's never been this troubled."

"What's wrong?" Hávi asked.

"*Wrong?*" Hvítvi asked. "Everyone's angry. No one liked

Jarl Illingr. They think you betrayed Father."

"*I never ...!*"

"You think that matters?" Hvítvi asked, his voice hissing with disgust. "Do you think that Mjóvi and Krókr care whether or not you betrayed Father? They wish that you had; then they wouldn't have to spread lies."

"Why do you keep them around?"

"I can't let them go, "Hvítvi asked. "Have them killed, yes, imprisoned in the dungeon, yes, but free to cause mischief? They have their uses, and in the past they've performed services that no one else could manage, but they're costly ... and too dangerous to unleash. Father keeps them tightly tethered here where they have to continually prove their loyalty. Even killing them would prove costly; it'd deny our family their unique services."

"What services?" Hávi asked.

"Arranging secret meetings with wealthy members of rival clans. Gathering information other clan-chiefs are trying to keep secret. Marry Jarl Illingr. Nothing that you can talk about, but believe me: they earn their keep."

"So I have to stay here, locked in this room, alone, all summer?"

"Not alone," Hvítvi said. "Things have calmed down enough that I can let you have some visitors, but it was close. All of Skadi's calling for Jarl Illingr's blood."

"*What?*"

"Did you expect anything less? No one wants to believe that Jarl Illingr was just giving you lessons in law. Mjóvi's told everyone that no woman, not even Hávi the Betrayer ..."

"*The Betrayer?*"

"That's what they're calling you. The morning after your foolishness, Mjóvi went into Skadi and gave a speech before the stocks decrying you as a slut and a whore, claiming that you shamed all of clan Austmaðr. Krókr has servants riding across the countryside *'gathering reports'*, but they're really spreading gossip. Even Hrafna and Brækir are angry, although they blame it all on Jarl Illingr."

"Have you ever talked to Jarl Illingr?"

"Yes, several times."

"I mean before this! Last week! Last year!"

"Why would I? He's father's enemy!"

"He's been kinder to me than you have! He's been friendly and understanding, more than anyone else in the castle! He's risked his life to help me, to keep me company, and even you don't …!"

Hávi silenced abruptly. Hvítvi had turned glacial white, and for the first time, his eyes moistened as if he were about to cry. She reached him in two steps, but he turned away from her, yet Hávi wouldn't let him hide right in front of her; whatever Hvítvi's big secret was, she wanted to know. Hávi gripped his thin shoulder tightly; against his feeble resistance she turned him around to face her, determined to learn why he always acted so strangely, when suddenly their eyes met, nose to nose, a gaze that lasted an eternity. Both froze, stunned. Fear filled Hvítvi's pink eyes as he stared into hers, fear and … *something else.* Then Hávi realized it: *she understood.*

A look of pure terror paled his white to bloodless pink. Face to face they held each other, his trembling hand reaching up to touch her elbow, her arm, her shoulder. Hvítvi was no strange old man come to steal her honor against her will. Hvítvi was a year younger than her but older in ways that she'd never comprehended before coming to Skadi. He lifted his soft, white hand, brushed his long fingers into her blonde hair, twisted one of her obstinate curls, and then grimaced and tried to turn away. The urge to kiss him swelled. Hávi knew that she should let him go, let him leave and never come back. He was her stepson, her husband's youngest boy, and nothing could ever happen between them, but Hávi knew that if she let him go now then she'd never see him again. He'd lock himself in his room forever, and she couldn't bear that, no matter what. He pulled against her with all of his pitiful strength, but she held him with ease, torn between casting him away and pulling him into the tightest embrace that she'd ever given.

Finally he quit struggling, closed his eyes, and turned his head as far from hers as he could. Hávi slowly loosened her grip.

"Don't leave me," Hávi whispered.

Freed, Hvítvi walked straight out of her bedroom without a backward glance. She didn't hear another door open; Hvítvi was standing in her outer-room, probably composing himself before he opened the outer-door and exposed his tear-streaked face to Tryggvi and Bíldr. Hávi wanted to run to him, but what could she say? Hvítvi was already struggling against the scandal that she'd caused; she couldn't give Mjóvi another reason to believe that she'd betrayed her husband ... especially not for his weak albino son. But now Hávi understood why Hvítvi had always acted so strangely around her.

Hávi gasped, unsteady, and suddenly collapsed onto her carpet, her bedroom spinning. *No! Not this! Not now! She couldn't ...!*

A sudden pain punched her stomach. Hávi gasped and placed a hand protectively over her growing belly, feeling the swelling mound of the baby squirming inside her. Hvítvi's brother was growing inside her womb. She was married, bound by law and custom. That she'd been sold into a marriage that she'd never wanted didn't matter: *she couldn't love Hvítvi!*

Days passed in unbroken silence. Thoughts of Völu and Hlöðu, Hávi's two oldest confidants, kept returning, but they were far away, and Tryggvi's constant presence during the long, tedious hours needled her. Tryggvi frequently glowered at Hávi, who only responded to her questions with silent shakes of her head, and then wandered around her room only to open the window and stare out it dreamily, and then she shut it and lay on her bed. Hávi tried not to whimper. Tryggvi knew that Hávi was keeping secrets from her and had fallen to sullen brooding. She quit asking questions, which helped as Hávi couldn't think while being bombarded with endless inquisitive suppositions. Hávi's silence toward her best friend felt coldhearted, but a single answer would only lead to more questions, and once she started unraveling that tapestry there'd be no end to it.

Damn Hvítvi! He was intriguing, mysterious, and unique, different from every man that she'd ever met. His albino paleness and poor health were the least of his differences; he thought deeply, was cultured and polite, but also capable of dishonesties beyond anything that Hávi could fathom. Hávi recalled all of the warm, masculine voices that used to call from her dreams, her youthful girlish-fancies; suddenly all of those voices sounded like Hvítvi. Hávi buried her face in her lamb's fur pillow. *Damn Hvítvi!* He was everything that she'd ever wanted ... and could never have.

His milky face haunted her. Their one moment of understanding, his peculiar eyes so close to hers, his breath blending with hers, floated in Hávi's waking mind and tormented her dreams. Would she ever see him again? Would he hide forever in his own room just to keep from meeting her again? What could she do if she saw him in public: speak with uninterested indifference about the weather? Die inside while pretending not to notice?

Hávi awoke each morning bathed in sweat, still feeling his dreamy touch. Where her aged, hoary husband invaded, Hvítvi delved. Where her husband violated, Hvítvi spanned. Intimacy without revulsion, closeness without repulsion, invitation without rebuff; feelings and longings that she'd never known awoke, desires that denied every ounce of reason. *She was married! He was forbidden!*

Slowly, after over a week in turmoil, logic won. Hávi couldn't love Hvítvi; Mjóvi and Krókr would raise the Skåne against them. She glanced at the two locked doors across from her bed: if that wealth were ever stolen then clan Austmaðr would lose everything and clan Hersir would get caught up in a civil war; thousands would die.

Breiðr arrived right after breakfast with Hávi's new granddaughter. Infants always gladdened Hávi, who couldn't believe that one of these would soon come out of her. The infant squirmed and made faces and then it started to cry. Breiðr nursed it, and pointed out the sudden increase in the size of Hávi's breasts, which had been large since she was thirteen. Hávi blushed, Tryggvi laughed, and Breiðr's visit proved delightful. They discussed the myriad topics that only women could; Breiðr worried only that her husband wouldn't be pleased to have fathered a daughter, but Hávi assured Breiðr that she'd bear him a son next year.

Breiðr stayed through dinner, Tryggvi gladly carrying two

trays to bring up enough food and ale for all three of them. After Breiðr left, Hávi chided herself; she didn't have to be trapped alone.

"Tryggvi, will you do me a favor?" Hávi asked.

"Of course," Tryggvi replied, but then she cast a wary eye at Hávi.

"I'm tired of sitting in this room all day ..."

"Please don't ask me to help you leave!"

"No, no," Hávi said. "Would you tell Mistress Hvassi and Master Kamban that I'd like to continue my lessons with them?"

"Oh, gladly!" Tryggvi beamed. "More company will brighten your days. Anybody else?"

"Yes," Hávi said, thinking of every face that she missed, even the servants in the kitchen who'd been so friendly toward her. "Just spread the word that Hávi Austmaðr's happy to greet anyone who still wishes to be her friend. Oh, and do you know who I'd like to talk to? Blönduhorn: could you send a message to Hrafna's tavern to tell Blönduhorn that I'd like her to come visit me?"

"Blönduhorn?"

Hávi nodded, but she didn't explain; Blönduhorn could help her in ways that no other woman could.

Chapter 19

Hvassi smiled as she examined the scrap.

"That's much better," Hvassi complimented Hávi, who had tried hard to keep her stitches even. Each time she pulled her tiny needle through the loose-woven fabric, two threads trailed behind it, and even if her needle was in the exact center of the thread when she'd started, by the time that she'd drawn both threads through the cloth, then one or the other thread would stretch, catch, or bunch up. Finally Hvassi showed her how to pull the needle to one side or the other with each pass to straighten out each stitch. It slowed Hávi's poor needlework even more; Tryggvi and Hvassi each made four straight, even stitches in the time that it took her to do a crooked one, but even Hávi could see her improvement.

"By next year I'll have sewn a whole line!" Hávi joked.

"It won't take you that long," Hvassi said, and she reached into her bag and pulled out half of a stick, a branch as thick as a dagger-grip, but cleanly split down its middle and sanded smooth, and its flat edge was carefully painted with a squarish red and blue crosshatching that ran the length of the six-inch branch.

"This is your first project," Hvassi said. "It's trim for the collar of a dress."

"It's wood," Hávi pointed out.

"This is the pattern that you're going to follow," Hvassi explained while Tryggvi suppressed a giggle. "See the thin knife-marks? That's how you count the weave of your cloth." Hvassi pulled out a narrow strip of tan cloth about a finger's width and an arm span long. Then she pulled out two skeins of embroidery thread, one bright red, the other deep blue, all of which she handed to Hávi.

"I'm not ready!"

"You'll learn from your errors," Hvassi said. "Just remember, whatever you make you're going to have to live with."

"What?"

"This trim's for you," Hvassi said. "I'm having another dress made, a pink dress, and this'll be the trim for it. Do your best; this will be the dress that you'll be wearing when your husband returns."

"But I'm still learning!"

"Then you'd better learn faster," Hvassi said. "You've practiced enough; it's time that you began sewing."

Hávi glanced fearfully at Tryggvi.

"And Tryggvi won't help you," Hvassi said firmly. "I can spot where one master seamstress drops off and another finishes; I'll know if Tryggvi helps you."

Hávi paused, looking askance at the materials in her hands, knowing that she wasn't good enough.

"I'll try," Hávi said, "but if I do, then you have to make me a promise."

Hvassi leaned back, her vast weight making the stout chair creak, and she eyed Hávi suspiciously.

"What promise?"

"That you'll talk to me ... *and be honest!*"

"Child, I'm always honest," Hvassi said. "I'm poor, old, and unmarried; what do I have to lie about?"

"Then ... you'll answer my questions?"

"That depends on your questions."

"Do ... do you ... still like me?"

"Dropped stitches, child! Why wouldn't I like you?"

"Be ... because of ... what happened ..."

"With Jarl Illingr?" Hvassi asked. "Fool girl, don't you remember? I caught you coming back from his tower the day that you pretended to be sick!"

Hávi and Tryggvi stared open mouthed.

"*Then ... then you know that I was ...!*"

"Trying to learn the den Skaanske Lov?" Hvassi finished. "Of course I knew it! I told you that you'd get caught, remember? I advised you to stop even though I knew that you wouldn't."

"*You knew ...?*"

"Silly girl, of course I knew," Hvassi said, shaking her head. "I was young once; I know how exciting exploring can be, discovering new places and testing your limits. You two thought that you could swim across a river, but didn't learn that the middle current is always strongest until you were caught in it." Hvassi chuckled to herself. "Now you've been caught. Hopefully you'll learn."

"Hvassi, this is serious!" Hávi exclaimed. "*Jarl Illingr's slated to be killed!*"

"I doubt if anything can stop that now," Hvassi said.

"But he's innocent!"

"*Innocent?*" Hvassi asked. "*Jarl Illingr?* The clan-chief that had his own brother hung?"

Hávi and Tryggvi gasped.

"Don't be fooled by his *'weak old man'* act," Hvassi said. "Jarl Illingr was a clan-chief, and while he was, he acted like all clan-chiefs do. I don't know all of the stories about him, but if half of the ones that I've heard are true, then he's been as ruthless as all the others. He's done things that would whiten your hair, if you knew about them. He knew what he was doing when he agreed to teach you; he wasn't teaching you law as a favor to your husband!"

"He knew that my learning the den Skaanske Lov would cause Jarl Austmaðr trouble" Hávi said. "He told me so."

"You see?" Hvassi said. "You may've been acting stupidly, but he wasn't; he planned to avenge his clan by using you."

"He did, at first," Hávi said. "But then, after a while ... well, he grew nicer."

Hvassi snorted. "He tricked you."

"He had two granddaughters," Hávi said, "and he said that he wished that they'd grown up like me."

"Yes, he had two granddaughters," Hvassi said, "and Jarl Austmaðr killed them both."

The next day Master Kamban *'thumped'* into her outer-room on his crippled leg and cane; Hávi and Tryggvi patiently awaited him. Felian, Kamban's attendant, entered behind him and quietly took a seat upon the stool which Tryggvi had set out for him. Felian carried a large carpetbag but kept his eyes respectfully lowered. As Master Kamban came in, Hávi stood and formally curtsied to him. Master Kamban smiled, then bowed as low as his bent back would allow. Hávi gifted him with a gentle smile; if he hadn't been cursed then he'd look just like everybody else. Master Kamban *'thumped'* his cane, then his crippled leg, over to the large chair that Hávi had placed by the table. Then he cleared his throat.

> *"Frigg, blessed queen of the womb,*
> *Freyja, before whom all men swoon,*
> *Gefion, Eir, Sif so fair,*
> *Make a son to be my heir."*

"I use that one every day," Hávi said.

Master Kamban smiled.

> *"Moon, son of Mundilfari, light of the night,*
> *Sun, daughter of Mundilfari, glow golden bright,*
> *Brains of Aurgelmir, float over land and sea,*
> *Bifrost, rainbow thy blessings; bright-color me."*

"Every Hersir child knows that one," Hávi smiled.

Master Kamban's smile faded.

> *"Odin, Thor, Balder, Tyr, Idun, Bragi,*
> *Freyr, Lofn, Hod, Vidar, Aegir, Vali,*
> *Ull, Forseti, Njord, Saga, Ve, Vili,*
> *Heimdal, protect me from the evils of Loki."*

"Oh, ravens protect!" Hávi exclaimed, startled. "So many sacred names! That's a fearful chant!"

"One of my most-powerful," Master Kamban said proudly. "Let's begin with that."

Master Kamban repeated his potent spell one line at a time. Again and again she recited it until Master Kamban was certain that she knew it, and then he called forth Felian and had him place his carpetbag at Hávi's feet; it was full of small cloth bags and what looked like a few weapons.

"Take something out of its bag," Master Kamban said. "Anything. Start with the red pouch, if you like."

Hávi pulled out the small, red cloth bag.

289

"Open it."

Hávi untied its laces and opened the bag. Inside it were old, dried leaves.

"Do you recognize it?"

"Should I?"

"Goats eat it every day."

Hávi pulled out the largest piece of dried leaf that she could see.

"It looks like ... a weed?"

"What does it matter what herbs look like?" Master Kamban scowled. "Little girls gather flowers for their mothers, some of which are deadly poisonous, but does that matter? Their mothers love only their bright colors and sweet scents. As a healer, you must overlook ostentatious, superficial qualities. You must learn to appreciate greater essences."

Hávi nodded, carefully saying nothing; surely she couldn't argue with a lame hunchback over the triviality of appearances. She glanced at the broken leaf in her hand, so dry that she could crush it into powder.

"It's dandelion," Master Kamban said. "Yes, common dandelion, a weed, but to a patient dying from infection it's more valuable than gold. Dried, crushed into a powder and boiled just right, it can save lives, if given in time with the right incantation."

"Farmers hate dandelions," Hávi grinned.

"Fools consider common things worthless ... as if rarity heightens value," Master Kamban smiled. "By that logic, hunchbacks and albinos would be prized children. Go on, pull out something else."

Hávi drew out another bag whose pungent scent she instantly recognized.

"Onion, also called cepa, helps those with colds and runny

noses, is good for the digestion, and gives fair complexion," Master Kamban said. "He who eats onions while fasting suffers no hunger-pains that day. Onion's good for dog's bite, if crushed with honey and vinegar and applied for four days. Salt and onion crushed together cures viper-bites. Onion's juice and woman's milk drives away earache. If one sniffs onion juice into his nose, it drives out harmful humors."

"I eat onion all the time," Hávi said. "I've had earaches."

"You didn't recite the incantation," Master Kamban smiled. "Treatments don't always work. Supposedly, if one washes his bald head in onion juice, hair will regrow, yet I've tried this with every incantation that I know, and you can see my results. If the gods choose to doom your patient, then no healing can save them."

Hávi opened another sack and pulled out a common dried thistle.

"Burdock, also called lappacium or hævindla, strengthens the stomach and belches out bad winds," Master Kamban said. "If one soaks in warm burdock juice, scabies and itches leave. Rinse your mouth with the juice: toothaches vanish. Boiled in wine, burdock roots drive stones from the bladder, and it's good for jaundice."

Hávi studiously observed each plant, trying to relate their individual characteristics to their healing properties. Master Kamban rattled on at length on every herb-pouch that she pulled out and actually laughed at a strange, very dried little vine with hard white berries that turned out to be mistletoe.

What Hávi had thought were weapons turned out to be tools, grim tools that she prayed she'd never have to use. One was a small, reinforced iron saw for cutting bones, and special knives for bleeding, each designed to extract a different type of humor. Hávi didn't understand how the shape of a knife would make anyone bleed differently, but Master Kamban was the expert so she had to take his word for it.

Master Kamban bragged of delivering Breiðr's baby girl; the revelation made Tryggvi gasp as, at Hávi's request, he described the procedure in detail. Tryggvi blanched and paled at his description, so Hávi sent her to the kitchen for a cool bottle of wine. Felian grinned as Tryggvi quickly departed; he seemed unfazed, inured by his long service to Master Kamban.

"Do you think that wise?" Master Kamban asked grimly.

"Do I ... *what?*" Hávi fumbled.

"Sending your servant away," Master Kamban said, his tone suddenly grave. "I like you, Hávi, but I don't wish to share Jarl Illingr's cell."

"What ...?"

"He should never have agreed to meet with you alone, no matter the reason."

"He's in a cell?"

"Yes," Master Kamban replied. "I examined him myself just yesterday. He's very ill."

"Ill?"

"Cold, damp prisons aren't good for young healthy men, let alone old men who've been trapped in a frozen tower for two years," Master Kamban said. "He has the sniffles and a violent cough ..."

"Did you cure him?"

"Mistress, there's no cure for his case," Master Kamban deepened his voice. "I gave him a hot drink of many herbs and a second blanket, but there's no hope as long as he stays in that dungeon."

"Dungeon?"

"Where did you think that they'd keep him?"

"Where's the dungeon?"

Master Kamban's frown deepened.

"That's forbidden knowledge," Master Kamban warned. "Only a handful know its entrance and I won't risk imprisonment by giving you information that can't help anyone. Jarl Illingr's fate is decided. He knows that. He asked for poison."

"You ... you didn't ...!"

"I didn't give him poison?" Master Kamban asked. "Of course not, but I refused to for my sake, not his. I understand that he pretended to be your friend ..."

"He is my friend!"

"Your *'friend'* has done you no kindness. His teachings couldn't help you ..."

"He told me that himself!"

"And yet he still taught you," Master Kamban said. "He fed you knowledge that would disgrace clan Austmaðr, once it was learned that you knew it, and he managed to get caught alone with you in his tower in the middle of the night. He knew what damage this scandal would cause. I was never his friend, but I knew him well; Jarl Illingr was a clever, crafty, resentful clan-chief. Revenge upon your husband was his greatest goal."

"It was, but he's changed," Hávi insisted. "He knows that nothing will restore clan Illingr."

"I won't argue with you, Mistress Austmaðr," Master Kamban said. "I think it best that we end our lesson for today."

"No!" Hávi said, but Master Kamban struggled to rise from his chair.

"Jarl Illingr did ask about you," Master Kamban said after he climbed to his feet. "He seemed worried that you were being punished for his crime."

Master Kamban limped toward Hávi, *'thumping'* on his cane. Stopping before her, Master Kamban bowed slightly, then reached down and placed his hand over Hávi's slight bulge.

"Have you felt him move yet?"

"I'm not sure," Hávi said. "I've felt something, but I'm not sure what it was. After the kalops ..."

"That'll pass after the birth," Master Kamban said. "May I have Felian examine you? My hearing isn't as good as it used to be."

Hávi nodded, and Master Kamban called Felian forth and had him rest an ear against Hávi's stomach.

"I hear two heartbeats, both strong," Felian reported.

"Very good," Master Kamban said. "All signs are favorable. My apprentice has been assisting me for four years; if anything should happen to me, you may trust that he's been taught well."

"Why should anything happen to you?" Hávi asked.

"Well, certain people in this castle who already don't like me may take quite an interest in the fact that you sent your servant out of your private chamber while I was in here," Master Kamban pointed out. "In the future, I'd prefer that you never do that again. If your servant can't bear hearing healer's talk, perhaps you should find another. Good day to you, Mistress Austmaðr."

"Please, call me Hávi."

"Mistress Austmaðr," Master Kamban stressed, and then he bowed slightly and *'thumped'* out the door.

Jarl Illingr sick and cold in a lightless dungeon: Hávi couldn't let him suffer, but what could she do? Wasn't she as trapped as he? Could Tryggvi bring him hot foods? No, Tryggvi didn't know where those dungeons were, and even if she did, no guard would let her in. Perhaps Bíldr would help her, she wondered doubtfully. Then, unexpectedly, while she could still hear the *'thumps'* of Master Kamban descending the stone stairs, someone knocked on her door. Wondering who it could be, Hávi opened her door. Outside, trembling in the hallway, stood Blönduhorn.

"You ... you summoned me, Mistress?" Blönduhorn asked.

Hávi smiled brightly.

"Please come in."

Blönduhorn looked the same, skinny as a starving snake, long yellow braids the color of the hearts of sunflowers, but her eyes were wide, her fingers trembling.

"Blönduhorn, you don't need to be afraid," Hávi said. "I didn't ask you here to get you into trouble."

"Yes, Mistress," Blönduhorn said fearfully.

Hávi sighed. There was no point trying to calm Blönduhorn; she was a simple peasant girl, as Hávi had been back in clan Hersir; despite becoming Mistress Austmaðr, Hávi didn't think that she could ever address Jarl Hersir's wife informally. Besides, she hadn't brought Blönduhorn here for herself.

"Let's go into my bedroom," Hávi said. "I don't want us ... to be overheard."

Timidly Blönduhorn followed Hávi through the door into her more-comfortable inner room. Their fire was dying, and Hávi could easily have restacked the burning logs, but she asked Blönduhorn to do it, and the younger girl gladly obeyed, grateful for a simple service that she could perform. While the young girl masterfully moved the hot logs with the poker, constantly flicking her head to keep both of her pigtails from dangling into the flames, Hávi considered; she couldn't plainly ask Blönduhorn; she'd have to be more subtle (*ironically, like Hvítvi, who'd truly kill her if he knew what she was doing*).

Tryggvi arrived with the wine.

"What happened to Master Kamban?" Tryggvi asked.

Hávi frowned at Tryggvi, then glanced at Blönduhorn, who was still building up the fire.

"We have a new guest," Hávi said. "Blönduhorn, have you ever met Tryggvi, my handmaiden?"

"No, Mistress," Blönduhorn said, and hesitantly she rose and bowed to Tryggvi.

"Enough of that; we're all friends here," Hávi said. "Tryggvi, pour the wine."

Blönduhorn looked worried as Tryggvi handed her a cup, but Hávi took one also, and all three girls sat. Blönduhorn insisted on sitting on the carpet despite Hávi's offer to fetch her a chair from the outer-room. Hávi examined her carefully: Blönduhorn was wiry, like most village girls, with long legs and pale skin and thin blonde hair, ungainly, unused to her sudden height.

"What I asked you here for was to learn about your brothers," Hávi said to Blönduhorn, whose features suddenly flushed with relief.

"Oh, they're fine," Blönduhorn assured Hávi.

"It's unfair how things happened," Hávi said. "I'd like to continue their education as soon as I can find another Law-speaker to teach them."

"Father would like that."

"I never betrayed Jarl Austmaðr," Hávi said. "I went to see Jarl Illingr about your brothers' lessons and things went awry.

You do believe me, don't you?"

"Yes, Mistress."

"Have you heard the stories that they're telling about me?"

"Yes, Mistress," Blönduhorn sighed, and then she gasped. *"I mean ...! No, Mistress!"*

"Blönduhorn, I don't blame you, I just want to hear what's being said. Everyone in Hrafna's tavern must be talking about it, and I've seen how you listen to conversations. People are careful what they say around your father and Brækir, but you slip between the tables quickly and quietly; you must know what they're saying."

"Yes, Mistress, begging your pardon," Blönduhorn said cautiously. "They ... they say that ... you and Jarl Illingr ... are ... that your baby's ... real father ... is ..."

"How dare they?" Hávi gasped, but then she reined in control of herself as Blönduhorn startled. "I should've expected that."

"False liars!" Tryggvi scowled. *"Anyone who'd believe that ...!"*

"They're just repeating the gossip," Hávi said. "The peasants in Hrafna's tavern didn't make up these lies."

"I never believed them!" Blönduhorn insisted.

"I know who's to blame ... and they live in the castle, not in the village," Hávi said. "Relax and drink your wine. I'm just glad to have your company. They've locked me up so that I can't deny their charges."

"That's terrible!" Blönduhorn said, "Mistress."

"Yes, it is, but you can be my voice," Hávi said. "What I say you must tell your parents and anybody else that wants to hear. Everybody goes to your father's tavern to hear the news; from you they'll hear the truth."

Hávi told Blönduhorn a simplified version of the events

that led her to getting caught in Jarl Illingr's tower chamber, stressing how she wanted to gift her husband with two Law-speakers trained by the best. Tryggvi sat silent through the telling, but her eyes widened several times as Hávi detailed parts that she hadn't known. Blönduhorn sat attentively through the carefully-edited speech, never taking her eyes off Hávi. Hávi finished quickly; she wanted to get to her main purpose, but Blönduhorn had to be very relaxed before she dared mention it.

Afternoon passed into evening as the three girls drank and chatted. Blönduhorn insisted on helping Tryggvi fetch dinner from the kitchen, and Hávi allowed it; Tryggvi was swaying from the amount of wine that she'd drunk, and neither Hávi nor Blönduhorn were sober. Yet Hávi kept insisting that both girls keep drinking, and as the wine disappeared, their moods lightened and their conversations grew increasingly jovial. Laughter preceded Tryggvi and Blönduhorn as they carried food and more wine up to Hávi's room. The guard's shout, warning them not to spill upon him, effused howls and cackles from both girls. Hávi decided that it was time.

"Refill our cups!" Hávi ordered Tryggvi while they ate moose-steaks and fish stew with onions and scallops. "I want to make a toast!"

Tryggvi filled all of their cups and then Hávi raised her wine high and said loudly and clearly:

"Hvítvi!"

Laughter burst from all three girls. Blönduhorn fell over onto her side, giggling, rolling back and forth on the carpet with one hand held high, a vain attempt to not spill her wine. Tryggvi, drunkenly sniggering, saved her from spilling all of it by snatching her cup and setting it on the hearth. Hávi tried to hold up her mug, and then slammed it onto her bedside table beside the remains of her dinner and fell back onto her fur pillows, unable to stop laughing. Ludicrous absurdities filled their chamber. Finally Hávi managed to sit back up and look at the other hysterical girls.

"When I first saw him I ... I thought he was a ghost!" Hávi blurted out, and all three girls fell back into fits of hilarity, Tryggvi falling off her stool onto the carpet beside Blönduhorn, who was clutching her sides, trying to contain giggles that shook her whole body.

"Enough!" Hávi gasped, wiping tears of mirth from her eyes as their laughter subsided, then threatened to re-erupt for the third time. "Stop laughing! I'm serious!"

Tryggvi and Blönduhorn abruptly stopped laughing, alarmed. Hávi realized that she was being too forceful; she'd drunk too much wine. Her head was spinning. Both of these girls lived in dread of her, as she'd grown up fearing Jarl Hersir's wife.

"Remember when I met Hvítvi in your tavern?" Hávi asked Blönduhorn. "You said that Hvítvi had once cut himself there ..."

"Oh, that was a terrible day!" Blönduhorn said.

"Hvítvi said that it was nothing ... that everyone exaggerated ..."

"Begging your pardon, no!" Blönduhorn insisted. "Hvítvi sliced himself deep, trying to cut some mutton, and three of mother's aprons were soaked with his blood before we staunched it enough for him to be carried back to the castle. I'll never forget that day; Hvítvi was white as your quilt. Many thought that he'd die. It took days for his wound to close and weeks before he was let out of his room. He still has the scar on his middle finger above the second knuckle."

"You must've been terrified," Hávi grinned.

"We all were," Blönduhorn replied, and Tryggvi nodded in agreement.

"I see," Hávi replied, but she thought she heard a deeper concern in Blönduhorn's voice, a personal worry for a beloved friend more than a concern for a stranger's child. "How long have you known Hvítvi?"

"Since he was very little," Blönduhorn said. "The other boys wouldn't play with him unless his older brothers insisted. He was a bastard, they said, a dwarf frost-giant, and they didn't want him touching them. Some said that one drop of his blood on their skin would deny them entrance to Valhalla."

"Hersir boys were cruel, too," Hávi said. "They terrorized us girls, and then laughed at us."

"All boys do that," Blönduhorn said.

"I got them back plenty," Hávi grinned wickedly. "I bloodied lots of Hersir-boys; one dropped a frog inside the back of my collar; his nose was broken before they drug me off him."

Blönduhorn and Tryggvi glanced at each other, as if doubting Hávi's tale, and then burst out sniggering.

"I got in trouble for that," Hávi chuckled. "I also got in trouble, what, only last year, when a boy slapped my butt and I dumped a pitcher of goat-milk over his head. The Hersir boys were so childish! Not at all like Hvítvi!"

All three girls started to chuckle, and then suddenly all laughter failed. Tryggvi and Blönduhorn looked startled, but Hávi fell quiet, suddenly serious.

"Tell me more about Hvítvi," Hávi ordered, and suddenly both girls looked nervous.

"Mistress, it's not my place ...," Blönduhorn began.

"I insist!" Hávi said, but at once she knew that she'd gone too far. This wasn't her plan! She hadn't counted on getting drunk, too tipsy to control herself. This had to work! *If she failed ...!*

"Hvítvi g-got th-the b-boys back ... once," Blönduhorn stammered, obviously worried, swallowing hard. "It was deep winter, and the Skadi boys refused to let Hvítvi join their snowball fights. One boy called Hvítvi a girl and they all laughed at him. Then, while they ran outside, Hvítvi snuck out the tavern's back door. The snow was really thick that year; people walked between the buildings through dug-out paths, the snow piled higher than their heads. Hvítvi harnessed up a horse to some anchors on ropes, and then he buried the anchors into the base of the snow-cliffs on both sides of the narrow trail. Finished, he snuck up behind the boys with an armload of snowballs and pelted them good. They chased him right into his trap, and when he slapped the horse's rump, it pulled the whole snow pile down atop them. Both walls collapsed upon the boys, and some were trapped. My father and some other men ran out and dug those boys out of the snow or they'd have suffocated; Hvítvi got in big trouble for that. Jarl Austmaðr was furious; two of Hvítvi's older brothers and three village boys had almost died, and it was spring before Hvítvi was let out of the castle again."

Hávi listened intently, imagining a young Hvítvi, unable to fight back, using his brains to best the other boys. Her imaginings made her smile and a warmth filled her, picturing Hvítvi as a young boy, her age, playing games with her in clan Hersir ...

'Stop it!' Hávi ordered herself. This was why she had to do this! *She couldn't ... daren't think of Hvítvi that way!* Hávi took a deep breath. Blönduhorn looked at least three years younger than she was, her skin soft and smooth, her yellow hair bright and sunny, but wearing only her soiled, worn

apron over her stained, ragged dress; she might as well be wearing a servant's garb.

Hávi pushed up, forcibly steadying herself to keep from falling, her balance almost gone as her bedroom drunkenly leaned. She grabbed onto her wardrobe, clung to it, and fumbled inside, then selected a tiny light blue dress with a white seal-fur collar. It was too small for Hávi; it must've belonged to one of Jarl Austmaðr's other wives; tiny Breiðr could fit in this dress now that she wasn't pregnant anymore.

"I think that this will fit you," Hávi said to Blönduhorn.

"Oh, Mistress, I couldn't ...!" Blönduhorn gasped.

"Tryggvi," Hávi ordered, deepening her tone to allow no argument, "dress Blönduhorn in this. *Now!*"

Soon Blönduhorn stood nervously, obviously more uncomfortable than ever, in the light blue dress with the white seal-fur collar. She'd never worn anything this fancy or luxurious, Hávi suspected, and feared to wear it now. Yet Blönduhorn said nothing, standing obediently as Tryggvi undid her pig-tails and straightened out her hair so that it fell smoothly over her shoulders. Hávi smiled; Blönduhorn was much prettier than she was.

"Go into the outer-room and await me there," Hávi instructed, and Blönduhorn immediately obeyed, although her frown couldn't be more sullen; Blönduhorn looked on the verge of tears. As soon as she closed the door behind her, Hávi turned to Tryggvi.

"Tryggvi, go find Hvítvi. Bring him here. If he asks, say that it's a surprise."

Tryggvi paled but stared back at Hávi.

"Mistre ... I mean, Hávi," Tryggvi said, her voice deeper than Hávi had ever heard before, "*you're going to get your hands burned again!*"

"Do as I say!" Hávi ordered, and she lifted her wine cup to her lips, then hesitated as Tryggvi stared at her adamantly before departing. Perhaps Tryggvi was right. *Was this a mistake?* The possibility hurt her spinning head. Hávi set her wine cup down; she didn't need to drink anymore.

Hávi stepped out into the outer-room with Blönduhorn. Tryggvi was gone and Blönduhorn looked worried, fidgety, as if she wanted to squirm out of the regal gown back into her barmaid's dress and then run home.

"You look beautiful," Hávi assured her.

Minutes passed in silence, and then a knock came to her door; Hvítvi entered. He glanced at Hávi, then spied Blönduhorn. In her fancy dress, her long hair flowing over her shoulders, beautiful Blönduhorn paled until she looked as snowy as Hvítvi except for two rose-bright cheeks.

Hvítvi frowned. His brows knitted. His hands balled into fists. Hávi felt tongues of fire scorching her fingers.

"Get out of that dress!" Hvítvi exploded, shouting at Blönduhorn, who screamed in fright. *"Bíldr! Take this girl back to her tavern as soon as she's dressed!"* Then Hvítvi snapped at Tryggvi. *"Change her back!"*

Terrified, Tryggvi jumped inside the room past Hvítvi, grabbed Blönduhorn and forcibly dragged the screaming girl back into Hávi's bedroom. Bíldr arrived in the doorway, one hand on the hilt of his sword, but he made no move to enter. Hvítvi stood in frozen silence, glaring at Hávi, who felt her hands blacken and crisp. *What had gone wrong? Why was he so angry?*

Moments later, faster than Hávi would've believed possible, Blönduhorn burst back into the outer-chamber, Tryggvi trailing, trying to tie her dirty apron strings as the frightened girl ran out of her reach and through the doorway.

Bíldr stepped aside as Blönduhorn dashed past him and fled down the stairs, and then, without even a nod at Hvítvi, Bíldr followed the young girl. Hvítvi said nothing but turned his pink eyes on Tryggvi, who needed no further prompting; Tryggvi bowed her head and swept past him.

Hvítvi closed the door behind her, almost shaking with rage. Then he turned abruptly to face Hávi, his suddenness reminding her of a striking snake.

"What're you trying to do?" Hvítvi demanded.

"I ... I just ...!" Hávi stammered.

"Are you trying to destroy their family as well as ours?"

"Destroy?"

"Are you drunk?" Hvítvi demanded. "Yes, you must be! Why ruin Hrafna?"

"I'm not trying to ruin them!"

"Well, that's what you're doing! First you drag Valla and Augi into your scheme with Jarl Illingr, and now ...!"

"You told me to ...!"

"Not with Valla and Augi! They're peasants! They've no business becoming Law-speakers!"

"Why not?"

"Because they're peasants!" Hvítvi shouted. "If they'd had more than one lesson then they'd be locked up with Jarl Illingr right now! Others've asked why I let the boys go free! I had to blow it off as another mistake of yours; only that satisfied them!"

"What?" Hávi demanded. "Valla and Augi weren't involved ...!"

"You involved them!" Hvítvi said. "You're Mistress Austmaðr! You can't play with people's lives like they're rag dolls!"

"Valla and Augi would've made good Law-speakers! Jarl

Illingr said so!"

"Yes, and look where he is now! Freezing in the dungeon, bitten by rats!"

"Rats?"

"Don't even ask!" Hvítvi shouted. "I didn't put him there! You did! Now you're trying to ruin Hrafna's family ...!"

"I'm not! I like them!"

"You've a funny way of showing it!" Hvítvi scowled. "Hrafna's tavern's been empty since you and Jarl Illingr were caught together. Many blame them for their sons' part in this. If they don't get some customers soon, then they may starve!"

"I'll give them some money ..."

"You can't! Hávi, they're peasants!"

"I was a peasant, too!"

"Yes, and if Valla or Augi marry some richly-endowed widow then they won't be peasants anymore, but until then, raising them up above their station will only cause problems. You can't disrupt the order of Skadi without repercussions. How do you think all of the other families felt when you favored Hrafna's family over theirs? You might as well have nailed the door to Hrafna's tavern shut. They'll be lucky to survive the winter, and if they suddenly appear to have an endless supply of coppers, then everyone will know where the coins came from. Hrafna will have to take his family and leave."

"No ...," Hávi tried to shout, but her confidence was shaky. *Had she ruined everything?* She remembered Helga and Hlöðu's endless gossiping about their neighbors' doings, and Gamli scowling at their nosiness back when he still talked. Doubtless the housewives in Skadi were no different.

"I ... I'm sorry," Hávi said.

"What good is *'sorry'*?" Hvítvi demanded. "Being sorry

doomed Jarl Illingr, Father's best Law-speaker, and now ...!"

"Can't I do anything?"

"You can have Jarl Illingr killed now: a quick death. You can beg Father not to kill him, but he will. Jarl Austmaðr can't afford to be perceived as weak or benevolent. Our enemies south and east are defending themselves more every year, and the Norwegians have to sail past us to get to the Rús. If they thought that they could conquer the Skåne, then we'd be a lot closer. Father must retain his reputation; all of our lives depend on him being perceived as tough."

Slowly Hávi crumpled. She'd ruined everything. If Blönduhorn had been seen wearing a royal dress then it would've been the gossip of the countryside. She should've never tried this. She didn't understand the rules. She wasn't raised to play games like these. She should've stayed in clan Hersir and raised goats. That's what she really was, no matter who she married; a simple clan-girl. Tears welled in her eyes.

"Don't do that!" Hvítvi said, but his voice softened.

"I ruin everything I touch!" Hávi sobbed. *"I should've never come here! Send me home!"*

Off-balance, about to fall, suddenly soft hands seized her arms, steadied her. Hávi burst into tears.

"Hávi, don't ..!" Hvítvi whispered, his voice pained.

Hávi looked up through bleary tears into his pink eyes. Clever and disciplined, smooth and cultured, Hvítvi was all that she liked about Skadi. Homesickness welled; she wanted to flee at once, taking only him. Fury no longer stared back at her, only sympathy. His high-cloud-white skin shined in the candlelight, his face so close.

"You can't go," Hvítvi said, probably a warning, but Hávi noted something more.

"I ... I couldn't leave ... you," Hávi said.

"N-no, Hávi," Hvítvi stammered. *"We can't ...!"*

Their eyes met, blue against pink. Hvítvi stared at her, disbelieving, and then suddenly their lips pressed. Hávi kissed Hvítvi hard, demanding more. Childish, little-girl-fantasized lovers, silenced since her forced-wedding, sang from the depths of her imagination. Birdsong twittered all around. Warm, golden light seemed to burst free.

"No!" Hvítvi hissed fearfully, and with all of his poor strength, he pushed away. In four quick strides, Hvítvi crossed Hávi's outer-room, yanked open her door, and then slammed it shut behind him.

Hávi stared at her closed door, and then collapsed onto her floor in a thunderstorm of tears; she ruined everything that she touched ... and now she'd touched Hvítvi.

Jay Palmer

Chapter 20

Hávi screamed as Tryggvi tried to drag her up off her cold outer-room floor. Tryggvi tried to insist on helping Hávi up, but between maniacal screeches, Hávi ordered her away, and finally Tryggvi obeyed. Hávi heard Tryggvi crying as she stepped out into the hallway and closed the door behind her, but Hávi was too wounded to feel another's pain. Hávi laid back on her cold, uncarpeted outer-room floor. She didn't deserve help. *She deserved to be locked in the dungeon, not Jarl Illingr!* She deserved nothing but the pain that she'd caused to others.

Unmoving save for her trembles, Hávi pressed her face against her hard wooden floor. She wasn't a jarl or clan-chief; she'd stuck her head up and gotten it chopped off, as she should've foreseen. *Mjóvi had been right!* If Hávi had obeyed Mjóvi and stayed in her room, never disobeyed her husband and never snuck out, then nothing would've been ruined. Hrafna's tavern would be thriving. The whole Skåne wouldn't be on the verge of revolt. Clan Austmaðr wouldn't be disgraced. Jarl Illingr would be safe in his tower. Jarl Austmaðr wouldn't be about to come home to a chaos that he could only settle with an execution.

Hvítvi wouldn't hate her.

Eventually the cold boards sucked all of the warmth from her flesh. Hávi shivered as she slowly pushed up onto her knees and grabbed the edge of the stout table to keep from falling. Her eyes cast about, fell upon the deadly swords and axes hanging on the wall. They called out to her; *one weapon could resolve all this.* One blade, one quick swipe, and it'd be over. Everyone could go back to normal, burying all of the blame with her. Perhaps even Jarl Illingr would be spared.

Hávi's hand lowered to her rounded bulge. Suicide wouldn't just kill her; inside Hávi's womb slept Jarl Austmaðr's next child, her son or daughter. He or she deserved to live. *Would her disgrace tarnish the life that hadn't even begun?*

Hávi struggled to shaky feet and clung to the stout table. Maps and scrolls, Jarl Austmaðr's treasured documents, lay piled upon it, untouched since he left. No point looking; Hávi couldn't read the mysterious rune-marked drawings of lands that she'd never see. Hávi stumbled into her bedroom, closed the door behind her, and then spied the light blue gown trimmed with seal-fur cast aside on her carpet: Blönduhorn; *Hávi had almost ruined her life as well.* Hávi stumbled to her bed, lifted her white quilt, and crawled underneath. The fire that Blönduhorn had built up now burned low, thin blackened logs spewing only a few bright tongues, casting accusing shadows of her horse-head bedposts upon her walls. Hávi pulled her quilt over her head.

Hávi didn't send Tryggvi away the next time that she entered. Tryggvi brought a tray of food and warm goat's milk; Hávi greedily drank the milk but left the food untouched. The glow at the window told Hávi that the sun was up but she had no idea what time it was. When a knock came at the door, Hávi told Tryggvi to send whoever it was away. Tryggvi reported that it was Hvassi, here to teach her needlework, but Hávi repeated her order and Tryggvi apologetically sent Hvassi away. The next day Master Kamban arrived with Felian, but he was dismissed as well.

Days bled into weeks. Hávi took to sitting by the window, watching the sea from a chair, usually wrapped in a blanket even when the day was warm. If she stood up then she could see down into the streets of Skadi, so Hávi stayed seated, unwilling to look upon other people. Sometimes she wished that she could go home to clan Hersir, but other times she was glad that she couldn't; Hávi didn't want to ruin her childhood home as she'd ruined Castle Austmaðr. She wished that she could send for Völu, but to what avail? Völu wasn't raised playing royal politics; Hávi preferred that her childhood cohort remember the Hávi that ran through their village laughing, not as a bitter, ruined wreck that cried each day.

Why had she kissed Hvítvi? Long hours of pondering offered no answer. She was married, his stepmother, and the scandal that it'd cause could topple the Skåne, perhaps all of Scandinavia. Mjóvi would ride this gossip on a wave of insurrection, a peasant revolt that'd tear down the walls of Castle Austmaðr. Yet Hvítvi's softness, his smooth, white skin and mysterious eyes haunted Hávi's dreams. She'd never met a man, especially not her husband, with whom she wished to mate. Jarl Austmaðr's invasions of her privates had tormented her, but she'd learned to endure, to comply without complaint. He was her husband. She was bearing his child. Few girls got to marry their childhood sweethearts. Hávi had never had a childhood sweetheart; she was married before she'd seen Hvítvi.

Slowly Hávi's stomach and bosoms swelled. Soon getting out of bed became a chore, and Tryggvi begged her to let Master Kamban examine her, but Hávi always refused. The summer waned, the hot days finally cooling, before the hard knock came on Hávi's door. Tryggvi came back with a message.

"Hávi, Master Kamban says that he needs to see you."

"What news?"

"He didn't say."

"I'll see him in the outer-room."

Soon Tryggvi opened the door. Hávi rose from her chair as he *'thumped'* inside, but Master Kamban waved her back down.

"Don't strain yourself with formalities," Master Kamban said, leaning heavily upon his cane. "Pregnant women need rest and I'd rather you hear this sitting down."

"Tryggvi, fetch a chair for ...," Hávi began.

"No need, no need," Master Kamban interrupted her. "I'm not here to intrude. I just have news that you'd best hear right away."

Hávi started to ask but fell silent, deciding to patiently wait.

"Hávi, I'm sorry to have to tell you this," Master Kamban bowed his bald head slowly, "but I bring bad news. It's about ... Jarl Illingr."

Hávi sat bolt upright, ignoring the wave of nausea that swept over her. *No, it couldn't be ...!*

"Jarl Illingr has ... died," Master Kamban said softly. "He was found this morning by his guards. I examined him, as I've been doing every few days since his imprisonment. There was nothing more that I could do."

Tears sprung forth, trickling down Hávi's cheeks. She gulped and then gasped, fighting to breathe through a constricted throat.

"H-how ...?"

"Who can say?" Master Kamban asked. "He developed a bad cough several weeks ago. I gave him more blankets and candles for his lantern; he used to stay warm in his tower by keeping a lit lantern inside his cloak. I gave orders to his guards to light his candle anytime that he asked for it, but when they found him his candle was out and his body was cold."

Master Kamban shook his head sadly. Hávi stared at him but there was nothing left to say.

"I'm sorry, Hávi," Master Kamban said. "I know that you thought of him ... as a friend."

Turning slowly, Master Kamban *'thumped'* out of the room, his head below his hump.

The sight that Hávi most-feared arrived on an overcast, drizzly day. Wrapped in her quilt against the suddenly-cool weather, wondering if the end of summer had finally come, Hávi sat before her window and stared at the sea. Ships sailed by every day, sometimes in small groups, and occasionally she spied the same three dragonships sailing past, always together; Hafr, Jarl Austmaðr's half-brother, protecting Skadi while the men were away. Large fleets, she knew, sailed south and east, or south-west to England, but seldom came this far north. Today a vast fleet filled the eastern horizon, which appeared so suddenly that Hávi momentarily feared that enemy raiders had come, but she knew in her heart that the even-more-dreaded day had finally arrived.

Hávi rose silently, smiled at Tryggvi, who'd fallen back to sleep on the foot of Hávi's bed, then she went into her outer-room and opened the door. A young man, practically still a boy, glanced at her nervously from the hallway.

"There's a fleet on the horizon," Hávi told him. "Go tell Master Hvítvi that Jarl Austmaðr has returned."

"I-I can't leave my post," the boy stammered.

"Fine," Hávi sighed. "Find Bíldr and give him the message. He'll know what to do."

Somehow finding another guard didn't bother the foolish boy; he left at once. Hávi stared at the empty hallway after the boy had descended the stone stairs; now she could leave her rooms without anyone knowing. Jarl Austmaðr had returned; she didn't need to obey Hvítvi anymore, but what good was that? Hávi feared to think what Jarl Austmaðr would say when he heard about what she'd done during his absence. She hoped that Hvítvi would be the one to tell him; if Mjóvi or Krókr were the first to whisper in Jarl Austmaðr's ear then their reports were sure to be poisonous. Hávi glanced down the empty hall toward Hvítvi's room; slowly she walked to his door and knocked. To her amusement, Bíldr opened the door. He stared at her, his frown obvious, though mostly hidden behind his bushy mustache.

"Jarl Austmaðr's back," Hávi said softly, and then she meekly returned to her room.

Twenty minutes later, Tryggvi, whom Hávi had awoken, was still brushing Hávi's hair when the knock came at her door. Hávi was wearing her black dress with the Austmaðr family crest on her chest, since she had never finished the collar that Hvassi had made her start. Tryggvi quickly placed her silver tiara in her hair and they answered the door together.

"I'm to escort you to the harbor," Bíldr said.

Hávi bowed in acquiescence, then followed him down the stairs. Tryggvi stayed behind, insisting that the room needed a rapid cleaning.

The bell rang repeatedly as Hávi entered the courtyard. Mjóvi, Master Krókr, and a dozen other castle elders stood about in the light, misty rain, and most of the castle stood nearby. Before them, in rows of two, the guards stood just inside the main gate. Bíldr led Hávi to the front, to stand right behind Hvítvi, but Hvítvi kept his back to her, his long white hair and slender back all of him that she could see. Hávi couldn't blame him. *What could they say?* All of this ceremony was purposeful; Jarl Austmaðr would know that something was wrong even before he got off his ship. As always, Hvítvi had arranged things precisely, keeping everything under tight control. If Hávi had been half as clever as Hvítvi then she wouldn't be dreading her husband's return.

The townspeople of Skadi, who'd come running out into the streets at the constant ringing of the bell, cheered when the royal procession appeared marching down the crunchy white sea-shell road. Most of the fleet was hidden by trees but the gap in the bay showed many tall, striped sails hiding the horizon. A long banner hung over the sail of the lead ship: crimson red, hanging from spar to deck, bearing the Austmaðr family crest. The townsfolk of Skadi cheered wildly.

Their sails lowered inside the bay. The lead ship slid beside the dock and several men leaped overboard, splashing into the salty water, then running comically, with bright smiles and outstretched arms, as women and children burst from the crowd and ran splashing out to meet them. Dozens hugged and kissed as small waves lapped over their knees, heedless of the wet or cold. Two men jumped onto the dock with stout ropes which they masterfully wound around thick wooden pylons.

Jarl Austmaðr, tall and mighty as ever, stepped off the rail onto the dock and raised both fists in triumph toward the gray, overcast sky. The whole crowd cheered, but Hávi noticed that no smile graced Jarl Austmaðr's face. He looked as serious as death.

Other ships filled in behind Jarl Austmaðr's, crowding the harbor, but they remained strangely silent, their rowers stiff and grim-faced. The sailors watched those fathers who had splashed ashore, and the cheering crowd, without mirth, their lowering sails the only movement upon their ships as their fierce dragonhead prows softly slid up onto the sandy shore.

Jarl Austmaðr walked to the edge of the dock. While the crowd cheered, he held up both hands to motion for silence; everyone stopped cheering. Jarl Austmaðr paused until even the laughing children were hushed, and then he spoke loudly so that all could hear, but his voice was tremulous and choking.

"People of Skadi! Great news I bring! Successful has this viking been! Profit has been earned, enough that each man in the fleet will have silver in his hands when he returns to his family! Few have fallen, yet each loss is grievous. For my part, the family Austmaðr has suffered as great as any. My dear, beloved son, Auðgi, met his end bravely, slain by the cowardly Rús in a violent ambush."

Gasps filled the crowd. Women began to weep. Brave men bowed their heads and many removed helmets, hoods, and caps. Soon even the excited younger children, not understanding the cause of the sudden upset, began to wail.

"Tonight let there be celebration!" Jarl Austmaðr continued, his deep voice booming over the muted sobs. "Tomorrow night, here on this beach, we shall bid farewell to all those whom we loved, whose spirits, as we speak, are winging their way toward fabled Valhalla on the steeds of the Valkyrie."

Some men cheered feebly, trying to lighten the fallen mood, but their voices failed, quickly overwhelmed as the crying escalated. Sterki stepped up behind his father, his red hair darkened by the overcast, rainy sky, and placed a hand of comfort upon his father's shoulder. No more was said; Jarl Austmaðr stepped down off the dock onto the sand as if each step cost a lifetime of sorrow. Eyes downcast, he approached Hvítvi and wrapped his great arms around his thinnest son in a great hug so tight that Hávi feared Jarl Austmaðr might hurt fragile Hvítvi, lost in his grief, but Hvítvi whispered something into his father's ear and returned the mighty hug as best he could and, interlocked, the two men walked back to the castle.

Hávi and all of the others stepped aside to let them pass, Sterki close behind his father and younger brother. Hvítvi carefully avoided her eyes, and if Jarl Austmaðr noticed Hávi then he gave no sign. Only Sterki's cruel glare glanced at her.

Auðgi dead?

Hávi swallowed hard. Auðgi, who was always laughing, the awkward, excitable bear-cub of a son, her second stepson, *dead?* Hávi stood unmoving as the elders, and then the rest of the crowd, followed Hvítvi, Jarl Austmaðr, and Sterki back up the white road. Then Bíldr marched Hvítvi's guards past her, and finally many townspeople walked by, but Hávi never moved.

Not Auðgi!

Suddenly an infant blocked Hávi's view of the white sands at her feet. Breiðr had stepped close before her, her newborn daughter in her arms. A strange man that Hávi didn't know, who must've come off one of the many ships, had his arm around Breiðr's shoulders.

"Mother, we must go back home," Breiðr said softly.

Hávi obediently followed Breiðr and her husband, her thoughts a confused tumult. The walk itself was strangely taxing, and finally Hávi stopped, gasping, exhausted. Breiðr's husband offered to carry her, but Hávi refused, leaning on him instead. She placed one hand protectively over her bulging stomach, which had started to cramp. Never had she felt so weak. Many times she'd seen pregnant women slowed to the point of being bedridden by the slightest effort and now she understood why; the pain of simply walking while carrying a baby stunned her. Hávi took a deep breath and struggled to continue.

Inside the castle, Hávi glanced around the great hall, but Hvítvi, Jarl Austmaðr, and Sterki had vanished. Muted whispers, barely audible over the whimpering and sobs, filled the great hall. Hávi felt stunned by the news of Auðgi's death, numb, confused. She'd never gotten to know him, and now her only chance was lost.

Breiðr made Hávi sit in a chair near the back of the hall and ordered a servant to fetch wine. Breiðr asked Hávi if she should send for Master Kamban, but Hávi refused; she wouldn't let a simple pregnancy slow her down, but when the wine came she drank it greedily. Besides, Master Kamban wouldn't relish *'thumping'* his way through a crowded great hall in front of most of the castle elders just to tell Hávi that she needed rest. Hávi asked Breiðr if she could hold her baby daughter, and contented herself to nestle the infant in her arms while the whole hall gossiped. Hávi didn't dare leave, knowing the rumors that it would prompt, but no one was going to talk to her with everyone watching. The babe in her arms was just the distraction that she needed.

Tears leaked from her eyes, guilt for not spending more time with Auðgi. She knew how dangerous the vikings were. She'd watched Hersir men roughly train their sons: armed raiders who landed on Hersir shores would ruefully pay the price. Were the Rús any different? Hávi suspected not; every man would defend his family from raiders, and raiding was the whole purpose of the viking. The whispers and sobs grew louder, but the hall seemed quiet without Auðgi's contagious laughter.

A tiny finger suddenly jabbed inside her nostril; Breiðr's baby had grabbed her nose, smiling and burbling, unaware that her Uncle Auðgi had just died. Hávi clutched the infant tightly; *she couldn't let this happen again.* She would know as much of this child, of all her stepsons and stepdaughters, and most especially know the child inside her, as best as any mother could.

Unacceptable laughter came from deep voices as a large group of men noisily entered, but one of the elder men, the one who'd told Hávi that he'd seen a sea dragon, snapped gruffly at them, and they fell silent. Into the great hall they carried eight large chests, past Hávi and across the hall; everyone stared at the chests even after they disappeared through the far doorway and up the stone stairs. Several minutes later they returned, their hands empty, and Hávi suspected that the chests lay in her outer-room, guards posted at her door.

A servant came and got Master Krókr, who promptly

vanished through a side door. *That must be where Jarl Austmaðr had vanished to.* Now Master Krókr could start poisoning Jarl Austmaðr against her, but Hávi wasn't worried; Hvítvi had gotten to him first and eventually she'd have her chance.

"Breiðr, I need some bed rest," Hávi said, and her stepdaughter took her granddaughter from her arms.

"Do you need help?" Breiðr asked.

"No, not yet."

"Don't be embarrassed," Breiðr said. "I know what pregnancy's like."

"I know," Hávi smiled wanly and she heaved herself up off the chair. "Breiðr, I'd like you to come visit me."

"I will."

"I want us to be friends."

"I'd like that, too."

Chapter 21

Hávi's bedroom door creaked open so slowly that she was surprised when Jarl Austmaðr entered. Hávi's husband had always been many things: old, strong, energetic, abrasive, commanding, decisive; never once had she seen him look tired. Stepping into their room, his shoulders slumped, his head drooping, Jarl Austmaðr looked exhausted. He didn't even raise his head to look at her, just stared at the carpet, his long, thick arms hanging limply. Four months he'd been gone, but he'd aged years.

"You've made my grieving worse," Jarl Austmaðr said.

His words drove deep into her.

"I grieve, too," Hávi said.

Jarl Austmaðr lifted his head. On his cheeks Hávi spied the first tears that she'd ever seen dripping into his long, graying beard. Once, after her wedding, she'd seen her own tears wet that beard, but never leaking from his eyes.

"Auðgi was ... a good son," Jarl Austmaðr said. "It's been

weeks, but I haven't been alone since then, had no peace to think."

"I'm sorry, too, about Jarl Illingr."

"I warned you to stay away from him!" Jarl Austmaðr suddenly shouted, his whole body trembling-taut.

"I know," Hávi said meekly, unmoving, hoping that her stillness would calm him.

"Hvítvi said that Jarl Illingr was teaching you law, that he'd latched on to that stupid request about women refusing marriage ...!"

Jarl Austmaðr shook his head. Hávi wanted to argue, to defend her quest and her friendship with Jarl Illingr, but this wasn't the time. Jarl Illingr had insisted that patience was her best shield; *he'd been right, as always.*

"I'm sorry," Hávi repeated.

"Stand up," Jarl Austmaðr ordered.

With no recourse, Hávi slipped off their bed and stood before him. Jarl Austmaðr stepped up and roughly placed his hand on her tender bulging belly, squeezing firmly, feeling the child growing inside her. Hávi winced slightly; she'd forgotten his ungentle touch.

"Is it a boy?"

"I recite the charm for a son every day, but only Frigg can say."

"How long before the birth?"

"Mid-winter."

Jarl Austmaðr turned away disgustedly, clenching his massive fists. What if he rejected her? Would she lose her child? *Her life?*

"Husband, come to bed."

Jarl Austmaðr determinedly walked to the window, flung open the shutters, and stared down into the courtyard.

"Mjóvi says that the people hate you."

"Mjóvi speaks with Loki's tongue," Hávi said. "So does Krókr. Ask Breiðr and Bíldr ..."

"Who?"

Hávi took a deep, calming breath before replying.

"Breiðr, your daughter, and Bíldr, Hvítvi's guard."

"What do they matter?" Jarl Austmaðr scowled. "A woman and a guard? Who listens to them? Mjóvi has many powerful ears ..."

"I only want the two attached to her head."

Jarl Austmaðr turned to look at her; Hávi met his stare resolutely.

"You've grown over the summer," Jarl Austmaðr said.

"I've learned that I have enemies," Hávi said. "So do you."

"Who?"

"We have the same enemies."

"Yes, but I decide how to fight them."

"Of course."

"And when to fight them."

"Yes," Hávi said, "but I would be honored ... to help."

Jarl Austmaðr turned away.

"Husband, our bed's been cold."

Hávi slept little that night. Jarl Austmaðr drifted off quickly, but his sleep was troubled. Auðgi's name whispered from his lips several times, and each time his body shuddered. He rolled and thrashed against their covers, once pulling their white quilt completely off her. Gently Hávi pulled him close and cuddled him as if soothing an injured child; Jarl Austmaðr never would've allowed it if he were awake. Then, just once, a different name was uttered.

"Sterki!" Jarl Austmaðr whispered, a soft hiss, and even while sleeping, his face twisted with rage.

The next morning Jarl Austmaðr awoke, dressed, and left their room in silence. Hávi wondered if she should remain hidden but she'd been locked in her room most of the summer. Hávi rose to dress and was unsurprised when Tryggvi entered.

"Mistress, let me ...," Tryggvi said, and she hurried to take the gown from Hávi's hands.

"I want to go out," Hávi said.

"Out where?" Tryggvi asked.

"To Skadi."

"Mistress, I don't think that's wise."

"I'll decide what's wise."

"The gates are crowded," Tryggvi explained. "Many have come to pay their respects for ... for Auðgi."

Hávi opened the shutters and looked down. First she saw Hvítvi, his snow-white hair gleaming in the morning light. Jarl Austmaðr stood beside him, just outside the gate, with a shock of red hair on his other side: Sterki, Hávi's least-favorite stepson. Half of Skadi seemed gathered outside of the gate. One or two at a time came forward to talk to Jarl Austmaðr, doubtlessly offering what condolences they could. Hávi glared, furious; *they'd come to offer sympathy to the Austmaðr family ... and she hadn't been included.*

"Let's go to the roof," Hávi said.

For a long time, peering over the high edge of the roof, Hávi watched Jarl Austmaðr accept unheard condolences. Twice the crowd parted as some wealthy noble in a fancy carriage rode up and someone important strode past the peasants. Jarl Austmaðr rose from his chair to greet these people and had them escorted into the castle. Finally Hávi took Tryggvi down to the kitchen, where she hadn't been in

many weeks; the cooks and helpers welcomed her but not as
warmly as before. Hávi and Tryggvi took some sweets and
headed to the nursery. Fróði, Auða, Grái, and Hrogn
cheered delightedly and gladly accepted her treats, then
returned to their play. Hávi was free to talk to Breiðr, but
their conversation was bland, muted by the listening ears of
the wetnurses.

That evening, Hávi arrived for dinner dressed in her new
red gown, brought back from the viking, she climbed the steps
of the high-table and slipped behind all of the crowded chairs
all the way to the center ... only to find Hvítvi seated on Jarl
Austmaðr's left, Sterki on his right, and every other chair at
the high-table filled. Hávi froze; *she'd been set up again.*

Jarl Austmaðr turned to her, defiance in his eyes. Hávi
understood at once; she was being publicly rebuked again.
Hvítvi, Sterki, and all the rest at the high-table looked at her,
as did every eye in the hall. Hávi paused a second, then
continued forward. Jarl Austmaðr was punishing her for her
scandal with Jarl Illingr, displaying his strength and authority
to all. He had to ... or his enemies would call him weak.

Reaching the center, Hávi bent down to whisper in her
husband's ear as if that had been her intent all along. He
tilted his head to listen and she moved her lips, but no sound
came; Hávi couldn't think of anything to say. She pretended
to mutter something, then stood up and slid back the way
she'd come, not even glancing back. It was her fault that
she'd been caught in Jarl Illingr's tower in the middle of the
night; *she'd earned this rebuke.*

Closely watched every step, Hávi walked all the way to the
women's table, and then she got the greatest surprise: at the
other end of the women's table sat Mjóvi. *Had she sat here
since her husband's death?* Hávi hesitated, then smiled

brightly at her. Mjóvi scowled and looked down at her empty plate, her frown fixed amid taut wrinkles. Without her late husband to torment, Jarl Austmaðr had no reason to keep Mjóvi at the high-table. Mjóvi was being publicly punished for her part in causing the scandal and there was nothing that she could do about it; *she wasn't the wife of a jarl anymore.* Jarl Austmaðr wasn't just humiliating Mjóvi, he was blunting her influence, demoting her in the eyes of the whole clan. Despite her own rebuke, Hávi almost laughed.

Not one word was spoken at the women's table. Usually a font of gossip and slanders, the women sat timid, exchanging nervous glances from Hávi, at one end, to Mjóvi at the other. Hávi sat smiling until their table was finally served, and then she ate with relish; their food wasn't hot but it was far warmer than it'd been before she'd talked to the cook. Mjóvi ate quickly, then rose, leaving half of her food untouched, and she swept through a side door without a word.

"What a pleasant dinner companion!" Hávi said casually, and the whole women's table erupted in sniggers.

Normal conversation returned to the women's table. Apparently the widow of a jarl wasn't as feared as the wife of a jarl, but the boldness of the ladies surprised her. Mjóvi was ruined, helpless, but like a cornered snake, Hávi was sure that she was now more dangerous than ever. Hávi ate in silence, listening but thoughtful. Jarl Illingr was dead, but he'd been her most-trusted confidant; she wouldn't let him die in vain. She kept thinking over everything that he'd ever taught her.

"When you're holding the key to changing our laws, you'll know it," Jarl Illingr had said. *But what had he meant?*

Jarl Austmaðr stumbled into their bedroom quite drunk several hours before sunrise; Hávi wouldn't have awakened if he hadn't fallen across her legs trying to crawl into bed. The next morning Hávi awoke first, but she knew better than to leave her bedroom while her husband slept, so she rose and opened their shutters. Rain was falling, a light drizzle, so no one was visible save for a few unfortunates hurrying across the muddy streets of Skadi. Hrafna's tavern looked as far away as her home in clan Hersir. She wondered if she'd ever taste västerbotten again.

Late that evening, Jarl Austmaðr summoned Hávi. Beside Hvítvi and Sterki, Jarl Austmaðr led a silent procession of everyone in the castle through the gates and down the white road. Many carried torches. Hávi followed behind Hvítvi, more aware of him than anyone else, but he pretended that he didn't see her. Breiðr walked beside her, Bíldr behind them with Mjóvi, Master Krókr, and all the rest of the castle guards and servants, cooks and washer women, blacksmiths, and woodcarvers. Master Kamban was absent; his presence would've only made things worse, but Felian walked silently among the crowd.

Darkness shrouded Skadi, a shadowy evening sky of few stars and a cloud-hidden moon, but the torchlight made everything look aflame. Many footfalls crunched and ground the broken shells, signifying their mournful passage. Ahead, Hávi spied bright lights; the townspeople of Skadi awaited them with a hundred more flaming torches, bright sparks flittering and flickering, rising on the wind, lining the white road. Hvítvi's snowy hair glowed.

Hávi bowed her head; *she knew what lay ahead.*

Among the torchbearers of the townsfolk, Hávi was unsurprised to see Hrafna, Brækir, and Blönduhorn, although they were outnumbered by faces that she'd never seen. Not all were silent; many women wept openly and grim sadness masked every face. Even some men's cheeks shined.

As they passed, the torchbearers fell in behind, and the great procession led all the way through Skadi, between the familiar houses and shops that Hávi had spent a month watching from her window. They passed by the well, the small hill with the stocks, and didn't stop until they were walking across sand.

The wide, dark harbor was empty of fishing boats, looking almost naked. The few stars and many torches glinted off its choppy surface, making the water flash as if aflame. A soft wind blew from the north. Only one large vessel floated in the whole harbor: a great dragonship with its sail unfurled, listing hard to starboard against the wind, but firmly lashed to the dock. Hávi had never seen less than two dozen ships in this harbor, even during summer when the men sailed most of the vessels away. The eerie sight sent a shiver up her spine.

More folks awaited upon the shore bearing torches, lighting the beach as the waters endlessly splashed and receded. All were warriors, Jarl Dúfunef foremost among them. Jarl Hersir stood before many of her kinsmen, the warriors of clan Hersir. All stood silent and grim-faced, rigid under the flaming torchlight.

Jarl Dúfunef stepped forward as Jarl Austmaðr stopped, facing his fellow jarls. The head of the procession stilled, but the remainder circled around them. Jarl Dúfunef waited until he was fully encircled and all movement ceased. In one hand he held a flaming torch, in the other his long, straight, helical horn with its thin, sharp point and heavily-etched twisted spirals. Slowly he raised both above his head and the crowd fell utterly silent, even the crying muffled.

"Auðgi!" Jarl Dúfunef shouted. "Auðgi, we honor you!"

A cow mooed from somewhere close by but Hávi couldn't see it. Jarl Dúfunef looked older than she remembered, still tall, strong, and fierce-looking, but grimmer, darker, as if his face refused to be illuminated by the hundreds of flickering torches. His rugged features no longer looked youthful; his thick black hair was even more streaked with gray, like an aged wolf. His pure white bearskin cloak shone in the torchlight. Behind him, each of his warriors stood wearing sealskin cloaks pinned with a sharp, carven tusk, but no one moved unless the wind blew the flames of a torch near their face.

"Auðgi was a great warrior and a true friend!" Jarl Dúfunef shouted so that all could hear. "I knew Auðgi since we were kids, young princes of respected clans, bold and proud. Auðgi loved to viking more than anything else. He was a great warrior. Many enemies now serve Hel in Niflhiem because they dared cross swords with him. I personally witnessed many of his kills and swear that few men could rival his courage. Yet, when I think of Auðgi, when I recall our fondest moments, it's not with a sword in his hand that I recall him, but with a tankard foaming with beer until he drained it in one draught. No one else ever made me laugh so hard that ale spewed out of my nose. Even when battles went against us, Auðgi never failed in his everlasting humor. Never have I met a man more like mighty Thor in temperament; Auðgi's eyes were always open wide and no man disliked his company."

Jarl Dúfunef took a deep breath and surveyed the assembled crowd before continuing.

"Auðgi was a man worthy of the greatest praise, a prince of clan Austmaðr, Jarl Austmaðr's fifth son, strong and energetic, worthy of his father and his people. Proud and lucky were the warriors that served him, who followed him into battle, who now mourn greater than any. Among the best Auðgi stood, not only of clan Austmaðr but of clan Dúfunef, clan

329

Hersir, and every other clan in Scandinavia. Auðgi was fearless, and of no man can any say better. What is life but a chance to excel, to prove one's worth above others' accomplishments? Auðgi met every challenge, not grimly, not intimidated, but gladly, laughing and daring any ordeal to best him. Auðgi praised lesser men, scoffing at his better-accomplishments, for so great was he that the victories of others never shadowed his heart. Auðgi never vied for praise or feared to be outdone. The few times that he was bested in wrestling he bought ales for his opponents, and of none but those dishonored did Auðgi speak ill. Though he has left us, though his spirit has wrapped its strong arms around the waist of a beautiful Valkyrie and flown to fabled Valhalla, even I, the leader of clan Dúfunef, shall always feel Auðgi in my heart and strive to be like him. Of that, upon peril of his life, let no man doubt."

Dread silence followed this challenge, and Jarl Dúfunef turned slowly, sternly surveying the crowd as if seeking doubt on any man's face. Then he turned to the great dragonship, which was listing heavily, its full sail catching the wind, and he bowed. Suddenly Hávi understood: Auðgi was on that ship, his body wrapped and laid on its deck laden with weapons and treasure.

As Jarl Dúfunef returned to stand before his men, his father, the previous Jarl Dúfunef, his aged-gray beard glowing red in the torchlight, patted his back and whispered to him, but Hávi couldn't catch his words. Jarl Hersir came next, striding to the center of the circle, standing alone on the wet sand. In his one hand he carried a torch.

"I didn't know Auðgi as well as Jarl Dúfunef," Jarl Hersir's deep voice boomed out, echoing across the water. "Auðgi was far younger than I and died too early. But what I knew of

Auðgi I liked, even admired. Like his older brothers, Auðgi was wise and clever, strong and proud. A great Jarl Austmaðr Auðgi would've made, had the mantle of leadership ever fallen to him. Auðgi cared for every person in his clan, his ship, and our fleet. Auðgi didn't try to command through ignorance; he knew that the wisdom of many was often greater than the wisdom of one, even of a leader. Auðgi knew how to listen, but even more, Auðgi knew how to enjoy life. The immortality that the gods kept from men Auðgi understood; he celebrated each day, not with innocence but with wide-eyed wonder, eager to make each day his. How great our clans would be if we all lived like Auðgi."

Jarl Hersir bowed slightly to Jarl Austmaðr, whose face Hávi couldn't see. Then he nodded to his men and they parted. A great black bull was brought forward. It mooed in protest, but two men pulled it by ropes and several pushed it from behind. Other animals were also brought forward, two horses, a young moose, two deer, and six goats. All of the animals were hobbled, hampering their attempts to flee, but not muting their moos, neighs, and bleats. Other men carrying swords instead of torches came forward, and as the Hersir men struggled the resisting beasts into place, facing the water, Jarl Hersir hooked his torch into the crook of his handless arm, lifted up a great hunting horn, and then checked to make sure that his swordsmen were ready.

"Odin!" Jarl Hersir shouted. "Odin, accept now these gifts! Feast and welcome our beloved lost son, Prince Auðgi Austmaðr, and accept him as your servant, einherjar, a noble in Elvidner, your hallowed hall of warriors. Blessed be Odin! Blessed be Prince Auðgi!"

Jarl Hersir put his hunting horn to his lips and blew a loud, deafening note. As one, sharp swords swept down. Severed heads toppled and blood gushed, some splashing all the way across the water onto the dragon's hull. People cheered a long, loud uproar of triumph mixed with wails of grief.

Other men came forward with small axes and large knives, and as the crowd watched, each beast was butchered, legs removed, and entrails cast into the sea. Bleeding sections were carried up onto the dock and loaded aboard Auðgi's funeral ship.

Hvítvi slowly turned around. His pink eyes, afire in the torchlight, sighted upon Hávi's tear-streaked cheeks; the anguish on his face struck her like a mortal wound. She wanted to reach out, to comfort him, but three clans stood watching, and she could only meet his pale, bloodshot eyes with her own. Neither could do nor say anything, and finally Hvítvi turned back and placed a hand on his father's shoulder. Jarl Austmaðr's arm rose and wrapped around his youngest son. Sterki, whose red hair flamed dark in the torchlight, glanced at the two of them but he quickly turned away.

Jarl Austmaðr released Hvítvi and stepped forward into the empty circle. Jarl Austmaðr walked slowly, heavily, and addressed the crowd without raising his head.

"Loki," Jarl Austmaðr said, his deep rumbling voice heavy with remorse. "Loki ... is why we're here."

Many in the crowd gasped and stared disbelieving. Hvítvi glanced at his brother, Sterki, who stood rigid, tense but unmoving.

"Loki didn't create evil," Jarl Austmaðr continued, shouting over the wind. "Loki was the half-son of a god, but evil found its home inside him. Odin knows that, at the end of this world, Loki will arise from his cavernous prison and break free of his magical bonds. Then shall all evil things arise, join Loki, and make war upon all that's good. Ragnarök shall rage, the final battle ... and maybe the end of life forever. Odin knew this long ago, and so he created the Earth and the sky, the sea, the clouds and the mountains, not for himself, not for gods or giants, but for us, for men. On that fateful day when Heimdal winds his great horn, the gods cannot stand alone. Odin needs warriors, brave and mighty, to face the evils of every world, and though even the gods may die on that day, it is with us, with men, that life and goodness may triumph over evil ... and survive."

Jarl Austmaðr paused. No one spoke. Only the wind grew stronger, buffeting the flames of the torches and Auðgi's great, creaking dragonship.

"I've lost my son," Jarl Austmaðr continued. "My fourth dead son, and heavily burdened am I for each. Yet I mourn not for them; I celebrate their victories, for each now resides with Odin in Valhalla. Each has become, though too early for my mind, what I always wanted most for them, and someday for myself. Each now trains on the wide, grassy hills of Valhalla to prove worthy of their selection by the Valkyrie, to face every evil that shall someday arise and challenge all of our gods and life itself. I know that every man here longs to join them in the end, to mount behind a Valkyrie and be flown to Odin's hall.

"Yet ... is every man worthy? Who is ... and who is not? Let every man here look to himself, face their darkest secrets, and recognize the good inside of them, the good that my son Auðgi held in such abundance. Let us cast out of ourselves any evil that we find, that someday we may be judged by the Valkyrie and not be found wanting. I pray you, every man, examine your thoughts ... and seek in your hearts for some echo of Auðgi's laughter. Let Auðgi's light drive out any darkness that you find. Odin made this world for us. It's our sacred duty, beyond all others, to be the kind of men who serve him best. Look into your hearts ... for the light of Auðgi."

Jarl Austmaðr bowed slowly as if crumbling under a great weight. Several deep breaths he took, and the crowd stood silent, anxiously waiting. Finally Jarl Austmaðr faced Auðgi's great funeral dragon. He held out his open hands. Hvítvi and Sterki took four torches from someone in the crowd, one in each hand, and walked forward. Both sons placed a flaming torch into one of their father's outstretched palms. Jarl Austmaðr lifted both flaming torches high. He stepped toward the sea, closer to the creaking funeral dragon, and then he threw. Both of his torches flew high, striking the huge sail, then falling atop the deck. Hvítvi and Sterki threw their torches next, and then Jarl Dúfunef and Jarl Hersir threw theirs. All of the torches fell aboard the ship, and from them arose a great flame.

Suddenly the whole crowd surged forward. Flung torches filled the windy night's sky, emitting countless sparks and whooshing rushes. Most landed directly aboard ship but a few splashed sizzling into the black waters. The flames grew higher and soon the flapping sail caught, burning as if it'd been soaked in oil. Lines were cast from the dock and the great dragonship floated free, blown by the wind. Hávi heard orders shouted from the center of the harbor, and the light of the rising flames illuminated a small knarr oared by a dozen men pulling on a rope tied to the funeral ship. Slowly they drew the great, fiery dragonship away from the dock as its sail ignited along one side. Flames raced skyward. By the time that they'd pulled it into the center of the harbor, Auðgi's funeral dragon was engulfed from its carven dragonhead to its curling tail, the oiled sail browning as fire slowly consumed it, lighting the harbor as brightly as the sun. Every torch had been flung at it, landing atop what must've been cords of oiled wood stacked beneath Auðgi's body. The air filled with the roasting scents of the sacrificed meats.

The oarsmen rowed hard, gaining speed, and quickly Auðgi's flaming ship crossed the harbor and headed out to sea, its red light flickering upon the high, thick clouds, lighting Auðgi's way to paradise: a flaming signal so bright that even the gods would see it.

Jay Palmer

Chapter 22

Little was spoken save for condolences. Jarl Austmaðr was reportedly wandering the hallways, even into the washing room, as if in a fog. Sterki alone seemed to chase after him, insisting that he drink heavily, and finally Jarl Austmaðr was so drunk that he couldn't eat dinner and had to be carried to his room.

An agonizing week passed. Hávi rejoined the cooks in the kitchen, helping prepare their meals, and twice she visited Hvassi and the other women in the sewing room, still struggling to cross-stitch a straight line. Jarl Austmaðr was rarely seen sober, Sterki never far from his side. By the time that he came to bed each night, usually carried by two strong guards, Jarl Austmaðr was too drunk to talk. Hávi regretted his insobriety, but even if he could talk, what could she say? Hvítvi had vanished into his chambers and had not emerged. She longed to speak to him most, to mend the rift between them before it became a chasm.

Finally, unable to stand it any longer, Hávi went and knocked on Hvítvi's door. Bíldr answered, staring questioningly down at her.

"I wish to go into Skadi," Hávi said.

"Why?"

"I purchased a chest for Jarl Austmaðr which should be finished by now," Hávi said. "I wish to present it."

"A message could be sent ..."

"I'd rather see to it myself," Hávi said, looking imploringly up at his mustached face. "I-I'd appreciate your company ... as escort."

Bíldr stared, surprised, then frowned. "Wait here."

A minute later, an older guard that Hávi didn't know slipped past her and closed the door behind him. Hávi waited a good five minutes and was about to knock again when the older guard came back with two other guards. They hurried past her into Hvítvi's chambers and then Bíldr came out, looking sour.

"Where's your handmaid?" Bíldr asked.

"Tryggvi's cleaning our room," Hávi said.

"I can't escort you alone."

Wise young man, Hávi thought, and she fetched Tryggvi, and then the three of them descended the stone stairs.

The sun outside was high, bright and warm but not hot; summer was quickly fading. Doubtless many were harvesting already, hurrying to bring in their crops before the first bite of winter. The countless tall wooden houses and shops gleamed as Hávi approached Skadi. She'd been locked up in the castle too long; she couldn't wait to taste västerbotten again.

Hávi's breathing became labored; in the daytime, walking into Skadi pregnant seemed more difficult than she'd thought possible, yet she kept going.

They visited the woodwright's shop first. The beautiful chest lay gleaming just inside his front door, finished and finely polished, a worthy gift, the most-ornate chest that Hávi had ever seen. The woodwright begged her forgiveness for not sending her a message, claiming that he didn't want to disturb anyone mourning for Auðgi. Hávi thanked him for his thoughtfulness, insisted on giving him an extra silver coin, and asked the woodwright to personally deliver the chest to the castle at sunset wrapped in a blanket. The woodwright promised obedience, and with many fair words they left his shop.

Hrafna's tavern wasn't empty. Several men occupied the table nearest the fire. One man had a sword drawn and was demonstrating a complicated move, bragging of some Rús that he'd killed. The other men smiled and laughed as they drank from their tankards: warriors boasting, as Hávi had grown up seeing around Hersir fires, yet upon seeing her they fell silent.

"Good day," Hávi greeted them.

The man with the drawn sword sheathed it quickly.

"Good day," he returned, and then he approached Hávi, quickly bowed, and without another word he swept past Hávi and out the door. One by one his companions did the same. After a barrage of *'Good days'* from each, Bíldr, Tryggvi, and Hávi stood alone, speechless, staring across the long tavern at Brækir and Blönduhorn, who stood by the kegs washing clothes in a barrel and hanging them to dry on thin ropes strung along one wall.

Hávi swallowed her pride. She'd just been insulted by peasants, confirmed unworthy as clearly as when her husband had publicly chastised her, yet she paused only a moment to conquer her fury. Mjóvi had accomplished her foul work; Hávi was the disgrace of the Skåne. Humiliated but determined, Hávi walked across Hrafna's tavern and sat down at the table before the small, dying fire. Bíldr and Tryggvi stood silently by the door.

Blönduhorn poured her an ale but Brækir took the tankard and set the drink before Hávi.

"Anything else, Mistress Austmaðr?" Brækir asked with ice in her screechy voice.

"Your company," Hávi smiled, motioning to the bench beside her.

"Mistress, I have work to ..."

"You will sit with me!" Hávi said loudly, menace in her voice.

Brækir paled, then pulled her wool shawl tight about her shoulders. She reluctantly sat beside Hávi, her lips tightly closed. Hávi hated using her position; once she'd been so common that Brækir would've boxed her ears for speaking so.

"Blönduhorn, bring your mother an ale and some västerbotten," Hávi ordered Blönduhorn, who hurried to obey.

"Brækir, I apologize," Hávi said. "I know what the rumors are saying, that I disgraced Jarl Austmaðr, our clan, and the whole Skåne, but it's all lies."

"If you say so, Mistress," Brækir said perfunctorily.

"How can you talk to me like that?" Hávi almost shouted. "After all that I've tried to do for your family ...!"

"Yes, Mistress," Brækir said. "Will that be all?"

Blönduhorn brought ale and the västerbotten and set them between Hávi and Brækir, then she stooped to build up the fire.

"Be off with you!" Brækir ordered.

"No," Hávi countered. "I wish Blönduhorn to stay."

Trembling, Blönduhorn stared up at Hávi and Brækir, obviously terrified, but Hávi continued to ignore her.

"Brækir, be honest with me; do you believe the rumors?"

"What rumors, M'am?"

Hávi glared, frustrated. Lies could be argued with, but ignorance couldn't be disproved; pretending ignorance had gotten Hávi and Völu out of trouble several times. Frowning, Hávi turned to Blönduhorn.

"Blönduhorn, do you believe the rumors?"

"Oh, no!" Blönduhorn insisted. "I'm sure that Auðgi died an honorable death."

Eyes flew open, Hávi shocked, Brækir horrified, and Blönduhorn terrified. Despite Hávi's late pregnancy, she jumped to her feet.

"What do you mean '*honorable death*'?" Hávi shouted angrily.

"*She means nothing!*" Brækir screeched as she roughly shoved Blönduhorn back toward the kegs. "*Fool child! Outside!*"

"*What did you mean?*" Hávi screamed. "*Come back here! Explain ...!*"

Blönduhorn burst into tears and ran off, heedless of Hávi's shouts. Reaching the back door, Blönduhorn banged it open and vanished outside.

"*What did she mean?*" Hávi demanded of Brækir. "*How could Auðgi not have died an honorable death?*"

Brækir said nothing. Hávi grabbed her arm and shook her as if she'd squeeze the truth from her. Suddenly Bíldr seized both women and pried them apart with surprising strength.

"That's enough!" Bíldr shouted. "Be quiet! Do you think that these walls don't have ears?"

Hávi pulled free of his grasp but glared stubbornly.

"Leave her be!" Bíldr insisted. "You care for this family; Hvítvi knows that, but if you force her to talk now then everyone under this roof will be killed!"

"Killed?" Hávi gasped.

"Murdered," Bíldr assured her.

Hávi staggered. *Curse of Loki! What was being kept from her this time?* Yet she looked up into Bíldr's stern face, saw his earnestness, and knew that he'd never lied to her.

"Murdered," Bíldr whispered, his eyes full of warning. "As I will be ... if I speak."

Hávi stared at him, then at Brækir, then to the door out of which Blönduhorn had fled, and she even glanced back at Tryggvi, whose tears drenched her cheeks as she trembled by the door. They all knew ... *a secret* ... and Bíldr was right: making any of them tell her would get them killed.

"Take me home," Hávi ordered Bíldr. "I want to speak to Hvítvi."

"Out," Hvítvi said.

Hávi stood defiant, ready to argue, but Hvítvi wasn't talking to her. Bíldr, Tryggvi, three other guards, and a young servant who was replacing the white cloth covers over all of the furniture obediently turned and left Hvítvi's outer-chamber. Bíldr gave Hvítvi a stern warning glare ... and then closed his door firmly.

Hávi and Hvítvi stared at each other. Into a silent abyss fell whatever feelings they shared; Hávi was Hvítvi's stepmother and had to remain in that role, but Hvítvi stood as handsome as ever, his long white hair gleaming like new snow, his straight nose and soft features highlighting his pale complexion against the whiteness of the room. *If only he'd smile!* His dark blue tunic alone made him stand out; otherwise he'd have seemed a ghost lost in his fog-chamber, but Hávi forced herself to concentrate on why she'd come, not the joy that she always felt in his presence.

Hávi's joy crashed like a wave on rocks when Hvítvi spoke.

"You're utterly mad," Hvítvi said. "You must be mad! Clan Austmaðr's about to fall into ruin ...!"

"Ruin?"

"... and you go shouting about it in taverns!"

"I didn't shout anything!"

"How far do you think your position protects you? How far do you think Father will let you go before he can't afford to keep you anymore?"

"What do you mean *'keep me'?*"

Hvítvi turned away, but Hávi grabbed his arm and forcibly spun him back.

"Don't do that!" Hvítvi hissed, pulling his arm free of her grip. "I know I'm not strong; you don't have to prove it."

"What's going on?" Hávi demanded.

"Nothing," Hvítvi said softly. "Nothing that you need to know of and nothing that you can do anything about. The less that you know the safer you are. Just talking about it's dangerous."

"Talking about what?" Hávi demanded. "About Auðgi ...?"

"Silence!" Hvítvi seethed. *"Do you want to kill both of us?"*

Hávi paused, horrified by the unexpected fear in Hvítvi's voice. Hvítvi scowled and stepped away, sighing as if under a heavy burden.

"Just tell me," Hávi whispered. "I won't say a ..."

"You've proven how well you can't keep a secret," Hvítvi

sneered. "Jarl Illingr's dead. Clan Austmaðr's shamed. Mjóvi and Krókr were virtually running the Skåne during the scandal. You don't know what's been happening; you were locked up in your room ..."

"You locked me in my room!"

"For your own protection, like I would protect a stumbling infant at the top of a stairs," Hvítvi scowled, his voice barely a whisper. "Clan Austmaðr was calling for your blood."

"Mjóvi and Krókr, you mean," Hávi whispered.

"Clan Austmaðr has enemies, wealthy lords and rival clans, which constantly watch for signs of weakness," Hvítvi said. "Their spies don't just listen to gossip; they spread bad news like a plague. Father's canceled all taxes on our lands just to appease the peasants, which means that we're living off the spoils of the viking. Our expenses won't allow us to do that forever. We've got to reestablish a perception of strong, calm leadership."

"How did Auðgi die?"

Hvítvi bowed his head and seemed to crumble before her. Tears leaked from his eyes and his breaths came in small gasps, almost sobs.

"If I tell you then I could be killed," Hvítvi whispered slowly. "You could be killed. Clan Austmaðr could fall."

"Please?"

Hávi reached out and took his hand but Hvítvi jerked it from her suddenly as if frightened to touch her.

"No!" Hvítvi whispered desperately. "We can't ... we can't touch ... we can't ... *anything!*"

Hávi bit her lower lip as the unwanted memory of Hvítvi's perfect kiss flashed through her mind. She could still taste his soft, desirable, pale lips. They were alone again, without witnesses, yet she couldn't think such thoughts; she

understood the dangers now, the destruction that they'd cause
...

"*Auðgi,*" Hávi whispered.

Hvítvi sighed deeply, then sank onto a white sheet-covered bench. Huge tears rolled down his cheeks as he gestured for Hávi to sit beside him.

"No one knows," Hvítvi whispered so softly that he had to speak right into her ear. "Father led a raid deep into a northern city near Germany as they were making their way home. Auðgi was with the family guard, protected, but he got separated. Auðgi vanished ... with Sterki."

"*Sterki ....?*"

"This is nothing but rumor," Hvítvi warned. "No one knows what happened. Sterki and Auðgi were alone ... and when our guards found them, Sterki was carrying Auðgi over his shoulder. Sterki said that they'd been attacked, and that Auðgi was wounded by a group of Rús hiding in the shadows of a barn. Sterki claimed that he killed the Rús, then brought Auðgi back to be healed. But ... Auðgi ... was beyond healing. He'd been killed by a sword just like the one that Sterki carried."

"*Fiend of Loki!*"

"*Silence!* I wasn't there, and I only heard the rumor because I have my own spies who sail with Father."

"What is known?"

"Only that the guards demanded that Sterki take them back and show them where he'd fought the Rús, but Sterki refused. When Father learned that Auðgi was dead ..., well, at first he demanded the same thing, but Sterki refused him; he publicly rebuked Father, and ... rather than beat him, Father relented."

"Why?"

"Because Sterki's all that he's got left!" Hvítvi hissed. "I can't rule the Skåne; without Auðgi, Sterki's his only choice! Father can't afford to lose Sterki, no matter what ...!"

"Even if he ...," Hávi whispered, lowering her voice so softly that she had to speak directly into Hvítvi's ear, *"...even if Sterki murdered Auðgi?"*

"Jarl Dúfunef asked that, and I think that Jarl Hersir supported him," Hvítvi said. "They're not happy. This isn't the first time; one of our older brothers died years ago by a stray arrow while Sterki was missing, but no one believed the rumors then. Those old rumors have resurfaced, but Father's resolute. There's no one left to rule clan Austmaðr except Sterki, so Father refuses to consider him guilty. I can't consider him guilty. You can't consider him guilty. And, for Odin's sake, don't even speak of this to Hrafna, Brækir, or Blönduhorn! They're just peasants, and Sterki would have no compulsion against having their throats cut in their sleep, they and all of their children. He'd probably burn down their tavern to hide their murders, and Father would have to look the other way again, although knowing what happened."

"Doesn't he care?" Hávi asked.

"Of course Father cares!" Hvítvi seethed. "It's eating him up. Why do you think that he's drinking so much? Why do you think that Sterki's hovering over him like a swooping raven? Father knows, but he can't admit it. He can ruin one son, but not when he's the family's only hope of maintaining rule. And that's why you can't leave the castle again."

"What?!?" Hávi demanded.

"Why do you think I've got guards protecting me day and night?" Hvítvi asked. "I'm not much of a threat, but you, *Mother* ...," Hvítvi stressed the word, "... are Mistress Austmaðr, bearing Father's child, possibly a new son; Sterki fears you most of all."

"But ... you let me go into Skadi today ...," Hávi said.

"You didn't know," Hvítvi whispered. "Now you do."

"But Sterki can't know ..."

"Are you willing to bet your life on that?" Hvítvi asked. "What if he just suspects? I can't know half of the things that I suspect. Never assume that any secret is kept; in times like this, assumptions get you killed."

Hávi closed her eyes, feeling the wetness of her unnoticed tears. *Poor Auðgi!* Sterki; what was her husband to do? Outlaw his own son and destroy clan Austmaðr? But Hávi couldn't say anything without revealing what she knew, then probably being forced to reveal from whom she learned it. Sterki had always despised her: hadn't he once threatened her and her unborn child? Jarl Austmaðr had promised to speak to him, but if Sterki would murder his own brother, how safe could she be?

Hávi opened her eyes, startled to find Hvítvi's pink eyes staring worriedly at her, inches from her face.

"Hávi, are you going to get us killed?"

Hávi couldn't answer.

Jay Palmer

Chapter 23

Drunk, Jarl Austmaðr stumbled into his bedroom late that afternoon. The front of his tunic was soaked; he looked like he'd spilled his whole ale horn down his front. As the door opened, he grabbed its lintel to steady himself, then stumbled inside the room, swaying as he walked, his eyes upon the stained carpet.

"What happened?" Hávi asked.

"Oh, just an accident," Jarl Austmaðr scowled, starting to unfasten his belt. "Fetch me a dry tunic, will you?"

Hávi helped him unfasten his belt and then peeled the soaked tunic off him. Jarl Austmaðr was little help; too drunk to stand still, too big for her to pull around, especially while she was heavy with child. Jarl Austmaðr swayed, tipped, and several times almost fell, but Hávi managed to strip him and used the back of his tunic to dry his chest. Then, gritting her teeth, Hávi pulled her husband into an embrace and kissed him.

"What's this?" Jarl Austmaðr asked, surprised.

"Why don't you stay up here for a while ... with me?"

"I told Sterki that I'd be right bac...," Jarl Austmaðr began, but Hávi cut him off.

"We've done nothing but sleep in our bed since you came home."

Jarl Austmaðr's eyes popped and he stared down at Hávi.

"But ... but I didn't think you .... you're already pregnant ..."

"With your son," Hávi said, and she took Jarl Austmaðr's large, rough hand and placed it against her extended belly. "Two more months and he'll be born."

"No ..., I mean, I thought ... you didn't ..."

"I'm your wife," Hávi said, and she pulled him toward their bed.

"But ... Auðgi..."

"I mourn him, too," Hávi said softly, "more than you know. I think I need it. I think you need it, too ..."

Jarl Austmaðr sat down on the edge of their bed and Hávi began unlacing and pulling off her dress. She knew the cause of his drinking, and although his aged flesh didn't repulse her as it used to, still an unwelcomed shudder ran up her spine.

Jarl Austmaðr made love to her with tears dripping from his eyes. Afterwards he actually sobbed as Hávi held him. Her husband was a clan-chief, a viking leader; he could never appear weak in public, but he'd loved Auðgi, his laughing, bear-like son, more than he'd ever admitted. Sobs racked his body, but didn't last long; he clenched both fists, every muscle taut, and Hávi struggled to hold his fury at bay, feeling the full strength of his body, attempting to restrain his crushing arms from injuring her unborn child. Jarl Austmaðr could easily break her bones if he tried, but she held him close, unresisting, and quickly his anguish failed. He pushed away from her the instant that his sobs subsided.

"Hey!" Sterki's voice shouted as a fist banged on their outer-door. "You fall asleep in there?"

Jarl Austmaðr winced as if stabbed, but Hávi pretended not to notice. She stared at her husband; he looked haggard, exhausted.

"Shall I send him away?" Hávi offered.

"No!" Jarl Austmaðr said with surprising emphasis. "No, I'll go. Sterki's been ... in a foul mood ... since his brother died. Stay away from him. Do you hear me? This isn't like with Jarl Illingr; *don't ever be alone with him!"*

"I won't," Hávi promised. "I won't disobey you ... ever again."

Jarl Austmaðr slowly rose, then shouted for Sterki to wait as he dressed. Biting her lip, Hávi watched him.

"Husband," Hávi said softly, "while you've been gone I've ... gotten to know Hvítvi. He's a ... good son."

Jarl Austmaðr paused but never raised his eyes off the carpet. With a heavy sigh, he left.

"Mistress!" Tryggvi cried urgently, ascending the stone stairs as Hávi descended.

"Is something wrong?" Hávi asked.

"It's sunset," Tryggvi said. "The woodwright's here."

Hávi hurried down to the great hall where the woodwright stood just inside the door, cap in hand, looking very nervous. Beside him, covered in a blanket, stood the magnificent wooden chest, hidden by a blanket thrown over it. Two older boys, the woodwright's sons, stood against the back wall, eyes wide, scanning every detail of the great hall so amazedly that Hávi guessed that they'd never been inside the castle before.

The hall was nearly full, and many of the guests were eyeing the three peasants and the large covered box.

"We'd best get this over with," Hávi said, seeing Jarl Austmaðr take his seat at the high-table. Sterki, she noted, sat right beside him; Hvítvi wasn't there. "Boys, pick it up and follow me. Don't uncover it until I say to."

"I'll wait here," the woodwright said.

"No," Hávi insisted. "You will escort me."

The hall slowly fell silent as Hávi led the small procession past the many tables, stopping only before the high-table. Jarl Austmaðr stared at her and the covered box. The woodwright seemed worried; he didn't escort Hávi but followed her closely, his sons behind him carrying the large covered box by its pole. When Hávi stopped, she gestured for them to bring the box forward and set it down, after which both boys went and stood behind their father.

"Most dutiful husband," Hávi spoke clearly, facing the high-table, her voice carrying across the hall. "I commissioned a gift for you, unknowing the grief of your return. I've no desire to interrupt your mourning, but I would present my gift, small though it may now seem."

Jarl Austmaðr's eyes raised and a brief smile passed over his face. He nodded, and Hávi echoed his nod to the woodwright, who bowed deeply and pulled off the blanket. A gasp rose from the assembled guests; the ornate wooden chest gleamed brightly in the firelight of the great hall. None could deny its craftsmanship. Several different woods had been used in its construction, and even the pole carrying it shined from a recent polishing.

"Take that away!" Sterki's harsh voice snarled over the gasps. "How dare you disgrace a grieving father ...!"

"No!" Jarl Austmaðr boomed. He glared at his son, who

stared back defiantly but said no more. Jarl Austmaðr pushed back his chair, scooted behind the seated guests, and then descended the steps and approached his wife. Hávi curtsied while the woodwright and his sons bowed deeply. Jarl Austmaðr took the pole out of its holders, then carefully examined the exquisite wooden chest, slowly opening and closing its many lids, sliding his fingers over its carved ravens, seals, and tiny inlaid wooden swords.

"Even amid my grief I can't help but admire such magnificence," Jarl Austmaðr said loudly enough for the whole hall to hear. "A fine gift from a faithful, dutiful wife."

The hall erupted in applause. Hávi smiled brightly, flushed with relief. Jarl Austmaðr turned to the woodwright and shook his sweaty, shaking hand, then further disturbed him by asking Master Krókr to find seats for the woodwright and his sons in the great hall. Master Krókr bowed and then led the woodwright and his sons to seats near the back, ignoring their protestations of being too humble to dine in the castle. Jarl Austmaðr examined the chest again, and then he thanked Hávi a second time. Hávi curtsied so slowly and deeply that even Mjóvi couldn't have faulted her.

"Leave it here while we eat," Jarl Austmaðr said, meaning the chest. "Let everyone get a chance to look at it."

"As you wish, my husband," Hávi said.

Jarl Austmaðr glanced up at the high-table, frowned, and suddenly he embraced Hávi in front of everyone. Hávi felt surprised until his voice whispered into her ear.

"You can't sit at the high-table; it's not safe."

Politely Hávi stepped back, curtsied again, and then she turned to take her place at the women's table. Mjóvi stormed out of the hall before Hávi reached her seat.

Over the next few days Hávi busied herself in the kitchen and sewing room, thanking both the cook and Hvassi for all of their teachings. Both laughed off her gratitudes, reminding her that this was her castle, not theirs, but both seemed delighted with Hávi's renewed determination. In the kitchen, Hávi chopped vegetables and churned butter tirelessly. In the sewing room, while trying to force a seam straight, Hávi once stabbed herself with a needle so hard that her blood flowed freely and the women had to pry her sewing from her fingers before she bled upon it. Then Hávi sent Tryggvi with a message to Master Kamban, apologizing for her impertinence and begging him to resume his medical instruction. Felian, Master Kamban's attendant, relayed a most-sincere greeting to Hávi and assured her that his master would be delighted to begin her lessons again. Hávi arranged for a lesson the next day in the Hall of Audiences, but then she frowned; there was still Hrafna's family that she'd wronged, and of course, Jarl Illingr, but he and his family were beyond all help.

Thoughts of Jarl Illingr reminded Hávi of something; he was dead, but were all of Jarl Illingr's teachings lost?

"Tryggvi, what's been done with Jarl Illingr's tower?"

"Done?" Tryggvi asked. "Why ... nothing."

"You mean it's all there?" Hávi asked. "All those papers and scrolls that he wrote?"

"I ... assume so."

"Could you get them?" Hávi asked. "Without being seen, I mean; get all of his papers and hide them somewhere safe?"

"Mistress, haven't you been burned enough?" Tryggvi asked warily. "Forgive me, but ..."

"That won't happen this time," Hávi promised, but in her heart she knew that she might be lying.

Hávi grinned as Tryggvi departed. Those papers held

everything that Jarl Illingr knew about the law. Now all that she needed was someone who could read.

"Yes, of course I can read," Master Kamban said.

"Could you teach me?"

The hunchback eyed Hávi suspiciously while Felian and Tryggvi shifted nervously on their stools.

"I thought that you wanted to learn healing."

"I do," Hávi assured him. "I just thought, if I knew how to write, then I could copy down ..."

"And then what?" Master Kamban asked. "Go searching through scrolls while someone's bleeding to death? Paper's useful in healing; blood soaks easily into paper and quickly clots over paper-covered wounds, but often healing allows no time for reading scrolls. Lives can be saved only if you know what to do."

"Master Kamban, you know as well as I that I'll never be let onto a dragonship," Hávi said. "I'll never go viking and seldom be allowed outside the castle. What's the point of learning healing if I never get to use it?"

"I'm not allowed on battlefields," Master Kamban said pointedly. "I never leave the castle, but there's plenty to keep me busy. I've birthed sixteen children, cared for many of the elderly, and accidents abound. On top of all that, there's Hvítvi; there'll be plenty for you to do."

Hávi spent the day learning several new healing chants. Master Kamban was disappointed that she couldn't recall all that he'd said about herbs; he went over it again, and Hávi struggled to memorize each word, identify each plant, and recall every medicinal use for each. Master Kamban said that he was impressed with her sudden devotion, and Hávi was glad to hear his appreciation. She'd spent all summer offending people and distancing herself; she had fences to mend.

"Valla and Augi?" Jarl Austmaðr asked. "Who're they?"

"Hrafna's oldest boys," Hávi said.

"Why them?"

"Who else?"

"Why not boys from a wealthy family?" Jarl Austmaðr asked. "We wouldn't have to pay for them."

"Wealthy sons would be loyal to their families. By choosing peasants, they'd be loyal to you."

Jarl Austmaðr laid his head back against his sheepskin pillow.

"That's a good point," Jarl Austmaðr said. "Are you still hoping to make them Law-speakers?"

"Clan Austmaðr needs good Law-speakers," Hávi said. "If we can't find them and we don't make them ..."

Jarl Austmaðr frowned.

"Valla and Augi," he said. "Do ... do you think that they're capable ...?"

Hávi swallowed hard: time for the truth.

"Jarl Illingr thought that they were good students ... and he was the best."

"Very well," Jarl Austmaðr said. "Clan Dúfunef has several wise scribes. I'll offer to trade some cows for one if I can't find a Law-speaker. But Hávi: *you will not learn to read!*"

"As you wish, my husband."

Valla and Augi began their lessons in reading and writing with Gylðir, a young man from clan Dúfunef, the very next week. Gylðir seemed too young to know how to read; he was several years younger than Hávi, but he seemed delighted with

his new duties. He'd even had some training as a Law-
speaker, although he'd never attended a Thyngr. To help
him teach the boys, Hávi gave him a large scroll written by Jarl
Illingr entitled *Interpretations of the den Skaanske Lov,* and
Gylðir thanked her profusely. He invited Hávi to stay and
observe his first lesson, but she knew that Jarl Austmaðr
would hear of it, so she declined. But, if she slowly gave him
every one of the scrolls that Jarl Illingr wrote, then eventually
Jarl Illingr's teachings would return to life.

Harvest drew off almost everyone. The guards, when not
on duty, earned extra money helping the local farmers, and so
the castle emptied for most of the fall.

Hvítvi stayed hidden in his room and Hávi relaxed, certain
that her feelings for him were just a passing phase, something
that she'd get over in time. When her mind wandered,
pleasant thoughts of Hvítvi swirled inside her, yet when she
recalled that he was her stepson, she forcibly banished them.

Hávi's worries grew as Jarl Austmaðr became seldom seen
without Sterki hovering close by like a red-headed wolf
prowling its prey. Her husband kept drinking heavily,
encouraged by Sterki, who also drank a lot and became more
belligerent as he drank; they often argued. Sterki's face was
seldom seen without a disgusted snarl even when he laughed,
and his nasty glare stung Hávi whenever they exchanged
glances. Hávi was certain that he'd kill her; Hávi's growing
belly, possibly a rival son, seemed to poison his mind. As
Hávi started to wear only dresses which allowed for her
bulging midsection, her fear of Sterki increased. He never
spoke to her, so there was nothing to prove his obvious
enmity, which Jarl Austmaðr alone, blinded by strong ales,
didn't see. Several times Hávi considered voicing her fears to

her husband, but what would Hvítvi say? Jarl Austmaðr
would demand to know where she'd heard the rumors of
Auðgi's murder, of which there was no proof, and Hávi
daren't refuse her husband.

The first snows came late, which pleased everyone. Hávi
finally had to submit to her bed; her stomach was so big that
she couldn't walk well and all movement drained her strength.
Yet inside Hávi could feel distinct fumblings: tiny feet kicked
and a miniature body squirmed. She gave up helping in the
kitchen and sewing room. She even gave up her lessons with
Master Kamban; although she could now identify every herb,
name their properties, and chant dozens of healing charms.
Hávi wondered why she'd never considered the possibility
that her child was a girl but somehow even these thoughts
couldn't dissuade her certainty that she was bearing a boy, a
son who'd grow to be ...

Tears burst from Hávi's eyes. Her son would be an
innocent, helpless babe. *Would Sterki allow her child to live,
to grow up, a rival to the title of Jarl Austmaðr?*

Tryggvi fretted over Hávi every minute and Master
Kamban started checking on her each day. Living mostly in
his own room, Master Kamban reported that he'd heard
nothing of what was happening inside the castle while Hávi lay
bedridden, but he also tended to Hvítvi every few days, and
from him Hávi learned that Hvítvi had taken to leaving the
castle with his guards and riding across the countryside,
although he knew that it was risky and horses made him
sneeze. But the snowdrifts weren't deep yet and he always
rode fast to the houses of friends that he trusted, surrounded
by enough guards to defend a small siege; Master Kamban
suspected that he was laying traps for anyone who might

attempt to ambush him rather than waiting for them to trap him. Every time that he got back Hvítvi had to spend a day or two in his steam-room before he felt well again, and Master Kamban praised Hávi for teaching him to rub heads; often he relieved Hvítvi's pains enough to let him sleep using her technique.

Jarl Austmaðr grew increasingly irritable as Sterki's presence became a constant irritant. Jarl Dúfunef once visited, and before the whole assembled feast, he ordered Sterki to leave him and Jarl Austmaðr alone. Sterki stormed off swearing vengeance, and Jarl Dúfunef asked aloud, while watching him stomp away, '*if anyone else had died while alone with Sterki*'. Sterki rashly reminded Jarl Dúfunef of Jarl Illingr's ears, and Jarl Dúfunef had to shout to restrain a dozen of his angry retainers while Sterki left the hall. Jarl Austmaðr said nothing during their argument, and then sat through dinner and long into the night while Jarl Dúfunef whispered in his ear.

Tensions grew daily as Hávi's stomach swelled. She rose from her bed three times every day to walk around her bedroom, sometimes to sit in her big chair by the window or the fireplace, which Tryggvi kept burning high to keep off any chills, although Hávi complained that her room was stiflingly hot. Hávi couldn't get comfortable anywhere and had to force herself not to snap at Tryggvi.

Mjóvi's evil hadn't quelled. No others came to see Hávi; afraid for her safety, Breiðr's husband refused to let her sleep in the castle. Many times Tryggvi stumbled into Hávi's room weeping uncontrollably; vicious tongues now argued where once great friendships existed. Castle Austmaðr had grown unpleasant, full of undeserved suspicions and violent tempers. Skadi, rumors reported, was even worse, ripe with feuds and thievery. No man left his door unbarred or walked about unarmed.

Worst of all, Sterki kept forcing his company on Jarl Austmaðr; echoes of their arguments rang through the halls. Hávi wished that she could help, but what could she do, burdened with a child as her birthing time grew closer? She became Jarl Austmaðr's only escape from Sterki, the one person that he could turn to that wasn't reminding him of what everyone suspected.

Chapter 24

"You can't tax peasants in the middle of winter!" Jarl
Austmaðr shouted.

"By spring, clan Dúfunef will be storming our shores!"
Sterki argued.

Aching, lying in her bed, Hávi gasped labored breaths
while Tryggvi held her hand and bathed her forehead with a
cool cloth. Jarl Austmaðr and Sterki were at it again, this time
in the outer-room, just on the other side of her door.

"Jarl Dúfunef isn't going to attack us!" Jarl Austmaðr
shouted.

"My spies say that he's amassing weapons and building
new ships," Sterki shouted back.

"Good! We can use them for the viking ..."

"He won't wait until the viking! Mjóvi said ...!"

"I don't care if Mjóvi overheard it herself! I helped raise
Jarl Dúfunef! His father and I grew up together ...!"

"His father's been locked in a dungeon!"

"I don't believe that, either."

"Are you willing to risk clan Austmaðr on an old friendship?"

"Your proofs are just hollow rumors."

"You're a fool!"

Their argument grew steadily worse. At times no words could be discerned as they shouted simultaneously, neither listening to the other.

"If I were Jarl Austmaðr ...!" Sterki shouted.

"You'd tear the Skåne apart!" Jarl Austmaðr shouted. *"You'd kill everything that our family's gained, just like you killed Auðgi!"*

Hávi gasped and Tryggvi stifled a scream. *So it had finally come out into the open!* But suddenly a great crash echoed, as if the heavy table had been toppled, and shouts came so loudly that the walls and doors shook. Shrill, violent cries shrieked through the stone walls, furious, and a sword-clang rang out. Three vicious steel-clashes resounded, then suddenly their door burst open. Sterki stood in their doorway, panting hard breaths as if he'd just endured a great struggle. Blood splattered the front of his rich, studded-leather tunic, and more blood dripped off the long steel sword naked in his hand. Hávi and Tryggvi screamed, unable to do anything else.

Screaming, Tryggvi jumped to block Sterki's path as he charged them, his bloody sword raised, but he merely shoved Tryggvi aside, crashing her hard into the fireplace stones. Sterki jumped at Hávi, who leapt off her bed with a strength that she hadn't known pregnant women possessed. Yet her bed was no barrier to Sterki, who paused only a moment, glaring murderously, before he lifted a booted foot and stepped up onto her bed, his empty hand bracing himself upon a wooden horse's head. Hávi backed up against the stone wall behind her, trapped, with no place left to go, screaming in terror. Bloodlust filled Sterki's eyes.

Tryggvi screamed, jumped upon the bed, and wrapped her arms around Sterki's knees. Almost toppling, Sterki cursed and kicked at her, and then he turned and stabbed with all of his might. Downward the point of his deadly blade stabbed right into Tryggvi's back. Hávi screamed as Tryggvi's blood spewed upwards, but Sterki paid Tryggvi no more heed than if she'd been a cockroach that he'd stepped on. Sterki pulled out his sword and turned its red-dripping point toward Hávi who, having no weapon, not even a stool to defend herself with, wrapped both of her hands protectively over her bulging stomach, protecting her child to the last.

Bíldr's cry startled her, and suddenly he charged her bed, yanking his sword from its scabbard. Sterki turned; each threw a deadly blow at the other: deafening sword-clangs rang throughout the castle. Three more guards rushed into the room as Bíldr and Sterki crossed blades. All raised their weapons but Sterki only jumped backwards, off the bed where Tryggvi's body lay, and crashed against the wall beside Hávi, who screamed and tried to flee, but his adamant grip seized her arm and flung her back against the wall. His sword point rose and pointed at Hávi's heart.

"Stop!" Hvítvi shouted from the doorway as Bíldr threatened to climb onto the bed. Hávi glanced at Hvítvi; pale in an old, faded-salmon tunic, spots of a dark, sickening red covered his tunic and hands. "Bíldr, come back! Don't threaten him!"

Bíldr obeyed, but Sterki stood frozen, his teeth bared like a rabid dog, his sword point hovering inches from Hávi's swollen breasts.

"Let her go," Hvítvi warned.

"Father attacked me!" Sterki shouted. "It's my right to defend myself ...!"

"You killed Father!" Hvítvi shouted. "You murdered him ... just like you murdered Auðgi!"

"How dare you?" Sterki shouted. *"With father dead, I'm Jarl Austmaðr!"*

"Let her go!" Hvítvi ordered. "Let her go, or I swear that you'll never leave this room alive!"

"Why don't you fight me yourself?" Sterki challenged. *"Coward! Ghostly freak!"*

"Let her go and you'll get a trial," Hvítvi said coldly. "You may still die, but it won't be today."

"Lower your blades!" Sterki shouted at Bíldr and the other guards. "I order you! I'm your jarl, clan-chief of Castle Austmaðr ...!"

Not one of Hvítvi's guards moved. Bíldr laughed coldly, tightening his grip on his sword.

"Murder!" cried a voice from the outer hall, and many other voices took up the echoing cry, but Hvítvi merely glanced at the crowd running from the hall into the outer-room, then crowding behind him to peer into Hávi's bedroom.

"Help me!" Sterki ordered them. "Men of clan Austmaðr, defend your jarl!"

No one moved. Mjóvi's voice screamed in the outer-room and Master Krókr's voice loudly demanded to know what had happened.

"Brother, let Mother go ... or die now!" Hvítvi ordered.

"Mother?" Sterki laughed wildly. "You call this bitchy whore our mother?"

"You won't leave this room with a sword, and if you kill

her then you won't leave this room ever! No one's going to help you! You can't escape!"

"I don't have to escape!" Sterki shouted. "*I'm Jarl Austmaðr!*"

"Get back!" Hvítvi shouted at the crowd behind him, and then he motioned one man forward. A single guard entered the room, a young man that Hávi had seen but never spoken to. He held a bow with an arrow nocked and ready.

A silence fell over the castle. Even the shouts in the halls outside silenced, allowing only sobbing wails to waft into the crowded room. Hávi pressed back against the cold, rough, hard stones of the wall, their sharp-hewn edges cutting into her back. Normally strong for a woman, but burdened by pregnancy and facing a desperate warrior taught swordfighting since his earliest years, a survivor of numerous vikings, Hávi stood helpless, Sterki's sword frighteningly poised to ram through her heart. Obeying Hvítvi's silent gestures, the young guard drew his long arrow back, then raised his bow and aimed at Sterki.

"Don't shoot unless I say so," Hvítvi whispered.

"*Think, fool!*" Sterki snarled at the young guard. "As Jarl Austmaðr, I can make you rich, a viking lord with ships of your own, wealth and plunder like you've never dreamed of!"

The young guard never even blinked.

"*Think!*" Sterki said desperately. "Side with me, and treasures beyond your imaginings will cascade through your fingers! A castle of your own! A whorehouse of your own!"

The young guard hissed between his clenched teeth.

"*My greatest treasure ...*" the young guard snarled, "*... was my friend Auðgi!*"

"Don't shoot!" Hvítvi hissed. "You heard him, Sterki! Drop your sword or I let him kill you. *Let Mother go!*"

"Why?" Sterki demanded. "You want this whore? Fine! Keep the bitch, but her child ...! I can kill her bastard!"

Hávi screamed as his blade lowered toward her huge, extended stomach, but its point never stabbed. The bow twanged. The arrow slashed past Bíldr and the other guards: Sterki's blood sprayed across the ruined white quilt and Tryggvi's body. Sterki cried out, fell back, and as his grip loosened, Hávi jerked free and dashed aside, crashing past her shuttered window into one of the treasury doors before her strength gave out; she collapsed onto the floor. Bíldr and the other guards jumped forward and a fierce scuffle broke out. They wrestled Sterki, who cried out as his sword clanged against the floor. Bíldr and the other guards pulled Sterki to his feet, alive, but with an arrow shot deep through his right arm just below the shoulder, nailing his arm to his ribs. Bíldr had a firm grip on the feathered shaft of the arrow, and each time that Sterki resisted, Bíldr yanked hard on the arrow.

Mjóvi's and Krókr's voices rose over the roar of shouting, but Hvítvi never moved, his frail presence blocking the door.

"*Sterki Austmaðr,*" Hvítvi said icily, and his soft voice cut through all the loud cries, "*I hereby charge you with the murder of Jarl Austmaðr, our father.* Bíldr, take him to the dungeon. Lock him in chains. Post every guard that you trust around him. Master Krókr, send word to Jarl Hersir, Jarl Dúfunef, and all of the others. Let word go out across Scandinavia: as Jarl Austmaðr's son, I command a Tynwald."

Audible gasps filled the room. Hávi stared at Hvítvi, recalling Jarl Illingr's words:

'Tynwald is how Swedish lands are ruled. Clan-chiefs and Swedish kings can call themselves anything that they want, but decisions that affect the whole country must be agreed upon by the Tynwald, our highest council, the closest thing that we

have to a government.'

But Jarl Illingr had also said: *'Councils can rule against you, and if that happens at a Tynwald, your last hope is lost.'*

"Tynwald," Hvítvi repeated. "There the doom of Sterki will be decided: chief and lord of clan Austmaðr ... or death."

Still struggling, Sterki was forced toward the door by Bíldr and the guards. Hvítvi stepped aside at last, allowing them to drag Sterki past the crowd of guards and castle-folk, through the outer-room and down the stone stairs. Sterki's curses echoed down each hallway, and everyone stared aghast, horrified and confused.

Hvítvi approached Hávi and silently held out his hand. Hávi's head spun, confused, and then she realized that she was on the floor, leaning heavily against a treasury door. Unreality seemed to a cast a fog of white steam about her. She didn't want to rise, didn't want to glance at her bed, to see the horror that lay upon it, or go into her outer-room where even more horror awaited, but Hvítvi calmly waited and slowly she lifted a hand. Hvítvi's puny strength helped very little, but as Hávi struggled to rise, every assistance helped. Without Hvítvi, Hávi would've laid on that floor until ... *forever.*

On unsteady feet Hávi glanced at her bed. Tears exploded; Tryggvi lay face-down, unmoving, upon the crumpled white quilt now drenched in blood. Hávi started to collapse but hands grabbed her, and then more hands came, and somehow she was half-carried from her terrible bedroom. In the outer-room, startled castle folk blocked most of the foul scene that she knew was there: Jarl Austmaðr dead on the floor, slain by Sterki ... for accusing him of killing Auðgi. Hávi cringed, dying inside. Jarl Austmaðr ... and Tryggvi ... and before that ... Auðgi; Hávi screamed in defiance ... and then blackness consumed her.

"Hávi?"

"H-Hvítvi?"

"She's coming around," said the strange voice. "I think that she wants you."

"You're the healer," Hvítvi's smooth voice echoed inside her head, glowing like a lantern in eternal darkness.

"For frights, you might be her best medicine," said the voice, and a strange image formed in her mind ... a hunchback, a healer ... *Master Kamban.*

"Hávi, Hvítvi's right here," Master Kamban said softly, reassuringly. "You're in his room. You're safe. Hávi, open your eyes."

Hávi squeezed her eyes tight. She didn't want to open her eyes. She wanted to fall back into darkness, into oblivion, to wallow forever in emptiness rather than face what lay outside. In the real world terrible things had happened, frightful things; awful nothingness was her only escape.

"Hávi, listen to Master Kamban," Hvítvi's voice said.

Hávi whimpered. Hvítvi was in the real world. He wasn't in her blackness where Hávi wanted to stay; the injustice burned. A soft hand gently pulled on her arm; Hávi resisted, but the comforting blackness fell away, leaving her exposed. The real world bloomed. Unwillingly Hávi opened her eyes.

A bald head lowered behind a hunched back; a prominent worried expression filled her vision. Behind him everything was white.

"Hávi, take it slow," Master Kamban said, and as Hávi focused on his face and words, she seemed to remember.

"T-Tryggvi ...?" Hávi stammered.

"Dead, I'm afraid," Hvítvi's voice came from beside her, and Hávi turned to look at him, his features almost lost in the whiteness of the room. Hvítvi's hand caressed her shoulder. "I'm sorry."

"Jarl ... Austmaðr?"

"Dead," Hvítvi said. "Sterki killed him before he ever came into your room."

The world tilted and whirled. Horrible thoughts stabbed through her mind, then fleeted past incomplete, leaving only confusion. Hávi stared at all of their faces, uncomprehending.

"She needs sleep," Master Kamban declared.

"No," Hávi said uncertainly, feeling unbalanced as if she were standing on a tiny dragonship bobbing on rough waters. "No, I ... give me a minute ..."

A fist pounded on the door. Everyone startled; two guards drew swords and took positions before and beside the door, ready to kill whoever entered.

"It's Bíldr!" spoke the familiar voice.

The guards unbarred the door. Bíldr entered and they closed and braced the door behind him.

"Sterki's chained up tight," Bíldr reported, holding up a black key. "This is the only key. I've got ten men guarding him; Auðgi's best friends. The rest of the guards are alerted; I've got friends at every entrance to the castle and others stationed inside, including the kitchen and on this floor. We're as safe as we can get without killing those that we don't absolutely trust."

"We can't go that far, not yet," Hvítvi said, glancing back at Hávi. "I've got to go for now but I want you to get some rest."

"No," Hávi managed to say, but she knew that he wouldn't leave without a reason. "Where ...?"

"I've got to send messengers," Hvítvi explained. "I'm

recalling men from the viking: Father's friends and Sterki's enemies. We'll need them to face the assault."

"Assault?"

"Hávi, clan Austmaðr has no chief," Hvítvi said. "People aren't going to sit by and wait for others to conquer the Skåne. We need troops and allies, quickly, or we'll lose everything."

"Lose?"

"The first thing that we'll lose is our lives," Hvítvi said. "Stay. Sleep. I'll be back."

Hvítvi left with Bíldr, but he gave orders to the other two guards to bar the door behind them and not let anyone else back into the room. Hávi watched them go, then turned to Master Kamban.

"What's happened?" Hávi asked.

"You know ... who died," Master Kamban said, leaning back in his chair, taking a deep breath. "Hvítvi has to secure the castle against an attack from outside while protecting us from enemies inside the castle."

"Enemies inside ...?"

"Mistress Mjóvi and Master Krókr aren't pleased that Hvítvi had Sterki chained in the dungeon."

"He killed my husband!"

"Sterki claims that Jarl Austmaðr attacked him, and Mjóvi and Krókr believe him."

"He lies!"

"Yes, but think how much power they'll wield if Sterki becomes clan-chief. Mistress Mjóvi and Master Krókr know that Hvítvi despises them; they can't let him gain control."

"What can we do?"

"Host a mid-winter Tynwald," Master Kamban said. "The longer that we wait the more difficult defending Castle Austmaðr will be."

"Can't we just throw Mjóvi and Krókr out?"

"Loki's beard, child!" Master Kamban exclaimed. "Add powerful leaders to an open rebellion? No, even locking them up would be risky. Either way, the odds are against us."

"Why?"

Master Kamban smiled, looking relaxed for the first time.

"Look at me," Master Kamban said. "What do you see?"

"Why ... a healer ..."

"Not many see that," Master Kamban said. "Even among those that I've healed, people see me as a twisted monster. Hvítvi's treated little better; oh, a lot of people tolerate him and speak politely because he's Jarl Austmaðr's son, but Hvítvi knows how they feel about him ... about us, people who look differently. We live with it all of our lives."

"But Hvítvi ...!"

"Hvítvi understands the precariousness of his situation," Master Kamban continued. "However good he might be, or however wisely he might rule, Hvítvi can't be Jarl Austmaðr; our soldiers would desert him, and then we'd be prey to the first invaders to beach on our shores."

"But Hvítvi would make a great Jarl Austmaðr!"

"Not if our warriors won't fight for him," Master Kamban said. "Not if all of clan Austmaðr falls because of his leadership. He can't fight. He can't lead troops in battle. There are lots of clans who'd love to conquer clan Austmaðr, not just to gain control of the Skåne but for the wealth that our clan's acquired. Our success has earned us bitter enemies and now, like it or not, we don't just appear weak: we are weak."

"But our men will fight to protect their families!"

"Or they could just grab their families and run," Master Kamban sighed. "Or they could switch to whichever side that they think will win."

"Don't we have allies?" Hávi asked. "Clan Hersir ...!"

"Yes, a powerful clan, and possibly clan Dúfunef, but not many others. All remember clan Illingr; there's still bad blood over that. This is greater than clan Austmaðr; if hostilities break out, then the clans could splinter: Sweden could face civil war."

"*War ...?*"

"That threat's our only hope," Master Kamban said. "If open war starts then every clan will fight for control, and it won't matter who wins because Sweden will be so weakened that Norway, Denmark, and even the Germans and Rús may simultaneously invade us. None of our clans would survive that assault, and if we can't avoid that, then nothing else matters. Fear of that scenario is what Hvítvi has to plead to the other clan-chiefs at the Tynwald to keep them from attacking."

"But ... then ... *who will be ... the next Jarl Austmaðr?*"

"Who knows?" Master Kamban replied. "Another question is ... *what will the new Jarl Austmaðr do with the last Jarl Austmaðr's hunchbacked healer, albino son, and pregnant widow?*"

Chapter 25

Hávi stared out of her window. Twenty armed guards stood inside the barred wooden gate ready to fight. Outside, angry peasants shouted and cursed despite the deep snow which continued to fall; a vast crowd, more than lived in Skadi, enough to challenge the full might of Castle Austmaðr, but too few to take the castle without heavy losses. The whole Skåne knew of Jarl Austmaðr's death. Most of the peasants gathered right before the gates, but some spread out along each wall as if besieging the castle. Hávi bit her lower lip and wished that she had some västerbotten.

Locked in her room, four guards just outside of her door, Hávi was a virtual prisoner again. Bitra, an elderly washer woman, had been assigned to be her servant, but Bitra feared Hávi and sat huddled under blankets before the fire, trying to warm her slender, aged wisp of a frame when not fetching Hávi food or water. Hávi ignored her, missing Tryggvi, ashamed that her mourning centered on her beloved, young handmaid rather than her aged, irascible husband. Hvítvi had sent Hávi one message: *'Stay armed'*. It seemed foolish; what could a heavily-pregnant woman do against armed warriors even with an arsenal? Still, Hávi had scavenged a sword from the outer-room and hidden it beside her bed and made Bitra bring her a large, sharp knife from the kitchen.

Garbed in white exceeding Hvítvi's paleness, Hávi suffered her mourning alone. Guilt and impropriety warred inside her; Jarl Austmaðr had been her husband and all of her thoughts should mourn him, but Jarl Austmaðr had been a strangely small part of her new life, more like the furniture in a room rather than the house to which her life belonged. Seldom had they spoken, and they'd been married only a few months before he'd sailed away, leading the viking. Despite her forced wedding, Hávi had to admit that she'd gotten lucky; Jarl Austmaðr had never beaten her, as some husbands did, and while he'd often seemed unconcerned, at times he'd shown deep caring, and thinking of him welled her sadness, an aching hole that could never be filled. She couldn't call her feelings for him love, but she'd been greatly fond of her late husband ... more than she wanted to admit.

Thoughts of Tryggvi brought instant tears to Hávi's eyes. Jarl Austmaðr had given her a new life, but Tryggvi had shared her life; little Tryggvi, her short, cherub-faced companion through everything that Hávi had endured since leaving clan Hersir. Tryggvi had talked with her, after a little coaxing, and shared her adventures, and warned Hávi before she jumped headfirst into trouble. Tryggvi had come so far from the timid, cowardly child that she'd been ... but now she'd grow no more.

Hávi's mind dwelt upon Hvítvi. Fear trembled her lower lip; more than eight months pregnant, Hávi could do nothing to protect Hvítvi, upon whom the fate of clan Austmaðr rested. The paltry forces gathered outside of their gate were just the visible face of a rearing rebellion. Hávi glanced at the two locked doors in her room, the gold-filled treasuries of clan Austmaðr; all of Scandinavia was preparing to fight over the ownership of the Skåne and the contents of these two stone-walled closets. Hvítvi wouldn't survive a full-scale assault. All that protected Castle Austmaðr was Hvítvi's wit and cunning, and Hávi recalled her own words, the arguments she'd shouted at her mother that fateful day long ago in Jarl Hersir's mansion about the Catholics *'who display golden cups and crosses in castles defended only by men wielding books'.* Could wit and cunning defend clan Austmaðr against spears, swords, and the greed of ambitious jarls?

Hávi couldn't stop thinking about Hvítvi, not just for clan Austmaðr. Clan Austmaðr was Hvítvi's life; if it fell then he'd surely be killed, but Hávi couldn't help thinking impure thoughts, improper for a newly-made widow of a great viking lord. *What would come of the feelings that she and Hvítvi shared?* Was their stepson-stepmother relationship unimportant now, or even more so? What if ... Hávi dared to think ... *what if she married Hvítvi?* Would their marriage make Hvítvi any more acceptable to the warriors of clan Austmaðr, or would the scandal of their nuptials inflame a war throughout the Skåne?

Someone knocked on her outer-door so softly that it almost went unheard. Hávi and Bitra both went to investigate.

"It's Felian," the familiar youthful voice replied, and Bitra unbarred the door.

Hávi gasped. Felian stepped inside wearing an iron cap, carrying a spear, and wearing a red guard's tunic with a large dagger on his belt. His youthful face belied his fierce garb.

"Felian, what happened?" Hávi asked.

"Hvítvi made me a guard," Felian said. "A lot of boys have been armed and set to watches. Even Master Kamban's helping; he's taken to Jarl Illingr's tower from where he can watch the harbor for enemy ships."

"Is there anything that I can do?"

"No, that's why Hvítvi sent me," Felian said. "I'm to tell you to stay in your room and don't come out for anything. Ships have been sent to clans Hersir and Dúfunef for support, and they'll deliver word of the Tynwald throughout the Skåne, and even to some distant villages outside of our lands. But winter's hit hard and the sea's rough; Njord alone may deliver our sailors safely. Yet, even if our messages are delivered to the ends of the Skåne, it'll take more than a week before the jarls can respond. Hvítvi can't afford half of a Tynwald or there'll be challenges, so he chose the full moon to host the Tynwald, and that's thirteen days away. Bíldr argued with Hvítvi; he doesn't think that Castle Austmaðr will still be here thirteen days from now, but Hvítvi says that no earlier date will do."

Hávi placed a hand on her sore, swollen stomach. If only she wasn't so pregnant! She would gladly fight for clan Austmaðr! Yet wishing wouldn't help; her fate was out of her hands.

Days passed in irksome nervousness. Twice Felian arrived with word from Hvítvi, always the same: *stay inside, brace the door, and stay armed.* Felian reported that horsemen had also been sent north and south to spread word of the Tynwald to the peasants, but in four days no news had returned, no riders or ships, no sign of support or invasion. The midday mob shouting outside of the gates became customary but only lasted two hours each day, and then they would wander back to Skadi frozen stiff.

Bitra wasn't as shy as Hávi had thought. Dour, glum Bitra confessed that she'd always loved Jarl Austmaðr and still couldn't believe that he was dead. Breiðr came to visit on the fifth day; her husband had decided that she was safer living inside the castle than among the mob of Skadi. She informed them that the sewing room was empty; even Hvassi was locked in her room praying to Freyja.

Two dragonships sailed into the snowy harbor on the sixth day. Hávi, Breiðr, and Bitra cheered; the yellow banner of clan Hersir hung bright upon them. A hundred warriors disembarked and marched through Skadi up the white sea-shell road. The crowd, which had started to march back to Skadi, stopped as the warriors drove between the protestors heedless of their jeers and challenges. Hvítvi's white figure appeared in the courtyard as the gates were opened for them and Jarl Hersir led Hávi's old clansmen into Castle Austmaðr.

Less than an hour later, a knock came to their door.

"Hávi!" Jarl Hersir called. "Open up!"

Bitra opened the door and Jarl Hersir came in, and beside him came a strange, slender young woman in a snow-covered purple cloak with a royal crest on it. Freckles dotted her face, her red hair shone, and her smile widened as she saw Hávi.

"*Völu!*" Hávi shouted, and she tried to get up out of her chair.

"Stay down!" Völu ordered, running forward and bending over to hug Hávi, her chill, familiar arms more welcoming than anything that Hávi could recall.

"Time for that later," Jarl Hersir said gruffly. "Hávi, I need to speak to you alone."

"I'll be back," Völu promised, giving Hávi's hand a reassuring squeeze.

"Bitra, take her to the kitchen," Hávi ordered. "See that she gets some food."

Völu looked shocked and glanced from Hávi to Bitra and back again, but Hávi gestured her away. This dismissal seemed to distress Völu even more, but under Jarl Hersir's impatient glare, Völu followed Bitra out the door.

"Hávi, what in Niflheim's going on here?" Jarl Hersir demanded.

"Sterki ...," Hávi began, but Jarl Hersir cut her off with a wave of his stump.

"I know that Sterki killed Jarl Austmaðr!" Jarl Hersir hissed. "Who's going to replace him? I'm not going to sacrifice Hersir warriors fighting for a lost cause!"

"Hvítvi ..."

"Hvítvi can't be Jarl Austmaðr," Jarl Hersir said. "Fear of a clan-chief protects his clan as much as his warriors."

"Ask Hvítvi," Hávi replied.

"I just did," Jarl Hersir said. "Hvítvi wouldn't tell me."

"Why not?"

"Hvítvi doesn't trust me."

"He let you inside the castle!"

"What choice did he have?" Jarl Hersir snarled. "Ask for our help, and then leave us outside to freeze? If he had, I'd be attacking this castle right now."

Incredulous, Hávi gasped.

"I mean it," Jarl Hersir said. "Clan Hersir may not be as big as clan Dúfunef, but we're closer and we got here first. Our other ship will be here in two days with more than a hundred more men. We can defend this castle for a while, but not against all of Scandinavia."

"We need you!" Hávi shouted.

"For what?" Jarl Hersir asked. "To forestall the inevitable?

If the Austmaðr bloodline's spent ..."

"Hvítvi would make a great jarl!"

"No one will follow him!"

"Give him a chance!"

"To do what? Die when another clan scratches his cheek and bleeds him to death?"

"Hvítvi's the smartest man that I've ever met!" Hávi insisted. "Hvítvi could be the greatest Jarl Austmaðr ever!"

"Half of clan Austmaðr's lands originally belonged to clan Bagal," Jarl Hersir said. "Jarl Refr's father swore a blood-oath against clan Austmaðr twenty years ago, and clan Refr's been waiting for a chance like this. Half of the clans in Scandinavia have grievances against clan Austmaðr, and they're not going to stop from attacking given a chance for revenge. Do you think that they're going to be frightened by a pale youth who could die just shaving his nonexistent beard? I won't throw away men fighting a battle that I can't win."

"What should we do?" Hávi asked.

"Sterki," Jarl Hersir said softly.

"Sterki murdered Jarl Austmaðr!"

"That's right, so people will fear him."

"Sterki murdered Auðgi!"

"Yes, I know."

"Sterki murdered Tryggvi!"

"Who?"

"Tryggvi, my handmaid!"

Exasperated, Jarl Hersir shook his head.

"Yes, Sterki's an untrustworthy scoundrel," Jarl Hersir said. "If there was anyone else who could be Jarl Austmaðr then I'd say outlaw Sterki now. But, *is punishing Sterki worth losing clan Austmaðr?* A civil war will tear our clans apart!"

"My husband ...!" Hávi seethed. *"My stepson! My*

handmaid!"

"Think, Hávi!" Jarl Hersir whispered fiercely. "You'll die next, and Hvítvi, and anyone who stands beside you! Clan Austmaðr must have a jarl ... or die. No amount of fighting's going to change that. Sterki's a blood-thirsty tyrant who'll stop at nothing to secure clan Austmaðr, which is all that may save it."

Hávi glared up at him past the thick, black hair hiding most of his face. Once she would've cowered before him, afraid to stare back; now she wanted to strike him.

"Hvítvi has a plan," Hávi whispered. "I don't know what it is, but I know Hvítvi. Trust him. When he can, he'll let us know what his plan is."

"Who that plan is ... or else it's not a plan," Jarl Hersir said. "Someone's got to lead clan Austmaðr. I don't want to get embroiled in a civil war, but I'll do what I must to protect clan Hersir."

They glared at each other stubbornly, then Jarl Hersir's gaze fell to Hávi's stomach.

"When's it coming?" he asked.

"Soon, I hope," Hávi said. "I feel like a walrus."

"I hope that it's a boy."

"It is."

"How can you tell?"

"It has to be."

Jarl Hersir nodded grimly and lowered his voice to a deep whisper.

"Hávi, if war's coming, if the end of clan Austmaðr has come, then I'd prefer that clan Hersir claim as much of the Skåne as we can. I make no excuse for this, but you have to understand: the first clan to start fighting will be decimated by the second and third clans. We don't have enough warriors to face all of our enemies; the last clan to join the fray, after the others clans are weakened, will likely emerge the owner of the Skåne. If Hvítvi can't convince me that he can win, I'll desert him."

Hávi stared at her old clan-chief. Jarl Hersir met her glare unflinching: he was determined, and even if she hadn't been heavy with child, she could never force him to change his mind.

Later, Völu came back and held Hávi's hand as she laid back on her furry pillow, and their friendship was reunited. Völu had changed her hairstyle; she still wore pigtails, but down her back, her red hair flowed long and free. She looked older, more mature; Hávi complimented her upon it, and then asked about Helga and Hlöðu. A deep frown darkened Völu's face, and she shook her head sadly.

"Hávi, Gamli died two months ago," Völu said softly. "He fell over and caught a chill on the hillside, and by the time that Hlöðu got him inside, Gamli had a fever. He died in bed four days later. The whole village came out to mourn him. Did you know that he'd captained a dragonship when he was young?"

"Yes, Gamli was a captain for three years, but then he got wounded," Hávi said, bowing her head, trying to hold back her tears. "Father sailed on Gamli's ship on his first viking. Father said that Gamli was never the same after losing his captaincy. Jarl Hersir was just a young man then, Father's age, when Gamli couldn't go viking anymore."

"They told great stories of Gamli," Völu said. "Jarl Hersir laid one of his own swords upon him before they buried him ... *Oh, Hávi!*"

Völu leaned forward and hugged Hávi as she burst into

tears. Hávi knew it'd been coming; Gamli had been very old and hadn't been able to dress himself in years. Still, Völu's news crushed her; *she'd loved her grandfather.*

"Helga's very happy," Völu continued. "She got Þistill, and he had a great viking."

"Mother's married?' Hávi gasped, futilely wiping her wet cheeks.

"Yes," Völu said. "Þistill's an old man, but he's strong and works hard. He resodded your roof all by himself within a week of marrying Helga."

"Did I know him?"

"I don't think so," Völu said. "Þistill's family are fishermen; they live farther up the river, outside of Hersir village."

"What about you?"

"Didn't you hear?" Völu smiled brightly. "I married Bifru!"

"What.?!? But you hate Bifru!"

"He doesn't dump buckets of water over my head anymore," Völu grinned wickedly. "He's very attentive to all of his husbandly duties."

"You're pregnant?"

"Not as much as you," Völu laughed, and Hávi tried to laugh through her tears.

"And I was afraid that you'd get stuck with Hálmi!" Hávi smiled.

"Not me!" Völu smiled smugly, *"Hálmi was married to ... Sleitu!"*

The room exploded with laughter, Hávi sniggering so hard that she had to clutch her ribs and feared that she'd hurt her baby. Then a knock came on her door and Bitra entered from the outer-room.

"Begging your pardon, Mistress Austmaðr," Bitra said. "Master Kamban's here to see you."

"Send him in," Hávi said, and Völu eagerly stood up and faced the door, then stifled a brief scream as the hunchback clambered into the room *'thumping'* on his bad leg and stout cane. Völu glanced fearfully at Hávi, who shot her a reproachful glare, warning her to be silent.

"Thank you for coming," Hávi said warmly to Master Kamban. "Those teas that you made eased my pain."

"Glad to hear it," Master Kamban said, *'thumping'* over to Hávi's bedside, from which Völu hastily retreated.

"I'm sorry," Hávi said, embarrassed. "Master Kamban, this is Völu, my best and oldest friend from clan Hersir. Völu, this is Master Kamban, my teacher, our most skilled healer, and my close friend."

Master Kamban turned and bowed as best he could to Völu, who bowed slightly, but both of their glances brimmed with venom.

"How are we feeling today?" Master Kamban asked Hávi.

"Very well, thank you," Hávi said. "I ... I don't suppose there's anything that I can do ... to hasten the birth? I'm sick of being pregnant."

"Then you should relax," Master Kamban said. "You could deliver any day, but you don't want to hasten it. Frigg grants her blessings in her own time, and it's unwise to infuriate her."

"Well ..., *the sooner the better.*"

"Before the Tynwald would be best if it's a boy, worse if it's a girl," Master Kamban said. "But you've done all that you can. Now you need to rest and build up your strength."

"I will," Hávi promised. "What news?"

"Hvítvi's decided to postpone your husband's burial until

after the Tynwald," Master Kamban said.

"Burial?" Hávi asked. "But ... why not ... a ship-fire, like Auðgi?"

"Auðgi wasn't a jarl," Master Kamban explained. "Jarl Austmaðr ruled for nineteen years and was respected by many. Hvítvi's ordered a mound be raised for him; the greatest honor. A whole dragonship will be buried with Jarl Austmaðr in its hold, to sail him to Valhalla. Treasure and weapons, everything that he'll need in the afterlife, will be buried with him, and a great fire will burn atop his mound for a week. Then a large, granite stone will be carved with runes and set atop his mound, a tribute to his memory forever."

"What ... what about Tryggvi? When will Tryggvi be buried?"

"Hávi, Tryggvi was buried this morning."

"What?!?" Hávi screamed. *" Why didn't anyone tell ...!"*

"You couldn't go."

"Why not?"

"For the same reason that you can't attend your husband's funeral," Master Kamban said. "You can't leave the castle. We'll tell everyone that your pregnancy has left you too weak, but the truth is that it's not safe for you anywhere in Scandinavia."

"How can you expect ...?"

"Hávi, ravens are gathering by the thousands," Master Kamban said. "Jarl Hafr's caught four foreign ships carrying messages about the gathering. One mentioned arriving two nights before the Tynwald; Hvítvi suspects that there may be an attack."

"What of clan Dúfunef?"

"No news yet," Master Kamban said, shaking his head. "Hvítvi's plenty worried; clans Dúfunef and Hersir are

Austmaðr's staunchest allies. If we lose either of them, then clan Austmaðr will fall."

Master Kamban thoroughly examined Hávi, who experienced no more discomfort or embarrassment than usual, save that Völu startled every time he touched Hávi's swollen stomach. But Völu said nothing, reducing her reactions to disgusted winces and cringing flinches; Hávi would speak to her later. Master Kamban, however cursed, was loyal to Hvítvi, and clan Austmaðr needed every loyal man.

As Master Kamban finished, giving Hávi the same instructions that he always gave her, he turned to Völu and bowed, then *'thumped'* out as Bitra held the door for him.

"He's a good man," Hávi said to Völu after he'd left.

"How can you say that?" Völu demanded. "He's a monster!"

"No more than Ørrabein," Hávi said.

"Ørrabein didn't get a husband."

"That's mean!" Hávi scowled. "I'll talk to Jarl Hersir. I'll see that Ørrabein gets ..."

"Are you mad?" Völu asked. "You can't order Jarl Hersir! Who do you think you are?"

"I'm Mistress Austmaðr," Hávi said so forcefully that Völu stepped back, wide-eyed. "I can do all kinds of things, and I don't answer to anyone but Hvítvi. Once we were equals, Völu, but this isn't clan Hersir and I don't milk goats anymore. I'm fighting for all of our lives, and if I fail ..."

"How can you fight?" Völu scoffed. "You can barely get out of bed!"

"I got out of bed fast enough when Sterki tried to kill me," Hávi said. "Right now the best way that I can fight is to bear clan Austmaðr a new jarl."

"You can't know that it's a boy!"

"It has to be," Hávi said. "Otherwise, we're all dead."

Chapter 26

"Messengers have arrived from clan Bagal," Breiðr said. "Jarl Bagal has offered to support clan Austmaðr, but Hvítvi won't pay his price."

"What price?" Hávi asked.

"All of the Skåne north of the Klar River."

"How much land is that?"

"That's half of clan Austmaðr's lands," Breiðr said. "Hvítvi says that he'd share lands with Hersir and Dúfunef before he bows to Jarl Bagal."

"Any sign of Jarl Dúfunef?"

"Not yet," Breiðr said.

"Hvítvi can't wait much longer," Hávi said. "The Tynwald's only a week away."

Völu wet her cloth in the bowl that Bitra was holding, wrung it out, and then dabbed at Hávi's forehead. Hávi couldn't sleep anymore and every movement strained. The women tried to comfort her but failed. Master Kamban came by twice a day but he, too, was helpless, claiming that Hávi's daily chants to Frigg were all that could ease her pains. Breiðr and Völu began to recite the chant with Hávi but it only annoyed her; she'd never believed that anyone could feel as tired as she did.

Suddenly horns sounded and a great clamor arose. Breiðr ran to the window and flung open the shutters; snow-clumps fell upon her as she thrust her head out.

"Ships!" Breiðr cried. "Clan Dúfunef's here!"

"As friends or foes?" Völu asked fearfully, and all the women exchanged worried looks.

"How m-many?" Hávi asked, holding her huge stomach.

"Four ships are in the harbor and more sails on the sea, hidden by the trees."

"Watch them," Hávi said.

"No!" Völu said. "Close that window! There's nothing that we can do about it and Hávi can't get chilled!"

"I'll be alright."

"No, Völu's right," Breiðr said. "I'll go down and learn what I can, then hurry back."

"I'll let you out," Völu said.

An hour later, Breiðr returned with glad news.

"Hvítvi and Jarl Hersir welcomed Jarl Dúfunef inside the castle," Breiðr reported. "They've taken oaths of mutual support. Jarl Hafr's fleet arrived with the last Hersir ship; we're as protected as we can get."

Hávi smiled and leaned back. Völu wet her lips with the cloth.

"It's not as good as it sounds," Breiðr said. "Hvítvi had to promise that no lands of clan Austmaðr would go to anyone but clan Hersir and clan Dúfunef, and he's already promised them large sections of the Skåne, totaling a third of clan Austmaðr's lands."

"Better that than lose all," Hávi said, but secretly she was worried; Hvítvi was compromising to keep them alive. Clan Austmaðr still needed a chief. *If she bore a daughter ...* "Tell Hvítvi," Hávi gasped, "that Mistress Austmaðr will attend the Tynwald."

"You can't!" Völu shouted as Breiðr and Bitra choked back their surprise.

"I can," Hávi said. "I'm not the first pregnant woman and I won't have my son's future decided while I lay a'bed. Tell Hvítvi ... that I'll be there ... or they'll hear my screams throughout the whole Tynwald."

"I'll tell, but I can't make him listen," Breiðr warned. "Meanwhile, would you mind if they moved the nursery into your outer-room? The castle's packed and Master Krókr's struggling to find places to house our soldiers. Half of Skadi's moved out, mostly out of fear, and both floors of Hrafna's tavern are being used to barrack the warriors of Dúfunef and Hersir."

"What about Hrafna's family?"

"Hrafna's a guard now and his family's left for the hills. Hvítvi's orders: only men who can fight remain; the arriving clans will need to shelter in their houses and many peasants hope to earn silver by renting out their homes. When all of the clans arrive, clans Hersir and Dúfunef will be moved inside the castle, and then we'll really be crowded."

Eight dragonships full of enemy warriors arrived three days before the Tynwald, a joint fleet of clan Bagal and clan Refr, but no fighting began. More ships joined them the next day from clans that Hávi had never heard of: Glóra, Jótun, Vörsa, Aurriði, Mjöksiglandi, and Tyrr. Some jarls arrived with only a personal guard; princes from Mostrarskegg and Carst of Norway and from clan Yngri of Finland, all wealthy sons of kings eager to form profitable alliances. Tensions grew inside the castle; not all of the clans in Skadi opposed clan Austmaðr, but unquestionably more warriors gathered outside of Castle Austmaðr than inside of it. Every clan-chief came to the castle with a guard of honor and were invited to the feast, but when Hvítvi permitted only two guards for each clan-chief, some accused him of setting a trap and refused to enter Castle Austmaðr.

Taking care of her stepdaughters and the castle children kept Hávi, Völu, and the other women busy. Young Fróði seemed greatly troubled by the happenings of the castle, no longer interested in her toys. Auða, who had a new, yellow dress, also seemed to have no interest in her toys, but she'd learned a new song and sang it over and over despite Fróði's complaints. Grái never went anywhere without her favorite rag doll in one hand and her special blanket in the other, and Hrogn wanted nothing but to go out and play in the snow and cried often when her pleas went unanswered. Hávi tried to distract Hrogn with sweets from the kitchen but soon even bribes failed.

Völu delighted the young children and invented games that kept them gleefully occupied. From Hávi, Völu got twenty copper coins which she flung across the room, making the children laughingly scurry to collect and return them all, and then Völu would fling the coins again. The children never seemed to tire of this game but got so tired that, after the usual bedtime complaints, they quickly fell asleep.

The night before the Tynwald, Hvítvi and three other guards came into Hávi's bedroom. Hvítvi ordered everyone into the outer-room, but Hávi refused and insisted that Völu be allowed to stay, vouching for her ardently.

"Very well," Hvítvi said to Hávi, "I couldn't allow you to stay without a servant anyway, and we need to talk. Völu, what you're about to see must go to your grave, which'll be soon enough, if we fail. No one's going to worry about which clan a woman is from once the fighting starts. If you stay by Hávi, you risk everything."

"I've stood by Hávi all of my life," Völu said, sounding more serious than Hávi had ever heard her.

"Good," Hvítvi said. "I need you both ready to ride at a moment's notice."

"Ride?" Hávi asked incredulously, placing a hand on her swollen belly.

"Bíldr's preparing a wagon, but there's no guarantee," Hvítvi said. "It's that, or hide you in the dungeon. A second's delay will kill us; if we have to run, we're defeated."

"What about the others?" Hávi asked. "The children, the servants, ...?"

"With luck, they'll be set free afterwards," Hvítvi said. "Everybody that we take will be one less chance for clan Austmaðr to survive. The most important thing is to keep Jarl Austmaðr's infant son alive; without him, we'll be dispersed like clan Illingr."

"What's happening?"

"We're bargaining for our lives with scoundrels and thieves," Hvítvi said. "Clans Hersir and Dúfunef will support Jarl Austmaðr's half-brother, Jarl Hafr, as clan-chief, but their price is treasure, land, and oaths of mutual support. Father would have a fit, but we've no choice. Some of the other clans have promised to support us for gold alone; I don't trust them, but I've got few options. Jarl Hafr's agreed to rule clan Austmaðr, but we'll have to support him; he's not too bright."

Hvítvi unlocked the closest treasury door and Völu gasped loudly, seeing the glints of gold and silver unexpectedly gleaming. Hvítvi ordered two of his men to pull out and open seven small chests, each of which were full of beautiful treasures, silver cups, jewelry, and countless coins of every shape and hue, which mesmerized Völu, who clapped her hand over her mouth to keep from screaming. Hvítvi sorted the treasure until three small chests were filled exactly as he desired, and then he had all of the other chests put back inside the treasury. He locked the doors when they were finished and had each guard pick up one of the three remaining chests of priceless treasure, and then he turned to Hávi.

"I'll send Bíldr to fetch you in the morning," Hvítvi said. "I need you at Sterki's trial. Don't unbar your door for anyone but Bíldr or me, especially not for Master Krókr. Your friend will have to stay up here; Sterki's trial will be dangerous, but I'll need you to testify of what you heard the night of the murder."

"I'll be ready," Hávi promised.

"Don't wear jewels," Hvítvi warned. "Just wear the tiara; this isn't the time for clan Austmaðr to appear rich. And don't mention Tryggvi; I know that you miss her, but her death ..."

"Her murder!"

"... her murder," Hvítvi acquiesced, "isn't relevant to this trial. Our Law-speakers shall bring her up if needed, not you."

Hávi nodded obediently.

Hvítvi stared at Hávi, and for a moment his ice-hard, pale features softened. He could say nothing, but Hávi hoped that Hvítvi's thoughts were of the two of them together. Yet Hvítvi only nodded, then swept from the room, and the guards carried out their heavy, priceless treasure chests.

Völu stared at Hávi, her eyes wide.

"I thought that I'd married well!" Völu said softly, her voice teeming with amazement. "You ... you're ... a queen!"

"Yes, a queen without a king," Hávi said sadly. "Usually that means death. If I'm going to die, then I'd rather have stayed Hávi Hersir."

"When ... when he opened that door ...!" Völu began, staring at the closed treasury door.

"Enough!" Hávi interrupted her, nodding toward the main door as Breiðr and Bitra came back in. Völu glanced at them and fell silent, but she continued to stare at the doors.

"What happened?" Breiðr asked.

"Nothing safe to know," Hávi said. "Hvítvi commands that I attend the Tynwald; I must be up and dressed by dawn tomorrow."

"Then you should get some sleep," Breiðr said.

"I want everything ready first," Hávi said. "Check my black dress, the one with the Austmaðr family crest; make sure that it's clean, and get out my tiara ... no, bring me my box of jewelry."

Breiðr fetched the jewelry box from the wardrobe while Bitra pulled out Hávi's black dress and examined it carefully. Völu gasped as Hávi opened the box; her priceless tiara was on top, but Hávi absently set it aside and sorted through the rest. Finally she took out a beautiful, golden ring set with a large, polished sapphire, an intricate silver necklace woven like mail with tiny rubies on leaf-shaped plates, and three silver coins that she fished out of the bottom.

"If things go badly," Hávi said slowly, "I may never come back to this room. If that happens, and anyone asks who you are, tell them that you're servants, wash-women, wet-nurses, anything that you like. Don't claim to know me or anyone else; I'll be unable to help you ... or myself, if it comes to that. Take these ..." Hávi placed the sapphire ring into Völu's hands, the ruby necklace into Breiðr hands, and made Bitra accept the silver coins. "I give these to you. If everything goes wrong, with these you may be able to survive, at least for a while. Hide them well; you may be searched. Try to escape in the confusion."

"Hávi ...," Breiðr said, "if there's anything that we can do ..."

"Just stay alive," Hávi said. "Trust Hvítvi ..."

"The albino?" Völu asked incredulously.

"That albino's more a man than any I've met," Hávi said. "If he asks you to do something, just do it."

"But ... but he's cursed!" Völu argued. "He ... *and that healer!"*

"I thought so, too, at first," Hávi admitted. "I was wrong, and I found out how wrong I was at great cost. Don't be like me; steep costs are more affordable to the wife of Jarl Austmaðr. Save the children, if you can; they're in more danger than any of you. But don't sacrifice yourselves. For some there may be no escape."

"Are you mad?" Völu demanded. "You expect us to sit here and ...!"

"I expect you to run," Hávi said.

"You talk like you're going to your funeral," Völu argued.

"My death ... or my salvation; I just don't know which.

Sterki's not the only matter that the Tynwald will debate; who'll be the next Jarl Austmaðr is what they're really here to see."

"But Sterki murdered ...!" Breiðr argued.

"What do rich men care about who murdered who, as long as it's not them?" Hávi scowled. "Men: we'd be better off if women ruled the world!"

Breiðr and Bitra gasped, but Völu burst out laughing.

"Mistress, take care!" Bitra whispered. "I've seen women whipped for saying such things!"

Breiðr nodded in silent, fearful agreement.

"I support you," Völu chuckled fearlessly.

Hávi reached out and grasped her beloved Völu's hand. She felt like a beached whale, huge and bloated, but she had friends. If only Tryggvi had lived, then she would've felt complete. But the night was deepening and tomorrow would be a busy day; she needed rest. Hávi sent Bitra to bed, then had Breiðr and Völu snuggle up on each side of her under her new quilt and kept her warm and comforted all night.

"It's Bíldr," the voice followed the early-morning knock on their door.

Völu removed the brace and opened the door. Hávi stood ready, Breiðr and Bitra beside her, each holding one arm. Her long black dress, which had always been too big for her, now strained at its seams to contain her pregnant body. The embroidered silver crown upon her chest shone over the golden rising sun, the ebony ravens promenaded by her now-huge breasts, and the black wolf's head with red eyes stared menacingly, stretched tightly over the mound of her swollen stomach. The twinkling tiara upon her blonde hair capped her regal appearance; Hávi stood as a solemn monument to her people, a proper widow of her clan, an undoubted queen rightfully bearing the proud Austmaðr family crest. Bíldr nodded appreciatively and took her arm as she stepped into the hall, but he didn't smile. As they descended the stone stairs Hávi wondered if she'd ever make it back upstairs.

The warriors crowded on the lower steps startled Hávi, but Bíldr patted her arm reassuringly and led her all the way down. Bifru, Völu's new husband, stood eagerly on the very bottom step, leaning on a long axe, and after seeing him, Hávi recognized many warriors of clan Hersir, all of whom stared at her as she stepped toward them.

"Good morning, Bifru ... clansmen," Hávi said.

"Uh ... g-good morning, Hávi ... I mean, Mistress Austmaðr," Bifru stammered, the only one of clan Hersir who dared address her openly.

"Thank you," Hávi said to Bifru. "You've made Völu very happy. I'm sure that she'll bear you many sons."

Bifru said nothing but attempted an awkward bow.

"We'd best hurry," Bíldr said to Hávi.

"Are all of the Hersir warriors inside the castle?" Hávi asked as she followed him.

"Yes, at every doorway," Bíldr said. "Clan Dúfunef's guarding the gate; they fill the courtyard. Our warriors are in the hall."

As she stepped inside the great hall, Hávi saw hundreds of Austmaðr warriors, even young boys and old men armed and helmeted, lining every wall save behind the high-table. Others filled every bench or stood crowded in the back. A glance at the high-table warned Hávi how serious this was; every man at the high-table was a jarl. Jarl Austmaðr's half-brother, Jarl Hafr, sat in the center, Hvítvi on his right, Jarl Dúfunef on his left. Jarl Hafr was very tall, much like his late brother, but with a full head of salt-and-pepper hair that hung long onto his shoulders and a jagged scar that cut across his chin; Hávi stared at him, seeing her late husband's eyes staring back at her. Jarl Hersir sat beside Hvítvi, and on both sides sat dour, fierce-looking men, all with a rigid determination that made the sight of them the most fearsome gathering that Hávi had ever seen.

"There's a place for you at the front table," Bíldr whispered, and Hávi noticed that the foremost table was full of the oldest and most respected men of Castle Austmaðr and one woman: Mjóvi sneered as she and Hávi's eyes met.

"Wait here," Hávi whispered to Bíldr.

"This is no time for dramatics!" Bíldr whispered back.

"Trust me."

She stepped forward, right in front of Hafr and Hvítvi, placed a hand upon her swollen belly, and performed as perfect a curtsy as her condition allowed. Watching her, Hvítvi leaned over and whispered something into Jarl Hafr's ears. He nodded, then suddenly pushed back his chair, stood up, and bowed to Hávi. Whispers broke out among the crowded hall but Hávi ignored them, forcing herself to smile brightly; she was there mostly for show. Hvítvi nodded slightly to her and she sat upon the crowded bench at the end of the Austmaðr table. Unfortunately, the only empty space was beside Master Krókr, who looked disgusted and turned away as she sat down, but several of the castle elders nodded to Hávi in silent greetings.

"Bring in the sword!" Jarl Hafr said loudly.

Benches scuffed against the stone-paved floor. Every person rose to their feet, and Hávi stood with them, looking toward the main doorway. Bíldr stood there holding out before him a beautiful sword, gold-hilted and jewel encrusted, and reverently he carried it into the great hall. All whispers silenced as he carried the glittering blade into the very center of the great hall and held it up for all to see, then turned and presented it to the high-table.

"I shall take this Tynwald sword!" cried an aged, trembling voice. It came from Jarl Dúfunef's father, the elderly man who sat beside his son. Bíldr presented the blade to him and the old man took the blade, held it up and looked at it, then passed it to his son.

"Has this sword drawn blood?" Jarl Dúfunef asked.

"It has," Bíldr answered.

"As jarl of clan Dúfunef, appointed by my father, I command this Tynwald!" Jarl Dúfunef shouted, and then he passed the priceless sword to Jarl Hafr, who instantly passed it to Hvítvi, who passed it to Jarl Hersir.

"I'm Jarl Hersir, as was my father, grandfather, and his fathers for eight generations!" Jarl Hersir shouted. "As clan-chief, I command this Tynwald."

Jarl Hersir passed the sword on down the high-table. Every man who was a clan-chief, one at a time, took the blade and cried out their command to hold a Tynwald. Hávi stared at each one, briefly wondering who the jarls were that didn't swear; probably close relatives and clan-nobles, but she watched their faces as they spoke, carefully noting each.

Jarl Glóra was an old man whose long beard had aged golden rather than silver or white. He had stern features, bright eyes, and his voice was as clear as tolling bells. Jarl Jótun was a dark, ferocious-looking man with an angry scowl that seemed etched upon his face, and over each of his shoulders protruded the pommel of a sword across his back. Jarl Vörsa was obviously the youngest, with long red hair and only a scraggily, youthful beard, yet he held his head high and looked proud. Jarl Aurriði looked discomforted, his pale features nearly a match for Hvítvi's whiteness, making his nervous twitches even more visible. Jarl Mjöksiglandi looked most like a viking lord; proud and strong, thick-set, his long, black beard full, forked, and braided, with both ends tucked into his belt. His gaze was intimidating, and he wore a leather hauberk and sat clearly unafraid under a thick golden crown. Jarl Tyrr, another elder, perhaps as old as Jarl Dúfunef's father, had many scars on his face, but he sat serenely, more relaxed than any other at the high-table, confident in his own element.

"I am Jarl Bagal, lord of the lake-lands," a clan-chief said, a tall man who would've stood an inch taller than Jarl Austmaðr had he been there. "I command this Tynwald, yet I also command the presence of the one jarl missing from this table: Sterki, the next Jarl Austmaðr!"

Angry shouts and curses filled the castle as many men cried in agreement or protest, but so chaotic was the tumult that no one could tell who was shouting what. Then voices rose calling for silence amid cries of *'Sterki Murderer!'*, *'Sterki Austmaðr!'* and *'Den Skaanske Lov!'*.

Finally quiet was restored, although many hands now clenched the hilts of deadly weapons. Jarl Bagal passed the sword all the way back across the table and into the hands of a thin, young-looking man with red hair drawn back into a braided ponytail wearing a slender silver crown.

"I am Jarl Refr," he said, his voice as high as Hvítvi's but filled with disgust. "For clan Refr, in support of clan Bagal, I command this Tynwald!"

Jarl Refr held the precious sword defiantly as if abhorrent to give it up, but as most of the jarls glared at him, Jarl Refr scowled and passed the sword back toward the center. Hvítvi took it and held it up.

"I am son and heir of Jarl Austmaðr," Hvítvi began, but again the hall burst into chaos.

"Liar!" several jarls cried, echoed by warriors from the closer tables. Warriors of clan Austmaðr shouted retorts, and soon the deafening cries became unintelligible. Long minutes passed before quiet restored enough for Hvítvi to continue.

"As I said, I am Jarl Austmaðr's son and heir, but not the only one," Hvítvi shouted, his high voice piercing the last of the shouts. "My older brother, Sterki, is also a son and heir, but he stands accused of murder and treason, and the crown of clan Austmaðr can't pass until this crime is tried."

"Treason!" Jarl Bagal shouted, and several voices cheered him, but he waved them silent. "Sterki's the eldest living son of Jarl Austmaðr! First let's decide who's the rightful Jarl Austmaðr before we objurgate the alleged murder!"

"Enough!" cried an angry, strained voice, and the elder Jarl Dúfunef pushed back his chair and stood. "A Tynwald doesn't begin until the commands of the gathered clan-chiefs conclude! You can't argue issues until the Tynwald starts!"

"The Tynwald's rituals can't conclude until all of the clan-chiefs command that it begin," Jarl Jótun spoke up, his grating voice shouting above the angry murmurs of the crowd. "We sit in Castle Austmaðr. We must have the Jarl Austmaðr's command to begin the Tynwald!"

"Yes," Jarl Refr agreed, "and by birthright, Sterki is Jarl Austmaðr!"

Many men jumped to their feet and cried in outrage. Swords were drawn and brandished threateningly, and many rose in preparation for a fight. Hvítvi shouted, but his weak voice was lost in the clamor, and Jarl Vörsa, pounding on the high-table with the pommel of a large dagger, only added to the chaos.

Jarl Mjöksiglandi rose slowly, not speaking. His dark eyes glared and he grabbed the thick braids of his black beard and held them, staring at the hall with the intensity of a steadfast lord, a power recognized across the Skåne. Slowly everyone fell silent.

"Clan Mjöksiglandi, distant though we are, has many reasons to be here," he said without shouting, but his deep voice carried to every ear in the hall. "None in clan Mjöksiglandi would weep to see clan Austmaðr fall, be led by a murderer, or by a weak, sickly clan-chief. Yet a civil war would leave all of us weak and force us to leave half of our viking forces at home. I'd say that Sterki is Jarl Austmaðr, but I don't want to encourage my sons to gain my crown by killing me." The hall burst into laughter. Jarl Mjöksiglandi maintained his composure and continued as soon as the laughter died. "Clan Mjöksiglandi suggests that Sterki be brought into this council, and then that both he and Hvítvi command this Tynwald."

Cheers and brays met this statement, but neither affected Jarl Mjöksiglandi, who stood chuckling as he lifted his ale-horn, drank deeply, then sat back down and calmly leaned to one side of his chair, surveying the crowd's reaction with a wry, content smile. Hávi eyed him worriedly; *whose side was he on?* Hávi had expected fewer arguments; what would happen if fighting broke out? Would the Austmaðr, Hersir, and Dúfunef guards around her be able to reach her before her blood was spilt? The Tynwald seemed more like a barely-controlled war than a legal council.

Hvítvi stood up and motioned to Bíldr.

"Bring in the prisoner," Hvítvi said.

Some cheered, but many scowled at these words. Hávi

managed a brief smile; Hvítvi was truly in his element, fighting with words, wit his best weapon. Calling Sterki a prisoner was more insulting than anything else that he could've said.

Sterki's appearance in the great hall brought every warrior to their feet. Some chanted *Jarl Sterki!* while shouts of *'Auðgi!'*, *'Murderer!'* and several less-polite terms echoed distressingly. Sterki strode in looking very much like a prisoner; dirty, wearing the same blood-stained studded leather tunic that he'd worn when he stormed into Hávi's bedroom and murdered Tryggvi. Yet Sterki seemed untouched by his imprisonment; he stepped firmly and purposefully across the hall. He walked right up to Hávi, who leaned back, frightened, wondering what he'd do, and suddenly he spun around. Tight leather thongs bound his hands behind his back, but instantly a big, sharp knife slid between his wrists and severed his bonds. Hávi glanced to her side; Master Krókr had cut Sterki free, and the first thing that Sterki did was take the big knife from Master Krókr's hand and slide it into his own belt.

Many cheered as Sterki turned to face the hall, free and armed. His bright, red hair and wolfish features stood out as proud and strong as any jarl.

"I'm Jarl Austmaðr," Sterki shouted, and the hall exploded so loudly that no one could tell who was shouting what. Chaos continued unabated, but finally Sterki raised a hand and all fell silent to hear him. "Every man here is, or has been, a warrior. We are a warrior-people. My weak, younger brother has challenged my birthright. I say, if he would challenge me, let him fight as an Austmaðr! Pick up a sword, face me, and let the victor reign!"

Derisive, mocking laughter echoed off the halls. Jeers and cries of *'Holmgangr!'* filled the hall and several swords were held out, pommel first. Sterki took one sword and turned to challenge Hvítvi. Hávi gasped; Sterki could carve Hvítvi like a dead chicken, and many of the derisive cries echoed with bloodlust. But Hvítvi never moved or even flinched. Sterki strode up to the high-table, sword tight in his raised fist, and looked as if he meant to jump onto the dais and stab Hvítvi, but suddenly Jarl Hersir and Jarl Dúfunef rose on each side of him, both lifting naked blades warningly. The crowd fell silent as Sterki hesitated.

"Yes, you'd like that," Hvítvi sneered. "Kill to gain ownership of the Skåne; why not? You've done it before. You murdered our father in cold blood. Your swordcut was thrust through his back; *was he even aware that he was being attacked?*"

"He turned as we fought!"

"Did Auðgi turn?" Hvítvi demanded. "What about Væni, our poor third brother? Where were you when that arrow killed him?"

"Fight me, you coward!"

"Slœkidrengr's our only brother that I know you couldn't have killed," Hvítvi scowled. "Or did you pay to have him killed?"

Sterki and Hvítvi glared at each other, furious red eyes pitted against pale pink, while the whole hall hung upon their brotherly feud.

"Gold!" Sterki shouted. "A chest of gold for every clan-chief that supports me ... to be delivered before you sail home!"

Several cheers sounded, but they quickly failed in the silence. Jarl Bagal stood up suddenly, holding a blade, and Jarl Refr joined him.

"Don't!" Jarl Hersir growled at them. "The castle's ours!

Your men will never reach you in time!"

"What are you going to do, kill us?" Jarl Bagal sneered. "Half of the warriors in Scandinavia are outside of your gates. Kill us and no one inside Castle Austmaðr will be alive by dawn. Sterki's the rightful heir."

"The crown of clan Austmaðr can't be earned by patricide," Hvítvi said. "Think what you're asking for; making an honorless murderer into the leader of the wealthiest clan in Scandinavia. What'll happen to you once you've helped him to power?"

"My friends will be rewarded!" Sterki said.

"With swords in their backs?" Hvítvi asked. "Arrows shot from shadows? That's how Sterki rewards his family! He'll give you lands and gold, then loot them from your corpses!"

"Enough!" Jarl Dúfunef cried, and he turned to Jarl Bagal. "You've both spoken. Hvítvi's weak and Sterki's a kin-slayer. Clearly neither of them can inherit! Spaki, who inherits when sons can't?"

"No!" Jarl Glóra said. "The Tynwald hasn't started! You can't call Law-speakers yet!"

"I'm a Law-speaker," Jarl Hersir said. "I'm not as good as some, but we all know the laws of inheritance: the oldest brother inherits if a man has no sons."

"Sterki's the eldest son!" Jarl Refr shouted.

"This isn't the first challenge to inheritance," Jarl Hersir said. "Neither of these boys are worthy of inheritance; Hvítvi's too weak and Sterki's accused of murder. That leaves Jarl Hafr, Jarl Austmaðr's only brother."

"Jarl Hafr's not in line!" Jarl Bagal shouted.

"That's why we need a Tynwald," Jarl Hersir said. "Without this Tynwald, civil war begins now. And we can't hold a Tynwald if you fishwives won't stop haggling over nonsense! Let's get started! Then we can argue the details!"

No one responded. Jarl Hersir stared at all of them, then grabbed Hafr's arm and pulled; Jarl Hafr rose to his feet.

"We should vote on whether Jarl Hafr can stand in for his brother," Jarl Bagal insisted.

"A Tynwald can't vote until it's been opened!" Jarl Dúfunef's father interrupted, and he reached past his son and cuffed Jarl Hafr.

"I command the Tynwald," Jarl Hafr said.

"Now we vote!" Jarl Refr said.

"You can't vote until testimony's heard," Jarl Hersir said.

"We've heard their testimony!" Jarl Refr said.

"Law-speaker Spaki, have we heard testimony?" Jarl Dúfunef asked.

Hávi and everyone else in the hall turned to a thin, bald man in a crimson robe whose beard hung to his waist.

"This Tynwald couldn't hear testimony until Jarl Hafr began it," Law-speaker Spaki said, "and now all trials must be held in order of assertion."

"You can't!" Jarl Bagal shouted. "Jarl Hafr isn't Jarl Austmaðr!"

"Accusations discussed at a Tynwald must be announced at Law Rock," Law-speaker Spaki said. "Has anyone here demanded a challenge of clan-inheritance at Law Rock?"

No one spoke. Everyone in the hall stared at each other, at Law-speaker Spaki, and at Hvítvi and Sterki.

"The only accusation made at Law Rock was by Hvítvi, before witnesses, against his brother, Sterki, for the murder of Jarl Austmaðr." Law-speaker Spaki said.

"Then I'll make the accusation right now!" Jarl Refr said.

"You can, if you wish to leave the Tynwald," Law-speaker Spaki said. "You can make your accusation now, but even if you do, Hvítvi made his accusation first. The murder of Jarl Austmaðr is the first case of this Tynwald."

"Is that true, Brunda?" Jarl Bagal demanded.

A short, fat man, just as bald as Law-speaker Spaki, but much younger, whose beard was dark red, looked up at the high-table, frowned and slowly nodded.

"All cases at a Tynwald must be heard in the order of their accusation," Law-speaker Brunda said.

"Sterki, your brother and uncle have commanded the Tynwald," Jarl Hersir said. "Do you concur?"

"I, Jarl Austmaðr, command this Tynwald," Sterki said.

Complaints erupted, but Jarl Hersir waved them silent, then nodded to the taller Law-speaker.

"The bloodied sword has been presented and the clan-chiefs have all commanded," Law-speaker Spaki said. "This Tynwald has begun."

Chapter 27

"Witnesses of the accusation must be heard first," Law-speaker Spaki announced.

"Let Hvítvi speak first," Law-speaker Brunda said.

"Hvítvi's not a witness; he made the accusation!" Law-speaker Spaki argued.

"Then he may witness himself," Law-speaker Brunda countered.

Law-speaker Spaki considered this, frowning, obviously not expecting it.

"Let the first witness stand and give testimony!" Law-speaker Brunda cried out, not waiting for Law-speaker Spaki to agree.

Hvítvi waited until Law-speaker Spaki shrugged, then stood.

"The very night after ...," Hvítvi began.

"You see?" Law-speaker Brunda shouted suddenly, interrupting Hvítvi, turning to face the hall and gesturing wildly. "You see how Hvítvi seeks to twist his testimony? Called upon to testify as to what he accused his only-remaining brother of at Law Rock, instead Hvítvi attempts to influence this Tynwald with his whole tale! The cursed-one seeks to confuse you!"

Nervous murmurs whispered throughout the crowd.

"Twist?" Law-speaker Spaki hissed loudly enough to be heard without shouting. "It's you who's twisting! You attack unspoken testimony and call him *'cursed'.*"

"He is cursed!" Law-speaker Brunda cried. "Look at him! Odin disfavored Hvítvi so much that he made him white as the snow that buries us each winter! In clan Bagal, such a cursed child would be sacrificed at birth to prevent him from raining bad luck on the whole clan. Can warriors safely support one whom Odin cursed?"

Muted cheers agreed and several shouted *'Freak!'* and *'Kill him!'.*

"Having never been a warrior, that's a question that you'll never be able to answer," Law-speaker Spaki retorted, speaking directly to Law-speaker Brunda.

Laughter followed; Law-speaker Spaki smiled brightly at the glowering, insulted Law-speaker Brunda, and the crowd loved it. Hávi sat shocked; she'd always assumed that a Tynwald would be a solemn, officious ceremony, but this was deadly and vicious, even comical. Jarls argued their cases with Law-speakers before a gathering of warriors, all of whom stood armed and ready to fight. Playing to the crowd seemed to be the only determination of success; failure could spark a war which could not only kill all of the jarls but begin a leaderless civil war.

"I accused Sterki of murdering ...," Hvítvi began, but again Law-speaker Brunda interrupted him.

"Murder!" Law-speaker Brunda shouted. "Murder of his father and his brother!"

"No!" Law-speaker Spaki shouted. "Again, this serpent-tongued Law-speaker seeks to confuse! How are we supposed to hear the witnesses if you keep interrupting?"

Law-speaker Brunda turned and faced Hvítvi.

"Do you believe that Sterki murdered Auðgi?" Law-speaker Brunda demanded.

"That's not the question!" Law-speaker Spaki shouted, storming over and glaring down at his opposite. "We need to hear what was accused by the witness, not by you!" Law-speaker Spaki turned and faced Hvítvi. "What were your exact words at Law Rock?"

"I ... said ..." Hvítvi said slowly, staring at Law-speaker Brunda, ready for any interruption, "... that ... Sterki ... murdered ... Jarl ... Austmaðr."

"Is that it?" Law-speaker Spaki asked. "Did you make any other accusations that night?"

"No."

"Jarl Austmaðr ... and no one else," Law-speaker Spaki repeated loudly to the crowd. "That's what this Tynwald was called for. Whether or not Sterki killed his brothers is irrelevant to this ..."

"Irrelevant?" Law-speaker Brunda cried. "Is it irrelevant to any man in this hall if a son kills his brother?"

"It's procedure ...!" Law-speaker Spaki started, but he was interrupted.

"I asked that question of any *man* in the hall," Law-speaker Brunda chided loudly. "There's no point in you answering."

Laughter erupted again; Hávi would've smiled if her life hadn't been on the line. Even Jarl Hersir and most of the men at the high-table seemed amused. Law-speaker Brunda obviously wanted to include Auðgi's death in the accusation as it couldn't be proven by witnesses.

"Who else witnessed this accusation?" Law-speaker Spaki asked, trying to regain control.

Four men came forward, Bíldr, an older guard, and two townsfolk, one of whom was Hrafna, who wore an iron cap, carried a long spear, and looked very unusual outside of his apron and tavern. Each swore, upon their honor, that Hvítvi properly accused Sterki of murdering Jarl Austmaðr, and Law-speaker Brunda didn't interrupt one of them.

"Only four?" Law-speaker Brunda asked when they all were finished. "Surely there were more people watching this accusation."

"It was late at night," Hvítvi said. "Some were women, but they were sent away before the Tynwald."

"Women!" Law-speaker Brunda laughed. "How convenient! What kind of accusation is witnessed by women?"

A sword sang from its scabbard.

"Are you calling me a woman?" Bíldr challenged.

"I just hope that this council will be spared the misery of listening to the testimony of women," Law-speaker Brunda sneered.

Hávi clenched her teeth to keep from responding; Law-speaker Brunda was just goading her, trying to keep her from speaking.

"But surely there were other witnesses," Law-speaker Brunda spoke up. "Let them come forward now."

To everyone's surprise, six tall, heavily-muscled men with thick, black beards rose from a table near the front and approached the center before the high-table. None spoke, but all glared evilly, bristling and fingering their weapons.

"Did you witness Hvítvi's accusation at Law Rock?" Law-speaker Brunda asked the tallest of them.

"Yes," he drawled, his deep voice grating like a plow being dragged through stones, slowly sweeping the whole hall with his eyes, challenging any who dared dispute him.

"Wait!" Law-speaker Spaki cried. "Who are these men? Where do they hail from?"

"They're merchants from clan Refr," Law-speaker Brunda answered.

Hávi choked, staring up at the six grisly, unwashed, heavily-scarred men. *Merchants?* They were obviously warriors!

"Merchants?" Law-speaker Spaki scoffed, and instantly the tallest of them half-pulled a large sword from his scabbard, but Law-speaker Brunda grabbed his sword arm. The huge warrior obviously allowed the weak, pudgy law-speaker to restrain him as only the strongest could force him to refrain. Law-speaker Spaki hesitated, looking up at the tall, fierce warrior, but continued. "Exactly what wares do they sell?"

"Swords," Law-speaker Brunda replied smugly.

"I see," Law-speaker Spaki said. "And how is it that six large, fierce-looking ... merchants ... managed to witness an accusation at Law Rock without being seen?"

"It was dark," Law-speaker Brunda smiled. "Or perhaps those witnesses who've already testified simply choose not to recall them."

Angrily Bíldr jumped forward, half-pulling his own sword, but Law-speaker Spaki quickly stepped in front of him and placed a restraining hand on his chest.

"No one calls me a liar!" Bíldr shouted.

The five other *'merchants'* half-pulled their swords, and

the sounds of drawing steel hissed throughout the hall. Hávi glanced around; every warrior seemed on the verge of fighting. Some of the jarls were shouting to calm their men, others stared eagerly and expectantly, awaiting the first clash of steel.

"Wait!" Law-speaker Spaki cried, alarmed. "Wait! This can be sorted out!"

"Yes, wait!" Law-speaker Brunda also shouted loudly.

Slowly the warriors relaxed their hard stances, still glaring at each other.

"Spaki," Law-speaker Brunda said directly to his rival, "you can't challenge testimony that hasn't been given!"

"They testified!" Law-speaker Spaki argued.

"No, they just said that they were there," Law-speaker Brunda pointed out.

"Exactly!" Law-speaker Spaki said. "They spoke at a Tynwald! They testified that they were there!"

"Before you challenge them, you should hear all that they have to say," Law-speaker Brunda said.

"Why should we listen to testimony of 'merchants' who can't prove that they were there?" Law-speaker Spaki demanded.

"Merchants don't pass through a city like Skadi without trying to sell their wares," Hvítvi said suddenly, before Law-speaker Brunda could reply. "Who saw you?"

"They'd already sold their wares," Law-speaker Brunda explained casually, as if dismissing a trivial matter. "They were headed home ..."

"Who did they sell their swords to?" Hvítvi asked. "Why didn't ...?"

"Quit badgering them!" Jarl Bagal shouted. "You sound like you look: *like a woman!*"

A few chuckles rose, but every warrior gripped their weapons, still ready for the fight.

"I know these men," Jarl Refr said wryly. "They're merchants ... and their word is good."

"Funny how we haven't heard their words," Jarl Dúfunef scowled. "All that I've heard is that pumpkin-faced Law-speaker talking for them."

"Yes," Jarl Vörsa said. "If these ... merchants ... wish to give testimony, I wish to hear it from them ... directly."

"By all means," Law-speaker Brunda agreed, turning to the tallest merchant. "What did you hear at Law Rock?"

The tall merchant scanned the high-table, then pointed at Hvítvi.

"That one," he snarled, "the cursed one; he said that Sterki murdered Jarl Austmaðr ... and Auðgi."

"Liar!" Bíldr shouted, and swords escaped their scabbards throughout the hall.

"No!" Jarl Dúfunef rose to his feet.

"Kill him!" Sterki cried at the warriors. "Don't let him call you a liar!"

"Stay your swords!" Jarl Hersir shouted and rose to his feet, lifting his heavy sword. "The first man who draws blood at this Tynwald faces me!"

Everyone paused, staring at the high-table.

"What was I wearing?" Hvítvi asked. "You witnessed my accusation; what was I wearing?"

"It was dark!" Law-speaker Brunda laughed, though his was the only mirthful voice in the hall. "They're here to witness what they heard, not what they saw!"

"Let them testify," Jarl Aurriði said irritably. "I didn't come here to fight."

"Where did you stay?" Hvítvi asked. "You couldn't have

slept outside in the freezing cold, and most of the village men are here, including the tavern-masters."

"We camped around a hot fire," one of the *'merchants'* said.

"Where?" Jarl Dúfunef demanded. "Where did you find dry wood? Where are the ashes of your fire ... so we can prove your tale?"

Snarls from the *'merchants'* were repeated across the hall. Hávi leaned back as they glanced at her; surely she'd be killed first if fighting broke out, as it obviously would.

Hávi stood up. She turned to face the high-table, then curtsied as best she could. Most men looked surprised to see her stand and some jeered, but Hávi lumbered across the space and stood beside Bíldr.

"Throw that whore out!" Sterki shouted.

"Master Hvítvi, I would speak," Hávi said, and more jeers and curses sounded, but Hávi only spoke louder. "I would like to prove that these good men are merchants."

Utter silence followed this declaration. Hvítvi stared at her, his eyes full of silent warning, and the rest of the jarls seemed amazed.

"By all means!" Jarl Mjöksiglandi spoke up, smirking. "If you can resolve this then I'd like to see how."

"But if you can't," Jarl Tyrr said, "then you leave! It's a disgrace inviting a woman to a Tynwald."

"As you wish," Hávi said to Jarl Mjöksiglandi, and she raised her voice to be heard by all. "These six men claim to be merchants, sellers of swords. I say: let them prove so. Many jarls have graced Castle Austmaðr with their presence, and my beloved late husband, were he here, would certainly wish to present these good jarls with presents. Alas, my husband is dead, so, as his widow, I would purchase gifts to present to our most-honored guests: swords, *your swords.*"

Hvítvi smiled, as did Bíldr and many others, but many stared daggers at Hávi.

"I pay well," Hávi said loudly. "A full gold coin apiece; far more than these common swords are worth. Surely no real merchant would refuse such a deal."

Sterki scowled and stomped off the three paces to face Hávi, ignoring the threatening poise of Bíldr's drawn sword.

"Sterki ...!" Hvítvi warned. "If you harm her then I'll have every guard here kill you!"

Sterki glowered at Hávi, his breath hot, his hatred almost steaming from his furious expression. Everyone froze.

"Archers!" Hvítvi cried.

Hávi glanced up, as did many others. In the tiny windows above the thrones on the high dais, arrow tips emerged, steel points aimed at Sterki. Behind them glared the eyes of deadly archers.

"If you win here then you may live to rule Austmaðr," Hvítvi said warningly. "If you lose, you'll be outlawed, but you'll live. If you kill her, whatever happens to clan Austmaðr, *you die!*"

Sterki glared murderously at Hávi, then turned and spat at Hvítvi and walked back to stand behind Law-speaker Brunda.

Jarl Mjöksiglandi burst out laughing, a deep, pure belly-roll of sheer amusement. Jarl Glóra also laughed, and suddenly everyone was laughing except Law-speaker Brunda, Sterki, and the six *'merchants'.*

Jarl Hersir set down his sword. From his belt-pouch he brought out a handful of gold and silver coins. Six gold coins he counted out, dropping each to ping as they bounced on the high-table.

"Six gold coins," Hvítvi said. "Five times the worth of those swords..."

"No real merchant would refuse that," Jarl Dúfunef said, "unless, of course, they're not really merchants, their testimony is false, and they lied to this Tynwald ...!"

Law-speaker Brunda fumed, frowning so deeply that his chubby cheeks puffed.

"You can't ask them to give up their only weapons ...!" Sterki argued.

"What do sword merchants need weapons for, except to sell?" Jarl Mjöksiglandi laughed, and he stroked his braided beard and he turned to the six men. "I'm convinced: sell your swords. The penalty for lying to this Tynwald will cost you far more; warriors in the stocks freeze to death when the snows are this deep."

The tall *'merchant'* glared, his black beard bristling, and he clenched his sword angrily. Everyone watched him; even Hávi was convinced that he'd swing his blade and start the war, but Law-speaker Brunda displayed more courage than he appeared to have by cuffing the mighty warrior's arm. The tall *'merchant'* lifted his sword high, growled loudly, and then dropped it to the floor. His sword clanged loudly on the flagstones, and some shouted obscene curses, but the tension relaxed almost instantly. Many sighed, and most scabbarded their swords and looked relieved.

The other *'merchants'* dropped their blades as well. Their clangs filled the air like ringing bells, and then they all turned away and headed back to their seats. Law-speaker Brunda reached up to try to scoop the gold coins off the high-table, but he proved too short; Sterki cursed at him and turned away in disgust. Law-speaker Spaki stepped forward and scooped the coins into Law-speaker Brunda's hands ... and everyone laughed.

"So, they are merchants," Law-speaker Brunda said, although his voice brimmed with disappointment.

"They certainly bought their lives today," Law-speaker Spaki agreed, looking up at the tiny windows where the arrowheads had been, which, out of each, a pair of eyes watched the proceedings. "But as to the value of their words, as with any testimony, only the council of jarls may judge."

Bíldr picked up the six dropped swords, which he piled onto the dais beneath the high-table, beside Jarl Dúfunef's feet. Hávi sighed; she was alive, at least for now, but the Tynwald was far from over.

Hvítvi rose again and spoke.

"Testimony of the accusation's been given," Hvítvi said. "The testimony conflicts, but the honor of the witnesses will be discussed in private. Let us proceed."

"Having proven that the accusation was justly made ...," Law-speaker Spaki began.

"That wasn't proven!" Law-speaker Brunda argued.

"That's not for Law-speakers to decide," Law-speaker Spaki stated. "After the accusation's concluded ..."

"The accusation isn't concluded!" Law-speaker Brunda shouted.

"After all witnesses to the accusation have been heard ...," Law-speaker Spaki paused, as if expecting to be interrupted, but Law-speaker Brunda, after a moment's consideration, waved him on, "the accused speaks next, to deny or confirm the accusation."

Law-speaker Brunda fumed at the wording, but didn't challenge Law-speaker Spaki's phrasing. All eyes turned to Sterki, who seemed angrier than ever, struggling to control his temper like a hissing snake awaiting the right moment to strike. With a deep breath, Sterki came forward, still clenching his sword, its point scraping the flagstones.

"I killed my father," Sterki announced coldly. "I admit that; he and I were alone in his room and I'm the only witness to his death. I didn't want to kill him; he attacked me. How many of you would stand helpless and not fight back? Father was drunk; everyone in the castle knew that. He'd been drunk since we came back from the viking. Auðgi's death unhinged him; he couldn't bear the loss of my beloved brother. I wish that there had been others to witness Auðgi's death. I risked my life to avenge him, and I expected Father to thank me for slaying his precious Auðgi's murderers, but no: Father blamed me for his death; not because he thought that I killed Auðgi, but because I was the older brother and I'd failed to protect Father's favorite son."

Sterki paused to let everyone consider this. Hávi frowned and leaned against the edge of the high-table; she'd be more comfortable sitting down but, despite the heaviness of her stomach, Bíldr's nearness made her feel safer. She breathed deeply, determined not to show weakness, but seldom had she felt as tired.

"Father and I were arguing," Sterki continued. "We often argued ... as if we could do anything else, as drunk as he was. Finally he started yelling at me, blaming me for ... for allowing Auðgi to be killed. I yelled back, tired of trying to explain what happened for the hundredth time to a drunkard who wouldn't listen, and suddenly Father drew his sword and charged me. You know how well he fought; it was him or me. I defended myself as any man here would've; three times he hacked at me, and if I'd missed a single block then I wouldn't be standing here today. The rest ... well, you all know the flurry of combat: it just happened. I was fighting for my life ... and I won. I killed my father, but I didn't murder him."

Sterki finished speaking, standing proud and defiant. Utter silence filled the hall and Jarl Hersir bowed his head. Hávi grimaced; Sterki had given a clear account of what had happened and left no holes to expose his lies.

"Father was stabbed in the back," Hvítvi said softly.

"He stumbled past me, drunk," Sterki said. "He turned his back just as I thrust."

"Then, what about the handmaid?" Hvítvi asked.

Sterki stopped and stared at Hvítvi, apparently not expecting this argument.

"Tryggvi, Hávi's handmaid," Hvítvi specified. "Father's body had barely hit the floor and you charged into Hávi's bedroom and tried to kill her, and when her handmaid tried to stop you, you murdered her in cold blood!"

"I ... I ...," Sterki stammered, but he quickly recovered. "I was in a bloodlust." Sterki turned to face the warriors in the hall. "You're all warriors, you know what it's like on a battlefield. I'd just killed my own father. The berserker-madness came upon me; I tried to kill the person closest to me."

"A woman?" Jarl Dúfunef scowled. "I've never heard of a berserker killing a woman."

"That was a murder without honor!" Jarl Jótun hissed, and many heads nodded in agreement.

"No accusation has been made regarding the handmaid!" Law-speaker Brunda spoke up. "Sterki can't be outlawed for a crime that he was never accused of."

"Law Rock's only a mile away," Jarl Dúfunef snarled.

"By all means, walk there," Jarl Bagal urged, and Jarl Refr laughed wickedly. "That may prove a long mile."

"True, the only crime that Sterki's been accused of is the murder of Jarl Austmaðr," Law-speaker Spaki said. "But note:

Sterki's confessed to killing his father before the whole
Tynwald. Of that there's no doubt, so let no man say that
Sterki's innocent of his father's death. As to whether or not it
was murder, that's for the council of jarls to decide. Was
Sterki truly endangered, a mighty warrior of many vikings who
just bragged of avenging his brother by alone killing many
Rús, so threatened by a drunken old man, his own father,
whom he admits was so drunk that he was stumbling, unable
to think clearly? Is that the terrible danger that so threatened
a viking warrior that he had to stab his own father through the
back? Three times their swords clashed; this was no sneak-
attack; at least, not by the father."

"Nor by Sterki!" Law-speaker Brunda quickly added,
speaking loud and fast. "If Sterki had wanted to kill his father,
to kill any man, he could've stabbed him without once
crossing swords! But many heard the shouts and clangs: they
were fighting; of that, there's also no doubt."

Murmurs rose in the back of the hall. Many considered
this and exchanged worried glances.

"I'm not a Law-speaker," Hvítvi said, "but I think that the
testimonies of the accusers and the accused are finished.
Next comes open court."

"Correct," Law-speakers Spaki and Brunda said
simultaneously.

"Very well," Hvítvi said. "Jarls have the right to speak first
and last."

"Start at the end," the elder Jarl Dúfunef said, "and send a
wench in; my ale-mug's empty."

As a kitchen maid was summoned to refill the horns and
tankards at the high-table, Jarl Refr stood up and spoke.

"I've known Sterki since my first viking," Jarl Refr said,
staring out across the hall. "Sterki's the kind of man that every

clan wants to lead it. He's brave, determined ..."

"This isn't about who'll rule clan Austmaðr ...," Law-speaker Spaki interrupted.

"I'll say anything that I want!" Jarl Refr shouted. "I'm a clan-chief and I won't be dictated to by a petty law-babbler!"

Law-speaker Spaki bowed apologetically to Jarl Refr, whose angry face was as red as his hair, and Jarl Refr continued.

"I say that Sterki was born to be clan-chief. He makes decisions quickly. He doesn't tolerate fools. He fights well. He knows how to lead troops, and under his leadership clan Austmaðr will prosper. In arbitrating this accusation, this Tynwald will be deciding the future of clan Austmaðr. Clan Refr, and many others, support Sterki as Jarl Austmaðr's only true heir. You know how crazy fights get; what does it matter who started it? It wasn't a cowardly murder; it was a duel between experienced warriors. Unless someone can prove otherwise, clan Refr supports Sterki."

Jarl Refr nodded to Sterki, who gave him a brief grin, then resumed his frown. Jarl Refr sat back down and Jarl Tyrr slowly stood up, his long, gray beard hanging thin with age.

"I'm disappointed," Jarl Tyrr said, crinkling up his scarred face. "Clan Tyrr has no love for clan Austmaðr, and we don't care if Sterki rules, is outlawed, or dies; every path bodes ill. There's no honor here. Clan Austmaðr will be ruled either by a cursed jarl, an idiot, or a suspected murderer. They even let women witness their Tynwalds. No real warrior will fight for any of them. I've heard no evidence that Jarl Austmaðr was murdered. We're too far away to claim a tract of its land, so we'll take our chest of gold now or a wergild later. I just want this over with tonight."

Jarl Tyrr sat back down and Jarl Vörsa stood up.

"This is my first Tynwald," Jarl Vörsa said, anger in his tone. "Father wasn't up for a long, cold voyage, but I can say what he'd say if he were here: *what kind of savages are you?* Brothers fighting, fathers murdered by sons ... in clan Vörsa we don't threaten family, and civility is upheld even in the most furious family arguments.

"I don't know these men who've testified. I don't know Sterki or Hvítvi. I knew Auðgi, and I'd hoped that every man in clan Austmaðr was like him. I'm sorry that my expectation was so wrong. I'm disgusted with the lot of you. If this is what clan Austmaðr is, then I say good riddance!"

Jarl Mjöksiglandi hammered his fist on the high-table as Jarl Vörsa sat down, and many in the hall, and most of the jarls, echoed approval, banging fists or clapping hands.

The old man next to Jarl Vörsa stood up next.

"I'm not a clan-chief," he said. "Jarl Vörsa's father sent me to keep an eye on his son; I'll be proud to report to his father how well he's proving himself."

Another round of applause, briefer but no less ardent, filled the hall. The next two men shook their heads when he sat down, declining to talk, and then Jarl Mjöksiglandi rose.

"I'll listen to the rest of the testimony before I draw any conclusions," Jarl Mjöksiglandi said. "However, Jarl Vörsa made an important point; I don't know any of these men who've testified and I'd like to hear any who'll vouch for them."

With dignity Jarl Mjöksiglandi sat down, and Jarl Dúfunef stood.

"We all live in Sweden," Jarl Dúfunef said. "Most of us live in the Skåne. Our enemies avoid our shores because we're one people, fierce, strong, and united. Do you think that Norway leaves us alone because they're nice people?

They fear us, as do the Rús, ..."

"They'd fear Sterki!" Jarl Bagal spoke up.

"Don't interrupt me!" Jarl Dúfunef shouted angrily. *"If you want your turn to talk ...!"*

"Don't order me!" Jarl Bagal half-rose.

"Bagal, sit down!" Jarl Dúfunef's father commanded. "After what Jarl Vörsa said, do you really want this Tynwald to sound like a bunch of gossiping fish-wives?"

Jarl Bagal glared and growled, but he sat back down and drank from his tankard. Jarl Dúfunef stood frozen, fuming.

"They fear us," Jarl Dúfunef's father whispered.

"Oh, yes," Jarl Dúfunef continued. "Our neighbors fear us, and we can't show weakness by warring amongst ourselves. Every clan here could find a reason to war with every other clan if they go looking for it. Clan Dúfunef says that we should be looking for reasons to *not* go to war with each other; we have all of Europe to fight with ... and steal from, if we want to get rich. Lands far wider than Scandinavia exist ... if we have the strength to take them. The only way that we'll survive to take what's ours is if we trust each other and have clan-chiefs worthy of that trust. Unlike most of you, I know Sterki. I don't trust Sterki. I don't like Sterki. Letting Sterki get away with murdering his father to become clan-chief weakens us all. None of our clans will survive if the largest of us can't be trusted not to stab us in our backs."

Jarl Dúfunef took a breath to speak on, but his father laid a hand on his arm and he reluctantly let whatever else he was going to say go unsaid, and he sat back down.

Hvítvi rose next, but he paused before speaking.

"I'm very proud of Jarl Dúfunef," Hvítvi said, looking even paler than usual, "not only for what he said, but for what he didn't say ... at his father's request. He didn't even argue with him; I wish that my family was like that. I apologize to Jarl Vörsa; clan Austmaðr's not as civilized as it used to be. I could try to blame all of that on my brother, whom I believe murdered my father and two of my brothers, and whom I witnessed murder an innocent, helpless girl. Yet I won't; I'll only say that even beasts of the forests don't kill their own family like this. I look forward to better days for clan Austmaðr ... and to a clan-chief who can lead us honorably."

Hvítvi stood a moment longer, then quietly sat back down. Jarl Hafr stood up. He didn't speak at first, but stared across the room to every section, taking in all their faces.

"I find all of this disgraceful," Jarl Hafr growled. "Warriors from all over the Skåne gathered to decide which of us are liars; my father, and my good brother's father, would've beaten our heads in just for needing to be here. Real warriors don't lie. I don't lie."

Jarl Hafr sat down to tumultuous applause, so much that Jarl Hersir, after rising, had to wait until the hall quieted before he could speak. When he spoke, Jarl Hersir's deep, even voice echoed to every ear in the hall, but his eyes never left Sterki.

"I knew Jarl Austmaðr better than any man here," Jarl Hersir said. "We played together as kids and Jarl Austmaðr risked his own life on a battlefield to bind my arm when I lost my hand. Attempt to kill his own son? *Sterki, you're a liar;* even drunk, Jarl Austmaðr wouldn't do that, and I've seen him more drunk than any of you, so drunk that he couldn't lean forward to puke. Sterki, you murdered your father and my best friend, and I'm sure that you murdered Auðgi, too. Lying about your murders only compounds your cowardice ..."

"You'll die, old fool!" Sterki shouted, his face crimson,

every muscle taut.

Jarl Hersir stared at Sterki, meeting his contempt with quiet resolve.

"A death-threat," Jarl Hersir said pointedly, emphasizing his words. "Wise men act as they will, but fools and liars always react as their nature demands. Whenever challenged, Sterki always resorts to the same scheme: *eliminate his challenger.* Murder is his only nature. Those who ally themselves with a murderer, be warned: it's not in Sterki's nature to coexist. If he becomes Jarl Austmaðr then he won't stop until he rules all of Scandinavia."

"Clan Hersir will certainly fall," Sterki promised.

Jarl Hersir and Sterki exchanged glowers.

"The day that you become Jarl Austmaðr, we're at war."

"Then we're at war!" Sterki shouted.

"Enough!" the elder Jarl Dúfunef shouted. "Aren't matters volatile enough? Hersir, sit down! There's no point in ... *poking the puppy!"*

Sterki cursed, but no one heard his words; laughter burst from everywhere, and several sarcastic shouts of *'Puppy!'* came from the back.

Several more jarls, not clan-chiefs, declined to speak, and then Jarl Bagal stood up.

"No one has more grievances against clan Austmaðr than clan Bagal," Jarl Bagal said. "Jarl Illingr might argue that, but he can't: clan Illingr's dead, murdered by Jarl Austmaðr ... and his widow. I see no difference between the son and the father. Jarl Austmaðr got pruned away just like Jarl Illingr's ear-tips. This Tynwald's unnecessary: Sterki inherited clan Austmaðr the instant his father died. No clan that's as murderous, as steeped in the blood of Scandinavians, as clan Austmaðr has any right to claim a moral high-ground.

"Clan Bagal supports a simple solution: clan Austmaðr has fallen. If clan Hersir and clan Dúfunef would join us, their share of the booty would outfit their vikings for the next five years. Clan Bagal and clan Glóra could reclaim the lands usurped from us, and the remaining Austmaðr lands we could divide up, or you can sell them to me; clan Bagal will pay yearly tribute for all Austmaðr lands. Let's do to clan Austmaðr what it did to clan Illingr, without civil war, and all of us leave here rich."

Jarl Bagal stared down at everyone from his impressive height, perhaps the tallest man in the room, certainly the tallest on the high-table dais. His expression denoted his seriousness as his eyes scanned the other jarls, measuring their faces for signs of agreement or anger. Whatever he saw, he sighed and continued.

"Clan Bagal has no interest in a strong clan Austmaðr. Sterki's trial's a joke; to see who becomes the next Jarl Austmaðr is our only reason for being here: the idiot half-brother, the cursed weakling, or the father-killer. Clan Bagal doesn't care who wins. Clan Bagal wants its lands back and will support anyone who'll swear to us, right now, or clan Bagal supports no one."

Jarl Bagal stood a moment longer, looking at Sterki, Hvítvi, and Jarl Hafr, and finally he sat down.

"I, Jarl Austmaðr, do swear to return the lands of clan Bagal," Sterki said, "but not until I'm crowned and every non-Austmaðr warrior's returned home."

Urgent whispers broke out, filling the hall with the hiss of a hundred steaming kettles. Jarl Bagal stood back up, glanced at Hvítvi and Hafr, and then announced:

"Clan Bagal supports Sterki as Jarl Austmaðr."

Some applauded, but most of the men shouted angrily. A

few shouted curses, but Jarl Bagal ignored them and sat down, grinning. Jarl Jótun quickly stood, his dark, ferocious countenance enhanced by his grim expression.

"How convenient!" Jarl Jótun scowled. "Clan Bagal's support is for sale like a whore's pleasures! What of justice? What of honor? What about our laws and traditions?"

Jarl Bagal lost his grin and slowly looked up at Jarl Jótun, deadly warning in his eyes.

"Clan Jótun will hear the rest of the testimony before it judges. I say this: already this court's been lied to, either by Hvítvi's men, who pretend that they didn't see the merchants, or by these merchants, who weren't there at all. Whoever lies to this council better never step foot on Jótun lands; they'll die in our stocks if I catch them."

Jarl Jótun sat down quickly as the hall fell silent: no man doubted his threat. Another jarl, not a clan-chief, stood up.

"If we don't follow our laws then what's the point of having them?" he said. "Inheritance laws are very clear: Sterki's the eldest; Sterki inherits all. However, no law says that a clan-chief can't be tried and outlawed for murder. If Sterki's outlawed today, then Hvítvi inherits as if his brother never existed. If Hvítvi wishes to hand leadership of clan Austmaðr over to Jarl Hafr or anyone else, that's his right. I say that Sterki's clan-chief, but that doesn't mean that he can't be outlawed by this Tynwald. This Tynwald has no authority to decide who the next Jarl Austmaðr is. Only one accusation has been legally made and our only business is the resolution of that accusation."

He sat down. Jarl Glóra, sitting at the very end of the high-table, stood very slowly, stroking his long, gold-flecked beard and looking thoughtful.

"Clan Glóra has suffered at the hands of clan Austmaðr,"

Jarl Glóra said. "Clan Austmaðr has suffered at the hands of clan Glóra. Clan Jótun once attacked clan Vörsa, and the rivalries between clan Mjöksiglandi and clan Dúfunef are older than either I or Jarl Dúfunef the elder, and we're the oldest jarls in the Skåne. Jarl Jótun speaks well about the den Skaanske Lov; the duty of every Tynwald is to uphold our laws, not to leverage the return of stolen lands." Jarl Glóra glanced darkly at Jarl Bagal, who looked away. "This is my twelfth Tynwald, and if my health doesn't improve then it may prove my last. My eldest son's been ready to take my title for a decade now and his brothers support him; I look with disdain upon the family Austmaðr for forcing this Tynwald on us in the middle of winter. Yet this council has a duty to keep our laws honorable ... and to keep lying tongues from twisting it into serpent's knots. People who follow twisted laws have no honor; it's the duty of a Tynwald to keep our laws honest and plain to keep our people honorable, worthy of respect.

"In clan Glóra, we don't pass the mantle of clan-chief by murder. If this council declares that Sterki murdered Jarl Austmaðr then we can't let him ascend to the throne of clan Austmaðr. We owe that precedence to all of the clans of the Skåne, to the den Skaanske Lov that we leave to our children, and, perhaps most important, to the sons of our clan-chiefs. A single civil war will seem trivial if we prove to our sons that inheritance through assassination is legal. The sons of clan Glóra know this; it's to the unworthy sons of Jarl Austmaðr that this lesson must be taught."

Jarl Glóra stared at Sterki and then turned his glare to Hvítvi; Sterki met his glare defiantly but Hvítvi nodded meekly. Hávi felt herself blushing; even if Hvítvi won, even if Jarl Hafr became Jarl Austmaðr, this disgrace would last forever.

Jarl Glóra sat back down. The crowd shifted nervously; no one spoke.

"It's time for open testimony," Law-speaker Brunda announced, and Law-speaker Spaki nodded in agreement. "Anyone present may speak now. Come forward, be recognized, and you may testify before this council. We ask that you be brief; we don't want to be here all night."

No one stepped forward, not wanting to be the first. Both Law-speakers scanned the hall, looking for any movement, when a high-pitched voice spoke up.

A single man pushed forward to the front of the hall. Hávi glanced up in surprise; it was Hrafna.

"State your name and home," Law-speaker Spaki instructed. "Then say what you will."

"I'm Hrafna," he said. "I own the largest tavern in Skadi, so I keep track of all strangers, which isn't hard as most travelers supp and bed in my tavern. I just want to say that I know Bíldr and the others that testified with me. All of my life I've known these men and I'd swear to their honor with my life. These other witnesses, these *'sword-merchants'*, I never saw them until today."

The crowd reacted strongly; someone in the back shouted *'liar!'*, but he was quickly stared down by everyone else. All of these men were warriors; they didn't tolerate deceivers. Many heads nodded approvingly.

Three times Hrafna bowed deeply, once to each side, and then to the center; being a tavern master adept at gestures of respect. The crowd seemed to approve his manner; many clapped his shoulders as he stepped back against the wall.

A dozen others came forward, all men of Skadi or guards of Castle Austmaðr, and each spoke praisingly of Bíldr and the others. Finally Jarl Mjöksiglandi rose.

"I've heard enough of the honor of Hvítvi's witnesses," Jarl Mjöksiglandi said. "The day's passing and I don't want to miss lunch listening to the same testimony over and over. Is there anyone here who would swear their life and honor for the *'sword-merchants'?"*

Jarl Mjöksiglandi paused and scanned the crowd. Law-speaker Brunda gesticulated for some to come forth from the crowd, but a full minute passed, and no one moved or spoke.

"Very well," Jarl Mjöksiglandi said. "Is there anyone else who has testimony about the actual killing?"

The moment passed slowly. Finally Hávi stood forward and faced Jarl Mjöksiglandi, curtsied as best she could, and addressed the council.

"Honored guests," Hávi said, sweeping all of them with her gaze. "I plead with you on behalf of my murdered husband. I am widowed early, not because of accident, sickness, or honorable death, but because my husband had a deep heart. Jarl Austmaðr loved Auðgi and, despite his certainty to the contrary, he couldn't accept that one of his beloved sons would be so base as to murder his own brother. He knew what such an accusation would do to clan Austmaðr, to the whole Skåne, if the only apparent heir to our clan were openly accused of murder. From the few lessons of the den Skaanske Lov that I forced Jarl Illingr to teach me, I understand what this means. All is to the shame of clan Austmaðr.

"I loved my husband. It took me some time to understand this; I didn't want to be married to anyone, and the first time we spoke was after our wedding. Eventually I loved Jarl Austmaðr as much as he loved his sons, all of his sons, and he'd lost three sons before I ever met him. His sons and clan Austmaðr were all that he cared about. For love of clan Austmaðr, my husband tried to deny the truth that he knew.

"I was the closest to the murder ... in the very next room ... and I heard all. I was in my inner-room, my bedroom, with Tryggvi, my handmaid, whom Sterki also killed. I heard the sword-clangs. I heard the shouts as they fought ... and my husband's death-cry. I heard their arguments before the fight began."

Hávi struggled to breathe, every eye in the hall intent upon her. She felt hot, dizzy, tired and uncomfortable, larger and uglier than she'd ever felt before. Every emotion that she had welled up inside her as tears filled her eyes. She struggled to remain calm, to appear in control.

"I know ... why Sterki murdered my husband," Hávi said slowly, letting her tears flow freely down both cheeks. "In Jarl Austmaðr's last words, he admitted ... *he accused* ... Sterki of murdering Auðgi."

Shouts rose, but Hávi heard only distant thunder. The great hall began to spin, and Hávi swooned into darkness.

Chapter 28

"Open the door!" Bíldr cried, kicking against her wooden door with his heavy boot. "Hávi's sick!"

The brace scraped and the door opened, Völu, Breiðr, and Bitra all screaming, but either their words were nonsense or Hávi was incoherent; the doorway that Bíldr squeezed her through seemed vastly too small, as if Hávi had transformed into a massive, sobbing bull walrus that someone was trying to thread through the eye of Hvassi's smallest needle.

"Jarl Austmaðr! My husband!" Hávi reeled from side to side, barely aware as Völu shouted *"Get back!"* and then strong hands curled around the backs of her knees and she was lifted and thrown into a snow bank ... no, it was white sheets: Hávi was in her bed.

"Lock the door behind me!" Bíldr ordered, and then he was gone.

It was too much. Exhausted, hammered by so many tragedies that Hávi couldn't separate them, Hávi cried as many hands held her, blankets piled overtop of her, and someone lifted her head and made her drink. Sweet wine poured between her lips. Tears flowed freely until a welcomed sleep overtook her.

"Hávi?"

Something strange bothered Hávi, like the wings of a tiny moth brushing against her face.

"Hávi?" asked the same deep voice.

Master Kamban's face swam into view. Hávi tried to reach up and hug him but her arms wouldn't move.

"Be still, Hávi," Master Kamban said. "Everything's fine."

Hávi shook her head, trying to clear it of the night-fog that misted her every thought. Bright sunlight beamed through her snow-covered window letting out the stifling heat; its brightness nearly blinded her.

"Wha ...? Is ...? What did they do ... to Sterki?" Hávi asked.

"Nothing yet," Master Kamban replied. "They've been awake all night discussing it."

"All night?"

"It's past midday."

"But ...!"

"Your only concern right now is your baby," Master Kamban said forcefully. "You've done all that you can. No woman approaching childbirth should suffer such burdens."

"I'm fine," Hávi insisted, although she felt weak as a kitten.

"Drink your tea," Master Kamban insisted. "Ladies, ..."

Master Kamban *'thumped'* backwards, carefully sliding his cane amid the women's long skirts as they rushed forward. Breiðr held out a cup for her and Völu lifted her head.

"I don't want tea ...," Hávi resisted, but she opened her

mouth to catch the hot drink as Breiðr poured it or it would've drenched her new, multi-colored quilt. Strangely, the tea cooled her.

"I'm too hot," Hávi said.

Blankets were flung back until only a white sheet covered her. Released, Hávi lifted her arms and stretched.

"How much longer is this baby going to stay inside me?"

"Oh, quit complaining," Völu said. "You're not the first pregnant woman."

"The longer the baby stays inside you the stronger it'll be," Master Kamban said.

"Better for ... for clan Austmaðr ... if it comes soon," Hávi said warily, for she had almost said *'Better for Hvítvi ...'*.

"Not if it's a girl," Master Kamban said. "If it's a girl, best if it's not born until all of the jarls go home."

"It can't be a girl," Hávi said.

"Frigg will do as she pleases," Völu said. "Finish your tea."

Hávi drank more tea, and eventually ate some dried fruits and a small cake, mostly to appease Breiðr, who seemed to fret that Hávi wouldn't have the strength to push out a son. Völu laughed at Breiðr's worries.

"I've seen Hávi outwrestle boys two years older than her," Völu said. "Once she almost beat up Bifru, and he's a mighty warrior."

"That was six years ago," Hávi said, but she smiled anyway. "Master Kamban, what's going on?"

"The council's deciding," Master Kamban said. "Sometimes it takes an hour and other times it takes days. The jarls are arguing, making deals, and probably threats."

"Will Sterki be outlawed?" Hávi asked.

"Who can say?" Master Kamban shrugged. "Hvítvi and Hafr will do their best. Jarl Dúfunef supports them, but each jarl will do what's best for them, not what's best for clan Austmaðr."

"Will they sell their support to Hvítvi?"

"Yes, but they'll also sell to Sterki."

"But ... isn't Sterki in the dungeon again?"

"Sterki's a son of Jarl Austmaðr; he's got as much right as Hvítvi to be part of the council. They're all in the great hall. The warriors have been moved into the courtyard where they're burning bonfires for warmth."

"Do you have any idea who's winning?"

"Felian's in the archer's room above the kitchen," Master Kamban said. "No one's supposed to be listening to the jarls debate, but ... well, Bíldr's got a few trusted men there, and I convinced him to let Felian accompany them. He's a good boy; too young to be a warrior, of course."

"What's he said?"

"Felian says that the jarls keep making speeches but no one's listening. Hafr suggested that Sterki should be put to death, but there was little support for that. Hvítvi demands that Sterki be banished for life, but Sterki insists that no clan in the Skåne will be safe when word gets out that a weakling was made Jarl Austmaðr. Hafr's not a good speaker; Hvítvi and Jarl Hersir keep trying to hush him up, but Jarl Bagal insists on hearing his opinion on every detail."

"What do you think will happen?"

"No one cares what a hunchback thinks, but I can't imagine that they'd execute Sterki; it'd start a war. No one doubts Sterki's turpitude, but justice doesn't pay in gold or lands. Honor is Hvítvi's problem; Sterki can give away most of clan Austmaðr and then take it back by force, once he's clan-chief. Hvítvi's warned them that Sterki will betray them, but promises of gold are more welcomed than cautions."

"So Sterki will be outlawed?"

"Will even that help?" Master Kamban asked. "Sterki can wait out his outlawry in clan Bagal or Refr and claim his birthright when it's over. He'll have to promise them half of clan Austmaðr to do it, but he will. Outlawing Sterki, unless it's for life, won't help much, just delay the inevitable."

Hávi felt like crying again. Sterki's promises couldn't all be hollow; the other clan-chiefs may choose to take what Sterki offers, even if they must fight to keep it, rather than weaken clan Austmaðr by accepting Hvítvi's offer, and then fight to conquer clan Austmaðr. What could Hvítvi offer but a continuation of the status quo with clan Austmaðr on top?

Hávi glanced at the locked treasury doors. Would even giving away every coin in clan Austmaðr soothe generations of bitter rivalries?

Pain! Hávi's stomach convulsed suddenly. She choked, then fell back onto her pillow gasping, but its intenseness was already fading. She laid back, tired, as Breiðr and Völu tried to make her drink more tea.

"No, I need to get up," Hávi said, pushing back the bed sheet.

"Get up?" Völu asked incredulously.

"I think she should," Breiðr said.

"If Hávi wants to stand, let her," Master Kamban said.

Slowly, with a great deal of help, Hávi climbed off the bed and lowered her great bulk onto her feet. She felt awkward, unbalanced, her bloated body tipping to every side, yet it felt good to stand. Hávi stepped toward the fireplace, wanting to hold onto its solid mantle, although Breiðr and Völu were each gripping an arm, struggling to support her. Then the strangest sensation that Hávi had ever felt slimed her: a warm dampness splashed down her legs, drenching her feet. Völu screamed.

"Don't be alarmed," Master Kamban said loudly, trying to quiet Völu.

"Don't worry, Hávi," Breiðr said softly without Völu's hysteria. "It's just your water."

"Dry her off, change her nightshirt, and put her back into bed," Master Kamban ordered. "I'll let Hvítvi know."

"Know what?" Hávi demanded.

"Hávi, you're about to give birth."

Master Kamban returned an hour later, Felian at his side. Felian still wore his oversized steel helmet and carried a tall spear, but they only emphasized his youth. Felian seemed aware of this and fidgeted uncomfortably; Hávi chose not to smile. Felian carried Master Kamban's large medical bag. Master Kamban *'thumped'* over to Hávi's bedside.

"What's happening?" Hávi asked Master Kamban.

"First, how do you feel?" Master Kamban asked.

"I'm fine," Hávi insisted. "How goes the Tynwald?"

"Poorly," Master Kamban said. "The jarls are still arguing about everything that they can, some using the Tynwald as an excuse to plan next year's viking."

"No decision?"

"Why should they decide?" Master Kamban asked. "Once Hvítvi's accusation is settled, they either fight or go home. The jarls are happy to sit around enjoying clan Austmaðr's hospitality since both Hvítvi and Sterki are giving them anything that they request in hope of winning their support."

"How long can they go on?"

"They'll stay until the food and ale runs out," Master Kamban said. "That won't take long ..."

"Those jarls can't eat that much!" Hávi said.

"No, but their armies can," Master Kamban replied.

"What?" Hávi demanded. "Hvítvi's feeding their armies?"

"Some," Master Kamban answered. "If Hvítvi won't, Sterki will. Sheep are being slaughtered by the dozen; Clan Austmaðr will have to tighten its belt until harvest, but that can't be helped."

"Did you talk to Hvítvi?"

"Only for a moment. Hvítvi ordered me to bring you something."

Master Kamban turned and nodded to Felian, who set down the big, medical bag and rummaged through it. When he stood up, his hands held four large daggers.

"One for each of you," Master Kamban said, and Felian handed a dagger to Breiðr, Bitra, Völu, and Hávi.

"It's this bad?" Hávi asked.

"Jarl Glóra seems to support Hvítvi, but Aurriði and Tyrr are supporting Bagal and Refr. Jótun and Vörsa seem to waiver and may be waiting until Mjöksiglandi decides. The rest don't seem interested in voicing any opinion. Jarl Hersir and Jarl Dúfunef made ardent speeches, and Hvítvi pointed out that Sterki, if he honors all of his bargains, has already sold most of clan Austmaðr."

"How can they do that?" Hávi demanded. "They know that Sterki's a liar!"

"Clan-chiefs do as they please, and what pleases them is profit. Sterki murdered kin, so he should be outlawed for life, but I'll be surprised if they can outlaw him for seven years, as if even that will be long enough."

"What do you mean?"

"Seven years is an insult to Jarl Austmaðr's memory," Master Kamban said. "In seven years Sterki could return, backed by the armies of other clans, to attack clan Austmaðr, which he is weakening right now. Your son will still be a child; we'll be engulfed in civil war."

"Then Sterki will kill us all eventually," Hávi said. "It's just a matter of when."

Eventually Hávi made them let her get out of bed and walk around. She really wasn't feeling bad; she was still young and as strong as some men, despite aching all over and feeling like she was carrying a basket of baby goats inside of her. Walking helped, but soon she tired and went back to bed. Völu made Breiðr and Master Kamban laugh with stories of Hávi's youthful misdeeds, including the fire that they'd built up in a smoke hut one winter, never expecting that a snow-covered grass ceiling might suddenly burst into flames. Bitra fetched them food from the kitchen, and Hávi insisted that Felian eat with them, despite his protests. For a day trapped in her bedroom, despite the constant aches, everyone had a great time.

Late that night Hávi's pains began. Hávi thought that she'd known pain; pulled muscles, bruises, and scraped knees dotted her childhood, but the first time that she screamed no one was more surprised than she. Völu prayed to Frigg, fearing that Hávi was dying, but Breiðr calmly held Hávi's hand and assured her that it would soon be over. Yet the sudden convulsions terrified Hávi, who'd never imagined such torment, like she'd pulled every muscle in her body and all of the Hersir boys were punching her stomach as hard as they could. Every time that she thought the pain couldn't get much worse it did, and soon Bitra pulled off her sweat-soaked sheet and covered her with a fresh one. Master Kamban began loudly reciting spells and invocations to the gods that he'd taught Hávi months before, and he encouraged her to recite them with him, but Hávi grew irritable as the pains twisted deeper. Slowly Breiðr's calm insistence that Hávi would be fine grew annoying, and Völu's wide-eyed fright at witnessing her first human birth infuriated her. Finally Hávi's patience failed and she cursed all of them. Then she burst into tears.

Suddenly Hávi realized what was wrong; she was bearing a girl, not a son. Hávi didn't know how she knew this, but her certainty overwhelmed her. Hvítvi needed a new brother, a cross between Jarl Hersir and Auðgi, a tribute to Hávi's father, Jorgen, a son whom Jarl Dúfunef could teach to fight and who'd grow up as wise and learned as Jarl Illingr, or Sterki would assume the crown and kill the beautiful albino, and then Hávi would have nothing, no hope, and no future. No daughter could become Jarl Austmaðr. Hávi had failed: she'd be shunned by her people. Hvítvi would throw her out of the castle and she'd be finally, utterly alone.

Ashamed, she kept her knowledge secret, ignoring Breiðr's worried questions and Völu's frantic expression. Perhaps she and her daughter would die in childbirth; then they'd be spared the embarrassment and shame of Hávi dooming all of clan Austmaðr.

The night lasted forever, and in the wee hours of the morning came the worst pain of all. Hávi pushed out her child with a scream that echoed throughout Castle Austmaðr. She reeled from the final agony, shaken to her core, but afterwards, the first sight that her eyes saw was a wide smile on the face of Master Kamban.

"It's a boy!"

Breiðr reached over with a wet cloth and wiped the blood off, and then Master Kamban lifted the small, red-pink shape and placed it in Hávi's arms. Hávi took her newborn into her grasp with incredulity unbefitting someone who'd grown up raising goats and watched dozens of kids born of squalling nannies. He was beautiful. The cry of her baby sounded a clear trumpet of happiness, overshadowing even the exhaustion of her agonized body. His tiny limbs flopped like a limp fish, and hesitantly, disbelieving, Hávi spread his tiny legs with her fingers, doubting her senses until she saw his token of manhood. She'd done it: *Hávi had born a son.*

"J-Jorgen," Hávi gasped, her breathing still labored. "J-Jarl Austmaðr he may be, but until then ... Jorgen."

Master Kamban nodded, then turned to Felian.

"The boy's name is Jorgen," Master Kamban said. "Tell Hvítvi first. Go!"

Soon the bell rang loudly, again and again, signaling the birth of a new jarl. Hvítvi and Jarl Hersir rushed into her room.

"Congratulations!" Hvítvi said so softly that he could barely be heard, but his relief echoed in his voice and seeped into Hávi's heart and thrilled every wounded fiber of her being. His thin, wry smile delighted her, and all of the pains that she'd suffered seemed suddenly irrelevant. She looked up into his pink eyes and smiled.

"Well done," Jarl Hersir smiled so widely that his teeth became visible through his thick, black beard and mustache. "Clan Hersir's so proud of you!"

Hávi grinned up at both of them, but her eyes lingered on Hvítvi.

"Your ... brother," Hávi offered, and she gently lifted the tiny figure.

Hesitantly Hvítvi held out his pale, milky hands. Hávi held tiny Jorgen until Hvítvi lifted his slight weight from her arms, and then she collapsed, exhaustion taking its toll. Hvítvi lifted Jorgen slowly, as if afraid that he'd hurt the newborn infant, when suddenly it gurgled and Hvítvi's white pallor ashened.

"Don't worry; babies do that," Master Kamban said. "Now we have work to do. Give Jorgen to Breiðr; we've got to clean up Hávi so that she can sleep, as she needs to."

"Thank you, healer ... my friend," Hvítvi said to Master Kamban, and to Hávi's surprise, Jarl Hersir clapped Master Kamban across his hump and hugged him with comfortable familiarity.

"Best healer in the Skåne," Jarl Hersir laughed heartily. "Remember that, Völu, when it's your time."

"Me?" Völu gasped. "I'm not going through that!"

Everyone laughed at her, and Hvítvi and Jarl Hersir both congratulated Hávi again, then departed. After the door was braced behind them, Master Kamban and Bitra scooted Hávi aside, along with her mattress, and Völu demonstrated her Hersir-born strength by heaving a fresh straw mattress over the exposed bed-ropes, then pulled off the old, soiled mattress after Hávi was transferred onto the fresh, stiff, spiky straw which was sewn inside of a newly-woven bag. With warm, damp cloths they cleaned Hávi off and then covered her with dry, unsoiled quilts, and Breiðr placed Jorgen on her chest, but Hávi barely had the strength to hold him.

"Jorgen's asleep," Master Kamban whispered softly to Hávi. "You should follow his example."

Hávi had never heard better advice.

Jay Palmer

Chapter 29

Tired, but feeling stronger than she had in weeks, Hávi descended the stone stairs with Jorgen, her precious baby, cradled in her arms. She was wearing her new, red dress again, which was so tight that she couldn't have worn it before birthing Jorgen. Bildr kept a firm grasp on her right arm, Breiðr on her left, as Hávi took each step. Felian and Bifru led the way, carefully carrying long spears pointed up, away from her. Hávi had asked Master Kamban to accompany her, but he'd politely refused; Hvítvi might welcome his presence, but unfriendly eyes would see the appearance of a hunchback at the presentation of a new Jarl Austmaðr as a sign of terrible doom. Sadly Hávi understood, but she'd hugged Master Kamban tightly, thanked him, and praised his healing skills with every kind word that she knew. Völu followed them down the stone stairs, eager to catch her first glimpse of the Tynwald, probably the only one that she'd ever see.

Cheers and applause broke out as Hávi stepped into the great hall. Everyone rose to their feet and most hands clapped while others joyously beat fists against their hard hauberks or hammered the pommels of their heavy daggers on the stout boards of tables. Hávi glanced at all of the smiling faces and spied only a few frowns: on Master Krókr, Jarl Bagal, and of course, on Sterki. The lines on Mjóvi's face were stretched as taut as bowstrings, her expression as pained as if every billy goat in the Skåne had just butted her.

Jarl Dúfunef waved for silence and then Hvítvi raised his father's huge drinking horn from a table covered not only with horns and chalices, but with many platters of food.

"Warriors of the Skåne!" Hvítvi called out to the whole hall. "Behold my new brother, son of Jarl Austmaðr, born of Hávi Hersir Austmaðr, father's lawful wife; I give you Jorgen Austmaðr!"

Shouts and whistles joined the exultation of the crowd. One man drew two swords and clanged them together repeatedly, and then the cheers only slightly diminished as hundreds of mugs were held aloft in honor, then drained in single draughts. Hávi beamed; never had she felt as welcomed in her adopted clan.

The cheer lasted long, and servants hurried forth with large pitchers of ale to offer refills, too few and too slow to reach every empty mug. Hvítvi and all of the jarls remained standing, even the elder Jarl Dúfunef. Beside her, Breiðr led Hávi to the center of the room where she turned her to and face Hvítvi. He smiled warmly at her, his pale skin shining in the brightly-lit hall. Hávi wanted to curtsy but feared that she might be too weak or that she might drop her precious newborn, so Hávi simply inclined her head as best she could, striving to conserve her strength.

"Enough!" Jarl Refr cried, his glare fixed upon Hvítvi. "Get it over with; then we can celebrate everything!"

The hall fell silent, troubled by this pronouncement. Hávi paled; anything that pleased Jarl Refr couldn't be good. Hávi glanced to the far side of the high-table; there stood Sterki, a wicked, wolfish grin curling his lips. Jarl Hersir shook his head sadly and Jarl Dúfunef scowled loudly. Fearfully, Hávi glanced up at Hvítvi, hoping for some sign, some clue to what was about to happen. To her surprise, Hvítvi wore his wryest grin.

"This Tynwald has reached its decision," Hvítvi announced, and the room tensed and fell utterly silent. Anxious hands grasped pommels and swordgrips, ready for anything, but Hvítvi continued calmly, relaxed. Only Hávi, who knew him well, could see the tension behind his appearance.

"Sterki, brother and eldest living son of Jarl Austmaðr," Hvítvi loudly addressed, and Sterki stepped forward proudly, defiantly. Hvítvi waited until Sterki reached the center of the hall and turned to face the entire council of jarls seated at the high-table. "Brother, this Tynwald has ruled that I lawfully accused you of the murder of Jarl Austmaðr at Law Rock on the very night of his murder, and of that murder, though no eyes but yours witnessed it, this Tynwald has ruled that you be outlawed."

Hávi's heart leapt at Hvítvi's words, but the silence that followed this declaration surprised her. Slowly she realized that Hvítvi had mentioned no duration for the outlawry; *would Sterki be banished for life, or would Hvítvi be forced to fight for the crown of clan Austmaðr after only seven years?*

"I personally disagree with the decision of the council," Hvítvi said softly with a subtle hiss in his breath that belied a tiny crack in the tremendous control that he was exerting. "Clan Austmaðr and Scandinavia deserve better than to honor a son who assassinates his own father to steal his crown and hide his other murders. Yet the council has voted and all of the jarls have agreed. The sentence of this Tynwald that I place upon you is outlawry ..." Hvítvi gritted his teeth as he spoke the words, "... *for six months.*"

Hávi's jaw dropped. The warriors in the hall reacted with equal disbelief. *Six months?* After the murder of Jarl Austmaðr, Auðgi, and Tryggvi, six months was an absolute insult! Hávi staggered, protectively clutching her tiny baby in her arms, and Bíldr and Breiðr grabbed her to keep her from falling. *Six months!* Sterki would return after next summer's viking free to challenge Hvítvi with all of the forces that he could muster and six months to plan, ready to take Castle Austmaðr by force. War would assault them before harvest, and even with help, prospects for clan Austmaðr were grim. Jarl Hersir bowed his head in defeat and Jarl Dúfunef looked so angry that he might storm out of Castle Austmaðr.

"*Outlawry ... for six months!*" Hvítvi raised his high voice over the few protests from the stunned hall and the stammered whispers that hissed like baby serpents. "Sterki, you stand judged by this council of jarls. Do you accept the judgment of this Tynwald and stand outlawed?"

Sterki smiled evilly up at his pale, thin, younger brother.

"I accept this judgment ... and stand outlawed ... for six months!" Sterki shouted, his every word dripping with sarcastic delight.

"As host of this council of jarls, I hear and witness your acceptance of sentence," Hvítvi said loudly. "This concludes all business of this council of jarls. As host and eldest, living son of Jarl Austmaðr, I declare myself Jarl Austmaðr and close all further proceedings. This Tynwald is over!"

Angry shouts erupted from the Austmaðr warriors. Many drew weapons, but every warrior of clan Bagal, Refr, Aurriði, and Tyrr drew weapons in defense of Sterki, standing as a wall between him and the lower tables. Bíldr drew his sword and bodily stepped in front of Hávi, shielding her in case fighting broke out, and Völu slipped up behind her, her hands knotted into fists. Breiðr grabbed her arm and pulled, but Hávi stood disbelieving, unable to move.

"Keep my crown polished," Sterki sneered at Hvítvi, much to the mirth of his supporters. "I'll be back for it soon!"

"You'll never wear father's crown while I live!" Hvítvi stared back at his wolfish brother, returning his glare with interest.

Sterki laughed, as did many others.

"I'll make that promise true!" Sterki shouted.

Hávi stared at Hvítvi: *was he mad?* Sterki was a hardened warrior and Hvítvi could barely lift a sword! When Sterki returned, Hvítvi would be only the first of the clan Austmaðr's rulers that he'd kill. The second would be ... Hávi gasped ... *Jorgen, her newborn son!*

Hávi slowly shook her head, feeling unbalanced, delirious, Sterki's evil laughter stabbing into her ears. Hávi glanced at Hvítvi, amazed that he stood so calmly, and then back to Sterki. *No! She couldn't let him kill Jorgen!*

Hávi glanced down, searching, and her eyes fell upon the thing that she needed most: under the high-table, right where Bíldr had piled them beside Jarl Dúfunef's feet, lay the six swords purchased from the *'sword-merchants'*, who were now standing protectively, with new swords, between Sterki and the warriors of clans Austmaðr, Hersir, and Dúfunef that filled the hall. But no one stood between Sterki and Hávi.

Ignoring Breiðr's attempts to pull her to safety, Hávi turned to Völu and gently pushed Jorgen, who started to cry loudly, into her arms. Völu gasped, but instinctively took the child. Hávi let go of her son, determined to save him. *Hávi's life was worthless compared to that of her son.*

Triumphantly Sterki turned to face the hall, his arms raised in victory. Jarl Bagal and Jarl Refr applauded, as did several other jarls. No one was watching Hávi. She placed her hands against Bíldr, and with the strength of a new mother's protectiveness, Hávi shoved Bíldr so hard and suddenly that he stumbled aside. Sterki's red hair gleamed brightly, the back of his head facing her; Hávi snatched up a sword from the top of the pile, swept it out, and raised it high. Hávi aimed at the back of Sterki's head, and she swung the sharp sword with all of her might.

Warned by shouts and expressions of surprise, Sterki spun around just as Hávi's sword slashed at him. Hávi never hesitated, but she'd never swung a heavy sword before and Sterki was a warrior tried by violent vikings; with incredible speed he ducked and lashed out; Sterki's hands struck like hungry snakes. Sterki caught Hávi's fist as it gripped the deadly swinging sword, and with a strength and mastery unknown by Hávi, Sterki redirected her hand ... and the sword whizzed over his head as he ducked. The heavy sword sliced nothing but air, but the momentum pulled Hávi's arm to its fullest extension and then wrenched the sword out of her grip. It flew free over the crowd, struck flat against several warriors in the front row, and then clattered harmlessly to the stone floor. Hávi froze, horrified; she'd tried to kill Sterki before ten clans of warriors and the council of jarls ... *and failed.*

"Illicit bitch!" Sterki cried, and his fist flew. Hávi saw his knuckles coming at her face. Pain that only childbirth equaled smashed into her; Hávi fell against the dais, slammed into one of the stout legs of the high-table, and crumpled to the floor. Dimly, through a blinding haze of agony, Hávi saw Sterki glare murderously at her, and suddenly he jerked a sword out of his belt. Sterki raised his sword; where Hávi had failed, Sterki wouldn't: *no one could murder like Sterki.*

"Wait!" Hvítvi shouted, his high voice piercing over all the others.

"She attacked me!" Sterki shouted back, not lowering his deadly sword. "You all witnessed! It's my right to kill her!"

"You have no rights!" Hvítvi shouted at Sterki. "You're outlawed, remember? You don't exist, and Hávi just tried to do what I was going to do anyway!"

Sterki hesitated, considering this announcement, pondering its meaning and implications, but Hvítvi gave him no time to think.

"I'm Jarl Austmaðr!" Hvítvi shouted fervently. "Many of you doubt my ability to rule, and I can't blame you, but right now I do rule, and this is proof of what I can accomplish!"

As Hávi lay helpless beneath Sterki's poised sword, Hvítvi stared at his brother with undisguised hatred.

"Archers!" Hvítvi shouted.

Sterki looked shocked, glanced upwards, and fear paled his expression until he was nearly as white as Hvítvi. Out of the three tall, narrow windows over the thrones on the highest dais, the barbed tips of deadly arrows pointed. Sterki cried out and turned to flee when the first arrow slashed through the air. Its long feathered shaft stabbed into Sterki's shoulder. Two more arrows rent the air over the high-table, both striking Sterki cleanly through his unprotected back. Sterki cried out and spun to face his brother even as he started to fall.

The warriors protecting Sterki glanced back and shouted angrily, unexpecting Sterki to be attacked from behind while they stood between him and a hall full of warriors. Sterki cried out as he tumbled backwards onto the hard stones, driving the bloody arrows even farther into his back. Mere seconds passed, and suddenly a fourth arrow shot forward and struck Sterki dead center in his chest. A fifth arrow followed it, true to its mark, and a sixth arrow whizzed through the air, stabbing into Sterki's stomach, landing with a sharp *plink* as if it'd penetrated clean through his body before its steel tip loudly rapped the stones beneath him. Sterki gave a last feral cry, and then collapsed.

Bíldr grabbed Hávi and jerked her to her feet with a strength that Hávi feared, and then he pushed her against Breiðr and Völu, and shielded all three of them with his body, his sword raised, ready to defend them with his life.

"Enough!" Hvítvi shouted. "Stay your swords! Let all fighting cease ... and the promises of clan Austmaðr, all the promises that I made, even to clan Bagal and clan Refr, will be honored! Let one more man be killed and all promises are void! I swear that I'll honor every promise: land to some, treasure to others, but all fighting must cease!"

"*Murderer!*" Jarl Refr shouted angrily, and many warriors grunted their agreement.

"Sterki was outlawed!" Hvítvi argued, facing Jarl Refr. "He accepted his outlawry before every man in this hall! A man outlawed can't be murdered: that's the law! No retribution for Sterki may be legally demanded ...!"

"Clan Refr won't stand for this!" Jarl Refr screamed.

"That's your decision!" Hvítvi challenged. "But if you fight, then you surrender any claim to the gold that I promised you!

Sterki's dead! Supporting Sterki can't help you anymore! It's your choice; leave our shores rich with gold ... or fight, and if you fight then you forfeit the claims of every clan. The door's yours! Let no man of clan Austmaðr, Hersir, or Dúfunef stay Jarl Refr! Make your choice!"

Jarl Refr glared daggers, his eyes red as blood, when suddenly a chair scraped backwards. Jarl Bagal turned and, without a word, ungently shoved past the others standing behind the high-table. Roughly Jarl Bagal pushed free, and then he stomped down the narrow steps off the dais onto the stone floor. Without hesitation or a single glance back, Jarl Bagal drove past Sterki's corpse and through the crowd of warriors of every clan. The men in the center aisle stepped back for him as Jarl Bagal walked rapidly across the great hall, his great cloak flapping behind him. Guards opened the twin doors as he approached and Jarl Bagal stormed between them, out of the hall.

Suddenly movement drew all eyes back to the front. The warriors of clan Bagal quickly stepped after their lord and followed him across the flagstones and outside.

"Enough," Jarl Mjöksiglandi said loudly, breaking the silence. "Clan Mjöksiglandi will stay no longer in this accursed castle where kin murders kin. Bring our promised tribute to our ships at once; clan Mjöksiglandi sails as soon as it arrives."

"It'll come by midday," Hvítvi promised.

Jarl Mjöksiglandi nodded, then pushed back his chair with undisguised dignity. The other jarls followed his lead; chairs pushed back against the higher dais and Jarl Jótun, Jarl Vörsa, Jarl Aurriði, and Jarl Tyrr all turned to follow as Jarl Mjöksiglandi led the way down the steps, off the dais, and across the hall. Many of the warriors grumbled at this, but each followed as their clan-chief departed.

Jarl Refr stood glaring, then cursed loudly and kicked back his chair so that it toppled off the dais and crashed to the floor. He jumped off the dais and stomped, like an angry child, the length of the hall and vanished outside.

"Seal warriors, into the courtyard!" Jarl Dúfunef shouted. "Bar the gate behind them!"

"Warriors of Hersir, into the courtyard!" Jarl Hersir bellowed. "Archers to the roof!" and then he turned to Hávi. "Bíldr, get the women upstairs! Hávi, bar your door and keep the shutters closed!"

Hávi offered no resistance as Bíldr and Breiðr hurried her up the stairs right behind Völu, who was carrying Jorgen. A moment later Breiðr slid their door-brace into place as Bíldr ran back downstairs.

Shouts erupted outside, cries of fury and screams of pain. Swords clanged and crashes thundered: *the battle had begun.*

Hávi stared at the closed shutters; she ached to see what was going on, but Breiðr sternly led her to her bed, Völu placed Jorgen in her arms, and Hávi resigned to wait. While Bitra cowered in the corner beside the fireplace, Hávi, Breiðr, and Völu sat on the edge of Hávi's bed, placidly listening as screams and curses and clashes of steel rose from the courtyard. There was nothing else that they could do; their fates were outside of their control.

Hávi began a chant, and all of the women joined in.

> *"Odin, father of us all,*
> *Thor, let your hammer fall,*
> *Heimdal, see now our foe,*
> *Gods of Asgard, lay them low."*

The sounds of the battle quickly died. Less than half an hour after it started, silence abruptly fell. All of the women stared at the closed shutter, but none dared approach it.

"We must've won," Völu said. "It'd take them longer to siege a castle."

A tense hour passed, and then Hvítvi's voice followed a knock on their door. Völu ran to open it; Hvítvi stepped into Hávi's room followed by Bíldr and four other guards.

"It's over," Hvítvi said.

"Who was fighting?" Hávi asked.

"Clan Refr," Hvítvi shook his head. "Jarl Bagal promised him that, if his men could force open the gates, that he'd lead all of the clans against us, and Jarl Refr could claim half of the wealth for himself. *The fool!* Jarl Refr sent his men leaping over the gate; the first twenty were instantly killed, and the rest fought like madmen. They managed to unbar the gate and shove it open wide."

Hávi gasped, but Hvítvi only smiled grimly.

"Jarl Refr and the last of his men charged inside the open gate, facing all of the warriors of Austmaðr, Dúfunef, and Hersir combined, and then Jarl Refr turned around, wondering why he was alone. Jarl Bagal stood there with three hundred warriors of clan Bagal, but he never attacked. They stood and watched as clan Refr was butchered, slain to a man ... everyone but Jarl Refr."

"W-W-Why?"

"Land," Hvítvi answered. "Jarl Bagal wanted land more than treasure, but with Sterki dead, he didn't get it. Clan Refr lives beside clan Bagal, and by goading Jarl Refr into sacrificing all of his warriors, clan Refr has no one left to defend it."

"Clan Refr will be just a memory by spring," Bíldr said.

"What will happen to Jarl Refr?" Hávi asked.

"He'll become like Jarl Illingr, I guess: a jarl without a clan," Hvítvi said. "I suspect that he'll simply be found dead soon; Jarl Bagal won't want him alive to accuse him at Law Rock. The last that I saw of him he'd stolen a horse and ridden off."

"He won't make it far," Bíldr said. "A single horse and rider in all of this snow? He'll never make it home."

"That may be for the best," Hvítvi said. "And now, I need to open those doors. Only Hávi may stay."

Breiðr, Bitra, and Völu needed no further prompting. As one they rose and hurried past Hvítvi, Bíldr, and the guards, and they closed the door behind them.

"You need to pay off the jarls?" Hávi asked.

"Yes," Hvítvi said bitterly. "Our treasury will be nearly empty after this. Jarl Hersir and Jarl Dúfunef will stay a few more days to witness as I name Jarl Hafr the new Jarl Austmaðr."

"Must you?" Hávi asked.

"Yes, and you must support this decision," Hvítvi said firmly.

"*I'll support anything that you ask me to,*" Hávi promised.

Hvítvi stared at her as if expecting some argument, but Hávi smiled. She couldn't blame his worry; Hávi's headstrong antics had given him plenty of reasons to believe that she'd never meekly accept anything, but Hávi now had everything that she'd ever wanted, and as soon as she and Hvítvi were alone then she'd give him everything that he wanted ... and more. Hávi would gladly be the wife that every man wanted ... to Hvítvi, the husband of her dreams. Of her other dreams, Hávi was sure that they'd come true in time. Jarl Illingr had told her that when she held the key to changing the den Skaanske Lov, then she'd know it. Hávi looked down upon the sleeping face of Jorgen, her beautiful son; Hávi might not be able to force rights for women into law, but her son, the future Jarl Austmaðr, would have resources that she could only dream of. Raised correctly, strengthened and educated, Jorgen could change the world. And soon daughters, Hvítvi's daughters, would become Jorgen's half-sisters, and Hávi would raise them to become mothers who trained their sons as she'd train Jorgen, and rights for women would spread across the Skåne, across Scandinavia, and eventually to all of Europe. Motherhood was the only tool that they needed, mothers educated in the den Skaanske Lov; Hávi could start that by teaching the fundamentals of law to every woman and girl in Skadi both as Jorgen's mother and as Hvítvi's wife.

Hvítvi unlocked the treasury doors and the guards began hauling out clinking chests and piles of treasure. Soon they were counting out fistfuls of wergild, tribute to be paid for peace. Their victory today would cost clan Austmaðr dearly, but new wealth would come, and then all would be right again.

Hávi cuddled Jorgen to her breast and sighed. In a world of men, she was finally getting everything that she'd ever wanted.

Saga 3

Viking Queen

Chapter 30

"*I will not marry Jarl Hafr!*" Hávi shouted.

Winter's sun shone low and coldly upon the wide, flat roof of Castle Austmaðr. Hávi's loud refusal was muted by the waist-high snow which had been shoveled away from the door just enough to make a cleared space where two people could stand.

"Lower your voice!" Hvítvi seethed. "You promised to do

what I asked."

"I thought that you'd marry me!"

Hávi and Hvítvi stared into each other's eyes, hers warm and blue, despite the frostiness biting their exposed faces and the angry glare she was giving him, his eyes colorless orbs showing pinkish pupils, surrounded by albino paleness, almost invisible against the whiteness of the snowfall. She was the widow of his aged father, while he was only a year younger than she, and they both shared the same deep emotion, but Hvítvi seemed determined to ruin even that.

"Are you trying to get us killed again? If anyone hears ...!"

"Why can't we marry?"

Hvítvi lowered his head, then looked out across the panoramic view. Westward, the nearby towers and crenelated walls of Castle Austmaðr loomed like stone teeth. Beyond them stretched forested foothills bordered by peasant farms, backdropped by the tall, glacier-capped mountains that separated civilized Sweden from the barbarous Norwegian lands. Eastwards, a white-paved road led to Skadi, a large city built around a sheltered harbor that opened onto the white-capped sea, whose frothing, dark green waves gleamed in the afternoon sunlight. Hávi and Hvítvi stood wrapped in furs and heavy cloaks against the bitter icy breeze that stung their noses and cheeks.

"Jarl Hafr shouldn't inherit," Hvítvi explained. "The only valid heir is Jorgen, but an infant can't lead the viking."

"You could be his regent."

"Leading the vikings is what made clan Austmaðr rich; someone strong must lead the viking. A regent and a leader would make two Jarl Austmaðrs ... and Jorgen would make three; we'd crumble in politics. Jarl Hafr's a great fleet-captain, but if he's named Jarl Austmaðr unwedded, then his eldest son becomes next in line; the only way that Jorgen can inherit is if you marry Jarl Hafr."

"Let his son inherit," Hávi said. "Then we can marry."

"To insure his inheritance, Sterki wanted to murder Jorgen before he was born ..."

"*Sterki was a murderer!*"

"Good leaders don't leave rivals free to usurp them. What do you think Jarl Hafr's sons will do to Jorgen ....?"

"How many sons does Jarl Hafr have?"

"Hafr has two sons from his late wife ... and eleven bastards from his ... serving girls."

"*Serving girls?*"

"Sluts: Father gave them to him in exchange for his support."

"*The man that you want me to marry has sluts?*"

"To save Jorgen's life, you must marry Jarl Hafr!"

Hávi glared at Hvítvi's odd pink eyes. Despite his albinism, Hvítvi was all that Hávi wanted, the man of her dreams, a man that she could love forever. Sadly, she'd only met him after being forced to wed his irascible father, Jarl Austmaðr, not knowing until she arrived in Skadi that her aged husband ruled the largest clan in the Skåne, perhaps in all of Scandinavia. Their troubled marriage hadn't lasted to see the birth of their son, as Sterki, Jarl Austmaðr's oldest, living son, had murdered to usurp his father's throne. But Hvítvi had ordered Sterki's death, killing his own brother with no more mercy than Sterki had shown to his many victims, including two other brothers and Hávi's beloved handmaiden, Tryggvi.

"No one need ever know," Hávi said. "We can take Jorgen and flee ..."

"Without Master Kamban I won't live long," Hvítvi said,

"and Master Kamban can't fend for himself; we need servants to augment our weaknesses. What village would welcome a hunchback and an albino? Even if I steal what little treasury clan Austmaðr has left, who'll defend us? And even if we could ... what of duty? Already thousands of our people are displaced by the land-grants that we paid to prevent civil war; must we abandon our whole clan to homelessness, poverty, and death?"

"I can't marry Jarl Hafr!"

"You must."

"Kiss me."

"Eyes may be in the towers."

"I see none."

"Regardless, they're there," Hvítvi said. "That's why I chose the roof; we can be seen but not heard ... or get caught together in Jarl Illingr's tower. You must marry Jarl Hafr ... no matter how we feel."

"You do love me!"

Hvítvi fell silent and calmed his expression; Hávi hated his vaunted self-control. Hvítvi could hide all of his emotions, an irritating skill with which he wisely managed all of clan Austmaðr. Hávi wasn't as skilled at managing; her foolishness had cost the life of Jarl Illingr, her secret teacher of Swedish law, whom she'd hoped would help her end the callous practice of forced marriages. Hávi had to keep Hvítvi talking: his emotions seeped out in his voice.

"You will wed the woman that you love ... to another man?"

"I'll do what I must ... for your son ... and for our clan ... *and so will you.*"

Suddenly Hvítvi started to shiver; his poor health couldn't endure severe cold. Hávi frowned; he'd purposed this discussion on the frozen roof to insure its shortness; the longer that he stayed here the sicker he'd get.

"I won't do it," Hávi said.

Hvítvi shivered visibly.

"S-s-shall w-we s-s-stand here and d-discuss it?"

"If you were any other man I'd throw you off this roof," Hávi said, and she seized Hvítvi by his fur cloak and dragged him inside.

In her bedroom, Hávi fumed.

"At least you'll still be queen," Völu, Hávi's best friend, said as she glanced at Jorgen, Hávi's newborn son and the future ruler of clan Austmaðr, asleep in his redwood crib, which was decorated with the same carven horse-heads as her bedposts.

"Queen Whore in a kingdom of sluts," Hávi scowled as she sat on her bed. "I can't do it."

"Isn't that what you said before you married Jarl Austmaðr?"

Hávi glared at Völu; they'd been companions since childhood. In many ways, Völu looked much like she had at nine; youthful, the same dark, red hair with long braids, an explosion of freckles, and bright yellow-brown eyes. Völu's pregnancy was only beginning to show despite her boney frame. Völu had taken over Tryggvi's duties as Hávi's handmaid, but Völu was never timid; unlike Tryggvi, Hávi could never intimidate Völu. Hávi glanced at her shuttered window and felt as if the walls of her bedroom were closing in about her.

"Jarl Hersir arrives tomorrow," Hávi said. "Perhaps he'll talk to Hvítvi."

Völu's doubtful expression clouded Hávi's hope; Jarl

Hersir was a practical, expedient clan-chief. Although Sterki had murdered her stepson and husband, Jarl Hersir wanted to support him as the logical choice to replace his father. A claw-digging shudder crawled up Hávi's spine: *women still didn't have the legal right to refuse a marriage, especially not if their intended was a maker of local laws.* Hávi's breath stuttered in rapid, frightened gasps: *the man that she loved was going to marry her to Jarl Hafr.*

Jarl Hersir stood irresolute in Hávi's outer room while Völu sat silently in the corner.

"Hávi, you know better," Jarl Hersir said, his ruddy lips almost hidden by his thick, black hair, which flowed from his head and chin so heavily that only his large nose and expressive eyes could be seen; the existence of his ears was a mystery. "You must marry Jarl Hafr to strengthen his claim to clan Austmaðr. In exchange, he's promised to name Jorgen as his foremost heir and the next Jarl Austmaðr. Without this marriage there will be challenges to his rule; Mjóvi and Krókr have been spreading discontent throughout the Skåne ..."

"They should be executed ...!"

"They would've been killed if they'd caused half of the scandals that you have, but they have powerful allies, and clan Austmaðr can't afford another disruption. I've stood by Hvítvi all that I can; clan Hersir can't support him if things get any worse. You need to do your duty; if you'd been born to politics then you'd understand that the needs of your clan outweighs your happiness. I've done things that I hate myself for ... as all clan-chiefs do. Tomorrow you'll wed Jarl Hafr ... or clan Austmaðr falls."

Five hours passed before Hávi stopped crying. She held

her head up, her frown fixed and furious, as Völu and Breiðr dressed her and escorted her down the stone steps for dinner. To their disgust, Mjóvi and Master Krókr stood whispering together at the foot of the steps between the doors to the great hall and the doorway to the kitchen.

Master Krókr, Sterki's staunchest supporter, was the tallest man that Hávi had ever met, although aged and fat; a mountain of a man long gone to seed. He was the castle seneschal, the chief servant, and saw to the daily routines of all the servants within Castle Austmaðr and in its wide fields. Mjóvi was the castle bitch, a dried-up prune of a woman, very slight, whose withered shell held the most-poisonous tongue in Scandinavia. Mjóvi was the widow of Jarl Illingr and the woman who least-mourned her husband's death, but she held the ear of every powerful woman in the Skåne and was the undoubted mistress of lies and gossip; if she'd been a nanny goat then Hávi would've butchered her on sight. With cruel, sadistic smiles on their faces, both of them glared at Hávi as she descended the stone stairs. Hávi started to flee back upstairs but Völu and Breiðr gripped her arms and forced her to keep walking.

The great hall brought no relief to Hávi's regretful heart; Jarl Hafr, Hávi's intended, sat comfortably in her husband's chair on the lower dais. Hávi strained to control her disgust; he was his brother's heir and tradition required him to sit in her husband's chair ... no matter how repulsive he was. She'd gain nothing by attempting to flee the castle; Völu, Breiðr, and the guards would stop her.

The great hall's ceiling towered twenty feet high supported by stone walls and tall, thick-trunked columns, each bearing four bright, flaming torches. Every wall was hung with colorful tapestries and brilliant banners. Past the thirteen rows of lower tables stood a dais three feet above the rest of the room. A long high-table topped the dais, and behind it rose another dais, towering over the high-table, and upon the higher dais stood two ornate, matching, high-backed, gold-polished chairs; one for Jarl Austmaðr and one for Hávi, although never once had she sat in that chair. In the wall above the thrones were three tall, thin windows which opened from another room, from which Hvítvi had archers shoot his murderous brother. Silently Hávi wished that someone's arrow would save her from a second forced marriage.

Hávi headed away from her husband-to-be and joined the women in the back of the hall at the women's table. Smiles greeted them; Hávi had saved clan Austmaðr by bearing a son to inherit from her murdered husband. While the castle women gossiped and swapped unlikely rumors, Hávi sat with her back to the high-table, although stealing occasional glances to spy Hvítvi, Jarl Hersir, and Jarl Hafr sitting centermost at the high-table, eating heartily and planning her future without a care for her feelings.

Several platters were finally placed on the women's table ... late, but at least they were still steaming. Only cold foods used to be served to the women; Hávi's intervention had insured that everyone in the castle received hot foods, which had made Hávi the castle hero until her fumbling antics had embarrassed her husband and cost Jarl Illingr's life.

Mjóvi appeared at the far end of the women's table grinning like a hungry goat in an herb garden. Few of the castle women liked Mjóvi, yet she sat among them without hesitation.

"What a wonderful day!" Mjóvi grinned thinly, her eyes alight. "A fine day for sailing."

Hávi and the other women exchanged worried glances at

this pronouncement. Völu alone looked confused; Völu had remained in clan Hersir when Hávi had been taken away, and Völu had only recently discovered the deadly seriousness of Castle Austmaðr politics.

Shrill cries of delight filled the great hall as the main doors opened. A strong, wintry breeze blew in; a large group entered: many men of different ages, ten young children, and a dozen strange, attractive women that whipped back snow-dusted wool hoods and exclaimed over the grandeur of the great hall. Several called out to the high-table, excited, joyous cries, and Jarl Hafr smiled and waved at them. All twelve young women ran forward, giggling like children. Several jumped up onto the edge of the dais and, to Hávi's horror, leaned over the high-table and kissed Hávi's fiancé.

"New serving girls!" Mjóvi exclaimed with wicked delight. "I'm sure that your betrothed shall never lack for ... *their services.*"

With a smile whose every tooth Hávi hated, Mjóvi rose and departed triumphantly. Hávi was half-risen to go after her when Völu seized her arm.

"Sit back down!"

"Let me go!"

"It's been years since we wrestled ...!"

"I pinned you then ...!"

"You weren't Mistress Austmaðr then."

"You're pregnant ...!"

"You just gave birth ...!"

"Mother ...," Breiðr prodded Hávi, urging caution with fearfilled eyes. Breiðr was Hávi's eldest stepdaughter in Castle Austmaðr.

Hávi remained standing and glared at Mjóvi, and as she neared the back door, Hávi whispered a terrible curse.

"Jorgamund entwine in entrapping folds,
Fenris bite and swallow her whole,
Hel to Niflhiem make her dead,
Loki's curse upon her head!"

Völu's eyes widened as several women stifled horrified screams, but Hávi stood and stared until Mjóvi's fragile, aged frame vanished through a door near the kitchen. Many men's heads swiveled from the newly-arrived, gleeful women bouncing on their toes to discover the source of the frightened tumult. Angrily Hávi sat back down; she was being humiliated by a dozen sluts and didn't need to make it worse.

"Master Kamban was supposed to be teaching you *healing charms*," Breiðr scolded.

Hávi sneered at her betrothed's giggling serving girls.

"Clan Austmaðr has never needed healing more."

Several women at the table sniggered. Völu glanced at the excited arrivals.

"Who do you suppose the children are?" she asked.

"Bastards, mostly," Breiðr said. "Hafr's wife only bore him four children before she died."

"Let's get out of here," Hávi said, and she started to rise.

"If you walk out now then you'll start another scandal," Völu said. "Sit down; you'll only disgrace yourself."

Uttering a string of profane curses, Hávi sat back down with an expression that could mortify baby goats. She glanced around; all of the castle women wore deep frowns, their brows lowered conspiratorially, casting dark glares at the new arrivals.

"I'll saw off Mjóvi's horns if it's the last thing that I do," Hávi promised, and then she winced at the shrill, excited voices before the high-table. *"And if Hafr expects me to tolerate those sluts then he might lose a horn as well!"*

Worn, faded tapestries and swirling, polished crosshatchings covered every wall of the small Hall of Audience, a fantastically-ornate chamber which was uncomfortably cold despite its roaring fireplace in the back wall. Even the torch sconces were intricately carved, the woodwork seemingly nailed to its colorful walls just to over-decorate the room. The decorations only existed to hide the many secret holes through which everything in the Hall of Audience could be observed; Hávi knew that she was being spied upon. She sat at the table holding her newborn infant Jorgen in her arms. On the table, two tall, brightly-glowing brass candelabras illuminated a tray of sweet pastries, a bottle of wine, a pitcher of ale, and several thick wooden mugs and silver goblets.

Jarl Hersir sat silently beside her, alternately nursing his large tankard and fingering the candle's slowly-melting wax while wearing a frown born of frustration; Hávi had been born on a goat ranch in clan Hersir and he'd married her off to his best friend, the leader of clan Austmaðr, but Jarl Hersir wasn't a relative; Hávi suspected that he was there mostly to restrain her temper. Jarl Hersir only had one hand; his other had been amputated by a Danish axe on his first viking, but Jarl Hersir was still a highly-respected clan-chief.

Hvítvi entered first, his albino-pink eyes lowered, followed by Jarl Hafr and two young men that Hávi didn't know. Hávi sat rigid but Jarl Hersir noisily rose and nudged her. With a Mjóvi-worthy frown, Hávi rose to her feet as Jarl Hafr proudly presented himself with a slight nod.

"Mistress Hávi Hersir Austmaðr, these are my sons, Skytja and Rauðkinn." Jarl Hafr said. "Boys, this is your new mother."

Hávi examined all three of them: Jarl Hafr was very tall, much like his brother, her late husband, but with a full head of salt-and-pepper hair that hung thick and long upon his meaty shoulders, and he had a jagged scar that cut across his chin. He shared his brother's brown eyes under spidery gray brows, his wide, musk ox nose, and sagging ears, but his aged, shaggy, identical beard was trimmed to only a finger's length. Yet the most startling difference was his expression; Jarl Austmaðr had always looked thoughtful and serious. By comparison, Jarl Hafr looked casual, almost-dreamy, as if half-asleep even while fully awake.

Both of his sons were large, fully-grown young men despite their boyish faces. Skytja, his eldest son, was taller and thinner than Rauðkinn, and Skytja bore a stout bow strung over his shoulder whose staves were so thick that Hávi wondered how anyone could draw it. He wore a yellow tunic and bright green trousers, had blonde hair, and held himself very erect with the calm confidence of a mountain. Rauðkinn was several inches shorter and darker than Skytja both in mood and appearance. He wore a black tunic over blood-red trousers and carried an axe with a long, narrow blade; designed for fighting, useless for chopping wood. His girth was wider than his older brother; physically Rauðkinn reminded Hávi of Auðgi, her murdered bear-cub of a stepson, although his deep-set eyes and nasty glower couldn't be more different from Auðgi's eternally-cheery disposition.

"Welcome to Castle Austmaðr," Hávi said formally to both boys, and then she hoisted the babe in her arms. "This is Jorgen, your new brother and the heir of Jarl Austmaðr."

Neither boy smiled although Jarl Hafr grinned widely. Both boys glanced at the infant, then returned their stares to Hávi.

"I'll be your brother as well," Hvítvi said. "We'll all be Austmaðrs after the marriage, but we stand in great difficulty; our recent troubles have damaged our family's standing and wealth. We must work together; separately we'll fail."

"Well, that's that ...," Jarl Hersir began.

"I thought that you had daughters, too," Hávi said suddenly.

After the briefest moment of surprise, Jarl Hafr spoke up.

"I have two daughters, and I hope that you'll take them both under your wings. I must warn you: each is a handful."

"And other children," Hávi added.

An uncomfortable pause followed.

"Perhaps this isn't the time ...," Hvítvi said in a crisp, warning tone.

"No, I welcome all the children of my ... late husband's brother," Hávi said. "I want to know all of them."

"I'll see that you meet them," Jarl Hafr said.

"And I noticed that your children didn't arrive alone."

Hávi's voice reeked with displeasure and Jarl Hersir's elbow bumped her admonishingly.

"I told you that Jarl Hafr always travels with his serving girls," Hvítvi said.

"In what ways do they serv...?" Hávi began.

"Hávi, I think that we're done here," Jarl Hersir spoke up, his loud voice filling the small hall. "Perhaps we should ..."

"Perhaps not," Hávi refuted.

"Don't worry," Jarl Hafr smiled widely, cutting off Jarl Hersir's failed attempt to distract Hávi. "Discretion is the heart of my girls; *I won't neglect my husbandly duties to you!*"

Jarl Hafr gave Hávi a sly wink.

"That's good," Hávi said, fighting to keep from punching him, "because if I ever find a slut in my bed ... *I'll kill them.*"

Dead silence met this pronouncement; Hvítvi and Jarl Hersir looked horrified. Jarl Hafr seemed confused, and Skytja and Rauðkinn exchanged surprised glances. Suddenly both boys broke out laughing while the grown men stood speechless. Still laughing, Skytja bowed to Hávi.

"Honored to meet you, Mother."

After a mirthful nod from Rauðkinn, both boys turned to leave.

"Good luck, Father," Rauðkinn slapped his father's back before they walked out of the Hall of Audiences.

In Jarl Illingr's cramped tower, Breiðr shivered while Völu piled all of their kindling on the tiny fire. The growing flames illuminated Hávi as she sat before the narrow desk holding Jorgen to her breast inside a wool blanket.

"Just like men: after the sons left, they just stared at each other," Hávi scowled. "I escaped as quickly as I could ... I claimed that Jorgen had to be nursed."

"What do you want with this chilly tower?" Breiðr asked.

"A place of my own," Hávi said. "A place to hide, to get away from everyone. Sharing my bed is bad enough; I don't want to waste any time with Jarl Hafr."

"You'll do your wifely duties if I have to tie you down," Völu said. "Most women can't find one husband and you're getting a second."

"If you're calling me lucky then you can pile yourself on those coals," Hávi said. "Between now and the wedding I want to remake this room ..."

"Tomorrow?"

"*Tomorrow?*"

"Yes, the cook's already started preparing the feast."

Hávi's face paled. "*But .... but ...!*"

Völu seized Hávi as she tilted, making sure that she didn't drop Jorgen.

"N-no ...!"

Hávi couldn't find Hvítvi anywhere; his chambers were empty. Völu followed her long into the night, searching everywhere that Hávi could think of, even onto the frozen roof, although they both knew that Hvítvi couldn't be there.

"He's hiding from me!" Hávi complained.

"What did you expect?" Völu asked. "He knows that you're looking for him."

Most of the castle was asleep; muted snores sawed through every closed door and the great hall, where many servants slept before its four wide fireplaces, echoing with the thunderous drone of a great nasal chorus. Twice they crossed through the familiar kitchen, disturbing the sleepy boy that remained awake to keep the low fires burning, then sneaking down every hallway that they could find, even locating several narrow, low-ceilinged stairs that Hávi had never seen before leading to small recesses and storage rooms filled with dusty barrels and crates, broken sea chests, missing-spoked spinning-wheels and broken farming equipment, and the huge clay jars and the countless baskets that Hávi knew were used by the cooks to prepare for the summer viking. Occasionally they ran into a guard pacing the halls, twice being asked why they were haunting the castle in the wee hours of the morning, but Hávi never revealed their purpose; if Hvítvi was hiding, surely these lesser guards wouldn't know where he was. Yet they never seemed to be alone; soft footsteps always echoed from not far away.

They stood quietly, Hávi's ear pressed against a suspicious door, as a strange man suddenly reached the bottom of a nearby stairs. All were startled; his eyes flew open as he spied Hávi and Völu staring at him, standing together in the lonely hall, which he glanced both ways to view in its entirety. Hávi didn't need Völu's sharp intake of breath to warn her; she'd never seen anyone like this man before. Thin and short, Hávi would've mistaken him for a castle youth if not for his long, ragged black beard or the wide hat that would've shadowed his face if he hadn't been holding up his lantern as he descended the steps. Both girls began stepping backwards before he turned toward them with grim, silent determination; his hand slipped into his dark tunic and drew out a long knife.

Both girls screamed loudly as he charged them, shrill screeches breaking the utter silence of the shadowy hallway. Running was futile; he raced unchecked, too fast to respond. His knife stabbed toward Hávi, but suddenly Völu bodily slammed him against a wall, and his blade missed Hávi's chest, stabbing through her forearm as he bounced against the wall's rough stones. He slashed at Völu, seeking to slit her throat, but Hávi shoved him down; his blade lightly gashed through Völu's dress right below her neckline: a mild injury. Völu's family were farmers and Hávi had grown up frequently butted by stubborn, full-grown goats, who'd quickly learned to flee after Hávi's hard boots had bruised or cracked their round, fragile ribs. In a chaos of terrified screams, fallen lanterns, and shouts for guards, servants and castle elders burst from their rooms to find the failed assassin lying upon the narrow hallway flagstones with Hávi and Völu alternately stomping upon his head.

"They'll both be fine," Master Kamban pronounced.

"You could've been killed!" Hvítvi snapped at Hávi.

"He probably expected to meet weak castle-bred girls,"

Bíldr chuckled.

Hvítvi didn't grin. Hávi and Völu wilted under his stare, which stabbed far more deeply than the assassin's knife. Hávi's forearm was heavily bandaged; her wound had penetrated clear through, but had not severed a major vessel. Völu's skin was cut to her breastbone, but thinly; several blood-soaked layers of paper were plastered over her chest. Master Kamban chanted several healing charms, which Hávi recited with him, although by rote; all of her attention was focused on Hvítvi.

"An assassination the night before your wedding," Hvítvi glowered. "More attempts to destabilize clan Austmaðr: our enemies are determined."

"Why kill Hávi?" Völu asked. "Jarl Hafr will still become Jarl Austmaðr."

"Marriage to Hávi will cement his legitimacy," Bíldr explained. "Not all look forward to his leadership; Hvítvi's father was more feared and respected."

The door burst open; Jarl Hafr stormed inside.

"What happened?" he demanded.

"Hávi was attacked," Hvítvi said. "An assassin attempted to spoil your marriage ..."

"How'd he get inside the castle?"

"We'll discover that as soon as we can," Bíldr said. "He's chained in the dungeon with five men watching him; however he got in, he won't get out."

"Why isn't he being questioned now?"

"Your bride and her servant are Hersir girls; we'll be lucky if he lives long enough to answer questions."

Jarl Hafr glanced at Hávi as if momentarily confused, but she returned his glare with the stoicism of Law Rock.

"Uncle, I'd like to assign Bíldr as Hávi's personal guard,"

Hvítvi said. "She's no longer safe, not even inside the castle."

"Are we still getting married?"

"Tomorrow at noon," Hvítvi said. "It's best if we do it quickly, especially now."

"Hvítvi, can I speak to you ... *alone?*" Hávi asked.

"No," Hvítvi said firmly, and without waiting for an argument, he walked toward the door. "Good night, Mistress Austmaðr."

Chapter 31

Hávi wanted to cry. She wanted to rage and hurl things, to stomp out a tantrum like she hadn't thrown since her mother wouldn't let her take a sharp hoe after Bifru, Völu's husband, for shoving a frog down the back of her dress when they'd both been eleven years old. Hávi wanted to scream and curse, but she couldn't; she wasn't a spoiled child any longer, and any disgrace that she caused would fall upon her unwanted fiancé and her adopted clan. If Hvítvi was correct, and his surmises usually could be counted on, Hávi's son's life depended on her wedding Jarl Hafr. Again Hávi was being forced to an altar that she didn't want, first by her obligations to clan Hersir, now by her obligations to clan Austmaðr. Refusal was irrelevant; Hávi had once publically suggested giving women the right to refuse unwanted marriages only to be laughed out of the great hall; *men would never grant women rights superseding their own.*

"You look lovely," Hvassi said as she stepped back to

survey her handiwork.

Hvassi was a huge woman; she had penetrating brown eyes, long graying hair, and rolls of flesh around her thick neck that looked like stacked necklaces of chins, but she was an unrivaled seamstress. Hávi felt like a prized goat about to be sold off; she stood in Hvassi's latest creation, a long dress of golden fabric trimmed with white and pink. The fabric clung tightly; Hávi hadn't lost much of her pregnancy-weight, having birthed Jorgen only a month before.

"Don't puke this time," Völu said.

Hávi would've grinned if she hadn't been so miserable. At her last forced-marriage, no sooner had Jarl Hersir pronounced Hávi and Jarl Austmaðr wedded than Hávi had vomited, too upset to contain her fury at marrying a total stranger thrice her age. She knew Jarl Hafr, but their only conversations had concerned preventing all of the other clans from turning against clan Austmaðr. This was a marriage of politics, nothing more, but it wasn't the wedding that Hávi dreaded; her second wedding night would be torture.

"That bandage throws off the balance," Hvassi frowned. "Does it hurt much?"

Hávi brushed her thickly-bandaged forearm; it hurt terribly, but Hávi wouldn't drink the herbal mixtures that Master Kamban had made for her; they'd lessen her pain but also steal her judgment.

"I'm fine," Hávi said. "How about you, Völu?"

Völu stood with her red hair flowing in wavy ringlets to her elbows; Völu glanced at the tight bandage that covered the thin gash that stretched from shoulder to shoulder just above her breasts.

"Losing my pig-tails hurts worse," Völu said, pushing back her thick, red hair with a sharp glare at Bitra, an elderly washer woman who'd insisted that Völu's customary pig-tails were inappropriate for Hávi's second wedding.

"The sun's high," Bitra said, her wheezy voice impatient. "They're expecting you downstairs."

Hávi sighed and forced back the moistness that welled in her eyes.

"Come," Völu said to Hávi. "Postponing doom doesn't make it any better."

The great hall cheered as Hávi appeared in the doorway. Every table was crowded, every aisle packed; all of Skadi had arrived to witness the wedding of their new Jarl Austmaðr. An overwhelming urge seized Hávi to flee back upstairs and bar her bedroom door, but she fought to quell it. *I can do this! I must do this!* Breiðr walked upon her right, carrying Jorgen, and Völu walked on her left carrying a bouquet of rare winter flowers. All three stepped into the riotous great hall amid celebration the like of which Hávi had never witnessed.

Hvítvi drew her eyes first; his albino whiteness stood out among all of the dark haired, sunburnt complexions that the rest of his family bore. She gave him a glare of blackest hate: *how could he do this to her?* Where would he be tonight while she was being forced to spread her legs to her late husband's idiot brother? But Hávi wasn't the naïve child that she'd been at her first wedding; she forced herself, step-by-step, closer to another imprisonment of the heart. *Clan Austmaðr needed this marriage. Her son's life required this marriage. She was the only one who didn't want this marriage.*

Grinning widely, Jarl Hafr stood before Hvítvi, towering over the albino. His salt-and-pepper hair was tied back in a ponytail, promenating the jagged scar that cut across his chin in the shadow of his neatly-trimmed beard. Hávi remembered the true Jarl Austmaðr's eyes as she'd approached him for the first time on their wedding day; keen, sharp eyes, which contrasted with the vacant stare of her husband-to-be. Hávi bowed her head as she walked to stand beside him; if she looked at his face then she couldn't go through with it.

"A glorious day!" Hvítvi shouted as loudly as he could. "A blessed day! A wedding day!"

Hvítvi began the ritual as soon as the cheering in the great hall ceased. Quickly he recited the call to the gods and goddesses to bless the *'loving couple'*; Hávi wondered who he was talking about. Turmoil filled her mind as she ignored her vows. *What did vows matter?* She had no right to refuse the vows which would transform her from a free widow into the unloved slave of a man that she hated. Hávi mumbled her replies, and lifted her eyes just enough to glare murderously into the pink orbs of her beloved Hvítvi. Hvítvi's recitation faltered as their eyes met; he seemed to lose his breath, his vaunted self-control cracking even as he wed her to another man. But Hvítvi quickly recovered; he raised his eyes to the ceiling and resumed reciting the vows that Hávi had to repeat: to love and obey, to honor and serve, with the first perspiration on his pale forehead that Hávi had ever seen. A desperate hope flared; *Hvítvi could end this, even now, and spare me for himself!* But Hvítvi didn't even wait for Hávi to finish her vows before he turned to Jarl Hafr and began speaking his vows. Hvítvi didn't want this marriage any more than Hávi did, but he knew his duty and possessed a self-control that Hávi could never claim. Jarl Hafr recited his vows proudly, each word like a booming thunderclap in her ears crashing with the severity of Ragnarök. Hávi lowered her eyes; *her doom had come ... again.*

Sand was sprinkled in their hair, oils anointed their foreheads, and branches of spruce and pine brushed against them; charms to guarantee that their non-existent love would remain evergreen. Hávi's stomach churned but she refused it staunchly; *she wouldn't vomit at two consecutive weddings!* The final prayer was spoken and the broom was brought forward; Bíldr ceremoniously carried it in and set it onto the floor at Hávi's feet. The knife-wound in Hávi's forearm suddenly flamed to life; *if only the assassin had succeeded then Hávi wouldn't have to suffer this!* But Jarl Hafr turned her around and took her arm tightly, the deadly broom just touching their toes. Tears burst from Hávi's eyes; they jumped into marriage.

Cheers avalanched on Hávi like Mjóvi's sarcastic laughter. It was over, done; after only a month being a widow, Hávi was married again. She opened her eyes and scanned the great hall, at all of the laughing, smiling faces, and her vision coalesced on a small doorway that opened in the middle of the left-hand wall; a dozen feminine faces frowned at her, each masked with sarcastic resentment; her husband's twelve sluts, his *'serving girls'* that Hávi hated just for existing. Duty to clan Austmaðr stretched a false, unwilling smile across her face, keeping up the facade for political requirements. Hávi imagined herself chopping up those serving girls with Rauðkinn's axe; it brightened her smile considerably.

"Blessings upon Jarl and Mistress Austmaðr!" Hvítvi shouted after waving for silence. "With this union, not only are the honors of marriage bestowed, but also the ennoblements of highest office are legally and justly inherited. All hail Jarl Austmaðr!"

Jarl Hafr, now Jarl Austmaðr, raised his fist as the room

exploded in cheers. At a slight pull of her arm, Hávi allowed her new husband to lead her to the side where they could ascend the short steps to the first dais where she could try to force down her wedding feast without choking, but to Hávi's surprise, after climbing to the top of the first dais, Jarl Hafr turned her to face the smaller, steeper stairs that Hávi had noticed many times but never ascended. With Jarl Hafr's hand on her elbow, Hávi hesitantly climbed the stairs to the second dais, the higher platform upon which she'd never stood. Nothing sat atop the higher dais but the thrones which Hávi had often wished to sit upon, but now wished that she'd never seen. She stepped up onto the high, narrow wooden platform, nine feet above the flagstones of the floor, and looked out across the cheering great hall from a perspective that she'd only imagined. Jarl Hafr led her to stand before one of the identical, high-backed, gold-polished thrones towering over the high-table. Upon each seat was a gold crown. Jarl Hafr lifted his crown and placed it upon his own head while the crowd's cheers escalated, and then he picked up her gold crown and ceremoniously set it upon her head. Hávi stared up at her new husband, disbelieving as he took her hand and, as he lowered himself, Hávi sat upon her throne. Together they stared out at their people as the great hall shook to the rafters with the cheers of their people: *their subjects.* Hávi had finally been crowned queen of the Skåne.

Jarl Hersir and a crew of warriors from clan Hersir, including Bifru, arrived in the middle of their wedding feast. Jarl Hersir carried in a large silver bowl as a wedding present and presented it with heartfelt congratulations. Skytja and Rauðkinn fetched a chair and room was made to squeeze Jarl Hersir between Jarl Hafr and Hvítvi, as was customary for a visiting clan-chief. Centermost at the high-table, Hávi hugged him pleasantly but not tightly; her affection for her former clan-chief was muted by his politics, which never seemed to work in her favor.

"I'm sorry I'm late," Jarl Hersir said. "News reached me just as I was about to set sail; another feud's broken out: clan Mjöksiglandi and clan Glóra."

"Madness," Jarl Hafr said. "Clan Glóra can't resist clan Mjöksiglandi."

"The fighting's already over," Jarl Hersir said. "We sailed south to confirm it: Jarl Glóra was captured, and only the gods know what Jarl Mjöksiglandi will do with him."

"The map of Sweden's changed again," Hvítvi said. "That's three times since Sterki's trial."

"Never before has the Skåne suffered so many losses," Jarl Hersir said. "Clan Refr is dead. Clan Tyrr has sworn oaths of subservience to clan Bagal. Sweden has lost over a thousand warriors in the last month; we've never been weaker."

"How will we viking ... and protect our shores?" Jarl Hafr asked.

"I was thinking ... just considering ... that clan Hersir may skip the viking this year ...," Jarl Hersir said.

"You can't!" Jarl Hafr argued.

"If we can avoid civil war," Jarl Hersir continued, "while the other clans decimate themselves, then we could restock, fortify, and build new ships; strengthen Hersir, Austmaðr, and Dúfunef ..."

"Clans are strengthened by generations," Hvítvi said. "It'll take twenty years for the Skåne to recoup its losses of the last month. Even if Hersir, Austmaðr, and Dúfunef united, we'd weaken Sweden when we conquered it; our spies have failed to sow rebellions in Norway or Denmark: we're vulnerable."

"We have to go viking ...!" Jarl Hafr said.

"If the new Jarl Austmaðr doesn't lead a viking then that'll be perceived as a weakness," Hvítvi reluctantly agreed.

"Better to be perceived as weak than to be truly weak," Jarl Hersir said.

"If they don't perceive us as weak then they won't attack," Hvítvi said. "Besides, we've emptied our treasury to buy peace; we can't afford to skip the viking."

Hávi sat frowning as the men continued their endless debate. If not for the terrible cost of their petty wars then they wouldn't need the vikings to fill their coffers. If men stayed home and tended to their farms and wives then Sweden would grow strong, and if every man married and bore sons, instead of running off to get killed, then their armies would be so great that no enemy could threaten them. If every woman married and bore ...

Hávi froze, terribly aware of the doom that awaited her upstairs. Not every man was worth marrying, and forcing women to marry just to increase the population was what had doomed her to her first marriage. Sweden had to be strong to remain free, but was freedom bought by the slavery of women? *If Hávi's ambitions bore fruit, if women did gain the legal right to refuse a marriage, would Sweden be weakened?*

Hávi stared at the warm platters and bowls covering the high-table. A large wooden bowl of kalops, Hávi's favorite stew, steamed invitingly, but Hávi wasn't sure if she could stomach a single bite. The baked köttbullar, covered with lingonberries, looked delicious, but she had no appetite. To her surprise, the cook had made Janssons Frestelse, which she'd learned to make while helping out in the kitchen; she'd helped peel and cut both the onions and potatoes into thin sticks, then sautéed the onions in butter while they cleaned and filleted the anchovies. Potatoes were layered in the bottom of their biggest pot, and then the sautéed onions and anchovies were added in consecutive layers, each covered with a thin layer of potatoes, and then the pot was filled with fresh cream, lidded, and baked until everything was tender and tasty. For dessert, the cook himself served Mandelfyllda, a pie of baked apples and breadcrumbs basted with almond paste and covered with a thin pool of custard; Hávi couldn't resist taking a few bites.

The hot glog arrived just in time. Hávi's forearm was starting to throb; she considered excusing herself, claiming that her wound ached, and wondered if leaving early would insult her new husband or if sitting alone in her room, waiting to be raped, would be worse than sitting at the high-table with every eye in the great hall watching her. Hávi decided to stay; left alone, she'd certainly bar her door ... or even take Jorgen and try to escape the castle: she couldn't be trusted alone. Völu certainly understood that; every few minutes Hávi glanced at the women's table where Völu and Breiðr sat with Jorgen, and one of them was always watching her. Several at the women's table were wet-nurses; she couldn't use Jorgen as an excuse to escape, and Völu wouldn't let Hávi out of sight, not even if Hávi ordered her away. In many ways, Hávi missed Tryggvi, her beloved handmaiden; Tryggvi would let Hávi get away with anything.

As Hávi leaned forward to drink the steamy, potent glog, suddenly Jarl Hafr's arm reached over and wrapped around her shoulder. He squeezed her affectionately and Hávi almost choked. A shudder ran through her; soon he'd touch her in unthinkable ways ... *how would she endure?* Hávi drained her steamy glog in one draught, despite that it burned her mouth, and then she demanded that a servant refill her cup.

"Mother, are you alright?"

Hvítvi's voice seemed to penetrate the blur around her but
Hávi couldn't tell. The great hall was spinning, its noise and
motion rotating into one chaotic tumult. Glog drippings
stained the front of her dress, although she hadn't noticed
them until she heard someone call her *'Mother'* and looked
down to see if Jorgen was nestled against her breast.

"She's drunk," said a voice that was horrid and snarling
like the growling-grunts of an angry pig.

Hands closed upon Hávi's arms and lifted her. Her chair
vanished and deep voices twittered around her like the
flittings of pesky insects. One pair of strong arms wrapped
around her ribs and half-carried her, bumping into everyone
that they passed, down to the flagstones. More insects joined:
the voices of Völu and Breiðr swarmed as a dozen hands
swept Hávi from the hall.

"Let's carry her," said a strange, clear voice. "Rauðkinn,
take my hands."

"Hávi, sit down," Bíldr said.

Hávi lowered onto something that felt like a rope swing.
She glanced around, expecting to see the trees that the rope
swing hung from, but seeing instead the smooth, handsome
face of Skytja, her newest stepson, pressed against her right.
Rauðkinn, his darker brother, was pressed up against her left,
and Bíldr, whose thick moustache was brushing against the
back of her neck, had his arms around her waist, and the
three of them floated her up the stairs like a cloud rising up
the side of a mountain. Hávi laughed and kicked out her feet
playfully.

"Hávi, sit still!" Völu scolded.

Hávi's bed swayed and tilted; she clung to one of its carved horse-heads. Jorgen was crying. Deep voices faded and several doors closed. An empty bucket appeared in front of her but Hávi pushed it away; she hadn't eaten anything.

"Never seen her like this," Breiðr said.

"Bitra will be back soon," Völu scowled.

Bitra's return coincided with a foul-tasting hot tea that Völu forced Hávi to drink despite Hávi's curses and refusals. The tea made her sick and soon the bucket was no longer empty. Still they kept forcing the tea into her mouth; it gave Hávi a terrible headache. They pulled off her fancy gold dress and put her into her bed, but the heavy blankets crushed oppressively down on her. Just when she thought that she couldn't feel any worse, their door opened and Jarl Hafr came in. Breiðr and Bitra whispered *'good night'* and Völu squeezed her hand so hard that a milk-cow would've brayed and kicked her, and then all three women departed.

Jarl Hafr was grinning ear-to-ear. He pulled back her covers, sat beside her, and his hard, ungentle hand suddenly squeezed her breast, which moistened with flowing milk. Hávi looked up into the smiling face of her new husband.

"I really hate you," Hávi said.

Jarl Hafr's smile widened.

"I don't like you either," Jarl Hafr said. "Women who think like men should be horsewhipped. My serving girls smear honey on their lips to make their kisses sweet. But a wench is a wench, you know; some girls squirm best when they're tied down. Do you need to be tied down?"

Hávi closed her eyes and said nothing. Jarl Hafr got up and walked about the room; she heard his breath blowing out candles and him opening the shutters, felt the cool air of the wintery night enter her room, and then heard a heavy belt unbuckle and large buttons unfasten. Soon Jarl Hafr's weight returned to the bed; Hávi gritted her teeth at his first touch, and tears burst from her eyes as Jarl Hafr lifted her nightshirt and touched her underneath.

His fingers clawed, but she said nothing and kept her eyes closed like a little child pretending not to be there. An eternity of agony followed. Jarl Hafr grunted like a rutting boar as he forced himself inside her again and again. Hávi sobbed the whole time; not until he finally rolled off her did he offer any attempt at comfort.

"There: you must've enjoyed that," he said. "If not, you'll get used to it."

Jarl Hafr wrapped all of the blankets around himself and went to sleep. Hávi forced herself to think of Jorgen; *if not for him then she'd kill her new husband.*

Hávi spent the night on the hearth of her outer room; with the thick brace on their door, no one would ever know that she hadn't spent the night sleeping next to her husband. He arose with the sun and only laughed when he found Hávi wrapped in a cloak on the floor. Without a word, he walked toward the outer door and left her prone and alone.

To Hávi's relief, Bitra entered almost as soon as Jarl Hafr left. She carried a bucket of barely-warm water, and Hávi was vigorously scrubbing herself before Bitra returned from the kitchen with a fresh, steaming bucket. Bitra offered to help, but Hávi sent her to awaken Breiðr and Völu. By the time that all three ladies returned, Hávi was dressed and ready to work.

Hávi led them to Jarl Illingr's tower and they began cleaning and reorganizing it. Soon three other servants were helping, and Hvassi provided many thick tapestries, faded but still very colorful, which they layered over the tower's cold brick walls. Felian arrived to help; news of Hávi's industriousness had spread throughout the castle. By late afternoon, the fireplace was blazing and Jarl Illingr's wide desk and bed were gone; the tower room boasted a tall, narrow wardrobe, two small beds with new, straw mattresses, pillows and comforters provided by the sewing ladies, a bowl of fragrant herbs from Master Kamban, several trays of hot pastries from the kitchen, and Jorgen's crib. The tiny tower chamber was quite crowded, but Hávi insisted that everyone who helped her stay and drink wine.

"What's going on up here?" Master Krókr bellowed.

Master Krókr pushed up through the open trapdoor and glared at everyone. All of the servants shied away, trying to hide their reddened faces, but there was nowhere to escape.

"They're here with my leave," Hávi said.

"Who gave permission to decorate this tower?"

"I did."

"I'm the seneschal of this castle ...!"

"I'm Mistress Austmaðr: I give you permission ... *to depart my tower."*

Furious, Master Krókr glared at everyone in the room before he departed in a huff, stomping back down the long, spiral stairs. Hávi listened to him leave in a silence broken only by the crackling of the flames in the fireplace.

"He won't let this go unchallenged," Hávi said to all of the servants. "Perhaps you should be somewhere safe when he returns."

The servants didn't hesitate; Master Krókr could make all of their lives miserable. Völu and Breiðr offered to stay, but Hávi insisted that they leave, even Bitra. Half an hour later, while nursing Jorgen, heavy footsteps announced several visitors and Jarl Hafr stepped up into the tower room and glared at her.

"Are you alone?" Hávi asked him.

"No," he said.

"Perhaps you should be."

Jarl Hafr considered, then nodded to whomever stood on the steps behind him, and footsteps descended. Jarl Hafr waited a moment, then stared angrily at Hávi. She faced him resolutely.

"If I sleep up here with Jorgen then I needn't know which sluts are in your bed," Hávi said.

"I'm Jarl Austmaðr: I'll have my wife in any way and at any time I want."

"You have sluts aplenty; why want me?"

"I don't."

Hávi clenched her teeth and said nothing, hoping that his own words would infiltrate his thick skull. Jarl Hafr glared at Hávi for several moments, glanced at the new furnishings, and then he descended her stairs one stomp at a time.

"You can't," Hvítvi said, startling Hávi, Völu, Breiðr, and Bitra as he stuck his head up through the open trapdoor; his soft footsteps had given them no warning that he was approaching.

All four women froze, and then Völu, Breiðr, and Bitra rose, but Hvítvi stopped them with a gesture and pointed toward the empty bed beside the newly-cleaned wardrobe that had replaced Jarl Illingr's desk. All three nervously sat.

"Not long ago an assassin tried to kill you," Hvítvi said. "Your bedroom's more secure than this tower. Also, the news that you're not sleeping in Jarl Austmaðr's bed will spread ..."

"His bed won't be empty."

"That doesn't matter ..."

"The rumor that Mistress Austmaðr shares her bed with a dozen sluts won't spread?"

"We have to prevent ..."

"You could've prevented this!"

Hvítvi glared at her while her companions paled.

"Hávi, another son would ..."

"How dare you!"

Hávi rose, fists clenched, her muscles taut, ready to beat Hvítvi into a bloody pulp.

"You're my stepson," Hávi hissed between clenched teeth. "If you were my husband then I'd obey any order that you gave me ... but you're not: *you can't order me!"*

Pink eyes drilled into blue. Tedious seconds ticked by, and then Hvítvi vanished through the trapdoor and his soft slippers padded down the stairs. For the first time, Hávi's heart didn't wrench when Hvítvi left. Her second forced marriage hung between them; *now Hávi didn't love any man.* That thought opened a deep chasm in her heart; jarls, seneschals, and mistresses: no matter who won ... Hávi had already lost.

Jay Palmer

Chapter 32

Days passed tensely as everyone settled into their new routines. Jarl Illingr's tower required lots of firewood to keep warm, but Hávi expertly banked it each night so that they didn't freeze. Völu and Bitra were skinny enough to share one narrow bed and Jorgen slept in his crib between both beds. At Hvítvi's orders, the castle blacksmith hung a large bell from the ceiling inside their tower and a hole was drilled into the floor beside the wall. A rope hung from the bell which passed through the floor; in case of trouble, Hávi or the guard on the stairs below her could ring the bell to alert the whole castle. The blacksmith also affixed an iron slide to the trapdoor so that Hávi could seal her room at night; to force entrance, an assassin would have to chop through the floor. Hávi thanked the blacksmith and provided him with sweets and frothing ales while he worked, but he mentioned that Master Krókr wasn't happy, and he quickly finished his work.

Trouble came of the sluts; Master Krókr arranged for a

second women's table next to the first, but a shouting match broke out the first evening that the sluts and castle women dined side-by-side. Hvítvi moved the tables apart, and then Master Krókr got Jarl Hafr's permission to move them back together, and Mjóvi joined the women at their table to reign in their objections.

The next day, Mjóvi was the only lady of the castle to show up for dinner. Hávi had dined in her tower room every evening since her wedding, and that night she held a picnic on the stairs of her tower for all of the women who refused to dine beside the sluts.

Hávi resumed her lessons in sewing and healing and frequently showed up in the kitchen ready to work. The cook eagerly welcomed her and soon Hávi was preparing sauces and basting the roasting meats; chores which the cook trusted to few others. Hávi learned new recipes and worked diligently; 'Hávi-cooked foods' became a phrase that implied excellent taste. Only once did one of the sluts appear in the kitchen, claiming that she loved to cook, and then a meat cleaver suddenly stabbed into the doorframe beside her while she was looking in another direction.

Snow fell thick that winter, such that travel from the castle to Skadi became difficult, but a wandering minstrel arrived and delighted them all with a new musical instrument from the southlands called a 'lute', which he played masterfully. Some nights he stood at the foot of the stairs to Hávi's tower and played while all of the castle women sat in the narrow hallway, on the flagstones, or on the steps leading upwards. Bíldr, Hávi's personal guard, always stood not far away, and Völu and Bitra obeyed orders to summon him anytime that Hávi wanted to go anywhere but the main rooms of the castle. Jarl Hersir arrived for a few days and Völu spent those nights with Bifru; Breiðr left her husband's bed on those nights to stay with Hávi and Bitra.

While Bíldr watched, Master Kamban took Hávi outside to the castle's butchery to teach her how to set a broken bone. He demonstrated with the severed leg of a newly-slaughtered horse, searing vessels closed with a hot poker, and complimented Hávi on not flinching from the blood or the smell. Smiling, Hávi explained that she'd butchered many goats in her youth. Völu also watched without flinching, but Breiðr turned green and fled puking.

Mistress Hvassi pressed Hávi until she actually finished a needlepoint project: the worst Austmaðr family crest that Hávi had ever seen. It was so poor that Hvassi agreed that Hávi couldn't wear it in public and started Hávi on a second attempt with even more supervision. Hávi still couldn't thread a needle without several tries, but Hvassi refused to ask the blacksmith to make needles with larger eyes.

Hvítvi was seldom seen in the castle; Master Kamban missed two lessons with Hávi because he was attending Hvítvi, who'd caught a terrible cold and spent much of the remaining winter in his hot-fog room, the thick steam keeping his fragile sinuses open. Master Kamban thanked Hávi repeatedly for teaching him how to massage heads to relieve Hvítvi's pain, and he recited the new healing chants that he'd invented to improve her technique. Hávi asked to visit Hvítvi, but Bíldr refused; rumors of Hávi in Hvítvi's chambers while she absented herself from her husband's bed weren't permissible. She contented herself with daily reports of Hvítvi's health from Felian.

Several of the new women were welcomed at the castle: Jarl Hafr's daughters, even those young daughters born of the sluts, were allowed to join the castle women, although their mothers weren't mentioned. Knarrarbringa was Jarl Hafr's eldest daughter, a big-boned, bossy, merchant-ship of a woman with huge bosoms. Mela was her only full-sister, a wild child with athletic tendencies for climbing trees and stone walls, and who swore that she could scale the outside walls of Hávi's tower, but the older women refused to let her try. She reminded Hávi of Hersir girls out-wrestling village boys. Mela had hair of a dark gold that looked brown at night but gleamed yellow in bright sunlight. Inn Bareyska's mother was a slut from the Hebrides. Eyverska was born of a slut from the Orkney Islands. Inn Flamska's mother was from Flanders. Urd and Spörr were both only nine, but they insisted on staying with their sisters rather than in the nursery, although Hávi's youngest stepdaughters, Fróði, Auða, Grái, and Hrogn had welcomed them and taught them all of the games that they knew.

Hávi seldom saw Jarl Hafr, but when she did, he always had a smiling slut or two on each arm. They never spoke, and Hávi's days and nights passed blissfully without him. Her refusal to tolerate his sluts had ingratiated all of the castle women save for a few old crones like Mjóvi. Hávi was hopeful; in the late spring, her husband and most of the men would sail away on the summer viking, and then their support might just expel the sluts from the castle. Perhaps even Mjóvi's sharp tongue could be blunted over the summer. Besides, Jarl Illingr had stressed that, legally, Hávi could do nothing alone. Because of the recent viking deaths, women made up two-thirds of the population of the Skåne; Hávi's support was strengthening.

Weeks passed into months and the snows began to melt. To Bíldr's frustration, Hávi insisted on taking all of her women-friends to Hrafna's tavern on the first sunny day of spring. Reluctantly Bíldr fetched two silver coins from Hvítvi, who passed along a message that such frivolities couldn't be repeated, and Bíldr followed as Hávi led a skirted procession of thirty women from Castle Austmaðr down the white, crushed-shell-paved road to the city of Skadi. The castle women, including Jarl Hafr's older daughters, marched laughing into the familiar tavern, followed by six frowning guards led by Bíldr.

Having received warning of their coming, Hrafna greeted them all, and a plate full of västerbotten was set before Hávi, who thanked him profusely.

"Nonsense," Hrafna waved away her gratitude. "Serving Mistress Austmaðr and her guests is the greatest honor that I have!"

Burly Hrafna was Hávi's favorite tavern-master; he was always cheerful and welcoming, even with strangers that he'd never seen before. Hávi insisted that all of the women try her favorite hard cheese and Brækir, Hrafna's wife, soon brought more. Brækir delighted at hosting most of the castle women, although she was overly-formal to Hávi, whose interference had almost cost her family everything. For her sons, Valla and Augi, Hávi had arranged to have Jarl Illingr teach the den Skaanske Lov, the law code of Sweden, although he'd only given them one lesson before Hávi was caught in his bedroom, and the subsequent scandal had cost Jarl Illingr's life. Gylðir, a young man from clan Dúfunef, and occasionally Law-speaker Spaki, now taught Valla and Augi four times a week. She was forbidden to attend their lessons; Hávi still bristled at this; she needed to learn the laws to change them, but Hvítvi had sworn that the lessons would end if she interfered again.

Blönduhorn alone didn't seem happy to see Hávi, although Hávi hugged her and praised her undeniable beauty before all. Hávi had once dressed Blönduhorn in one of her gowns and paraded her before Hvítvi, hoping to blunt Hávi's attraction to her own stepson; an attempt that had failed utterly. Lithe and youthful, with long, straight, blonde hair with mismatched braids, Blönduhorn was Brækir's niece, scarecrow-thin and usually smiling. Hávi regretted Blönduhorn's obvious uneasiness around her and apologized again for dragging her to the castle.

Hávi had to force Hrafna to accept her silver coins while he bowed and insisted that he was too humble to charge Mistress Austmaðr. Their visit to his tavern was followed by a brisk walk through Skadi, peering into all of the shops, but it was still too cold to walk all of the way down to the harbor, so the women returned to the castle before the sunset, laughing and celebrating their camaraderie.

Preparations for the viking began early; Hávi was one of the first to know of it as she worked in both the kitchen and the sewing room. Soon all of Castle Austmaðr buzzed like a beehive.

"Hávi," a strange, bitter voice called as Hávi started to climb the steps to her tower. Hávi startled to see one of her husband's hated sluts walking toward her.

"How dare you?" Hávi snarled, looking down upon her. "Begone, slut!"

"My name is Gellir ..."

"I don't care!"

"None of us asked for Jarl Hafr," Gellir said. "Your first husband purchased us ... and slept with each of us before he sent us to his brother."

Hávi glared at Gellir: Gellir was short and round but showed no trace of softness. She had black hair and angry eyes, but kept her obvious strength restrained. She met Hávi's glare undaunted.

"I just wanted you to know," Gellir said. "Like you, we do what we must, not what we choose."

Gellir walked away without another word. Resolutely Hávi watched her depart, Völu and Bíldr standing quiet, frowning, but obviously reluctant to interfere. With an accusatory glance at both of them, Hávi resumed climbing her tower steps.

Gellir's words kept Hávi awake most of the night. Hávi didn't doubt her claims; her late husband didn't have Jarl Hafr's dominating needs, but Jarl Austmaðr took advantage of every situation. He was too wise to forget discretion; going viking every summer, Hávi doubted if he'd let captured women go free if they could warm his bed or please his men. Hávi had never wondered what life was like for the sluts; *hadn't she prostituted herself by marrying Jarl Hafr for the good of clan Austmaðr?* Yet it was too late; if Hávi befriended the sluts now then she'd lose the support of all the castle women. Her legal goal, if she could attain it, would help all women. Justly or not, Hávi had to despise the sluts.

One morning, while wearing thick mittens and transferring freshly-baked chicken-bread from its oven-trays to the cooling-shelves, Hávi glanced up to see Jarl Hafr enter the huge kitchen. Ignoring the other cooks, he approached her directly.

"Wife, our guests arrive today. Your presence at the high-table is required."

Unable to refuse, Hávi nodded silently as the kitchen staff stared in frozen alarm; Hávi hadn't sat beside her husband since their wedding night. Jarl Hafr glanced at Hávi's appearance, covered in flour and sweating from the heat of the ovens.

"I trust that you'll dress appropriately."

That evening Hávi entered the great hall in all of the splendor that Hvassi and Breiðr could manage, Bitra having spent almost an hour braiding, piling, and pinning Hávi's hair into a swirling, uncomfortable mound trailing thin orange ribbons. Every table in the hall was filled, the foremost table lined with the seal-skin cloaks which identified the warriors of clan Dúfunef. Both Jarl Dúfunefs, father and son, sat at the high-table talking with Hvítvi, Jarl Hafr, and Jarl Hersir. Unexpectedly, Master Krókr sat close by them with many of the castle elders. Hávi ascended the lower stairs and squeezed past the men to the empty chair beside her husband. To her surprise, her empty chair sat between her husband and Hvítvi, who looked warily at her as she approached. Hávi sat beside him, then laid a familiar hand upon her husband's arm and cast Hvítvi a deadly stare.

Hvítvi paled to his purest white, then resumed talking to Jarl Hersir, who aimed a warning glare at Hávi. Hávi sipped at her ale and asked a passing servant for hot glog, and then she began nibbling at the sweets piled upon the high-table.

"My brother had it right," Jarl Hafr said. "Churches are the key to Europe's unity; we need to keep attacking them."

"Fear is what we need most," the older Jarl Dúfunef agreed. "They must fear us more than their only god."

"Warriors are what we must deny them," Jarl Dúfunef the younger said. "Every male child can grow up to avenge their fathers. Every woman who can bear sons must be slain."

"We can't kill everyone," Hvítvi said. "If our enemies think that we'll kill them whether they fight us or not then they've nothing to lose by fighting. That's why we can't burn every city to the ground; they'd have no choice but to unite and invade us."

"We can't fight all of Europe," Jarl Hersir agreed. "We need for all of the viking leaders to focus their attacks on our enemies' borders. If their borders are weakened, then they can invade each other, and we can profit from their disunity."

"Brilliant!" Hvítvi said. "Even the Norwegians might help."

"Father sent a ship around to the western shore but it never returned," Jarl Dúfunef said. "We don't know if our message was received, sunk, or pirated."

"Pirated, probably," Jarl Hafr said. "I know Norwegians; I've fought them while you've vikinged. They're savages."

"They say the same about us," Jarl Hersir said.

"We've received replies from the Danes and the Finns; every first viking should be on a border," Jarl Dúfunef said.

"Excellent," Jarl Hafr said. "This will be the year that our enemies turn on each other."

Plans and contingencies mounted unabated as dinner was served. Hávi had helped prepare most of their dishes and she'd become extremely-discerning about their taste. The loganberries were no longer fresh, so much of their natural sweetness had lessened; Hávi wondered if a light honey-sauce would enhance their flavor until new berries could be harvested. The freshly-baked tuna, flavored by a steaming barley stew, rich with baked onions, was delicious. After all of her work, Hávi had hoped to have some of the new chicken-bread, but that was being stored for the viking; she resolved to have some cooked as soon as the men departed.

Before they finished eating, Jarl Hafr had planned the conquest of Europe all the way to Rome, which Hávi only knew of from Jarl Illingr's maps. Most of the men had fallen silent while Jarl Hafr raved on; such plans were virtually impossible.

While everyone was drinking, Hávi absently let her elbow rest upon Hvítvi's slender arm. Her stepson instantly tensed, then slid his hands into his lap and gave Hávi an admonishing glare. Hávi smiled sweetly back at him; he may be able to marry her off but he couldn't deny his attraction to her ... or scold her in public. Sitting at her husband's side, Hávi could do anything; she yawned widely and stretched her arms so that Hvítvi had to duck. Watching intently, Jarl Hersir tried not to laugh.

"Don't drink too much, Mother," Hvítvi whispered to her. "You wouldn't want a repeat of your wedding night."

Hávi stiffened and glared at Hvítvi; *how dare he? He'd thrown her into her husband's bed ... and then ...!*

"You got drunk that night, remember?" Hvítvi continued.

Hávi fumed; she'd forgotten. Hvítvi was being his usual charming self, reminding her of that horrible night. Hávi resisted the urge to hit him; half of the Skåne would be talking about it tomorrow: another scandal, yet she balled up her fist, ready to punch.

"Hávi ...!" Jarl Hersir hissed, his thick brows lowered so far that they almost obscured his eyes. "Perhaps you should retire for the ...."

"Perhaps not," Hávi snapped.

Jarl Hersir ignored her and spoke up to Jarl Hafr.

"Most-noble host, I fear that I bear private news for your wife about her family in clan Hersir. Before she retires, may I walk with my clan-child?"

502

"Of course," Jarl Hafr said, casting Hávi a disgusted glance.

Breiðr and Völu followed at a discrete distance as Jarl Hersir walked beside Hávi.

"Hávi, I know how terrible this has been for you, but all of Scandinavia, including your mother, can sleep tonight because of your sacrifice."

"All of Scandinavia is laughing at me: a queen supplanted by whores."

"You've a strong son that'll grow up to be Jarl Austmaðr. He'll never starve or be poor as long as you keep up this pretense."

"Jarl Hafr's a pig."

"He's Jarl Austmaðr now ... and he deserves your allegiance both as your husband and as your clan-chief. Your first Jarl Austmaðr wasn't without faults."

"He didn't disgrace me."

"You disgraced him."

"Not on purpose. If he'd get rid of those sluts ...!"

"Then what? If you take a pig out of its pen, does it stop being a pig? If he got rid of the sluts today, would you love him tomorrow?"

"I'll never love him."

"Everyone knows that. Look, we'll be viking in three days ..."

"I'll hope for the best ...!"

"Hávi, you can't say that; just thinking about it's treason. Besides, if Odin calls Jarl Austmaðr to him this summer, then his eldest son will have to inherit."

"Skytja seems competent ..."

"Someone tried to assassinate you to hurt clan Austmaðr.

What do you think they'll do to Jorgen? They'll never leave him alone; every day he'll be the rightful clan-chief that had his crown stolen but is too small and weak to take it back. Your enemies will send their kids to taunt and torment Jorgen until he's as twisted as Sterki. When he's grown, they'll promise him men and ships to help him reclaim clan Austmaðr; Skytja and Rauðkinn know this. Do you think that they'll ever trust him, assuming that they let him live?"

"We could return to clan Hersir," Hávi said.

"Clan Hersir has its own problems; we don't need yours."

"I'm clan Hersir!"

"My wife is Lady Hersir because I won't let her call herself *'queen',*" Jarl Hersir said. "She wants to, but once you declare yourself a queen then you escalate every problem and add new ones; what do you think she'll do if a real queen comes to clan Hersir? How many of clan Austmaðr's enemies will follow you? No, Hávi; Jorgen can't come to clan Hersir. We don't have castle walls or enough men to protect him."

"So ... Jorgen must be Jarl Austmaðr ... or ...?" Hávi asked.

"Jorgen is half-Hersir; having him become the ruler of clan Austmaðr will give clan Hersir a power and influence that we've never had. Why do you think that I arranged for your first marriage? If Jorgen dies then clan Hersir suffers, too. Your marriage makes us allies; if clan Austmaðr falls, then clan Hersir might fall, too."

Days passed in a busy madness. Master Kamban's healing lessons had to be postponed while Hávi worked in the kitchens and Völu started helping her, chopping vegetables and churning butter. Breiðr and Bitra became trapped in the sewing room; Hvassi was commanded to provide a new sail and a hundred knitted socks and wool caps for those going viking. Everyone in the castle crawled to their beds after midnight and was awakened before dawn to continue preparations.

The dawn of the sailing day brightened, gray and cloudy. Accompanied by Völu and Bíldr, Hávi walked in the traditional procession to the harbor with the castle elders; behind, not beside her husband. A year before, Hávi had kissed her husband before the whole Skåne; now the idea repulsed her. Hávi slowed and let others pass her; Mjóvi walked ahead of her as if Hávi didn't exist.

Again the many fishing boats had been removed, replaced by mighty dragonships. All of the warriors were still working, loading food and supplies for their months away. Wives and children watched their busy menfolk, preparing to say good-bye, terrified that they may never see them again. A grim mood silenced all talk; Jarl Hafr used to guard the coast, not lead the viking for all of the clans of the Skåne. They needed a profitable viking, but Jarl Hafr was untested.

Again the sacrifice was brought forward. A magnificent bull, bigger than last year, was led to stand upon the sands. Hvítvi held out the great sword and Jarl Hafr took it smiling; the sacrifice was considered a powerful omen for the success of the viking.

"*Odin! Odin!*" some of the men started shouting, and soon every man took up the roaring chant. "*Odin! Odin! Odin! Odin! Odin! Odin!*"

Jarl Hafr stepped up beside the massive bull and raised the huge, heavy sword high over his head. The shouts of *'Odin!'* escalated, a deafening roar echoing across Skadi. Jarl Hafr raised his voice and shouted to the sky.

"Gods of our fathers, I call upon thee,
Grant us riches or Valkyrie!
Gods of Asgard, by fire and ice,
Accept now this sacrifice!"

Jarl Hafr took a firm grip on the wide, raised blade, flexed his muscles and, with a high-pitched scream, Jarl Hafr slashed downward.

The bull's head didn't fully sever. Several inches of throat-skin remained, holding fast to the great sword as the bull collapsed with a final thrash that jerked the sword out of Jarl Hafr's hands. The bull's blood, whose forward-spray was always measured, had instead spewed in all directions, and painted Jarl Hersir, Jarl Dúfunef, and Jarl Hafr, who stood shocked and ashamed, his blood-drenched hands empty, the sacrificial sword fallen onto the sands.

"Oars out! Sails up!" Jarl Dúfunef shouted angrily, and the men turned silently away from the sacrifice, eager to leave the disgrace behind. The villagers, all of Skadi, stood shocked and appalled; *never before had a Jarl Austmaðr shamed them.*

Minutes later, Jarl Hafr was hidden by the men on his ship as all of the dragonships were sailed out of the harbor. No one cheered, waved, or wished them well; the gods had cursed the viking.

Chapter 33

That night, Hávi insisted that Völu, Breiðr, and Bitra join her for dinner in the great hall. The castle had been uncomfortably quiet all day; Hávi hoped to set the mood for the entire summer by hosting the evening meal as it used to be before Sterki had murdered his father. Hávi, Völu, Breiðr, and Bitra all dressed formally for dinner, however, upon entering the great hall, they found most of the tables empty; only a few servants had come. The high-table sat empty.

"Where's everyone?" Hávi asked.

"No one wants to be seen, I suppose," Völu said.

"An ugly start to the viking," Breiðr said. "The peasants will fear them cursed."

"Never say that!" Hávi snapped. "If we start saying it then others will repeat it."

"It's too late to stop that," Breiðr said.

"What we need to do," Hávi said firmly, "is give them

something else to talk about."

"What?" Völu asked.

"Us," Hávi said. "The four of us ... sitting at the high-table."

Objections rained, but Hávi wouldn't be gainsaid. With Völu's reluctant help, since neither Breiðr nor Bitra could outmuscle them, they drug the frightened women up the short stairs onto the lower dais, and soon shocked servants entered to find the four women seated at the center of the high-table, all looking nervous. Bíldr came running in through the main door and stared disbelieving as Mjóvi and Krókr hurried in from another door, and all of the servants in the great hall suddenly fled. Bíldr cursed aloud and then departed; Hávi knew what was coming next.

Ten minutes later, Hvítvi walked into the great hall as casually as if it were a normal evening. He paused and yawned slightly, glancing about with apparent disinterest, although Hávi knew that he was fighting to remain calm. Secretly she envied his control as he gracefully walked to the center space before the high-table; only they, Mjóvi, and Master Krókr remained in the hall. Hvítvi faced Hávi and drilled his pink eyes into her blue.

"Explain this."

Hávi took a deep breath and tried to appear as calm as Hvítvi.

"You'll have to punish me," Hávi said confidently. "This will be a scandal; the talk of the Skåne."

"Why?"

"News of the sacrifice has already circulated," Hávi said. "If people start talking about me, about how I was publically humiliated by you, then they'll have something else to talk about ... something besides the botched omen."

Hvítvi stared at her long and hard, unmoving, before he turned his head to glance at Mjóvi and Master Krókr.

"What do you think?" Hvítvi asked them. "A good plan?"

"It's disgraceful!" Mjóvi seethed. *"Again she injures clan Austmaðr!"*

"Possibly," Hvítvi said. "Mistress Austmaðr sacrifices her dignity for the sake of her clan: that'll give idle tongues abundant food for wagging. Hávi, this is shameful: you're banished to your tower for a week."

"Yes, Master Hvítvi," Hávi said, and she bowed her head in acquiesce.

"Now, I think," Hvítvi finished.

Without another word, all four women rose and exited the great hall. Hávi didn't dare glance behind her, but she did spy Mjóvi and Master Krókr glaring daggers at her. Hávi gifted them with a bright smile and then followed the others out of the great hall.

The next day, Hávi regretted her sacrifice; from her high, third-story window, Hávi could see Skadi buzzing with women furiously shopping; after the men sailed, every woman with any wealth descended upon the craftsmen and purchased all of the treasures that their husbands would never let them buy. Most of the craftsmen made their biggest profit on that day, and Hávi had dreamed of dining in Hrafna's tavern and trying to make amends with Brækir and Blönduhorn after a day of spending Austmaðr silver. Even Hvítvi might agree that Hávi being seen spending money would undercut the rumors of Austmaðr's empty coffers, however true they might be. But Hávi's confinement provided an excuse for Mistress Austmaðr to not spend money that they didn't have; it was probably for the best.

Felian arrived on the third day demanding that Hávi accompany him. Hávi explained that Hvítvi had banished her to her tower, but Felian insisted that Master Kamban needed her or someone would die. Hávi and Völu ran with him, leaving Breiðr and Bitra lagging far behind. Felian led them down several narrow hallways to an open door.

Master Kamban knelt beside the bed of an elderly woman, his lowered head almost hidden by his deformed back. She looked weak, too pale to be sleeping, and her few breaths were soft and ragged. Hávi knelt beside her teacher and examined the woman while Master Kamban chanted exuberantly.

> *"Kindly Hel open thy gates*
> *Accept this maiden who awaits*
> *Gently welcome into your hall*
> *She whose sweetness the Norns now call."*

Hávi glanced at Master Kamban as she took up the familiar chant. The bald hunchback's frown told her everything; there was nothing that they could do.

"Hávi, it's time that you introduced yourself to the gods to whom Mistress Kamfi now ascends," Master Kamban said. "You've learned much about healing; now you must learn its ultimate truth: eventually all patients travel this road."

With great difficulty, Hávi assisted Master Kamban to stand on his heavy crutch, and then he *'thumped'* backward, gesturing to her first patient. Hávi hesitated, then turned to Mistress Kamfi. She was incredibly old; Hávi couldn't recall having ever seen her before. She wasn't surprised; many castle elders avoided the common rooms due to their failing health. Master Kamban had taught Hávi almost everything that she knew about healing, but she'd never gotten to practice. Now she grimaced; her first patient had nothing to heal. If Master Kamban had given up then nothing that Hávi knew could help.

Hávi noticed several other people crowded into her tiny room, all elders like Mistress Kamfi. Some she'd dined with in the great hall, and they looked pleadingly at her. Hávi took a deep breath; Master Kamban had taught her well.

Kneeling before the aged woman's bed, Hávi bowed and pressed her fists together, then raised her arms and called to Hel, the Goddess of Death. Loudly she repeated the chant that Master Kamban had taught her, emphatically reciting each word as if to embed her chant into the ears of her listeners forever. Whether the half-goddess Hel heard her or not, Hávi wasn't sure; Hávi had heard stories of divine intercession all of her life, but she'd never seen any evidence that the gods cared for anything but suffering and death. If death they craved, then Mistress Kamfi would feed their lusts; Hávi chanted so forcefully that Hel would have to hear.

> *"Idun's apples golden life*
> *Mimir's waters set to rights*
> *Blessed gods, we pray to all*
> *Deny now the Norn's call."*

Long her chant lasted. Several times Master Kamban came and examined Mistress Kamfi while Hávi held both of her hands over different parts of her patient: feet, legs, stomach, heart, and head, always renewing her chant. It was harder than she'd imagined, and Hávi was exhausted before Master Kamban raised his manly voice over hers.

> *"Gods of peace and Gods of war*
> *Accept this life which is no more*
> *Welcome the spirit departing this shell*
> *Kindly greet her, blessed Hel."*

Two elderly women burst into tears, and an elderly man

tried to comfort both of them at once. None glanced at Hávi but Master Kamban, who rested a reassuring hand on her shoulder and gave her a slight nod. Hávi rose off her sore knees and glanced about; many elders crowded the narrow hallway outside the tiny room, and over their heads towered Bíldr and Völu, standing silent and respectful. Sweaty, Hávi staggered toward the door. As she stepped into the hallway, several elders touched her arms and spoke softly.

"Thank you, Mistress Hávi. You eased her passing well."

Their tangible gratitude startled Hávi; she humbly accepted their praise. Völu pushed through them to take Hávi's arm and assist her away.

"Hávi, you ... shouldn't have come down here without me," Bíldr whispered, but his voice was filled with reluctance.

"That ... that was good," Völu told Hávi.

"Where's Jorgen?" Hávi asked.

"With Breiðr."

Moments later, Master Kamban joined them.

"We're not done," Master Kamban said. "We need to give them time to grieve properly and then we must attend the body. This is part of healing."

Hávi nodded weakly.

An hour later, at Master Kamban's direction, Hávi asked the mourners to depart so that the healers could finish their task. All of them thanked her again and each walked away solemnly. Felian returned with two buckets, reminding Hávi of her morning baths. At first she wondered what the water was for, and then she feared the answer.

"Dear friends," Master Kamban said to Bíldr and Völu, "I beg your pardon, but the prayers that I must speak now are for healer's ears only."

"I can't leave Hávi unguarded this far from her tower,"

Bíldr said.

Bíldr consented to watch from the end of the hall and Völu accompanied him. As soon as they were alone, Master Kamban spoke in a whisper.

"Felian, what did you think of Hávi's performance?"

Felian looked embarrassed.

"Master, she's our Mistress ...!"

"Healers must be above such trivialities as rank; even kings die. Evaluate your Mistress."

"Everything was ... correctly spoken."

"Keep going."

"Hávi's prayers were very ... impassioned."

"Excellent. Continue."

"Well, I mean, if I had to find fault, and I wasn't looking to ..."

"Tell me truly," Hávi urged Felian.

"It ... wasn't ... convincing."

"Exactly," Master Kamban said. "No matter how strong some appear, all humans are delicate. Our strongest poisons always work, but our strongest medicines usually fail. Most times, life hangs in an uncertain balance; our job is to tip the scales in our favor.

"Mistress Kamfi was very old and sick; nothing that you could have done would have healed her, but what of those watching, those who'll someday look to a healer as death comes for them? At such times, if there is any hope, their belief in your healing skills may be all that holds Death at bay. Every chance that healers have, they must prove their mastery. Were the gods swayed to divine mercy by your performance today? You must dig deeper, Hávi. You must truly beg for their help, and you mustn't hide your pleas from those watching. Only greatness draws the attention of the gods, who alone can defy Death. All who watch your prayers, gods and mortals, you must convince."

"I ... I thought I ..."

"You did well," Master Kamban said. "Didn't she Felian?"

"Most assuredly!"

"If you hadn't been worthy then I'd have taken over," Master Kamban said. "You must witness my next deathwatch; mine earn high praises."

"But why?" Hávi asked. "I've seen a farmer lose his arm and return to work only weeks later. Why can one man survive a severed arm and another die to a cold breeze?"

"Answer her, Felian."

"We're tools of the gods," Felian said. "Odin needs warriors to fight beside him at Ragnarök; the rest of us are irrelevant. Some gods, especially the goddesses, granted to each of us special gifts, which they can increase or remove based on how we please them."

"But which god is watching you now?" Master Kamban asked. "If you live to please Heimdal, who benefits travelers, what if his arch-rival Loki is watching? You can't pray to two enemies and hope that either will heed you."

"Then what can we do?" Hávi asked.

"The same as everyone else: pray, and hope that your prayers are answered. And when you're called upon to heal, then you must pray twice: for yourself and for your patient." Master Kamban glanced at the prone, shrunken body of Mistress Kamfi. "Her spirit has departed and begun its long journey. When we send her body to join it; it must be clean and properly dressed so as not to offend Hel. You two must clean her; Felian, don't do all of the cleaning; Hávi must learn."

Touching Mistress Kamfi was even worse than touching

Master Kamban, which Hávi had at first feared to do as he was a hunchback, obviously cursed. But that was long ago; Hávi no longer feared to touch her wise teacher, especially since the massages that she'd taught him had helped relieve Hvítvi's paralyzing headaches. But Mistress Kamfi was cold and limp, and Hávi's fingers recoiled from her. The frail, small body proved difficult to move; undressing, washing, and then redressing her took all of her and Felian's strength. Then one of the castle elders arrived with a new linen shroud, and Hávi and Felian struggled to wrap Mistress Kamfi properly so that a seamstress could sew it closed.

That evening, Hávi scrubbed herself so hard that her skin was red and raw before she toweled herself dry. Völu washed also; both felt soiled by the death. Breiðr bathed Jorgen while Bitra fetched them food; Hávi was still confined to her tower, although certain that Hvítvi knew what she'd done today.

Hvassi couldn't climb the steps to Hávi's tower chamber and Völu doubted if she could squeeze through the trapdoor, so Hávi descended to her bottom step and Völu fetched them both chairs, amazing Breiðr upon returning carrying a heavy oak chair in each hand. Hávi laughed; she and Völu's physical upbringing often astounded the weak, castle-born royals. But Hvassi scolded Hávi for her newest poor embroidery, taking it away and ordering her to start over.

"Hvassi, as much as I ...," Hávi began.

"You're not going to quit," Hvassi said. "Every time that I see Hvítvi he asks how you're progressing. I've told him that I can make a decent seamstress of you, and I will if it kills both of us."

"But I'm terrible!"

"You have divided ambitions," Hvassi said. "Look at what you've already done: studied law, learned cooking, trained as a healer, mastered castle politics, and borne Jorgen, the next Jarl Austmaðr: no woman's ever attempted so much."

"I had to learn those things," Hávi said.

"Exactly," Hvassi said. "You learned because you had to. You could've decided not to try, and then you'd have failed. You need to make sewing a priority equal to the others; you could embroider if you were really determined."

"Maybe I do too much," Hávi said.

"I think that you need a bigger challenge," Hvassi grinned. "Every year Jarl Austmaðr and Jarl Hersir exchange tokens of unity between their clans; this year you'll embroider that token."

"No ...!"

"What you sew will go back to clan Hersir as a symbol of your skills. Everyone'll see it; your mother, your friends, ..."

"Sleitu," Völu said.

Hávi glared at Völu; while they were growing up, both of them had hated Sleitu.

"I'll bring you a fresh cloth, new skeins, and a complex design," Hvassi said, "and I'll show it to Mjóvi myself."

Hávi complained to no avail; Hvassi used Hávi's failure as a scrap to show her three new stitches, all of which she'd need to accomplish the new token. The only two that Hávi had ever learned was the cross-stitch and the chain-stitch; now she had to learn the running-stitch, the back-stitch, and an unbelievable nightmare called the French-knot that only a few of the seamstresses had mastered. Hávi watched and listened glumly, delighted when Bitra carried Jorgen down to be nursed. Hávi tried to use Jorgen as an excuse to end the lesson, but Hvassi insisted that Hávi could watch and learn while she nursed, and soon Völu took Jorgen so that Hávi could prove her abominable needle-mastery.

Hours later, her fingers bleeding from countless needle-pokes, Hávi ascended to her tower while Bitra fetched food for them all. No one spoke, unwilling to comment on Hávi's disastrous new stitches.

"I want to speak to Hvítvi," Hávi said to Bíldr.

"Why?" Bíldr frowned, though it was mostly hidden by his bushy mustache.

"It's a family matter."

That afternoon, Hávi was escorted into the Hall of Audiences. Hvítvi sat near the fireplace in the back, which was lit despite the warmth of the day. He wore a pale blue tunic and a wide scarf of butter-yellow, but his bloodless face was haggard; Hvítvi had been sick. Bíldr and Völu accompanied her and stood just inside the door as Hávi approached him. His appearance startled her but she was determined not to be sidetracked.

"Hello, Aunt," Hvítvi said weakly.

Hávi glared at the sickly albino.

"Are you happy?" Hávi asked.

Hvítvi looked up, surprised.

"Why should I be unhappy?"

"You married me off, as you desired. You locked me in my tower for a week. You sent Hvassi to torment me with needles. Are you happy?"

"Many women learn needlepoint."

"Many milk goats."

"Only one is Mistress Austmaðr."

Hávi glanced at the offensive decorations.

"I asked to speak to you privately, and you meet me in this ... *coliseum?*"

"What do we need to talk about?"

Their stares met, blue against pink, and both seemed determined to win their silent struggle.

"You insult me!"

"How?"

Hávi glared at her pale stepson; she'd loved him as no woman had ever loved a man, even though they'd only kissed once, and then only because Hvítvi's weakness had left him helpless in Hávi's strong arms. But he'd denied her, forced her to marry another, and abandoned her to rape and public humiliation; Hávi stormed out of the Hall of Audiences and back to her tower. *She couldn't believe that she'd ever loved Hvítvi.*

Early the next morning, Hávi, Völu, and Bitra were awakened by Felian, who knocked on their trapdoor until they unbarred it. All expected him to take Hávi to Master Kamban, but to their surprise, Felian insisted that Master Kamban wanted only Völu, Bitra, and Jorgen. Hávi objected, but Felian pleaded and apologized so profusely that soon Völu and Bitra carried Jorgen down the stairs after him, leaving Hávi alone.

Confused, Hávi sat in her tower for ten minutes before the stairs below her softly creaked. Hávi jumped to latch her trapdoor, which Bíldr always insisted that she keep locked; the last thing that she needed was another assassination attempt. She grabbed the hanging rope, ready to ring the bell, if needed, but no sooner had she barred her only entrance than a gentle knock sounded.

"Hávi," said Hvítvi's voice.

Hávi pulled open the trapdoor with such force that she wasn't sure if she wanted to pull Hvítvi inside or kick him down the tower stairs. Hvítvi looked as calm as ever, passive before Hávi's temper that rose like a tall ocean wave. Hávi hated his equanimity; she reached down and grabbed his tunic and pulled him up into her tower.

"Hávi, please ...!" Hvítvi began, but then Hávi kicked the trapdoor shut and slammed him against the thick tapestries covering her stone wall.

"I ought to snap you like a twig," Hávi growled.

Hvítvi looked shocked, helplessly pinned against the hanging, whose padding had protected him from the hard, stone walls.

"Is this why you wanted to see me?" Hvítvi asked. "To kill me?"

"You know that I could," Hávi said.

"Yes," Hvítvi scowled. "And you know how I feel about having my weaknesses taken advantage of."

"Advantage? You made me spread my legs for that ...!"

"Not so loud! No one must know that I'm here."

"Your body at the base of my tower won't be a secret."

"Don't make hollow boasts; you won't throw me out the window."

"Don't be so sure."

"I came to talk."

"What can you possibly say?"

"I'm sorry."

"Mate with Mjóvi and then tell me how sorry you are!"

"I'm fighting for our clan ..."

"I seem to be your favorite weapon."

"What would you have me do?"

Hávi bit her lip, torn; half of her wanted to beat Hvítvi into one giant bruise and the other half wanted to crush him against her until they merged forever.

"Jarl Illingr would've advised you to understand everything

before deciding anything," Hvítvi said.

Snarling, Hávi released Hvítvi.

"You're only mentioning him to evoke guilt," Hávi said. "You're manipulating me the same way that you manipulate everyone."

"Whereas you use your Hersir strength to pin me to the wall; we each use our skills to survive."

"My skills can kill."

"Ask Sterki about mine."

"What do you want?"

"You asked to meet me."

"*I can't talk in that hall!*"

"Hávi, I only used that hall to show others that we talked; it's just a pretense. What did you want to talk about?"

"I want some money."

"For what?"

"Hrafna's tavern, maybe some shopping."

"I'll have Bíldr bring you some. I appreciate what you did, sacrificing your freedom for our clan."

"Did it help?"

"Everyone in the Skåne knows the truth. Mjóvi's spies seeded several lies, but no one believes them. I've told half of Skadi how Father ordered you to ask for women's rights; the stories helped supplant the rumors of the failed sacrifice."

"I meant what I said about rights for women."

"I know, and I'm not opposed to it, but there's nothing that I can do about it now."

"You could advise me."

Hvítvi paused and looked thoughtful.

"My advice is to wait; the right actions at the wrong time would negate everything that you've done."

"*Done? I haven't done anything!*"

"Why ... you got all of Scandinavia talking about women's rights; it's still a common topic in taverns. *Didn't you know ....?*"

Hávi startled, and slowly Hvítvi smiled.

"I don't have all day," Hvítvi said. "I fed some lies to one of Mjóvi's spies around midnight; she and Master Krókr were awake all night plotting against us. Bíldr has all of the guards searching for another assassin; that's how I was able to sneak up here without being seen. Is there anything else that you need?"

Hávi paused, her emotions raging in every direction. *Still a common topic in taverns ....?*

"So ... you've been helping me?"

"Of course!"

"Why?"

Hvítvi's paleness flushed pink.

"What ...? What do you ...?"

"Why have you been helping me? What do you care if I suffer?"

Hvítvi looked confused, almost hurt.

"I should leave."

"I don't think so."

"Hávi ... Mother ..."

"I'm not your mother."

"Aunt, legally ..."

"Legally you're not here."

Hvítvi stared at her and then reached for the trapdoor. Hávi caught his arm in her firmest grip.

"The truth is what I want," Hávi said. "All of the truth ... all of the time. No lies. No manipulations. If you care for me ..."

Hvítvi bowed his head. Hávi seized his long, white hair

and turned his head to face her.

"If you love me ..."

"Hávi, please ...!"

"Where were you while I was lying naked with Hafr?"

Hvítvi looked frightened.

"The truth!" Hávi insisted.

Tears leaked from Hvítvi's eyes as Hávi held him firm.

"I was alone," Hvítvi said. *"Crying.* Does the truth help?"

Hávi glared; *was he telling the truth? How could she know?*

"You can't imagine how horrible it was," Hávi said. "But you can atone for it."

"Hávi, no ...!"

Hávi pulled him toward her. Hvítvi resisted, but Hávi felt him using only half of his meager strength; he was as torn as she. His white hair knotted in her fist, Hávi forced his pale lips against hers. Hvítvi struggled, tight-lipped, pushing against her with increasing resistance, but slowly his refusal faded. His closed lips yielded, his gentle hands started to cling, and his softness melded with hers. They kissed, firmly but gently, and Hávi's head spun lighter than any intoxication. Regrets twinged inside of her; she shouldn't be doing this, but she couldn't stop. He'd made her suffer rape; *did he deserve anything less?*

Hvítvi's resistance returned as she locked a hand about his wrist and forced it to her breast. Hávi was wearing only a light, summer nightshirt; his touch even through her thin fabric thrilled her. She rolled his hand over her breast as milk dampened its fabric.

"Hávi, stop ...!"

Hávi pushed Hvítvi toward her bed and used her toe to latch her trapdoor. Released, Hvítvi glanced anxiously around, but the only other exit was the window; he was as trapped as Hávi had been when Jarl Illingr last sat in this tower. Hávi reached down, pulled off her nightshirt, and cast it onto Völu's empty bed. Hvítvi's head shook in silent refusal, unable to voice his alarm.

"Shout," Hávi said, proudly bared before him. "Scream. Ring the bell and summon the whole castle."

Hvítvi glanced at the rope and followed it up to the hanging bell; if he pulled on that rope then half of the castle would catch them together. Hávi smiled; Hvítvi couldn't get caught in Hávi's bedchamber, especially not with her naked.

"Hávi, clan Austmaðr could fall ...!"

"I love you. No one need know."

Hvítvi stood horrified, still as white marble as Hávi approached.

"We can't ...!"

Hvítvi stepped up onto Hávi's bed and pressed his back against the colorful tapestries. Hávi climbed up onto her bed, trapped him in her warmest embrace, and pressed against his trembling body. Hvítvi returned her kisses with a passion that she hadn't known he possessed. Soon his hands began to explore without prompting. Hávi moaned and clung tightly, pulled him down, and drug him into paradise.

All too soon it was over, Hvítvi gasping, biting back cries that neither of them could scream. Hávi felt him fill her and replied in kind, cascading showers of relief and fulfillment throughout her every fiber. A rightness of the universe that she'd never experienced washed over her, but Hvítvi looked ashamed and quickly pushed free.

"We shouldn't have ...," Hvítvi said as he reached for his clothes.

"I expect frequent visits," Hávi said. "And don't forget the money for Hrafna's tavern; I feel a celebration coming."

"What if you get pregnant? How will we explain ...?"

"We'll say that Jarl Hafr raped me the night before he sailed."

"What if it's an albino?"

Hávi couldn't answer him, but she couldn't regret it, either; if it was an albino then she'd bear it proudly, glad that the farce was over. Hvítvi quickly dressed and departed in silence, his pink eyes staring accusatorily as he descended through the trapdoor. As pleasured as her body felt, Hávi lay in turmoil, naked upon her bed with Hvítvi's rich scent covering her.

She wondered if she'd ever see him again.

Chapter 34

Hávi whistled all the way to Hrafna's tavern. Bíldr, Völu, and Breiðr stared at her but asked no questions; Hávi had told no one, and suspected that Hvítvi would remain equally silent. Revelation of their tryst would destroy clan Austmaðr, but Hávi didn't care; two days had passed since Hávi, a woman married to one husband while nursing the child of another, had for the first time in her life willingly mated. Never had Hávi felt so happy.

Bíldr alone didn't look pleased; his lips, mostly hidden by his thick mustache, frowned as he walked silently, his hand on his sword-pommel to keep his scabbard from banging against his hip. Two older guards trailed at a respectful distance. As they approached Hrafna's tavern, Hávi determined to have a serious talk with Brækir and Blönduhorn; their animosity had lasted too long.

The white shell-paved road crunched beneath their feet as they strolled down the long hill from the castle into Skadi.

The blue sky promised a warm day as spring faded into a fragrant summer. Blossoms had sprouted all over, and in the distant fields, old men and the wives of those gone viking weeded and watered the newly-planted crops; harvest promised to be plentiful. Skadi looked as serene as always; mothers hurrying about dragging squalling children, the baker wheeling his cart, and kids, including Valla and Augi, running about laughing. As they approached the tavern, Valla and Augi stopped and bowed deeply to them. Hávi lightly curtsied.

"Hello, boys," Hávi said. "How are your lessons going?"

"We know everything," Augi said proudly.

"Better not let Gylðir hear that," Valla warned.

"I hear that Gylðir is very pleased, and so am I," Hávi said. "He says you're both quite on your way to being Law-speakers. Jarl Illingr would've been proud."

Both boys smiled and bowed again with amusing formality; they were learning well. Hávi, Völu, and Breiðr smiled at the boys, then they turned to enter the tavern.

Suddenly the sound of rapid hoofbeats approached, although no riders could be seen. Bíldr tensed and yanked out his sword; seldom did any ride fast through a busy city.

"Get inside Hrafna's! Hurry!" Bíldr shouted.

A group of riders thundered into view, charging out from between two buildings at a full gallop. Hávi gasped; all of the riders held drawn steel weapons.

"Valla! Augi! Run to the castle! Bring help! Run!" Bíldr shouted.

Terrified, both boys ran up the familiar white-paved road as the riders closed upon the others.

"Too many!" Bíldr shouted. *"Into Hrafna's! Now!"*

Grabbing Hávi's arm, Bíldr pulled her through the door

and barred it. The wooden brace fell into place only seconds before a harsh boot crashed upon it. The door shook; Hrafna paled and dropped the plate that he'd been carrying.

"*Upstairs!*" Bíldr shouted. "*Völu, take her!*"

Hávi didn't resist as Völu drug her and Breiðr to the ladder that led to the trapdoor in the ceiling, which flung open as half a dozen youthful faces, including Blönduhorn, looked down.

"*Climb!*" Völu shouted, and she pushed Hávi to go first.

More crashes shook the door as Bíldr and the guards pressed their shoulders to it. Hávi climbed almost to the top before Hrafna slammed the brace into the back door near his ale-barrels. Moments later, that door shook, too.

"*Get up there!*" Bíldr shouted. "*Bar every door!*"

Suddenly an axe bit through the wooden door. Hrafna cried out and Blönduhorn screamed.

"*Go!*" Bíldr shouted.

Hávi ascended into a wide, low-ceilinged attic filled with seven small children and Blönduhorn, who looked terrified. Both of them helped pull Breiðr and Völu up into the attic as the back door burst open. Many strange men burst into Hrafna's tavern before Völu slammed the trapdoor shut.

"*Put the wardrobe over it!*" Völu shouted.

Blönduhorn helped as the women dragged the heavy wardrobe over and toppled it onto the trapdoor with a huge crash. All of the children were screaming, but their cries couldn't overwhelm the many clashes of steel or a man's scream; Hávi's guards were fighting for their lives. Long moments passed while Hávi, Völu, and Blönduhorn stacked two beds on top of the wardrobe; Breiðr tried to quiet the terrified children, since her strength paled before the others'. Hrafna's voice cried out in pain.

"Uncle!" Blönduhorn shouted, but there was nothing that she could do.

Something hammered on the trapdoor and all of the children screamed louder.

"Hold it down!" Völu shouted, and she and Hávi fell onto the top-most bed, adding their weight to the pile. They screamed for Breiðr and Blönduhorn to join them, but both looked too scared to move.

The trapdoor hammered repeatedly, and then an axe chopped into it, but they could only hold it down and scream.

"Blönduhorn!" Hávi shouted. *"Are there any weapons up here?"*

Blönduhorn shook her head mutely while the little children's highest-pitches pierced their ears. Loud chops echoed through the tavern; soon they'd cut through. Strange voices shouted to hurry while the axe chopped. The sound of breaking wood resounded alarmingly; soon ripping cloth was followed by the axe chopping through the thin back of the wardrobe.

Suddenly new cries and clashes of steel filled the tumult. Angry shouts replied, followed by foul, shrill curses. The axe stopped chopping; Hávi and Völu exchanged wary glances. Long moments passed, but no clue arose, only more cries and deadly clangs.

"Mistress Austmaðr!" called a voice unexpectedly.

"Shut up!" Breiðr and Blönduhorn shouted at the children so fiercely that they froze, tears leaking down smooth, horrified faces. The sudden quiet was deafening.

"Who calls?" Hávi shouted.

"I'm a guard," the voice answered.

"Where's Bíldr?"

"Bíldr's dead."

An eternity later, Hávi knelt beside Bíldr; he wasn't dead, but he was close to it. Ignoring Hvítvi's orders, Hávi had refused to leave the tavern and ordered Master Kamban to be carried from the castle in a wagon; Felian had joined them minutes after the guards had arrived. Covered in blood, Hávi had dressed the wounds of all of the guards who'd rushed from Castle Austmaðr, including one man who'd lost his sword-hand. Never had Hávi recited healing chants so forcefully, so ardently, shouting to the gods until tears flowed from her eyes. Master Kamban had done all that he could for Bíldr and was concentrating on Hrafna; Völu comforted Blönduhorn as she held her bleeding uncle's hand. Like Bíldr, Hrafna had suffered many wounds, and both had been stabbed through the chest. Valla and Augi stood beside them. Both of the guards that Bíldr had led were dead. Five of Hávi's savage attackers were dead and all of their fellows wounded, but Hávi ignored their pleas for healing.

Hrafna's tavern looked like a battlefield; half of Skadi arrived to stare aghast at its blood-splattered walls. Many townsmen had helped subdue Hávi's attackers in the end; two attackers had died from arrows from the woodwright's bow.

Brækir arrived amid the chaos, hysterically pushing through the crowd.

"*Hrafna!*" Brækir cried, falling to her knees beside Blönduhorn.

Hrafna weakly opened his eyes.

"*G-g-g-good w-wife,*" Hrafna stammered, blood leaking from his mouth.

"Don't talk," Master Kamban ordered, pressing an herbal mixture to his worst wound. "Conserve your strength."

Hrafna ignored him, reached out and took Brækir's hand.

"*B-b-better w-wife than I ... d-d-deserve,*" Hrafna said, staring into his wife's frantic expression.

The effort proved too much; Hrafna's eyes closed and his head rolled forward onto his chest. A rattling sigh escaped Hrafna's lips.

Brækir and Blönduhorn burst out wailing.

"*Where's Hvítvi?*" Hávi demanded.

"That's none of your business," Mjóvi scowled. "If you weren't trolloping around Skadi like one of your husband's sluts ...!"

Hávi seized Mjóvi and lifted her off her feet in the center of the great hall before a crowd of shocked guards and servants. Furious, Hávi shook the old woman like a disobedient child.

"*Tell me where he is or I'll rip your arms off!*"

No one looked more shocked than Mjóvi, who hung helplessly in Hávi's strong grip, her feet dangling above the flagstones. Hávi glared at Mjóvi, and when no answer was forthcoming, Hávi set her back down and grabbed the old woman's thin arms with both of her hands as if she'd snap her fragile bones like kindling.

"*Hávi!*" Völu shouted. "*What if she doesn't know?*"

Völu grabbed Hávi's wrists and pulled them free from Mjóvi's arms; Hávi reluctantly released the old woman's frail limbs.

"*Next time,*" Hávi promised Mjóvi grimly.

With a prune-faced glare, Mjóvi stormed out of the great hall.

"Mistress?" an older guard spoke softly although his deep voice resonated across that hall. "Hvítvi is personally overseeing the questioning of your attackers."

"Where?"

"No one's allowed to know."

"Where?"

The guard hesitated, and then put a finger to his lips, motioning for silence. The whole room obeyed, not one person speaking or moving. In the sudden silence, a dim, shrill scream wafted through the castle, muted by its thick stone walls.

"Where's that coming from?" Hávi demanded.

The guard shook his head.

"Nowhere that you want to see, and my life's forfeit if I show you."

Hávi listened intently, trying to trace the faint sounds.

"Mother, no!" Breiðr whispered.

Only Völu followed as Hávi slowly walked down Castle Austmaðr's many hallways. Their footsteps drowned out the faint, agonized cries and they often paused to listen.

"Hávi, don't do this," Völu whispered. "There're some things that women shouldn't ...!"

Both stopped as footsteps approached; several of Jarl Hafr's sluts stepped out into the hallway, startled when they spied Hávi and Völu. Silently one of them gestured for the others to retreat.

"Wait!" Hávi ordered. "Who are you?"

All three stared apprehensively.

"Your names," Hávi demanded. "What are your names?"

"Berbeinn," one slut said, motioning to herself, then she pointed at the others. "Köttr. Mána."

"Go back to your rooms," Hávi said. "There's been another attack. Tell all of your ... sisters ... to arm themselves. No one's safe anymore."

All three of the sluts attempted a cursory curtsy and then fled back the way that they'd come. Völu watched them go, then stared quizzically at Hávi.

"Shut up," Hávi said. "You didn't see that."

Searching further, Hávi and Völu found that the muted screams came from a large room with many stacked beds built into its walls; a guardhouse inside the castle. Beside a thick carpet that had been rolled away was a small iron trapdoor in the center of its floor: screams and muted shouts reverberated through it.

"Hávi, you'll get in real trouble for this!" Völu warned.

The trapdoor was already unlatched. Hávi lifted the heavy iron plate and a noticeably loud scream came from the narrow steps beneath it. Hesitantly Hávi stepped down the long narrow stone stairs, almost a vertical ladder, into the coolness of a cave: this was the hidden dungeon of Castle Austmaðr, the prison where Jarl Illingr had died.

Hávi found a thick, wooden door blocking her way, but it was also unlocked. Hávi noticed Völu following her before she stepped into a cool, narrow, low-ceilinged, unlit hallway. The only glints of light shone around another closed door ahead. Hávi approached it cautiously; the screams echoed loudly in the hall.

Opening the door, Hávi saw a horrible sight: Hvítvi, Master Krókr, and five guards were standing around three naked men tightly-chained to the wall of a circular dungeon. Torches lit the room and one guard held a torch out before the naked prisoners, all of whom bore massive white blisters blackened by flames. Their groins shocked Hávi; all of their hair was burned away and their manhoods looked like charred sausages.

All faces turned toward them as the door creaked, most

faces horrified to see them, the prisoners looking up expectantly.

"*Get out of here!*" Hvítvi shouted angrily.

"*Disgrace!*" Master Krókr shouted.

"Which of these men killed Hrafna?" Hávi demanded. "Who harmed Bíldr, my friend?"

"*We'll deal with this!*" Hvítvi shouted. "*Get back ...!*"

Hávi pushed into the ghastly chamber, seeing several other doors with tiny grilled windows lining its curved walls. Master Krókr scowled and the shocked guards stood unmoving as Hávi walked up to the helpless prisoners.

"*Mercy!*" cried the prisoner closest to her, pulling at his adamant chains.

Nastily Hávi spat in his face, and then she held out her hand for the torch.

"*No!*" Hvítvi shouted. "*This is no place for women!*"

Hávi gave Hvítvi an angry glare, and then spat in the faces of the other two prisoners.

"I'll send for Master Kamban," Hávi said. "I don't want these ... *things* ... to die prematurely."

"*Go!*" Hvítvi ordered.

Hávi obediently walked out, taking Völu with her.

"You see?" Hvítvi said before she was gone. "Even our women enjoy your suffering. *Now talk!*"

Master Kamban refused to leave Bíldr.

"He's bad," Master Kamban said, replacing a blood-soaked bandage and tossing it onto a large pile of red, discarded cloths. "He may yet die."

"What can I do?" Hávi asked.

"I need more water," Master Kamban frowned. "Felian's been made a guard again."

"I'll get it," Völu offered, and she quickly left.

"You should be in your tower," Master Kamban said to Hávi. "These attackers might not have been alone. Are you armed?"

Hávi shook her head.

"Carry a knife from now on. Store some spears by your bed. Have your redhead and other women armed, too."

Hávi glanced around the tiny room; no windows. One wall held a large, discolored, copper plate; the wall's bricks were the chimney of a fireplace in a room below. A tall shelf stood covered in bowls, ceramic jars, and many, small wooden boxes, and a low, rickety bed pressed against one bare stone wall.

"Is this your room?" Hávi asked.

"When I don't have a patient in my bed."

"You don't have your own fireplace?"

"Few do. We need to roll him onto his side."

Hávi helped; Bíldr was unconscious and limp as a raw steak.

"Will he live?"

"I pray so," Master Kamban said. "Only the gods know; he's got a dozen lethal cuts."

"This is one of those times, isn't it? When a patient's belief in their healer ...?"

"Every time is one of those times."

Völu arrived with two buckets of fresh water while Hávi and Master Kamban attended Bíldr, praying so ardently that both cried real tears. Then Master Kamban gave Hávi a long, sharp dagger, ordered Völu to stay with Hávi and keep his door barred, and left them to enter the dungeon.

"It wasn't your fault," Hvítvi said. "It's mine; I never

should've let you leave the castle."

"You can't keep me locked ..."

"I must," Hvítvi said. "I can't risk another attack."

"I'm sorry about Bíldr. Master Kamban says ..."

"I get hourly reports ...!" Hvítvi interrupted. "Sorry; he's my best friend."

Hvítvi staggered, then sat down and pressed a hand to his paler-than-usual forehead.

"Are you alright?"

Hvítvi didn't reply. They were crowded into his private chamber with Völu, Master Krókr, and several guards.

"She should be locked in her tower to keep her from wandering," Master Krókr snarled, glaring at Hávi. "Or better yet: in her room ... where she belongs."

Hávi glanced at Castle Austmaðr's towering seneschal but kept her attention on Hvítvi; on the other side of the closed door was Hvítvi's hot-fog chamber, a sealed room backed by four hot fireplaces which was kept filled with steam, which Hvítvi needed when his sicknesses overwhelmed him.

"Hvítvi, is your head hurting?" Hávi asked.

"My head always hurts," Hvítvi said, "but I've no time ..."

"Here ..."

"No."

"I'm a healer!"

Master Krókr snorted with disgust, but Hávi lifted Hvítvi off his chair and set him onto the floor between her feet. Forcefully she began massaging Hvítvi's head as she'd learned to do caring for her grandmother, who was highly-allergic to cats. She rolled his soft, pale flesh beneath her strong fingers, pushed into his thick, milky-white hair and felt for the crevices of his skull where sinus pressures hid. Hvítvi writhed softly under her probing squeezes but he didn't resist. Hávi began to chant a healing charm.

> *"Mjollnir, let thy pounding cease,*
> *Hraesvelg, let your wings not beat,*
> *Loki's serpent, no acid fall,*
> *Let peace now reign over all."*

"This isn't helping," Master Krókr said.

"It's helping Hvítvi, and we need him most," Hávi said. "What did you learn from those men that attacked me?"

"Nothing that Mistress Austmaðr should know!" Master Krókr snapped.

"I'll find out anyway," Hávi assured him, and then she glanced at the worried guards. "After I'm done, Hvítvi should rest in steam for several hours."

The guards nodded uncomfortably under Master Krókr's disapproving glare.

Chapter 35

Felian spent twelve hours of every day guarding Castle Austmaðr, whose gates were closed and barred, and eight guards challenged every visitor who approached. Hávi cried over Hrafna; she wasn't allowed to attend Hrafna's funeral but sent Völu with a huge bouquet of flowers and a small bag containing a tiny gold ring, three silver coins, ten coppers, and Hávi's most-heartfelt condolences. Völu reported that Hvítvi had ordered the wood-cutters to give Hrafna a warrior's pyre as he'd died defending Hávi, and prayers to Odin named him Hrafna Einherjar, a rightful-warrior of Valhalla. Valla and Augi were appointed as guards and kept inside the castle, save for their father's funeral, although both Gylðir and Spaki were now teaching them the den Skaanske Lov every day, and both boys could recite many stanzas from memory. Hávi considered using them to continue her legal education, but she had to admit that now wasn't the time.

Castle Austmaðr became Hávi's prison; guards tromped in

pairs down every hallway day and night, even up the spiral steps to Hávi's chamber, where she'd yell at them to be quiet every time that she was awakened. The summer passed slowly, each day a repetition. Bíldr gradually recovered, but Hvítvi sickened and had to spend many hours in his hot-fog chamber attended by Master Kamban. Hávi suspected that Hvítvi's illness was due to stress; strange ships were reported sailing past Skadi and many suspected that they were Norwegians.

Hávi and Völu demonstrated to Breiðr and Bitra how to fight with knives, but they were pathetic. Still, Hávi insisted that they carry knives and she stored two bows and quivers of arrows in her tower along with two spears and a large scramsax. She and Völu could each shoot arrows from her high window over the castle wall, although neither were good shots. Their only attempt at aiming almost hit one of the guards defending the gate, and Master Krókr upbraided her before all of the cooks for nearly killing one of their much-needed protectors.

To everyone's amazement, Hávi asked all of the women to join her for supper in the great hall. It was Bíldr's first visit to the hall since he'd been wounded; he walked in very weakly, having only arisen for the first time the day before. Hávi entered the great hall on his arm, supporting him more than he was supporting her, and the entire great hall, crowded for the first time in weeks, rose to its feet and applauded; Bíldr was credited for saving Hávi's life in Skadi. Bíldr blushed but held his head high as Hávi escorted him to sit at the foremost table, and then she assumed her customary seat at the center of the high-table. All of the castle elders deferred to Hávi's presence; Hvítvi's chair was the only empty seat at the high-table. As she sat, Hávi raised her hand to gain everyone's attention, and the hall fell silent in anticipation.

"Gellir, will you arise and approach the high-table?"

Shocked gasps sucked in all of the air as every eye focused on the back table filled with Jarl Hafr's sluts. Short, round, black-haired Gellir rose slowly, fearfully, with eyes wide like a trapped fox. Many of the sluts urgently shook their heads, but Gellir hesitantly walked to stand before the high-table. Hávi stared imperiously down upon her. Slowly Hávi removed the wide gray scarf that she wore over her shoulders, wrapped tight about her throat. As the scarf was set aside, revealing her low neckline, all spied that between her bulging cleavage poked the short handle of a gem-studded dagger whose sheath dove between Hávi's tightly-pressed breasts.

"Gellir, can you fight ... with a knife?"

Murmurs erupted throughout the hall: *was Hávi challenging Gellir to a knife-fight?* Gellir paled and stared at Hávi's deadly dagger; *to win this fight she'd have to kill Mistress Austmaðr.*

"I don't like you, Gellir, or any of your sisters," Hávi said. "I didn't approve of your coming, I don't approve of you being here, and I don't like what you do. I know that none of you chose your profession, but I can't overlook its practice. But both assassination attempts weren't to kill me but to kill clan Austmaðr; if we continue to squabble amongst ourselves then our enemies will surely prevail. Our men are strong and valiant, but I and my ladies now carry daggers everywhere we go; I want every woman in Castle Austmaðr to carry or keep a knife close beside her at all times. Many castle women are unskilled with weapons; I would that those who can fight be prepared to defend those who can't. I ask again: *can you fight with a knife?*"

Short and round, Gellir stood below the high-table, but

suddenly she seemed to grow, to rise as Hávi's words penetrated her fears. Before the crowded hall Gellir hesitated, and then she suddenly bowed deeply to Hávi.

"You are Mistress Austmaðr," Gellir said loudly, her powerful voice carrying to every corner. *"Your wishes are our commands."*

Gellir walked proudly back to the slut's table as Hávi ordered the servants to begin serving. No one applauded this request or the truce that it implied, but whispers filled the hall like hissing snakes. Hávi began eating at once, trying to put the moment behind her. She chanced a glance at the women's table; even Völu looked shocked. Only Hvassi, dining at the women's table at Hávi's request, smiled and nodded approvingly.

The next day, Bíldr had two guards carry a chest of rusty daggers from the armory down to the great hall. Many were very old with broken handles or notched, corroded blades, but soon every woman wore a small dagger at her belt, under her skirt, or matching Hávi: poking up out of ample cleavage. Hávi expected harsh criticisms, but none came; Master Krókr held his tongue and contented himself to disapproving frowns since even Mjóvi carried a tiny silver dagger.

Bíldr reported that Hávi's would-be assassins had been hired by a local beggar who'd disappeared right after the attack; the blackguard had paid them well and promised them more gold; someone wealthy had been financing him. Hávi had expected no less. Bíldr refused to let Hávi see Hvítvi, claiming that he was resting in his private-room. Master Kamban confirmed this, explaining that Hvítvi was healthier than usual, just not up for visitors. She hoped that Hvítvi wasn't sick, just hiding from her. Then a summons came from Felian that Master Kamban needed her: *Hvítvi was very ill.*

Hávi ascended the stone steps at a run which even Völu, now obviously pregnant, couldn't match. The open doorway to Jarl Hafr's chambers held four sluts staring at the commotion in the hall: several guards, a few elders, and Master Krókr stood at the top of the stairs. The blaze in the hallway fireplace was crackling and spitting; not a good sign. Felian pulled Hávi past them all into Hvítvi's rooms.

Master Kamban patiently sat in the foyer of Hvítvi's room.

"Thank you for coming," Master Kamban said to Hávi. "Felian, go out to the herb garden and fetch three sprigs of mint and rosemary, even if they're not fully-bloomed."

"Yes, Master," Felian said, and he departed at once.

Confused, Hávi stood uncertainly; Master Kamban never dared risk being caught alone with her ... and he looked unexpectedly calm.

"Hávi, be discreet," Master Kamban said, and he gestured to the hot-fog room.

Worriedly Hávi opened the door; the latch hissed and steam puffed in all directions. Hávi instantly broke out in a sweat as she entered the strange, hot world of moist white. Swirling thick mists hid everything; somewhere in here, probably on the wide bench, writhing in agonized helplessness, was Hvítvi. She feared that he was dying; he wouldn't summon her for anything less. Hávi pushed into the fog and found the bench, but it was empty.

"Thank you for coming," Hvítvi's voice spoke.

Hávi spun around; wearing a snow-white tunic, Hvítvi looked like a ghost, almost invisible in the fog.

"I thought that you were sick!"

"Two days ago I was," Hvítvi smiled. "One of the few

advantages of being sickly is that you can recover quickly when you're used to it."

"The whole castle thinks you're at Death's door!"

"It was the only way that I could see you."

Hávi startled; Hvítvi had arranged another deception ... *for her.*

"I can't ... stop thinking about you," Hvítvi said. "About ... what happened ... in your tower."

"Oh?" Hávi replied uncertainly. "Are you angry ... or ...?"

"Or," Hvítvi assured her.

"What did you want to talk about?"

"Actually, I didn't want to talk."

Hvítvi took Hávi's hands and lifted them to his head. Guiding her hands, he slid her fingers into his hair, and then their lips met. Forcefully, desperately Hvítvi kissed Hávi. Thoughts swirled like the thick mists; Master Krókr and half of Castle Austmaðr stood in the hallway outside, having watched her enter. If anyone found them entwined then they'd both be slain, and clan Austmaðr would be broken and scattered by morning. When she'd met him, Hvítvi was Hávi's stepson, and now his uncle was his stepfather, Hávi's husband; he was her nephew. But desires overwhelmed her reason; Hávi pushed Hvítvi back only long enough to fling her dress off her shoulders.

The heat of the mists paled like Hvítvi's skin in the milky cloud. Ecstasy met their merging and repeated throughout; Hávi and Hvítvi struggled to restrain their groans, glad that the four loudly-crackling fireplaces surrounding them hid most of their noise. Soaking wet on the long bench, Hávi's mind reeled in a fog thicker than its moisture, her delight dampened only by fear of what one rumor of their passion would destroy.

Afterwards, Hvítvi fetched thick, dry towels and Hávi wrung out her damp dress as best she could.

"You need to look like you've been healing me," Hvítvi said. "Tell everyone that I'm finally asleep and that I look much better. Tomorrow I'll make a brief appearance looking haggard; I'm well-practiced at that. Your healing skills will be credited ..."

"Master Kamban knows about us?" Hávi surmised.

"We have no secrets," Hvítvi smiled grimly. "Our lives depend on each other."

"When will we ...?"

"I don't know when, but we'll be together again: I promise."

They kissed tenderly before she left.

"Why are you smiling so much?" Völu demanded.

Hávi startled from a reverie that she shouldn't be having ... not while others were watching.

"She's been like that for days," Breiðr said.

"Why shouldn't she?" Bitra asked. "Master Kamban himself couldn't heal Hvítvi; one hour with Hávi and he's up and around the next day."

"I was scared to death," Hávi lied. "I thought that he was going to die."

"He must've been very ill," Breiðr said.

Völu gave Hávi a deep-brow glare and pursed her lips.

Völu's belly swelled as summer deepened, and Master Kamban frequently attended her, feeling her bulge and giving her special herbs. Hávi was jealous; her pregnancy had been a nightmare of morning sickness and foods that she couldn't eat, but Völu never once showed any sign of pregnancy other than her growing stomach. Soon Völu was huge and Master Kamban announced that the birthing would come soon. Her water broke in Hávi's tower and Hávi carried her downstairs; at sunset, Völu bore a beautiful daughter with bright red hair. Völu named her Rauðrefr, which means *'little red fox'*, and all of the women delighted and fawned over the tiny infant girl. Hávi had never been more proud of Völu.

Rauðrefr was placed in Jorgen's crib, since Jorgen was now crawling and had explored every crevice of Hávi's tower. He hadn't walked yet, but Breiðr kept expecting it; they had to keep the trapdoor closed to keep Jorgen from falling through it. Hávi and the other women had begun taking Jorgen to the nursery every day, and his stepsisters delighted to play with their little brother.

Only a week after Rauðrefr was born, sooner than expected, wondrous news reached the castle; the viking had returned early; from the high windows, many faces spied their mighty dragonships sailing into Skadi's harbor. Hvítvi chose an honor guard to accompany him and many castle-folk into Skadi, but he insisted that Hávi remain protected inside the castle. Hávi felt excluded but had no desire for a public reunion with Jarl Hafr.

"Damn Jarl Dúfunef!" Jarl Hafr shouted as he walked into the great hall between Hvítvi and Master Krókr.

Loud squeals of joy contrasted with his curse as a dozen sluts ran forward and insufferable minutes of hugging and kissing and *'welcome homes'* ensued. Irritated, Hávi sat centermost at the high-table, half of the castle-folk seated on benches, the kitchen servants ready to serve the end-of-viking feast. But kisses didn't lighten Jarl Hafr's mood; his sluts drew back alarmed as he stormed past them snarling and muttering garbled oaths. Hvítvi and Master Krókr followed; all three walked past the high-table without a word or glance. Hávi stared perplexed and concerned: *something hadn't gone right.*

Suddenly Knarrarbringa pushed through the crowd, knocking people aside with her vast bulk, tears wringing from a face flushed with misery. Several elders complained, but to no avail as Knarrarbringa shoved past them and ran out of the great hall. Then Mela ran inside through the main doors, scanning the crowd as Knarrarbringa vanished through a side door. Mela ran up to the high-table, glancing in every direction.

"Where did she ...?"

"Your sister ran that way," Hávi directed her. "She looked upset ..."

"Her ... one of Father's guards ... *Svarfaðr didn't make it!"* Mela hurriedly explained. *"He died!* Mistress Hávi, you're a healer; *you have to help her!"*

"Help ...?"

"Knarrarbringa's pregnant!"

By the time that Hávi pushed past the elders and descended from the dais, Mela had vanished. They shared a small room opposite Hvítvi's on the top floor, but it was empty, and Hávi couldn't find them anywhere. She tried to search, but Völu, cradling Rauðrefr, refused to allow it; she wasn't supposed to wander without Bíldr, and he was still too weak to chase after them. Hávi ordered some servants to look for either daughter, but Mela and Knarrarbringa had disappeared.

Jarl Hafr appeared for his return-home feast sometime after sunset and sat in his chair, but he said nothing. Hvítvi and Jarl Hafr's sons sat beside him, but not one word passed between them. Hávi only once caught Hvítvi's eye; he glared at her warningly, almost-imperceptively shook his head, and then he stared at his untouched food.

"Nothing went right," Bifru said, carefully holding Rauðrefr in his arms, sitting on the bed in Hávi's tower as Völu smiled upon him and their new daughter. "Jarl Hafr wouldn't listen to Jarl Dúfunef or Jarl Hersir. Every raid had to be his way ... and several were utter disasters. Every night the clan-chief's argued, and every day we lost more men. That's why we're back early; Jarl Dúfunef and Hersir threatened to abandon him off the coast of Germany."

Breiðr and Bitra stood, watching the joyful couple, but frowning at the melancholy news.

"What of plunder?" Hávi asked.

"Very little, and they squabbled over every coin," Bifru said. "I've never seen the men so dispirited. We lost five ships, two from clan Dúfunef. If only Auðgi had lived! He knew how to keep alliances."

"*Alliances?*" Breiðr asked.

"Sweden's falling apart, fractured by feuds. Clan Austmaðr defends our coasts; without us, there'd be civil war. None of the jarls like Jarl Hafr; he's a pale shadow of his brother. If something doesn't happen soon, we're all doomed."

"Hold still, Knarrarbringa," Hávi said.

Master Kamban's hand probed her belly. Knarrarbringa startled and recoiled from the hunchback's intrusive touch, but Mela held her tightly. Knarrarbringa's eyes were wet and red.

"Here," Master Kamban said to Hávi. "Touch here."

Hávi stepped forward; Knarrarbringa seemed less frightened by her touch as she pressed her fingers into Knarrarbringa's wide abdomen, feeling for anything unfamiliar. Then she touched the same solid shape that Jorgen had been.

"It's big," Hávi said.

"Nearly six months, I'd say," Master Kamban said.

"Six months?" Mela exclaimed.

"Women of girth can conceal a pregnancy longer," Master Kamban said.

"Wh-what am I ... going to do now?" Knarrarbringa asked.

"Jorgen was born after his father's death," Hávi said. "You'll do as I did ... with all of our help."

"But ..."

"You're my stepdaughter, Breiðr's sister, and your child will be an Austmaðr," Hávi said firmly, emphasizing each word. "You're family. We'll help."

Knarrarbringa burst into tears and Hávi hugged her, and then pulled Mela into a three-way embrace.

"Thank you, Mistress Hávi," Mela said.

"Mother," Hávi corrected.

"You and your baby appear to be very healthy," Master Kamban decreed. "I'll have the kitchen prepare you my special tea."

"Is ... isn't there a charm ... to insure a son?" Knarrarbringa asked.

"Hávi will teach it to you," Master Kamban said.

> *Nettles prick and tulip's stem,*
> *Roses' thorns the manhood gem,*
> *Frigg, let my battle be won,*
> *Odin's wife, grant me a son.*

Hávi recited the chant until Knarrarbringa was mumbling along with her, and then promised that she'd help her speak it every day. They left both girls in their chamber and Hávi walked beside Master Kamban as he slowly *'thumped'* down the stone stairs on his crutch and game leg.

"She's young and well-built," Master Kamban said. "She'll be fine."

"She's been able to conceal it; no small feat," Hávi said.

"I'm concerned about my herb supply," Master Kamban said.

"I could harvest ..."

"Not all of my herbs grow in Sweden," Master Kamban said. "Some of my more-exotic medicines come from France; they only grow in hot climates. They have to be bought from merchants ... and they're not cheap."

"Surely we can afford ..."

"Master Krókr says that we can't," Master Kamban said. "Some are for Hvítvi."

"I'll tell him."

"He knows."

"Hvítvi wouldn't refuse ..."

"He already has."

"I'll talk to him."

"Please do."

Hávi had never realized how difficult stairs were for Master Kamban; it took them nearly ten minutes to descend two flights. At the bottom of the stairs, Hávi thanked Master Kamban again and sent him to rest. Silently she determined to bring his patients to him, if possible; one misstep from the top stair and she'd lose her beloved teacher.

The next day, Bíldr appeared, half-carried by Felian, up

the spiral stairs to Hávi's tower. Bitra opened the trapdoor
for them; Breiðr and Völu were elsewhere with their
husbands. Hávi welcomed him and had Felian set Bíldr on
her bed to rest while Hávi sat beside Bitra. Bíldr paused to
catch his breath; Hávi's stairs were still a challenge for him
although he was growing stronger.

"Mistress, Hvítvi has ordered me ... to instruct you to
pack," Bíldr said. "We may not ... need to move you, but ..."

"Move?" Hávi asked. "Where?"

"He's not sure," Bíldr said. "To clan Hersir, if Jarl Hersir
... will allow it."

"He won't," Hávi said. "Why?"

"The viking was a disaster," Bíldr explained. "Jarl Hafr's
convinced ... that Jarl Hersir and Jarl Dúfunef spoiled the
viking ... to ruin him. If hostilities break out ..."

"War against Hersir and Dúfunef ...?!?"

"It's madness, but no matter who wins, you'll lose," Bíldr
said to Hávi. "Just be ready: if Hvítvi commands it, then you
and Völu may have to flee for your lives."

"Hávi can't leave the castle!" Bitra argued. *"There's been
two attempts on her life already!"*

"If things get any worse, life inside Castle Austmaðr may
be more dangerous than outside of it ... for all of us."

The next day, a servant arrived to summon Hávi to Jarl
Hafr's bedroom. Accompanied by Völu, Hávi ascended the
stone steps and entered her old outer-room, which was greatly
changed since she'd last slept on its hearth during her ill-fated
second wedding night. Gone were the table and shelves
littered with maps and scrolls and the crossed swords and axes
that decorated its walls; Hávi's outer-room was draped with
bright linens and crowded with three new wardrobes, two

wide beds, four cribs, and the cries of squalling infants. Jarl Hafr's sluts sat upon their beds and all of them stared apprehensively at Hávi as she re-entered the rooms that were rightfully hers. Hávi ignored the pregnant appearance of three of the sluts, who hid their faces and looked ashamed. Even Gellir looked worried as she and Hávi exchanged glances, and then Jarl Hafr's voice boomed from his bedroom.

"Hávi!"

Hávi's old bedroom also looked crowded, stuffed with two new wardrobes and the table from the outer-room. Jarl Hafr stood glaring at Hávi as she entered. Hvítvi and Master Krókr stood beside the windows, Bíldr almost hidden between the wardrobes, leaning back against one of the locked treasury doors. The familiar huge fireplace and bed with its four horse-head posts looked the same, save that four pillows lay across its head and another four pillows lined its foot; *did her husband sleep with all of his sluts at once?* But Hávi's attention focused on the bed where her sobbing stepdaughter Knarrarbringa sat.

"What's the meaning of this?" Jarl Hafr demanded. *"I expected you to keep my daughters protected!"*

Hávi took a deep breath and reined in her disgust and relief; *she wasn't the one in trouble.*

"Master Kamban examined her," Hávi said. "She's six months pregnant; she was carrying her child the first day that she entered Castle Austmaðr."

"Is this true?" Jarl Hafr shouted angrily at Knarrarbringa.

Sympathy filled Hávi as Knarrarbringa's sobs turned to wails under her father's derisions. Hávi stepped forward and took Knarrarbringa's hand.

"Come with me, child," Hávi said. "We'll take care ..."

"And now her husband's dead?" Jarl Hafr continued to shout. *"We need to marry her off! But who'll want her?"*

"This isn't the time ...," Hávi started.

"I decide what time it is!" Jarl Hafr bellowed.

Hávi glared at her worthless husband.

"The other jarls won't have her, not bearing another man's son," Hávi said. "But there are some here in Castle Austmaðr whose loyalty has been proven countless times through years of unwavering service. Marriage to a daughter of Jarl Hafr ..."

"I'm Jarl Austmaðr!"

"Marriage to a daughter of Jarl Austmaðr would be a great elevation worthy of their service, ennobling them as family of the Skåne's ruling clan."

"Who?" Jarl Hafr demanded.

"I can think of several," Hávi said. "Let me talk to Knarrarbringa alone; we may be able to settle this quickly."

Pulled by Hávi, Knarrarbringa feebly rose from the bed and limped, tear-faced, across the new carpet which had replaced the rug stained by Tryggvi's blood. But, as she escorted Knarrarbringa, Hávi gave a stern, knowing glance to Bíldr, who paled and looked as if his slowly-mending wounds had dehisced.

Knarrarbringa and Mela spent several evenings in Hávi's tower. At Hávi's request, a funeral bonfire was built on the sands before the harbor, and all of Skadi attended, honoring all of those lost in foreign lands. Under heavy guard, Hávi was allowed to attend, but she remained silent as many came forward to speak of the men that she'd never know, including Svarfaðr, Knarrarbringa's dead lover, whom Jarl Hafr reluctantly spoke well of at Hvítvi's insistent prompting.

One evening, much to Knarrarbringa's surprise, Bíldr was sitting in Hávi's tower when she and Mela arrived. Bíldr jumped to stand and grunted from the exertion.

"Welcome," Hávi said. "Knarrarbringa, Mela, I believe that you know Bíldr, Hvítvi's best friend, confidant, and my personal guard."

Bíldr blushed as Knarrarbringa and Mela worriedly curtsied, and Völu and Bitra offered them their seats on the extra bed.

"Bitra, could you fetch some more wine for my guests?" Hávi asked. "Völu ...?"

"I'll help," Völu offered, and she and Bitra vanished through the trapdoor.

Knarrarbringa, Mela, and Bíldr exchanged nervous glances as Hávi lifted Jorgen, who'd been making an ardent dash toward the trapdoor, into her lap. She sat back and held her son comfortably.

"Knarrarbringa, you never told me of your previous home," Hávi prompted. "Where did you live?"

"Castle örn," Knarrarbringa said hesitantly.

"It's not as big as Castle Austmaðr, just a wide tower defending the town of Nidgi," Mela quickly added. "But it's nice; nestled beside a big lake."

"Do you know of Castle örn?" Hávi asked Bíldr.

"Been there once ... many years ago," Bíldr said reluctantly, clearing his throat and brushing his thick moustache with his fingers. "I had an uncle ... lived in Nidgi; he's ... long gone."

"How interesting!" Hávi exclaimed with exaggerated exuberance. "You must tell me all about it."

Bitra and Völu never returned. At Hávi's insistence, Bíldr and Knarrarbringa described fishing on the lake and roaming through Nidgi. Both swore that they'd never seen each other before although Hávi doubted it; both blushed bright pink under her many questions. Bíldr tried to insist that Hvítvi must need him, but Hávi assured him that Hvítvi would send for him and that he couldn't deny her guests the pleasure of his company. Mela spoke very rarely; several times Hávi caught her eye and nodded approvingly. Mela seemed content to sit quietly and look comfortable.

A week later, at the stroke of noon, the great hall rang with cheers.

"Do you, Bíldr Ulfson, take Knarrarbringa Austmaðr as your wedded wife?"

Hvítvi looked less pale than usual, but Jarl Hafr looked red-faced, torn between relief and anger.

"Waste of a daughter!" Jarl Hafr muttered under his breath, but only Hávi stood close enough to hear it.

"I do," Bíldr vowed loudly.

"Do you vow loyalty and faithfulness to this woman alone, defense of your house, and support for her and all of your family?"

Bíldr vowed ardently.

Hávi came forward holding out a living circlet of tulips and daffodils woven amid willow leaves and bound by fresh ivy, slender vines with budding leaves that encircled each flower's long stem. Hvítvi took the circlet and held it up before everyone, and then lowered it onto Knarrarbringa's head, crowing her like a queen; Knarrarbringa blushed scarlet.

Hvítvi recited the ancient words, a tongue so old that few could translate it. Hávi caught the old names of the gods, Wotan instead of Odin, Fræj instead of Freyja, but she paid scant attention to the rest, focused only on the newlyweds.

Upon request, Skytja sprinkled sand into their hair while Hvítvi kept speaking, and then Breiðr slowly circled them, brushing them with boughs of pine and spruce, blessing their love to remain evergreen. Hvítvi dipped his fingers into a bowl and flicked sprinkles of water at the bride and groom.

After his vows were spoken, Rauðkinn carried the broom forward and set it at their feet. Bíldr and Knarrarbringa took hands amid the expectant silence and jumped high; Hávi wondered how Knarrarbringa could jump so strongly while six months pregnant.

Cheers deafened them all; the great hall cascaded in one joyous noise. Servants ran to fill raised horns while Bíldr shook hands with Jarl Hafr, who never once smiled. Then everyone rushed forward to shake hands with Bíldr. Hávi hugged Knarrarbringa, and then Mela, who stood beside her sister holding a huge bouquet of bright daffodils and colorful carnations.

After signaling the crowd for silence, Hvítvi spoke loudly.

"Finally I welcome my best friend to the family Austmaðr as my true step-brother, legal and recognized. Welcome, brother Bíldr!"

While many cheered, Jarl Hafr scowled and Skytja and Rauðkinn fidgeted restlessly, as did several of Jarl Hafr's many younger sons, bastards born of his sluts: young Körtr, who was very short and had long blonde hair, Víga, who looked unusually angry for a ten-year-old, Jóturn, who was very large for being only six, strawberry-haired Stjarna, and tiny, wide-eyed Fagri, who was too young to know what was happening. Lafskegg, Holta, and Mág cried; all three were babes still held in the arms of their slut-mothers.

Hávi's many stepdaughters watched from the other side, smiling but not gleeful. Standing beside the stepdaughters from Hávi's first marriage, Breiðr, Fróði, Auða, Grái, and Hrogn, all of Knarrarbringa and Mela's stepsisters attended: Inn Bareyska, Eyverska, Inn Flamska, and two babies named Urd and Spörr. Bíldr and Knarrarbringa's joyous wedding was the first gathering of all of Hávi's kin in clan Austmaðr. Bíldr seemed happy; he and Knarrarbringa had gotten to know each other under Hávi's insistent supervision. While they as yet shared no love, both were content with the arrangement; Knarrarbringa's child would have a worthy father and Bíldr became Hávi's family. Hávi smiled; her family had become large and strong, swelling with the promise that somehow all would end up well.

At midnight, during Bíldr and Knarrarbringa's glorious wedding night, Loki himself sailed into Skadi.

Chapter 36

Screams in the night suddenly erupted from the distant moonlit city. Shouts arose unexpectedly, dim but long, echoing from the dark shoreline. Distant crashes of axes upon doors and the violent clangs of swords awakened everyone with a window; Hávi sprung to her tower window and threw open its shutters.

"What is it?" Bitra cried.

"Ships!" Hávi said, looking eastward at the starlight reflecting off many tall masts. *"The harbor's filled with dragonships!"*

"Dúfunef?" Bitra asked. "Hersir?"

"I don't think so," Hávi said as a woman's scream pierced the twilight. "I think it's ... *invaders!*"

Carrying Jorgen in her arms, Hávi and Bitra hurried down the spiral steps to find frightened guards running through the castle. Many wore hastily-donned mail and were still buckling on belts, struggling not to drop armloads of weapons.

"What is it?" Hávi demanded.

"Norwegians!" a guard shouted.

"Defend the walls with every man that we have!" Jarl Hafr shouted as several guards strapped a thick coat of leather plates with heavy bronze scales onto him, barely evading the deadly, naked sword that Jarl Hafr was waving about.

Hávi and Bitra slipped into the great hall, trying to keep from getting run over.

"Back to your tower!" Jarl Hafr shouted at them. *"Fighting's men's work!"*

Hvítvi stood on a table shouting orders at the guards; he glanced at Hávi but ignored her; giving orders that he didn't have time to enforce was pointless. The guards obeyed Hvítvi instantly without question; *what a great Jarl Austmaðr Hvítvi would've made!* But Hávi had to admit that there was nothing that she could do; her presence at the wall would only worsen their defense. All of Sweden was weak, and Castle Austmaðr was the key to the Skåne; if they lost, then Sweden lost.

Hávi and Bitra went back to their tower, but Hávi made Bitra hold Jorgen while she fetched their packed bags of clothes, and then they sat anxiously on the lowest steps; if Hvítvi wanted her then this was where he'd come for her, and Hávi intended to be waiting for him. But the crashes and shouts of battle horrified her; thunder reverberated from the Norwegians battering their gates, fighting to get inside.

Impatiently Hávi ran upstairs just to glance out of her window; Castle Austmaðr's gates were crowded with hundreds of savage strangers with spears and torches, forcing their way forward under huge round shields. Hávi grabbed one of the bows that she and Völu had stashed there and shot an arrow into the darkness; she couldn't tell if she wounded anyone, but she felt certain that her arrow landed outside of the gate. Arrow after arrow Hávi fired into the press of bodies and shields that pushed forward as they fought to scale the sharp-pointed fence that Hávi had thought impenetrable and trampled across those unlucky fools who'd impaled themselves upon the deadly stakes hidden in the ditch before their barricade. Many attackers hammered at the gates, against which the Austmaðr guards pressed from the inside, fighting to keep its stout wooden braces from breaking. Hávi kept shooting arrows into the frenzied press.

Moonlight and torches illuminated the scene; the invaders outside the gate easily outnumbered the protectors defending Castle Austmaðr. *If they broke into the castle then no one would escape!*

Firing her last arrow, Hávi grabbed her largest dagger, stashed it in her skirt's drawstring, and flew back down the spiral stairs. Just as Hávi reached the foot of the stairs, Hvítvi came running up.

"Hávi, come!" Hvítvi shouted. *"Bring Jorgen!"*

Hávi and Bitra started forward, but Hvítvi stopped them.

"Bitra, give Jorgen to Hávi," Hvítvi shouted. "Go back up to Hávi's room and wait for her to join you."

Both Hávi and Bitra froze at this command; *Hvítvi was ordering her to her death.*

"Hávi, take Jorgen and follow me!" Hvítvi shouted. *"No time for arguments!"*

Hávi took Jorgen, but ordered:

"Stay right behind me, Bitra!"

Carrying Jorgen, Hávi ran behind Hvítvi, frequently glancing back to make sure that aged Bitra was only a step behind. She kept scanning the hallways for Völu, but couldn't see her and couldn't waste time searching; Jorgen's life depended on her following Hvítvi.

Hvítvi led her out of the back door near the outer barracks that Tryggvi had shown her on her first morning in Castle Austmaðr. Across the wide grounds, next to a small, open door in the back of the palisade, a dozen horses awaited. Atop the horses sat Jarl Hafr, Skytja and Rauðkinn, Bíldr, and several other important men of Castle Austmaðr. Hvítvi reached his horse and mounted; only one empty horse remained.

"What's she doing here?" Jarl Hafr demanded.

"Hávi, mount up!" Hvítvi shouted. "Bitra, I'm sorry but we can't take you."

"She can ride behind me ...!" Hávi said.

"Your horse won't last!" Hvítvi argued. "It's three days ride to clan Dúfunef or Hersir; we'll come back in six days."

"Six days?!?" Hávi exclaimed.

Suddenly a cry came behind them; out of the door from which they'd exited Master Kamban came hobbling, struggling to hurry on his crutch and game leg. As the crippled hunchback tried to catch up, all of them watched him stumble and fall down the short steps.

Hávi screamed, dropped her clothes bag, and then forced Jorgen into Hvítvi's arms. While several men shouted at her, Hávi ran back to the castle and grabbed her mentor's arm, pulling hard to assist him to his feet. Master Kamban couldn't survive without them and Hvítvi couldn't survive without him; *they couldn't leave him behind!*

As she struggled to raise him, suddenly a loud crash was followed by a chorus of victorious cries. Hávi righted Master Kamban just as a hundred savage Norwegians charged around the corner of their castle, many chasing the few fleeing Austmaðr guards that had survived the destruction of the gate.

Hávi tried to run but they swarmed between her and the horses: *Hvítvi was cut off.*

"Go!" Hávi shouted as she saw terror whiten Hvítvi's pale face. *"Get Jorgen to safety!"*

Hvítvi started to ride right through the press of Norwegians dividing them, but Bíldr seized his reins and pulled him away; *he'd never make it and Jorgen would be killed.* With no alternative, all of the riders turned and galloped their mounts out the palisade door and away from Castle Austmaðr. Helplessly Hávi watched as Hvítvi and Jorgen, her lover and her son, rode off and left her behind.

Several Norwegians attacked them, startled by the appearance of a hunchback and a woman in the dark chaos of a starlit fight.

"Swedish monster!" one of their attackers shouted, and he charged Master Kamban.

"No!" Hávi cried. *"He's a healer!"*

A heavy, round shield knocked Hávi aside as the man who'd shouted ran a sword through Master Kamban's chest. Master Kamban cried out and staggered back, then fell limply onto his hump. Hávi screamed and tried to reach him, but many hands grabbed her, mostly on her arms, but several clutching her breasts.

"Enough of that!" the man who'd stabbed Master Kamban shouted. *"Slaves into the great hall until all of the defenders are slain. Hurry!"*

Hávi pulled her right arm free and dug into her skirt-band to reach her dagger. With a savage cry as feral as any beast, Hávi lunged forward and drove her blade to the hilt into the chest of Master Kamban's murderer. His Norwegian death-cry mingled with shouts from every man, and then something struck Hávi hard across the back of her head.

Sobs awakened Hávi, whose throbbing head tortured her. Völu was holding Hávi with one arm and Rauðrefr with her other, Breiðr and Bitra pressed close against them both.

"J-Jorgen?" Hávi asked.

"Jorgen escaped," Bitra said. "Hvítvi took him."

"*You should've gone with them!*" Völu scolded as Hávi sat up.

Hávi felt the back of her head; a lump the size of her fist protruded from her skull; her lightest touch upon it was excruciating. Her hair was soaked from the wet rag that someone had been holding against her. She was lying on top of a lower table in the great hall, which was filled with countless frightened women: wives and daughters from Skadi, castle elders and servants, and Jarl Hafr's sluts. Only a few of the oldest, frailest men of clan Austmaðr were visible, but strange, fur-clad warriors guarded every door in the great hall; the women were penned in, trapped: *captured.*

Hávi glanced around; Gellir looked terrified, with most of her sisters clinging to her. Mjóvi stood centermost of the castle elders. Most of the women of Skadi were clustered in the center between the two groups. Only Brækir, Blönduhorn, and their small children stood alone.

"What's happened?" Hávi asked.

"Clan Austmaðr's ended," Breiðr sobbed. "All of our men are dead ... or fled. We're all that's left."

Hávi scanned the great hall. All of the women were crying as harshly as her head was pounding. Hávi's spirit crushed; Master Kamban had only been one among the many who'd fallen. Shaking her head, Hávi forced herself to stand.

"We're ... not through yet ...," Hávi said. "As long as we're alive, we've ..."

"You!" Mjóvi screeched so loudly that every eye turned toward her. Mjóvi pushed back several elderly women surrounding her and charged forward. *"You did this! You've weakened Austmaðr again and again ... and finally killed it!"*

"Be silent, you old crone!" Hávi shouted. "You've done more to weaken clan Austmaðr than I! But now we have to take care of ..."

"Hold your lies!" Mjóvi shouted. *"You're the worst thing that's ever happened to Sweden!"*

"That's not what your husband said!" Hávi shouted, and several women gasped at the insult.

"Was that while you were sleeping with him?" Mjóvi challenged.

"No one was sleeping with him ... especially not his barren bitch!"

Mjóvi glared murderously. Hávi took a deep, controlling breath, fighting for patience while flashes of agony tortured her head.

"All of our men are gone, and until they return ...," Hávi said.

"You lead nothing!" Mjóvi spat.

"I'm Mistress Austmaðr!" Hávi shouted at her. *"I'm the wife of Jarl Austmaðr and mother of the heir apparent ...!"*

"Not anymore!" Mjóvi snapped. *"There's no more Austmaðr, thanks to you, and as for that bastard brat of yours, he won't live a day if he returns to Castle Austmaðr! I'll kill him myself!"*

"That's treason!"

"The only treason was bringing a Hersir to live among decent Austmaðrs!"

Völu started forward, but Hávi pushed her back, then glared at Mjóvi with blackest hate darkening her eyes.

Hesitating only a moment, Hávi walked away from Mjóvi. Behind her, Mjóvi stood defiant, glaring at her retreating foe, but Hávi didn't exit; Hávi walked to the nearest fireplace, reached down, and picked up a small axe.

"No one threatens my son!" Hávi snarled, and she lifted the axe menacingly.

Breiðr tried to intervene, but Völu held her back. Mjóvi stood insolently glaring until Hávi stepped close, and then she backed away cautiously.

"You wouldn't dare!" Mjóvi challenged.

"Lying bitch!" Hávi accused with grim determination. *"You've done everything that you could to destabilize clan Austmaðr! Now you threaten the life of my son before every woman here! With all of our men gone, I rule clan Austmaðr, and if I do anything before we're all killed, I'm going to rid clan Austmaðr of you!"*

Hávi raised her ax and strode forward, her long legs chasing Mjóvi step by step as she backed away. Women gasped and their guards shouted warnings but, focused on her prey, Hávi ignored them all.

"Bitch!" Mjóvi shouted. *"Mad-woman! Usurper! Traitor!"*

Hávi's first swing proved her experience at slaughtering goats. Mjóvi's skull split with surprising ease. Copious red sprayed, bathing Hávi and all of those nearby. Every woman screamed, even Völu, some in horror, others in disbelief. Hávi had struck twice more, snarling hatred such as she'd never experienced, before one of the guards ran forward and snatched the axe from Hávi's hand. Mjóvi had crumpled into a morbid, profusely-bleeding ball; Hávi's final blow had caved in the base of her skull.

Blood-drenched, Hávi turned to face the incredulous

guard.

"*I am Queen Hávi Hersir Austmaðr! I want to talk to your leader! Now!*"

Breiðr and most of the women sat on the benches, too stunned to stand, and fearfully stepped away as Hávi approached. Völu and Bitra cleaned Hávi up as best they could, tearing scraps from their own gowns to wipe her off, and Hvassi pulled an old banner off a wall and laid it over Mjóvi's still-bleeding body. Most of the women stared uncomprehending and whispered, casting disbelieving glances at their queen. Gellir stared aghast at her, unable to speak, but silently she stepped forward and took Hávi's hand; into Hávi's palm Gellir passed a small dagger.

Flanked by two armed Norwegians, Hávi ascended the stone steps, still covered with blood, with Gellir's small dagger deep inside her cleavage. Into her old bedroom the guards led her. Both treasury doors were hacked apart, their shattered remains hung from bent, ruined hinges. All of clan Austmaðr's treasure lay piled in the center of the room. The wardrobes had been ransacked; the floor was carpeted with the crumpled gowns of the sluts. Five men crowded the bedroom, one man lying bleeding on her bed.

Hávi pushed through the men and examined the wounded man: besides several arrows *(she hoped that one was hers!)*, the man had been stabbed through his thigh and blood poured from his wound. They'd torn his pants away at the hip but only pressed a soaked, balled-up wool skirt to his cut. Instantly Hávi snatched a discarded outfit from the floor and started to bind his wound.

"*I thought that you were Queen Austmaðr,*" one of the

men growled.

"I'm a Swedish queen," Hávi said as she worked. "I cook feasts, embroider, heal, and I've studied the den Skaanske Lov, although I'm not a Law-speaker. This man's artery's been severed: I need to make a tourniquet or he'll die. Even if this works, he might lose his leg."

The men exchanged surprised glances as Hávi bound one of Jarl Hafr's thin undertunics around the man's upper-thigh and then drew a large dagger from one of the men's belts and used its blade to spin her tourniquet tight enough to cut off the flow of blood to his leg.

"Master Kamban was the best healer in the Skåne ... and one of your fools killed him," Hávi said. "I need hot water ... and herbs from his room to soak out any infection."

"You'll get it," the man said.

"Do you lead these savages?"

"I'm Jarl Gullskeggr."

Hávi glanced at him; *'gullskeggr'* translated to *'gold-beard'*, but his beard was black; he looked young and very strong.

"You've murdered my people, Jarl Gullskeggr," Hávi said. "I hate you."

"Yet you heal my captain."

"I want something."

"What?"

"Safety for my women."

"That's asking a lot."

"Is it worth this man's leg?"

"I'll consider it; I have other wounded men."

"You've got all of our wealth; leave the wounded and I'll guarantee their safety."

"We'll leave tomorrow."

"And my women?"

"Slaves fetch high prices; I can't leave them."

Hávi reached out, seized the knife holding the tourniquet tight, and yanked it out, slitting the tourniquet in half. The man cried out and grabbed both ends, frantically trying to hold the severed cloths together.

"*Replace that or I'll have all of your women raped!*"

"You'll do that anyway."

"*Obey me or I'll kill you.*"

"Better dead than a slave."

"Women don't defy me."

"I'm a queen."

Jarl Gullskeggr paused to consider.

"Heal my men and you'll be left behind unharmed."

"I need my servants."

"Two servants."

"Five."

"Agreed."

An hour later, Hávi had replaced the tourniquet and made three others, in addition to bandaging and binding numerous wounds, and sewing some gashes closed, some of which would never fully heal. A line of wounded men waited in the hall outside; Hávi had fetched Master Kamban's herbs and tools and took over Hvítvi's chambers; the wounded sat upon Hvítvi's couches and groaned as Hávi cleaned out their cuts and removed arrow-tips.

As she worked, Hávi's mind raced; she doubted if they'd leave her behind even though they'd promised; Jarl Gullskeggr didn't look pleased during their bartering. She needed to delay them; if the women were still here in six days then clans Hersir and Dúfunef could retake the castle and rescue them. *But would they come? What was left of clan*

Austmaðr to rescue? Men dead, wealth stolen, and their women sold off to slavers in foreign lands; why should Hersir and Dúfunef risk their men's lives?

Six days! They could be anywhere in six days, and Jarl Hafr wouldn't even look for them!

Jarl Gullskeggr stepped inside Hvítvi's outer-room, curiously opened the door to Hvítvi's hot-fog room and peered inside as the remaining steam hissed out.

"Close that," Hávi said. "The steam's for healing certain conditions which your men don't have."

"We have sweat-lodges in Norway," Jarl Gullskeggr said, and he closed its door. "I've ordered that none of your women are to be raped; that should compensate for your skills. In exchange, your cooks are making us supper."

"I appreciate that," Hávi said.

"I told your cooks that you'd be tasting our food before we eat it."

"My cooks don't use poisons."

"You'll be able to prove that," Jarl Gullskeggr said. "You will dine with me."

After the worst of the wounded were tended, Hávi descended to the great hall where all of the women were nervously seated at the tables in the center, surrounded by laughing, boasting Norwegians. With the women were many children, including Jarl Hafr's daughters and her stepdaughters from the nursery. Despite her bloody state, as Hávi pushed her way toward them, several Norwegian scoundrels reached out to paw her, but she ignored them.

"Völu, Bitra, Breiðr, Hvassi, Knarrarbringa, Mela, Gellir, Brækir, and Blönduhorn," Hávi said loudly. "Come with me."

All of the ladies appeared stunned, especially those whom Hávi had named. All hesitated, but Hávi's glare warned them; they rose to follow as Hávi turned and walked through the press of men.

"Where do you think you're going ...?" one Norwegian guard challenged her.

"Jarl Gullskeggr ordered me to sup beside him," Hávi said. "I need my servants to dress me."

"All of them?"

"We're Swedes."

The man looked bewildered as Hávi led her procession out of the great hall and stopped them just outside the kitchen.

"Völu, fetch me something fancy to wear," Hávi said. "Gellir, go with her. Join us in Hvítvi's room."

"You'll need water for washing," Gellir said.

Minutes later, Völu and Gellir entered carrying several of Hávi's best gowns and two buckets of water.

"They ransacked your tower," Völu said. "All of your jewelry's gone."

"That doesn't matter," Hávi said. "Blönduhorn, watch at the door and make sure that no one's listening."

Terrified, Blönduhorn didn't move until Brækir nudged her, and then she ran to open the door a tiny crack and peer out.

"Bitra, you talk to the other servants," Hávi said. "Breiðr, you talk to the older children. Hvassi, you talk to the castle women. Gellir: the sluts. Brækir: the women of Skadi."

"What do we tell them?" Hvassi asked.

"If they're coming, clans Hersir and Dúfunef will be here in six days," Hávi explained. "Jarl Gullskeggr wants to sail tomorrow. He plans to sell all of us as slaves."

"What can we do?" Völu asked.

"We've got to keep them here," Hávi whispered.

"How?"

"We're going to be raped no matter what," Hávi said. "If Jarl Gullskeggr doesn't let his warriors rape us, then whoever purchases us as slaves will."

"You want us to be raped?" Brækir asked.

"No," Hávi said. "I want us to be married."

Led by her procession of women, Hávi entered the great hall with her head held high, completely cleaned and wearing her best dress. She poised before Jarl Gullskeggr, her *'servants'* behind her; as one they curtsied to Jarl Gullskeggr. Hávi couldn't help wondering what Mjóvi would say if she saw this, but she forced the thought away; *Mjóvi would never spread another lie.*

While her *'servants'* rejoined the women, Hávi ascended to the first dais and sat in her chair beside Jarl Gullskeggr. Platters of food lay before her; Hávi freely helped herself to large portions and then began eating, and with wary glances at her, the Norwegians began serving themselves.

"You're quite an amazing woman," Jarl Gullskeggr said.

"All Swedish women are amazing."

"You could go far in Norway."

"In a hut or a cave?"

"Norway is far more civilized than Sweden," Jarl Gullskeggr said. "Our kings are mighty warlords. Our castles are impregnable."

"That hardly proves civility."

"Civility is adherence to local customs. Our customs aren't yours; you'd have to know both to judge which is better."

"A civil man would leave our women to mourn their dead husbands," Hávi said. "Our lives will be bad enough; we've legal problems that you wouldn't understand."

"Such as ...?"

"The den Skaanske Lov grants Swedish women the right to own land for three months; this allows time for the men to return from the viking. With our men dead, we women now own all of the lands of clan Austmaðr. If you leave us behind then we'll have to send to other clans for new husbands; in three months, any unmarried woman will lose all claim to her properties."

"So ... any man that you marry legally inherits Castle Austmaðr?"

"Yes, including half of the Skåne, so all of the local clan-chiefs will send their sons," Hávi said. "I'll have to pick the strongest leader or the others will start a civil war."

"I heard that your cowardly husband rode away."

"I saw him before he deserted me; as a healer, I doubt if he'll survive his wounds. Even if he did, he was my true husband's brother; I never wanted to marry him. He abandoned me; if he returns, I'll appreciate watching him die."

"Swedish women are blood-thirsty. In clan Gullskeggr, women must remarry within a moon-cycle or lose their lands ... and none learn law."

"You undervalue your women," Hávi said. "You miss out on the advantages that some women could give you."

"Perhaps so. I'll mention this to my father, but he won't believe it."

"Your father's a clan-chief?"

"Clan Gullskeggr commands fifty miles of coastland to the mountains. I was born in a castle that dwarfs this."

"I heard that all Norwegians are barbarians."

"So says every nation about its neighbors. Norway's a wondrous land."

"Do you have any brothers?"

"Seven; I'm sixth in line."

"So you'll never wear a crown?"

"Not in clan Gullskeggr, but I seek lands to conquer."

"Swedish clan-chiefs will never tolerate Norwegians on their borders."

"But if I married you, then I'd legally own these lands ... by Swedish law!"

Jarl Gullskeggr gave Hávi a sly, appreciative glance, as if silently estimating her true worth. Hávi frowned at him, but secretly bit her tongue to keep from smiling; *he'd taken her bait.*

Chapter 37

"*I so swear my obedience and fidelity to Jarl Gullskeggr,*" Hávi vowed.

Jarl Gullskeggr smiled but Hávi didn't. She hated what she was doing to herself and all of her women, but they understood; five days remained before any hope of rescue. Some captain kept ticking off vows that Hávi recited by rote; marriage was a tool that men used to enslave women, nothing more. Hávi's third wedding was as unwanted as her others.

Hávi stood still as sand was sprinkled into her hair, her forehead was anointed with oil, and a circlet of flowers was placed on her head. No fir or cedar boughs were brushed against the couple to keep their love evergreen; it didn't seem to be a Norwegian custom. But the prayers to Odin and his many gods and goddesses went on forever, far more serious than any prayers that Hávi had ever heard at a wedding. Finally a broom was brought forward and placed at her feet.

'This marriage will end soon with one of us dead,' Hávi

thought, and then she took Jarl Gullskeggr's hand and jumped over the broom; the men cheered and the women wept.

A minute later, Jarl Gullskeggr took the arm of a tall, mature man who could've been his father but had long, golden hair and bright, blue eyes. Jarl Gullskeggr drew the man to stand before Hávi in the center of the great hall.

"This is Jarl Skjal, my most-honored captain," Jarl Gullskeggr said.

Hávi looked at him closely; nobility rested easily upon him, his braided beard hanging over a coat of steel mail trimmed with brass rings. Wide silver broaches decorated his shoulders. He stood proudly, and Hávi curtsied slightly to him, and then walked toward the women. Her eyes fell upon Völu.

"Noooo!!!" Völu hissed between clenched teeth.

"Völu, I'll give you to any man here," Hávi whispered. "Show me the one that you prefer ... or come and be wed."

Horror filled Völu's eyes like a baby deer caught between wolves. She glanced to both sides; hundreds of leering warriors stood ready, expectantly, each hoping that they'd be chosen.

"Bifru isn't dead ...!"

"Do you think that they care?" Hávi hissed between her own clenched teeth. *"If they can't wed you then they'll enslave you, and you'll be raped by a hundred common soldiers. I'm sure that they've a Dala and Hálmi somewhere; do you want poorly-cured goat-skins?"*

Völu clutched Rauðrefr tightly to her chest as Hávi pulled her forward. Völu walked reluctantly, terrified of going, more-terrified of refusing. Hávi pulled her to stand before Jarl Skjal and Jarl Gullskeggr.

"This is Völu Hersir, daughter of Jarl Hersir and his only

heir," Hávi announced loudly so that all in the great hall could hear. "She and I grew up together; she was only here by unlucky happenstance. Völu just gave birth, so she must be treated with great gentleness, but she is a wealthy and most-worthy widow."

Jarl Skjal bowed deeply to Völu and then took her hand. Jarl Gullskeggr looked pleased and motioned them toward the Norwegian who had conducted his and Hávi's wedding.

"Karl, come forward," Jarl Gullskeggr called, and a muscular, young man with bright, blonde hair stepped from the crowd. "Karl is my nephew and a most-noble warrior."

Hávi breathed deeply and steeled her nerves before she turned back to the women.

"Breiðr ...," Hávi called softly.

Slowly Jarl Gullskeggr brought forth his most prominent warriors, announced them as captains or sons of wealth, or just as great warriors, and Hávi went among her women and selected a bride for each. Hávi almost regretted having killed Mjóvi before she could doom her to the worst of the lot, but she selected Mjóvi's friends to wed the oldest and ugliest warriors. Many of the women sobbed horribly, and some had to be drug forward by soldiers; their weddings proceeded while they blubbered and trembled and their new husbands looked disgusted. But Jarl Gullskeggr insisted that every woman, especially those owning property, be married, and Hávi reluctantly complied. Hávi begged her new husband to allow an exception for Blönduhorn, but upon seeing her, Jarl Gullskeggr insisted that she wed his young cousin, who was very handsome and seemed delighted by his pretty virgin bride. Hvassi was wed to a man almost matching her immense girth. Knarrarbringa and Mela were wed to the sons of Norwegian jarls. Brækir was wed to a tall, muscular warrior who seemed thrilled to become the owner of his own tavern. Hávi introduced Gellir and her sluts as high-born ladies-in-waiting and honored them as prizes for any man, even a king. After their own nuptials, eight ship captains simultaneously performed wedding ceremonies, and still couples had to stand in line to be married; the weddings lasted all night.

In the wee hours of the morning, the last of the weddings concluded. Jarl Gullskeggr rose from his seat at the high-table and escorted Hávi up the narrow steps to the upper dais. Unexpectedly he held up Hávi's tiara, and the whole great hall fell silent save for the sniffles of the unhappy women.

"I hearby crown myself Jarl Gullskeggr! All of the lands once claimed by clan Austmaðr are now mine. These marriages give us legal claim over Castle Austmaðr and Skadi, and soon over all of the Skåne. There will be challenges to our rule, but I'll send messengers to the Swedish rabble offering truces in exchange for recognition of our claim. Where we came as penniless raiders, we entrench as wealthy nobles and townsmen; all that clan Austmaðr was, we now are. I'll send to my father for more warriors at once, and any Swedish clan that refuses to accept us we shall slaughter and claim as our own!"

Jarl Gullskeggr lowered Hávi's tiara onto his head as the rafters rose with thunderous cheers. Many warriors beat their fists against their chests, hammered on the tables, or clanged two swords together; anything to make noise. Hávi couldn't help but smile as she leaned close to her new husband.

"When we get upstairs, I'll pick out a more-suitable circlet for you," Hávi whispered.

Jarl Gullskeggr glanced at her questioningly.

"That's a tiara; a woman's crown."

Jarl Gullskeggr snatched the tiara off his head and tried to look inconspicuous, but standing before the tall thrones of clan Austmaðr atop the high dais with every eye in the great hall watching him, his attempt was useless.

"Shall we sit?" Hávi asked.

As one they sat upon the tall-backed thrones, and Jarl Gullskeggr quietly handed the tiara to Hávi, who placed it in her lap where everyone could see it. Some of the women smiled at this; Jarl Gullskeggr had just passed his selected symbol of power to Hávi before all of his men and all of her women. Despite her shock at being wedded a second time, Völu managed a wicked grin.

Hávi entered her old bedroom more reluctantly than ever; *the goddess Freyja would certainly disapprove of her wedding another while her husband lived.* This was no proper, legal wedding; Hávi was prostituting herself in the dim hope of staying alive. Even if this worked, all of Castle Austmaðr and Skadi would ever-after be called whores, but better another scandal than to be sold as slaves. Perhaps Jarl Hafr would use this as an excuse to divorce her. She wondered where Hvítvi and Jorgen were; if Hvítvi's illnesses overcame him in the wild, without a healer to tend him, then he could die, and Hávi feared to think what Jarl Hafr would do to her infant son.

Jarl Gullskeggr placed a hand on her shoulder and pushed her gently; Hávi hadn't realized that she'd stopped in her doorway. She knew what was going to happen, what she'd have to endure, but she had no choice. On their wedding nights, all jarls required the same to prevent scandal and shame. *Did even one of them care how their reluctant brides felt?*

Hávi steeled herself; she was the leader of all that was left of clan Austmaðr and he was the lord of the barbarians that had raped her country and was doing the same to its women. *She had to do this!*

Hávi turned to face her husband like a hungry wolf about to devour its helpless prey. As he closed their door, she seized his fur collar and pulled his face toward hers. Hávi kissed with the appetite of a woman desperate for her man; harder and more urgently than she'd dared kiss her weak, beloved Hvítvi. At first, Jarl Gullskeggr recoiled, surprised, but then he eagerly responded, returning her lusts with ardent, forceful demands. Jarl Gullskegger was easily as strong as her aged first husband and nearly as youthful as Hvítvi, a hard-muscled warrior tried by viking and war and used to commanding; thick, black hair covered his chest and stout forearms, and his hands possessed a crushing strength that could easily bruise, but restrained just short of harming her breasts. Clothes flew, cast aside, and both fell onto Hávi's bed like savage animals, kissing and mauling in frenzied passion. Hávi forced herself upon him, her acidic disgust overwhelmed by his powerful masculine supremacy evoking depths of physical desires that Hávi had never known. He rolled atop her and Hávi surrendered to his dominance, writhing and gasping and clenching his bulging biceps to draw him in ever deeper; his manly physique strained even her rugged peasant upbringing. Hávi snarled and bit as pleasures that she'd never felt gushed through her, lost in maddening passion.

They collapsed together, gasping and biting back cries. Hávi's chest heaved, her heart pounded, and powerful feelings clouded her mind and shrouded her screaming, silent objections. Jarl Gullskegger was her enemy; she couldn't mentally submit to him, but her body longed for his ecstasy, the summits that he'd driven her to, the pleasures that his strength and youth had aroused.

"*Wife, you ... are amazing,*" he gasped harshly.

Hávi fought to think of something to say, but her will was hijacked; only yearnings responded. One lonely thought arose, like wafting smoke tantalizing her brain: *her hated husband wouldn't be back for five more days.*

At breakfast the next morning, Hávi counted the Norwegians: slightly more than three hundred had survived the invasion. Almost a third of them were now married; less than a hundred women had been captured. Hávi assumed that the rest of Skadi's wives and daughters had hidden and then fled to the distant farms, hills, and forests. She wondered what was happening outside of the castle, if the farmers outside of Skadi had been attacked and their women violated, but Hávi had no way of knowing.

Jarl Gullskeggr, now wearing a man's silver crown, sat beside her. Half of the morning had passed before breakfast was prepared; doubtless the cook and his male helpers were dead, and many of the men insisted on enjoying their wives' pleasures before they were sent to the kitchen. To Jarl Gullskeggr's increasing astonishment, Hávi had joined the workers in the kitchen and assumed command; only an hour later, she sat at the high-table eating the eggs that she'd cracked, beaten, and cooked.

Hávi startled to see Brækir and Blönduhorn seated at the women's table.

"I'd have thought that your men would've wanted to see their homes in Skadi," Hávi said.

"They do," Jarl Gullskeggr said. "But I'm no fool, wife: your neighbors won't welcome our presence."

"I know," Hávi said meekly, wondering how much of her plans he'd guessed. "But surely you could let them out, a few at a time, with orders to return within an hour?"

All afternoon, Hávi watched out Hvítvi's window as wives escorted their new husbands into Skadi to inspect their marriage-purchased property. Hávi's teeth clenched in frustration; with their husbands dead, her women had legally owned all of Skadi for a few brief hours. Even if clans Hersir and Dúfunef sailed up and slew these invaders today, there weren't enough single men left to marry all of her women; by law, those wives whose husbands had died would lose all of their lands and houses to their clan-chief, her idiot-husband, after three months. By midwinter, Jarl Hafr's holdings would double due to her women's suffering; doubtlessly he'd be pleased.

Many of the wounded required further healing; Hávi changed many bandages and applied thick layers of healing herbs and chanted loud prayers over the leg of the captain that she'd tourniqueted; yellow bile spewed from his cuts as she probed their swellings. Hávi required six men to hold him as she cleaned his wound with strong mead, the only alcohol that she had; she doubted if he'd keep his leg.

At Hávi's request, Völu, Bitra, Breiðr, Hvassi, Knarrarbringa, Mela, Gellir, Brækir, and Blönduhorn joined her; they had to keep up their pretense of being her handmaids. Only Völu and Brækir had the stomach to help her heal; the other's hid in Hvítvi's bedroom until Hávi was finished. After washing and changing her soiled clothes, Hávi ordered Völu, Mela, and Blönduhorn to light all of the fires to heat up Hvítvi's hot-fog room, insisting that they use plenty of green wood which would pop, sizzle, and crackle; she didn't want to be overheard.

With Blönduhorn watching at the outer door, Hávi drew the others into the overly-hot chamber and ladled water onto the backs of the fireplaces, making the rocks hiss as the steam rose thickly.

"Four more days," Hávi whispered to her conspirators. "We have to endure these barbarians until then."

"Can I keep mine?" Hvassi grinned.

Hávi ignored her as the white mists swirled.

"We need a plan," Hávi said. "When our men return, I want all of our women somewhere safe until the fighting's over."

"We don't know when they'll come ... or where we'll be," Völu said.

"The Norwegians aren't allowed to sleep outside of the castle," Brækir said. "My ... he complained about it when he saw my ... our bed."

Brækir burst into tears and the women on both sides held her comfortingly.

"We'd be on our way to slavers if we hadn't done this," Hávi reminded her.

"My husband's dead!" Brækir sobbed. *"You ... you ...!"*

Hávi froze, taken aback by Brækir unexpected vehemence.

"Hávi wasn't responsible for Hrafna's death!" Völu defended.

"Where are Valla and Augi?" Brækir seethed. *"They should've been home ...!"*

"The Norwegians killed all the older boys in Skadi," Breiðr said sadly.

"We've all lost men that we loved," Mela said, and she took Brækir's hands and held them.

"I'm sorry, Brækir," Hávi said truthfully. "But we've got to save those of us left."

Brækir cast Hávi a Mjóvi-worthy glare, then lowered her tear-filled eyes.

"Whatever we do, we must plan carefully," Hvassi said. "If our new husbands even suspect ...!"

That night, Hávi didn't need to act like a slut; her husband's lecherous aggressiveness let her remain totally subservient and still his overpowering masculinity triggered surges of pleasure that she had to bite back to keep from screaming. Guilt overwhelmed; she didn't love him and planned to kill him, yet his ravages of her body thrilled her every fiber. She tried to think of Hvítvi, whose gentle caresses whispered promises of faithfulness and deep devotion, the truest love that she'd ever known. But her body responded to Jarl Gullskeggr like a dancer to music; thoughts of Hvítvi were drowned out by the loud drumming of her heart and the heaving of her bosom; all lesser sensations were forgotten in favor of all-consuming ecstasy.

"Mistress, may I speak with you?"

Hávi looked at the elderly, gray-haired, castle woman; she'd seen her many times although they'd never spoken. Fear filled the elder's aged eyes.

"I'm Járnsíða; I wash clothes," she whispered. "I need to speak to you ... privately."

"Is it urgent?" Hávi asked.

"Very."

Hávi put down the bowl of pepper-spiced honey with which she was basting chickens and hurried out of the kitchens; the other kitchen-women said nothing but continued with their chores. Hávi wondered what new trouble had found her; already she was chief cook, chief healer, and castle seneschal. To Hávi's surprise, Járnsíða walked quickly to Hávi's tower and ascended to the very top.

"Isn't someone living up here ...?" Hávi asked.

"Their wives promised to get them away, but we can't talk until we're sure," Járnsíða said nervously.

They pushed up the trapdoor and entered Hávi's tower; little had changed save that a great axe rested against one wall.

"I've a message to you from Master Krókr," Járnsíða whispered.

"He's not dead?" Hávi startled.

"No," Járnsíða said. "The hunchback's assistant ..."

"Felian's alive?"

"He came upon me last night when everyone was asleep," Járnsíða said. "He recognized me and we snuck away to talk. Master Krókr and almost a hundred of our men fled into the guardhouse when all was lost. They hid in the dungeon; one man sacrificed himself to conceal its entrance. They've no food, no water, and no way out."

"Who was with them?"

"I don't know. I told Felian what I knew ... which wasn't much."

"Thank you, Járnsíða," Hávi said. "You may have just saved us all."

The wounded captain's leg spewed black bile and his toes had turned green.

"He's going to lose it," Hávi said. "If not, he'll die."

"Can you do it?" Jarl Gullskeggr asked.

"I've never done anything like this," Hávi said. "Master Kamban had, but ..."

"You've taken his place. I have several men who can help; I'll send for them at once."

"I can't guarantee ..."

"Do your best."

Two long, heavy, fresh-cut tree trunks were carried inside the castle and up to Hvítvi's outer room. Three of Jarl Gullskeggr's toughest warriors, huge, burly men whose faces showed only scars and hate bound their frightened captain to both logs, one across his back with his bound arms outstretched, the other down his side with his good leg bound securely to it. Hávi had sorted through every tool that she'd found in Master Kamban's room and taken all of the knives and the short, sharpened saw. A dozen, red-hot irons sat ready in the blazing fire, awaiting their need.

"Have any of you ever done this before?" Hávi asked them.

"We've assisted," one man growled.

"Maybe you could ..."

"We only assist."

Lastly, one of them bound a furry pillow to the back of the wounded captain's head by a thick rope that ran through the captain's mouth. Hávi wondered why; it must be terribly uncomfortable, but she didn't ask.

"He's ready," one of the men said.

Hávi fought to control her trembles. As she lifted a narrow, sharp knife, the men knelt down upon the captain, further holding him, despite the many stout ropes wrapped around him. Short, rapid moans escaped the captain; he was sick with fever from the poisons of his dying leg. Hávi took a deep breath, placed her knife against his naked thigh ... and cut.

Blood spewed and the captain convulsed, screaming as

best he could, muzzled by the rope upon which his teeth gnashed. Hávi seized a red-hot poker and seared the biggest artery closed, and the captain jumped so hard that both logs and all three warriors bounced upon the floor. She kept cutting as fast as she could, first severing the muscles so that they weren't fighting her, while trying to ignore his agonized shrieks. She had no herbs or alcohol left; she had used all of it on her other patients. She prayed ardently but silently; her face was painted with her patient's blood, which would spew inside her mouth if she opened it. She'd butchered many goats, but never until they were dead. Three more hot pokers had to be used, each evoking howls that would ring in Hávi's ears forever. Finally Hávi set the grisly saw to his bloody bone and began slicing, a rasping, reverberant grind that shuddered though her whole universe. An eternity of horror drove remorseful spikes through her soul.

Finally the ruined leg fell free; all that remained was a blackened stump which Hávi had to finish searing, then bandage. The captain was shaking, the guards holding him grunting with their efforts to restrain him, every knot binding him pulled too taut to untie. Hávi was soaked to the skin from head to foot; she finished her task quickly, then ran into Hvítvi's hot-fog room and vomited.

"Alive?" Gellir asked incredulously.

"Járnsíða; a washer-woman, said so," Hávi said. "They're trapped in the dungeon; they have no food or water, and we have to save them."

"How?"

"We need to empty the guardhouse."

Gellir looked puzzled, then anger flushed her face. *"We're not sluts!"*

"That's my husband you've been sleeping with!" Hávi snapped, but then she forced herself to regain her composure.

"Why us?"

"Who else?" Hávi asked. "But I promise you; if you do this ... then no woman in clan Austmaðr will ever disdain you again."

Gellir sighed heavily.

"When?"

"Soon, or they'll starve. I've a whole, roasted pig to send to them, and a barrel of ale, but I need the chance to get it to them."

"What if they won't ...?"

"You need to make sure that they do."

In the kitchen, Völu and seven others stood ready; each carried two buckets for washing floors, but under their rag-covers, their buckets were filled with pork slices swimming in ale. Hávi nodded to them, then hurried out, wiping her hands upon her apron. She opened a door and nodded to Gellir and her sluts; all of them glared back. Hávi stood back as the sluts walked past her toward the guardroom. Hávi followed slowly; the lesser guards were too common to have earned wives, and several complaints had been voiced about the shortage of women. As Hávi peeked into the guardroom, she saw Gellir and her girls swarming over the delighted guards. The laughter of the girls sounded forced, but their promises of pleasure clearly enticed. Gellir gave the guards the directions that Hávi had instructed, and then all of the sluts followed Gellir as she ran lightly, playfully out of the guardhouse. Hávi dashed into an alcove as they exited, and a minute later, all of the guards chased after the sluts.

Hávi waited until they'd left, then ran into the empty

guardhouse and pushed aside the thick carpet; the trapdoor beneath it was unlatched. She yanked it open and ran down the stairs.

"*Krókr! Felian!*" Hávi hissed in the utter darkness.

"*Hávi?*" asked a voice.

"Where's Krókr?" Hávi demanded.

"Here!" came Master Krókr's voice.

"Food and drink are coming," Hávi said. "Eat sparingly; we're expecting clan Hersir and Dúfunef to arrive in three days but we can't be sure; it may have to last longer. I don't know if we'll be able to bring more."

"Where's Mjóvi?" Master Krókr asked.

"Dead," Hávi said flatly, and she didn't go into details. "Jarl Hafr and Hvítvi rode to get help. The Norwegians have taken the castle and married ..."

"We know that," Master Krókr said. "When do we ...?"

"When they rush out to defend the walls," Hávi said. "We'll come and get you."

"*Hávi?*" Völu's voice whispered from the trapdoor.

"Here's your food," Hávi said. "I've got to go ..."

"Wait!" Master Krókr ordered. "How are we supposed to ...?"

But Hávi didn't wait; she ran up the steps past Völu and the others: Gellir was depending on her.

"Husband!" Hávi shouted, and Jarl Gullskeggr looked at her as she ran up. "Your guards! They're raping my women!"

"*What?*" he demanded.

"Unmarried guards; *they threatened to hurt them if they told their husbands!*"

"*Where?*"

Hávi followed as Jarl Gullskeggr led a growing party of

warriors through the castle. Hávi had chosen a distant storeroom; every guard that they passed joined them as they strode rapidly down the narrow hallways and steep stairs. Jarl Gullskeggr knew what troubles this would cause among his men; no warlord can allow dissention in his ranks. Twenty-five men followed as Jarl Gullskeggr stormed up to the storeroom door and kicked it open.

"What's this?" Jarl Gullskeggr shouted.

A dozen shrill screams filled the air as Gellir and her girls, some with their clothes clenched in their hands, held before them to shield their mock-modesty, ran past Jarl Gullskeggr and pushed through the crowd of surprised warriors. Quickly Hávi led the sluts upstairs to Hvítvi's room; she didn't need to be there while Jarl Gullskeggr dealt with angry husbands or guilty guards; it would only save Swedish lives if the Norwegians killed each other.

Völu, Bitra, Breiðr, Hvassi, Knarrarbringa, Mela, Brækir, and Blönduhorn stood waiting in Hvítvi's blood-drenched outer room as Hávi led the sluts inside; Bitra, Brækir, and Blönduhorn were washing the walls with bloody rags. All of them looked offended as Gellir and her sluts entered.

"Did they ...?" Hávi started.

"We gave them the buckets," Völu said. "We didn't wait to talk."

"Valla and Augi!" Brækir sobbed. *"My sons are alive! Hávi, I'm sorry ...!"*

Brækir pushed forward and threw herself into Hávi's arms, weeping against her breast. Hávi held her tightly, and felt a refreshing relief wash over her: *Valla and Augi were alive!*

"That pork should hold the men for a few days," Hávi said. "If clan Hersir and Dúfunef arrive, then we can attack the Norwegians from outside and inside the castle."

"How will they know?" Breiðr asked.

"They won't," Hávi said. "Not until the fighting starts."

"Then all that we can do now is wait until our bastard-husbands are killed," Völu said.

"What if they can't retake the castle?" Mela asked.

"They have to," Hvassi said. "They're our only hope."

"No, they're not," Hávi said, and she gestured to the sluts. "We can't be held hostage to their whims. Gellir and her ... *girls* ... just helped us greatly; they started serious dissention in their army. We have to continue that; if each of us can get any two Norwegians angry at each other ..."

"... then they'll be at each other's throats before we're rescued," Völu finished.

"What if we're not rescued?" Hvassi asked. "What if Jarl Hafr's pleas fail, and Jarl Dúfunef isn't coming? Jarl Hersir could believe that clan Austmaðr's a lost cause; without the other clans, we won't ever get rescued."

"What can we do?" Knarrarbringa asked.

"Cause trouble," Hávi said. "We have three days left; from now until then, we fight a woman's war."

To Hávi's surprise, Blönduhorn attacked first. At supper in the great hall, which was peculiarly quiet after a dozen guards had been caught half-naked with other men's wives, Blönduhorn walked into the great hall on the arm of her handsome young husband, kissed and left him at his seat near the front, and was on her way to the women's table when suddenly her shriek alarmed the whole castle. As hard as she could, Blönduhorn slapped a surprised Norwegian warrior whom she'd brushed against in the crowd, and then she cupped her hands protectively over her breasts and looked appalled. Voices cried out as Blönduhorn's husband drew steel and charged the flabbergasted warrior, who was still stammering his innocence, his words lost in the calamitous tumult. Jarl Gullskeggr and all of the men at the high-table jumped to their feet and shouted for order as men struggled to pry the combatants apart. Hávi smiled wryly; *her women were good at this.*

"When I'm finished, your new tunic will make you look like a captain," Hvassi said to her large new husband. "A big man like you should lead others; *why haven't you been made a ship's captain?*"

Hávi couldn't overhear his whispered answer, but she heard Hvassi scoff at it.

"I hate this castle," Brækir said to her husband. "If we could sleep in town, then you'd have a whole tavern to yourself, a big, warm bed with lots of privacy, and all of the beer that you could want; *why can't we sleep in our house?*"

Brækir's husband didn't look pleased.

"I'm Jarl Hafr's eldest daughter," Knarrarbringa said to her husband. "Hávi's not Hafr-blood; *with my brothers dead, I should be queen, and you should rule this castle.*"

Hávi smiled; every woman in the castle was seeding discord. Their husbands looked increasingly unhappy.

Tensions filled Castle Austmaðr as the days ticked past. Several fights broke out and some Norwegians were severely disciplined. Each night, Jarl Gullskeggr paced angrily for half an hour before coming to bed.

"Tell all of the women to arm themselves," Hávi

whispered to her cohorts in Hvítvi's hot-fog room while the wood crackled and hissed. "*Find those blades that they carried after I was attacked in Skadi; when the bell rings tonight, if they get the chance, strike hard!*"

Jay Palmer

Chapter 38

No rescue came. Still flushed from ardent mating, Hávi crawled out from under her covers and crept to her window after Jarl Gullskeggr had fallen asleep. She'd hoped that clans Hersir and Dúfunef would arrive with the dawn, but the whole day had passed ... *were they coming at all?* The harbor beyond Skaði showed no movements save for the gentle swaying of the naked masts of the invader's dragonships. For long hours Hávi watched, despairing; the Austmaðr men in the dungeon weren't enough to take back the castle. Perhaps, if they could all sneak into those ships and overpower any guards, then the women could escape, but the guards posted at the gate would surely raise the alarm. The food that Hávi had given their men in the dungeon must be long gone; soon they'd starve to death.

Near dawn, chilled from watching all night, Hávi saw a shadow dim the reflected starlight filling the gap in the harbor's mouth. Shapes moved behind it, and an echo of distant hoofbeats rumbled. Hávi jumped to the window, pulling her quilt tight around her, and she accidentally threw the shutter open too hard; it banged loudly onto the outer stone wall.

"*Wha ....?*" Jarl Gullskeggr sat up blinking, alarmed by the noise. He glanced about through sleepy eyes and focused on Hávi standing nervously by the window. "*What're you doing?*"

"Sorry," Hávi said quickly. "I was ... hot ... opened the window."

"Oh," he said, and he laid back down and rolled over.

Hávi stood frozen; she should go back to bed before he suspected something, but she had to be sure. She looked out at the harbor; dragonships were sailing quietly into Skadi and the murmur of approaching hoofbeats grew.

"What's that noise?" Jarl Gullskeggr asked.

"Thunder," Hávi said. "Go to sleep."

Hávi closed the shutters and slipped under her covers, hoping to give them every possible second. Hvítvi was out there, possibly carrying Jorgen, beside Jarl Hersir and Jarl Dúfunef. The lives of every woman in the castle depended on them.

"*That's not thunder!*" Jarl Gullskeggr sat up suddenly, and then he glared angrily at Hávi. "*What've you been doing?*"

Jarl Gullskeggr jumped up, ran to the window, and pushed open the shutters. Desperately Hávi reached out; the dagger that she used to carry was stashed by her bed. Her fingers closed upon its handle and Hávi leapt out of bed. Jarl Gullskeggr was leaning out the window, looking in every direction.

"*Swedes!*" Jarl Gullskeggr cursed, and he turned to face Hávi.

Hávi stabbed hard before he was even aware that she was there; warm, wet blood gushed over her hand. Then a meaty fist struck her face and Hávi flew backwards across the room.

"Betrayer!" Jarl Gullskeggr gasped, yanking Hávi's blade out of his stomach and clutching at his blood-spurting wound. *"I'll kill ...!"*

But Hávi ignored her pain and jumped to her feet. Beside the treasure piled in the corner, Jarl Gullskeggr kept his sword propped against the wall; Hávi drew his own blade and faced him.

"That won't help you," Jarl Gullskeggr growled.

"If I can amputate a leg ... then I can kill you," Hávi said.

Gritting his teeth against the pain, one hand clutching his spewing wound and the other holding Hávi's knife, Jarl Gullskeggr lunged forward. Hávi swung hard, but he moved with the mastery of an experienced fighter; he caught her blade in the crook of his dagger and knocked her against the fireplace. He raised the dagger, then coughed and doubled over; grunting in pain, he fell to his knees.

"Bitch ...!" he hissed.

Hávi rose and raised his sword.

"Queen Bitch," Hávi said, and she swung again.

With great effort, Jarl Gullskeggr blocked her heavier blade a second time, but the exertion collapsed him into a gasping, writhing pile of bleeding helplessness; Hávi's dagger had wounded him deeply.

"I ... could've ... given you ... everything ...," Jarl Gullskegger seethed.

"You were the best lover that I've ever bedded with," Hávi said, "but it's not enough."

Hávi swung his sword as she'd chopped firewood as a child back in clan Hersir. Her swing met his neck, and all of the blood in Jarl Gullskeggr's body spewed into her fireplace, whose coals sizzled and steamed, extinguishing its flames. Hávi stood gasping in the sudden darkness; *her kinfolk were coming!*

Hávi grabbed a loose nightshirt and pulled it on, ignoring the blood that painted her. She ran out of her bedroom and down the stone stairs. Hávi passed two startled guards at the bottom of the stairs, dashed into the dark, empty kitchen, exited through another door, and then ran toward her tower, hearing the guards give chase behind her. Reaching its steps, Hávi jumped for the long, dangling rope and pulled it as hard as she could. The bell in her chamber far above rang loud and clear in the silent night and Hávi kept pulling hard, ringing the bell as loudly as she could.

Both guards arrived, having followed Hávi, and stared at her as she frantically rang the bell. Suddenly several loud cries echoed through the castle: death cries from stabbed husbands, and both guards drew and brandished their weapons. Hávi froze; the time for secrecy was over.

"Jarl Gullskeggr sent me to sound the alarm!" Hávi shouted at the guards. *"Swedes fill the harbor!"*

Both guards paled, and then they turned and ran off. Shouts filled the castle, cries of alarm and screams of pain, and some of the voices were women's; not all of the assassinations were successful. Two men came running down the stairs from the tower and Hávi pressed against the wall to let them pass.

"To arms!" the Norwegians shouted. *"Man the walls!"*

Hávi crept up the stairs just far enough that she could watch those running past the foot of her tower, awaiting her chance. Two women, Mela and a townswoman whose name Hávi didn't know, came running down the spiral stairs.

"We're sorry!" Mela said. *" We couldn't ...!"*

"You did right!" Hávi said. "Now go back and hide! Protect yourselves!"

"What about you?"

"I've got someplace to be!"

Without waiting to see what the women did, Hávi ran back down the stairs and into the chaos of the hallways. Norwegians ran cursing, pushing to get through doorways, carrying weapons in both hands. Hávi jumped to get out of their way, slipped past where she could, and ran for the guardroom. It was empty, as she'd hoped; the Norwegians were gathering in the courtyard to guard the broken gate and keep out her rescuers. Hávi kicked aside the thick carpet and pulled open the hidden trapdoor.

"Hurry!" Hávi shouted down into the darkness. *"Hersir and Dúfunef have come!"*

Tramps of rushing boots stomped up the narrow stairs into the guardhouse as a murmur of cheers was urgently hushed.

"What time is it?" Master Krókr demanded, wielding a sword like a warrior.

"Almost dawn!" Hávi answered.

"Good!" Master Krókr said.

"Where are they?" another asked.

"Dragonships fill the harbor and horses approach from both sides," Hávi said.

"Close the doors!" Master Krókr shouted. *"Bar them! We should wait until the fighting starts, and then charge at their backs!"*

"Hávi!" Felian's voice shouted, and his hand clutched her arm. "You've done well, but now you need to hide!"

"What?" Hávi demanded. "No, I ...!"

"Jorgen needs his mother!" Felian insisted. "Hávi, hide in the dungeon."

"I've been up here fighting ...!" Hávi argued. *"I killed their leader ...!"*

"You've done your part well," Felian said, his boyish face incongruent with his manly expression. "Now let us do ours."

Cursing, Hávi descended the narrow steps, but she refused to let them close the trapdoor. Master Krókr ordered for everyone to be silent, and they listened as muted shouts and angry commands wafted in from outside.

"Not yet," Master Krókr said.

Ten minutes later, a vast cry rose; a horde of men were charging the gates.

"Now!" Master Krókr said. *"Quietly! Kill before we're noticed!"*

The warriors rushed from the room in a great clamor of shuffling feet. Hávi didn't wait for an instant; once they were gone, Hávi jumped from the dungeon and ran out into the hallway, spied the last of the men running into the great hall, and then Hávi dashed up the stone stairs. Clangs of steel rang out in the courtyard and screams filled the castle. Hávi pushed open her bedroom doors, ran past Jarl Gullskeggr's corpse, crashed into her shutters and flung them open, staring down at the battle below. Dúfunef sealskin cloaks and warriors from clan Hersir ran forward carrying a long tree-trunk and crashed it into the crudely-repaired gate. The frail gate shook but held, pressed by thirty men on its inside. Then Master Krókr and his Austmaðr warriors swarmed in from behind; no one even noticed them until spears stabbed and swords and axes struck upon unprotected backs. Close-fighting broke out as angry cries mixed with death-wails; Hávi couldn't tell who was who in the dim light before dawn.

The second crash of the battering ram smashed the gate wide open, and vengeful Swedish warriors rushed inside. In moments, all fighting ceased; the defeated Norwegians yielded to the inevitable. Weapons were thrown down and hands held up imploringly; the remaining surrendered: *Castle Austmaðr was won.*

Hávi ran down the stairs. A few, frightened women stood in the hallways; they followed Hávi into the great hall where Völu and Breiðr stood waiting by the main door, staring out at the carnage.

"Stay inside!" Hávi shouted at them as she tried to run past, but Völu and Breiðr caught her.

"No, Hávi!" Völu shouted. *"Not yet!"*

"Hvítvi!" Hávi shouted. *"I have to find ...!"*

"You can't run past your husband looking for someone else!" Breiðr hissed, bodily blocking Hávi's exit.

Hávi stopped; they were right. Jarl Hafr was out there somewhere; she had to uphold the dignity of clan Austmaðr.

"I need to know that Jorgen's safe," Hávi insisted.

"The fighting's over," Völu said. "If he's safe now then he'll stay safe."

Völu was right; Hávi calmed herself and smoothed her bloodstained nightshirt. Outside in the courtyard, the Norwegians were disarmed and forced to kneel in the dirt surrounded by armed Swedes. Dawn rose slowly, diminishing the morning stars as black sky faded to blue.

Hávi saw tall, hairy Jarl Hersir first, but he was absorbed in managing the prisoners as his men searched each prisoner one at a time, relieving them of anything of value. Where hidden sheaths were found, the prisoner was beaten; soon prisoners began pointing out their hidden daggers rather than let them be found. Jarl Dúfunef noticed Hávi first; he bowed slightly to her, and Hávi motioned him over.

"Greetings, Mistress Austmaðr."

"My most gracious welcome, Jarl Dúfunef."

"We feared that we'd find no Swedes alive."

"Our lives were bought at great cost."

"I eagerly await your tale."

"I'll have a victory feast prepared."

"No hurry; we've much work to do."

"What will happen to the prisoners?"

Jarl Dúfunef gave Hávi a queer look.

"There are things that you must know," Hávi whispered.

Jarl Dúfunef nodded slowly.

"I'll pass the word."

The prisoners were herded into a corner of the courtyard, away from the broken gate. Many guards were placed around them, ordered to kill if any prisoner so much as complained. Hávi sent Völu to gather all of the women, as she refused to leave until she saw the white albino among the warriors discussing the prisoners, and only then did she truly calm down.

The kitchen was soon crowded, everyone preparing the feast. Breiðr had baskets of turnips carried out into the hallway, and she and many women sat upon the stone stairs and sliced vegetables on wooden boards. Hávi was too busy giving orders to do anything, but every woman, castle-women, wives from Skadi, and Jarl Hafr's sluts all worked together, side-by-side. Hávi excused herself for only a moment, ran up to her room, and seized Jarl Gullskeggr's small chest of treasure that he'd brought from his ship into the castle. Leaving the wealth of clan Austmaðr, Hávi carried the heavy chest into Hvítvi's hot-fog room, placed it under his bench, and covered it with a shawl. Then she hurried back down and found Bitra.

"Bitra, I need you to do me a favor," Hávi whispered into her ear. "Go upstairs and light big fires in all of the fireplaces surrounding Hvítvi's room, start it steaming, and make sure that his bucket is filled with fresh water. Touch nothing else in his room. *Nothing ...!*"

Bitra obediently ascended the stairs while Hávi returned to the kitchen. Although it was still morning, Hávi prepared a full feast, and sent Knarrarbringa and Mela to inform Jarls Hafr, Hersir, and Dúfunef when the food was ready. Gellir and her girls volunteered to serve ale, and Völu, Breiðr, Brækir, and Blönduhorn helped them. Warriors streamed into the great hall from the courtyard, led by their jarls, and as soon as they were seated, a mug or cup of ale was placed before them. The girls called each warrior their '*savior*'. Jarl Hafr stared dumbfounded as Völu and Gellir smiled brightly at each other; Völu noticed his amazement and purposefully hugged Gellir tightly as they passed carrying empty pitchers back to be filled.

Suddenly women streamed into the great hall carrying every plate, platter, and bowl in Castle Austmaðr. Warriors cheered and leaned aside to let the steaming foods be placed on their tables. The high-table was served first, but sparsely; minutes later every table held something for hungry mouths. Then, as the women turned to return to the kitchen, Hávi entered, wearing only an apron over her bloodstained nightshirt, looking so disheveled that Mjóvi would've called her a disgrace and an insult. But every woman paused when she entered, and suddenly thunderous applause greeted her; women bowed or curtsied deeply to her and warriors rose to their feet and applauded as loudly as they could. Hávi accepted their praise, then climbed to the first dais and slid behind the surprised men, especially the jarls, and took her place beside her husband. She politely acknowledged her husband with a nod, but she smiled brightly when she looked at Hvítvi.

Jarl Hafr glanced distrustfully at Hávi; no one had applauded his entrance, but Hávi ignored him and sat with all of the dignity that she could manage. Hávi felt exhausted and thrilled; relief washed over her, but she'd endured a terrible strain and hadn't slept all night; she needed rest, but her chief duty was about to come, an opportunity that might never come again.

"Hávi, why are you covered with blood?" Jarl Hersir asked.

Hávi smiled but didn't respond right away.

"That's but a part of a very, long story," Hávi said, and she looked to see one of Jarl Hafr's sluts walking past the high-table. "Kaða, could you fetch me some wine? I have a long tale to tell."

"Anything you request, my queen," Kaða curtsied deeply.

Jarl Hafr gaped astounded.

All three jarls, Jarl Hafr's sons, Bíldr, and Hvítvi sat amazed while Hávi described every detail from the moment that she ran back to help Master Kamban to her opening of the trapdoor to summon Master Krókr and the Austmaðr warriors hiding in the dungeon. Half-an-hour passed while she spoke, and every ear close enough listened intently. Hávi emphasized how all of the women sacrificed their virtue to keep the raiders here long enough for the men to return, and how all of the women worked together to care for each other and all of the children, and to destabilize Jarl Gullskeggr's men with petty squabbles and discord. She reported that

Völu had counted thirty-two Norwegians, including Jarl Gullskeggr, who'd been slain by their wives that very morning, and how three women had been killed attempting to murder their husbands. Hávi assured Jarl Hafr that the raiders had stolen clan Austmaðr's whole treasury, but thanks to the women, it was still safe upstairs in their bedroom.

Jarl Dúfunef rose, when Hávi finished her tale, and raised his frothing horn. At once, every warrior in the hall rose and lifted their ales, including those at the high-table.

"Men of steel, I command you to drink to a warrior unparalleled: Queen Hávi Hersir Austmaðr!"

Seldom had such cheers filled the great hall. Women came from the kitchen to join in the celebration, although warriors crowded every table so fully that there was no place for the women to sit. Alone seated while all others stood, Hávi blushed at their praise, then smiled as twenty women came running in to curtsy before her, and then ran back toward the kitchen.

When the cheering subsided, Hávi asked for news of Jorgen; Hvítvi assured her that he was safely in the loving care of the women of clan Dúfunef, and would be arriving as soon as a ship could be sent for him. Relieved, Hávi asked for the tale of their adventure, but no one wanted to speak. At Jarl Hafr's command, his son Rauðkinn reluctantly related their tale, but it was no equal to the heroism of Hávi and the women; they'd split evenly; Jarl Hafr, Hvítvi, Bíldr and several others rode off to clan Dúfunef, while both sons led the rest to clan Hersir. He tried to make their adventure sound dramatic, but both groups had arrived starving to beg for help against foreign invaders who'd already beaten them.

Rauðkinn praised Jarl Hersir and Jarl Dúfunef for uniting to defeat their common foe, and described their fear that the castle and Skadi would be empty when they returned. But Rauðkinn ended weakly; all of the men at the high-table sat staring at their ales while he talked.

"Hávi, we're undecided as to what to do with the prisoners ...," Jarl Dúfunef began.

"The prisoners have to be killed!" Jarl Hafr said.

"These prisoners married your widows ... and your wife," Jarl Hersir said harshly, and Jarl Hafr jerked tensely as if he wanted to draw his sword.

"We needn't decide quickly," Hvítvi added.

"If they return to Norway alive then they'll tell lies about us," Jarl Hafr said.

"No lie could surpass the truth," Jarl Dúfunef said.

"We've got to kill them!" Jarl Hafr insisted.

"What do you say, Hávi?" Jarl Hersir asked.

"Who cares what she thinks?" Jarl Hafr demanded. *"I'm Jarl Austmaðr ...!"*

"Clan Austmaðr only exists because Hávi saved it!" Jarl Dúfunef said.

"Father!" Skytja interrupted. "Please; I'm curious to hear what my stepmother would suggest."

Jarl Hafr snorted disgustedly and drank hurriedly, spilling ale down his front. Hávi took a deep breath before beginning.

"We women have sacrificed all that we had, our honor and our bodies, to save clan Austmaðr, its lands and its wealth. I'm content, but they deserve reward, not punishment. Their husbands are dead, and never will there be enough unmarried Austmaðr men to wed them; most will remain widows for the rest of their lives. They inherited their farms and homes when their husbands died; the barbarous Norwegians married them just to gain their lands. Now, after three months, they'll lose their lands and homes to their clan-chief because they have no husbands ... if you kill the Norwegians. There's no one else for them to marry; to keep their lands ... they must keep their husbands."

"No!" Jarl Hafr argued, but no other man spoke.

"Hávi ... *Mother*," Hvítvi said softly, controlling each word with great effort, "these Norwegians have witnessed our weakness; if word spreads, then next year every nation on the North Sea will invade us."

"I see," Hávi said. "So you'll reward those who saved clan Austmaðr, who've lost their husbands, sons, and virtue ... with poverty and homelessness."

Brooding silence met this pronouncement; ashamed, all of the men bowed their heads. None of them had taken the risks or suffered the degradations of the least woman in Castle Austmaðr. These women had saved everything, and now had everything to lose.

"Mother, you've proven yourself to be the wisest of us all," Rauðkinn said, ignoring his father's baleful glare. "I'd ask the advice of my greatest warriors before any battle; today I ask yours."

Hávi gritted her teeth and forced herself to remain calm, and then spoke with quiet demureness.

"If women had the right ... to own land ... permanently ... then they wouldn't need foreign husbands."

Chapter 39

The prisoners were crammed into the stinking dungeon, which was still fouled with the wastes of those who'd hidden in there for six days. Hávi insisted that each prisoner be given a large mug of water to drink before they were locked inside; several women, including Hvassi and Blönduhorn, begged Jarl Hafr for mercy upon their husbands. Jarl Hafr refused, but Jarl Dúfunef assured all of the women that no harm would come to their husbands until they'd decided what to do.

Heated debates consumed the day into night, but Hávi retired early in the afternoon. She asked Bíldr to accompany her and her servants, and then stopped when they were out in the hall.

"Ladies, could you give us a moment?" Hávi asked.

Worried looks exchanged between the women, but they stood off far enough for Hávi to whisper unheard by any but Bíldr.

"I need to speak to Hvítvi ... in private."

"You know that he can't ...," Bíldr whispered.

"It's important."

"Everyone's watching him. Now isn't the time ..."

Hávi sighed heavily and stumbled a little.

"You're exhausted," Bíldr said, and he turned to summon Hávi's friends.

"Wait," Hávi said. "Tell Hvítvi ... I know that I can trust you ... tell him that I hid something in his steam room ... something that he should keep secret. It was Jarl Gullskeggr's."

"I'll tell him," Bíldr said. "Now off to bed."

Awakening to Rauðrefr crying for her mother's nipple, Völu gladly reported that Jorgen would be arriving soon and that the jarls hadn't reached any decision; the Norwegian prisoners were still locked in the dungeon. Breiðr gave Hávi some troubling news; the captain whose leg she'd amputated had died in the night. Hávi couldn't mourn the invader's death, but regretted that she hadn't been able to heal him, certain that Master Kamban would've succeeded.

"Hávi, you mustn't blame yourself," Völu tried to comfort her. "I've never really looked up to you, you know; we were equals in clan Hersir, but now ... Hávi, you're the greatest woman that I've ever known."

Hávi hugged Völu tightly.

"Just be my friend; that's all I need," Hávi said.

Felian arrived to summon Hávi.

"Hvítvi requests your company on the roof," Felian said.

"The roof?"

"Yes, Mistress."

Hávi smiled widely.

"Was he alone?" Völu asked.

"No, Mistress; Hvítvi meets with Jarl Hersir, Jarl Dúfunef, and Master Bíldr."

Hávi's smile vanished and Völu glared knowingly at her.

"Tell them that Hávi will be right there," Völu said. "Breiðr, Bitra, could you give Hávi and I a moment alone?"

"But ..."

"Just a moment."

Breiðr and Bitra departed with Felian, who frowned sourly. Völu waited until they were gone, and then she closed the trapdoor.

"Hávi, what're you doing?"

"Doing ...?"

"You and Hvítvi."

"Me and ...?"

"You never take your eyes off him, and even his name makes you smile."

"You're mad!"

"Do you love him?"

"No, I ...!" Hávi choked; she couldn't get the words out.

"Freyja save us!" Völu gasped. *"Hávi! How could you ...?"*

"You can't know!" Hávi hissed. *"Please ..!"*

"He's your son!"

"Stepson!" Hávi argued. "Nephew ... I don't know what he is!"

"He's your funeral if you get caught!"

"We're careful."

"If I realized it then you're not careful enough!"

"You can't tell ...!"

"How have you managed to stay queen keeping secrets like this?"

"I have to go ..."

"I'm going with you."

"No, you ..."

"From now on, you're not going anywhere without me!"

Hávi scowled as Völu followed her up the stone stairs, down the long hallway, and up the steep steps to the roof. The gray sky blasted them with a chill breeze under dark, low clouds; summer was over and winter was fast approaching. On the wide, expansive roof, Jarl Hersir and Jarl Dúfunef greeted Hávi; they glanced questioningly at Völu while Bíldr stood as impassively as ever. Wrapped tightly in a thick cloak, Hvítvi smiled as Hávi stepped out, but his grin faded when he saw Völu's glare, a deep frown on her usually-jovial, freckled face.

"Hávi, there's no good solution here," Jarl Hersir said. "Women own property? Men will fight to take it from them, and every clan-chief will waste warriors protecting them. I agree that the women deserve reward; perhaps some silver ...?"

"Letting the Norwegians live isn't possible," Jarl Dúfunef said. "If any of them return home, then they'll spread news of our weakness throughout Scandinavia."

"Without husbands or homes, what good is silver?" Hávi asked. "You're dooming the women."

"They'll be taken care of," Jarl Hersir assured her.

"By who?" Hávi demanded. "By Jarl Hafr?"

"Jarl Austmaðr," Jarl Hersir corrected her.

"Jarl Austmaðr was my first husband; he never botched the sacrifice, ruined the viking, or lost the castle ...!"

"He's a buffoon," Jarl Dúfunef agreed. "He's not fit to be a jarl, let alone a clan-chief, but what would you have?"

"I ..."

"Quiet!" Hvítvi hissed.

Hávi started to object, but Hvítvi shushed them. An inner door closed and footsteps approached; Jarl Hafr climbed the steep steps and emerged onto the roof.

"What's going on here?" he demanded. "What's the meaning of this?"

"We just ...," Jarl Hersir began.

"Plotting behind my back?"

"We wanted to convince your wife that what she asked for is impossible," Jarl Dúfunef said.

"Her opinion carries no weight!" Jarl Hafr snapped. "I'm Jarl Austmaðr; I make all decisions!"

"You lead one clan in a nation of clans," Jarl Dúfunef said. "Other clan-chiefs have their own authority."

"Not on Austmaðr land!"

"Fine," Jarl Dúfunef said. "I'll just take my ships and leave: all of my ships."

"The captured ships are mine!"

Suddenly Jarl Dúfunef seized Jarl Hafr's fur collar roughly.

"Listen, you imbecile!" Jarl Dúfunef snarled. *"I supported you, and you've made pig-shit out of everything that you've touched. Half of your warriors are dead!"*

"Conscription crews have been sent ..."

"So you'll weaken all of your lesser castles and villages to protect your main castle?" Jarl Dúfunef asked. "Clan Mjöksiglandi or Bagal would be storming your borders within hours if they suspected! And they've been weakened by invading clan Glóra, Vörsa, and killing off clan Refr! I lost two whole ships because of you ...!"

"That wasn't my fault!"

"If you don't start cooperating then all of Sweden will fall!

And before I let that happen, Jarl Hersir and clan Dúfunef shall unite and wipe out clan Austmaðr and divide your lands between us!"

"How dare you?" Jarl Hafr shouted, and he pushed Jarl Dúfunef back. *"I'll have my guards ...!"*

"My guards outnumber yours!"

"Either of his sons would be a better leader than ...," Hávi started.

"Silence!" Jarl Hafr shouted, and he swung his fist at Hávi, but Jarl Hersir easily caught his punch in his one huge hand.

"If you'd landed that punch then we'd be at war," Jarl Hersir warned, his deep voice almost a growl. "Hávi saved us. You've ruined the Skåne."

"I rule the Skåne!" Jarl Hafr shouted.

"I'm leaving," Jarl Dúfunef said. "With my men and my ships, including half of the captured dragons. Jarl Hersir owns the other half; he can do what he chooses with his."

"No," Hávi said as Jarl Dúfunef tried to push past her. "You can't leave."

"Why not?"

"Because more Norwegians are coming."

Utter silence met this declaration.

"What do you mean?" Jarl Hafr demanded.

"Jarl Gullskeggr knew that you wouldn't welcome Norwegians in Sweden," Hávi said. "He hoped to hold the castle until winter set in, and he sent a ship with messengers back to Norway requesting more troops."

"When did you plan to tell us this?" Jarl Hafr demanded.

"When you stopped ordering her to be silent," Jarl Dúfunef replied. "Hávi, are you sure about this?"

"I heard him give the orders."

"Again Hávi's saving us," Jarl Hersir said. "We can

ambush them; let just one ship escape to report how strong Sweden is."

"If she's telling the truth ...," Jarl Hafr scoffed.

"Father-in-law," Bíldr spoke up for the first time, "I've known Hávi since she first came here; she's never once told a lie."

"We'll deal with the reinforcements when they arrive," Hvítvi said. "Our only issue here is to decide how to reward the women who saved clan Austmaðr. Hávi's right: silver will do little; we can't afford to pay them enough or feed them from our limited stores, nor can we allow their Norwegian husbands to live."

Surprised, Hávi looked up into Hvítvi's face. Hvítvi met her stare, then lowered his head and sighed dramatically.

"We have to let women own property," Hvítvi said.

"Gylðir and Spaki were killed," Valla said.

"We've no Law-speakers?" Jarl Hafr growled.

"We have Valla and Augi," Hvítvi said.

"They're kids!"

"They're all that we've got," Hvítvi said. "Without Hávi, we'd have none; she arranged for their training."

Jarl Hersir, Jarl Dúfunef, Skytja, and Rauðkinn looked down upon Valla and Augi; Hávi kept a tight grip on a shoulder of each boy.

"What's required to pass a local law?" Rauðkinn asked.

"You have to declare a Thyngr," Valla said.

"Any jarl and ten heads of households can declare a Thyngr," Augi added.

"Do laws made at a Thyngr affect other clans?" Jarl Dúfunef asked.

"Only laws made at a Tynwald affect more than one clan,"

Valla said.

"Laws made at a Thyngr can be undone at a Tynwald," Augi said.

"Excellent," Jarl Hafr said. "I can command this, and we'll hold a Tynwald in the spring to reverse it."

"A Tynwald requires appointed representatives from the majority of the clans in Sweden," Valla said.

"And all changes to laws at a Tynwald must be voted upon," Augi said. "Local laws can be ratified by a Tynwald, and then they can't be changed."

"So the jarls at a Tynwald could force a clan to keep any laws that it makes at a Thyngr?" Skytja asked.

"Yes."

"How can other clans enforce one clan's internal laws?" Rauðkinn asked.

"That's not the point," Valla said. "Clans require the support of its people; forcing a clan to keep a law that it won't enforce makes its leaders look foolish."

"It's a way of undermining a clan-chief's authority," Augi explained.

"These boys sound like Law-speakers to me," Skytja said.

"We can't make laws that we can't afford to keep!" Jarl Hafr insisted.

"If you don't plan to keep them then you shouldn't make them," Jarl Dúfunef said.

"Then we don't make them!"

"You've no choice," Jarl Hersir said. "For Hávi's sake, and for the sake of her son, your legal heir, you will command this law, or Jarl Dúfunef and I will divide your lands right now; you don't have the troops to stop us."

"Hávi, please stop them!" Blönduhorn came running in,

followed by several other women, and she fell to her knees in the middle of the hall, reaching up desperately, pleadingly, to Hávi , tears drenching her cheeks.

"What ...?" Hávi asked.

"They're going to kill them!"

"Our husbands," Hvassi explained. "Bíldr's summoning the guards."

"They're our enemies ..."

"He's kind and gentle!" Blönduhorn cried. "*I love him!*"

"My husband's no prize, but he's better than none," Hvassi added. "Four other women also wish to keep their husbands."

"Four out of a hundred?" Hávi asked. "What do the other women want?"

"Brækir never gave her husband a chance!" Blönduhorn sobbed.

"They want Bíldr to ... to do what he's doing," Hvassi said. "Can't we just keep the six husbands ...?"

"Would you risk the safety of Sweden upon these men?" Hávi asked.

"I would," Hvassi said.

"Do you think that the jarls would?"

"They have to!" Blönduhorn whimpered, her cheeks dripping. "*They have to ...!*"

A large crowd gathered in the hall, drawn by Blönduhorn's frantic wails. Hávi looked around for faces that she knew.

"Mela, Gellir, take Blönduhorn to my tower, please, and stay with her," Hávi said. "Felian, fetch them some cold wine from the cellar; I'll be up there as soon as I can."

As Felian ran off, Mela and Gellir helped lift Blönduhorn, who was almost limp in their arms, and they hustled her off to Hávi's tower. Hávi and Hvassi watched them depart in silence.

"Is there any hope?" Hvassi asked quietly.

"This isn't just about security for Sweden," Hávi said. "Hafr, Hersir, and Dúfunef have agreed to reward us with the right for women to own property indefinitely. According to Jarl Illingr, no women have had this right since Rome fell. Would you keep this right from all women just to spare your husband?"

"I would," Hvassi said, "but I can't expect others to support me."

"I'm sorry," Hávi said.

"Do you know how long it's been since I cried?" Hvassi asked.

Hvassi stood unmoving before Hávi, a great pillar of a woman, bigger around than Hávi could reach. Hvassi never moved, but tears began to stream from her eyes. Hávi wrapped her arms around her as far as she could, held her tight and let her tears drench her shoulder. Long minutes passed, the crowd silent while Hávi held Hvassi.

"I can't save them," Hávi whispered. "I wish that I could, but ... I'll do what I can."

The iron trapdoor in the guardhouse was closed and latched. Hávi stared at the men resolutely, defiantly.

"Hávi, you shouldn't be here," Bíldr said as the guards gathered around them.

"I promised their wives that I would," Hávi said. "It'll only take a moment."

"You can't warn them."

"I won't."

Slowly Bíldr nodded, and then he walked to the wall and removed a large stone which had looked like part of the wall, but slid out easily.

"This is part of the dungeon's ventilation," Bíldr explained. "All of their fresh air enters through here." Bíldr put his lips to the hole and shouted. "Norwegians! I have a message for six of you!"

"We're listening!" came the reply from the dark, narrow chimney.

Bíldr stepped back and motioned for Hávi to speak.

"I bring a message," Hávi shouted into the hole, "from the wives of Magr, Orðlokarr, Blákinn, Löngubak, Pái, and Skökull: their wives love them and have pleaded for their release!"

No reply met this pronouncement. Hávi and the others stared at the dark, silent hole, and then Bíldr placed a hand on Hávi's shoulder and drew her back.

"What's to become of us?" a voice wafted up through the chimney.

No one answered it.

"Pour the oil," Bíldr whispered to his guards.

Several guards stepped forward with large, clay jars filled with oil, and another man stood ready with a torch.

"You're going to ....?" Hávi whispered.

"The fire won't reach them," Bíldr whispered. *"The flames will consume their breathable air."*

Hávi stared at Bíldr, horrified, and then she fled from the guardhouse.

Jay Palmer

Chapter 40

At Hávi's request, Hvassi, Blönduhorn, and the other four wives were served a great meal in the sewing room with the best foods and strongest wines in clan Austmaðr. No others joined them; they wept openly at the news of their husband's deaths. Hávi comforted them as best she could, but to little avail. Hávi assigned two kitchen-servants to bring them as much food and drink as they desired, and then Hávi left them; she had to attend the formalities.

In the hallway outside the sewing room, Hávi paused to steel her nerves; *the Thyngr was about to begin.*

Hávi met Bíldr, who stood with his wife Knarrarbringa, in the hallway near the kitchen. Bíldr followed Hávi as her official guard, Knarrarbringa behind him, and they entered the great hall together. A large murmuring crowd filled the hall with muted expectancy. The high-table was only partially-filled; *none of the men wanted this.* Hávi and Bíldr ascended the narrow steps; married to Jarl Hafr's daughter, Bíldr earned a seat near the center beside Skytja and Rauðkinn, but Knarrarbringa had to sit at the women's table. To Hávi's surprise, Bifru, Völu's husband, sat at the far end of the high-table beside two others that Hávi didn't know.

Applause broke out as Jarl Hafr entered, followed by Jarl Hersir, Jarl Dúfunef, and Hvítvi. Most of the applause came from the back of the hall where women were crowded around the back tables; the warriors only applauded perfunctorily. The jarls assumed their customary seats at the high-table and silence fell in the hall.

"Bring in the sword!" Jarl Hafr commanded, although his frown couldn't be deeper.

A tall, broad-shouldered warrior ceremoniously entered carrying an ornate sword before him; Hávi had seen him many times but never asked his name.

"Has this sword been bloodied in battle?" Jarl Hafr asked him.

"In honorable combat," the warrior replied, and he lifted the sword up before the high-table. Jarl Hafr reached out and took the sword.

"I, Jarl Austmaðr, command this Thyngr."

Jarl Hafr passed the sword to Jarl Hersir.

"Due to our recent losses, heads of households from clans Hersir and Dúfunef will assist our brethren neighbor. I, Jarl Hersir, command this Thyngr."

Hávi didn't even reach for the sword as it was passed by her; she'd been allowed to sit at the high-table on condition that she say nothing.

"I, Jarl Dúfunef, command this Thyngr."

The sword was passed all the way down the table; four men whom Hávi didn't know commanded the Thyngr, and then the sword was passed back and three more men commanded the Thyngr; Bifru spoke last, and then the sword was passed back to Jarl Hafr, who held it up as if in supplication to the gods, and then set it onto the high-table before him.

"By law and custom, this Thyngr of clan Austmaðr is convened," Jarl Hafr said.

Scattered applause met this, but Jarl Hafr glared angrily at those clapping and silence quickly fell.

"Let the Law-speakers come forth," Hvítvi said.

Many laughed as Valla and Augi came forward; neither could see over the high-table and several men in the back stood up to look at them. One pair of hands clapped loudly; from the women's table, Brækir cheered her sons, but she stopped clapping and looked embarrassed when no one else applauded.

"Law-speakers Valla and Augi," Hvítvi said, "has our Thyngr been properly convened?"

"Legally, yes," Valla said. "Each man was chosen because he leads a household and Jarl Austmaðr is the rightful local clan-chief."

Several men at the high-table looked unexpectedly impressed by Valla.

"Let's get this over with," Jarl Dúfunef said. "We've only one order of business ..."

"Two," Jarl Hafr corrected.

Everyone in the hall stared at Jarl Hafr, but he sat as impassive as Bíldr.

"Two?" Jarl Hersir asked.

"One at a time," Jarl Hafr said.

Worried glances were exchanged; even Hvítvi's pale face darkened with concern.

"V-very well," Hvítvi said. "Law-speaker Valla, please read

the new law."

Valla lifted a small scroll and read it loudly.

"By command of this Thyngr, women of clan Austmaðr within lands of clan Austmaðr have the right to own property in their own name for the remainder of their lives. Possession of all lands and buildings owned by women shall pass unto their husbands upon marriage or unto their sons upon their recognition of manhood by their clan-chief. Upon their death, lands owned by women with no legal age-appropriate sons shall be claimed by their clan-chief."

Total silence met this reading. Hávi barely dared breathe; she'd wanted women to have the right to refuse any marriage against their will, but ownership of property was a good right; a step in the right direction. And, as Jarl Illingr had taught her, the decision to support this law had been decided before the Thyngr. Hávi fought not to smile, fearful of disrupting the moment.

"Jarls and accepted heads of households," Hvítvi spoke as loudly as he dared, "have any of you failed to hear this law?" No one spoke. "Do any of you object to this law?" No one spoke. "Law-speaker Augi, has this law been legally commanded?"

"A vote must be taken for any law to be approved," Augi said.

"Very well; all those who support this law, speak now."

Everyone looked at Jarl Hafr, but he didn't budge.

"I support this law," Jarl Dúfunef said.

"I support this law," Jarl Hersir said.

One by one, every head of household followed suit, voicing their support. Finally all were done, and every eye focused on Jarl Hafr.

"Reluctantly I support this law," Jarl Hafr scowled.

"Law-speakers Valla and Augi, has this law been passed?" Hvítvi asked.

Valla swallowed hard as if suddenly afraid to speak.

"This law is law," Augi said.

Cheers rose from many women, but their celebration was muted; no man cheered, and many cast warning glares at the celebrants. Hávi allowed a weak smile, but inside she was dancing; *she'd changed the den Skaanske Lov! Jarl Illingr would be proud of her!*

Hvítvi waved his arms for silence, then spoke to everyone.

"Is there any further business for this Thyngr? No? Then ..."

"I have business before this council," Jarl Hafr spoke up.

Silence fell as Jarl Hafr pushed back his chair to stand with deliberate slowness. He cleared his throat and stared out at the hall as if personally challenging every man.

"Master Krókr, come before the council ... and bring your witnesses."

Master Krókr came forward accompanied by five men, servants that Hávi had seen working the fields of the castle. The servants walked nervously in the wake of Master Krókr's heavy, confident strides.

"My seneschal has just returned from Law Rock," Jarl Hafr said. "He has legally made an accusation against someone in this room ... one of our own people ...*for murder.*"

Gasps met the pronouncement. Eyes opened wide and every face at the high-table looked shocked.

"Murder," Jarl Hafr repeated. "Murder of a great, noble lady who dedicated every day of her life to clan Austmaðr; for the murder of ... Mistress Mjóvi Illingr ... Master Krókr accuses ... *Mistress Hávi Hersir Austmaðr!*"

Screams drowned out countless gasps as half of the hall jumped to its feet. Jarl Hersir and Jarl Dúfunef stared at Jarl Hafr; murderous glares from men who murdered every summer. Jarl Hafr slowly sat back down, ignoring them all.

"Father ...," Skytja started.

"Be silent!" Jarl Hafr snapped.

"I won't be silent," Jarl Hersir said, barely controlling his whisper. "Clan Austmaðr would be dead if not for Hávi!"

"I didn't make the accusation," Jarl Hafr said.

"He's your servant!" Jarl Dúfunef growled.

"My seneschal is free to ..."

"Liar!" Jarl Dúfunef shouted and he rose to his feet.

"Betrayer!" Jarl Hafr jumped up.

Both drew swords as the crowd shouted, but Jarl Hersir seized Jarl Hafr's sword-arm from behind.

"Not at a Thyngr!" Jarl Hersir cried. *" You'll both be outlawed ... and lose your clans!"*

Jarl Hafr froze as Jarl Dúfunef lunged, but he masterfully stopped his flashing blade a hair's width from Jarl Hafr's throat; only great warriors possessed such skill.

"You dare threaten a jarl in his own hall?" Jarl Hafr shouted.

"Do nothing!" Hvítvi shouted at both of them. "An accusation's been made, but it's not legal yet."

"We're taking a break!" Jarl Hersir shouted to the whole hall. "The Thyngr will reconvene in one hour!"

No one left, all staring aghast at the high-table, at two jarls poised to fight, and at Master Krókr standing serenely before the council. Moments ticked by, and then a hundred whispered conversations broke the dead silence.

"Hávi, you should retire," Jarl Hersir said.

"No ..."

"You'll be summoned before the Thyngr resumes," Jarl Hersir said. "Please. We need to have a meeting of jarls, only jarls: upstairs: now."

"What do we have to discuss ...?" Jarl Hafr demanded.

"Your future!" Jarl Hersir snarled.

"Valla, Augi, you come with me," Hvítvi said.

Hávi sat silently objecting, but she knew that she had to obey. Jarl Hersir wouldn't betray her, and no one liked her husband. As Hvítvi hurried both Law-speakers out of the hall, Hávi took a deep breath and then made a show of standing with lady-like poise and demurely exited without a word. Völu, Bitra, and the rest of her friends followed; Völu started to speak but Hávi hushed her.

"I need to be washed and changed," Hávi said at the foot of her spiral stairs, and Bitra took Blönduhorn to help her fetch hot water.

"It's insulting!" Völu said as they climbed the steps. "He owes you everything!"

"Does a man thank his sword for killing an enemy?" Hávi asked. "Women are tools to Jarl Hafr, nothing more."

"You never should've married him," Völu said.

"Weren't you going to *'make me perform my wifely duties'?"*

They pushed through the trapdoor and climbed up into the tower.

"This is serious," Breiðr said as she rummaged through Hávi's wardrobe. "The accusation's been made. You could be outlawed for seven years."

"Austmaðr won't last seven days without Hávi," Brækir said.

"What can we do?" Völu asked.

"Nothing," Hávi said. "We have to trust the council."

"They can't outlaw you; half of them aren't even Austmaðr."

"If my husband outlaws you then he'll sleep alone for the rest of his life!" Völu said.

"Bifru wouldn't do that," Hávi managed a grin. "I'd have to go back to clan Hersir where he'd see me every day."

"If Jarl Hersir allowed it," Völu said.

Breiðr chose the green dress that Hvassi had made and Bitra and Blönduhorn arrived with hot water. They all helped bathe Hávi, who felt like she did back when Mjóvi kept her under her thumb. They were sitting on their beds still cursing Jarl Hafr when Bíldr came up the stairs.

"Hávi, they're ready."

Hávi entered the great hall to several cheers but mostly to angry stares; no one was happy. She ascended the stairs while her companions filed to the back to stand against the wall; several women offered their seat to Völu, but she refused. The high-table looked as it had before, each man seated, some with their arms crossed, and not one smile evident. Hávi scooted behind them to sit at her chair.

"Let the Thyngr commence," Hvítvi said. "Law-speakers, come ..."

"Wait!" Gellir shouted, and she strode down the center of the great hall toward the high-table with the determination of a juggernaut.

"How dare you speak ...?" Jarl Hafr shouted. *"Get ba....!"*

"I speak for the women!" Gellir shouted, stopping before the high-table and glaring up at Jarl Hafr. "If anything happens to Hávi ...!"

"Be silent!" Jarl Hafr bellowed.

"No man in clan Austmaðr will find a woman in his bed!"

Gellir shouted. "*No man!*"

All seemed shocked by this, but then some men laughed and some women applauded, and cheers rewarded Gellir as she turned and strode back to join the women.

"Thank you, *serving girl of Jarl Hafr,*" Hvítvi said, evoking more howls of laughter. "Before we debate this issue, we must hear the accusation and testimony from its witnesses. Master Krókr, will you speak first?"

"I will," Master Krókr said, rising from a table in the front. "Before the Thyngr began, I went to Law Rock with witnesses and shouted this accusation three times: *Mistress Hávi Hersir Austmaðr murdered Mistress Mjóvi Illingr.* All of the women here witnessed the murder ...."

"This isn't the time for evidence," Hvítvi interrupted. "Before witnesses of the murder can be brought forward we must verify that the accusation was legally made. Thank you, Master Krókr. Please introduce your witnesses to the accusation and let them describe what they heard."

Master Krókr grabbed one of the men standing beside him and pulled him to the center before the high-table.

"This is Svína," Master Krókr said.

"Welcome, Svína," Hvítvi said. "Are you of clan Austmaðr?"

"Never been off our lands," Svína said meekly. "I raise pigs for the castle."

"Very well. Tell us what you witnessed."

"Master, it's just as Master Krókr says; we followed him to Law Rock and he accused Mistress Austmaðr of killing Mistress Illingr."

"You heard him say this?"

"Yes, Master; three times."

Four more servants, Völubrjótr, þynning, Lútandi, and

Trumbubein, gave testimony to the accusation, each swearing that Master Krókr had said exactly what he'd reported. Hvítvi welcomed and listened to each, then thanked them for testifying. Hávi glanced at Hvítvi, hoping to catch his eye; *he was up to something.*

"Master Krókr, all of the witnesses are loyal servants of clan Austmaðr and support your testimony, which everyone here accepts as honorable," Hvítvi said. "Now tell this council; what relation was Mistress Mjóvi Illingr to you?"

"She was my friend and a staunch supporter of clan Austmaðr," Master Krókr said.

"She wasn't your sister, niece, or cousin?" Hvítvi asked.

"No, but she was ..."

"No relation at all?"

Master Krókr glared at Hvítvi.

"The loyalty of Mistress Mjóvi Illingr deserves to be honored!" Master Krókr said.

"No one doubts the word of such a loyal seneschal as yourself," Hvítvi said to Master Krókr. "Thank you. I believe that everyone at the council trusts that your account of the accusation is accurate."

Hávi startled; *what was Hvítvi doing? If the accusation was legally-made ...!*

"Law-speakers Valla and Augi, come forward," Hvítvi said, and the two boys hesitantly approached the high-table. "You've heard the accusation and all witnesses to it. Did Master Krókr make this accusation legally?"

"He did it right," Valla said, "but ..."

Valla glanced fearfully at Master Krókr, who glared down from his vast height.

"He couldn't!" Augi said loudly.

Master Krókr started forward, but Hvítvi shouted.

"Wait! Hear them out! Augi, what do you mean?"

"He did it right, but he wasn't her kin or her lord," Augi said.

"Do you have to be kin or lord?" Hvítvi asked.

"Law Rock is where legal accusations are made," Valla quoted. "Not anyone can make an accusation; women and children can't, and men can only make accusations that concern them. Where an accusation involves several men, only the oldest or the closest living adult male relative may make the accusation. If someone has the sole right to make an accusation, but is too afraid to voice it himself, then no accusation is made; the den Skaanske Lov makes no allowance for cowardice."

Several voices cheered, but Hvítvi waved them silent.

"Does that mean that only Mjóvi's oldest, living relative can make an accusation for her murder?" Hvítvi asked.

"Yes." Valla said.

"No!" Augi said. "Of all promises, oaths, contracts, and marriages, if a person is without kin, then their clan-chief assumes the status of their head of house, and may rule for them."

"That's right," Valla said.

"So," Hvítvi said, "Master Krókr made his accusation properly, but since the death of Jarl Illingr, Mjóvi's only head of house was Jarl Austmaðr, and only he could ..."

"*No!*" Jarl Hafr argued. "*I can delegate to my servants any duty that I wish!*"

"We on this council aren't bound by your wishes," Jarl Dúfunef said.

"All on this council are bound by the den Skaanske Lov," Jarl Hersir said. "Are there any who dispute the legal learnings of these boys?"

"*I do!*" Jarl Hafr shouted.

"Have you Law-speakers to dispute their recitations of the den Skaanske Lov?"

"*They are my Law-speakers!*"

"Then you should listen to them," Jarl Hersir said. "Even clan-chiefs aren't above the den Skaanske Lov."

"According to the den Skaanske Lov," Hvítvi said, "only Jarl Austmaðr is rightfully allowed to make accusations over Mjóvi's death. Jarl Austmaðr, have you made an accusation at Law Rock?"

"*I sent my seneschal!*" Jarl Hafr shouted. "*It's the same as if I'd gone there myself!*"

"I call for a vote," Jarl Dúfunef said. "Speak, members of the council: was the accusation against Mistress Hávi Hersir Austmaðr legally made?"

Jarl Hersir spoke first.

"I say no."

Nine more councilmen spoke, each voicing the same objection, and Jarl Hafr's face grew redder at each recitation.

"*Very well!*" Jarl Hafr shouted. "*I'll make the accusation myself!*"

"If you wish," Hvítvi said.

"*I accuse Hávi Hersi....!*"

"Accusations can only be made at Law Rock," Valla interrupted.

"*Loki kill you both!*" Jarl Hafr shouted at the boys.

Jarl Hafr pushed back his chair and shoved his way along the back of the high-table, down the steps, and he stormed toward the main doors with such vehemence that everyone crowded aside to make room for his tirade.

"*I'll be back in ten minutes!*" Jarl Hafr shouted. "*Then this accusation will be legally made!*"

Jarl Hafr pushed open the doors and vanished into the courtyard, shouting for a horse. Everyone watched him go in utter silence. Jarl Dúfunef snorted derisively and several men chuckled, but Hvítvi waved for them all to be silent and waited until they heard hooves gallop off down the white, shell-paved road.

"Skytja, my brother," Hvítvi said. "With our ... father departed, leadership of the Thyngr passes to one of us. You are his true son; shall we end the Thyngr before he returns?"

Skytja frowned at Hvítvi.

"I'm sure that he'll be right back."

"Yes," Hvítvi said, "but he didn't take any witnesses, so again the accusation will be illegal."

Skytja sighed and bowed his head.

"Brother, we owe everything to Hávi," Rauðkinn said. "I say we end this Thyngr."

Skytja shook his head, then bowed in surrender.

I declare this Thyngr ended.

"No!" Master Krókr shouted. " *We'll go after him ...!"*

He grabbed his servants and started toward the door.

"I don't think so," Jarl Hersir said. *"Warriors of clan Hersir, to the gate: let no one depart!"*

"Seal-warriors, join them!" Jarl Dúfunef shouted.

Without hesitation, most of the men in the great hall rose, and a great laughter erupted as they marched out the main door into the courtyard. Under the warrior's deadly glares, even tall Master Krókr paused, and his witnesses cringed.

"Don't try to keep Jarl Austmaðr out when he gets back," Hvítvi shouted to them, "but I suggest that no one who values their skin remain in the great hall when he returns."

More laughter erupted, but many turned to inconspicuously depart before Jarl Hafr returned.

"I think that we'd best set sail,' Jarl Hersir said to Jarl Dúfunef.

"I can't wait to get out of here," Jarl Dúfunef said.

Hávi left with the others, joining the crowd urgently trying to slip through the main doorways into the crowded hallway. Many tried to congratulate Hávi, but she hushed them.

"It's best that we not speak of it," Hávi said. "This castle has many ears."

Everyone heeded her advice, but all departed smiling.

Chapter 41

Hávi and her closest friends celebrated in her tower all night.

"I didn't win," Hávi said. "Master Krókr will see that Jarl Hafr makes the accusation properly."

"But the Thyngr's over!" Völu argued.

"He can command another," Hávi said. "Now that Jarl Hersir and Jarl Dúfunef have left, Jarl Hafr can gather ten heads of Austmaðr households and host another Thyngr ..."

"Clan Austmaðr would revolt ...!" Bitra said.

"It can't," Hávi said. "I can't let it ... even if I must be outlawed."

"That's not fair!" Breiðr complained.

"We got the right to own property," Hávi said. "For now, at least."

"Some women would rather have husbands."

"Women can be more choosey now."

"There're no men left to choose," Bitra said. "The villages

were already in short supply ...."

"Men with skills are what we need," Breiðr said. "Few can replace the woodwright or the blacksmith. Their wives may own their shops, but they can't run their husbands' businesses. It'll take generations to repair the damage that Jarl Hafr's done."

"Felian says that he was furious, finding the great hall empty when he returned. Jarl Hafr shouted for five minutes before a servant dared approach him."

Suddenly rapid footsteps pounded Hávi's tower stairs. Closer it rose, and then three sluts poked their heads up through the open trapdoor.

"Mistress, help us!" Kaða cried.

"Please!" þyna begged.

"It's Gellir!" Vaggagði said. *"He's beating her!"*

Gellir's cries echoed through the empty hallways. Hávi hurried up the stone stairs and ignored the young guard that tried to block her entrance. Pushing into her bedroom, followed by Kaða, þyna, and Vaggagði, Hávi found Gellir on the floor beside her old bed, Jarl Hafr standing over her weeping, prostrate form wielding a brutal length of coarse, thick rope. Gellir's clothes were shredded and blood leaked from countless abrasions on her bruised, reddened skin. Her screams cut off as she spied Hávi in her doorway.

"Stop!" Hávi shouted at her husband. "Leave her be!"

Jarl Hafr spun, recognized Hávi, and his sadistic glare reddened to murderous.

"You ...!" Jarl Hafr cried, and he swung his rope.

The screams amplified. Hávi jumped back, out of his range, but he chased her into the outer room, and before she could flee, his heavy length of rope caught her shoulder and knocked her off-balance. Hávi tripped, and then tried to turn, but his rope hit her again: tightly-braided tree bark as thick as her wrists which hit like a young, billy goat butting into you with its horns sawn off. Hávi stumbled, then fell, and the rope pounded across her face.

"*Bitch!*" Jarl Hafr shouted. "*Humiliate me ...!*"

Hávi huddled to protect herself, shielding her head with her arms, aware only of heavy stinging thumps and her own screams. Blows fell upon her back as she rolled, and then struck her arms; Hávi tried to rise, but his blows knocked her back down; Jarl Hafr may be an idiot, but he was a warrior trained to viking.

"*Stop it!*" Hvítvi's voice shouted, but then a thud sounded that didn't strike Hávi; Hvítvi cried out and fell. Jarl Hafr raised his heavy rope again: *he could kill Hvítvi!*

"*Skytja!*" Hávi shouted. "*Rauðkinn!*"

Jarl Hafr turned his blows back upon Hávi, who collapsed onto the floor, crying out. Kaða, þyna, and Vaggagði continued to scream and Gellir's voice shouted inarticulately, but Hávi lay helpless as blows rained on her.

"*Father!*"

Skytja and Rauðkinn charged into the room.

Hávi barely remembered being half-carried down the stone steps. Her sleeves were tattered, her swollen, bruised flesh protruding through wide, ragged rents in her ruined green dress. Wine was poured down her throat and onto her scrapes; Hávi screamed as they washed out her wounds. Felian was summoned by Völu, who treated her as Master Kamban would've. Upon seeing Hávi's bleeding back, Völu threatened to '*kill that bastard idiot*'.

"No!" Hávi whispered between painful gasps. "He ... will

... banish ... you."

"He should be banished!" Völu shouted.

"The ... den Skaanske Lov," Hávi forced the words through gnashed teeth. "Legally, a ... man ... can beat ... wives and servants."

"Then we need more rights!" Völu shouted.

Despite her pain, Hávi smiled.

The next day, Hávi ordered several women to start the kitchen fires for a large midday meal; nothing had been cooked the night before. Hávi dressed in her apron to help cook, but Bíldr came for her before she left her tower.

"Hávi, Hvítvi wishes for you to attend him," Bíldr said.

"Where is he?" Hávi asked.

"In his special room," Bíldr answered.

Hávi smiled, but she forced a frown when Völu and Bíldr glared angrily at her.

"Felian's with him," Bíldr said. "Hvítvi's very ill."

Hávi ran up the stone stairs, only Völu and Bíldr able to match her strides. She pushed through the doors into the thick steam without hesitation and found Hvítvi laying on his bench, a towel wrapped around his middle and Felian leaning over him.

"He's hurt bad," Felian said.

Hávi knelt; Hvítvi lay unconscious, and the only sign that he was alive were the barely-audible groans that escaped snow-white lips; he looked like he'd been bled dry. A pile of wet, bloody rags lay beside the bench.

"How many times did he get hit?" Hávi asked.

"Only once, but it was more than his fragile bones could take," Felian sad.

Felian showed Hávi the wound under the bloody bandage that he was pressing to Hvítvi's hair; Hávi felt his scalp and found a huge swelling upon the top of Hvítvi's head, inches above his forehead, which matched many of her injuries. But she was a tough goat-rancher; Hvítvi couldn't endure a tiny scratch. Blood leaked between his stark, white hairs.

"Keep pressing that bandage," Hávi said. "Press hard."

"It hurts him," Felian said.

"Better pain than death."

Hvítvi cried out as Felian pressed the rag to his head. Hávi held Hvítvi still with ease.

"It's alright," Hávi said. "We'll take care of you."

Bíldr came in and watched their ministrations through the thick, swirling fog.

"Is his skull cracked?" Bíldr asked.

"No way to tell," Felian answered. "We can't take the bandage off to check: he'll bleed to death."

"He hurts a lot," Hávi said. "Völu, fetch wine."

"No!" Felian said. "Wine thins the blood and he'll leak worse; dandelion tea is what he needs ... and chamomile for the pain."

Völu returned in ten minutes with the tea; it was weak and only warm.

"Bitra's making stronger tea," Völu said, breathing heavily in the thick steam.

"Völu, Hávi needs to be in here," Bíldr said. "Some might find your presence here improper."

"If you've got anyone who can throw me out then they're welcome to try," Völu said.

Bíldr looked affronted, but Hávi cut him off.

"Fetch me some dry clothes," Hávi said to Völu. "I'll be soaked before I'm through."

Völu darted Hávi an evil glare.

"Mind your business!" Völu snapped at Hávi before she left.

Hours passed nervously; Hvítvi paled so much that at times the steam hid him, but they refused to uncover his wound. Felian and Hávi took turns holding him; Hávi suggested that they tie his bandage on but Felian feared that it might harm Hvítvi's jaw when he cried out. Together they cared for Hvítvi as best they could; *if only Master Kamban were here!* Hvítvi passed into sleep but awoke crying out several times. He appeared too weak to lift his head. Hávi wanted to hold him as she'd held him before, to comfort him with hugs as tight as Hvítvi could endure, but Felian and Bíldr were watching.

"Gellir is being tended by the sluts," Bíldr reported. "They've taken over an empty room on the lowest floor and barred its doors; if Jarl Austmaðr finds them ..."

"Jarl Hafr," Hávi corrected. "He's not fit to be called Jarl Austmaðr."

"He rules our clan, like it or not," Bíldr said. "Either of his sons would be a better choice, but then Jorgen would be imperiled ... and so would Hvítvi."

"Surely you don't suspect ...!"

"I suspect everything."

Hávi arrived late for the evening meal in a yellow dress, her face dark with scabs and bright with bruises; everyone who saw her gasped. Several elders demanded to know who hurt her, but Hávi only turned and glared at her husband, who quickly choked down his supper and left the great hall without a word.

Hvítvi's wound left him bedridden for weeks. Hávi

attended him every day but never alone; Felian, Bíldr, or Völu always accompanied her, observing their every exchange with silent intrusiveness. Hvítvi's cuts lightly scabbed over after only two days, although his abrasions leaked for several days afterwards. But Hvítvi had lost too much blood; at first he struggled to maintain a weak consciousness and no color existed in his face at all.

Snows dumped upon the countryside as winter came early. Skadi was blanketed, and the gate guards protecting Castle Austmaðr were placed at high windows and ordered to watch from there; Skytja didn't want them outside freezing to death. Jarl Hafr argued with his eldest son, but their only resolution was to place Rauðkinn in charge of the castle guards.

Rauðkinn accepted this post and commanded that the guards stay warm and watch from the windows.

Gossip fueled the rumor-mill. Despite the thick snow, Jarl Hafr had returned to Law Rock with twenty guards and, with half of Skadi watching, repeated his accusation. Valla and Augi were forced to bear witness; *Hávi was legally and rightfully charged with murder.* When the next Thyngr convened, Hávi's accusation would be their first order of business. Hávi wondered if she'd be outlawed, like Sterki, and if her husband would try to kill her before she could flee. But, as she cuddled Jorgen in her arms, she never once regretted killing Mjóvi.

But Jarl Hafr couldn't host a Thyngr; none of the largest households would support him. Since being given the right to own property, most of the wealthiest households were headed by women, and they publicly announced their willingness to attend the Thyngr so that they could support Hávi. Jarl Hafr bridled at their derision and commanded a gathering of heads of households that worked for him, but with even less success. One shepherd informed Master Krókr that, if allowed to vote, he'd outlaw Jarl Hafr and keep Hávi; the shepherd was immediately dismissed, but upon learning of his declaration, the widow of the woodwright took him in and married him three days later. Four more castle workers married wealthy widows that week, leaving Castle Austmaðr seriously shorthanded.

"Dúfunef!" Jarl Hafr cursed loudly and often. *"This is his fault! Jarl Dúfunef ruined the viking to weaken us and now he's twisted our laws to insult me!"*

"Father, we wouldn't be alive without Jarl Dúfunef," Skytja said.

"Besides, we need his seal-warriors," Rauðkinn said. "If we lose them then we won't get to viking at all."

"We don't need clan Dúfunef to viking!" Jarl Hafr argued.

"No," Rauðkinn agreed, "but we need them to live peaceably beside us. If we leave clan Dúfunef behind, then we'll have to leave half of our troops at home to protect the castle."

Jarl Hafr growled and drank deeply from his horn.

"You're right," Jarl Hafr said. "Clan Austmaðr will never be safe while clan Dúfunef endures."

"Father!" Skytja shouted.

"Madness!" Rauðkinn scowled.

"We can't say such things!" Skytja said. "Clan Austmaðr's strong, but we can't stand alone."

"I'm Jarl Austmaðr!" Jarl Hafr bellowed. *"I say what I please!"*

"Then you speak without me," Rauðkinn said, and he dropped his half-eaten chicken leg and left in a huff. Jarl Hafr shouted at his son to come back, but he didn't.

"You're relieved of command of the castle guards!" Jarl Hafr shouted, but Rauðkinn had already departed.

One wintry evening, Hávi awoke to bootsteps ascending her stairs. Hávi startled; guards didn't patrol at night anymore; Castle Austmaðr didn't have enough guards left. Hávi didn't recognize these bootsteps: more than one set approached, walking slowly, furtively. She glanced to make sure that her trapdoor was bolted and then at the rope hanging from its bell. Finally Hávi drew the long dagger that she kept by her bed, the dagger that Master Kamban had given her.

Knuckles rapped gently on her trapdoor.

"Who is it?" Hávi asked.

"Your stepsons," Skytja's voice came through the wood. "Please; we need to talk."

Völu opened the trapdoor and Hávi's stepsons climbed up into her tower. Bitra was sitting beside Hávi on one bed and Hávi gestured to both boys to sit on the other. The light of the candles showed expressions of worry on every face as Völu stoked up the fire and then stood atop the closed trapdoor.

"Welcome to my tower," Hávi said to her stepsons.

"Thank you for seeing us," Skytja said, although he fidgeted nervously. "We ... we're sorry that we never ..."

"You're always welcome here. How can I help you?"

"We don't know if you can ...," Skytja said.

"No one else can," Rauðkinn said. "If you can't ..."

Nervousness tainted both of their voices. Hávi remained silent and waited for the boys to continue.

"It's Father," Skytja said. "He won't listen to reason."

"He's ruining clan Austmaðr," Rauðkinn said. "He keeps saying things that'll get us killed."

"Killed ...?" Hávi asked.

"Killed ... by Jarl Dúfunef," Skytja said.

"Jarl Dúfunef doesn't like your father, but he's a wise clan-chief."

"Very wise," Skytja said.

"Too wise to allow others to threaten him," Rauðkinn said.

Hávi stared disbeliving at her stepsons; *even her idiot husband couldn't be that stupid!*

"Father's been talking about it for days," Skytja said. "He blames Jarl Dúfunef for everything; the viking, the invasion, ..."

"Hvítvi was the only person that he listened to," Rauðkinn said.

Hávi raised her eyebrows questioningly.

"Oh, Father hates what Hvítvi says, but Hvítvi's advice is hard to refute," Skytja said.

"I don't know what help I can be," Hávi said. "Your father's accused me of murder."

"He says that you humiliated him," Skytja said.

"We don't agree," Rauðkinn added.

"Thank you," Hávi said to both of them.

"Father wants to host a Thyngr, but I think that we've talked him out of it," Skytja said. "Don't thank us: we finally convinced him that outlawing you in clan Austmaðr isn't enough."

"We told him that Jarl Dúfunef would gladly take you in if Jarl Hersir refused," Rauðkinn said. "We convinced him that he needs to outlaw you at a Tynwald ... or not at all."

"We don't want you outlawed," Skytja quickly added. "Eventually Father will find ten commoners who'll support him; he'll never get enough votes at a Tynwald."

"Besides, clan Austmaðr would lynch him," Rauðkinn said.

"What can I do?" Hávi asked.

"We don't know," Skytja said.

"We were hoping that you'd tell us," Rauðkinn said. "You've done so much ..."

"Your father beat me ...," Hávi said.

"Mother ...," Skytja said, "we can't be heard publically speaking against Father. He speaks to no one but us ..."

"And he isn't pleased with us," Rauðkinn added.

"If he thinks that we talked to you then he'll accuse us of betraying him," Skytja said. "We're barely able to restrain him as it is; if he quits listening to us, then he might proceed with his plan."

"What plan?" Hávi asked.

Skytja and Rauðkinn exchanged a worried glance.

"Clan Dúfunef," Skytja said unwillingly, looking ashamed. "Father's been ... making plans ... *to invade clan Dúfunef.*"

"That's insanity ...!" Hávi exclaimed softly, fighting to control her voice.

"We agree," Skytja said.

"Completely," Rauðkinn said.

"Clan Austmaðr has suffered great losses! Clan Dúfunef has hundreds of seal warriors ...!"

"Nearly a thousand, if we attack their shores," Skytja said.

"They'd slaughter us," Rauðkinn said.

"Your father can't believe ...!"

"He has several plans; to attack by night, or after they sail for the viking," Rauðkinn said.

"Or he could begin the viking, then force a division, and sail back while they're away," Skytja said.

"No plan would work," Hávi said. "Even if every seal warrior died tonight, clan Austmaðr doesn't have the troops to defend a second territory. Clan Bagal would decimate us if we spread our defenders that thin ..."

"We know," Skytja said.

"That's why we need your help," Rauðkinn said.

"Why should Hávi trust you?" Völu asked suddenly.

"*Völu!*" Hávi snapped.

"Think about it!" Völu hissed. "If anything happened to their father then they'd be the next Jarl Austmaðrs! *They're trying to get you to do their dirty work ...!*"

"*Be silent!*" Hávi hissed back at her.

"We don't want to be clan-chief," Rauðkinn interjected.

Everyone fell silent, Völu snorting with obvious disbelief.

"Rauðkinn's right," Skytja said. "We weren't born to be chiefs. Hvítvi's the last of six brothers; we've assumed since we were little that we'd never be chiefs. Sterki ruined our plans as much as he ruined yours."

"We want to be dragon-captains and go viking," Rauðkinn said. "Father always kept us with him, sailing up and down the coast, while the warriors sailed south and east. We want to raid other lands."

"Clan Austmaðr must have a chief," Hávi said. "I'm already charged with murder; I won't risk a charge of treason by suggesting that another should be clan-chief."

"We can't turn against Father either," Skytja said.

"Jorgen's still a baby," Hávi said.

"Clan Austmaðr may not survive until he grows," Skytja said.

"I've been through this before," Hávi said. "Who would you see made clan-chief if something happened to your father? Hvítvi's brothers are all dead because of that question."

"We'd support Hvítvi," Rauðkinn said.

"But no one else would," Skytja said. "And we can't let Father be killed; no crew would obey us if we dishonored our own father."

"Have you talked to Hvítvi about this?" Hávi asked.

"Yes, but ... did he believe us ...? You know how he is," Skytja said.

"I can never tell what he's thinking," Rauðkinn said.

"All I care about is my son's life," Hávi said. "I don't know what to do about my ... Jorgen's stepfather. I'm the last person that he'll listen to."

"We know," Skytja said. "We just wanted you to know ... that we aren't ... unsupportive of you."

"I wish that we'd talked before," Hávi said.

"We didn't know how you felt," Rauðkinn said.

"We can't be seen talking, especially not here," Skytja said. "Another scandal is the last thing that we need."

"I'm proud to be your stepmother," Hávi said.

Hávi insisted on hugging both of them before they quietly crept down her stairs, furtively following Bitra, who descended to make sure that their path was clear.

"Do you trust Skytja and Rauðkinn?" Völu asked Hávi when they were alone.

"I think so," Hávi said. "I need to ask Hvítvi how much I should trust them."

"Not alone, you won't," Völu said.

"He's still sick!"

"Kisses won't make him better."

"Völu!"

"Tell me that I'm wrong!"

645

Chapter 42

Purple, black, and green colored Hvítvi's white forehead, the rest of him paler due to loss of blood; Jarl Hafr's bruise discolored Hvítvi's head for a month. At Hávi's request, Bíldr sent out a hunting party to follow the tracks of a large moose that'd been seen scavenging for food near a local farm; the thick snow made trailing him easy, but one of their horses was killed when the wounded moose retaliated, before spears and arrows finally dropped him. Both the moose and the horse were cooked in the kitchen; Hávi oversaw their preparation and presented both as a guerdon for Hvítvi's recovery.

Jarl Hafr scowled, sitting between his sons, and Hávi wondered if he'd ordered them to sit there to keep Hvítvi away from him, or if Skytja and Rauðkinn had arranged it to shield Hvítvi from their father. Hávi sat on their opposite side, stealing glances past her husband at Hvítvi; she suspected that he'd arranged her seating, too.

In the middle of Hvítvi's celebration feast, Jarl Hafr stood up and motioned for silence.

"The snows are melting," Jarl Hafr said. "We need a successful viking this year; we're going to have a successful viking or heads will split. The kitchens will begin preparing food so that we can start early; our enemies won't expect to be attacked while they're still planting. Clan Hersir and ... clan Dúfunef ... will join us when they can. My sons, Skytja and Rauðkinn, shall captain their own ships, and we'll return when we can't carry any more plunder."

Scattered, wary applause met this pronouncement. Rauðkinn looked stunned, but Skytja managed to maintain a semblance of a smile, although his tooth-gnashed smirk looked counterfeit. Hvítvi alone nodded approvingly, but Hávi knew not to trust Hvítvi's outward appearances; taking her cue from Hvítvi, Hávi joined in the applause. Many castle women joined in the applause when Hávi did, and Hávi discretely nodded to them. Gellir, she noticed, and her husband's other sluts were seated together right beside a tableful of castle women; their rivalry was gone, voided by their mutual hatred of Jarl Hafr. Yet he was their rightful clan-chief; if Hávi was going to see him replaced then she'd have to do so in some way that avoided another scandal ... and she'd have to know who'd replace him before she allowed it; Hávi couldn't endure a fourth forced-marriage.

The flurry of activity before the viking occupied much of the next few weeks. Hávi heard rumors of discontent; the fields were still frozen and some farmers had broken plow-blades trying to get their planting finished early. Experienced sailors fretted over the dangers of sailing the cold North Sea, wary of temperamental, spring storms. Warriors openly questioned the wisdom of attacking enemy coasts without waiting for the other clans to join them.

Knarrarbringa and Mela approached Hávi as she toiled in the kitchen. Völu, who was trying to keep Jorgen and Rauðrefr from crying, followed them as they ushered Hávi into a corner.

"Mother, we have a problem," Knarrarbringa said in her deepest, most-serious voice.

"What is it?" Hávi asked.

"Valla and Augi asked us to talk to you," Knarrarbringa said. "It's ... about Blönduhorn; *she's pregnant.*"

Hávi startled.

"Are you sure?"

"Brækir's sure," Knarrarbringa said. "A lot of other women are worried; many suspect that they're facing the same ... predicament."

Suddenly Mela started to cry.

"Mela ...?" Hávi asked.

"Mela," Knarrarbringa said. "We're not sure, but ..."

"How many?"

"At least a dozen that we know of," Knarrarbringa said. "Several of the sluts ... and Hvassi."

"Hvassi ...?!?"

"Hvassi suspects but she isn't sure," Knarrarbringa said. "None of us know. Mela ..."

"I can feel it!" Mela sobbed.

"It's alright," Hávi soothed, wrapping her arms around her. "We'll all help you ..."

"But Father ...!" Mela argued.

"He'll be leaving for the viking soon," Hávi said. "There's no need to tell him yet."

"Many sons will grow up without fathers," Knarrarbringa

said dejectedly. "Some women are married; how can they tell their husbands ... *that they'll soon bear the son of another?*"

"Their suffering is nothing compared to what we endured," Hávi said. "Leave it to me."

"No," Hvítvi said. "Blönduhorn can visit the castle, but you can't go into Skadi; we can't risk another assassination attempt."

"The women are worried about how their children will be treated," Hávi said.

"Hávi, we need this," Hvítvi said. "I was more-worried about this aspect of women owning property than any other; a woman with enough wealth could avoid a husband. We need new sons more than ships or gold."

"*The sons of Norwegians ....?*"

"If they'll fight for clan Austmaðr, then I don't care if their fathers are Moors," Hvítvi said. "Tell the women not to worry; their children will be accepted regardless of their birthright. Also, inform them that any woman who isn't pregnant should become so; a man will be provided if they have none."

"Where will you find enough men?" Hávi asked.

"I don't know," Hvítvi said.

"Who'll teach their sons to fight?" Hávi asked. "The unmarried women worry that ..."

"I'll ...," Hvítvi began, but then he glanced at Bíldr and Völu. "Please excuse us; I need to speak to Hávi alone."

"*No,*" Völu said.

Hvítvi raised his pale eyebrows.

"I'm not asking ..."

"*I'm not leaving the two of you alone.*"

Hvítvi glanced at Bíldr, but he stood equally resolute, although he looked more discomfited. A long silence ensued while accusing stares dueled.

"They know us well," Hávi said to Hvítvi. "They suspect things ... of which they have no proof."

"Bíldr ...?" Hvítvi asked.

"Clouds may hide the morning sun, but I know when it's risen," Bíldr said. "Brother, we can't afford another scandal."

Hvítvi stared at all of them with his intense, pink eyes before responding.

"How many suspect?" Hvítvi asked.

"Only those that choose to," Bíldr said. "Mjóvi's evil outlives her; she should've been killed sooner."

"Don't say that," Hvítvi said. "Don't mention Mjóvi; Jarl Austmaðr's accusation at Law Rock was legally-made. Hopefully it'll be the first case of the next Thyngr, no matter when it occurs."

"Hopefully ...?" Hávi and Völu asked.

"Yes," Hvítvi said. "I've found no evidence, but it's possible that the last assassination attempt was financed by ... Jarl Austmaðr."

Hávi and Völu looked shocked.

"They didn't need to know that," Bíldr said. "We can't accuse Jarl Austmaðr without testimony against him."

"Hávi needs to know," Hvítvi said. "Jarl Austmaðr knows that Hávi might not be outlawed; he may prefer that she simply die mysteriously."

"I'll ...!" Völu began.

"You'll do nothing!" Hvítvi snapped at her. *"I decide what actions will be taken!"*

Völu swallowed hard, then nodded her acquiescence.

"We're all being watched," Bíldr said. "Several know that we're here; if Völu and I are seen waiting out in the hall ..."

"We could talk in your hot-fog room," Hávi said.

"No!" Völu said.

"You two are our most-trusted advisors," Hvítvi said, looking from Völu to Bíldr.

"Then take our advice," Bíldr said. "Don't be alone."

Hvítvi sighed.

"Perhaps it's for the best," Hvítvi said reluctantly. "Bíldr knows about ... what you left in my secret room ... what you stole from Jarl Gullskeggr. Does Völu know?"

"No," Hávi admitted, and Völu cast a glare at her.

"Jarl Gullskeggr left a small but very valuable chest of coins that he brought from Norway," Hvítvi explained. "Hávi hid it in my chambers while the castle was being retaken; Jarl Austmaðr knows nothing of it. I'll use those funds, if I must, to finance training for the sons of the unwed mothers; it's the best use of it that I can think of. Inform the women that their bastards will be legally equal to any son of clan Austmaðr."

"Hvítvi, could you command a Thyngr?" Völu asked.

"It wouldn't be legal," Hvítvi said. "As the first accuser, Jarl Austmaðr would have to attend, and no one could deny his right to sit on the council; we can't host Hávi's trial without him."

"What happens if Hávi's ...?" Völu started.

"If Hávi's outlawed then Jorgen loses all claim to the throne of clan Austmaðr," Hvítvi said. "That's what Jarl Austmaðr wants the most: for his own sons to succeed him."

"Skytja and Rauðkinn don't want to be clan-chiefs," Hávi said.

"Will they still feel that way five years from now?" Hvítvi asked. "Ten years? How old will Jorgen have to be to fight them, if they should change their minds?"

"I think that Skytja and Rauðkinn can be trusted," Hávi said.

"I agree," Hvítvi said. "But how far will you trust anyone with Jorgen's life? Once they're ship captains, will they abandon their ambitions to be fleet captains for an infant stepbrother?"

"Tell me what to do," Hávi said.

"Stay safe," Hvítvi said. "Protect Jorgen and yourself. Keep up the preparations for the viking, even if it bankrupts us."

"Bankrupts ....?" Hávi asked.

"Why viking early?" Hvítvi asked. "It makes no sense. Meetings across an ocean are problematic at best, nearly impossible to predict. Attacking enemies with only a part of our force is insane. Sailing early leaves the homeland vulnerable to attack by other clans; why risk it?"

"What do you think Jarl Hafr is planning?" Hávi asked.

"I don't know," Hvítvi said, "but I think ... I fear ... that he intends to invade clan Dúfunef."

Evidence appeared in the countless rumors that filled the castle. Jarl Hafr commanded a meeting with all of the castle guards and promised them land, houses, and women, if they obeyed him without question. All were ordered to keep their swords sharp and be ready to leave at a moment's notice, even at night. All of the men wondered at this; never before had any viking been launched before dawn; why sacrifice to Odin if he's asleep? Worries filled every mind and whispers spewed from every lip.

Preparations continued, sealing barrels of lutefisk and pickled herring, salted meats, and lightly-ground grains. Hard breads filled dozens of baskets and piled to the ceiling on several tables. Ale barrels were emptied into smaller kegs and stored in the cool basement beneath the kitchen. The sewing room rushed to finish another sail and knitted socks and scarves; never before had they such need of warm clothes. The wind off the glaciers was still icy and the last of the snows lingered.

Skytja and Rauðkinn pressed their father for his plans, but Jarl Hafr refused to reveal them.

"Every man loyal to our clan will follow me no matter where I lead them," Jarl Hafr insisted.

Felian, Valla, and Augi appeared on the stairs to Hávi's tower. Völu escorted them up, followed by Bíldr.

"We've been ordered to join the viking," Felian informed Hávi.

"What?!?" Hávi exclaimed. *"You're just boys ...!"*

"Jarl Austmaðr is taking every man that he can," Bíldr said.

"Jarl Hersir never took boys before their fifteenth year," Hávi said.

"Messengers were sent to Skadi and all six Austmaðr villages," Bíldr said. "Every man and boy able to lift a sword or draw a bow is ordered to Castle Austmaðr in eight days."

"Eight days?" Hávi asked. "That's insane! They shouldn't be leaving for three weeks!"

"In eight days the moon will be full," Bíldr said.

"Why should that matter?"

"A full moon makes it easier to ... *sail at night.*"

Suddenly Hávi understood: leaving at night wouldn't matter if they were sailing for weeks across the sea. Leaving at dusk, sailing by night, would matter only if they were sailing north up the coastline ... to attack clan Dúfunef.

"Subtly isn't my husband's best attribute ... assuming that he has any," Hávi said.

"My ears don't need to hear that," Bíldr warned.

"These boys are too important to risk in battle," Hávi insisted. "Felian and I are our only healers, and Valla and Augi are trained Law-speakers."

"They're friends of yours," Bíldr said. "They support you ..."

"You mean ...?"

"Our enemies might not be the only threat that these boys face," Bíldr said.

Tensions escalated as the final days ticked by. Jarl Hafr could be heard shouting angrily at his sons, demanding their loyalty no matter what. Castle-folk clustered in corners, whispering furtively. The sluts vanished; Gellir told Hávi that they were hiding in a room under the great hall, fearful of her husband's increasing tirades.

"When he finds us, he demands sex, then refuses, or quits early," Gellir told Hávi. "He yells at us for no reason."

"Just do as he says," Hávi sighed. "Come to me if he gets violent again."

"Hávi," Gellir said, "you know that ... we ... we know that everyone calls us *sluts* ... but if we had a choice ..."

"I know," Hávi said.

"We support you, Mistress," Gellir said.

"You're women of Castle Austmaðr," Hávi assured her. "I'd defend you like I would Völu."

The morning before the appointed day, men arrived by the hundreds. Most were recognized warriors, hardened by viking and battle, but many had seen too many summers or were untried youths. Nearly a thousand arrived; Castle Austmaðr's great hall barely had enough standing-room. Jarl Hafr insisted that all of them be fed, even opening kegs that had been sealed for the viking to provide food and ale. That last night he feasted them well, and then gathered them all in the courtyard.

"Men of Austmaðr, I haven't brought you here in vain," Jarl Hafr shouted to be heard. "Treachery threatens us, not from our natural foes, but from those in whose faith we trusted. My spies have reported that an imminent invasion is being prepared against us by those who once called themselves our brothers. We can't leave our homelands to be stolen in our absence, nor can we lie sleeping while their dragons sail into our lands with axe and torch. We must attack on our terms ... on their lands. It's no crime to attack in defense of one's clan, and our intent is to leave none alive to threaten us.

"Disloyalty can't be tolerated today; the threat that imperils us is too great. All of you, even my sons, know that our very future depends on this night, and death alone shall reward any who defy their clan-chief.

"All who are loyal: now we must put aside past alliances. To secure our homes, we must expand our border, take back the lands that were blackmailed from us, and add new lands; those lands will be yours once we've taken them: your farms, your castles, and your women, to do with however you please. My bed hosts half a dozen women every night; so will all of yours tomorrow. Tonight we sail to the lands of those who'd betray us while we sleep. Clan Austmaðr shall double in size and wealth ... and that wealth shall be yours!"

Some cheered wildly, but many looked askance. Jarl Hafr gave them no opportunity to argue.

"Arise, warriors of Austmaðr! March to our ships, and a glorious victory!"

Jarl Hafr led the way across the courtyard and out the gate.

With heavy sighs, Skytja and Rauðkinn followed their father.
Hávi, watching and listening from inside the great hall, wanted
to protest, but Hvítvi, holding the great sword of sacrifice,
motioned for her to be silent. To Hávi's surprise, Hvítvi
hefted the heavy sword with great difficulty and then followed
Skytja and Rauðkinn across the courtyard without voicing a
single objection. As the sun lowered toward the mountain
peaks, a thousand aged and youthful warriors of clan
Austmaðr obediently followed.

They're going to do it! Hávi thought wildly. *Clan
Austmaðr is attacking clan Dúfunef!*

Hávi followed in the procession, Völu at her side, after
motioning for Gellir and the other women to remain in the
castle. Their line crunched loudly down the white shell-paved
road to Skadi, whose women and children came out,
confused by the nightly march. Their walk seemed to take
longer; the men marched with their heads downcast.

Hávi clenched her teeth to keep from shouting; *they know
that he's leading them to their doom!*

The tall-masted dragons bobbed in the harbor, awaiting
only their crews. Master Krókr stood upon the sands before
them, holding onto the tether of a great black bull. Their line
fanned out; the warriors formed a great half-circle around
Master Krókr and the bull, meeting at the water's edge.

Hvítvi held out the great sword and Jarl Hafr took it. Jarl
Hafr lifted the great sword and test-swung it several times,
measuring its weight and balance; he couldn't afford another
mistake. The sacrifice was considered a powerful omen and
this would be doubly so.

"Odin! Odin!" Master Krókr started shouting, and soon
every man and boy, even some of the women and children
from Skadi, took up the roaring chant. *"Odin! Odin! Odin!*

Odin! Odin! Odin!"

Hávi hoped that he'd fail again; perhaps then the men would abandon him and return to their homes. But Jarl Hafr stepped up beside the massive bull and raised the huge, heavy sword of sacrifice high over his head. The shouts of *'Odin!'* escalated, a deafening roar echoing across Skadi. Jarl Hafr raised his voice and shouted to the sky.

> *"Gods of our fathers, I call upon thee,*
> *Grant us riches or Valkyrie!*
> *Gods of Asgard, by fire and ice,*
> *Accept now this sacrifice!"*

Jarl Hafr took a firm grip on the wide, raised blade, flexed his muscles and, with an expression of determination never before seen on his face, Jarl Hafr slashed downward.

The bull's head severed clean off. Blood gushed forward, a long spray that was certain to signify a good omen. Hávi bowed her head; *her last hope had failed.*

The warriors cheered the successful sacrifice.

"To your ships!" Jarl Hafr shouted. "Oars out! Sails up! For clan Austmaðr!"

Men started forward, many wading into the water toward their awaiting dragons. No wives ran forward to hug them.

"Invaders!" someone shouted. *"Look to the sea! Invaders!"*

Everyone froze, staring across the waters in the bright light of the rising moon. Far across the harbor, sailing closer, towards its mouth, many, tall dragonships approached, powered by sail and oar. Two, mighty vessels led them, fierce dragon-prows leading taut sails upon which familiar crests billowed in the failing sunlight. Every man recognized those crests, the emblems of their neighbors to the north and the south.

Fourteen dragonships of clan Hersir and clan Dúfunef sailed into the harbor of Skadi armed for war.

Jay Palmer

Chapter 43

"Draw bows!" Jarl Hafr shouted. *"Defend ...!"*

"Father, no!" Skytja shouted. *" We're unprepared!"*

"Back to the castle!" Rauðkinn shouted. *"Everyone, inside our walls!"*

Hávi and Völu ran away to keep from being trampled as the men followed Rauðkinn, heedless of his father's shouts, which went unheard as the crunching-tramps of their boots filled every ear. Hávi and Völu sheltered against the outer wall of Hrafna's tavern as the warriors of clan Austmaðr ran past them.

"What're you doing?" Völu shouted to be heard. *"Hávi, we've got to get back!"*

"No!" Hávi shouted back. "Let's wait for Jarl Hersir and Jarl Dúfunef."

"We can't!" Völu shouted. *"Hávi, Jorgen's inside the castle!"*

A stifled scream caught in Hávi's throat; *her husband had*

nothing left to lose. A thousand men inside Castle Austmaðr and two enemies outside of it; this battle would decide which clan would rule the Skåne. No matter how it ended, in the confusion of war, her infant son couldn't hope to survive. Hávi and Völu ran into the press and hurried behind the last of the warriors.

"Bar the gates as soon as all of our men are inside!" Jarl Hafr shouted as he and Skytja ran into the courtyard.

"Archers to the roof!" Rauðkinn shouted. *"Men without shields, inside the keep! Defend the castle!"*

"Rauðkinn!" Hávi shouted. *"We can't fight them!"*

"It's too late for that," Rauðkinn said. "Red, take Hávi to her tower and see that she stays there."

Hávi resisted, but Völu yanked her harder than she'd expected; Hávi was drug inside the castle.

"Hávi, what ...?" Gellir and many other women ran up to her.

"Take shelter!" Hávi ordered. "Don't come out until I call you!"

Without a moment of hesitation, Gellir turned and shouted to all of the women.

"Hide yourselves ... by order of Queen Hávi!"

Although their expressions revealed worry and doubt, every woman fled from the great hall. Hávi let Völu pull her; together they ran for her tower.

"Mistress?" Bitra asked as they pushed up into Hávi's room and sealed the trapdoor behind them.

Jorgen was nursing at Breiðr's breast. Hávi stared at her son, then visibly relaxed.

"Mother?" Breiðr asked.

"Jarl Hafr purposed to invade clan Dúfunef," Hávi said.

"That's lunacy!" Breiðr exclaimed.

"Clans Dúfunef and Hersir must've heard of it," Hávi said. "They just arrived armed for war."

"But they're our allies!" Breiðr argued.

"Jarl Hafr broke the truce," Völu said.

"We have no allies," Hávi said. "They won't give Jarl Hafr a second chance to betray them."

"Few will survive this," Bitra said. "No matter who wins ..."

"We lose," Völu agreed grimly. "Hávi and I are Hersir and Austmaðr; we lose twice."

"Open the shutters," Hávi said. "I want to see."

Obediently they opened the oiled sheepskins and the wooden shutters. Hávi peered out as Völu, Bitra, and Breiðr crowded behind her. Inside of the courtyard stood several hundred men armed with shields and spears. Hávi leaned out and saw a hundred bowmen lining the roof, all with arrows noched and ready.

Up the white-paved road from Skadi came a solitary figure: Bifru, Völu's husband; all of the women gasped. Bifru wore a steel helmet and carried a large round shield, but he walked forward with one hand held up, his open palm visible to all. Bifru shouted loudly to be heard by everyone in the castle.

"Men of Austmaðr, hear now and attend these words of your honored neighbors! No blood need be shed tonight! Come forth, Jarl Austmaðr, unarmed and alone, to face the judgment of those who placed you in power and succored you in your time of need. Jarl Hersir and Jarl Dúfunef await your explanation for your intended betrayal."

No one moved. No one spoke.

"Come!" Bifru shouted. "Allies we've been for three generations! Prove now your trust and present yourself for examination, or upon the dawn, we shall take Castle Austmaðr and slay all who resist us!"

No reply met Bifru's demands. Slowly he lowered his hand.

"So be it!" Bifru said, and he shook his head sadly. Slowly he turned and walked away.

"Shoot him!" Jarl Hafr's voice echoed up from the courtyard, but not one bow twanged.

Skadi blazed all night, illuminated by torches that lined the shell-paved road which seemed to glow in the darkness like a huge, white snake against the black of night. The full moon revealed Hersir and Dúfunef tents filling the streets of Skadi; easily three thousand warriors preparing for the dawn. Great losses they'd suffer taking the walled castle, but the warriors of clan Austmaðr didn't want this fight; Hávi had no doubt that clan Austmaðr would be dead before noon.

All night, the women sat fretting, huddled around the fire which Völu kept roaring. Their pieces were all set and fixed; nothing remained but the end of the game.

"Let's get some sleep," Hávi said.

"But ...!" Völu argued.

"Whatever happens, we'll deal with it better if we're rested," Hávi said.

Dawn stole into the world like a thief anticipating triumph. Quiet filled the morning sky until the sudden blare of many warhorns winded as the sun broke the horizon. Völu was instantly awake; her husband was among those that marched to besiege her new home. Bitra and Breiðr sat up, awakened by the unexpected trumpeting. Then Völu noticed that she was alone in her bed: *Hávi was missing ... the trapdoor was unbolted and open ... and Jorgen was gone.*

"Hávi!" Völu shouted. *"Hávi!!!"*

A thousand shields marched up the hill from Skadi and spread out, wide and threatening, backed by many behind them; never had Völu seen so many bodies all in one glance. The armies of clan Hersir and clan Dúfunef approached slowly, confidently, determined and without fear. Civil war had begun, and Hávi was nowhere to be seen.

"Hold the gate!" Skytja's voice wafted up from the courtyard, which was filled with armed men.

"Prepare to shoot!" Rauðkinn's voice echoed from the roof. "Hold until I ... *Wait! Bows down! Don't shoot!*"

A lone figure appeared walking outside of the outer wall along the wooden palisade. All gasped and stared; it was a woman, a lone woman holding a small, crying baby in her arms, walking slowly beside the spiked trench toward the white road. Völu recognized her instantly.

"Hávi!" Völu shouted.

Völu ran down the stairs, leaving Bitra and Breiðr screaming in fright. She crashed into warriors packed in the great hall and knocked several aside as she shoved to get through.

"Let me pass!" Völu cried frantically. *"Let me pass!"*

The men squeezed aside to make room for Völu, who drove through them like a weakened juggernaut. She pushed through the door into the courtyard only to find the men crowded even thicker before the gate.

"Hávi!" Völu shouted.

"Völu!" Skytja shouted. "What's Hávi doing out there?"

"I don't know!" Völu shouted, and she pushed to stand beside Skytja and his father. "She snuck out! Let me through!"

"That gate can't open!" Skytja said.

"Shoot her!" Jarl Hafr shouted to the rooftop. *"She's betraying us to our enemies! Shoot her!!!"*

Völu doubled up her fist and punched Jarl Hafr right in his face.

Hávi clutched Jorgen protectively to her chest and forced herself to keep walking. The first rays of the morning sun illuminated three armies but failed to dissipate the dawn's chill. The tall grass beside the deadly trench was thick with dew, forcing her to take smaller steps, but she kept going, ignoring the moisture soaking into her soft boots and creeping up her skirt.

The right wing of the advancing army halted as they spied her. Many faces looked shocked, but Hávi didn't stop. Slowly she approached the front of the castle and the white-paved road. The whole army hesitated, and Jarl Hersir, Jarl Dúfunef, and Hvítvi came out and stood before their troops as Hávi advanced.

Hávi reached the white road and turned toward Skadi. All eyes focused upon her, especially those that she knew so well. Before the halted army, she paused, clutched Jorgen tightly, and curtsied three times with such elegance and perfection that even Mjóvi would've been impressed.

"Hávi ...?" Jarl Hersir asked.

Hávi said nothing, just preceded forward. With a gentle wave, Hávi motioned them aside, and both jarls and Hvítvi, and then both armies, split down the middle, leaving a wide, clear path for Hávi. Without a word, Hávi walked between them.

"Keep the troops here," Jarl Dúfunef said behind her.

"Where's she going?" someone asked.

Footsteps crunching the broken shells warned her; she

glanced back once to find Hvítvi, Jarl Hersir, Jarl Dúfunef, and a small group of others following her.

In Skadi, many women and young children stood outside of their homes. Hávi never said a word, just continued onward through town.

Hávi passed stock hill and marched up to the next hill. Before her rose the tall pillar of stone inscribed with runes of the den Skaanske Lov: *Law Rock.*

This had to work! Never before had she considered what she was about to do, and everything that she'd learned about the den Skaanske Lov told her that this wouldn't work, but it was too late to change her mind and too much rested on this last toss of invisible dice. Hávi stopped and waited as a crowd of the women of Skadi, led by both jarls, Hvítvi, Bifru, and several other men of high-rank, closed in behind her. Then, taking a deep breath, Hávi faced Law Rock and shouted as loudly as she could.

"I divorce my husband!"
"I divorce my husband!"
"I divorce my husband!"

Hávi turned to meet incredulous stares from everyone.

"Hávi," Hvítvi said softly, *"women can't divorce their husbands!"*

"Women can't make accusations at Law Rock!" Jarl Hersir said.

"Fine," Hávi said. "Go back. Siege Castle Austmaðr. Start Sweden's last civil war."

Suddenly Jarl Dúfunef broke out laughing. His deep, untroubled guffaws echoed in the silent morning while everyone else stood dumbfounded.

"*A Tynwald?*" Skytja asked.

"Yes," Bifru said, standing four feet from the gate to Castle Austmaðr. "Hávi has made an accusation against her husband at Law Rock."

"Women can't make accusations!" Skytja insisted.

"Are you a Law-speaker?" Bifru asked.

"No, but ...!"

"Neither am I. The first purpose of any Tynwald is to determine if an accusation has been legally-made."

"But Hávi's accusation can't be legal!" Skytja argued.

"Then that's what the Tynwald will determine," Bifru said, "or ... we can start fighting right now."

"But that would take weeks to arrange!"

"We know that you were planning to invade clan Dúfunef; if you agree to postpone until after the Tynwald then we won't slaughter you today."

"Wait!" Jarl Hafr shouted. "Hávi's accused of murder! If there's a Tynwald, then my case holds precedence ... and if she's outlawed then she can't make any case!"

"That's what Hvítvi said," Bifru said, "and Jarl Hersir and Jarl Dúfunef agreed with him."

"This is crazy!" Rauðkinn said.

"It's up to you," Bifru said. "All parties must declare and accept pledges of peace. Jarl Hersir and Jarl Dúfunef will pledge to depart the castle immediately once the Tynwald is over, and only then may hostilities commence."

"Never!" Jarl Hafr shouted.

"*Father!*" Skytja and Rauðkinn shouted.

"Why delay the inevitable?" Jarl Hafr demanded.

"To spare lives!" Rauðkinn said.

Jarl Hafr snarled at his son and drew back his fist.

"*Don't make us do a Sterki,*" Skytja warned.

His face reddened by fury and embarrassment, Jarl Hafr pledged before all of their warriors to remain in clan Austmaðr until after the Tynwald. Jarl Hafr openly accused Hvítvi of betraying him, but Hvítvi explained that he knew nothing of Jarl Hafr's plans; Jarl Hersir and Jarl Dúfunef refused to explain how they happened to arrive in Skadi Harbor minutes before Jarl Hafr set sail. Three ships of messengers sailed to summon the other clan lords; the Tynwald would begin in six days.

Skytja and Rauðkinn offered Jarl Dúfunef and Jarl Hersir a place to stay inside of Castle Austmaðr, but both declined. They departed immediately after the pledges; Jarl Hafr was glad to see them go. He took Valla and Augi up the stone stairs and into his room.

"He wants to insure that Hávi will be outlawed," Skytja guessed. "That will clear any charges against him."

"Does Hávi have a chance?" Rauðkinn asked.

"Hard to guess," Hvítvi said. "Few jarls will care if she's outlawed, but many will object to a murderess going free."

"What about my accusation?" Hávi asked.

Hvítvi shook his head.

"Our laws forbid it."

"Are you sure?"

The uproar died quickly, but the gossip mounted. Hvítvi and Bíldr headed up the stone stairs while Skytja sent home the warriors who lived nearby and arranged for lodging for those from distant villages. Headed toward her tower, Hávi suddenly stopped, making Völu and Bitra bump into her back.

"Blönduhorn!" Hávi exclaimed.

669

"What about her?" Völu asked.

"She's pregnant; I almost forgot. Völu, could you do me a favor? Run into Skadi and ask Blönduhorn if she'll join me for supper tonight."

"Why?"

"Well, Brækir is very influential in Skadi, and with Blönduhorn pregnant, and Valla and Augi consumed with the upcoming Tynwald, we'll need the support of the townswomen."

"They already support ..."

"We need to be certain," Hávi said. "Ask them both if they'll join me for supper tonight."

"Very well," Völu said. "They'll come if I have to drag them here."

Hávi thanked Völu, and then started up the stairs to her tower. Bitra followed her silently, then startled when Hávi abruptly stopped again.

"Mistress ...?"

"Shhhhhh!" Hávi hissed. *"Did you see that?"*

"See what?"

"The bell-rope: it just moved! Someone's in our tower!"

"I didn't see ..."

"It could be an assassin!"

Bitra's eyes flew open. Silently Hávi motioned to her, and they furtively hurried back down the stairs.

"Go find Bíldr!" Hávi whispered. "Hurry! I'll get Skytja and Rauðkinn."

"But ...!"

"Run!"

Bitra hurried toward the stone stairs. Hávi watched her go, then slowly followed her, making certain that she wasn't seen.

Minutes later, Bíldr came running out of Hvítvi's room, Bitra chasing after him as fast as her aged legs would allow. From inside of the narrow hallway to the roof, Hávi watched them both descend the stone steps.

Without knocking, Hávi entered Hvítvi's room. His outer-chamber was empty; Hávi glanced inside his hot-fog room, but it was also empty, only hot and humid with very little mist. Hávi crept to Hvítvi's other door, listened carefully at it, and then opened it.

Hvítvi sat on his tall bed before his window staring silently outward at the blue sky. He turned as his door opened and his expression displayed the first pure shock that Hávi had ever seen him reveal.

"No intruder ...?"

"Bíldr will search, but find nothing."

"Völu ...?"

"Sent into town."

"Hávi, we can't risk ...!"

"What happens if I'm outlawed?"

"The best that we could hope for is that Dúfunef and Hersir conquers clan Austmaðr easily. They considered dividing us up after the Norwegians attacked; this invasion attempt was too much ..."

"You tipped them off ...?" Hávi asked.

"Somebody had to," Hvítvi said. "Jarl Hafr planned his invasion very carefully ... in the Hall of Audiences."

"Can I divorce him?"

"Our laws make no allowance ..."

"Is it against our laws?"

"That's what the Tynwald will decide," Hvítvi said.

"Your chest of gold, Bíldr, Völu, a ship; you and I could

escape ..." Hávi said.

"I can't sail," Hvítvi said. "Rocking makes me deathly ill and oceans are notoriously cold; I may not survive. Besides, Bíldr's married to Knarrarbringa, Völu to Bifru; how many must flee their homelands for our sake?"

"I love you," Hávi said.

"Hávi, you know how I ..."

"Say it."

"Why?"

"I need to hear it."

Hvítvi rose from his bed and approached her. They wrapped their arms around each other and kissed long and desperately.

All too soon Hvítvi pushed free. Hávi released him; Hvítvi hated having his weakness pointed out. But Hvítvi only pulled free long enough to lift the brace and set it into its brackets behind his door.

"I love you, Hávi," Hvítvi said.

Hvítvi made love to her slowly. Hávi had thought that Jarl Gullskegger's strength and endurance were unequaled, but the slow, tingling ecstasy that Hvítvi carried her to thrilled her beyond conception. His every touch was so soft that Hávi yearned for more. His kisses weren't demands and urgencies; Hvítvi's kisses were tender promises of eternal faithfulness and enduring affection. Hávi's head spun from his soft caresses, reeled from his penetration, and melted under his constancy. No forcefulness evidenced, but gentleness sublimed her every quivering passion, culminating in a steady tenderness like the sea kissing the sand, rocking forever inside of her. In her heart, Hávi knew that she could never again endure the touch of another man. They merged simultaneously and become one.

Chapter 44

Both Bíldr and Völu were furious. Hávi evidenced no care for the rapidly-approaching Tynwald or her impending outlawry; everything was perfect in her world. Five days passed in luxuriant splendor.

"You'd best start worrying," Völu scolded Hávi. "Sterki was outlawed and he never made it out of the hall."

"My worries won't change anything," Hávi said. "Jarl Hafr has Valla and Augi virtually imprisoned. Clan Austmaðr doesn't have any wealth left for bribes."

"A hundred women watched you split Mjóvi's skull," Völu said.

"Hvítvi loves me."

"I'm going to slap you if you say that again."

"Some can't support us," Bíldr said. "Jarl Ríki refuses to enter clan Austmaðr. Jarl Refr is dead. Clan Tyrr has sworn oaths of subservience to clan Bagal and pays them tribute. Clan Vörsa attacked clan Bagal, but lost. Clan Bagal can't retaliate because clan Tyrr will rebel if they send off their remaining troops."

"Clan Bagal's weak?" Hávi asked.

"Not so weak that they've turned agreeable. Jarl Bagal and Jarl Vörsa almost came to blows on sight of each other."

"Who else is here?" Völu asked.

"Jarl Mjöksiglandi," Bíldr said. "But clan Mjöksiglandi was invaded and seriously injured by clan Glóra. Mjöksiglandi retaliated; Jarl Glóra lives imprisoned in Jarl Mjöksiglandi's chief fortress, just like Jarl Illingr. Clan Glóra was conquered, but clan Mjöksiglandi lacks the troops to maintain their hold."

"Why'd he spare Jarl Glóra?"

"No one knows," Bíldr said, "but it's rumored that Jarl Glóra now mucks out Jarl Mjöksiglandi's stable."

"Who can support us?" Hávi asked.

"Jarl Jótun just arrived. Clan Jótun hasn't fought anyone; they fortified the narrow passes to their villages and allow no one to enter their lands. By staying out of it, clan Jótun is threatening to become the new power in Sweden."

"What about Jarl Aurriði?"

"Jarl Aurriði denies our right to host a Tynwald. He says that Sweden's fractured and can no longer call itself one people."

"That's only seven jarls," Völu said. "A Tynwald requires ten."

"Ten heads of households, preferably jarls," Hávi corrected. "Only one representative from half or more of the clans is needed. As the hosting clans, Austmaðr, Dúfunef, and Hersir are each including one family-head to sit on the council."

"Who?"

"Master Krókr."

"Easy to guess who included him," Völu said.

"Barnakarl, an elder from clan Dúfunef."

"Never heard of him," Hávi said.

"Bifru."

Völu gasped and clutched her breast.

"Jarl Hersir insisted," Bíldr said. "He's known Hávi since they were kids."

"No others?"

"We were lucky to get them," Bíldr said. "Most hope that civil war breaks out during the Tynwald."

"Is that possible?"

"It's likely."

Thunder boomed and lightning flashed across the blackened sky. The morning of the Tynwald arrived in a downpour to keep away all but the most-determined, yet warriors crowded the great hall or stood outside in the rain, many under wide roundshields, men of different clans hurling curses at each other. The servants in the great hall stoked up all of the fireplaces to heat the great hall while they rushed food and ale to all of the tables.

Völu, Breiðr, and Bitra bathed Hávi and dressed her in a new gown that Hvassi had made, white with yellow trim like the petals of daffodils. Bíldr arrived armed with a sword and shield, wearing a coat of mail and an iron cap.

"It is that bad?" Hávi asked.

"If trouble starts, my job is to defend your backs while you flee," Bíldr said, *"which you will do!"*

"I won't leave without ...!"

"You're a married woman and you'd best not forget that today!"

Hávi swallowed her pride and meekly nodded.

Bíldr led them inside the great hall and to the table closest to the door. Hávi noticed that she and Völu were the only two women present; they shared a table with many, young warriors who supported Hvítvi. The jarls hadn't arrived yet; Hávi sat silently and stared at the empty high-table.

The dull roar of conversations fell as Jarl Hafr led the way into the great hall. All of the jarls followed him; they took their seats at the high-table. On the end closest to Hávi sat Jarl Jótun, whose wry smirk bore the only resemblance to a smile. Jarl Vörsa sat beside him, casting dark glances at everyone. Jarl Mjöksiglandi looked the least happy, and he pulled apart his braided, forked beard as he sat down. Bifru looked like a nervous man pretending to be calm; he glanced once at Völu and then kept his gaze averted. Jarl Hersir looked the same as he had the whole time that Hávi had been growing up: a tall, thick bush of black hair and beard out of which a careworn face peered.

Skytja sat proudly beside his father, his shoulders back and his head high. Jarl Hafr sat center wielding the most-determined look. Rauðkinn sat opposite him resting one hand on his axe, which he hooked on the high-table's edge. Master Krókr sat beside him, looking stern and defiant. Jarl Dúfunef sat next, looking most-displeased at his placement beside Master Krókr. Barnakarl seemed to be the most-calm; he was a gray-haired elder with a long, thin beard who looked unconcerned about the impending trials. Jarl Bagal sat on the farthest end, as far from Jarl Vörsa as he could sit, and he looked the angriest.

Hávi almost screamed as she missed him: *Hvítvi wasn't there.*

Valla and Augi entered the great hall amid utter silence. As Law-speakers, they held the greatest power, a fact discomforting everyone, especially them. Hávi wondered if their learnings would outlaw her. Hávi glanced up at the narrow windows over the highest dais; *would the same fate that had ended Sterki's life claim her?*

Hvítvi entered next carrying the ceremonial sword. A troubled murmur whispered through the hall; the bloodied sword honored their warrior-traditions, yet pale, white-maned Hvítvi had never fought. Apparently aware of their objections, Hvítvi glared straight forward without a trace of weakness, more-serious than Hávi had ever seen him. With murder in his eyes equal only to the moment when he'd ordered his brother's execution, Hvítvi held the ceremonial sword high and set it onto the table before Jarl Hafr.

"This sword is bloodied ... but you aren't," Jarl Hafr snarled at Hvítvi.

"You bloodied me," Hvítvi said defiantly.

"This hall is for warriors! You've no place here!"

"Valla and Augi aren't warriors," Hvítvi said.

"They're Law-speakers."

"Yes, Law-speakers for the accuser," Hvítvi said. "I am the Law-speaker for the accused."

Hávi's heart leapt; *Hvítvi would defend her!*

"You're no Law-speaker!" Jarl Hafr sneered.

"I declare that I am," Hvítvi said. "Only the one whom I speak for may refuse me. Is that not the law?"

Jarl Hafr glared at Hvítvi, then glanced at Valla and Augi. Both boys looked frightened, but nodded. Jarl Hafr scowled.

"I, Jarl Austmaðr, command this Tynwald," Jarl Hafr shouted, and he handed the sword to Skytja, who passed it on to Jarl Hersir.

Every jarl and head of house commanded the Tynwald, ending with Jarl Bagal, who set the blade before him rather than pass it back.

"Enough ceremony; this Tynwald is begun," Jarl Hafr said. "The murderess must be outlawed."

"That's not the order!" Hvítvi said. "You can't declare a verdict before the trial!"

Everyone looked at Valla and Augi.

"The accuser speaks first, and then the witnesses," Valla said.

"Very well, then I'll speak and Master Krókr will witness ..."

"You can't," Hvítvi said. "In this Tynwald, you're a council member and must bear judgment upon all that you see: you can't judge and accuse, and Master Krókr can't judge and witness. So your case against Hávi must wait until the next Thyngr, and this court must move on to its next case ..."

"No!" Master Krókr shouted. "Augi said that we could do both!"

"He's right," Augi said meekly.

"Speak up, boy," Jarl Mjöksiglandi said, leaning over the high-table to look at them. "Who's right?"

"Ummm ..., Augi's right," Valla said. "Members of the council can speak like any other man at a Tynwald."

Hávi's throat constricted as Hvítvi sighed and turned away. Hávi trusted Hvítvi, but Jarl Hafr had been correct: *Hvítvi was no Law-speaker.* Valla and Augi had been closeted away since the decision to hold a Tynwald to keep anyone but Jarl Hafr from conferring with them. Since the only other Law-

speakers in clan Austmaðr had been killed by the
Norwegians, the case against Hávi was certain to be the
strongest. Despite Hvítvi's wisdom and cunning, he might not
be equal to saving her.

"I accused Hávi Hersir Austmaðr of the murder of
Mistress Mjóvi Illingr," Jarl Hafr said. "I accused her at Law
Rock three times before many witnesses, including both of
these Law-speakers, who swore to me afterwards that I'd
made my accusation legally. My witnesses included ..."

"Enough!" Jarl Bagal said. "Our only Law-speakers can
testify? Why should we listen to a parade of witnesses ...?"

"Law-speakers don't determine the validity of witnesses,"
Hvítvi said.

"I agree with Jarl Bagal," Jarl Mjöksiglandi said. "Let's
finish this and move on; I want to sail home tonight."

"But ...!" Hvítvi started.

"Peace," Jarl Hersir spoke up, waving his one hand.
"Before I decide if any other witnesses need to be heard, let's
hear from our Law-speakers: boys, did you witness the
accusation against Hávi, and was it legally made?"

"It ... i-it ...," Valla stuttered.

*"Jarl Austmaðr said that he'd kill our family if we didn't
outlaw Hávi!"* Augi shouted.

Chaos exploded in the great hall. Angry shouts erupted
from many mouths, especially those at the high-table, most of
whom jumped to their feet. Hávi tried to stand but Bíldr's
hand forced her back down, his shield raised protectively.

"Liar!" Völu screamed. *"Cheat!"*

Jarl Dúfunef pushed back his chair, climbed up onto it,
and stepped up onto the high-table, staring down at Jarl Hafr.

"You dishonorable ferret!" Jarl Dúfunef shouted. "You
bring all of us here ... weeks before the viking ... after a failed

invasion ... under a pretense of justice ... *all the while lying to us?!?"*

"Sit down!" Jarl Jótun shouted at Jarl Dúfunef, and he stared until Jarl Dúfunef climbed down off the table, and then he turned to Jarl Hafr. "Jarl Austmaðr, I didn't come here to be your tool. You will order these boys to speak only the laws as they learned them, now, or clan Jótun shall declare this Tynwald unrepresented."

Most of the jarls exchanged confused looks.

"Unrepresented," Jarl Jótun said to Valla and Augi. "Do you know what that means?"

Valla and Augi spent a moment whispering to each other before they responded.

"If a member of the council withdraws from a Thyngr leaving insufficient members, then the Thyngr is disbanded and can render no judgments and enact neither new laws nor changes to existing laws," Valla said. "If a Tynwald is shortened to nine council members then it is reduced to a Thyngr. The host of the Thyngr may appoint additional jarls to join the council, but its decisions will only be the rulings of a Thyngr, not the den Skaanske Lov."

"Exactly," Jarl Jótun said. "The host of the Thyngr may appoint additional jarls ... not heads of households ... and there aren't any. If any clan leaves, then this Tynwald is over."

"Are you a Law-speaker now?" Jarl Vörsa asked.

"We have Law-speakers in clan Jótun ... and we don't twist their words by threatening their families."

"Enough!" Jarl Hersir said. "Valla and Augi, you will recite our laws as Jarl Illingr would've; a Law-speaker's reputation comes from his faithfulness to the den Skaanske Lov. You, your mother, and your entire family will be welcome to move to clan Hersir after the Tynwald, if you feel threatened. Now tell the truth: what did you witness at Law Rock?"

"Jarl Austmaðr made his accusation three times before many witness," Valla said.

"Augi, do you concur?" Jarl Hersir asked.

"Concur ...?"

"Do you agree with your brother?"

"Oh, yes; we witnessed the accusation and it was legal," Augi said.

"Very well," Jarl Hersir said. "Is there anyone in this hall who would refute this testimony?"

No one spoke.

"Then that's it," Jarl Bagal said. "Let's mediate and resolve ..."

"Wait!" Hvítvi said. "Other witnesses have the right to speak."

"What other witnesses?" Jarl Bagal demanded.

"Everyone in the hall has the right to be heard," Hvítvi said.

"But it's been determined that the accusation was legal!" Jarl Mjöksiglandi said. "What's left to be proven?"

"Our laws say that others may speak if they wish it," Hvítvi said.

"Who would speak?" Jarl Dúfunef asked.

"Me," Hvítvi said. "If a council member can accuse and judge, then a Law-speaker should be able to speak."

"Speak then," Jarl Dúfunef said.

"I say that what this council decides today is more than a determination of murder," Hvítvi said. "Sweden is many clans but one people; the den Skaanske Lov is all that we have to unite us, to keep us together and protect us from our enemies, our worst of whom has already invaded our shores.

Surely we can expect more ..."

"This testimony has no bearing upon this case!" Jarl Hafr shouted. "Are we to waste our ears on every prepared speech ...?"

"I have the right to be heard!" Hvítvi said.

"No, you don't!" Jarl Hafr said with a wide grin. "You're my nephew, my wife's stepson; I'm the head of our house. Valla, Augi; does Hvítvi have the right to speak?"

Both boys sighed heavily. Valla spoke reluctantly.

"Over wife, sons, and daughters, of all promises, oaths, contracts, and marriages shall rule the father or husband, and invalid shall be any promises, oaths, contracts, and marriages without his approval."

Hvítvi stared at Valla disbelieving.

"As your stepfather, I speak for our family," Jarl Hafr said. "Testimony is the sworn oath of the testifier, and I say that my stepson Hvítvi has nothing to say."

A stunned silence fell upon the hall. Many exchanged nervous glances but none moved or spoke.

"*Valla?*" Hvítvi asked. "*Augi?*"

"Thus ... speak our laws," Valla said as if ashamed.

"Never before has anyone been barred from testifying," Jarl Dúfunef growled. "Are we a council of warriors or Lawspeakers?"

"Hvítvi's neither ... apparently," Jarl Hafr said, and several in the back chuckled at this.

"Let's consider this matter in arbitration," Jarl Mjöksiglandi said.

"No ...," Hvítvi said, but Hávi noticed the sweat on his brow; he was losing her case.

"Have you other witnesses?" Jarl Hersir asked.

Hvítvi glanced around desperately.

"Yes," Hvítvi said, though his voice held little earnestness.

"Call him forward," Jarl Hersir said.

"I can't," Hvítvi said. "My witness isn't a man; I call forth to give testimony ... *Völu Hersir.*"

Völu's eyes flew open. Shock covered every face.

"We're not here to listen to women!" Jarl Hafr said.

"Other women have testified before Tynwalds ... in this very hall," Hvítvi said. "Völu's the only person here who witnessed the murder that Hávi's accused of. She alone can testify to its occurrence."

"We know that Hávi murdered Mjóvi!" Jarl Hafr shouted.

"Then Völu's testimony will support your accusation," Hvítvi said.

Nervous glances exchanged; Hávi stared at Hvítvi: *was he trying to get her outlawed?*

"Völu, as your clan-chief, I command you to come forward," Jarl Hersir said.

Slowly Völu rose. She glanced at Hávi, then at Hvítvi, and then at her husband on the council; Bifru looked worried for the first time since the trial began.

"Start at the beginning," Hvítvi instructed Völu, pulling her to stand before the high-table.

"Well, the Norwegians had attacked," Völu said nervously. "They took the castle and forced all of us women into this hall. Many were hysterical; Hávi tried to calm us, but Mjóvi started screaming at her ..."

"What did Mjóvi say?" Hvítvi asked.

"She said that ... well, she claimed that Hávi had caused the Norwegians to invade ..."

"Is there anyone here ...," Hvítvi interrupted, "who believes that Hávi Hersir Austmaðr caused the Norwegians to invade?"

No one spoke. Many frowned.

"Keep going," Hvítvi said to Völu. "What else did she say?"

"She ... Mjóvi said that Hávi was unfit ... to be queen," Völu said. "They called each other a bunch of names ..."

"Did she say anything about Jorgen?" Hvítvi asked.

"Yes," Völu said. "Mjóvi said that Jorgen was unworthy of becoming Jarl Austmaðr."

"Anything else?" Hvítvi asked. "Think carefully!"

Völu lowered her eyebrows, wrinkling her forehead.

"Mjóvi threatened Jorgen," Völu recalled.

"Are you certain?" Hvítvi asked.

"Yes: Mjóvi said that he'd never live to grow up ... even if she had to make sure of it herself."

"Thank you, Völu; you may sit down," Hvítvi said, and then he addressed the council. "You've heard the testimony of a witness to the crime; Mjóvi threatened to kill Hávi's son, the heir of Jarl Austmaðr, before a hundred witnesses."

"Enough!" Jarl Hafr said to Hvítvi. "As your father, I command that you say no more!"

"Stepfather, not father," Hvítvi corrected. "You may prevent me from testifying, but I'm not testifying; Völu testified, and over her only Jarl Hersir holds command."

Jarl Hafr and Jarl Hersir exchanged a momentary glare.

"Jarl Hersir, you lost your left hand on your first viking," Hvítvi said. "Can anyone say that the enemy who maimed you was attacking your hand, but not you? No, to attack any part of a man is to attack all of him; every warrior in this hall can testify to this."

"Which means that you can't," Jarl Hafr interjected, but no one minded him.

"Jarl Austmaðr sits between two sons," Hvítvi said.

"Would any say that an attack upon one of his sons isn't an attack on his family, and thus an attack on him? Must not sons avenge a father that's attacked ... or even challenged? Mjóvi threatened to kill Jorgen, Hávi's son, the heir-apparent, and thus she threatened Hávi herself; that means that Mjóvi challenged Hávi, so this was a fight, not a murder. Would any man here do less for one of their sons?"

The silence of absolute stillness filled the hall.

"Law-speakers," Jarl Jótun said. "Share with us the verses of challenge."

"Warriors may challenge each other at any time for any reason," Augi recited. "None may interfere with a fight properly challenged. Challengers may Holmganger until the first drop of blood, or fight to the death, or until either yields. Death or injury by a proper challenge isn't murder, but may be declared invalid by a Thyngr or Tynwald after an accusation at Law Rock. A killing or injury after a yield is murder and may be accused at Law Rock. The results of a challenge may not be avenged until arbitrated by a council at a Thyngr or a Tynwald ..."

"That's enough," Jarl Jótun said. "The law states that warriors may challenge each other; these women aren't warriors."

"No women are!" Jarl Hafr agreed.

"What is a warrior?" Hvítvi asked. "If a farmer challenges another farmer, and they pick up weapons, then they become warriors, do they not? Mjóvi isn't the only death that Hávi caused; with his own sword, Hávi killed Jarl Gullskegger, the leader of the Norwegians who conquered this castle ... and without her, clan Austmaðr would be dead. Was that not the act of a warrior? The purpose of every Tynwald is justice; if only warriors can challenge, then can a father who isn't a warrior avenge his son's death ... or the threat of his son's murder? Can only warriors fight?"

"The question is ...," Master Krókr spoke up, "was this a fight or a murder? Mistress Mjóvi wasn't armed."

"If a man says that he'll kill you, do you wait for him to go home and get his sword and put on his helm and mail?" Hvítvi asked. "Mjóvi threatened to kill an infant; can't warriors kill with their bare hands? Jorgen was Hávi's only son ...!"

"Enough, Hvítvi," Jarl Hersir said. "You aren't testifying; we heard Völu. Is there anyone here who would refute Völu's testimony? Anyone who witnessed the killing?"

"I think that warriors should consider all testimony made by women as suspect," Jarl Hafr said.

"That's your right," Jarl Hersir said. "However, you're not the whole council ..."

"I'm three of the council's votes ...," Jarl Hafr said, resting his hands on his son's arms.

"I think otherwise," Skytja interrupted.

"I'm your father!"

"My vote is mine," Skytja said.

"As is mine," Rauðkinn added.

"You'll do as I say!" Jarl Hafr shouted.

"If I hear right, then you command our promises, oaths, contracts, and marriages," Skytja said. "Our votes are our own."

"I like this Law-speaker thing," Rauðkinn said. "The den Skaanske Lov seems to be the final authority; I think I'd like to learn it."

Jarl Hafr scowled at both of his sons.

"Is there any more testimony?" Jarl Hersir asked. "Does anyone in the hall wish to speak?"

No one spoke up.

"This case is in arbitration," Jarl Hersir said. "The council will convene in private."

As one, the entire high-table rose and left the great hall, some with black scowls, others showing no emotion whatsoever. Only Jarl Jótun left grinning.

"I should be there," Hvítvi scowled, watching them leave. "Jarl Austmaðr used Valla and Augi to bar me from the council at the last minute."

"Jarl Hersir won't let them convict Hávi," Völu said.

"Jarl Hersir's only one vote," Hvítvi said.

"Jarl Hersir wanted to support Sterki after he murdered Jarl Austmaðr," Hávi said. "He'll do what's best for clan Hersir, not for me."

"What's best for clan Hersir is if one of its descendents leads clan Austmaðr," Hvítvi said. "But Jorgen's youth dims that hope; it might not be enough."

"What if they outlaw me?" Hávi asked.

"Mjóvi wasn't your immediate family, so they can't outlaw you for life. But she was nobility and a clan member; they could outlaw you for seven years."

"Seven years!?!" Hávi gasped.

"Hávi should leave the great hall until the council returns," Bíldr said. "Each clan has warriors here and few love clan Austmaðr."

Reluctantly Hávi allowed them to escort her out of the great hall, but only as far as the kitchen, where the cooks were occupied but not busy, mostly just keeping the cooked foods hot until after the trial.

"You couldn't cook anyway," Völu said to Hávi. "You can't get dirty today. Maybe we should wait in the sewing room ...?"

"That's too far away," Hávi said. "I want to be here when

my fate's decided."

"Sterki wished that he was here, then wished that he wasn't," Völu reminded her.

A long, slow hour passed, and then word came; the council was returning. Bíldr had to restrain Hávi to keep her from running into the great hall, making her walk slowly behind him, and he walked with his shield raised. The hall was filled with whispers as they entered; a hundred conversations speculating on the outcome of the deliberations reached a crescendo as the jarls climbed the short stairs. Jarl Hersir alone remained standing, and he faced the whole hall.

"The first case is decided," Jarl Hersir said in his deep, booming voice that carried to the farthest corners of the great hall. "Jarl Hafr's accusation against Hávi Hersir Austmaðr for the murder of Mistress Mjóvi Illingr was legally and properly made. This council must now pass sentence upon Hávi Hersir Austmaðr." Jarl Hersir paused to look at Hávi. "*The sentence is ... seven ...*" (Hávi gasped!) "*... goats;* seven goats to be paid to Jarl Austmaðr, and having known Mistress Mjóvi myself, I think that Hávi is over-fined."

Cheers filled the hall while Hávi gaped in amazement.

"*I ... I won?*"

"*Seven goats ...!*" Bíldr laughed.

Hvítvi bowed his head in such relief that a pale pink colored his cheeks.

"Hávi, you have been fined seven goats," Jarl Hersir continued, and under his bulbous nose, through his matte of thick mustache and beard, Hávi saw his wide smile. "If you can't afford this fine, then clan Hersir ..."

"No!" Jarl Dúfunef interrupted. "Clan Hersir has enough glory having birthed Mistress Hávi; clan Dúfunef shall pay this fine, and let this be an end to it!"

More cheers followed, and most at the high-table were struggling to maintain some semblance of decorum. Jarl Hafr scowled deeply, casting dark looks at everyone, but refusing to look at Hávi. Most of the council members seemed delighted by his defeat.

"Enough!" Jarl Mjöksiglandi shouted at the revelers. "This Tynwald has further business!"

Quickly the cheers died, although Völu didn't stop hugging Hávi.

"This case is nonsense," Jarl Bagal said.

"I am a witness to this accusation and it was legally made, whatever its merits," Jarl Dúfunef said. "Jarl Hersir stood beside me ... and many of our most-trusted advisors."

"You can't declare an accusation legal!" Jarl Vörsa said.

"Women can't make accusations," Jarl Jótun added.

"Let's go through the process," Jarl Mjöksiglandi said, "and somebody bring me ale."

Servants rushed to refill every horn and cup on the high-table as Hvítvi rose and approached the center.

"As her Law-speaker, I'll speak for Hávi," Hvítvi said. "Hávi made this accusation at Law Rock three times: *'I divorce my husband'.*"

A murmur of disquiet filled the hall; many men glanced nervously at each other.

"Hávi's accusation is wattle," Jarl Hafr said. "Valla, Augi: who can make accusations at Law Rock?"

"Not anyone can make accusations at Law Rock," Valla said, although he sounded more reluctant than a baby chick jumping into a snake's mouth. "Women ... can't."

Scattered applause met this recitation; some warriors cheered. Jarl Hafr glared at Hvítvi as if defying him to challenge his real Law-speakers. Many at the high-table relaxed as if this matter were concluded. Jarl Bagal stood, as if to depart.

"*Wait!*" Hvítvi shouted.

"For what?" Jarl Bagal demanded. "You heard the boys ...!"

"*You have to consider ...!*" Hvítvi pleaded.

"There's nothing to consider!" Jarl Hafr shouted. "As women can't make accusations at Law Rock, Hávi's accusation isn't legal!"

"I don't want my wife divorcing me," Jarl Jótun chuckled, and many laughed with him.

"Mine can divorce me anytime that she wants," Jarl Vörsa said, and more warriors laughed.

"Are we done yet?" Jarl Mjöksiglandi asked.

"*No, we're not,*" Hvítvi insisted.

"Do you deny the den Skaanske Lov as Valla and Augi have recited it?" Jarl Bagal asked Hvítvi.

"Hvítvi, it's over," Jarl Dúfunef said.

"*No, it isn't,*" Hvítvi said, "*and I can prove it.*"

All fell silent and stared at Hvítvi. Jarl Bagal sat back down, looking curious.

"As you know," Hvítvi said, "Tynwalds are our highest court and have three powers: Tynwalds can make new laws, enforce existing laws with punishments, and change laws. Valla, Augi; what is the process for changing an existing law?"

All eyes moved to the young Law-speakers, but Valla only blushed.

"Existing laws can only be changed by a Tynwald," Augi recited. "To change a law, an accusation which defies the existing law must be made and arbitrated by a council of jarls."

"Exactly," Hvítvi said. "As a woman, Hávi's accusation defies existing law."

Many warriors shouted angrily as Hvítvi's words sank in. "Hávi didn't challenge that law!" Master Krókr shouted. "She didn't say *'Women have the right to accuse'!*"

"She didn't have to ...," Hvítvi began.

"I say that she did!" Master Krókr shouted.

"Then you may deliberate that with the jarls on the council," Hvítvi said. *"Which means that you must deliberate Hávi's accusation."*

"Insanity!" Jarl Bagal shouted. "Are we to deliberate ... what? ... whether or not we should deliberate ...?"

"The laws of our fathers are our laws," Jarl Mjöksiglandi said. "Hvítvi, your wisdom is as great as your weakness, but here you must prove to me that this isn't nonsense before I waste my words on it: why should I consider Hávi's accusation as legal? What benefit to clan Mjöksiglandi would come of this ... dishonorable and unprecedented alteration to the den Skaanske Lov?"

"None," Jarl Vörsa said. "Clan Vörsa will hear no discussion of women making accusations."

"Even deliberating this accusation will be perceived as a weakness," Jarl Bagal said. "Norway has already invaded us. If we give legal status to women ...!"

"Hvítvi, consider the wisdom of what you do," Jarl Hersir said. "If these deliberations will aid Sweden, then you must prove it."

Hvítvi stared back at all of the members of the council, but no words came from his lips. He glanced about the hall seeking some sign of hope, but none came.

"I'm sorry, Hvítvi," Jarl Hersir said. "This case is ..."

"Wait!" Hávi shouted, and she slowly stood up. *"I ... I can*

prove this."

Not a sound filled the hall as Hávi stepped up beside Hvítvi.

"Hvítvi was never trained as a Law-speaker," Hávi said, "and Jarl Hafr ..."

"Jarl Austmaðr!" he shouted.

"... my husband has kept Valla and Augi from him to protect his position, but I was trained as a Law-speaker. I was chastised, publically-shamed, and punished for my learning, as everyone here knows. But while I was taking lessons, I learned from the best: Jarl Illingr, who was the most-respected Law-speaker in the Skåne."

Jarl Hafr rose to object, but one hand from each of his sons pulled him back down.

"Why should you change the den Skaanske Lov?" Hávi asked, glancing to each man on the council, even at her husband and Master Krókr. "What is the den Skaanske Lov? Many believe that the den Skaanske Lov is our laws, the list of rules declared by our fathers so that we may live in a civilized society. I thought that, too, but Jarl Illingr taught me that I was wrong. You, members of the council, jarls and warlords: you don't need laws. You have wealth, power, and command armies; how can a dispute between farmers require the den Skaanske Lov? You hold their lives in your hands, upon the swords that you command, and all who live beneath you must obey or be slain. It's for dealing with each other, jarl to jarl, and clan to clan, that the den Skaanske Lov exists. The den Skaanske Lov provides the means to mediate disputes that must otherwise be decided by feuds, wars, and invasions ... including civil wars! While the den Skaanske Lov stands, Sweden stands. When the den Skaanske Lov falls, then we Swedes break apart into rivaling clans ... and will be devoured by our enemies. Our existence as one race depends on the den Skaanske Lov!

"The den Skaanske Lov was never meant to be rigid and unchanging, but fluid, malleable, becoming whatever it must to keep Sweden whole. But the real power of the den Skaanske Lov isn't laws or armies or jarls; the real strength of the den Skaanske Lov is the justice that every Swede knows that they can expect. It took a long time for me to understand this, and still I'm not sure if I grasp it entirely: the support of every Swede for the justice guaranteed to them by the den Skaanske Lov allows those thousands of peasants, warriors, clansmen ... and clanswomen ... to support and obey their feudal lord, their clan-chief. Without that support, the support of your own people, we'd have no Sweden; there is no Sweden. The den Skaanske Lov exists for all of us ... or it doesn't exist at all!"

Hávi took a deep breath and strove for control.

"I never disgraced my first husband, the real Jarl Austmaðr, Jorgen's father, save by speaking against his wishes with a man who was his mortal enemy," Hávi said. "If nothing else, let my testimony stand as proof that my liaisons with Jarl Illingr were just that: lessons in the den Skaanske Lov. But if you would do more than just follow the laws of your fathers, if you would understand and share the burden of their purposes, then you must consider my accusation; not just for me, for Sweden."

"You know why I married Jarl Hafr; I sacrificed myself, my honor, and my body, to a man who has thrice brought Sweden to the brink of civil war; once by his ruined viking, a second time by allowing his castle to be taken, and again by plotting to invade his closest neighbors. Now he forces this Tynwald, which would use the den Skaanske Lov to tear us apart rather than bind us together. I need not divorce him for myself; I haven't shared his bed for months and feel pity for those forced to rut with him; Jarl Gullskegger was thrice the husband that Jarl Hafr is."

"*Bitch!*" Jarl Hafr shouted. " *Whore!*"

"Where next shall he lead you?" Hávi demanded. "His invasion of a neighboring clan failed before he sailed from his own shore! What failure will he prompt tomorrow? Pray that it isn't the den Skaanske Lov; it's all that's keeping you together. To save yourselves, all of your clans, and all of Sweden, I beg you: consider my divorce; *my divorce will save you.*"

Hávi scanned the face of each man at the high-table, even her husband, and then walked back to her seat. Völu patted her arm and Bíldr stared at her with wonderment. Thousands of silent glances exchanged throughout the great hall; Hávi's words had struck deep.

"Valla, Augi," Jarl Hersir said softly, "tell us what you can of divorce."

Slowly Valla stepped forward.

"With approval of his father or clan-chief, a man may divorce his wife by making an accusation of divorce against her at Law Rock," Valla said. "Divorce is granted only upon deliberation of the council at a Thyngr or a Tynwald. A marriage contract is nullified by a grant of divorce; all bride-prices or bride-payments must be returned as if the marriage had never occurred. Where the marriage is made of different clans, sons remain with the clan of their father and daughters go to the clan of their mother. The council may declare a fine upon the grant of divorce to offset any damage to reputation or loss of property perceived by either part."

"If you deliberate this," Jarl Hafr warned, "then I'll declare this Tynwald unrepresented ... and it ends."

"You may do that," Jarl Jótun assured Jarl Hafr, "however, a Tynwald need not be attended by a jarl of every clan; if you chose to withdraw, and take your seneschal with you, then I'll suggest to every other council member that we all retire to clan Dúfunef, whom you meant to invade, and there we shall hold another Tynwald ... and decide the future of clan Austmaðr without you."

Jarl Jótun and Jarl Hafr glared at each other.

"Deliberate," Jarl Mjöksiglandi said. "We have no choice. Jarl Hersir, what say you?"

"Deliberate," Jarl Hersir said.

"What are we deliberating?" Jarl Bagal demanded. "Divorce, women making accusations, or whether we should be deliberating any of it?"

"That last must be the first of your deliberations," Hvítvi said. "The only question is ... *will Jarl Austmaðr unrepresent this Tynwald if we deliberate?*"

"Father, don't ...," Skytja warned.

"Please, Father," Rauðkinn said. "This deliberation will happen; don't let it occur without Austmaðr input."

"Hvítvi," Jarl Hersir said, "as the only living half-brother of Jorgen by blood, I request that you attend these deliberations; I require your wisdom."

Hvítvi nodded.

Slowly, reluctantly the council rose and started to file out. Bíldr seized Hávi and pulled her swiftly through a side door before the last of the council had even departed.

"To your tower," Bíldr ordered Hávi. "No argument! Lock the latch. I'll see that you're summoned before the council returns."

Hávi was too exhausted to argue. She'd done her best; it

was out of her hands now. Völu had to support her as they climbed up the winding stairs, and Völu bolted the trapdoor behind them.

"What happened?" Breiðr demanded.

Breiðr and Bitra sat silently while Völu described everything. When she told how Hávi wouldn't be outlawed, Breiðr seized Hávi in a hug and Bitra started to cry. But both were shaken when Völu described the deliberations that were occurring as they spoke.

"Hávi looks like she needs some wine," Breiðr said when Völu finished. "Bitra, come with me."

Opening the bolt, they vanished through the trapdoor and hurried down the steps. Völu relocked the trapdoor while Hávi picked up Jorgen and held him protectively.

"Be ready to flee," Hávi said to Völu. "If we fail, then I can't stay; Jarl Hafr will kill me."

"Men won't give women rights that supersede their own," Völu warned.

"I know," Hávi said, and tears fell from her eyes as she held out her son. "Take Jorgen. Raise him as your own. Never let him know who his parents were. Keep him safe ... as I'll never be."

"They'll have to go through me!" Völu promised, but she reluctantly took Jorgen.

"No," Hávi said, crossing her arms in empty despair. "Say nothing; just take Jorgen on Jarl Hersir's ship and never return. Jarl Hafr won't survive long; he's too stupid and he's enraged his neighbors. Sweden will fall to civil war. Flee to the hills if you must; before this is done, no clan in Sweden will survive."

Dusk approached and darkness consumed the cloudy sky

save for the few twinkling stars and the waning moon. No rumor of the deliberations came, and Breiðr reported that the clan-chiefs had commandeered the whole third floor. All night the deliberations continued, and each moment Hávi feared the worst.

Bíldr's familiar boots echoed on the spiral stairs, but Hávi refused to let Völu unbar the trapdoor until he called for them. Then Hávi followed him down, Völu, Breiðr, and Bitra following them; not one face evidenced hope. At the foot of the stairs, a large gathering of women met them: Hvassi, Gellir, all of the women of Castle Austmaðr, and many from Skadi. All offered support and prayers as Hávi stopped to hug a few.

"Come," Bíldr said to Hávi, and then he added to the others: "The council's decision might best be revealed without a hall full of women."

"We'll be in the sewing room," Breiðr said. "Good luck, Mother."

Breiðr kissed Hávi, then led the women away. Hávi followed Bíldr, only Völu in her wake.

The council of jarls entered the great hall with expressions of greatest unhappiness. Hvítvi came with them. Not one of them glanced at the gathered warriors, who fell silent in dread anticipation. To Hávi's surprise, Hvítvi ascended the stone steps and sat between Skytja and Rauðkinn; *Jarl Hafr hadn't returned.*

"A decision has been reached by the council of jarls," Hvítvi said after all of the others had sat down. "This matter wasn't deliberated kindly and no one's pleased, but each side has gained something, so all have sworn to uphold this decision, unpleasant as it may be."

Hvítvi paused as the warriors shifted nervously.

"As I'm not a warrior, I've been chosen to announce this decision," Hvítvi said. "By nearly-unanimous agreement, the council has agreed that the greatest threat to our clans comes not from our enemies ... but through foolish leadership. To protect ourselves and undo the mistake that we caused, *this council has voted to amend our laws ... to render ... unto women ... the right to make legal accusations ... and to divorce their husbands.*"

Angry curses rose from the hall and weapons were raised, but Jarl Hersir stood and challenged them all.

"What would you have us do?" Jarl Hersir demanded. "Sacrifice our race to spare our pride? Abandon the den Skaanske Lov?"

"Besides," Jarl Bagal said, "if one Tynwald can grant women rights then another can take them away."

"Peace!" Hvítvi shouted, his voice shrill and raspy beside Jarl Hersir's. "The outcomes of future Tynwalds are not our concern. Today, it is the decision of this Tynwald to grant a divorce to Hávi Hersir Austmaðr; *Jarl Hafr is no longer Jarl Austmaðr!*"

Almost everyone cheered at this; Master Krókr buried his face in his hands.

"The title and leadership of clan Austmaðr falls upon the only legal heir, Jorgen Austmaðr," Hvítvi said. "I have been appointed as his regent; I'll determine all administrative functions until Jorgen is of legal age to claim his own. Skytja and Rauðkinn shall assume command of our warriors; Skytja shall command all guards within Castle Austmaðr and Skadi, and Rauðkinn shall command all forces of the six other villages of clan Austmaðr. Clan Austmaðr will no longer lead the viking; Jarl Dúfunef has been unanimously declared to be the fleet-commander, and Jarl Jótun shall assume responsibility for protecting our coasts while the viking is underway; he'll collect tribute of gold from every clan for this."

Hvítvi paused, still frowning, and then he looked straight at Hávi.

"To this agreement, a terrible stipulation has been added," Hvítvi said reluctantly, as if it were tearing his heart in two. "For this decision to be agreed upon, *it has been overwhelmingly voted that Mistress Hávi Hersir Austmaðr shall be outlawed from clan Austmaðr for the remainder of her life.*"

Hávi and Völu gasped.

"I'm sorry," Hvítvi said to Hávi. "You must return home, to clan Hersir, and swear that you'll never again participate in any legal planning or activities; they can't afford for you to give women any more legal rights."

Hávi rose and slowly approached to stand before Hvítvi, looking up at him.

"Outlawed ... for life?" Hávi asked.

"Outlawed from clan Austmaðr," Hvítvi said. "And ... Jorgen must remain ... here ... to be raised to assume his throne."

"I'm to lose ... my son?"

"Not lose ...," Hvítvi said.

"My son is my life!" Hávi argued. *"Everything that I've done ... I've done for him!"*

"Your son must remain here ... but you can't," Hvítvi said. "Hávi, this stipulation isn't negotiable: the council is adamant."

"Who'll raise my son?" Hávi demanded.

"Whoever you want," Hvítvi said. "Völu, your mother, Breiðr, ..."

Hávi felt tears rise but she pushed them back; *she couldn't give in!*

"I will," Hvítvi said softly, reluctantly, bowing his head. "I'll raise Jorgen ... as if he were my own."

Hávi hesitated, then steeled herself.

"No," Hávi said.

"Think before you say that," Hvítvi said. "This is the only resolution that we can agree upon. If you refuse, then no divorce is granted; Jarl Hafr retains command, and civil war begins. The rights that you've earned for women will vanish with the den Skaanske Lov. You needn't be separated forever; Jorgen can come for visits, at least once a year. When he's grown, he'll have the authority to challenge your outlawry, and perhaps overturn it. Until then ... you must live apart."

Hávi gritted her teeth and trembled with frustration. What Hvítvi was asking was impossible! Unthinkable! Yet what choice did she have? If civil war began, then Jorgen's life would be at permanent risk, a threat to, or a tool of, every jarl in the Skåne. *Was one life, even hers, worth the price of peace across Sweden?*

How could she live without her son?

"I ... I need time," Hávi said.

"You don't have time," Hvítvi said. "The Tynwald's about to end; we must have your answer now. Hávi, I'm sorry."

"You're giving me no choice!"

"I never meant to," Hvítvi said. "This isn't my choice, either."

Hávi's mind raced; they were taking her son away from her by peace or by war. If she refused, then clan Austmaðr would be conquered and Jorgen would grow up the only heir to a dead clan.

"You bastards!" Hávi shouted. *" You've talked all night ... and this is all that you've got?"*

Hvítvi bowed his head. All of the council fidgeted. Every muscle in Hávi tightened and knotted; she had no choice, but to make this choice would kill her.

"I, too, have a stipulation," Hávi said.

"Name your stipulation," Hvítvi said.

"I won't have Jorgen raised by anyone but me ... or his father," Hávi said. *"If you would raise my son ... then you, Hvítvi, must marry ... me!"*

Gasps filled the great hall. Hvítvi raised his head and met her defiant eyes, pink into blue, and Hávi could almost see the thoughts race behind his calm, controlled expression. But Hvítvi turned from her to Skytja and Rauðkinn and whispered something that Hávi couldn't hear. Skytja and Rauðkinn glanced worriedly at Hávi, but both nodded. Hvítvi addressed the rest of the council.

"My honored stepbrothers have no objection; does anyone?"

"Are you serious?" Jarl Mjöksiglandi asked.

"He's mad if he does," Jarl Vörsa said.

"He's a fool if he doesn't," Jarl Dúfunef grinned.

Hvítvi raised his tired voice so that everyone in the hall could hear.

"Let it be known to all that Mistress Hávi Hersir Austmaðr and Master Hvítvi Austmaðr are pledged," Hvítvi said. "Tomorrow, before she departs, we shall be married before you all ... and Jorgen shall be crowned as the new Jarl Austmaðr. *Now, Hávi: do you accept these terms?"*

Slowly Hávi bowed her head.

"I will ... obey my husband's wishes," Hávi said, *"if he visits me often!"*

Riotous cheers exploded and everyone jumped to their feet. Only Master Krókr frowned; the Tynwald was over ... and Jarl Hafr had lost. All of the jarls stood and applauded; Jarl Hersir insisted on shaking Hvítvi's hand.

At midday, under a bright, blue sky, dressed in sunlight yellow, Hávi entered the great hall for her fourth and final wedding. Since before her first wedding, she'd dreamed of giving women the right to refuse a marriage that they didn't want; Hávi had never achieved that goal, but the right to own property, the right to make accusations, and the right to divorce a husband; *Hávi had fought well and hard.* Other women would have to preserve what she'd gained and perhaps acquire other rights still denied to their sex, but Hávi wasn't afraid; she'd be their example, a story spread by women everywhere and passed down to their daughters, perhaps someday reaching Norway, England, and even Rome.

Hvítvi stood in midnight purple, highlighting his paleness more than ever, awaiting her at the front of the hall. Men and women filled the hall, squeals of delight erupting from the smiling faces of all. Castle women, townswomen, and sluts stood together cheering her entrance; Hávi smiled at all of them.

Hávi clutched Jorgen tightly as she entered the great hall; despite her nuptials and impending wedding night, Hávi refused to be parted from her beautiful child for even a moment. Tomorrow she'd have to say good-bye to her precious baby; how she'd do that she still didn't know. But she wouldn't be gone seven years; in four months the viking would begin, and while the warriors were gone, she'd find a way back ... *and a way to stay.* The women would protect her ... *even if she had to live here while outlawed ..*

"Come, Hávi, before our feast gets cold," Jarl Hersir called to her, waving her forward as he'd done so long ago at her first wedding. All of the other jarls stood behind him, beside Skytja and Rauðkinn, both of whom insisted on still calling her *'Mother'*. Only Jarl Hafr had departed, cursing his sons and everyone else for betraying him. Master Krókr had stayed, but fled to his room; without Mjóvi or Jarl Hafr to support him, his influence was greatly reduced. Hávi glanced across the room at all of the faces; most of the women Hávi knew and loved; now they loved her as well.

Hvítvi's smile beamed. He took Hávi's hand in his own; Jarl Hersir started by binding their wrists ceremoniously with a golden cord. Then sand was sprinkled in their hair, water flicked, and boughs of evergreen firs were brushed around both lovers. For the first time Hávi listened to every word of her vows, glad to finally put meaning into them, and attended joyously while Hvítvi proudly pledged his life and love and devotion to her. Unlike the eternity of her former ceremonies, Hávi's fourth wedding didn't last long enough: all too soon Bíldr stepped forward, carrying the broom that would seal their lives together; Bíldr's smile was so bright that even his bushy mustache couldn't hide it. Together Hávi and Hvítvi turned to face the joyous crowd and Bíldr placed the broom at their feet. Finally Hávi was ready to jump into a whole new life.

Clutching Jorgen tightly, Hávi and Hvítvi jumped over the broom into wedded bliss. The great hall cheered and Hávi shifted Jorgen onto one arm and slipped her other hand around Hvítvi's back while he waved to everyone, accepting the many blessings being shouted at both of them. Sliding her strong hand up Hvítvi's slender neck to seize the back of his head, Hávi suddenly pulled Hvítvi towards her and kissed him hard and passionately before representatives of every clan in the Skåne. Hávi was finally married by her own choice to the man whom she loved most, and she wanted everyone to know it.

THE END

ABOUT THE AUTHOR

Born in Tripler Army Medical Center, Honolulu, Hawaii, Jay Palmer works as a technical writer in the software industry in Seattle, Washington. Jay enjoys parties, reading everything in sight, woodworking, obscure board games, and riding his Kawasaki Vulcan. Jay is a knight in the SCA, frequently attends writer conferences, SciFi Conventions, and he and Karen are both avid ballroom dancers. But most of all, Jay enjoys writing.